Blossoms
of Winter

a novel by
Don Pardue

Library of Congress Control Number: 2004098413

ISBN 0-9755892-0-2

First printing - November, 2004

Additional copies of this book are available by mail. Information / Ordering sheet located inside novel.

Printed in the U.S.A. by
Morris Publishing
3212 East Highway 30
Kearney, NE 68847
1-800-650-7888

ii

Dedication

To Donna and Victor whose sustaining support and creative input made possible the telling of this story; and to my wife, Barbara, for her mountain of tolerance.

~ Cover design by Victor Pardue ~

~ Editing by Donna Pardue Thompson ~

A Journey of Memories

The patchwork of passing seasons pressed onward in an unrelenting cadence, melding into years; then clusters of years became the changing seasons of life. The ghostly, blossoming memories of the springtime of youth were gathered up, then swept away by the restless breeze of life's summer. They rode the crest of the turbulent wind, collecting phantom playmates on their melancholy flight across the unbroken annals of time; then, after breathing warmth into the frost-laden autumn years, they alighted at last, coming to rest in the welcoming embrace of the lonely soul of winter…

Don Pardue

The creation of something new is not accomplished by the intellect but by the play instinct acting from inner necessity. The creative mind plays with the objects it loves. **Carl Jung**

Chapter 1

In the southwestern sky, the murky, billowing thunderhead towered upward, its anvil top spreading ahead of it. Like a gigantic flash bulb, the lightning flickered deep within the interior of the darkened clouds, silhouetting their swollen contours, and the distant rumble of thunder promised rainfall to the parched land. As the storm grew nearer, mounting gusts of cooling wind delivered the stimulating scent of wetness, and the sun hid its face.

The storm's premonition of rain was an empty promise, for the capricious clouds gradually drifted eastward, and the sun reappeared. The aroma of rain grew fainter, the breezes subsided, and the sound of rolling thunder became more muted. The plants of the scorching fields drooped listlessly as if kneeling in prayer for the quenching savor of rain.

In the city, the shimmering streets regained their swelter, and the flat rooftops of factories sizzled from the blistering assault of the merciless sun. Once again, the reviving rain had bypassed the city as the entire Midwest languished in the strangling clutches of a late summer drought.

Rob Beauvais was sitting in an old-fashioned swing on the front porch of his rented apartment in Ft. Wayne, Indiana. Gazing eastward, he lazily eyed the retreating thunderstorm. The rusty chains supporting the swing groaned rhythmically as he swung gently back and forth. He was fanning himself with an outdated magazine, for he was sweating profusely. It was early September, 1954, and the city was sweltering in the midst of the late summer heat wave. His wife, Madge was in the tiny kitchen in back of the small three room apartment trying to scrape

1

together something for dinner. From habit, Rob looked at his watchless, left wrist for the time. He wasn't yet accustomed to the fact that he had pawned his wristwatch a few days earlier. Rob rolled up the magazine and rose slowly from the porch swing. As he strode across the small porch, the worn, gray planks squeaked beneath his feet. He opened the screen door, which had numerous tears in the bottom of the screen, probably made by a pet dog sometime in the distant past. He had left the main front door open in order to keep the apartment cool, but it was a futile measure. The inside of the tiny apartment was like an oven, with the holes in the screen door offering easy passage for flies.

Rob stuck his head inside the small living room and looked at the clock sitting on a table...*3:45*, he noted. *Dean should be back at anytime.*

He closed the screen door and returned to the porch. This time he seated himself in a chair on the opposite side of the swing so that he would be facing the direction from which Dean would be returning. He unrolled the magazine and began to fan himself. His eyes were fixed on the narrow, shaded street, in the hope of seeing Dean. The intense heat rising from the asphalt formed a shimmering mirage, resembling a lake.

At last he saw his brother rounding the corner a block away from the apartment.

As he watched Dean walking toward the house, Rob thought that he detected a bit more of a spring in his step than when he left. When his brother was about a half block away, Rob called to him.

"Did you get it?"

Dean continued walking and didn't answer him, but responded with a "thumbs-up" gesture and a big grin on his face. He finished his walk to the apartment and quickly ascended the concrete steps to the front porch, seating himself in the swing facing Rob. He pulled from his back pocket a handkerchief and wiped his sweating face before saying anything.

"Jesus, it's hot," he said. "I thought we were going to have a good rain." His tee-shirt and the top portion of his khaki pants clung to his sweating body. The twenty blocks round trip he had made in the summer heat to the Western Union office had exhausted him, and he breathed heavily.

Rob sat silently, continuing to fan himself, patiently waiting for Dean to say something else.

After catching his breath, Dean announced, "Well, I've got some good news and some bad news. Which do you want first?"

"For God's sake, give me the good news." Rob's face showed impatience. "I can't stand to hear anything else bad right now."

2

"The good news is Al sent the money. The bad news is that he couldn't send the hundred I asked for. He could only afford seventy-five," explained Dean.

Rob frowned. "But didn't he owe you two hundred?"

"Yeah, but he said seventy-five was all he had," Dean answered, apologetically.

Rob grinned. "Hell, that's not too bad, but is it gonna be enough for you to get to Chicago? Get a room, buy cigarettes and eat?" Rob finished his question with a worried expression on his face. They both fell into silence.

Dean studied his brother before he answered. Rob, the oldest of the five brothers, was looking older than his 33 years. He was a heavy-set man of medium height, weighing about 200 pounds—about 20 pounds too heavy for his muscular frame. Rob was a ruggedly handsome man resembling his mother more than his dad. He had inherited his mother's straight nose, even teeth, and black wavy hair. However, he was going bald, like his father. His round face displayed small scars around his gray eyes, some caused by punches he had taken in numerous fights, others from blows he had endured years ago in the boxing ring. Dean thought to himself that Rob, sitting there in his sweaty tee-shirt with his muscular arms, resembled a prize-fighter.

Dean finally broke the silence. "Seventy-five dollars will have to be enough. Man, we sure got into a mess this time. Who'd a thought that neither of us could find a job. Three weeks in Ft. Wayne, trying every sign painting shop in town, and still no luck. I was even willin' to take that shoe salesman job 'til it fell through. What's for supper? I'm hungry as a bear."

Rob's wife, Madge, appeared at the front door, holding the screen door open.

Rob remarked, "Careful, don't let the flies out!"

Madge smiled at Rob, and noticing that Dean had returned, said in a weary voice, "Oh Dean, you're back. Just in time, too. Supper's ready."

Dean smiled at Madge. "Excuse me, but I've gotta wash some of this sweat off my face before I eat." He then walked through the apartment into the tiny bathroom adjoining the kitchen. The room had an old rust-stained commode that inevitably kept running when it was flushed. Across from a small shower stood a tiny old-fashioned sink, and above it hung a rather small mirror with a diagonal crack across one corner. The small light on the ceiling was a naked bulb with a long pull-chain. A single, thin coat of paint covered the walls, transparently revealing

3

the wallpaper that had once garnished the room.

He splashed water on his face, washed his hands, and pulled a comb from his pocket. When he looked into the mirror, he saw how badly he needed a haircut. Long locks of curly black hair fell over his forehead and half-covered his ears. Like his brother Rob, Dean was also handsome, but in a different way. While Rob had rugged, manly features, Dean's face reflected a more classic, almost effeminate quality with a straight nose and full lips. Like Rob, his eyes were steel gray. Rob sometimes said that Dean was "sissy-looking", an accusation that might very well cause a fight if Dean was within ear-shot of the remark. His face was less full than Rob's, but he had his brother's muscular build, and was about an inch taller. He was twenty-three, ten years younger than Rob and 20 pounds lighter in weight.

He combed his hair and decided that before he left for Chicago in the morning, he would definitely have to shave. He stepped out of the bathroom and into the kitchen, waiting for Rob and Madge.

Rob relinquished his seat on the porch and said sarcastically, "What are we havin', filet mignon?"

Madge laughed, and she and Rob went inside, letting the tattered screen door slam behind them. They walked through the dark, musty living room into the small kitchen. Grease stains were on the wall above the gas range, and beneath it on the floor, patches of wooden planks were beginning to show where years of traffic had worn away the cheap linoleum. The kitchen was barely illuminated with a single light bulb, casting a gloomy light in the room. To provide more space, a small oak table and three unmatched chairs hugged a corner of the kitchen. The room reeked strongly of disinfectant and grease. Because they had left Tennessee so hastily, Madge had neglected to pack her box of pot and pans. With no money to buy more, they had resorted to cooking with empty food cans and eating with plastic spoons and forks. The brothers chose the two chairs facing each other and wearily sat down. Madge hurried to the stove and began busily fussing over the simmering food. A thin, dark- skinned attractive woman with straight brown hair, Madge was quick-witted and easy-going. She had a bad temper at times but was generally forgiving and tolerant of the faults of others; a very convenient trait, indeed, since she was married to Rob.

"What have we got, Madge?" asked Rob.

"Well, we have bacon, biscuits, and we were goin' to have gravy, but while I was on the porch calling you to supper, the plastic spoon melted into the gravy."

4

Rob asked, "Think it changed the taste any?"

"Surely you're not going to eat it!" exclaimed Madge.

Dean laughed, "Plastic won't hurt you. At least it's sanitary. Hell, plastic might taste better than the gravy. No offense intended, Madge. What have we got to drink?"

"Water," Madge replied.

Madge set out three paper cups of ice water and dished out the bacon and gravy on three paper plates. She then took some hard, left-over biscuits from the oven and served them on another paper plate. She sat down between Rob and Dean, facing the kitchen wall. Madge began to munch on the bacon and left-over biscuits, but she didn't eat any of the gravy. Occasionally, between bites, she brushed away the flies.

Dean suddenly exclaimed, "Damn!" A large fly had landed in his gravy, and the three of them looked at the squirming insect with disgust. He carefully lifted the fly out with his plastic fork, and noticed that it had stopped wiggling.

"I think it's dead," said Dean.

"Maybe the plastic in the gravy killed the little bastard." Madge laughed.

Rob looked at Madge and sympathy showed in his eyes. "I guess you're tired, aren't you honey? Working all day and then coming home and cooking supper for two lazy louts."

Madge replied wearily, "Supper was no trouble. Nothing much to fix."

Madge didn't resent working. She realized that Rob and Dean had been trying desperately to find any kind of job. In order for the three of them to survive, she had found a low-paying job as a clerk in a small store within walking distance of the apartment. Her sister, Claudia, who lived across town, also helped by loaning Madge a small amount of money for groceries. Claudia wanted to offer further help, but she and her husband, Dale, were also struggling financially.

The first week, the brothers drove Dean's car when looking for work, but after the second week, they had no money for gasoline and the battery was low. Abandoning the car made it necessary for the three of them to walk everywhere. Job-searching on foot during a time when the city was in the grip of a heat wave proved to be an insurmountable task. Sometimes they would walk 40 or 50 blocks each day before arriving back at the apartment, feeling defeated and exhausted. Despite their frustration, Rob and Dean refused to give up, eventually seeking any kind of job.

Their landlady who lived upstairs often gave them the want ads from her daily newspaper. With a ball point pen, Rob would draw a circle around each job possibility. Then, looking on a city map, the brothers would try to locate the addresses that were within a reasonable walking distance of the apartment.

It appeared that a relief in their desperation came when Rob managed to sell a freelance sign to a lawyer. The specifications for the sign required that the dimensions be 24 inches by 48 inches, painted with a white background and black lettering. The sign was to be mounted on metal posts, placed in the ground, and set in concrete. Rob and Dean had the necessary tools, including sign kits with a large selection of brushes. The problem was that they had no paint or material for construction of the sign, no hole digger for setting the posts, and no money with which to buy them. The sign location was 18 blocks from their apartment. To ensure that he got the job, Rob priced it at $75 dollars; however, it was worth twice that amount.

Taking these obstacles into consideration, Dean asked his brother the obvious questions: "Rob, how are we goin' to get the materials for the job? Another thing—it's to be set in concrete. How're we goin' to dig the holes, or take the cement to the job site? It will take at least two bags and each bag weighs 94 pounds. And where are we goin' to get the metal posts for the sign? We don't even have a car to haul the materials!"

"You worry too much, Dean," Rob said in a comforting voice, "we've always figured out a way, haven't we? Remember what Dad always says: 'When the going gets tough, the tough get going'."

To solve the problem of background materials for the sign, Rob discovered, to his delight, two shelving planks in the top of the bedroom closet in their apartment. Each plank measured 12 inches by 60 inches. With some sawing here and placing there, the planks could measure exactly 24 inches by 48 inches—the precise dimensions that the specifications required. However, one difficult problem was figuring how to quietly pry the planks out of the closet without the landlady in the apartment above them thinking that the house was being dismantled. They discussed various possibilities of accomplishing this—a feat that would require some creative thinking. They finally came up with a plan.

In order to muffle the sound of the prying, Rob had to increase the volume on the radio. Then, with the small crowbar from his tool kit, Rob would tug, but the nail would make a loud, "SQUEAK" as it was removed. So at the same time, Dean had to cough loudly, synchronizing it with the squeak, hoping that his cough would obscure the sound of the nail being loosened. This repetitive process was carried on in hope that the landlady would only hear background music accompanied by frequent bursts of coughing.

Rob also found in the closet about a half gallon of white enamel that could be used for the sign background. Dean had in his sign kit a pint of black enamel that could be used for the lettering. With these basic, scraped-together materials, they were ready to start painting the sign. Now, they were left with the problem of finding some post-hole diggers, buying the cement, and obtaining some metal posts.

The landlady had a brother who loaned them some hole diggers, and Madge drew a small advance from her job for enough money to buy the two bags of cement. But that still left the most difficult item of all: the metal posts upon which the sign was to be installed.

The brothers set out on foot, each in a different direction, roaming the alleys within a twenty block radius, searching for some kind of metal pipe that could be converted into posts.

Eventually, after a couple of days of prowling, Dean found a rusty length of pipe about 20 feet long, which he laboriously worked on for two hours with his dull hacksaw, cutting the pipe until he had two posts of the required length. Rob lettered the sign while Dean wire-brushed and painted the two lengths of pipe with black enamel. They could install the sign with the bolts and an electric drill from their toolbox. An extension cord, which was borrowed from the landlady, could be plugged into an outlet at the lawyer's office.

With all the necessary elements collected, the brothers set out on foot to carry them to the job site—18 blocks away.

Carrying the materials to the job site would take more than one trip. On the first trip they carried the sign, posts, tools, and extension cord, with the brothers swapping their burdensome loads every three or four blocks. On the second trip, and another eighteen blocks in the merciless heat, each man had to carry a 94 pound bag of cement on his back. When the sign was completed, the brothers stood back and inspected it. To Dean's surprise, the sign looked great. No one would ever suspect that it had been constructed from scrap material.

Both men stood proudly admiring the sign. When Rob had initially accepted the job, its completion seemed an impossibility to Dean. The two men felt that they had just climbed a mountain, reaching the top. At that moment, Dean felt that they could accomplish any task set before them. If they were resourceful enough to accomplish this, they could survive almost any ordeal, no matter how difficult.

When the lawyer came out of his office to inspect the sign, he impassively studied it without any immediate comment. He was an expensively dressed, overweight, bald man with an overbearing demeanor. He finally looked at Rob and said, "The sign meets with my approval. You may leave your bill with my secretary inside."

Instead, Rob reached into his pocket for his pad of statements that he had purchased from the ten cent store. He tore the top copy out of the book and presented the man with the bill.

The lawyer looked at the bill and said coldly, "We'll have to mail you a check. You should receive it by the first of the month. Give the bill to my secretary."

Rob smiled at the man. "Sir, if it's not too much trouble, could you pay us now? We have a little cash flow problem."

The lawyer appeared irritated. "Your check will have to be issued through regular channels, sir. Our policy regarding payment is that we'll mail you a check by the first of the month."

Rob was beginning to become angry. He and Dean had almost no money left; their situation had begun to look desperate. Rob said, "Sir, I don't give a damn about your 'policy regarding payment!' All I know is that you ordered this sign and we did it. You inspected it and approved it—and you owe us $75 dollars, and we won't leave here until we get it!"

"But sir, as I told you, our policy regarding payment is…"

Rob took a step toward the lawyer, and the man peered into Rob's angry face.

Then the lawyer decided to change his "policy regarding payment." Rob and Dean went home with $75 in their pockets.

*   *   *

The brothers finally developed a stoic attitude in regard to their job search. They would do what they had to do. They would take one day, even one hour at a time and just put one foot in front of the other, sometimes plodding together, sometimes separating and walking in different directions. Walking by factories, through the slums, along skid row, always through the insufferable heat. Sometimes they would walk by taverns, dark and inviting inside, where they could smell the ice cold beer, where an open, welcoming door offered an exhilarating rush of cool air that enveloped their sweating bodies as they passed.

When the financial situation became so desperate that it appeared they wouldn't have anything to eat, Dean had reluctantly pawned his guitar. When that money was gone, he called his brother, Alvin, in

8

Tennessee, asking him to wire some money from home. It hurt his pride to ask for money from his brother, but after all, Al owed him.

*   *   *

After dinner, Madge threw away the paper plates, saved the paper cups, and cleaned up the kitchen. The brothers retired to the front porch to talk and make plans. Rob sat down in the porch swing while Dean took a chair facing him, wiping his sweaty forehead with a handkerchief.

Rob said, "Dean, I'm sorry I didn't walk with you to the Western Union office, but that long walk yesterday put a hell of a blister on my left heel."

"That's okay", replied Dean, "no use in both of us walkin' all the way down there. Damn it's hot!" He wiped sweat off his forehead with his hand.

They were silent for a long while. Dean studied the narrow street in front of the apartment as the men lolled lazily on the porch. Across the street, a mongrel dog hiked his leg, urinating on a fire hydrant.

Then Rob said, sadly, "Well, Dean, I guess you'll be leavin' for Chicago. Goin' tomorrow?"

Dean answered hesitantly, "I… guess so. Don't have the money to hang around here very much longer."

Again, the brothers became silent. They were reluctant to elaborate on the unpleasant subject of Dean's upcoming departure.

Dean's mind wandered. He noticed that the mangy dog, having finished marking his territory, walked slowly down the shady sidewalk, with its tongue hanging out, dripping saliva.

He quickly changed the subject. "I know you've got a blister, but do you feel like walkin' about three blocks?"

"Why?" Rob asked.

Dean grinned. "Well, there's a liquor store over on Grand Avenue. And we could buy some cigarettes. Hell, we ain't smoked in a week!"

Rob looked skeptically at him, "Man that really sounds tempting, but you need all the money you've got if you're going to Chicago. Madge and I can make it, hopefully, with her workin' 'til I can find something. She can pay the apartment rent and buy a little food 'til things get better, but you'll be on your own, with very little money. They don't give a damn about a Tennessee hick like you in Chicago."

Dean replied confidently, "Hell, Rob, Chicago's a great workin'

9

man's town. You and I had good jobs there last year. Come on, let's go to the liquor store."

Rob's face reflected an expression of sheer bliss. "Hell, let's go! But we can't buy but one bottle—and some cigarettes."

Both men simultaneously abandoned their seats, immediately energized by the thought that they were going to get a brief respite from the ordeal they had endured for the past month.

Rob said, "We better let Madge know we're takin' a walk."

He turned to the ragged screen door and yelled, "Madge—Dean and I are goin' for a little walk. We'll bring back some cigarettes."

"Buy something for breakfast. I'm not that worried about cigarettes!" Madge also smoked, but considerably less than Rob and Dean.

The brothers were light-hearted for the moment. They both quickly descended the porch steps and started walking up the broiling sidewalk, with Rob favoring his left foot.

Rob asked, "Dean, are you sure we can afford this? I feel guilty spending your Chicago money."

Dean retorted, "Well, if you feel so damn guilty, why don't' you go on back to the apartment, and I'll go get me a bottle and some cigarettes. Might just buy me a hamburger too. That plastic gravy didn't stick to my ribs much."

Apparently, Rob didn't feel that guilty because he didn't even slow his pace. Even with his blister he was keeping up with Dean, who was quickening his pace and taking longer strides.

The street was lined with large oak trees that offered shelter from the blistering sun. The dry, fading leaves with hints of color were beginning to suggest an approaching autumn. Although the daylight was beginning to fade, the heat was suffocating. From the exertion of their rapid pace, the men were now sweating profusely, causing their wet shirts to cling to their backs.

They stopped and watched for traffic when they reached the corner of the second block. A pretty brunette lady driving a Cadillac stopped at the traffic light, rolled down her window, and tossed her cigarette butt onto the street. She glanced at Rob and Dean with a look of disinterest, and as the light changed, she pulled away.

As the cigarette butt rolled toward the two men, they could see that it was king-size and had hardly been smoked at all. Rob casually bent over and picked up the butt. Looking at it with interest, he noticed that the tip had a small lipstick stain.

Dean glanced at Rob with an inquisitive look. "You gonna smoke that?"

Rob replied with a smile of ecstasy. "Damn right! Nothing wrong with this cigarette. It's gotta be germ-free. Did you get a load of the dish who was smokin' it?"

Dean considered his brother's comment. "We're gonna buy some smokes in about five minutes. Can't you wait?"

"No need to wait. I want to smoke now."

Dean shrugged with resignation. "Well, hell, okay—give me a drag."

Rob looked at his brother suddenly with an expression of exaggerated indignation. He half turned his body, holding his cigarette as far away from Dean as possible, as a child might do when refusing to share a cherished toy with a pleading playmate.

"Find your own cigarette!" exclaimed Rob, in feigned anger. He laughed, took a deep draw from the cigarette butt and inhaled deeply. "AAAAH.... God, that's good," He then took another deep drag, holding the smoke in his lungs for a longer time before exhaling it. He then handed the cigarette to Dean.

"Here," said Rob, grudgingly. "You sure you want to smoke after me? If you didn't want to smoke after that beautiful creature that threw it out, why would you smoke after a dirty pig like me?"

Dean didn't answer. He simply took the cigarette from Rob. They shared the smoke until they saw the neon sign hanging over the sidewalk, *West Side Liquors*.

They walked up to the entrance of the store and peered into the window. It was an upscale establishment, better than they had been accustomed to frequenting. Seeing the plethora of bottles lining the shelves in the store excited them. They quickly stepped inside.

The cool interior of the liquor store felt cold compared to the outside heat. Rob was already dreading going back outside into the suffocating, humid air. Because he was the older brother and, therefore, the spokesman, Rob strolled ahead of Dean to the counter where a tall, balding, bespectacled man confronted him.

"Good evening, sire," greeted Rob, "would it be possible to speak to the manager of this establishment?"

The man warily eyed the two men. "I'm the manager. How may I help you sir?" the man asked, with a practiced air of dignity. Judging from the manager's articulate, pompous demeanor, it was obvious to Dean that this was a humorless man.

With a counterfeit, aristocratic voice, Rob asked, "Sire, may I see a list of your best imported wines?" His voice carried an acumen common only to discerning connoisseurs.

11

The store manager looked intently at Rob, whose question was completely out of character with his appearance, being that his tee-shirt and jeans were soaked with sweat, and he badly needed a shave. Undaunted, the clerk's impassive expression was virtually unchanged except for a slightly raised eyebrow. After all, he reasoned, this customer could possibly be an eccentric millionaire—someone who dressed this way because he was so rich that he felt no need to impress anyone with his appearance.

Peering skeptically at Rob through the bottom of his spectacles, he began reciting a list of his finest wines.

"Sir, we have a delicious Cabernet Sauvignon, and we have Chardonnay, Pinot Noir and this Riesling has a very fine bouquet."

As he reeled off several more excellent choices of wine, Rob's face displayed an intense interest. He suddenly interrupted the man. "Sire, I believe that I have made my decision. It was a rather difficult choice, considering all the selections you have described. I prefer the *La Boheme,* right there."

Rob pointed to the bottle he desired. It was probably the cheapest wine in the store, mostly consumed by "winos" and derelicts.

"How much is that quart— right there?"

Unmoved and trying his best to retain a modicum of professionalism, the manager said, "Sir, that bottle of wine will cost you a $1.89 cents."

"What do you think, Dean?" asked Rob.

"A little expensive, but I guess it's okay unless he has something cheaper," answered Dean. "We better get two of them though."

Rob amended his request. "Sire, you'd better give us two bottles— I almost forgot about my distinguished companion here, he'll need one too."

Without emotion, the manager obediently took two bottles of the cheap wine off the shelf and handed them to Rob. Dean handed his brother a five dollar bill, which Rob handed to the manager. He gave Rob the change from the five and said, "Thank you, Sir." Dean noticed that he didn't say "Come back".

When they were nearly out of the store, Rob suddenly turned back toward the manager and inquired in a decorous manner, "Sire, could you direct me to the nearest alley?"

From habit, the man started to answer, and then abruptly stopped himself. He merely rolled his eyes, turned, and walked away. Dean noticed when the man looked back over his shoulder, his face registered a look of disgust.

Throughout the wine transaction, Dean had never changed his expression. Both Rob and Dean had a penchant for the outrageous, and it was an unspoken rule between them that it was forbidden for either of them to act as if anything was out of the ordinary. They never displayed any sign of shock at what the other did, no matter how outlandish the behavior.

Their way of coping with dire circumstances was to find some humor in any situation, or to display an unperturbed attitude. It was as if they were mocking the sad state-of-affairs in which they had placed themselves.

When they walked out of the liquor store, the outside air seemed hotter than ever. As they started for the corner with the two bottles, Rob said, "Hey, I wasn't kidding about taking a drink in the alley. I noticed one right behind the liquor store before we turned the corner to go in."

Dean studied Rob's expression, noting that he appeared only half-serious.

"Come on, Rob, we'll have a drink when we get back to the apartment. Besides, we need to stop at the market and get some cigarettes—also something for breakfast in the morning. I can't start for Chicago with a belly full of plastic." Dean had stopped calling the breakfast substance "gravy".

They stopped at a market where Rob waited in front as Dean went inside. Soon he returned with a carton of *Pall Mall* cigarettes, a pound of bacon, a loaf of bread, a pound of coffee, and two cans of pork and beans.

Rob poked his head into the sack that Dean was carrying. "Man, you're really splurgin'" He feasted his eyes on the carton of cigarettes. "At the rate you're spendin', you're goin' to run out of money before we get home."

"I'll have enough," answered Dean, "besides, I can't go any longer without a few drinks and a cigarette or two, and something in my stomach that's fit to eat."

The men quickened their pace as they headed back to the apartment. They hurriedly opened a pack of cigarettes, each taking one. They walked in silence the rest of the way, each in excited anticipation of opening the first bottle of wine.

After they had ascended the three steps onto the front porch, Rob yelled through the screen, "Come on out Madge, we got cigarettes. And bring some paper cups—we got some wine."

They each took a seat on the porch— Rob in the swing and Dean directly across from him.

Madge appeared at the door. "Did you buy us anything to eat?"

"Oh, I forgot to mention that," answered Rob. "We got a few things for breakfast."

Madge looked at both men accusingly. "So your booze and cigarettes are more important to you than eating?"

"Oh, I was going to mention the food," Rob countered, apologetically, "but I was just tryin' to keep my priorities straight."

Rob removed the wine and cigarettes and handed the bag of groceries to Madge. Dean spoke up. "We didn't get much, Madge, just enough for breakfast. I didn't know what you and Rob wanted to eat after I'm gone—also, I forgot what brand of cigarettes you smoke. I'm going to leave you guys a little money, so you can buy whatever you want after I'm gone. Tomorrow's Sunday, so you'll have time to shop."

Madge took the bag of food and disappeared into the apartment.

"How are you gonna leave us any money?" queried Rob. "You just had $75 dollars to start with. What if your car breaks down?"

Dean considered his brother's question. "Well, if it breaks down, I won't have enough money to get it towed in and fixed anyway. If that happens, I'll just abandon the son-of–a-bitch and start hitch-hikin'."

Rob commented, "I think there's some kind of law against abandoning your car along the highway."

Dean looked at Rob with an incredulous stare and answered sarcastically, "Oh, don't worry about that. If it breaks down, I'll just push it all the way to Chicago. After all, there are no hills in this God-forsaken part of the country. And you know that neither of us would ever break *any* kind of law."

"Seriously, Dean, how much money do you have left?"

Both men were fanning themselves as Rob rocked slowly back and forth, the supporting chains squeaking with each sway of the swing. Dean pulled a handkerchief from his pocket and mopped the sweat from his face. Replacing the cloth, he extracted his wallet, opened it, and counted the money.

"I have $63 dollars left and some change. We've only spent about four bucks on the wine, the rest on groceries and cigarettes. Hell, can't we do a little less bullshittin' and a little more drinkin'?"

"I thought you would never ask," Rob grinned, picking up one of the quarts and unscrewing the lid at the top. "Don't need a corkscrew for this wine."

Dean reached across and handed Rob two large paper cups. Rob poured wine into each cup until they were both about three-fourth full. He then held the two cups at eye level against the setting sun, comparing the contents, in order to ensure that each of them had the exact same amount. He poured a few drops from one cup into the other, to even them up. Then after comparing them again, he seemed satisfied. He handed one of the cups to Dean.

At that, Madge came out the door. She looked at the brothers. "Is this a private party, or can anyone join in? How about a drink for the lady of the house?" She had a paper cup in her hand.

Rob replied, "Oh, excuse me honey, here have a drink of wine." He poured her a drink, a bit smaller than his and Dean's. She sat down in the porch swing next to Rob, and set her drink on the porch rail. Madge had showered, and her hair was still slightly wet. She had a towel in her hand, and she had changed into some thin pajamas. After resting her bare feet in Rob's lap, she began to vigorously towel her hair with both hands. "You guys should take a shower. It will help you cool off."

Dean swallowed a generous portion of wine from his cup, but Rob was less hurried in his consumption. He held the cup of wine under his nose, sniffing it.

"A rather nice bouquet," Rob commented, ostentatiously. He then took a very small sip, rolling it on his tongue, gently smacking his lips together. He looked up questioningly, as if he were trying to recognize the vintage. His face displayed a patronizing expression, as if he were a connoisseur of fine wines. "AHHHH, nothing like a fresh wine!" He said, pretentiously. "A very good year....1954."

"What month?" asked Dean, with sarcasm.

The men lit cigarettes, deeply inhaling the smoke. They sat for awhile in deep thought.

Finally, Dean looked at Rob and grinned. "We oughn't to drink but a quart tonight and leave the other quart for an eye-opener in the mornin'. We got to make this wine last us. We don't want to chug-a-lug this wine like we used to do in Miami last year."

Dean was referring to a habit that they developed when they worked together in a sign shop in Miami, Florida. Each morning on their way to work, the brothers would buy a quart of cheap wine at a liquor store, divide it equally in two paper cups, and race each other to see who could finish the wine faster. When they arrived at work, they were not completely intoxicated; however, they were pleasantly high.

On one of those mornings shortly after the brothers had started working, the owner of the sign shop began peering over Rob's shoulder as

Rob lettered a sign on an easel. He began sniffing the air around Rob's head and asked, "What's that smell? Have you been drinking?"

Rather than respond with a lame excuse, Rob looked annoyed and replied, "Look, I don't ask you what you have for breakfast, do I?"

Luckily for Rob, the owner of the shop was very fond of both Rob and Dean, and he too had an unusual sense of humor and an appreciation for the ridiculous. He roared with laughter, and later often told the story to many of his friends. Also, both brothers were very skilled and dependable workmen. It would have been financially unwise for him to fire either of them.

*   *   *

Madge finally took a small sip of her wine. Her face displayed an ugly grimace, as though she were going to regurgitate.

"Good, huh?" asked Dean.

"My God, this stuff is awful!" Madge complained.

"But you'll have to admit, it has a nice bouquet." Rob held his index finger up and his eyes widened, as if to underscore the point.

Dean took another drink and lit another smoke. "I figure I can let you and Madge have twenty dollars, Rob. That'll leave me $43."

"No, I won't take that much. Tell you what, I'll take $13. That'll leave you exactly $50 dollars to leave with. Certainly not a fortune, but maybe enough to get you to Chicago if the car holds up."

"Hell, let's not worry about the car tonight. I'll worry about that tomorrow, when the time comes to worry about it. If I worry about it tonight, I'll just be worryin' about it twice." Dean was amazed at his own wisdom.

They all sat in silence as they occasionally hit the wine. Dean was beginning to feel the booze and was in a garrulous mood. He could hold less liquor and became more talkative than Rob. The tingle in his stomach gave him a feeling of contentment and bravado. It was the first alcohol he had tasted in weeks and it was beginning to have its effect.

"Hell," Dean said confidently, "I bet I'll have a job in Chicago by Monday morning. Why don't you and Madge go with me? It'll be like old times!" He was suddenly bubbling with enthusiasm.

Rob looked over at Madge. "A couple of drinks of wine and he's already crazy as hell." Then with a patient smile on his lips, he looked at Dean. "Careful, old buddy, we can't afford to get drunk tonight. You've got a long trip ahead of you tomorrow. Besides, the last time we

16

got drunk together, as I remember it, I had to kick your ass."

"That's not the way I remember it," Dean retaliated.

Madge interrupted them, "If you guys are gonna start talkin' about fightin', I'm goin' inside. You know that you two love each other more than anything. Dean's leaving tomorrow, and here you are talking about fightin'. You're really gonna miss each other. Dean's gonna be lonely, all by himself in Chicago, and things won't be the same here without him. It'll be the first time you've been apart in more than two years."

Rob laughed, "Madge, we're not about to fight, I was just raggin' him a little bit. And don't start goin' sentimental on me." Rob lit another cigarette and poured himself another half-cup of wine. He raised the cup and proclaimed, "Cheers," and gulped down the contents. He too was beginning to feel the wine.

It was now getting dark. The sun had fallen behind the large oak trees that lined the narrow street, casting long, ghostly shadows on the houses and lawns. The clouds in the western sky were blazing with a last display of brilliance. Rob and Madge, seated in the swing and facing westward, watched the orange orb descend beneath the western horizon, leaving the atmosphere all around them bathed in an amber glow.

Dean was not offended by Rob's remarks. He felt too warm inside to take offense. Anyway, he was not in the mood for a fight. For the first time in months, he felt sentimental. He suspected that Rob had the same feeling, but Rob had always been reluctant to show any sentimentality. Even so, the brothers were close and could read each other's feelings, even when their moods went unrecognized by others.

Dean lit another cigarette and poured himself another half-cup of wine. The bottle was now more than half-consumed.

"Why do you think Dad was so mad when he told us to hit the road?" queried Dean.

"What do you expect?" asked Madge, "With you two beating each other up over nothing, and Lord, your poor mother, her heart was breakin' for both of you."

Rob and Dean were tied together by a strong bond which existed from their love and respect for each other; however, there was a benign sibling rivalry between them that became more overt when they were drinking together. Throughout their lives they had vied for attention and approval from their father.

Rob thought for awhile about what Dean and Madge had said.

"You know Dean," Rob began, "I don't really blame the old man. Think about it. Here he was with his sign shop doing a good business, with Elwood working for him. Everybody was happy. Things were going smooth. Then we show up, out of nowhere, as we do about once or twice a year. He puts us to work, when he really doesn't need us, and we repay him by getting drunk and getting into a fight. We embarrassed Dad, scared the hell out of Elwood, and broke Mom's heart. Hell, we deserved the old man firing us and telling us to hit the road."

"Man, that booze must be hitting you, too," remarked Dean. "That was quite a speech. And I'm a little surprised that you take up for Dad, like that. Hell, we're his sons, just like Elwood is."

"Yeah, but Elwood is loyal to Dad and Mom. He was raised the same as we were, but he doesn't raise hell the way we do. He's meek and obedient. Mom feels closer to Elwood than to any of us."

All three of them sat quietly for a while.

The sun had now gone down. It was completely dark and the street lights had sprung to life. The heat began to gradually lose its stranglehold on the city, at least until tomorrow.

Dean reflected on what Rob had said.

"Rob, what were we fightin' about anyway? I think I was drunker than you, so I don't remember—do you?"

Rob smiled, "Hell, I don't know. Something trivial. The strange part is, you and I were friends the next mornin' and everybody else was mad as hell, except for Mom. She was just sad, and cried when we packed up to leave. Maybe you and I just work off our frustrations every now and then by fightin' each other. Some people get upset when they see two guys beatin' the shit out of each other. They're just narrow-minded, I guess. No sense of humor." Rob grinned mischievously as he uttered the last words.

Madge rose slowly from the porch swing, leaving the cup with the remainder of the wine on the porch rail. She stretched her arms expansively outward and yawned. "Well look, you guys, I'm bone tired and sapped from the heat. I'm going to bed now and leaving this philosophizing to you two. Dean, I won't tell you goodbye right now. I'll wait 'til in the mornin', provided that you don't leave too early, and judging from the way you two are hitting that wine, I don't believe you'll be leaving at the crack of dawn. Well, good night."

"Good night Madge," they said in unison. Madge went inside and when the screen door slammed behind her, it seemed much louder in the quiet of the evening.

Both men were silent. Dean picked up the wine and looked at the bottle. There was only about a fourth of it remaining.

Rob said, perceptively, "I know what you're thinkin'. You're thinkin' 'let's open the other bottle of wine!' Well, if we do, what will we do in the mornin' for an eye-opener?"

"Hell, we'll buy another bottle," reasoned Dean.

"Have you forgotten that tomorrow is Sunday? The liquor store will be closed."

"Well, we'll walk back down to the liquor store right now and buy another bottle from that snobbish asshole," Dean answered. "They won't be closed yet."

Rob replied, "If we do— and don't think I'm not tempted— you'll feel like hell drivin' up that hot, lonely road tomorrow. Let's finish this one bottle and call it a night."

"Let's compromise," suggested Dean. "We'll finish this one bottle, and open the other one and drink only about one fourth of it. That'll still leave us with a hell of an eye-opener in the mornin'. Hell, I just want to drink enough in the mornin' to feel better. I don't want to start driving my car to Chicago completely stoned."

Rob smiled. "Yeah, well that makes pretty good sense. You must not be completely drunk to make such brilliant suggestions."

Since they both agreed on the compromise, Dean hurriedly poured the remaining wine of the first bottle into the two cups. They felt much more comfortable knowing that this was not their last drink of the evening. Their last drink meant they would retire for the night. Then, in the morning, with very little conversation, Dean would be gone. Without saying so, they both wanted to make this night—their last night—linger a while longer.

After another drink, Dean broke the silence. "You said that Elwood was Mom's favorite. I guess he's Dad's favorite too."

Rob hesitated before replying.

Finally he said, "No Dean... *you're* his favorite. He loves Elwood because Elwood is so loyal to him, and clings to him. He loves Elwood like he is still a little boy."

"Well, why in the world does he tell me to hit the road... why does he stay mad at me, no matter what I do, even when I'm not drinkin'?" Dean asked, with frustration.

Rob answered, "Let me tell you something that I've known for a long time. You and I both were Dad's favorites. He expects more out of us than Elwood, Alvin, or Clay. He didn't expect much out of his other sons, but he expects—or rather, *demands*—plenty out of you and me. He thinks we are the smartest, most talented, courageous sons he's got.

I'm not sayin' we *are*, understand… I'm just sayin' that's what he thinks. But we weren't able to live up to his expectations. Hell, I doubt that anybody could. Anyway, he's given up on me. He hasn't given up on you, yet."

"What makes you think he favors me over you?" Dean asked. "He kicked me out, same as you."

Rob said, "The day after our fight, Dad followed me to the car as I was packin' and told me that the whole mess—the fight, and the way you and I are livin', wanderin' all over the country—was my fault. He said that I had led you astray, and that all of your life, people had been leadin' you astray. He said that you would amount to more than any of his sons if people like me would quit leadin' you astray. Hell, he's given up on me. He told me so. And I've given up on him."

"You know what's ironic?" Dean inquired. "Dad is the most independent man I know. He never let anybody tell him what to do. Hell, he's the original rebel. He never even let his step-mother dominate him—and you know the stories that Dad and Uncle John tell about her. He's unique. Luckily for him, and for the world, he channeled his rebellious nature into positive things. And here you and I are, just like him in our rebellious nature. Hell, he taught us to be the way we are, then punishes us for bein' that way. Don't you think that's ironic?"

The wine was really affecting Dean's thinking now, and he was amazed at his own philosophical ramblings.

Rob answered, "Dad wants the best for all his sons. I don't doubt that he loves us. But there's no livin' with him. He wants to control everybody around him, even Mom. He's able to control Elwood, and sometimes Al, but I think Clay will rebel, just as you and I did." Rob stopped the porch swing, rested his elbows on his knees, and clasped his fingers together. "You know, Dean, there's an inconsistency in Dad's thinking. He says most people are like sheep, that they are followers, with no mind of their own. Yet, he wants his sons to be his sheep, and him to be the shepherd." Rob continued, "But of all his sons, it's you and I, who are the most unlike sheep, and it is you and I who get chased from his house."

They peered into the night in silence. The quiet of the evening was broken only by the incessant chirping of the creatures of the night. Finally, Dean spoke, "Why do you think that we have such a hang-up about what Dad thinks? What about what Mom thinks?"

Rob answered, "Hell, I don't know, I'm no psychologist. Maybe we both ought to be worrying about what we think of ourselves. In regard to Mom, she loves us all unconditionally."

From the second bottle, Rob poured another drink into the two cups. "Dean, this has to be our last drink for tonight. We need to go to bed, so you can get up in the mornin'. We need to put some gasoline in your car and get it started. I hope it'll run."

Dean's speech was beginning to slur. The cheap wine with its 20 percent alcohol content had affected him more than it had Rob. "Okay. We'll go to bed soon. That couch in the livin' room looks pretty inviting. By the way, this place isn't exactly the *Taj Mahal*, is it?"

"Well, what do you expect for $60 dollars a month? *Buckingham Palace?*"

The two men sat in silence. In order to postpone their last night together, both hesitated in taking their last sip of wine.

Rob spoke. "Dean, when you get to Chicago, don't go to work for that cheapskate, Hyman Moore. He worked you for less then union scale last year, and that'll get the union on you. Hell, we've been painting signs for Dad since we were ten years old. We're first-class sign painters now. Go to a legitimate union sign shop."

"You think I can be that picky? I've got to go to work—quick—first day, if possible. I'm gonna run low on rent money. Oh, that reminds me," Dean said, pulling his wallet from his pocket, "Here's you a little money to run on." He handed Rob a twenty dollar bill.

Rob replied, "I told you I'm not gonna take twenty. Madge is workin'. I said I would take thirteen. That'll leave you fifty."

"Hell, Rob, seven more dollars ain't gonna make me or break me. Besides, I'm gonna quit drinkin' after tonight." Dean quickly reconsidered his last remark. "That is, after I take me an eye-opener in the mornin'."

Rob thought for a moment and then made a suggestion, "I just had an idea. Do you remember Tom Allred? Madge and I used to have an apartment in the same building with him on Adams Street, on the west side of town. 3263 West Adams Street. You visited us there last year a few times. Remember? He's a nice guy. Drive out there when you get to Chicago and I'll bet he'd put you up for a week, 'til you get your first payday. Watch out for Old Man King, though. He owns the apartment building and I got into it with him over something."

"Did he run you out of the apartment?"

"No, he hates me, but he's afraid of me," declared Rob. "I'll take the twenty if you'll promise to go see Tom Allred. That'll save you some money. Just steer clear of Old Man King."

"Okay, that's a good idea," answered Dean. Both men became silent for a few minutes. It was getting late. The narrow street in front of the apartment had little traffic, only a car every few minutes. The dim street light at the corner of the block barely illuminated the men's features as they sat facing each other on the small porch.

"Well, let's drink up," suggested Rob.

"A toast to my grand departure for Chicago, tomorrow," Dean slurred.

The brothers raised their paper cups, tilted their heads back, and in unison, tossed down the last drink of the evening.

Both men stood.

Rob said, "You'll have to go after some gasoline for the car in the mornin'. There's a five gallon water can on the back porch, with a sprinkler on the spout. Take the sprinkler off, and it'll make a good gasoline can."

"Okay," replied Dean, "wake me up in the mornin'. I've got to shower and shave before I leave." He knew that Rob was not a late sleeper.

"Well, good night," said Rob.

"Good night," Dean answered, "see you in the mornin'."

Rob opened the screen door for his brother, and then followed him through the door. He closed it gently, so not to awaken Madge.

Certainly, travel is more than the seeing of sights;
it is a change that goes on, deep and permanent,
in the ideas of living. **Miriam Beard**

Chapter 2

"Dean, wake up! C'mon Dean—Rise and shine!" Rob's cheerful voice reverberated through Dean's brain.

Dean was sprawled on the faded, lumpy couch in the living room. Rob had awakened him from a deep, dreamless sleep. For a brief moment, he looked around the room with puzzled eyes in an attempt to orient himself to his surroundings.

Then, his eyes began to show a flicker of recognition. Rob had turned on the bright lamp on the table near Dean's head, the glaring light penetrating his eyes. He held his right hand over his eyes, shielding them from the light, but also hiding his anger that they reflected. It irritated him to see his brother's cheerful demeanor in the early morning after a night's drinking. Rob had even turned on the radio.

Slowly, Dean threw back the blanket that covered him. Rob must have draped it over him, he reasoned, since he had fallen asleep as soon as he flopped on the couch the night before.

"How do you feel?" Rob asked.

"I feel fine," lied Dean. "How do you feel?" Rob ignored the question.

Neither of them liked to admit that they ever had a hangover. Dean had often noticed, with some resentment, that Rob seemed impervious to hangovers.

Rob's appearance and the sweetish aroma emanating from him indicated to Dean that his brother had already showered, shaved, and applied shaving lotion. It discouraged Dean to realize that those same chores awaited him.

"What time is it?" Dean asked, in a fabricated, cheerful voice.

"Ten after eight. You can make it to Chicago easy in about four or five hours. You overslept, but I figured you could use the sleep."

Dean could smell the aroma of fresh, brewing coffee. He usually loved the smell when he awakened, but this morning it was nauseating. From past experience, he knew that cheap wine leaves a terrible hangover. In an attempt to appear chipper, he rapidly got up from the couch.

"Got to shave and shower," he said, "and lay out some clothes."

"Want some coffee first?" asked Rob.

"No, I'll wait 'til after I shower."

Dean retrieved his shaving kit from his suitcase beside the couch and headed into the bathroom.

Rob walked into the kitchen and poured himself some coffee. He lit a cigarette and sat down at the kitchen table with his coffee, slowly sipping it. He, too, had a slight hangover, but not nearly as dreadful as Dean's. *A couple of good snorts of wine will remedy that*, he thought. He was glad that they had bought the second bottle, and he was particularly grateful that they had saved most of it. Rob craved the wine more than the coffee that he was drinking, but he felt honor-bound to wait until Dean was ready to drink with him.

Rob slowly stood and walked through the musty living room to the front porch. He decided that he would empty the ashtrays and generally clean up the porch from the night before. As he lifted the ashtray from the porch rail, he noticed an almost full cup of wine that Madge had left from last night. He picked up the wine and drank it, feeling a bit guilty that he was cheating Dean out of his portion. He sat the ashtray down.

Rob settled himself in the porch swing, noticing that the air was already beginning to feel stuffy. It was going to be another scorching day. It was Sunday morning, and the street in front had no traffic. At this early hour, the neighborhood seemed deserted. He didn't see a soul on the sidewalks, and the loneliness of the street only echoed the emptiness he felt at that moment. He sat still with the swing immobile, contemplating the day that lay ahead of him.

His hangover was fading now; the wine was doing its job. He felt almost normal physically, but emotionally, he was melancholy.

At that moment, Madge appeared at the screen door. "Well good mornin', bright eyes." she said cheerfully, "What are you doin' out here all alone?"

When she saw that Rob was in a reflective mood, she remarked, "A penny for your thoughts."

"Oh, I wasn't thinkin' anything, much. Just waitin' for Dean to get showered and dressed. This is his big day, ya' know."

"You're gonna miss him, aren't you?"

"Who?" asked Rob.

"You know damn well 'who.' Dean, that's 'who'."

"Miss him?" growled Rob, "Why, hell no! Dean'll do fine in Chicago. It may be lonely for a couple of days for both of us, but we'll both be fine. Anyway, we both need a break from each other."

Madge didn't pursue the line of questioning any further.

Rob stood and walked toward the front door as if some thought had just occurred to him. Suddenly, he stopped, and said, "Madge, while Dean is showerin', I'm gonna get that can off the back porch—walk and get him some gasoline. There's a gas station a couple of blocks over."

"While you do that, I'll start some breakfast," answered Madge.

*   *   *

Madge was in the process of preparing breakfast when Dean stepped into the kitchen, combing his thick shock of black hair. He had already dressed in clean khaki pants and a yellow, short-sleeve shirt—clothing that Madge had washed and ironed. He was now clean-shaven and smelled strongly of cheap after-shave lotion.

"My, but don't you look better" Madge complimented. "Smell better, too."

"Thanks, Madge—where's Rob?"

"He went to get you some gasoline. He should be back any minute. Only had to walk two blocks over."

"Is he that eager to get rid of me?" Dean asked jokingly, as he seated himself in a kitchen chair.

Madge turned the bacon over in the skillet that she had borrowed from the landlady. She briskly brushed away a pesky fly.

"Rob really hates to see you go, but don't expect him to show it."

"I wish I could leave you some more money, Madge, but I'm cuttin' it kinda thin as it is," Dean said, apologetically.

"Oh, we'll get by. Rob'll find work. He always does. Rob's got me to help him, but you don't have anybody."

When they heard the slamming of the dilapidated screen door, they knew Rob had returned with the gasoline. He strolled through the living room into the kitchen. He noticed Madge was working on breakfast, and Dean, seated at the table, was dressed and looking much better.

"Madge, who is this stranger, seated here at the table?" asked Rob, cheerfully, in reference to the improvement in Dean's appearance.

Dean quipped, "The way you guys are raving about how great I look today—I must have looked like hell yesterday."

Rob laughed, "You looked okay yesterday. It's when I woke you up this morning' that you looked like hell."

Madge said, "I'll have breakfast ready in about ten minutes. We're havin' bacon and beans. Do you guys want me to pour you some coffee?"

"No," answered Rob, "But since you're in a pourin' mood, you can pour both of us a cup of wine—and make sure they're equal. I don't want to get into a fight with Dean before breakfast."

Madge followed Rob's instructions. She poured equal portions of wine which she then handed to them with no comment.

"Let's go out on the porch, Dean, and get away from the flies," suggested Rob.

Rob sat down in the swing, while Dean took his usual porch chair, directly across from, and facing his brother.

"Let's drink up," said Rob, enthusiastically. Both men raised their cups, downing about half of the wine in the first few swallows. Psychologically, Dean began to feel better, even before he physically felt the effects of the wine.

"Dreadin' your long drive?" asked Rob.

"No, I just dread getting' the car started."

They both sat silently for a while, each of them firing up a cigarette.

At last, Rob said, "Well, it's gonna seem a little strange without you, Dean. I won't have anybody to help me carry cement when you're gone."

Both men uncomfortably chuckled.

"Rob, it is really time that I leave. In the past, we both have had good jobs, good apartments, and plenty of money. We've been on our asses here for the first time since we started moving around the country together."

"Dean, maybe you ought to stay here and tough it out a little longer. We'd eventually get jobs."

"Well, that may be so. But without me here, you and Madge can make it just fine, with her workin'. Another thing, it would be a lot less strain on Madge with her washin' and ironin' my clothes since we've been here. And you two don't have any privacy with me here."

Rob didn't reply.

"Another thing," continued Dean, "I want to go back to work. Start makin' a little money."

"Breakfast is ready," Madge called from the kitchen.

The brothers abandoned their seats and strolled through the house into the kitchen. Madge had fried the bacon and heated the canned pork and beans. She had already served them on three paper plates, along with three steaming paper cups of coffee. In the center of the table stood a stack of white bread on a single paper plate, and the cheap bottle of wine.

As the three took their customary seats at the table, Dean noticed that his appetite had returned to some extent, as he was no longer nauseous. The cup of wine had done a remarkable job.

"Looks great, Madge," complimented Dean.

Rob sampled a bite of the bacon and exclaimed, "My compliments to the chef!"

They finished their breakfast and sat for a brief while in silence, sipping on their coffee.

Rob suddenly stood, picking up two paper cups and the bottle of wine. "Dean, why don't we retire to the front porch for a little round of serious drinkin'?"

"Go easy on that stuff!" Madge warned, "Dean has to drive all the way to Chicago."

"Spoilsport," answered Rob, sarcastically.

Dean followed Rob to the front porch where they both alighted in their usual places. Rob poured reasonably equal amounts of wine in the two paper cups. "Dean, as you know, I seldom listen to a woman's advice, but occasionally they do come up with something that makes a little bit of sense. For instance, that remark Madge just made about goin' easy on the wine. Maybe we ought to take it kinda slow. You don't need to be in a hurry. It's only 9:45. Hell, you don't need to leave here until around noon."

"I agree," replied Dean, "I don't want to leave town drunk."

Both men took a small drink of wine and lit cigarettes. The drink they took was more like a sip, not solely because they wanted to keep Dean sober, but also to ensure that the wine would last for awhile, to enable them to make plans and say their goodbyes.

They sat silently, facing each other, leisurely smoking. Rob rocked gently in the swing while Dean slouched in his chair, his legs crossed, relaxed. They both were in a reflective mood.

Madge had not made an appearance on the front porch since breakfast. She intuitively realized that the brothers needed some time alone before Dean left them.

Rob finally spoke, "Dean, you know what I told you last night, about

Dad sayin' that I have led you astray? Well... maybe I have, to some degree. I'm not implying that you are easily led, now, by any means." Rob was apologetic in his tone of voice. He knew that Dean could be offended if anyone suggested that he was easily led. "I'm just sayin'... well, hell, I'm ten years older than you. To Dad... well, and to me, too, you're still my kid brother—I mean little brother—I mean, *younger* brother. Hell, you know what I'm tryin' to say." Rob was finding himself at a rare loss for words. He was trying to be honest with his brother, but because Dean was so sensitive about his ego, he was finding it necessary to sound evasive. Rob certainly didn't want his final day with his brother to end in a fist fight.

Dean looked at Rob intently. He felt a bit sorry for his brother in his bumbling attempt to make his point. They were both in a sentimental mood, and since Dean was soon leaving, he found himself in a forgiving state-of-mind. He recognized the impossible task that Rob had set for himself: To be honest and say things from his heart without sounding overly sentimental, while at the same time, not damaging Dean's pride.

Understanding this, Dean smiled. "Rob, I know what you're tryin' to say. Hell, you don't have to dance all over hell and half of Georgia to say it. It don't even sound like you when you mince words like that." Rob looked relieved.

Dean continued, "You haven't led me astray, Rob. Hell, I've probably led you astray. You don't know all about me, or how I feel. I'm probably meaner than you are!" He said these last words with pride. The morning sun was now bearing down mercilessly on the city, and the men were once again sweating. On the street, traffic was beginning to gradually increase with people on their way to church.

It was time for another drink of wine. This time, Dean poured it, only a half-cup for each of them. He handed his brother the cup, and Rob lit a cigarette.

"While we're bein' honest, Dean, I've got something else I want to say. I was just thinkin' last night when we were talkin'—about Dad, the shop, and Elwood, that maybe-and this is just a thought of mine- maybe you ought to forget Chicago. Maybe you ought to head that car back the way we came, right back to Tennessee. I'm not sayin' that you definitely should, I just brought it up as a possibility."

He looked at Dean cautiously, trying to discern his reaction. Rob was again uncharacteristically "dancing all over hell and half of Georgia", and for the same reasons as before. He also knew that if he posed the possibility to his brother in anything stronger than a mild suggestion, that Dean would more likely do the opposite.

Dean didn't answer immediately. He lit another smoke, and took another small sip of wine. He thought about the relationship that existed between them. He had often noticed that when the two of them were joking, working together, or were discussing routine situations, they were very outspoken, sometimes even rude. But when the conversation between them became serious or sentimental, each of them had a problem with being brutally honest. In fact, the entire family of brothers shared the same trait.

Dean looked forgivingly at his brother. "Rob, you know I can't go back to Tennessee. Not now. Someday I probably will, but when I do, I'll have enough money in my pocket; I'll be drivin' a nice car, and wearin' good clothes. And then it'll be just to visit."

Rob delicately persisted, "But if you went on back, Dad would welcome you, if you went back without me. I guarantee he would. He always takes us back, even me, sometimes."

"Just like the prodigal son, huh? He would put his best robe on me, and kill the fatted calf," Dean replied sarcastically.

"Well, he might put the ice on you for a while, to teach you a lesson, but he'd be glad you came back." Rob was trying his best to be diplomatic.

"I'm goin' to Chicago, and that's that." Dean declared, a bit irritably.

Rob knew that any other attempt at persuasion would make Dean determined to differ even more. He also knew that his brother felt that the suggestion was an insinuation that he couldn't make it on his own, that he needed his father in order to survive. Rob dropped the subject.

By now, both men had recovered from their hangovers, except Dean had a slightly sour stomach. In fact, they were beginning to feel the effects of the wine, but not to the point of drunkenness. Their pledge to slow down on the pace of their drinking was paying off. The bottle of wine was now about three-fourth gone.

Dean peered at the bottle of slowly disappearing wine. It occurred to him that the wine in the bottle was like the sand in an hour-glass. When the wine was gone, he would also be gone.

Both men sat in silence, each dreading to broach the subject of Dean's impending departure.

"Well, Rob, let's drink that last cup of wine. I've got to get ready to hit the road. Got to get the gasoline in the car and see if it will start."

"Why don't we eat lunch before you go? Madge can rustle up something."

"I don't feel like eating. I'm not a bit hungry."

"Well, why don't you go in and pack? I'll put the gasoline in the car," Rob suggested.

"Pack?" asked Dean, "I have never unpacked! I've been livin' out of my suitcase. I'm already packed. I don't have many clothes. I'm gonna buy me some when I get my first payday."

Rob took the bottle from the porch rail and poured the final drink in each of their cups, emptying the bottle.

This time he again went through the routine of ensuring that each cup contained equal amounts. He handed Dean his final cup.

After a brief period of quietness, Dean said, "Before I finish my last drink, I'm goin' in and tell Madge goodbye, and thank her for keepin' my clothes in order and for cookin' for us."

Dean opened the screen door and went inside. Madge was in the process of setting food out of the refrigerator, beginning to prepare for lunch.

"Madge, don't fix any lunch for me. I'll be leaving right away."

"You're not stayin' for lunch?" she asked. "When are you leavin'?"

"Just as soon as I get the gasoline in the car and load my suitcase."

"You and Rob didn't get into an argument, did you? Is that why you're leavin' so quick?" asked Madge worriedly.

Dean laughed, "No, Madge, Rob and I are great buddies. The mood just hit me, and I've got to get rollin'."

Madge looked sadly at Dean. "Rob's gonna be sad after you leave. He might be hell to live with for a few days. I'll be sad too, and I'll worry about you. Both of you."

Dean smiled at Madge. "I just came in here to thank you for makin' me feel at home, and for keepin' my clothes washed and ironed—and to tell you goodbye."

When they hugged each other, Madge's slim body seemed very small to Dean.

Madge said, "I'm not followin' you back out—I'm just stayin' inside. I don't like goodbyes that are strung out."

"Neither do I," replied Dean. "Goodbye Madge. Thanks again for everything."

"Goodbye, Dean. You take care of yourself."

Dean turned suddenly and picked up his suitcase. He glanced one more time at the apartment interior, and then returned outside to the front porch where Rob was picking up the can of gasoline. Dean gulped down his last drink of wine, then they both walked down to the curb where the car was parked, and Dean threw his suitcase in the back seat.

As Rob removed the gasoline cap and began pouring the fuel into the tank, Dean warned, "Save a little to prime the carburetor. She might not start."

Dean raised the hood of the car and removed the cover from the carburetor. He opened the door and entered the driver's seat, "Okay, Rob, pour about half of that gasoline into the carburetor and let me try it."

Dean hit the starter button, but the engine barely turned over. The battery was almost dead.

"Pour the rest of the gas in it and put the cover back on it," yelled Dean. "We'll have to push her off." Dean got out while Rob was closing the hood.

Dean said, "Once we get her started, I'll be okay. The battery will recharge after a few miles. The trouble is, once we get her kicked off, I'll have to keep her goin'. There'll be no turnin' around and stoppin' for any goodbyes."

The two brothers stood about three feet apart, looking at each other. Both of them smiled.

"Dean, I want you to promise me you'll take care of yourself. Try not to get into any fights—unless it's absolutely necessary."

"I promise," answered Dean.

When it came time to say goodbye, there was an awkwardness between the brothers. Men seldom hugged each other, particularly in the Beauvais family.

Dean awkwardly extended his right hand and Rob took it in his, but with his left hand clasped over the top, sandwiching Dean's outstretched hand between his, and Dean did the same. It was as near to an embrace that the two men dared. Both men sensed the clumsiness of the gesture, and were slightly embarrassed by the stiff formality of a handshake between brothers with such close mutual feelings.

"So long, Pal." said Rob.

"Yeah, see ya, Rob."

Dean climbed into the car and closed the door, while his brother got behind and began pushing. He turned on the ignition, held in the clutch, and put the car in second gear. When Rob had the car to sufficient speed, Dean let out the clutch and the motor kicked in with a roar.

"Write me!" He heard Rob yell over the roar of the engine. Dean acknowledged by waving back to him. As he pulled away, a plume of blue smoke billowed from the exhaust pipe. And looking in the rearview mirror, Dean could see through the dissipating smoke, Rob waving to him.

The greatest griefs are those we cause ourselves.
Sophocles

Chapter 3

The ever-diminishing image of Rob disappeared from sight. Dean drove the car slowly for two blocks, then turned right onto the main boulevard. He sighed in disbelief when he saw the number of traffic lights that lined the busy street. First gear was no longer operational, and the car had to depend on second gear to resume its movement. After each stop, he accelerated slowly, but now the slipping clutch was accompanied by a shuddering vibration of the vehicle.

He noticed on his right, about a half-block ahead of him, a service station. He wondered if it was the same place where Rob bought the gasoline earlier this morning. Slowing the car, he considered filling up his tank, but reconsidered. Pumping gas now meant shutting off the motor, but continuing forward meant feeding energy to the weak battery. Plus, the thought of using the overworked clutch so soon seemed impractical.

The Sunday morning traffic was sparse. He glanced at his watch, noting the time was 11:50. He had managed to avoid the Sunday morning church traffic. It was sheer luck, for he hadn't planned the time that he would leave. He rarely planned anything in his life, except when he found it absolutely necessary.

As he moved further from the downtown area of the city, he increased his speed. His windows were lowered, offering him some relief from the heat. As he approached the suburbs, the traffic began to increase. Another leisurely glance at his watch told him that it was 12:15. After-church traffic, he figured.

Ahead on the right, he spotted a service station—"Broadway Garage". Feeling confident that the battery had recharged, he braked, swung the car into the station by the gasoline pumps, and shut off the engine. When he stepped out of the vehicle, he felt the stifling heat of the surrounding air envelope him. The incessant heat intensified the effects of the wine he had consumed earlier.

The service station was a dilapidated building which catered mostly to auto repair customers. A short, red-faced, middle-aged man ambled toward Dean's car. The man was wearing a gray work outfit that was badly stained with oil and grease. An oval patch above the left shirt pocket displayed the name "George".

When the attendant came nearer, he stared curiously at Dean for a brief moment. The strong odor of alcohol emanated from the man. "What can I do for you, kid?" he asked, in a thick, northern accent, suggesting that he was originally from the Northeast.

"Fill 'er up and check the oil. Clean the windshield too, if you don't mind."

Pulling an oily rag from his back pocket, the man wiped perspiration from his forehead. "Jesus Christ, it's hot! What weight oil does your car use, kid?"

"Put in 40 weight, because she uses some oil. Also, give me your cheapest gasoline."

While the attendant serviced his car, Dean went inside to the restroom. When he returned, the man had already pumped the gas and was closing the hood.

"I had to put in two quarts, kid. Better take along two or three extra quarts in case you run out. Right front tire's slick too. The other three ain't too good. Where you headed, kid?"

"Chicago," answered Dean.

When the attendant had finished servicing the car, he started to clean the windshield, which was splattered with a generous amount of bird droppings that had dried to a hard crust. "Jesus Christ—you want me to put my hands in that? Look at the shit on that windshield!"

"Look, mister, I didn't shit on it! The birds did it! Leave the damn windshield alone if you don't want to wash it! And stop callin' me 'KID'!" The attendant didn't answer, but dutifully continued to wash off the bird droppings.

Still feeling sadness about his departure from Rob, Dean was not in the best of moods. However, since the attendant had continued cleaning the windshield, it was apparent that he meant no offense. Perhaps he

33

was angry for having to work on Sunday or maybe he was merely suffering from a hangover.

With no desire to be unnecessarily cruel, Dean said apologetically, "Hey, look mister, I didn't mean to be so cranky. Things haven't been goin' so well for me lately. I'm sorry... I should have cleaned off that mess myself."

"Don't worry about it, kid," the man answered, unperturbed.

As he was finishing the windshield, the man couldn't help but see inside Dean's car the scarred, cheap suitcase that was held together with tape. With empathy, he asked, "Down on your luck, kid?"

"Is it that obvious?" Dean handed the man a ten dollar bill and put the three quarts of extra oil in the front seat of the car.

Having smelled the strong odor of alcohol on the attendant, Dean figured that he was a drinking man. He smiled and asked, "Say pal, do you know where a guy can buy some beer on Sunday? I'm kinda hung over today."

The man didn't immediately answer but took the money from Dean. "Come on in kid. I'll give you your change."

He followed the attendant inside the garage where another man with greasy clothing was working on an old Buick, hoisted high on the garage rack. The inside of the repair shop was dank and dimly-lit. The musty odor of grease and oil pervaded the interior of the dark room.

"Have a beer, kid," he invited, fetching a can of beer from an ice cooler and opening it for Dean. "It's a long, hot grind—all the way to Chicago." He handed Dean the change along with the can of beer.

"Thanks," said Dean, gratefully. He accepted the ice cold beer and raised it to his mouth, draining at least half of it before taking the can away.

"There's a place that sells beer after twelve noon on Sunday about three blocks down on the left. Place by the name of *Anderson's Market*," the man said, obviously trying to be helpful.

"Thanks a lot," answered Dean. "Oh—I'll need a roadmap."

"You won't need a roadmap, kid. Stay on this road and it runs right into Route 33. Thirty-three north will take you all the way to South Bend. Then turn west, go to Gary. After Gary, just watch for signs that say, 'Chicago'."

"Thanks for everything—the beer, the directions, and especially for cleaning that bird shit off my windshield," Dean said, and the two men shared a laugh.

"Don't mention it, kid." He eyed Dean with an expression of interest.

"If you don't mind my asking, how old are you, kid?"

"Twenty-six," Dean lied. "Why?"

"Thought you were about eighteen or nineteen."

It offended Dean whenever people saw him as a teenager; he wanted to appear mature, older than his twenty-three years. He secretly wished that he appeared to look as old as Rob. Underestimating his age was a common mistake made by many, and Dean was embarrassed by it. However, he realized that the man didn't mean to offend him.

Dean finished the beer, and tossed the empty can into a nearby trash barrel. The attendant casually opened another beer and handed it to him.

"You look a hell of a lot like my son, kid. But he was only 19."

"Was?" Dean asked.

"Lost his life in Korea—September, 1951. Battle of Pork Chop Hill. He was my only son; he was my whole life. Hell, for a minute there, when you drove up, I thought you were him," said the man, reflectively.

Feeling sadness for him and at a loss for words, Dean muttered, "Gosh, I'm sorry, mister."

The attendant fished his wallet out of his pocket and pulled out a faded photograph. He handed the snap-shot to Dean. "Here's a picture of him in his uniform, made shortly before he was killed." Dean noticed a slight tremble in the attendant's hand as he handed him the picture.

Dean inspected the photograph with considerable interest, his curiosity aroused because the man had mentioned the resemblance of his son to Dean. He noticed a similarity, but the likeness was only moderate. He guessed that the man probably saw a resemblance to his son in many faces he encountered.

"Nice lookin' young man," remarked Dean, awkwardly. Still struggling for the right words, he muttered, "You're right, he does look a lot like me—only better lookin'."

The attendant grinned impishly, "Had your temper, too, kid. We was gonna open a garage together. I had big plans for us, but he enlisted the day after graduatin' high school. Didn't even tell me about it until the day he left. I just hope he didn't leave 'cause he was tired of workin' on cars."

Dean was touched by the shared intimacy between two men who had only met, each without even knowing the other's name. Since it seemed appropriate, he thrust out his right hand. "My name's Dean Beauvais."

The man returned the gesture, taking Dean's right hand in his. "George DeAngelo." Dean felt the strength of the attendant's firm grip.

"Were you in the service, kid?"

"Spent two years in the Air Force during the Korean War. Never saw any combat though. Stayed right here in the States. I was stationed not far from here—Chanute Air Force Base in Illinois. Say, I may be keepin' you from waitin' on customers," Dean said, eager to get on the road.

"Nah, not any customers to speak of, on Sunday. Besides, Charley there can wait on 'em."

He seemed reluctant to end the conversation with Dean. In some curious way that he did not comprehend, he felt that sharing small talk with this stranger who bore a likeness to his son assuaged his grief, and soothed the longing that he felt for his son.

"My son was in the infantry. I never felt that we had any business over in Korea to start with," lamented Mr. DeAngelo, "I'd feel better, maybe, if I felt it was a good reason for my son dying. I'm proud of him just the same."

As Mr. DeAngelo's red-veined eyes were fixed on the image of his son in the photograph, Dean studied the man's features. His hair was thinning, and his ruddy scalp and rotund face displayed great beads of perspiration.

Mr. DeAngelo was a portrait of misery, Dean determined, and although he felt compassion for the man, he decided that he couldn't tolerate any further sadness for today.

Dean lifted the can of beer to his lips, swallowing the remaining contents, and flipped the empty can into the trash barrel.

"I've got to hit the road, Mr. DeAngelo. I'm sorry about your son, but things will get better for you, in time. It's been a pleasure to meet you, sir." Dean again extended his hand. "Thanks again for the beer."

The two men exchanged handshakes. "So long," George answered. "Take care of yourself, kiddo."

Dean climbed into his car and hit the starter button. The immediate roar of the engine told him that the battery had been recharged. His hand shoved the lever into second gear, and the clutch in the old Ford shuddered as he pulled slowly away. He turned around to wave to Mr. DeAngelo, but the man was oblivious to him. He was still looking sadly at the picture of his son.

It is good to have an end to journey toward, but it is the journey that matters in the end. **Ursula K. LeGuin**

Chapter 4

The inrushing air from the lowered windows, though hot, felt good on Dean's face. He turned northwest onto Highway 33. The two beers that he had consumed in Ft. Wayne had rejuvenated him, and after purchasing a six pack of beer at the market suggested by George DeAngelo, he was finally on the road.

Although lonely for Rob, he felt a sense of freedom that exhilarated him. The stream of air that blew through his tangled, bushy hair indicated to him that he was again *on the move*. He was on a journey to a new place where new experiences awaited him.

For the past two years, Rob and Dean had lived a nomadic existence; however, it was Dean who had always initiated the moves. He had a restlessness inside of him that Rob didn't share. Not wanting them to separate, Rob always agreed to move with him. He was not a follower; he simply was apathetic in regard to where he lived. Although Madge didn't share his sentiments, one place was as good as another to Rob.

As Dean left the suburbs into open country, he rolled up the window in order to temporarily stem the flow of air. He tapped a *Pall Mall* cigarette out of the pack and lit it, then rolled the glass down again. He considered drinking one of the beers from the six pack, then decided against it since he could still feel the effects of the beer he had just finished. Puffing on the cigarette, he wished that the radio in the car was in working order. He loved music, but being without his guitar, and now the radio, left Dean feeling empty.

He hoped that his crippled vehicle would survive the trip to Chicago. He had purchased the car in Chicago last year with the firm belief that he had found a genuine bargain. The car was a pale green, 1949 Ford two-door sedan, and when the salesman had shown it to him, it looked to be in good condition. He had bought the car for about two-thirds the cost of comparable vehicles, and he had boasted to Rob at the time of how he had really got a great deal from the salesman. Naturally, the car turned out to be a "lemon". Now, as Dean reflected on the transaction, he was dumfounded by whatever method of wizardry that the car dealership had used to visually transform a complete pile of junk into the beautiful car he had bought.

As the miles of asphalt disappeared beneath him, he made a mental assessment of his car's condition: First gear of the transmission had been stripped shortly after he bought the car. The windshield wipers only worked sporadically, and the sound on the radio was a grating blast of static. Rust had invaded the entire under-surface to the extent that the rear floor boards were completely rusted through in places; the rocker panels under both doors were totally eaten away by rust. The worn-out motor drank oil thirstily, and the slick tires were worn almost threadbare, particularly the one on the right front. However, the worst problem was the slipping clutch. Luckily, his journey was across flat land, eliminating the problem of ascending any hills with his disabled clutch.

Dean considered the decrepit condition of the car. He decided to postpone his worrying until something bad actually happened. He would drive as carefully as he could and keep oil in the engine. He figured that the chance of making it was 50-50. Pretty good odds, in Dean's way of thinking.

The effects of the beer, as well as his mood, had begun to wane. He decided that it was an appropriate time to pull over to replenish himself with beer and his engine with oil.

Looking ahead to a leftward curve in the highway, he noticed the road held a large expanse of shade, which was cast by a towering oak tree on the right. Slowing the vehicle, Dean pulled the ramshackle Ford into the shade of the tree, off the pavement, and onto the broad road shoulder. The large oak tree stood majestically alone in a bare, untilled, pasture field that was enclosed by a barbed-wire fence. A dozen head of Holstein cattle grazed near a small, distant pond. More cattle stood in the cool water, taking a respite from the midday heat.

Dean plucked a can of motor oil from his front seat and stepped outside of the car into the smoldering heat. He stood erect, stretching himself expansively to alleviate the stiffness he felt from sitting for hours in the car seat. Striding to the front of the car, he raised the hood and checked the oil. Noting that the dipstick showed that the oil was low, he poured in a quart. Rechecking the oil, he seemed satisfied, so he closed the hood.

After taking a can of beer from his car, he stepped between the wires in the fence and seated himself on a large, decaying log beneath the protective shade of the huge tree. Pulling a beer opener from his shirt pocket, Dean opened the can. Because the beer was getting warm, the contents began to spew. He placed his lips over the hole in the can and drew the escaping beer into his mouth. He then took a long drink from the can and fired up a cigarette. He was in a listless, pensive mood as he reclined lazily on the old, fallen log. As he languished in the shade, he missed the gratifying ritual of playing his guitar.

Traffic on the road was light, with people in their passing vehicles paying little attention to him as he relaxed at his new drinking spot. As he sat idly in the shade, he heard the faint quarrelsome buzzing of insects, and smelled the humid aroma of the steamy weeds on the heated earth. The muted, complaining call of squawking crows could be heard somewhere over a distant corner of the pasture field. *It is peaceful here*, thought Dean.

Leisurely, he took another swallow of the beer. Sometime in the near future, he would quit drinking. This was not an empty promise he had made to himself; he knew this fact with a certainty. Unlike Rob, Dean had never been a regular drinker. Often, he would spend months at a time without tasting alcohol. However, he inevitably started again, and he would then usually drink with a vengeance, sometimes for days. Then, he would abruptly stop, as a violent storm would mysteriously and suddenly cease.

Feeling the effect of the alcohol, he experienced a kind of serenity in the protective umbrella of the massive oak tree. Since he was in no particular hurry, he decided to rest there for awhile. Taking another sip of the beer, he became engrossed in thought.

He began to reflect on his past two years with Rob. He already missed Rob, and he was sure that Rob also missed him, although he probably would never admit to it. He knew, and actually had known for a long time, that it was time for them to separate. In some ways, they were good together. Both were creative and resourceful, and when working together as a team, they were sometimes capable of accomplishing amazing things.

In some ways, however, Rob and Dean were bad for each other. Their continuous association with each other reinforced the fatalistic attitude entrenched in both men. Each of them had become enamored with the incongruous behavior of the other.

In addition, his constant presence with Rob and Madge had put a strain on their marriage. Madge was fond of Dean, but she had actually wished that he would go.

The night before Dean's departure, Rob had asked him to stay. But it was a lame invitation upon which his brother hadn't placed much emphasis. Half-wishing that Dean would stay, Rob knew in his heart that it would be best if he didn't.

*   *   *

Dean finished his beer, then tossed the empty can in a patch of ragweed. He stood and gazed lethargically across the sun-drenched pasture while drinking in the tranquility of the rural view. He was saddened to leave this peaceful haven and to resume his grueling drive.

Re-crossing the barbed-wire fence, he climbed into his car. The recharged battery gave the engine an immediate start, and Dean drove onto the highway, the decrepit old car shuddering as he slowly accelerated.

Still reminiscing about Rob, he recalled the things that Rob had taught him in his youth. Much of Dean's skills in art and sign painting had been learned from Rob and their father. Rob had been a middleweight amateur boxing champion in the *Golden Gloves*, and during his years in the armed forces, he also carried the same boxing title in the Navy. Years later, he taught Dean some of his boxing skills, which enabled Dean to also win the amateur championship in the middleweight division. Their father was immensely proud of both of his sons' boxing success.

However, Rob's affinity for the sport was greater than Dean's. Rob fought with an aggressive style in which he was willing to take a punch, if necessary, in order to deliver a blow to his opponent. Dean, on the other hand, was more of a defensive fighter. Since he didn't like being hit, he relied more on boxing skills rather than aggressiveness. Although Dean won eight of the nine fights that he fought, he didn't particularly enjoy boxing. Engaging in the sport was mainly done to make his father proud of him, an honor that he regarded higher than any championship title.

The fact that both brothers had been skillful boxers tended to aggravate the sibling rivalry that existed between them. Disputes were often settled with their fists.

Moving about over the country with one another meant that Dean and Rob fought each other in many places. They lived together in Miami, Chicago, Upstate New York, Louisville, Charleston, Ft. Wayne, and Knoxville. Movement to most of these places was usually instigated by Dean—a trait that had begun to try Madge's patience. True to his vagabond nature, Dean was a modern-day hobo.

Dean thought back to his youthful years when he first began to experience the urge to roam. As a teenager, he was seized by wanderlust. Even before entering the service, his restlessness had compelled him to strike out on hitchhiking trips with a like-minded boyhood friend, Jake Stone. Unlike his other cohorts, Jake was well-liked by Dean's father, Will, and was like a family member to the entire Beauvais clan, particularly to Dean and Elwood. Dean figured that his father's acceptance of Jake was because of the similarity of their natures; for Will Beauvais had little regard for those whose nature differed from his.

Jake's personality reflected many of Will's characteristics: He was a rebel in spirit who disdained social injustice; in addition, his view of life's problems was one of simple clarity. With a pronounced sense of right and wrong, he shared Will's simplistic view of the world. Slender in build and balding at an early age, even Jake's physical characteristics were similar to those of Dean's father. Jake, however, had long ago abandoned his vagabond ways, but Dean had retained his proclivity for rambling.

Since Jake displayed the cautious nature of Dean's father; Dean enjoyed scaring him. He remembered an incident that occurred when, as teenagers, he and Jake were swimming in the lake and a storm approached. Lightning flashes grew closer to them, and as they swam further from shore, Jake yelled, "Let's get out of the water!"

Dean grinned and replied, "It's impossible for that lightning to strike us!"

Fearfully, Jake shouted, "Don't talk like that! We're liable to drown!"

"It's impossible for us to drown!" Dean teased.

Instantly, Jake turned and frantically swam toward the shore. As Dean reflected on the incident, he regretted the folly of his own behavior. Will felt that Jake, unlike Rob, exerted a positive influence on Dean; in contrast, he felt that Rob was the instigator of many of Dean's fights. As Dean reminisced, he chuckled to himself when he recalled some of the comments Rob made when he found himself involved in an altercation. Rob had a fondness for uttering outrageous statements in the most inappropriate situations. Once, during a fracas in Chicago, a man had thrust a knife into Rob's back. When Rob turned around to face the man, he again stabbed Rob, this time in the chest. Weakened from the loss of blood, he was taken to the hospital.

Upon inspecting the wounds on both sides of Rob's torso, the examining doctor asked, "My God! Did it go all the way through?"

As if irritated with the question, Rob answered, "Hell no, it was just a knife, not a sword."

The doctor laughed, and so did Rob, until he passed out from the loss of blood.

Dean recalled another incident when Rob's comments seemed ridiculous. A heated argument broke out between them, and while Dean was driving the car along a residential street in Chicago, Rob struck him in the face. Dean suddenly steered the vehicle off the street, through a picket fence, and into the front yard of a stranger's house. The brothers simultaneously abandoned the car and became engaged in a fist fight. Suddenly an outraged man ran from the house and exclaimed, "What the hell are you guys doing fighting in my yard?"

Rob stepped back from his brother, holding his outstretched hand in front of him, as a signal for Dean to momentarily stop the fight. As Dean backed away in compliance, Rob turned to the irate man and said, "Surely, you don't expect us to fight out in the street! Do you want us to get run over by a car?" Rob's tone carried the implication that the man was making an unreasonable request.

Dean remembered Rob's past repeated displays of emotional indifference during stressful events. A couple of years earlier on another of the brothers' aimless trips, Dean was driving down a traffic-congested street in Miami, as the brothers quarreled over some trivial matter. Frustrated by the stalled traffic in front of him and angry at Rob, Dean decided to throw a scare into his brother. Suddenly, he steered the car to his right and drove the entire length of the city block on the sidewalk, while pedestrians scattered in every direction. However, Dean's daring act was in vain, for when he looked over at his brother, Rob's face reflected a bored expression. Seated in a relaxed position with crossed legs, Rob was nonchalantly in the process of cleaning his fingernails.

*   *   *

Dean's car picked up speed as he smiled at the memory of his brother's outlandish response. He realized that behind Rob's façade of indifference was a more profound side to his character. The brothers were emotionally close enough for Dean to see beneath the veneer of nonchalance presented by Rob.

It occurred to Dean that their father also was aware of the deeper side of Rob. *Maybe*, thought Dean, *that was why Dad was so tough on him*; *perhaps he saw Rob as a man who was wasting his potential.* He wondered if he had incurred his father's uncompromising wrath for the same reason.

Rob's creativity, tenacity, and sheer guts convinced Dean that he was a true survivor. With that realization, he felt much better about abandoning Rob in Ft. Wayne.

Dean was now entering the outskirts of South Bend, causing him to slow the car. He estimated that South Bend was approximately the halfway mark in his journey to Chicago. He decided to drive through the city, waiting to check the oil on the other side in the western suburbs.

As he drove through the downtown area, he noticed the buildings were taller, and the inner city was larger than in Ft. Wayne. Ahead he spotted the directional sign, with its arrow pointing left and reading "South Bend". Slowing the car, he turned left onto the desired route; then, as he gradually increased his speed, the abraded clutch shuddered in protest.

On the right side of the highway, a sign reading, "University of Notre Dame", pointed in the direction of the school. Since he had always been a fan of the *Notre Dame* football team, he felt privileged to be at the "Home of the Fighting Irish". He had always loved football, having played for two years in high school and one year in college.

He had only attended college for one quarter, and he cringed at the memory of it. After he was discharged from the Air Force, he tried out for football at *Southern Wesleyan College* and was awarded a football scholarship.

It was a rare opportunity for him, but, unfortunately, Dean's only interests were football and girls.

To the surprise of many, Dean had made the highest marks on the college entrance examination of all the enrolling students. He wasn't surprised, or even impressed with himself, for he knew that he and all four of his brothers were intelligent. Although quite unusual, all five of the brothers had been double-promoted in grade school—Rob and Elwood had this honor bestowed upon them twice.

Because of Dean's entrance examination score, the school faculty, especially the dean of the school, expected great things from him. Since he was older and had been in the armed services, the other football team members admired him; and consequently, because of his popularity with the other players, he was elected freshman class president.

Dean made the starting line-up on the team and was blessed with an abundance of potential girlfriends. He seemed to be unable to comprehend that he had everything going for him.

At first his team mates attempted to emulate his behavior, admiring his wit and sense of humor. But when he began to fail various subjects, he became less popular with some of the team. College classes bored him, and the monotonous drone of lectures sedated him, causing him to become lost in daydreams which carried his mind into the world outside the classroom windows.

When in high school, football had been one of his passions, but it no longer held any fascination for him. His years in the military had somehow changed him. His disdain for authority figures caused him trouble with his coach when he chose to disregard team rules that he considered to be stupid. Ultimately, his fellow players, who felt a loyalty to the coach and to the team, had come to have little regard for Dean.

The crowning blow came when the dean of the school requested that Dean report to his office. In a stern lecture, he admonished Dean for his failing grades.

"Son, you came here to our school showing more promise than most of the students we've had in years. You had everything going your way: Top score on your entrance exam, a football scholarship, class president… Everyone was proud of you, but you respond by thumbing your nose at this fine school. My advice to you is for you to go back where you came from, wherever it is that people like you go. You're wasting your time, and more importantly, OURS."

Dean was stunned and embarrassed, but he displayed no emotion. "Well sir," Dean replied flippantly, with a broad, exaggerated grin, "I didn't ask for your advice, but I'm going to take it anyway. I'll be glad to get out of this mental institution of higher learning."

With insolence, he rose from his chair, pretentiously saluted the man, and lazily ambled from the room.

Seemingly unperturbed, Dean was actually mortified. He felt shame to the depths of his soul, for he knew in his heart that the dean of the school was right on target about him. The most puzzling aspect was that even Dean himself didn't understand his own behavior. *Maybe if Dad had been more supportive of my going to college*, thought Dean

Dean tapped a cigarette from his pack and lit it. He opened another beer, again catching the spewing froth of the tepid liquid in his mouth. By busying himself with these trivial activities, he hoped to distract his mind from the painful memory of his college experience.

Since he was now out of the suburbs of South Bend, he decided it would soon be time to stop and check the oil. Also, as soon as he finished the beer, he would need to find a restroom. He decided to press on for a few more miles.

He began to ponder his and Rob's behavior pattern. Rob had served in the U.S. Navy in World War II aboard the battleship *U.S.S. California.* He had survived seven major battles in the South Pacific, one of which involved Japanese suicide planes crashing into the battleship. The terrible assault killed scores of men; many who were close friends of Rob's. With the help of the other sailors, it became Rob's grisly, unspeakable duty to collect the remains of the dead. Some of the victims had been blown into small bits: a finger here, a toe there, part of a man's head in some other place. In some instances it was necessary to scrape burned, blackened flesh from the deck of the ship. These bits and pieces of human remains, too burned and mangled to be identifiable, were tossed into a common bag.

When Rob returned from the war, he was actually suffering from combat fatigue, although people didn't know what to call the condition at the time. He became cynical and carried within himself a fatalistic outlook on life.

Day-to-day existence of mundane chores held no meaning for him. His behavior became erratic, sometimes destructive. In one instance, seemingly without reason (except for the fact that he had a dislike for marines) he turned over a telephone booth, with telephone and marine toppling down with it. The senseless act resulted in Rob taking a severe beating by the marine and two of his friends.

Dean realized that his brother's indifferent attitude toward life was probably a consequence of his terrible war experience. While this rationale helped to explain Rob's capricious behavior, Dean had no excuse for himself.

*   *   *

He had now driven westward well beyond South Bend. The increasing number of houses along the highway indicated to him that he was entering the residential area of some community or town. Ahead, on the right, a small sign read, "Pinola—City Limits". Noticing a *Sinclair* service station ahead, he slowed the vehicle, rolled over the hose that rang a bell, and parked the car by the gasoline pumps.

As the attendant approached the car, Dean stepped out of the vehicle and generously stretched his limbs in order to eradicate the stiffness he had acquired from his prolonged sitting position. It was only when he stood fully erect that he suddenly realized how desperately he needed to urinate.

"Fill her up with regular," ordered Dean, "and put in some 40 weight. Got a restroom?"

"Yes sir, on the right side of the station," the attendant pointed as he spoke.

Returning to the car from the restroom, Dean lit a cigarette. Noticing that the attendant had finished servicing his car, he reached for his wallet. "How much do I owe you?"

"Four seventy-five," answered the attendant, "I had to put in two quarts of oil."

He paid the man and climbed into the car. He liked to stop along the way, but he dreaded starting out again because he could visualize the damage being inflicted to the threadbare clutch.

He started the car and pulled away from the station with the worn clutch chattering. When his car gained momentum with the increasing speed, the shuddering of the clutch began to subside, and the old jalopy began to cruise along smoothly.

The temperature had dropped a bit, and although it was still hot, the air was less humid. He estimated that he would be entering Chicago's south side in a short while. He opened another warm beer, this time without catching the spewing liquid in his mouth. Uncaring, he was content to allow the gushing contents to spill out over his fingers onto the tan, ragged upholstery of the front seat.

Reminiscing as he drove, his thoughts again turned to the wretchedness that Rob had experienced in the war. He couldn't help but compare Rob's military experience with his own.

Dean had joined the U.S. Air Force in September, 1949. Unfortunately, he was inclined to rebel against authority figures. The tradition and structure of the military is predicated upon obedience and strict adherence to rules, some of which make little sense. Hence, it is not an appropriate place for a man who has a predisposition to defy authority.

Basic training was the most demanding part of military service. Since Dean considered it a challenging test of his manhood, he predictably excelled. After basic training, he was sent to *Chanute Air Force Base* in Illinois. His activities there were more like civilian job duties. It was an easy life—too easy, and Dean found it to be a dull existence.

The Korean War began in 1950, and although many military men went to fight in the war, Dean remained in the States. He became bored with his easy life while many of his peers were dying in Korea. However, because of the war, stricter rules were imposed on the service men at home. A mixture of boredom and strict regulations is a dangerous combination. Because of his hostile attitude, Dean had several fights while he was in the service.

True to his nature, he did an excellent job in the performance of his duties, but his relationship with his superiors was not good, especially with officers. Since he had high marks on the entrance examination, he had the opportunity to attend officers' candidate school; however, he turned it down because of his dislike of officers. Instead, he counted the days until his discharge as he performed the same mundane tasks.

Maybe it was for the best, Dean thought. Yet when he compared his military record with Rob's horrific experience in World War II, and the loss of some of his own friends dying in the Korean War, he felt a pang of guilt.

The idea of Mr.DeAngelo's young son dying in Korea caused sadness in Dean. *Perhaps planning his son's life for him had only driven him away from his father*, he thought. He increased his speed as he drove through the western suburbs of Gary. In a short while he would drive through Hammond, which was only a stone's throw from the south-side of Chicago.

Dean had ambivalent feelings concerning his military role during a time of war. He had great admiration for men who were brave enough to fight, even die, in war. Conversely, he possessed a deep sense of the futility about the wrongness of war. World War II was a necessary evil, but to Dean, waging war rarely made sense, particularly in the case of the Korean War. His guilt was not based on the fact that he did not fight in the war; it was his flippant, rebellious behavior in the military at the time when other men were giving their lives that troubled him. He felt that the least he could have done was to take the military more seriously, as a gesture of respect for men who were fighting the war; after all, they didn't start the war. *It is the politicians, not the soldiers, who create wars;*

but it is common men like George DeAngelo's son who die in them.

Four years had passed since Dean was in the service, and time had assuaged his guilt to some extent. He had matured in some ways, and it caused him to regret many of his past attitudes and behavior. Even at the tender age of twenty-three, he had been exposed to many experiences and circumstances that had begun to alter his thinking.

He was surprised that he had already passed through Hammond. Being in deep thought with the constant stretch of asphalt before him had caused him to barely notice the city. He was now in the south side of Chicago, and having driven this same route before, he knew how endless the drive seemed before he was to turn west on Madison Street. The effect of the alcohol had diminished, causing him to experience a slight headache. As he drove through the endless neighborhoods, the putrid odor of the stockyards invaded the atmosphere around him.

As he pressed northward, his thoughts turned to women, and he wondered if he would ever marry. At the youthful age of twenty-three, he still had plenty of time to find the right girl. However, he and his brother Elwood were the only brothers who were still single; even Clay, the youngest son in the family, had recently married.

In spite of his youth, Dean was street-wise, and having a wizened knowledge of the cruel ways of the world gave him a cynical outlook on life. Yet, he was emotionally immature, especially in regard to women. This, compounded with the fact that he had no sisters, made women an interesting enigma to him.

His mother, Sarah, the only female in Dean's male-oriented family, had always played a subordinate role to her husband, Will. Her inner strength was over-shadowed by the constant presence of six males in the family. Life had been difficult for Sarah. She had once dreamed of having a daughter, but instead she gave birth to five, high-spirited sons. As a result, the sons had little exposure to the feminine side of the human race. Dean's understanding of women stretched only to knowledge he had acquired in order to seduce them. Other than his mother and his aunts, he had little regard for women.

Dean decided that if he ever married, he would have to meet his bride-to-be in someplace other than his hometown, Tyler City, Tennessee. Due to the self-inflicted damage to his reputation, few respectable Tyler City girls would associate with him. Occasionally, a curious hometown girl would be attracted to him, as a lark, because of his reputation, but usually the girl's irate parents would quickly put an end to the relationship.

After a seemingly endless drive through the south side, he finally reached Madison Street and made his way westward. Because of his leisurely pace and frequent stops, he was arriving at his destination later than he had expected. A glance at his watch told him that it was 7:08. Since the Sunday traffic wasn't heavy, he figured he could arrive at Tom Allred's apartment around 7:30. He hoped Tom would be home. Although Rob had told him that Tom was a nice fellow, Dean dreaded asking him if he could stay for a few days.

Proceeding to the 3200 block on Madison Street, and eventually turning onto Adams Street, he spotted the number 3263 on the front of the apartment building. He steered the weary old Ford to an empty space in front of the apartment building and parked the vehicle.

Don't smother each other. No one can grow in the shade.
Leo Buscaglia

Chapter 5

Gazing intently at the reflection of his face, Dean inspected his image in the mirror. He noticed that his face was still smooth from his early morning shave. Pulling a comb from his shirt pocket, he combed his dark strands of hair.

After lighting a cigarette, he sat idly in his car before entering the apartment building. He dreaded his initial meeting with Tom Allred. With a sigh of resignation, he got out of the car, then stretched to rid his constricted body of stiffness. He noticed that the heat had subsided considerably. He looked curiously at the two-story apartment building. Constructed of grey stone, the structure appeared to be in good repair. Both the first and second stories of the building were furbished with a small front porch, each accommodating an array of inexpensive furniture.

Dean ascended the front steps onto the porch. He opened the front, glass-paned door, and entered a dimly-lit corridor that emanated the musty smell of antiquity. He climbed the stairs leading to Tom's apartment, and finally was standing in front of his door. Attempting to look his best, Dean fastidiously tucked the tail of his shirt into his pants, straightened his collar, and dusted his clothing. He rang the doorbell and waited for a response.

The door opened and a middle-aged, balding, overweight man appeared. He was wearing a sleeveless undershirt and blue jeans. He had a rather small, flat nose, and bulging lips that protracted to cover his crooked teeth. He was approximately five-eleven in height, but his slouching posture made him appear shorter. Dean hadn't seen the man but once, a year ago, and had forgotten what he looked like. Upon seeing him again, Dean's memory of Tom Allred's appearance quickly returned. The man's puzzled expression made it obvious to Dean that Tom didn't recognize him.

Dean displayed an elaborate smile and extended his right hand. "Hi, Tom. I'm Dean Beauvais, Rob's brother. Remember me?"

For a moment, Tom looked bewildered. "Whose brother?"

"Rob Beauvais's brother. Remember? I met you about a year ago. Rob lived in the next building over."

Tom's expression changed to one of recognition. Exposing his crooked teeth, he returned Dean's smile and accepted his extended hand.

"For Christ sake! What are you doing back in Chicago? I thought you and Rob had moved to Tennessee!" His pronounced northern accent sharply contrasted Dean's southern drawl.

"Well, we did—but I've moved back. Rob stayed in Ft. Wayne. Hell, it's a long story."

Tom curiously eyed Dean, wondering what he was doing here, for the men were only acquaintances. Both men stood awkwardly for a moment, then Tom broke the silence.

"Well, come in! I'll have the old lady fix us something to drink."

Tom had became an uncomfortable, reluctant host. Custom dictated that it was his social obligation to pretend that Dean was his friend; it had placed both men in an awkward position.

Tom took long strides into the dining room, but quickly changed his mind and began walking toward the living room. "Come on in, Dean."

As Dean entered the living room of the apartment, he smelled the unmistakable aroma of cabbage being cooked. The apartment was rather neat and uncluttered, but bland. A couple of cheap, lithographic prints adorned the white plastered walls, and the planked floor was mostly hidden by an oval shaped rug embellished with a pattern of flowers. Furniture in the austere room was sparse: A plain wooden table with two chairs, a couch and matching easy chair, and a television set comprised the entire contents of the room.

"Have a seat…what'd you say your first name was?" asked Tom. His expression showed a trace of embarrassment for not remembering the name.

"My first name's Dean. Where would you like for me to sit?"

The tantalizing aroma of sizzling ham drifted from the kitchen, blending with the pungent smell of the cabbage. Dean hadn't eaten since he left Ft. Wayne and he was famished. He hoped that Tom would at least invite him to dinner.

"Sit right there on the couch, Dean, I'll go get the missus."

Dean wearily took a seat on the large couch. It was a faded brown, fabricated from some kind of rough material, and worn from considerable use; however, it was quite comfortable to him.

Tom returned from the kitchen with an opened can of beer in each hand. Handing Dean one of the beers, he sat down heavily in the easy chair facing Dean.

"Oh, I forgot to ask, do you drink beer?"

"Well, not as a rule," lied Dean, "But I am a little thirsty after that long trip. Thanks, Tom."

"The old lady will be out here in a minute, as soon as she takes out the ham. You can stay and eat with us, can't you?"

"Well, I hadn't really planned on it," lied Dean, again. "But, I guess I could. I really only came here to talk to you about somethin'."

Before Tom could answer, his wife came through the open kitchen door, drying her hands with a towel. She was a grossly overweight woman, but her appearance was neat; she was wearing a house dress with a printed vertical stripe pattern, and a white apron covered her protruding stomach. Her even features, although now somewhat bloated, suggested that she had once been pretty. Her black hair was gathered, pulled to the back of her head and twisted into a bun.

"Honey, this is Dean Beauvais, Rob's kid brother—do you remember Rob, used to live next door? And Dean, this is Stella, my wife."

Dean stood up and shook hands with Stella. "I'm pleased to meet you, Ma'am."

"Hello," said Stella.

Dean noticed that her face remained expressionless throughout the introduction.

"Set an extra plate, Stella, Dean's gonna eat with us." Tom uttered the words as a command.

"All right," droned Stella. Showing no emotion, she walked back into the kitchen.

"Now what were we talking about before she busted in?" asked Tom, with annoyance.

"I...uh...said I wanted to talk to you about something," Dean answered hesitantly.

"Whatcha' got on your mind?" Tom was anxious.

Dean dreaded asking Tom the inevitable question. Haltingly, he began talking. "Well, Tom, I was talking to Rob before I left him in Ft. Wayne, and he said…"

"What the hell's Rob doin' in Ft. Wayne?" Tom interrupted.

"Well—he's lookin' for work there…Anyway, he said, knowin' I was comin' to Chicago. Well, you see, I'm not too well-heeled with money, and I don't really have a place to stay…but I'm sure I can get a job, real quick… anyway…Hell, Tom, I'll just lay my cards on the table. I'm on my ass."

Tom's expressionless eyes studied Dean, as he had been intently listening, trying to determine what Dean was trying to say. Then, with a suggestion of humor, his eyes came to life, and Tom laughed.

"Hell, pal, join the club. I ain't worked in four weeks!"

Dean's heart sank. It appeared that Tom and Stella were as destitute as Rob and Madge.

"Damn, Tom, I'm sorry to hear that. How are you and Stella gettin' by?"

"Well, we're barely skinnin' by. Stella's not in good enough health to work. I had a few dollars saved up, so we've got plenty to eat for the next few days, but if I don't get work soon Stella and I will be up shit creek, without a paddle, and then we'll have to use our hands." Tom chuckled at his own remark.

"How'd you lose your job?" asked Dean.

"I just got laid off—from *Chicago Tool and Die*. They said they'd call some of us back, but it may not be 'til the first of the year. And with winter comin' on, with those heat bills. Jesus, I don't know…" Tom's voice trailed off.

"How are you payin' the rent?"

"Well, I ain't. Mr. King's been nice enough to carry me for a month, but his patience will only go so far. I'm just a month behind, though. I been lookin' for work everyday. I don't have a car, so I have to ride the El, or walk. I'm goin' again tomorrow." Tom's face projected worry.

"I know how you feel," answered Dean. "Rob and I both have been doin' some unsuccessful job huntin' in Ft. Wayne."

"I've been out lookin' all day," complained Tom. "Just got home a few minutes ago. That's why we're havin' such a late dinner. How long has it been since you've eat?"

"This mornin' when I left Ft. Wayne."

"Jesus, you must be starvin'. You can eat with us tonight. Where you stayin'?"

"I ain't," said Dean, "I've…still got to find a place."

"Well, if you don't mind sleepin' on the couch, you can stay here tonight then look for a place in the mornin'." offered Tom, congenially.

"That brings me to what I wanted to talk to you about. I was hopin' that if you let me sleep here for a week, I'll pay you some money when I get paid Friday. That would help both of us." explained Dean.

"Do you already have a job?"

"No, but I'll get one tomorrow. I always do get a job here in Chicago on the very first day."

"Jesus Christ! You're on your ass. Don't even have a job, and no place to stay? Hell, you're ready to start livin' on the street, man! What if you don't get a job by the end of the week? It would be you, me and Stella all squattin' here, and Old Man King would throw us all out on the street!" Tom was more frustrated than angry.

"I'll make you a deal, Tom. Let me eat and sleep here tonight, and I'll get a job tomorrow. If I don't get a job tomorrow, I'll just keep goin', and you won't see me again. I know I'll get a job!"

"Well, I don't want to sound cruel, but if you don't land a job tomorrow, it would be better for all of us if you did hit the road," Tom said apologetically.

"Dinner is ready," Stella's voice droned from the kitchen.

The men stood and walked through the open door to the kitchen. The character of the room echoed the same neat, but mundane motif as the living room. A dinette-style table surrounded by four matching chrome chairs was nestled in a corner of the small kitchen.

The table had been set, with the cabbage, ham, sliced bread, and stewed potatoes in the center. Stella poured milk from a half gallon carton into the glasses and placed the container in the center with the food.

All three took a chair, and without offering to pass any of the food to either Stella or Dean, Tom grabbed his plate and immediately began to eat. He glanced at Dean. "Dig in!" he said. The sound of his voice was muffled by the gigantic glob of cabbage between his teeth. The ravenous noises projected from his mouth could have been heard in the living room. As he stared at Tom in amazement, Dean noted that Stella sat silently, seemingly unaware of Tom's gluttonous grunts.

The ham smelled delicious, but the cabbage, now fully cooked, gave off the putrid odor of cattle flatulence; however, Dean was so hungry that he feasted on the food.

They finished the meal in silence, and Dean rose from the table and thanked Stella for the dinner.

"You're welcome," she answered with a dispassionate expression.

"Thanks, Tom," said Dean.

Juice from the cabbage oozed from Tom's mouth and dripped from his chin. Tom only nodded to Dean, for the enormous clump of food in his mouth thwarted his ability to speak.

Dean excused himself, and walked back into the living room. Making himself at home, he turned on the television set, and reclined lazily on the couch. The melodious voice of Rosemary Clooney floated through the apartment: "Hey, there, you with the stars in your eyes…" He lowered the volume and switched the station to the evening news.

While lounging on the couch and awaiting Tom's return, Dean patted his shirt pocket in search for his butane lighter. With a flip of his wrist, the silver cover flung open. He lit a cigarette, clicked shut the cover, and returned the lighter to his pocket.

Dean detected the muffled voices of Tom and Stella as they talked in the kitchen. A moment later, Tom entered the room and walked to the television set, lowering the volume even more. He then took a seat facing Dean, in the easy chair.

"Listen, Dean," he began falteringly, "are you sure you can get a job pretty quick? It's not just wishful thinkin'?"

"I guarantee it!" Dean replied, confidently. "I worked in Chicago last year and got a job the first day that I went out lookin'. Hell, I changed jobs two or three times just for the variety of it. I never got fired from any of them, I just wanted a change."

"Well, the old lady and I talked about it, back there in the kitchen. We agreed that it's not fair to give you just one day to get a job. I'll propose a deal to you. You can stay here 'til Friday, then if you don't have a job, you'd better leave because Old Man King will start complainin'."

"Tom, I really appreciate it. I promise you, come Friday, when I get paid, I'll make it up to you." Dean assured him.

"Well, that's not all of the deal I was goin' to propose," explained Tom, hesitantly. He paused for a moment, collecting his thoughts to ensure that he properly worded the upcoming proposal.

"Now you don't have to do this, if you'd rather not, but I think it's a proposition that will help the both of us. If you do get a job, when you get paid Friday, let me have enough money to pay a month's rent, or whatever you can afford. In return, you can stay here for a whole month. Stella will wash your clothes and cook your meals, and you can see what a good cook she is."

Dean didn't immediately answer. He truly felt that he could quickly find a job, but he wasn't fond of a situation that placed him in the position of again being an intruder for an entire month. It would also confine his sleeping quarters to the living room, on the couch. On the other hand, the proposal had its positive aspects: Good food, clean clothes—plus, it would spare him the unpleasant task of locating a place to stay. Also, Dean realized that the arrangement would cost him less money.

Deciding that the good outweighed the bad, Dean answered, "Okay, Tom, it's a deal." Initiating a handshake, he thrust out his right hand as a gesture to clinch the verbal contract between them.

When Tom shook Dean's hand, his face carried an expression of relief. "You won't be sorry! This will help us both. In order to give you some privacy, Stella and I will spend a lot of our time in the bedroom. We got a TV in there. Most of the time, you'll have the livin' room all to yourself."

It was still early in the evening, but Dean was tired from his trip. He wished that Tom would retreat to the bedroom very soon. As if he had read Dean's mind, Tom announced, "Look, I'll get you some sheets and a blanket, and you can have some privacy. There's a bathroom with a shower on the right in the hall leadin' to the bedroom. Make yourself at home."

Tom left the room to get the bed furnishings while Dean showered and shaved in the bathroom. When Dean returned to the living room, the couch had been neatly prepared with sheets, a blanket, and a large, fluffy pillow. Tom had already left the room. Dean turned off the television set and changed from his sweaty clothing to a clean tee-shirt and a pair of lightweight cotton pants. He removed his socks, then turned off the overhead living room light.

As he lay down on the couch, he heard Tom's voice call from the hallway, "Goodnight, Pal. I'm goin' to sleep late in the mornin' because I'm sort of tuckered out from so much job huntin' today. Do you want Stella to fix you some breakfast?"

"No thanks, Tom, I want to get an early start. Tell Stella not to get up for me. Goodnight."

Placing his head on the soft pillow, Dean fell asleep immediately.

The next morning as he drove eastward along the 3100 block of West Madison Street, he searchingly scanned the buildings on the north side of the street. Suddenly, his eyes focused on the building he sought—MADISON SIGN COMPANY—in large letters, identifying his destination. After signaling left, he steered the car into an alley on the right side of the building and parked the car in a lot behind the sign shop.

Dean knew this area well. Two years earlier, he and Rob had worked at *Madison Sign Company* for a couple of months; however, they had abruptly quit their jobs with no advance notice to the owner. The brothers' unannounced departure from the job was again precipitated by Dean's restless propensity for wanderlust. He knew that the owner would be justified if he felt anger toward him, and he dreaded confronting him.

The owner of the shop, Leon Dupree, was an amiable, likable man about fifty years of age. He and his more-than-often nagging wife lived upstairs in an apartment above the sign shop. Since it was rumored that he was homosexual, many artisans among the sign painting community spoke disparagingly of him. It made no difference to Dean, however, because he had a personal liking for the man, and Leon had always treated him fairly.

Deciding that he had nothing to lose but his pride, he entered the back door of the shop. Sign shops in that day had a unique smell. Considered to be a harsh odor to some, to Dean it was a fragrant aroma that caused a wave of nostalgia. The familiar, scented mixture of turpentine, linseed oil, and enamel paint incensed him. It brought back a remembrance of his father's shop, and the way his father's clothing used to smell when he came home from work. As he inhaled the aroma, Dean felt a brief moment of homesickness.

Madison Sign Company was a small shop that usually employed about five or six people. He saw two men toward the front of the shop, painting on a large banner. Descending the stairway on the right was Leon Dupree.

As Leon reached the bottom of the stairs, Dean approached him. As he walked toward the front, Leon glanced at Dean, but showed no recognition of him.

"Leon!" yelled Dean.

Leon stopped in his tracks and turned toward him.

"Leon, I'm Dean Beauvais. Remember me? I used to work here a few years ago… Rob's younger brother."

Leon studied Dean for a moment, then his eyes revealed a flicker of recognition.

"Oh, yeah, how are you Dean?"

As the two men shook hands, Leon asked, "What are you doing up in these parts? I thought you went back to Tennessee. How's Rob?"

"Rob's fine. Got a good job down in Ft. Wayne, Indiana," Dean lied. "I thought you might need a good sign painter."

"Whom do you suggest?" Leon looked at Dean sternly.

"Well—me, actually. I know Rob and I left you with no notice a couple of years ago, but…"

"How do I know you wouldn't do it again?" Leon interrupted.

"Well, you don't know, but I don't intend to. But if you don't want to take a chance on me, I'll get a job someplace else."

Leon's harsh stare gradually melted into a sympathetic smile. "All is forgiven, Dean. Hell, flying the coop without notice seems to be a characteristic of most sign painters. I'm loaded up with work. When can you start?"

"Now!" answered Dean, excitedly.

"Well, you can get almost a full day in," said Leon, "we just got started."

Dean finished out the day, and even drew $20 dollars from Leon at the end of the work day.

Dean worked the full week at *Madison Sign Company* while staying at Tom Allred's house each night. Tom's wife, Stella proved to be a good cook, although she was no more talkative than a fence post. She dutifully kept Dean's clothes cleaned and pressed without any complaint, or without her face ever revealing any expression. At first, Dean thought that she had a dislike for him, but the faint smile that she had revealed at some of his ridiculous remarks convinced him otherwise. He decided that Stella was basically a sad person, perhaps because of her life with Tom.

When Dean arrived at Tom's house on Friday evening, he was happy. He had received his payroll check and had already cashed it. Tom was seated in the easy chair in the living room while Stella was in the kitchen, preparing dinner.

"Any luck today Tom?" asked Dean.

"Same old story," replied Tom, sadly, "Nobody's hirin'."

Dean pulled his wallet from his back pocket and counted out five $20 dollar bills.

"Here's a hundred. Will that be enough to keep Old Man King off your back? That's all I cleared after deductions. Is that okay?"

"That will be fine," answered Tom with a broad smile, "but I don't want to take all you've got."

"Don't worry about it, Tom. I drew $20 dollars from the boss earlier in the week, and I had a little money on me when I hit town. I've got enough to get by."

"Well, pal, you won't have to worry about room and board for a month, and Stella will keep your clothes in good shape, too."

"You know, Tom, it makes me feel uncomfortable to have Stella washin' my clothes. Madge did it for me in Ft. Wayne; I suspect that

Stella's not too happy about it."

"Don't worry about it. The deal's between you and me, and she's got no say in our deal. Besides, I'm sure she don't mind. Come on in the kitchen. Stella's got dinner ready, we been waitin' for you."

Except for the expulsion of voracious sounds exuded from Tom as he ate, dinner was always consumed in silence. At each dinner, the behavior was a replica of the prior meal; while Tom relentlessly gorged himself, Stella sat dispassionately silent, as Dean quietly stared at Tom in disgust.

After dinner that night, the men dispatched themselves to the comfort of the living room while Stella silently attended to her kitchen duties. Firing up a cigarette, Tom turned on the TV set and began to watch "Gunsmoke." He then fell heavily into the easy chair as Dean reclined lazily on the couch. It suddenly occurred to Dean that if Stella wished to watch television in the living room, there was no place for her to sit. Dean then sat up straight, confining himself to half the couch.

"Tom, do you think Stella wants to watch TV with us?" asked Dean.

"Nah, she hardly ever comes in here. Spends most of her time either in the kitchen or bedroom," replied Tom, lazily.

Dean leisurely lit a smoke, and casually looked at an 8 by10 photograph encased in a metal frame that rested on a small end table. The picture was of a pretty, slim brunette woman about 25 years old, standing in front of a flower shop. She was holding a floral arrangement in her hands as she flashed a toothy smile. Upon closer inspection, he was surprised to discover that the image in the picture was Stella.

"Tom, I couldn't help but notice that picture of Stella. How long ago was that?"

"Hell, I don't know. Maybe, 20… 25 years ago." answered Tom. "She was working at a flower shop then. When I first met her, she had some hare-brained idea about starting her own floral shop. I didn't think I would ever get her to shut-up about it."

The western episode on TV ended. As Tom changed the station to a John Wayne movie, he yelled to his wife.

"Stella! Bring me and Dean another beer."

Obligingly, Stella came into the room with two open cans of beer, handing one to each man.

As she turned to leave the room, Dean asked politely, "Would you like to watch TV with us?" As he spoke, he moved closer to the side of the couch to show Stella that there was room for her in the living room.

"No, thank you," answered Stella. She spoke in the same apathetic monotone as she walked away into the bedroom.

After consuming several more beers, Dean and Tom silently watched television until after midnight, only occasionally making a casual comment about the program or some other trivial matter. About 1:00 a.m., the men retired to their beds. Since tomorrow was Saturday, both men planned to sleep late.

Dean awoke Saturday morning to the aggravating clamor of loud noises in the living room. Annoyed with the disturbance of his early morning sleep, he elevated his body to a sitting position on the couch, glaring in the direction of the noise.

The table had been moved to the center of the room where Tom and another man sat facing each other. The two men were playing stud poker for small change, and each time that he drew a desired card, the man facing Tom would discharge a resounding shout. Dean was hesitant to censure the men for their rudeness, for after all, it was Tom's apartment; however, in spite of himself, he glared angrily at them.

The man facing Tom was a short, bald man of about 60, with small, beady eyes. In his mouth he held the stub of an unlit cigar. He took note of Dean's indignant stare and looked directly at him.

With a sneer, the older man muttered, sarcastically, "Well, looky here! Sleepin' Beauty's awake!" To Dean's way of thinking, the remark was adding insult to injury.

"Who the hell are you?" asked Dean angrily.

"Well, I would say that the most logical thing would be for me to be askin' you that question," retorted the beady-eyed man.

In an attempt to defuse the situation and to give Dean a warning, Tom politely interjected, "Dean this is Mr. King, my landlord. Mr. King, this is Dean Beau…."

"I don't give a shit who he is!" interrupted Mr. King. "He's acting like a smart-ass to me in my own house! You're Rob Beauvais's brother, ain't you? He's a real ass-hole!"

"Yeah, Rob said he knew you," commented Dean, "told me all about you!"

"Yeah, I can just imagine what he said about me," growled Mr. King, angrily.

"Oh, he didn't say much… He just said, 'Watch out for Old Man King—he's a real PRICK'!" Dean said casually, with a grin.

Instantly, Old Man King leaped up from his chair. Reaching into his baggy pants pocket, he pulled out a snub-nose 32 caliber pistol. He was shaking so violently with anger that Dean feared that King might shoot him, maybe even accidentally.

"Get out of my house, you son-of-a-bitch!" he screamed with rage. Dean looked at Tom, trying to interpret his attitude about the argument, but with a helpless shrug, Tom only hung his head.

"Tom, I gave you all the money I had... where am I gonna stay?" asked Dean. With his head still lowered, Tom didn't answer.

Dean yelled in anger, "Mr. King, the money Tom gave you for rent came from me! Somebody either owes me some money or a place to stay!"

Lunging forward, Old Man King held the barrel of the pistol within inches of Dean's face. "Get out of my house NOW, you son-of-a-bitch!"

"I'll need to gather up my stuff," explained Dean.

"Screw your stuff! I said NOW!"

With Mr. King pointing the gun at him, Dean picked up his shoes and suitcase and headed for the door. Looking back as he walked through the door, he saw Tom sitting at the table, his head hung and his eyes peering down at the table.

If all difficulties were known at the outset of a long journey, most of us would never start out at all. **William F. Buckley Jr**.

Chapter 6

Where do I go from here? For a long while, Dean sat in his parked car in front of Mr. King's apartment building. Frustrated, angry, and still in a mild state of shock over his abrupt expulsion from Tom's apartment, he found himself in a quandary concerning his immediate plans.

He had done little to incur Mr. King's extreme wrath, and it was now obvious to Dean that the landlord held strong resentments stemming from his past altercation with Rob. Since the old man had shown up with a gun in his pocket, Dean considered the possibility that Tom and Mr. King had conspired to cheat him out of his money; then he quickly dismissed the suspicion from his mind. After all, he considered Tom a decent man, and besides, he doubted that Tom possessed the imagination to concoct such a scheme.

Lighting a cigarette, Dean made preparations to drive away. With only fifty dollars in his pocket, he hadn't enough money to finance his food and lodging until next Friday's payday. He pondered the possibility of returning to Ft. Wayne, but quickly ruled it out; after all, his current financial status was proof that his Ft. Wayne experience had been a mistake.

Still perplexed about his course of action, he started his car, pulled slowly away from the curb, and began driving. He could always think more clearly when he was moving. Without planning his route, he found himself heading downtown. Looking to his left, he saw that he was passing *Madison Sign Company*. Sadly, he realized that he was leaving Leon Dupree again without notice.

Dean drove for over an hour. He was in the south side of the city, leaving town by the same route that he had entered it the week before. Spying a market sign on his right, he wheeled in close to the gasoline pumps and a loud bell sounded as he slowly drove over the long rubber hose. The attendant appeared and began filling the car with gasoline and oil as Dean went inside to purchase a carton of cigarettes and two six-packs of beer.

He returned to his car and maintained his southward course. He had to think more rationally about his predicament, and reluctantly he finally decided that his best course of action was to return to Tennessee, and his father. Even if his dad viewed his return with skepticism, he felt that his father would give him a job, if only part-time. Anyway, it was far better than the life he had been leading, and, it would be great to see his mother and Elwood again. Suddenly, he felt a deep yearning for home. Having made his decision, his spirit felt a buoyancy that caused him to increase his speed.

Traffic became thinner as he moved farther south. He opened a beer and lit a cigarette as he began recalling the events of the past two weeks. While travel and experiences in life supposedly make people wiser, Dean's recent exposure to the world had only posed more questions in his mind. He had always thought that he had learned something about human nature, but the questions that now plagued his mind left him confused:

If Mr.DeAngelo loved his son so much, why had he stifled his ambitions instead of setting him free to pursue his own dream?

Why are homosexuals like Leon Dupree despised when they have hurt no one, while politicians who send our sons to fight their wars admired?

What happened to the pretty, smiling Stella that I saw in the photograph? If she had aspired to own a small business, why did she give up her dream so easily? She and Tom didn't seem desperately unhappy; they appeared numb, but comfortable in their numbness. Afraid of changing or taking a risk, they stayed complacently nestled in their protective cocoon of sameness.

His thoughts again returned to his father. Will had accused Rob and others of leading Dean astray; however, that assertion provoked him more than any other opinion held by his father. To Will, being easily led was synonymous with weakness, a trait that was intolerable to him, as well as to Dean.

*   *   *

Dean finished his beer and carelessly tossed the empty can into the back seat. He drove further away from the city. Ahead on the right shoulder of the road, he saw a hitch-hiker. Feeling the mood to talk to someone, he pulled the car over just beyond where the man stood. In his rear-view mirror, he could see the reflected image of the man grow larger as he trotted to the car. The hitch-hiker opened the passenger door and tossed a shabby bag over the seat.

"Where you headed?" asked Dean.

"Bloomington, Indiana," answered the stranger, sliding into the front seat as he slammed the door.

"Where's Bloomington?"

"A little town about 45 miles southwest of Indianapolis," he replied.

"Well, you're in luck. I can take you as far as Indianapolis, then you'll have to head west. I'm goin' on down to Knoxville, Tennessee."

The hitch-hiker was a slender man, dressed in army fatigues. His upper lip brandished a reddish moustache, reflecting the color of his straight, wind-blown hair. His thin, brooding face was plain, but not ugly. He appeared to be about twenty-eight to thirty years of age.

"I sure appreciate this ride, pal. Do you live in Tennessee?"

"Well, yeah, sometimes," answered Dean, realizing that he really didn't know where he lived.

"Been in Chicago?" asked Dean.

"Yeah, took a job there, made good money operatin' a printing press, but I got homesick and decided to go back home to Bloomington and work for my dad. He owns a small print shop. I didn't work quite a month in Chicago."

"Yeah, well, I'm goin' back home to work for my dad, too. He owns a sign shop. I'm a sign painter by trade," explained Dean.

"Well, you look pretty young to be a journeyman sign painter. How old are you—about twenty?" asked the man, casually.

"Hell No! I'm twenty-six," lied Dean, with agitation.

"Well, you're lucky" replied the hitch-hiker in an easy-going manner. "I'm just twenty-five, and most people think I'm at least thirty."

"Do you like workin' for your dad?" asked Dean.

"Yeah, I do. I don't make much money workin' for him, but life is comfortable in Bloomington, and I'm content there. Hell, man, Chicago scares me, it's too big."

"So, do you get along well with your dad?" Dean realized that he was prying.

"Yeah, we get along great. Always have. Even when I was a kid, my dad used to do stuff with me and my buddies—you know, played base-ball with us and things like that."

"Well, that's good," remarked Dean, "when I was a kid, my dad used to run all my friends off when they came around. I had one pal...a guy by the name of Jake Stone. My dad kinda liked him...Come to think of it, he's a lot like my dad. But, anyway... Dad didn't want us to go to other kids' houses either. Actually, it was like we had an invisible fence around the property. We knew we couldn't go beyond that fence, and our friends knew that they could never enter."

"Why'd he do that?"

"Hell, I don't know, it's hard to explain. He thought we were too good for other kids."

"Too good in what way?" The hitchhiker was curious.

"Well, not too good financially, that's for sure. Not morally either, because some of the kids who came around were good kids. He just thought we were *too good*, that's all. Maybe intellectually, or talent-wise, or we had more potential than other kids. It was almost like a certain kind of snobbishness... Hell, I don't know, I told you it's hard to explain," Dean answered with frustration.

"And that pissed you off?"

"Hell, I'm still pissed off when I think about it."

Being a private person by nature, Dean rarely discussed intimate feel-ings with others. However, this man seemed likable and intelligent. Dean felt that perhaps sharing feelings with another person who had a different perspective on life might be of some benefit. Strangely, he felt emotionally safe in sharing intimate thoughts with a total stranger, a man he would probably never see again.

Turning his head and offering his right hand, Dean smiled and said, "By the way, I'm Dean Beauvais."

Grasping Dean's hand and returning his smile, the man replied, "Phil Cameron, I'm glad to meet you."

"Want a beer?" asked Dean.

"Sure."

"Open us a couple of cans." Dean handed Phil the beer opener. "The beer's in the back seat, next to that excuse for a suitcase. It's probably warm, so don't let it spew on you."

Both men lit cigarettes and sat silently smoking and sipping their beers for a long while as the old car chewed up the miles of asphalt. Phil finally spoke, "You said your dad was protective of you when you were a kid, not lettin' you play with other kids... Did he try to make a sissy out of you?"

"No, it wasn't like that," explained Dean, "just the opposite, in a way. One of the first things I remember about my dad was when I was about four or five years old, he made me go back and knock the hell out of a kid who had pushed me down. The kid was my best friend, and I had let him get away with pushin' me. I wasn't afraid of him; I just didn't want to fight him because he was my friend. Dad taught all of his sons that taking crap off anybody dishonored the family name. Mainly, though he just thought that outside influences were bad for all of us boys. The most important thing in my father's life is the family honor. Dad is a man of high principles. He'd whip the hide off of us if we ever lied, cheated, or stole anything from anybody."

"Were you and your brothers good kids?"

"Well, Mom and Dad taught us some good traits. My dad didn't allow any cussin' around the house, and we had to earn every dime we got for spendin' money. We were honest, loyal to the family, and we didn't lie—well, not too much. But we fought each other a lot. We were full of mischief toward each other. But we fought like hell with anybody outside the family in order to take up for each other. Dad was a champion of fairness and justice. If anyone picked on someone in the Beauvais family, he felt that justice was served only when we beat the hell out of the person who picked on us. If the person who picked on one of us was too big, Dad would send my older brother, Rob, to finish the job. What about your family?"

"Well, I have a sister. She's married now, and got a couple of kids. Our family always got along with each other, and everybody else too."

"Do you like operatin' a printing press?" asked Dean.

"Yeah, it's okay. I like workin' with my dad. Do you like sign painting?"

"It's okay, but I'm kind of tired of it. I've been paintin' signs since I was about eleven or twelve. I wish I could do something more creative, like be an artist, or a musician, or maybe a writer."

"Ain't a sign painter an artist?"

"Well, sign painting is akin to art, but I'm bored with it. I'd like to do something that makes me feel really alive inside. Don't you ever wish you had a profession that's exciting?"

"Hell, work is work." commented Phil. "I'm not too excited about any particular line of work, but I'm content with being a printer. I just want to get in my 40 hours and have a good time on Friday night and weekends. Doesn't sound like you're too content with sign painting."

"Well, bein' content is not enough. I've just got this kind of energy inside me that sometimes makes me feel like I'm going to explode. Maybe that's what makes me roam all over the country. Hell, I must have had a dozen jobs in the last couple of years. But to be honest, I'm getting' weary of going from place to place. All of the places turn out to be the same, and that energy I feel keeps buggin' me."

"Well, if you're so full of energy, why don't you get a job that's physical, maybe construction work?" asked Phil.

"That's not the kind of energy I'm talkin' about." argued Dean. "It's an energy that comes from somewhere inside me. It's kind of like an itch that you can't scratch. I can't cure it by painting signs."

"Hell, man, nobody really enjoys work. Besides, everybody's not creative like you," replied Phil, with a touch of sarcasm in his voice. "We can't all be artists, you know."

"I'm not inferring that artists are the only people who are creative," answered Dean, with frustration. Creative opportunities exist in nearly every line of work. Look at all the modern technology we have. You wouldn't even have a job if somebody hadn't invented the printing press. We wouldn't have electricity, telephones, or automobiles. Inventors, engineers, musicians, and printers—like you, can be creative. Teaching is also a very creative profession."

"Hell, teachers don't make any money." said Phil. "A good offset press operator makes more than a teacher."

"It ain't a matter of making money." explained Dean. "My grandfather was a teacher, but he had to farm part-time to provide for his family. He could've made more money farming full time, but he loved to teach. He did something that was rewarding to him. That's what I'm talking about. I'd like to work at something that I love so much that I don't even notice when it's quittin' time."

"You're dreamin'," replied Phil, with a grin, "there ain't no such job, at least not for me. Hell, you're lucky to have a sign painting job with your dad. Maybe you're spoiled. Hell, maybe all of us in America are spoiled. Look at how some people live in other countries, some of them are starvin'. I'm content just to have a job and work my 40 hours. Then, on Friday nights, my dad and I drink beer and shoot pool, then we watch ball games on Saturday, and I'm content with that."

"My dad is one of the most creative men I've ever met," said Dean. "He's invented things, though he never got them patented. He's a damned good landscape artist, and he's proud of us, his sons, for having the same talents. But what does he expect us to do with those talents? He'd be happy if his sons, especially me, would work all of our lives for him in his sign shop, then take it over after he dies. He just wants to build a Beauvais dynasty."

"You're lucky to have a job," Phil lectured. "You're just bein' unrealistic with all this creative talk. You need to learn to be practical and happy with what you have."

Dean realized that he and Phil were diametrically opposed in their philosophies of life. He changed the subject.

"Hell, we're gettin' too serious." Dean smiled at his passenger. "Open us another beer, Phil."

Phil opened two more beers, handed one to Dean, and fired up a cigarette. Taking a break from their lively conversation, the two men sat silently for several miles.

Finally, Phil said apologetically, "I hope I didn't get you riled up with what I said. I didn't mean any offense by it."

"You didn't offend me," Dean said. "Hell, that's the most I've talked to anyone in weeks. I hope you didn't get sick of my yakkin'." He now felt a tinge of embarrassment about his long-winded speech.

The men were now nearing Indianapolis, and darkness was slowly descending upon them. Ahead, to the south, faint flashes of lightning lit up the darkening sky, defining the rounded shapes of the towering cumulus clouds. Dean began to dread driving into the distant storm.

Turning to Phil, he said, "I hope that storm misses us. It won't be long until we hit Indianapolis where you'll have to head west. It'd be tough hitch-hiking in a storm."

"Oh, I'll find some place to dart into, if it hits." Phil seemed unconcerned.

Dean looked at Phil, curiously. "You said that the job you had in Chicago paid well. How come you're hitch-hikin' instead of ridin' a bus?"

"Well, I only worked for three weeks, and I had to join the union. Had to pay all the money up-front. With my furnished room and eatin' out, I ended up broke. If I had stayed, I would have made real good money in a few weeks, but I got to missin' home. I just lit out, flat-broke, hitch-hikin'. I just don't feel comfortable anywhere except Bloomington."

"Well, I don't feel comfortable anywhere." Dean complained.

As they moved southward, the lightning flashes ahead grew brighter and more frequent. The approaching storm provoked an uneasiness in both men, causing them to fall silent as occasional gusts of wind whipped the car.

"I'd rather be hitch-hikin' then trying to drive this old trap through a storm." Dean looked ahead at the darkening sky.

They were now moving through the outskirts of Indianapolis, and since they were no longer in open country, the trees and buildings on each side of the road formed a barrier against the buffeting wind. The incandescent streaks of lightning were now accompanied by delayed drumming of thunder as the storm grew nearer to them. Ahead, the Route 37 sign pointed to the right.

Phil nodded his head, "Hey, this is where I get out. I gotta take Route 37. It'll take me home. With luck, I'll be there soon."

It was now beginning to sprinkle rain as Dean pulled the car over near the route sign, and luckily in front of a small restaurant.

"You'd better go into that restaurant 'til the storm's over, or you'll get soaked," advised Dean. "Maybe you can get something to eat and wait out the storm."

"I don't have enough money to eat," replied Phil, as he reached into the back of the car to retrieve his bag.

Dean drew five dollars from his wallet and handed it to Phil.

"Here, take this. They're liable to run you out of that place if you don't spend some money."

"Hey, pal, I don't want to take your money."

"Take it!" Dean commanded, pressing the money into Phil's hand. "Got cigarettes?"

"I got three or four."

Dean dug a pack of cigarettes from the carton and handed it to Phil.

"Hey, I feel guilty taking your money and cigarettes," Phil said, apologetically.

"Let's just say it's payment for all that bullshit you had to listen to." Dean grinned at him.

"Hey, man, thanks a lot. I haven't' eaten since six o'clock this mornin'."

As Phil stepped out of the car, the rain began to fall in a deluge. His voice competed with the booming roar of the rain on the car roof as he yelled, "I gotta run, I'm getting' wet. Thanks again."

Picking up his bag, Phil dashed into the restaurant, waving at Dean as he entered the door.

*　　　　　*　　　　　*

As Dean drove the car through the city, the storm abated, to some extent. The rain was steady, but only moderate, and the lightning flashes and the distant echoes of thunder were less frequent. The frayed wipers squeaked laboriously in their effort to clear the windshield of the steady rain. With each acceleration of the car, the wipers slowed in their recurrent beat. Night had fallen, and it was almost completely dark. He resumed his journey, looking forward to getting back to Tennessee.

He drove steadily for hours, crossing the state line, through Louisville, and deeper into Kentucky. He was happy to be back in the south, but he dreaded crossing over the Cumberland Mountains with his worn-out clutch.

He drove on with his thoughts wandering back to Chicago. Remembering his ruckus with Mr. King made him angry again. The old man had called him a 'son-of-a-bitch', and while northern people commonly used the term rather casually, with no consequence, southern men took exception to it; in the South, calling a man that name would almost invariably lead to repercussions.

Dean was aware—with the exception of Elwood, that he and all of his brothers had bad tempers. Realizing that his temper could someday cause a calamity, he decided that in the future, he would try to exercise more control over it. He knew that he had been very lucky, for he had never been hurt badly in a fight. He decided that unless there was absolutely no way to avoid it, he wouldn't ever fight again. Actually, he hated confrontations.

Looking to the southwest, he again saw faint flickers of lightning playing in the distant clouds; and after several seconds elapsed, the muffled thunder echoed deep within the dark thunderheads. Another storm was approaching.

As the storm drew nearer, strong, intermittent gusts of wind rocked the car and sheets of rain swept the road. The strong, fresh smell of ozone was in the air, as the lightning illuminated the recessed caverns within the clouds in the distance. The storm was rapidly moving toward him.

Suddenly, the full force of the storm struck with a vengeance. The rain, mixed with hail, began to fall in a cloudburst, cascading down on the roof of the car in a deafening roar. The blinding bolts of lightning and the ear-splitting crack of thunder were now in unison, and the reverberating cannonade of thunder shook the earth. The rivulets of water in the road and the sudden bursts of wind made it difficult to control the car, and the windshield wipers labored uselessly.

Dean was in the desolate part of a Kentucky rural area, and his dim lights were unable to penetrate the heavy rain. As he could no longer see to drive, he decided to pull over somewhere.

Ahead, on the left, a dim, reddish glow shone through the mist, illuminating the sodden air. As he drew closer, he saw that it was a tavern. He swung the car into the parking lot and stopped close to the door. Parked in front were two motorcycles and a single car. It was a lower-class tavern; a long, low building constructed of painted white concrete blocks. In the paned window in front, a red neon sign read, *Bluegrass Club*. Behind the building was a trailer. He was familiar with this type of arrangement; usually, the trailer was the living quarters of women employed by the tavern for the purpose of attracting male customers, a common practice in the South.

He got out of his car, and in an attempt to avoid getting soaked, he hurriedly dashed into the tavern, closing the door behind him.

The interior was comprised of one large room with a small kitchen behind the bar. A group of booths lined both the left and right sides of the long walls. An expansive hardwood dance floor filled the center of the room. A jukebox was tucked into the front corner of the left wall, and the nasal whine of Hank Williams echoed through the room, "Hey, Good Lookin…"

As he looked around the room, he noticed a huge man behind the bar. The tavern was almost deserted; only two men and a woman occupied the middle booth on the right side of the room. Dean strode to the left side, took a seat in the back corner booth and lit a cigarette. The warmth of the room felt good to his rain-soaked body.

He sat in the dark corner and noticed the woman from the booth was now walking toward him. *A bar maid*, he thought. She stopped at his booth and struck a provocative pose.

"What will ya' have, honey?" she asked in a saccharin voice.

"I'll have a Budweiser."

She was a small, pretty woman, with short, blonde hair. Her lipstick was bright red, and she wore a close-fitting dress, with the short length revealing her shapely legs.

She stood by the booth longer than necessary and did her best to display a sexy grin. As she walked away, she swayed her hips with a practiced effort. When she returned with the beer, she placed it in front of Dean, then slid into his booth, facing him.

"Are you sure you're old enough to buy beer?" she asked teasingly.

"I'm sure."

He was tired, and not in the mood to argue the point, and neither was he in the mood to talk to the bar maid.

"I don't believe I've seen you in here before, have I honey?"

No, I'm just passin' through. I really just came in here to get out of the storm and let my clothes dry out a bit." He wished the woman would rejoin the two other men in the booth and leave him alone.

"Want to buy me a beer, honey?"

"Look, I've got to go in a minute or two. I don't have time to sit and drink beer. Anyway, I'm about broke." explained Dean, trying to be honest.

"Got a quarter for the jukebox?" she asked. "You ain't too broke for that, are you?"

Smiling tiredly at the woman for the first time, Dean slid a quarter across the table to her. She picked up the money and prissed to the jukebox.

With a casual glance, he noticed the two men glaring at him from across the room. He now realized that they didn't approve of his talking to the girl. Just as he turned his head away to avoid their hostile looks, the girl slid into his booth and faced him again. The jukebox began to issue the mournful wails of the country song, "Lovesick Blues."

"Want to dance, honey?" She flashed a sexy smile.

"Excuse me," he answered, "I've gotta go to the restroom."

He hoped the woman would be gone when he returned.

When he walked back into the room, the girl, whirling alone on the dance floor, was slithering closer to his booth, displaying her sexual wares with suggestive body contortions.

Dean slid back into his booth and noticed that one of the men from across the room was walking toward him. He was a huge man, weighing maybe 220 pounds, with his stout body sporting a leather jacket. Atop his massive head, at a jaunty angle, he wore a black biker's cap. As the man neared Dean's booth, he gently pushed the barmaid to one side and removed his jacket, carelessly tossing it into the booth beside Dean. Below his short tee-shirt sleeve, his left forearm displayed a tattoo of a fire-breathing dragon.

He stopped directly beside Dean's booth and grinned sarcastically. As Dean turned his head and looked the man directly in the eye, he noticed that the man's countenance bore a resemblance to the face of a hog. The tip of his nose resembled the end of a double-barreled shotgun.

Dean hoped that there was some way to avoid fighting this man. He felt a stab of fear, not of a fight, but of his predicament. Unless he dispatched this man quickly, which appeared doubtful, considering his size, the police might be summoned. Dean felt all alone in a strange, isolated place. For a moment, his thoughts welcomed the police, but since he had very little money, it dawned on him that he could be arrested for vagrancy.

The man's grin expanded, exposing large, widely-spaced teeth. "Me and my buddy over there have been arguin' about somethin'," he said, enjoying his rehearsed rhetoric. "We've been tryin' to decide which one of us is goin' to throw your sissy ass out of here." His remark carried the implication that either of the men could easily accomplish the task.

Dean looked directly into his eyes, his expression showing total unconcern. From experience, he knew that to show fear was to lose half the battle.

Smiling back at the man, Dean replied, courteously, "Well, while you two are tryin' to make up your minds, do you mind if I finish my beer?"

"Oh, he's a smart ass, too!" shouted the man. "Look, asshole, I mean for you to get out NOW! You ain't finishin' nothin' in here."

Dean shrugged and began slowly coasting across his seat, "Okay, pal, you win."

The man was only about three feet from him, and as Dean stretched out of the booth, his crouched position enabled him to put all of his weight into the punch that he delivered.With the speed and force of the blow, his right fist disappeared into the pit of the man's wide stomach. Upon realizing that his next move determined his survival, Dean hammered his opponent's huge face with a dozen ruthless punches. Blood spurted from the man's snout-like nose, as he reeled backward, trying to catch his breath.

As Dean continued his advance, his face met the end of a shotgun barrel wielded by the large bartender. He spoke to Dean with his voice calm but emphatic, "Get out of here now, and you'll live. You don't, and I'll kill you!"

Complying with the bartender's wishes, Dean started for the door, noticing that the other man who had been in the booth was gone. *The man probably didn't want to get involved,* Dean thought.

"Put some miles between you and this place," ordered the bartender, "this guy may come after you. I saw that he was pushin' trouble on you, and I'll hold him here for awhile. He's one of my regulars, but he's always lookin' for trouble."

"Thanks," Dean stepped outside.

The storm had moved out, but moderate rain persisted. With the dim-red, neon sign lightning his way, he briskly made his way to his car. As he opened the car door, he heard a scuffing noise. Just when he sensed someone was behind him, a crushing blow rained down on the top of his head with a flashing light exploding behind his eyes, accompanied by a shrill ringing in his ears.

Almost unconscious, he dropped to his knees. To his surprise, no additional blows followed. As his consciousness fully returned, he slowly rose from his kneeling position and looked around…His assailant had fled.

Dean slowly got behind the wheel and drove away. His ears were still ringing, and he stifled an impulse to vomit. He felt a warm liquid ooze over his forehead into his eyes and realized that his head was bleeding badly. With his left hand, he felt the large gash in the crown of his head. It had taken several seconds for the flowing blood to make its way through his thick crop of hair to his face and neck. The blood now began to flow freely, spilling onto his shirt and lap. He became cold and began to violently shiver. Suddenly, he felt that he might faint.

He pulled into a small lane on the right and parked under a large willow tree. Lightheaded and dizzy, he smacked at all the knobs on the dashboard until finally the lights and motor shut off. He slowly retrieved the handkerchief from his back pocket, and as he held it tightly against the wound on his head, he fell over in the front seat.

After waking from the fainting spell, Dean looked at his watch…11:50, only about fifteen minutes had elapsed. Feeling the gash on his head, he noted that the blood was now beginning to clot and had almost stopped its flow.

He sat in the car and stared into the darkness. Realizing that he could not be far from the Tennessee state line, he entered the highway and resumed his journey. To alleviate the throbbing in his head, he opened a spewing beer and swallowed the entire contents. Considering that his adversary from the *Bluegrass Club* might be searching for him, he glanced repeatedly into his rear-view mirror. After drinking another beer, he lit a cigarette and deeply inhaled the smoke; the headache was beginning to subside.

Recalling the incident at the tavern, he cursed himself for not realizing that the second man in the booth had been waiting for him outside the tavern. Dean theorized that the man had probably been hiding behind the car with a beer bottle or a rock.

The passing storm had ushered in cooler air, causing him to shiver in his wet clothing. In his effort to get warm, he turned on the heater, one of the few things in the car that worked. He drove through a long stretch of desolate Kentucky country and at last crossed the state line into Tennessee.

Realizing that his bloody appearance must be hideous, he looked for an all-night service station where he could clean himself up in the restroom. After driving for several more miles, he spotted a place on the left and parked his car near the restrooms located on the side. Hurriedly, he removed a shirt and a pair of pants from the suitcase and made his way to the side entrance. He pushed on the bathroom door and was pleased to find that it was unlocked. Facing an attendant and asking for the restroom key was something that Dean had not wanted to do, especially in his condition.

After using his wet handkerchief to wash the blood from his face and neck, he undressed and threw his bloody clothes into the trash barrel. He looked at himself in the mirror as he dressed in his clean clothes. Then, before returning to his car, he carefully combed around the matted hair that covered the cut in his scalp.

He drove the car to the gasoline pumps where the attendant serviced the car with gasoline and oil. Luckily, the station manager hadn't seen him in his bloody clothing.

"How far to Knoxville?" asked Dean.

"I'm not really sure of the miles, but you're about an hour away." answered the attendant. "By the way, did you know that the cords are showin' on your right front tire?" he asked.

"No, I really hadn't noticed," lied Dean.

He pulled slowly away from the station with the lame clutch shivering in complaint. Early Sunday morning traffic on the road was light; once again by accident, he had chosen a fortunate time to make his journey. In an effort to suppress his returning headache, he opened one of the last two beers and swallowed large gulps of the liquid; for the beer was no longer a beverage to him, but instead, a medication.

His earlier exhilaration about returning to Tennessee had turned to gloom. While in Ft. Wayne, he had boasted to Rob, saying that when he did go back home, he would be well-dressed with money in his pocket and driving a good car. Instead, he was broke, dressed like a bum, and driving a trap. To make matters worse, he had just been bashed in the head. And only a few hours ago, he had vowed to himself that he would make a better effort to control his temper; but now he felt like killing someone.

It seemed to Dean that trouble followed him. As he recalled the past month, he became more depressed than ever. His father had told him to leave, but having no where else to go, he was now returning home in total humiliation.

Although bad luck had plagued him in the past, good fortune also smiled upon him; for the crippled car miraculously made it over the Cumberland Mountains, through Knoxville, and into Tyler City.

It was after 4:00 a.m. when Dean parked his car in front of the Beauvais home. Stepping gingerly from the car, he quietly pushed the car door shut. He knew that his parents never locked the front door at night, except when it was necessary to bar entrance to an errant son who had broken the 10:30 p.m. curfew. Opening the front door, he silently stepped into the spacious living room, gently closing the door behind him.

The welcoming, unmistakable aroma of home that engulfed him nearly reduced him to tears. The lamp in the right rear corner cast a soft light over the large room, as his eyes took in the familiar arrangement of inexpensive, but tasteful furniture. His father's desk and chair were in the right front corner, an easy chair near the center of the room, and the large, comfortable sofa toward the back of the room. The walls displayed three of his father's most recent paintings.

The atmosphere of the room exuded a warmth, stirring emotions he had never before felt.

As he tip-toed toward his sleeping place on the sofa, his mother, Sarah appeared in the open doorway leading from the dining room. A light sleeper, she had apparently heard Dean as he entered the house, and being completely unafraid of prowlers, she had decided to investigate the unexpected noise.

Sarah was barefoot and wearing a white, cotton nightgown, with its length reaching her ankles. She was an attractive woman of medium height, and although she was slightly overweight, she carried it gracefully. Her short, graying hair, which had once been black, was undone and flowing freely about her gentle face.

As she walked into the lighted room, she squinted without her glasses in an attempt to recognize him.

"Hi, Mom," said Dean, softly.

"Why, it's Dean!" exclaimed Sarah, smiling. Upon hearing his voice her eyes displayed an instant expression of recognition. She walked quickly to him with outstretched arms.

"My rambling man has come back home!" she said, as her eyes filled with tears.

Dean stepped forward and took her in his arms, hugging her almost too tightly. As he held her, he felt the warmth and plumpness of her body and smelled the well-remembered fragrance of perfumed soap and talcum powder.

As his mother embraced him, he felt a comfort that he hadn't experienced in months. He felt protected from the cruel world with which he had been involved. He hoped that his mother would never know about the past incidents of his life.

Stepping back from him, Sarah asked, "Are you hungry? I can make you something to eat."

"No, Mom." He smiled at her. "I'm just tired."

"Shhh," whispered Sarah, with her finger to her lips, "Don't wake Will."

"If I can stay here a few days 'til I get on my feet... Tell Dad I'll move on," he whispered.

"You can stay here as long as you want to, and I can promise you that. Thank God, you're home."

Dean knew that his mother held a passionate, unconditional love for all of her sons. Again hugging her, he said softly, "Go back to bed, Mom. I'll probably sleep a little late."

"Wait a minute, Dean, I'll need to get you some blankets and a pillow. You can sleep on the couch tonight because Will wouldn't like it if you woke Elwood. You can sleep in Elwood's room with him tomorrow night."

His mother left the room, returning soon with sheets, a blanket, and a pillow. She quickly arranged the couch as his bed.

He hugged his mother again.

"Mom, you'll never know how glad I am to see you."

"I think I know," answered his mother, smiling.

"I love you Mom."

"Goodnight, honey, I love you, too. I'm so glad that you came home."

He watched as Sarah turned and wearily walked away toward her bedroom. As she disappeared beyond the door, he felt a deep sense of love for his mother and a bitter remorse over the worry he had caused her.

Dean undressed and crawled under the covers on the couch. After thanking God for bringing him home, he immediately fell into a deep sleep.

Life's a voyage that's homeward bound.
Herman Melville

Chapter 7

It was 6:00 a.m. and still dark outside when Will Beauvais awoke. He was wearing pajamas when he stepped out of bed and slipped on a pair of comfortable house shoes. The tantalizing aroma of brewing coffee indicated that Sarah was already up and puttering with the routine kitchen chores.

Without bothering to get dressed, he walked from his room through the small dining area into the living room where he knew that Dean was sleeping. Although Dean and Sarah had been reasonably quiet the night before, Will had heard his son when he entered the house. Consequently, he hadn't been able to go back to sleep until about 5:30, only to re-awaken at 6:00.

After turning on the dim lamp in the corner, he walked to the couch and peered down at his sleeping son who was lying on his side, snoring. Looking more closely, he noticed that the pillow that cradled his head bore traces of dried blood. Will stood by the couch for a long while, studying Dean.

He turned off the lamp and strode to the front door, gently opening it to avoid awakening his son. He walked to Dean's car and in the half-darkness, noticed the decrepit condition and muddy exterior of the vehicle. He carefully opened the car door and the inside light came on, illuminating the interior of the car. Will's inspection of the car's interior confirmed his worst fear; the upholstery of the front seat displayed large splotches of dried blood, and the back seat contained the ragged suitcase and several empty beer cans.

After gingerly closing the car door, he quietly re-entered the house.

Walking stealthily through the living room, he slowly crept through the dining room, and into the large kitchen. Tucked into the corner was a small oak table with four chairs, one of which was occupied by Sarah. Since it was too early to start breakfast, she was leafing through a *LOOK* magazine while sipping on her coffee. With a worried expression, she watched as Will poured himself a cup of coffee. He then seated himself beside her in one of the oak chairs.

"Well, I guess you know that Dean came back home early this morning." Sarah spoke very softly to avoid awakening either Dean or Elwood, who was asleep in the small bedroom that adjoined the kitchen.

"Yeah, he woke me when he came in," answered Will, "and I didn't get much sleep after that. I was awake when you came back to bed, but I didn't want to talk about it with you until I digested the situation a little more. What do you think he is doing here? Why do you think he came home?"

"Well, I guess he got tired of roaming. He also probably wanted to be with Elwood again. You know how close they are…They're closer than any of the boys," replied Sarah.

Will considered Sarah's answer. "You're right. They are closer than the others. How in the world could two people who are so different be so close to each other? Elwood is gentle and obedient, but Dean is wild and rebellious."

Sarah and Will sat in silence for a long while, thinking. She noticed the expression of sadness on Will's face. Although he usually appeared younger than his age of 63, Sarah noticed in his pale blue eyes a tiredness and an indication of worry, making his general demeanor appear older. His posture was usually proudly erect when sitting in a chair, however, Sarah noticed that he was now slumping as he sat, making him appear shorter than his height of 5'8".

Will was smaller in stature than any of his five sons. He was medium in build and had a wiry muscular body shaped by a lifetime of hard work. The dark, graying hair, receding from his forehead displayed hints of future baldness, a characteristic common to most of his male ancestors in the Beauvais family. A pronounced Roman nose harmonized with his bony face and his large ears slightly protruded. His prominent chin suggested determination, an appropriate characteristic for a man with his tenacity.

Sarah finally spoke, hesitantly, "I'm so glad that Dean is back home with us." She looked at Will in order to discern his reaction.

"Sarah, I can't allow him to stay…at least not permanently. Maybe long enough for him to get on his feet."

"Well, why shouldn't he stay? He's still our son, the same as Elwood. He's wild, sometimes, but I think he's mixed up…confused about life. When I first saw him last night, it made my heart sing. Dean is basically good. He has a good heart." Sarah smiled.

"Well, even if he started behavin', there's not enough work for Elwood and him. It wouldn't be fair to Elwood to share the work with Dean." Will explained.

"Then you could go out and sell more jobs—bring in more work," reasoned Sarah.

Will looked at Sarah, with skepticism. "And about the time we got a shop full of work, we'd wake up some morning and with no warning, Dean would be gone."

"Will, he's our son. Elwood would gladly share the work with him. He doesn't care about the money. Can't you just give him a chance?" Sarah pleaded. "Please don't be mean to him when he wakes up."

"Sarah, I don't intend to be mean to him. I'll treat him like a son should be treated."

"Well, this time I've got a feeling that he has learned his lesson," replied Sarah, "I really feel that he will be all right now."

Remembering the blood he had seen on the front seat of Dean's car, Will decided that he wouldn't tell Sarah about it. He sipped on his coffee as they both sat silently.

Finally, Will spoke. "Even though he is younger than Elwood, Dean has been hardened by the world, while Elwood is as innocent as a lamb. I'm afraid Dean would be a bad influence on Elwood, the way that Rob was bad for Dean."

For the first time in the conversation, Sarah abandoned her pleading attitude. With a stern look toward Will, she replied in a kind, but firm voice. "I don't think that any of our sons are that easily influenced. But assuming as you do, that they are, then isn't it just as possible that Elwood would be a good influence on Dean?"

"Sarah, Elwood worships Dean. I'm still afraid that Dean will be a bad influence. I love Dean just as much as you do, and he can stay for a few days until he accumulates a little money. I told him not to come back here until he changed his ways. I can't go back on my word, or it means nothing. When he gets on his feet, I want him to leave."

"How do you know he hasn't changed his ways?" asked Sarah.

Will was again tempted to tell her about the blood on the car seat, then decided against it. Anyway, she would soon see the blood stains on

Dean's pillow.

"I'm sorry, Sarah. I want him to leave."

"And I want him to stay!" There was a hint of defiance in Sarah's voice. "Will, I have never tried to over-rule your decisions about our boys, and I would never speak up against your decisions in front of the family. But I'm telling you now," she said calmly, but with resolution, "I want Dean to stay."

Will was perplexed, for he had seldom seen Sarah act this way. Frustrated and unsure of where the conversation might lead, he felt that they had reached a stalemate. Although Sarah didn't appear to be angry, and was gentle in her demands, she seemingly had put her foot down about the matter.

Unsure of his next move, Will stood and pushed his chair aside. "Don't fix me any breakfast. I'm going to town for awhile." He then left the room.

Each time that he felt stymied or angry in regard to a problem, Will had a long-standing habit of driving away in his car. He then would sit alone for hours, until he reached a decision. He was always slow and deliberate in making up his mind, but once his decision was resolved, it became unalterable—it was as if it had been set in concrete.

Sarah sat at the kitchen table, sipping her coffee. After a few minutes, she heard Will's car pull away from the house. Realizing that Elwood would soon awaken hungry, Sarah began preparing breakfast. She decided to let Dean sleep as long as he wished. She would cook a meal for him when he awoke. As she removed the bacon from the refrigerator, she heard a muffled noise from Elwood's bedroom, a room known to the Beauvais family as the "Bull Pen". Clay had jokingly given that name to the room because of its appearance. The austerity of the rather large chamber gave it a resemblance to the "bull pen", or holding room of a jail, a large cubicle where prisoners receive visitors. Apparently, Clay had first-hand knowledge of the appearance of a jail cell. From the time that Clay had named the bedroom, the label was adopted. With every future reference to the room, each member of the Beauvais family referred to it as the "Bull Pen".

Just as Sarah placed his breakfast on the table, Elwood came through the Bull Pen door into the kitchen. He was still wearing a pair of baggy pajamas, and before he sat down at the table to eat, he immediately went to his mother, embracing her in a powerful bear- hug. Lifting her so that her feet were well off the floor, he shouted, "Good morning, Sairy," calling her by the pet name he had given her. He then kissed her roughly on her smooth cheek before releasing her.

Sarah gasped, then said with a laugh, "Elwood, you just about squeezed the daylights out of me!"

"Where's the Cap'n?" asked Elwood, cheerfully, with his usual morning optimism.

"Will had to go into town for a few minutes." Sarah said.

Since Elwood was unaware that Dean had returned home, Sarah remarked, "Eat your breakfast, Elwood. After breakfast, I have a surprise for you."

"Don't tell me," joked Elwood, "but I'll bet you brought me a good lookin' woman." He purposely squinted one eye, opened the other eye widely in an exaggerated stare, and winked idiotically at his mother.

"You wouldn't even know how to act around a woman," his mother teased with a smile, knowing that Elwood had never had a date with a girl.

"I'll be back in a minute, and I'll show you your surprise." Sarah turned and walked from the room as Elwood sat down to his breakfast. Of Sarah's five boys, Elwood, the middle son in age, now 25, was most unique. He was different from his brothers in appearance, temperament, and personality. As a grown man, he stood six-two in height and weighed 320 pounds. He was fair in complexion, and his large head displayed a thick crop of straight, black hair. He had inherited his father's Roman nose and his mother's large brown eyes. Because of his poor vision, he wore thick, horn-rimmed glasses.

Unlike his brothers, Elwood was even-tempered, predictable, and easy-going. He was extremely intelligent, and considered a genius by his former teachers. His quick wit and humor not only attracted many friends, but also defusing many a potential family squabble.

Inheriting many of his mother's traits, his disposition lacked the male-dominant characteristics of his brothers; instead, Elwood had a balanced personality that incorporated the tenderness displayed by his mother.

*   *   *

Because of Elwood's voracious appetite, he quickly consumed his breakfast, helping himself to second portions from the platter of bacon and eggs that his mother had placed in the center of the table. As he was washing down his last bite with coffee, Sarah walked into the room, smiling at him.

"If you're through eating, go into the living room. Your surprise is in there."

Unsuspecting in regard to the nature of the surprise, Elwood rose from his chair. He again squinted one eye and displayed a grotesque, foolish grin. Then, walking like an ape, he lumbered toward his mother.

In spite of herself, Sarah laughed. "Now stop acting silly Elwood! And don't try to hug me again. You nearly broke my ribs the last time you did it."

Elwood hugged her, only gently this time. "Okay, Mom, what's the big mystery? What's this big surprise you're talkin' about?"

Sarah methodically began to clear the dishes from the table. Smiling slyly, she said, "Go into the living room and find out." She now pretended that she had only a slight interest in the 'surprise.'

Although Elwood seldom drank, he joked, "I'll bet you bought me a fifth of *Jack Daniels*." He wiped his mouth on the arm of his pajamas and walked briskly to the living room.

Upon entering the room, he immediately saw Dean, who was still asleep on the couch. Instantly, he stopped and stared downward at Dean. Having followed Elwood, Sarah walked past him and switched on the dim corner lamp.

"Shhh," whispered Sarah, "Don't wake him up."

"It's Dean," said Elwood, excitedly, "When did he get back?"

"About 4:00 this morning." She looked fondly at Dean.

Earlier, Sarah had seen the blood on Dean's pillow and had replaced it with another, sparing Elwood the unpleasant sight of it.

Elwood was dumfounded. All he could manage to do was to stare at him. "Dean's back home!" he uttered in disbelief.

Placing her forefinger to her lips, Sarah whispered, "Be quiet—don't wake him. Let him sleep."

Both of them studied Dean for a long while as he slept. Quietly, Elwood pulled up a chair beside the couch. Finally, he sat, continuing to stare at Dean.

"Don't wake him, Elwood. He'll be up before long."

"Does Dad know he's home?" whispered Elwood, anxiously.

"Yes, he knows."

"Is he gonna let him stay?"

"Yes, he's going to stay," answered Sarah. She turned and walked back toward the kitchen.

Suddenly energized, Elwood quickly rose from his chair and began to walk the floor. After pacing several times, he returned to his chair, sat down, and began to rock his body from side to side, a nervous habit that he had acquired as an infant.

At that moment, he heard his father's car pull into the parking area in front. As he listened, Elwood heard Will enter the shop which adjoined the house. Elwood stood, walked across the room, and entered the shop.

"Good morning, Cap'n," he exclaimed, cheerfully. He didn't mention Dean, deciding to let his father broach the subject.

"Oh, hello, Elwood." Will had a stern look on his face. It was always easy to discern Will's mood by his expression; his face consistently mirrored his state-of-mind. Obviously, he would have made a lousy poker player.

Without any mention of Dean, Will began to assign Elwood's work for the day.

"Elwood, you can finish this sign on the easel, then, later, we've got a truck coming in that we have to put some lettering on."

Elwood could no longer tolerate the suspense.

"I guess you noticed that Dean came home," said Elwood, casually. With curiosity, he closely eyed Will, in an attempt to read his face.

"Yeah, I noticed." Will's expression revealed worry.

"Well, maybe he can help me with this sign—the one on the easel?" suggested Elwood. His question carried the assumption that Will would give Dean a job, and let him stay.

"I'm afraid that we don't have enough work for both of you," replied Will.

"I'll help you sell some more work." It was obvious that he wanted Dean to stay. His father didn't immediately answer, and both of them fell silent. As Elwood began mixing his paint in preparation to begin work, he suddenly blurted out, "Are you gonna let him stay?"

"He may not even want to stay… He may just be passing through. If he needs money to keep moving on, I'll give him a few days' work."

"But what if he wants to stay?" Elwood was persistent.

"Do you want him to stay, Elwood?"

"Yes, I do. I'll share all my work with him."

"What about what I told him?" asked Will, "I told him not to come back…What will the whole family think of me if I don't mean what I say?"

Being the only son who dared question Will's judgment, Elwood replied, "Oh, Dad, you said that when you were mad. Nobody's gonna hold you to something you said when you were angry. I think everybody in the family will think more of you if you'll show some compassion… I know that I will."

"Is that how you really feel?"

"Absolutely!"

Respecting Elwood's opinion more than any of his other sons', Will conceded, "Okay, he can stay, but he'll be taking part of your work."

Elwood's face radiated a broad smile. He put his beefy arm around Will's shoulders and allowed his hand to drop onto his father's chest. With his index and middle fingers, he deftly fished a cigarette from Will's shirt pocket, a gesture he performed several times each day; although he smoked, Elwood seldom bought his own cigarettes.

He was the only son who would ever put his arm around his father, but the act was a natural expression for Elwood, and the gesture gave his father a warm feeling. Will also had grown fond of the way Elwood pilfered cigarettes from his pocket, but he often playfully reprimanded him for the presumptuous habit. Feeling this warmth, Will suddenly felt a desire for his son's understanding.

"Elwood, I guess you might think I'm hard on Dean sometimes—and Rob, too."Will explained, "But when both of them got into that fight, right here where we live, it was disrespectful to our home. I've always tried to raise you boys to respect our home because it is the most sacred place in my life. I never had any of this when I was a boy. There's something almost sacrilegious about dishonoring a man's home, because a man's home is his castle."

"I know, Dad. I'm proud of you for giving Dean another chance," complimented Elwood.

Will picked up his gray felt hat, positioned it on his head, and turned the front brim down, a sign that he was again leaving.

They walked to the front door and Will remarked, "Go ahead and start that sign, Elwood, I'll see you after while. I'd like to give Dean a little time to get up and get his head on straight before he sees me. He'll probably feel a little sheepish, at first."

Elwood paused at the front door and finished his cigarette as he watched his father's car drive away.

Immediately, he headed back into the living room, making no pretense to start working. He took the chair by the couch where Dean slept and again began rocking as he studied his sleeping brother. After a few minutes had passed, he decided to awaken him. After all, it was nearly 9:00, and he knew that Dean wouldn't want to sleep away the day.

Extending his arm to Dean's shoulder, he gently shook his brother. Dean's upper body suddenly sprang up, and he sat awkwardly on the couch, wild-eyed. The look of puzzlement in his eyes gradually changed to one of recognition as he stared at Elwood. He threw the blanket aside, and both men simultaneously rose to their feet; Elwood immediately embraced him, causing Dean to lose his balance and fall backward onto the couch, with Elwood in his awkwardness, falling on top of him.

"Damn, Elwood, you didn't have to tackle me," he protested, "I'm still weak from just wakin' up."

Both men stood, and Elwood hugged him again. Dean laughed and said, "I guess you know you're breakin' my ribs."

Having heard the commotion, Sarah appeared in the doorway, smiling, "Are you two boys fighting? I heard all the noise. Are you hungry, Dean?"

"Yeah, Mom, I'm hungry as a bear."

"Me too," said Elwood, enthusiastically. "Let's have breakfast, Dean!"

"You've already had breakfast, Elwood." Sarah reminded him. "Anyway, you're supposed to be on a diet." She began folding the blankets from the couch. "Dean, how is Rob doing? I'm glad he's got Madge with him. Where are they now?"

"They are fine, Mom. I'll tell you all about it later. I've got to shower first." Dean headed for the bathroom. "Where's Dad?"

"He went to town for something. Hurry up, Dean; I'll be in the kitchen. We've got a lot to talk about," said Elwood, excitedly.

As Elwood sipped coffee at the kitchen table, Sarah went into the Bull Pen to straighten his bed. At last, dressed in clean work clothes, Dean walked into the kitchen. He poured himself some coffee and took a chair beside his brother. Both men filled their plates from the platter of bacon and eggs that Sarah had placed in the center of the table. In spite of his usual voracious appetite, Elwood was more in the mood for talking.

"I talked to Dad this morning. He wants you to stay here and help him and me in the shop."

Dean didn't immediately answer. Since he was famished, he was more interested in eating than talking. In his enthusiasm and lack of manners in the consumption of his breakfast, he reminded himself of Tom Allred's gluttonous style of eating.

"I want you to stay, too. I'll need somebody to help me on the pictorial work that we have to do." Elwood continued.

Between bites of food, Dean mumbled, "What makes Dad think I want a job? What makes him think I'd want to stay here? After all, he

86

ran me off. Maybe I just came to see you and Mom."

As Dean continued to eat, Elwood studied him closely.

Finally he spoke. "Dean, Dad may not show it when you first see him, but he really wants you to stay here with us. If anyone knows Dad, I do. I know you're proud, and Dad telling you to hit the road was hard for you to swallow, but don't you think Dad has a point?" Elwood began rocking nervously. "Come on, Dean, be a man. Leave Dad a little room to save his pride. He may give you a little lecture, but he'd really feel sad if you left. If what I'm telling you wasn't true, I wouldn't be telling it to you. Have I ever lied to you before?"

Dean washed down his last bite with coffee and smiled at his brother. "You worry too much, Elwood. Whatever Dad says to me, I've got comin'. Within reason, of course."

"Then let's not talk about it anymore. It's settled!" Elwood beamed.

"Ain't you supposed to be workin'?"

Elwood hurriedly gulped down his food before he answered. "I might just take the day off. I've got pull with the boss. Come on, let's go out front and smoke."

Each carrying a cup of coffee, they ambled through the house and out the front door, both claiming a seat in a lawn chair in front of the shop building. Relaxing in his chair, Dean lit a cigarette, and after stealing one from his brother's shirt pocket, Elwood did likewise. The brothers sat quietly for awhile, sipping on their coffee and smoking.

After the Depression, Will had bought a house that rested on five acres of land. Later, with the help of his sons, he built a sign shop in which he operated the family business. The portion of the building used for the shop was comprised of one large room. It had a double wide, sliding door on the northeast side of the building, large enough to allow trucks to enter. On the southwest side of the structure, Will had built the Beauvais dwelling, which was attached to the business, combining the shop and their living quarters into one large complex. To the dismay of Sarah, Will sold the attractive home in which they had formerly lived. She loved the house and wished to keep it separate from the shop. However, in business matters, Will always made the final decision.

In front of the shop by Highway 11, Will had erected a lighted sign that displayed the name of the business: ***Beauvais Signs-Established in 1930***.

*　　　　　*　　　　　*

The front of the shop building was shaded in the early part of the day, offering comfort to Dean and Elwood on this warm, autumn morning. Dean's eyes looked off to the west, following the outline of the rolling hills, now speckled in colors of gold, orange, and red. The illumination of the golden-yellow leaves of the large maple trees shading the sides of the building had never seemed so intense. The two brothers sat in silence, only hearing the occasional plunks of walnuts bouncing on the shop's tin roof.

Dean snuffed out his cigarette and spoke, "You know, Elwood, I used to feel stifled here at home, working in the shop, but now it is really refreshing to be back here."

"What changed your mind about it?" asked Elwood.

"Well, if you'd been where I've been for the past four or five years, and compared the atmosphere and surroundings of this place to others, you'd know what I mean."

"Have you been in terrible places?" asked Elwood.

"No—not terrible, exactly. Just average places, I guess. But until I saw how other people live, I didn't realize what a wonderful place that Mom and Dad have created here. I've not been able to appreciate the warmth of it until now."

Since Elwood's travel had been limited, his exposure to other life styles was confined to what he had read in books. With aroused curiosity, he asked, "What do you mean? What's so different about how other people live?"

"Well, for instance, this couple I stayed with for awhile in Chicago—Tom and Stella Allred. Their apartment and lifestyle was so depressing that I couldn't help feeling sad—all the time I was there."

"Why? Was their place dirty and cluttered… or what?"

"No, that's not it. Actually, it was rather neat and clean. There was just something lonely and lifeless about them, and the place. There was hopelessness about the whole situation."

"What do you mean? Did they argue a lot or something?"

"No, not at all. They didn't seem to have the energy for that. Tom was an unemployed tool and die maker. He was afraid to try a new trade, so he's probably still unemployed. And his wife, Stella, was once a beautiful woman with dreams of her own, but she had given up on everything… her dreams, her appearance, and even her marriage. Each day was a carbon-copy of the day before. Go to work, watch TV at night, and go to bed, then repeat the same routine tomorrow. They never showed any love or affection for each other. All the romance and excitement had gone from their marriage. They were totally without passion in their lives. It occurred to me that there may be millions of Toms and Stellas in the world."

Elwood studied Dean's thoughts. "Hmm... sounds pretty dull to me. But we all have to work, and sometimes there isn't time for anything else."

"That's true," replied Dean, "but we should love what we do. If we can't find that passion in our jobs, then we have to dig deeper, and we can't let others stop us. At one time in the past, there might have been some hope for Stella, but Tom stifled all of the life out of her. She's like a walkin' zombie. I hope Dad's domineering personality doesn't do that to Mom."

Elwood interrupted, "Dean, that'll never happen to Mom. She's really the guiding force of our family. She kinda stays in the background, but she is a strong influence on Dad. Mom has too much creative drive and tenacity to ever become like this Stella you're talking about. It's true that Dad makes all the financial decisions, and about where we live, without discussing it with Mom. But when it comes to us, their sons, Mom is just as involved in the decision-making as Dad. Did this Tom and Stella have any children?"

"No, thank God. They might have turned out like Tom and Stella...God forbid."

"Well, maybe not," commented Elwood, "Maybe if they'd had kids their lives would have been different, more exciting. And maybe Stella should have been more assertive. Some women need more balance in their personalities instead of always accepting the traditional female submissive roles."

"Anyway," continued Dean, "When I walked back into our house last night, after seeing how the Allreds lived, I couldn't help but notice the contrast. There's something warm and inviting about our place. Dad's oil paintings hanging on the walls...walls with nice warm colors instead of stark white, and Mom's fresh flowers on the dining room table, and the flower garden and grapevines that she tends to in the back yard. Even the smell of the shop adds color to our home...the aroma of the turpentine, linseed oil, and the overall blend of odors, but most of all, the love that Mom and Dad show for each other—and for all of us. You know... even the rowdiness and mischief between all of us brothers shows that there's life about this place. There was a feeling of death about the apartment in Chicago...Anyway, you just had to be there to understand it."

"I do understand it. I would rather live one good day with passion than to live a month without it, like Tom and Stella." The men sat in silence until Elwood changed the subject. "Dean, you and I are going to make some music! Ray Houser, Clay, and I are organizing a quartet, and we need a baritone. With the way you play the guitar—why, we could sound as good as the *Mills Brothers*, or the *Ames Brothers!*"

"I don't have my guitar anymore," said Dean.

"What happened to it?"

"I had to pawn it in Ft. Wayne for rent money. Hell, it was just a cheap guitar, anyway. I'll buy another one, only better."

"Well, we need your singing voice, that's for sure." Elwood was excited.

"I don't have a singin' voice," confessed Dean, "You're the one with the voice."

Elwood grinned, "Maybe you don't have a solo voice, but you've got a great harmonizing voice. And the way you play the guitar, we'll be great! I'll get the guys together and we'll practice tomorrow night…maybe even tonight."

"Sounds good to me," replied Dean.

Elwood looked at his brother. "Dean, why don't you and I start going to church together?"

"Nah, Elwood… I don't care much for self-righteous church members. They're not my kind of people."

Together, the brothers looked up as a man walked into the front, paved parking area. His slow, limping gait immediately revealed his identity to Elwood and Dean. It was Jim Burns.

Elwood leaned toward Dean and whispered, "Speaking of colorful, look who's coming here."

In height, Jim Burns was about as tall as their father, Will. He was slightly overweight, and his round, ruddy face was embellished with a purple, heavily-veined nose. A crop of prematurely graying whiskers surrounded his face and lips where an unlit cigar stub protruded from his mouth. His sweat-stained felt hat hung at a rakish angle, partially covering a shock of unruly hair that badly needed cutting. He was wearing dirty, ragged overalls that were as old and worn as his brogan shoes.

He limped his way across the parking lot, stopping in front of Dean and Elwood, and carelessly dropped a seedy bag that contained his belongings. The blended stench of alcohol and stagnating sweat drifted from him when he stopped near the brothers. As he stood, he shifted his weight in order to favor his impaired leg, which was a result of injuries he had received during the war. With his right hand, he vigorously scratched his crotch. Being almost blind in his right eye, he simultaneously closed it while opening his left eye even wider. Cocking his head to the right, he looked at the brothers with a one-eyed stare. Exposing his yellow teeth, his generous grin had the appearance of a sneer. Elwood was entranced by Jim Burns, and often imitated him, a habit that sometimes irritated Will.

"Whar's the Cap'n?" asked Jim, with a sneering grin.

"He went to town, Jim," answered Dean. Elwood studied Jim, fascinated by his demeanor.

"Where have you been keeping yourself, Jim?" asked Elwood. "We haven't seen you in a while."

"Oh, I jes' bin hyar and about," replied Jim. "Bin pickin' up a little work, now an' agin."

Dean asked, "What kind of work, Jim?"

"A little contrac' work. I don't keer to work on a rag'lar basis."

"What do you need to see the Captain about?" asked Elwood, studying him.

"Jes' wanted to ask him sumthin'. Have ye got a light fer my seegar?"

Dean flicked his lighter, holding the flame to the end of the cigar stub, but to no avail. The stub was too soggy.

"Shit," muttered Jim, in disgust. "I picked this seegar up off the street, an' the damn thing's got soggy from somebody else's spit. I'll find me another." He nonchalantly tossed the sodden cigar butt away.

"Want a cigarette?" asked Dean, pulling the pack of *Pall Malls* from his pocket.

"Nope. Never smoke seegarettes, jes' seegars. Jes' chew on 'em, mostly. When will the Cap'n be back?"

"Gosh, I don't know, Jim. He never tells us when he's comin' or goin'," responded Dean.

"Well, ye need to ask him sumthin' fer me," said Jim. "Ask him if he's collected on that big election billboard he painted down in Bat Holler. I'll be stayin' with my cousin, down there close to Bucktown. Fred Simmons—the Cap'n knows whar he lives. He needs to let me know by tomorra."

"Why do you need to know if he has collected on it or not?" queried Elwood.

Squinting his right eye, and peering intently with his bulging left eye, he displayed a mischievous grin. "Cause I got a contrac' on that sign."

"A contract?" asked Elwood, "What kind of contract?"

"A contrac' to blow the damn thing up with dynamite! I'm gonna

91

blow the damn son-of-a-bitch to hell!" Jim burst into laughter that sounded like the ranting of a hyena.

Elwood grinned broadly, completely spellbound by Jim Burns.

"Can't tell ye who contracted me to do'er, but I'm gonna do'er!" said Jim, again cackling with laughter. "As ye know, I like the Cap'n...I trust him, an' don't wanna do 'im no dirt. I wanna make sure he's collected on that thar sign, afore I blow it to hell and back!" He laughed crazily again, this time in unison with Elwood.

"The Cap'n's allus bin good to me," continued Jim, "I wanna treat him right. Not many men aroun' as good as the Cap'n. Used to give me a little work, now an' agin."

"I hope he didn't give you any contract work." Dean commented, dryly. Elwood roared with laughter.

"Speakin' of contrac' work, I dynamited four signs down by Springwater. Made fifty dollars on that little job." Elwood was now completely enraptured with Jim Burns.

"Started to burn 'em down, but dynamite's quicker...and a hell of a lot purtier, and more fun!" proclaimed Jim, proudly.

"Well, I gotta git along. Tell the Cap'n what I said," He picked up his shabby bag and limped away. Elwood and Dean laughed as they watched him disappear from sight.

After his laughter subsided, Elwood spoke. "Poor guy. The war screwed him up. You know he was a bright, clean-cut guy when he was about twenty. Dad felt sorry for him because he was from a poor family, and used to give him a little part-time work as a helper. Dad said he was once a pretty good sign painter, and he had a lot of creative ideas. He still likes Jim, and in some ways, is sorta fascinated by his behavior. He'll do any kind of dirty deed for money, but he's loyal to Dad."

"Another casualty of war," lamented Dean. "Just like a service station attendant that I met in Ft. Wayne. He lost his son in the Korean War. That poor man is a pitiful case now. And you know how the war messed with Rob's mind."

Elwood thought about Rob and some of the horror stories that he brought home from the war. He had told the family some of the painful ordeals that he went through, but he only discussed it one time. From that point on, when he mentioned the war, he only reminisced about the positive experiences he had encountered.

Wanting to stay on a more cheerful subject, Elwood thought of Jim Burns again. "Let me tell you a good story about Dad and Jim Burns." Elwood smiled as he spoke.

"You know how fearless Dad is. The only fear we ever knew him to have is a fear of storms—ever since he was a child. Well, you know how he is particularly afraid of lightning. Anyway, one day he hired Jim Burns to help him letter a sign on the side of a water tank in Knoxville…about 200 feet high. A bad storm came up, and lightning began flashing all around them. Dad told Jim that they better get down off the tank. Jim said, 'Hell no, I'm not getting' down. I DARE that lightning to strike us!' Dad got down quick, scared to death. Jim stayed up on the water tank for a long time, cursing the lightning."

Knowing his father's fear of storms, Dean laughed heartily. At the same time, he felt a pang of pity for Jim Burns.

Dean changed the subject. "I hope Dad's not too mad at me. You know, he hardly ever gets mad at you Elwood."

"He gets mad at me when he's in a bad mood and I imitate Jim Burns," said Elwood. "But when he's in a good mood he laughs about it. By the way, I'm not going to tell Dad about Jim Burns' plan to dynamite that sign Dad painted. It would just put him on the spot. He would just worry about whether or not he should report it to the police. You know how honest he is. Besides, he's already been paid for the sign. Let's just let sleeping dogs lie."

The brothers looked up as Will's car pulled into the parking area. Both of them stood as he got out of his car and walked toward them.

"Hello, Dean."

Groping for the right words, Dean stammered, "Hi, Dad…It's good to see you again."

Will walked into the shop as Dean and Elwood followed. When all three were inside, Elwood walked away, separating himself from his father and Dean. Will slowly turned to Dean.

"Dean, you and I need to talk."

In order to offer them privacy, Elwood walked toward the living quarters. "Dean, I'll see you in a few minutes."

*   *   *

"Sit down, Dean." His son immediately complied.

Will was unhurried as he prepared his thoughts before talking to his son. After taking a seat facing Dean, he reached into his shirt pocket and fished out a cigarette which he always smoked in a holder. Dean anxiously watched his father as he performed his invariable ritual: He methodically massaged the cigarette between his thumbs and forefingers until it was completely malleable. After inserting it into his cigarette holder, it hung like a limp rag. Lacking sufficient rigidity to keep it in the holder, it usually fell to the floor soon after being lit; as a result, in the past, Sarah's carpet had suffered a multitude of ugly burns.

His deliberate, measured attitude was unnerving to Dean as he silently sat, watching his father take abbreviated puffs on his cigarette. Dean began to grow increasingly impatient and uncomfortable, wondering how bad the lecture was going to be. He desperately wished that his father would get on with it. Finally, Will spoke:

"Is your head okay? Were you hurt bad? You don't have to tell me what happened—I just want to know if you're okay."

"I'm okay…I wasn't hurt much."

"Dean…I need to know what your intentions are. Where do you go from here?"

"I…don't plan to go anywhere…I'd like to stay here, if you'll let me."

"I mean where do you go from here with *your life?*" asked Will.

Dean had asked himself the same question. He detected a faint glimmer of compassion in Will's eyes. He realized how much he loved his father, although he had never told him. He began to feel shame about his past behavior. He knew that he owed his father an apology; however, he realized that his act of contrition shouldn't be interpreted by his father as groveling, which would be seen as insincerity and weakness by Will. His mind labored, searching for the appropriate words. He decided to simply speak from his heart.

"Dad, although my past don't show it, I really want to make something out of my life. I really love…. this family, this place. I'd like to stay here, and work for you if you'll let me. I'm sorry I acted like I did. Rob's sorry, too. We talked about it together in Ft. Wayne."

"Is that where Rob is? Ft. Wayne, Indiana? Is he alright?"

"Yeah, Rob's doing okay." Dean lied. He didn't want to worry his father with Rob's situation.

"Dean, how do I know that you'll do better?"

"Well, I can only promise to you that I'll try my hardest. By the way, Dad, working at all the sign shops where I've been, I've learned a lot about the sign business. I'm a first-class sign painter, now!" Dean boasted.

"I'd rather know that you're a first-class person, Dean." A look of compassion had replaced the harshness in his father's eyes.

At that moment, the door swung open and Elwood entered the room. Emulating Jim Burns, he walked with a pronounced limp. He was wearing a floppy hat, and as he neared Dean and Will, he squinted his right eye as his left eye bulged out at them in a grotesque, one-eyed stare. He exposed his teeth contorting his mouth into an idiotic sneer.

"How ye doin' Cap'n?" With his right hand, he dug at his crotch. Taken completely by surprise in the tense moment of their conversation, Will and Dean momentarily peered at Elwood with an incredulous stare. Then, suddenly, they simultaneously erupted with laughter

Music hath charms to soothe a savage breast,
To soften rocks, or bend a knotted oak. **William Congreve**

Chapter 8

Rules of the Shop and House

1. *No drinking on the premises*
2. *No visitation by drunken friends*
3. *No cursing or vulgar language*
4. *No fighting except in self-defense*
   (The man who hits the first lick
   is the man who starts the fight,
   and will immediately be fired
   and expelled from the house)
5. *Must be in bed by 10:30 p.m.*
6. *Wake-up time is 7:00 a.m.*
7. *Must report to work at 8:00 a.m.*
8. *Supper is 6:00 p.m. (Be there)*
9. *No back-talk to parents*
10. *No immoral women allowed*
   Will Beauvais

After entering the shop to begin working, Dean and Elwood stood together reading the sign that their father had posted on the wall the day after Dean's arrival. A neatly hand-lettered poster, it bore the unmistakable lettering style of Will Beauvais. Shaking his head with disgust, Dean turned to his brother.

"Well, Elwood, now you know what I mean when I say that the shop and house are tied together in more ways than one. Obviously, that sign is directed toward me."

Elwood smiled at Dean. "It's not directed *specifically* toward you, Dean...It's meant for all of us brothers. It's only been a few days since Al and Clay got into a fight here in the shop...And after all, remember that you and Rob got into a fight here awhile back."

"Well, just read the rules! They look like they're tailored to fit me!" complained Dean.

"I hate to say this, Dean...But if the shoe fits wear it!" Elwood replied.

Turning his gaze back to the sign, Dean said, "That last rule doesn't fit me. I've never brought an immoral woman to either the house or the shop."

"Read it again, Dean. Dad doesn't mean for us to not bring immoral women to the house or shop...He means 'no immoral women allowed'...*Period.* No immoral women in our lives, anywhere, or anytime."

"Damn!" exclaimed Dean, "What am I supposed to do for female companionship? Surely he doesn't mean that!"

"Knowing Dad, I'm afraid he means exactly that." Elwood grinned foolishly, "Maybe you ought to get yourself neutered...Anyway, you know how dad feels about loose women."

Dean frowned. "Hell, there's probably not a woman in Tyler City who could live up to Dad's strict set of values. Elwood, I might decide to work here, but I'll probably live somewhere else. I can't live by those strict rules."

Elwood looked worried. "Dean, Dad might allow you to live somewhere else, but I doubt it. I think he feels that any son working for him should live here at home."

Dean again peered at the sign. "You don't see those kinds of rules on the wall of most sign shops."

Elwood laughed. "Well, I don't suppose that most sign shops have too many employees like the Beauvais brothers."

The brothers slowly walked away from the list of posted rules and began working together, preparing to letter a sign. Suddenly, they turned toward the sound of the opening front door.

"Well, if it ain't the world traveler, come home to roost!" Clay exclaimed, cheerfully.

On the second day of his working at Beauvais Signs, two of Dean's other brothers, Clay and Alvin, stood at the open front door. Having heard from their mother that Dean had returned home, they stopped by the sign shop to see him.

When their brothers entered, Dean and Elwood stopped working, as both brothers, smiling, approached Dean.

"How are you doing, Dean?" asked Alvin, displaying a broad grin.

"Is that the best welcome you guys can give your favorite brother?" remarked Dean, as he smiled at Alvin and Clay. "What are you two guys up to?"

Suddenly, Clay knelt to a crouch, a gesture quickly followed by Dean. They began to pretend that they were boxing each other, both throwing fake punches into the air.

"Better watch it guys," joked Alvin, "Dad will run both of you off for fightin'."

As he faked another punch, Clay accidentally up-ended a can of paint on Elwood's table. Clay must have been born under an unlucky star; for frequent mishaps and weird occurrences were common to him.

After the brothers shared a laugh, Clay asked, "When did you get home, Dean?"

"A couple of days ago."

"How's Rob?" asked Al.

"He's okay. He and Madge got an apartment in Ft. Wayne, Indiana."

"Is he comin' back, too?" Clay was curious.

"I don't think so… at least not right now."

"Goin' to be around long?" Clay asked, aware of Dean's predisposition to roam the country.

Dean grinned, "Until Dad runs me off again."

"Well, knowing you, that won't be long," said Al, "I think I'll just tell you goodbye now."

The four brothers laughed.

Clay, at age 21, was the youngest of the Beauvais brothers. Standing six-two, his appearance was very similar to that of Elwood, except that he had his father's blue eyes, and weighed about 200 pounds, which he carried well on his muscular frame. He was a body-builder and had often worked out in the gym with Dean. Clay was very intelligent, and shared with his brothers the Beauvais attraction to ridiculous behavior and humor. Although likable and easy-going, Clay had the worst temper of all the brothers.

"I can't visit with you for very long," said Clay, "Al and I just dropped by to see you. We've got to go look at a house we're goin' to paint."

"You and Al are paintin' houses?" Dean's question showed surprise. Alvin spoke, "Yeah, we're workin' together some of the time…whenever I can get Clay to work."

Clay laughed, then suggested, "Say, Dean, maybe you and Elwood and I can join Ray Houser tonight for some singin'… That is, unless Dad has run you off before then." The brothers laughed again.

"I'd like to get together tonight, if Elwood wants to," said Dean.

Then, Clay stepped over between Elwood and Dean and started singing, "Down by the Old Mill Stream."

Dean and Elwood immediately joined him, as their three voices blended into perfect harmony. Al, standing a few feet away, looked at his watch with impatience.

On the second stanza of the song, Sarah came into the room, her face radiating an elaborate smile. The brothers finished the song, then broke into laughter.

"We've still got it, Mom," Elwood boasted to Sarah.

"You sure do," complimented Sarah, smiling, "It sounded wonderful. It sure livens up the place to hear you boys singing together again, and to see everybody happy."

"Yeah, Mom! We've still got it!" Clay echoed Elwood's words.

"Well, I don't want to get too close to you because I don't want to catch it," complained Al. Irritated, he again looked at his watch checking the time. Obviously, he wanted Clay to disentangle himself from the singing session so that they could go to work.

Al, the second son born into the family, was 30 years old—three years younger than the oldest son, Rob. In appearance, he was about Clay's size, but with his long legs and broad hips, he projected an awkwardness in his stance and movements. His brown eyes, complexion, and facial features were much like those of his mother.

Showing his impatience, Al paced the floor. Again looking at his watch, he said grouchily, "Clay, is there any way on God's earth that I can get you to leave here, so we can go to work?"

Except for Al, everyone in the room laughed. They all knew that Al's anger was always brief; he would be playfully laughing about something within a short time.

Elwood walked over to his mother and hugged her, lifting her off the floor as he usually did when petting her.

"Put me down, Elwood!" said Sarah, and they all laughed.

Clay playfully punched Dean again on the shoulder. "Listen, I've gotta go before Al explodes. Call me, Elwood, if you want to get together tonight." Turning to Sarah, he said, "Bye, Mom."

Al then called out, "Bye, Mom. See ya, Elwood... I'll be seein' you soon, Dean."

After receiving their goodbyes, Al and Clay headed for the door. Looking back over his shoulder, Clay said, "Dean, if you stay home this time, we'll start working out together again. I can bench press 250 pounds now."

"Well, if you can do that, I can bench press 255 pounds," bragged Dean.

Elwood and Dean worked until five o'clock that evening in the shop. They showered, had dinner with Will and Sarah, and got dressed for their evening meeting with Clay and Ray Houser. As they left the Beauvais house in Elwood's red 1951 Ford pickup truck, Elwood was charged with excitement over Dean's return home, and the possible renewal of their singing group. The totality of his joy in life was his camaraderie with his parents, brothers and friends; for although he was 25 years of age, he had never had experienced the love for a girlfriend. Although his father paid him reasonably well for his work, he had little need to draw his wages: he cared nothing about money, usually allowing Will to hold the bulk of his earnings, collecting only enough from his parents to enable him to engage in simple pleasures with his friends. Luckily for Elwood, his dad was completely honest when holding his money, scrupulously keeping an accurate record of his withdrawals. Unlike his brothers, Elwood was completely content with his simple life style of mingling with his friends while living with his parents at home.

"It's good to be back home, Elwood, especially working and being with you," said Dean. "I'd like to keep working in the shop, but after staying a few weeks at Mom and Dad's house, I'll probably get me a small apartment of my own."

"Why?" asked Elwood, "We can sleep together in the Bull Pen. There's two beds in there. Why would you want to leave?"

"Because, sooner or later, Dad and I will lock horns. You know I can't obey all his rules."

"Don't do that, Dean," pleaded Elwood, with a disappointed expression. "You don't think I'd cramp your style, do you?"

"No, that's not it," replied Dean. "Hell, let's not talk about this tonight. I'll stay with all of you for awhile...I shouldn't have brought it up right now. But if I lived somewhere else, what I do in my personal life, away from the shop, would be my business. But if I'm living with Dad and break one of the house rules…well, I'll get run off, and there goes my job, too. The shop and house are tied together… in more ways than one."

As Elwood drove the truck into the outskirts of Tyler City, he checked the time. Noting that it was 6:30, he said, "We're too early to meet Clay at Ray Houser's house. Do you want to drive around for awhile? Maybe drive over to the park?"

"Sure," answered Dean, as he lit a smoke. Elwood reached into his brother's pocket for a cigarette, and Dean lit it for him.

"Uh…Dean, do you want some beer?" asked Elwood, who only occasionally was a moderate drinker.

"No, I don't want any beer tonight."

"Well, I don't want to cramp your style… If you want some beer, don't hesitate because of me. I want you to feel comfortable."

"Hell, Elwood, if I wanted beer, I'd get it. I wouldn't ask your permission." commented Dean, with a show of irritation. "I'm not a damned alcoholic, where I can't go one night without beer."

"I notice you have gotten into the habit of cussin' a lot," observed Elwood, "Don't do it around the house…You know how Dad doesn't allow it in the home, or shop."

"Elwood, don't worry about it. Every time I get around Dad—or Mom, my cussin' glands just seem to shut down, automatically." Dean grinned at his brother.

"I just don't want you and Dad to get mad at each other. I don't care how much you cuss." Elwood swung the pickup truck into the curb at the City Park and shut down the engine.

"Dean," continued Elwood, "I saw the blood on your car seat before you put a blanket over it. Did you get into a fight somewhere recently?"

"Yeah, I got into a little tussle up in Kentucky when I was drivin' home. It happened in a bar where I stopped to get in out of the storm."

Elwood was fascinated with the image of Dean in a fight. Although he was awkward and lacking in the agility and physical prowess of Rob and Dean, Elwood never backed away from a conflict. However, because of his sound logic and congenial manner, he had managed to avoid physical confrontation with others. It was foreign to his nature to stoop to violent behavior in order to defend his or his family's honor. Paradoxically, although he had a personal aversion to violence, he felt an admiration for the fighting abilities of Rob and Dean.

"Did you win?" asked Elwood, with interest.

"I don't know. The fight didn't get very far before the bartender stopped it. I guess you could say I lost. I was the one who ended up with his head bashed in."

"Did you get hurt bad?"

"Naw, just a flesh wound, you might say," Dean replied, in an attempt to be humorous.

"Were you scared?" asked Elwood.

"Hell yes, I was scared. I was scared shitless. Wouldn't you be scared? A 250 pound monster attacks you in a lonely bar, in God-knows-where, Kentucky. Not only that, I'm driving a car with slick tires and a worn-out clutch. Plus, I was down to my last dollar, and it all happened in the middle of a violent hail storm. And all over a little whiny bar maid who wasn't fit to take to bed."

"Was she pretty?" asked Elwood, with fascination.

"Who?"

"The bar maid! You said she wasn't fit to take to bed. She must have been ugly."

"No... actually, she was kind of pretty, if she hadn't dressed herself up like a whore. But, I didn't exactly have women on my mind, Elwood."

"But I bet if you'd been in a different situation that you would have taken her to bed." Elwood was engrossed in the story.

Dean grinned at Elwood and with his fist playfully poked him on the shoulder. He realized that more than likely, Elwood had never had a woman.

"Elwood, why are you so fascinated by that whore? I believe you're the most sex-starved man I've ever met."

Suddenly realizing that Elwood was embarrassed, Dean felt sorry for him. He remembered how proud that Elwood had been of him because of his boxing skill and his participation in college football; but his brother's clumsiness and obesity had precluded his participation in sports. Consequently, he had vicariously enjoyed sports, even fights, through the exploits of Dean. It also appeared that it was the same in regard to sex.

"Elwood," asked Dean, guardedly, "have you...ever had a date with a woman?"

"You know the answer to that, without asking." Elwood seemed ashamed.

"Elwood, you need a woman." Dean said, emphatically.

"I don't want that kind of woman." Elwood protested.

"Oh, I'm just talking about a woman that cooperates. Anyway, I was just tryin' to show you that I care about you," continued Dean, with a puzzled expression.

"Shut up about it! Okay?" Elwood looked away from Dean.

"Okay, Pal…whatever you say. I just want you to be happy. I sometimes get concerned about you. You know, kinda like I can tell that you're concerned about my drinkin'."

"Well, now that you mention it, why do you drink so much? Can't you get by without it?"

"Sure, I can get by without it. I'm not drinkin' now, am I? Sometimes I quit for months… You know that."

"Then, if you can do without it for months, why don't you just keep on going without it, and quit?"

"Hell, I don't know…I just don't crave it for months, but then, I get in this strange mood, and then…Oh, hell, I don't want to talk about it! I don't like to be pinned down, or make promises."

To show Elwood that he wasn't angry with him, he laughed and with his elbow gently poked him in the ribs.

After filching another cigarette from Dean's pocket, Elwood said, apologetically,

"Dean, about the subject of women and me…I didn't get mad at you, I'm just not appealing to women. Who'd want me? Look at me… I'm so FAT!"

For a long while, there was silence between the brothers. Dean decided against further pursuit of the subject.

There was an incongruous situation existing between the two brothers. Elwood was two years older, and more intelligent than Dean. Possibly, his intellect exceeded that of all his brothers. Although he had never attended college, he was well-educated. He possessed an insatiable thirst for knowledge. By the time he was a grown man, he had read literally hundreds of books in countless categories.

Conversely, his education about life had been confined to books and his limited experiences in Tyler City. Dean, with his extensive travels and exposure to various types of people, actually appeared to be the wiser brother. His street-wise knowledge of the world compared to Elwood's naiveté made him seem to be an older and more experienced person who was protective of his younger sibling.

He knew that Elwood hero-worshiped him. Dean wished that his brother could live a meaningful life through his own experiences rather than through the acts, deeds, and romances of others. He suddenly realized that arranging a date for Elwood would be a shallow, temporary solution to his yearning for female companionship. With his depth of character, Elwood needed to ultimately establish a relationship with a woman with common interests to his own, as his father had done when he found Sarah.

Dean knew in his heart that the woman who eventually married Elwood would be lucky indeed to wed a man as loyal and lovable as he. Realizing that Elwood, because of his obesity, hadn't the confidence to pursue a relationship with a woman, Dean felt that he should attempt to influence his brother to improve his appearance by losing weight.

"Elwood, you may be right, I probably do drink too much." He commented, casually. "I might just quit for good."

"How did you reach that conclusion?" asked Elwood.

"Oh, I was just thinking, just because we are a certain way, doesn't mean we can't change our ways. We can always try to deny ourselves things we know are bad for us."

"Well, I wish you would, Dean. I didn't want to tell you this, but you've worried the heck out of me, but I didn't want to lecture you about it." Elwood appeared excited over the prospect.

"Okay, I'll make a deal with you," Dean proposed, "I'll quit drinkin', startin' right now. In return, you go on a diet. We'll put twenty bucks on it, and the first one to break the rule has to pay up."

"Dean, don't you know I've tried to diet a hundred times? Anyway, people can't quit habits on bets, or New Year's resolutions. You're smart enough to know that!"

"Excuses, excuses, excuses!" said Dean. He was smart enough to know that Elwood's assertion was true, but he figured that if he could get him started on a diet that maybe after losing a few pounds, he might have the confidence to approach a woman. Then, possibly, he would have a stronger motivation to continue the diet.

"That's a foolish bet, Dean. Forget it! We both know that won't work. You can't stop drinking, either by betting on it."

"Watch me!" Dean challenged.

Elwood started the truck and backed out of his parking space. "Time to get movin' and meet Clay and Ray." Elwood drove away.

"By the way, Elwood, I can't believe that Clay and Al are workin' together! God, what a match-up! They never did get along. That's like mixin' fire with gasoline."

"They're working together painting houses," said Elwood.

"Sometimes, on certain jobs, they'll work for a day or two with Dad and me. There's not enough work at the shop to work them full-time. Anyway, neither of them gets along well enough with Dad to work for him on a regular basis."

"Damn!" said Dean, "It's just a matter of time 'til they lock horns. That partnership ain't gonna last!"

"I know what you mean," agreed Elwood. "Clay's already beat the heck out of Al a couple of times. You know how Al is not skilled at fighting. But he's not afraid of anybody. Too bad, since he can't fight."

"Well, I didn't think that Clay was too good at fightin' either."

"He is now. He was working at the lock and key factory when a supervisor reprimanded him. Clay proceeded to floor him, then sat right there until the police came and put him in jail."

"Gosh, that don't sound like the Clay I know. Except for some of his temper tantrums, I never knew him to be rebellious."

"He's changed. Just a month or two ago, he rebelled against Dad, here in the shop. He's started drinkin' a lot, too."

"Oh, no! Clay's started drinkin'? I ought to kick his ass!"

"I don't know if you could do that anymore. He might just kick your ass. You might be able to get the best of him, but you'd have to kill him to do it. He has absolutely no fear."

"Well, that's too bad. I'm worried about Al and Clay workin' together. I don't think that's gonna work out. Anyway, how long are either of them gonna be content with paintin' houses?"

"They won't for very long," answered Elwood, "They're just doing it for the money."

"I'll bet Clay will eventually leave Tyler City, just like I did." Dean concluded.

"Well, Dad is really going to be disappointed if all of his sons leave. His dream was for all of us to live around here. He wanted to build up the shop into a big business and turn it over to us. You know that two or three acres he owns behind the shop? He had it divided up into five lots, one for each of his sons."

"That'll never work, Elwood. What if some of his sons want to follow their own road map? Maybe some of us want to do something else with our lives…chase our own dreams and live somewhere else. When a man starts tryin' to force a son to do somethin' he doesn't want to do with his life, sometimes bad things happen."

"Well, Dad's just trying to show his love for us," claimed Elwood. "He's proud of his shop, his family, and his home. When he was growing up, he never had a home or a family. He wants to keep his family together. That's why he's giving us all adjoining lots."

"All the King's Men in a row, forming the 'Beauvais dynasty'. Then, maybe after we're all married, living side by side, Dad can dig a big moat around the property, keeping us all inside while keeping everyone else out of the castle." Dean appeared to be irritated.

Elwood looked sternly at his brother. Being more familiar than the other sons concerning the motives of his father, he said, "Dad means well. I wouldn't feel uncomfortable living on one of the lots and working in the shop, maybe permanently."

"Maybe you're like the hitch-hiker I picked up on the way back to Tennessee," suggested Dean. "He had a good opportunity in Chicago, but he didn't feel comfortable living and working anywhere except with his dad. That's okay, I guess, if you're happy with it. I'm not knocking it. It's just that I don't think that Dad should automatically assume that it's gonna be that way."

Elwood pulled the vehicle to the curb in front of Ray Houser's apartment on Fifth Avenue. Having married only six months earlier, Ray had only recently rented the place.

As the brothers stepped from the truck, Clay came out of the Houser apartment door to meet them.

"Where have you been? We've been waitin'," inquired Clay.

"We're only about 5 minutes late," replied Elwood.

Clay and Dean spoke to each other and exchanged grins as the three brothers entered Ray's apartment. Seated on the living room couch were two family friends, Jake Stone and his pretty brunette girl friend, Heather Tomlin. Upon the brothers entry, the couple stood.

"Hi, Jake!" greeted Dean, "It's good to see you! Who's that pretty girl with you? Hi, Heather!" Both Dean and Elwood hugged the couple.

"Are you going to sing with us?" Elwood inquired.

"Are you kiddin'?" asked Jake. "It's good to see you guys! Especially you, Dean. Are you back home to stay this time?"

"Who knows?" joked Dean. "Maybe."

Jake smiled. "When are you gonna quit roamin', Dean? We heard you were back in town and decided to come and hear you guys sing. Elwood said you were going to practice tonight."

Jake and Heather reclaimed their seats on the couch as the Beauvais brothers remained standing.

Comprised of three rooms and a bathroom, the apartment was relatively small; however, the living room was rather spacious. As the brothers continued to talk to Jake, Ray entered the room, smiling. He was a slim man with an olive complexion and a head full of thick black hair. He stood at five-ten, the same height as Dean.

The brothers walked toward him, and Ray extended his hand to Dean. "Hey, pal! It's good to see you again. Now we can finally start making some music. We're calling our quartet 'The Vagabonds'."

Clasping Ray's hand, Dean said, "It's good to be back, Ray. I'm afraid I'm a little out of practice in the singing department. How are we goin' to work this out? Clay's a first tenor, Elwood's a second tenor, and you and I are both baritones. Who's gonna sing bass?"

"You and I will both switch back and forth, between baritone and bass," said Ray. "We'll just key everything a little higher."

The men turned their eyes toward the kitchen as Ray's wife, Bonnie, along with another woman who was obviously her sister, entered the room. Both women were attractive with flaming red hair, and they bore a distinct resemblance to each other. Ray introduced Bonnie's sister, Rhonda, to the Beauvais brothers.

After Bonnie had served coffee, the women sat on the couch as the quartet practiced their repertoire, mostly songs made popular by the *Mills Brothers* and *Ames Brothers*: "Nevertheless," "Til Then," "Paper Doll," and many others. Dean accompanied the singing with Ray's guitar. The conclusion of each song was followed by vigorous applause by Bonnie and her sister. However, Elwood stole the show with his rendition of "September Song." Singing the lead as the other three members hummed the background harmony, he crooned the song with his smooth voice, demonstrating a kinship to the sweet, melodious tones of Perry Como. As he was singing, Dean noticed the reaction of Bonnie's sister, Rhonda, as she sat spellbound with her face exuding an idyllic expression. She had been totally captivated by Elwood's rendition of the romantic, melancholy song. When he finished, she walked toward Elwood. Stopping in front of him, she looked into his eyes.

"That was the most beautiful version of that song that I've ever heard," she complimented, as she raised her hand to his shoulder. "You have a lovely, beautiful voice."

Completely embarrassed by the woman's physical and emotional closeness to him, Elwood was at a loss for words. His blushing face carried an expression of surprise, for he had never before experienced such a look from a woman.

"Thank you…I'm—glad you liked it," he stammered.

The quartet practiced for at least two hours before they finally said their farewells. Clay drove away to his apartment as Elwood and Dean struck out for home in Elwood's truck.

"Well, that was a good session," concluded Dean, obviously in a good mood. "You know, Elwood, I'm happier now than I've been in a long time. Maybe I could stay with you and Mom and Dad. Anyway, I'm not too well-heeled with money for apartment rent right now."

"Dad will only charge you $15 dollars a week for room and board…You can't beat that. Then, you get to eat Mom's great cooking." Elwood seemed animated.

"I might just give it a try. By the way, Elwood did you see the way that redhead went for you, back at Ray's apartment?"

"Aw… it wasn't me that she responded to. It was the song. She's obviously the sentimental type that gets all emotional over a sad song." Elwood smiled.

"Are you kidding?" asked Dean. "Hell, I saw the way she looked at you! Can't remember the last time a woman looked at me like that." In his clumsy way, Dean was trying to instill some confidence in his brother.

Embarrassed, Elwood quickly changed the subject. "Remember, Dean. No cussing around Dad and Mom."

Dean laughed. "Elwood, you're right about my cussin'. It really shows ignorance in a person. I'm gonna try to stop it, whether or not I'm around Mom and Dad. Speakin' of cussin'…Do you remember how Clay used to cuss when he was about five years old?"

Elwood chuckled. "He used to rip off the word, 'goddammit' when he got mad—which was often. Dad didn't want to whip him because he was sickly, so he would put him in the basement as punishment. You know how dark the basement was, with all those spiders. Poor Clay was terrified of spiders."

"I can't blame him. I'm scared of spiders, too," admitted Dean. "I'd rather have been given a whippin' than that."

In remembering the method of punishment, Dean laughed. "I remember one time Dad put him in the basement for cussin', and Clay would plead with Dad, 'please let me out…please let me out. I won't cuss anymore. Please…I won't cuss anymore. GODDAMMIT! Let me out of this shit hole!'"

The brothers laughed at the memory. Then Elwood changed his mood. "It sounds funny, but actually, it's sad. That was pretty cruel of Dad. And you know… Dad used to really whip the hide out of Rob when he was little. Remember that?"

Dean remarked. "Hell, yes, I remember it. That's why I was obedient to Dad. I saw what could happen if we got sassy with him. But Rob was headstrong and stubborn, and he just wouldn't back down. And he paid for it …Dad made sure of that."

"Remember the trouble between Dad and Rob on that one Halloween night?" asked Elwood.

Dean laughed, "Oh yeah, and Dad didn't know what to do with Rob. He was too big for Dad to give him a whippin'. The neighbors kept coming to the house and telling Dad that Rob had turned their outhouses over. Dad took up for Rob at first, though."

"I know, I remember Dad asking them…'Did you see my son do that?'" replied Elwood. "Nobody saw him, but when Mr. Worley pointed out that the Beauvais toilet was the only one left standing within a radius of a mile, Dad headed straight for Rob."

"Man, we were all pretty rowdy when we were growing up. We must have put a lot of gray hairs in Mom and Dad's heads." Elwood shook his head at the memory.

"Well, we were not really mean, just high-spirited, especially when we got bored. We pulled most of our stunts when Dad was away," claimed Dean. "We especially pulled some good ones when Dad took that extra job in Oak Ridge."

At one time, Will had taken a sign painting job for Sloan and Wilson Construction Company. Since the business was employed by the government to help build the new nuclear plant in Oak Ridge, there was plenty of work. It paid top wages with good overtime pay, and Will saw it as an opportunity to make some extra money. At that time, business was slow at Beauvais Signs. Alvin and Rob had taken sign painting jobs in Knoxville. When Will went to work at Oak Ridge, Elwood and Dean were left there to run the shop. Elwood was twelve years old at the time, and Dean was ten. They worked together after school, keeping the business open by designing and lettering the few signs that came into the shop. They were adequately skilled in the production of simple jobs. On evenings and weekends, Will worked with them, keeping records and sometimes correcting mistakes that his sons had made.

None of the Beauvais brothers were lazy. When they weren't painting signs, they worked for local farmers. Often their time had been spent doing chores at home, tending to the farm animals or working in the garden. They had highly active imaginations and found inactivity boring. Consequently, during idle times in the shop, Dean and Elwood spent their time concocting methods of making Alvin miserable. Some of the elaborate schemes devised by the boys were quite creative.

Thinking back to their childhood pranks, Dean laughed. "Remember when you organized the Beauvais Army? You always made yourself the General and made Clay a Private. I think I was always a Major."

"Oh, Lord, yes," replied Elwood. "Remember when I would send Clay on 'military missions'?"

The brothers laughed, and Elwood continued. "Poor Al, we always made him the enemy, and you would always summon Clay to 'make an assault on the enemy'."

"Yeah," Dean replied. "And Al was lying there one time with that terrible toothache. Remember that? And we told Clay to go throw a pitcher of ice water on him. Al's temper really showed that day."

Elwood chuckled, "Well, it turned out that Clay was wounded in action! He must have been at least 50 yards away when Al hit him with that apple. Man what a shot!" Laughing aloud, Dean said, "When Clay came back to the shop crying, you painted a chevron on his bare arm and made him a Corporal."

Elwood added, "Yeah, I awarded him a Purple Heart. Remember how I painted it on his chest?"

Dean punched Elwood on the shoulder and laughed, "Remember when you were also the victim of an ice-water incident? Clay really got you that time…He got you when you were lying in bed in your jockey shorts!"

Elwood replied, "Yeah, and I think half the town remembers that one."

Dean laughed, "I can't believe you would chase him all the way to his school bus with nothing on but your jockey shorts! Hell, you even chased him into the bus! How embarrassing!"

Elwood's face reddened, "Well, embarrassment never stopped a Beauvais brother from getting revenge. You know that, Dean. Wonder what made Clay do that to me?"

Dean remarked, "Actually, it was a 'little mission' that I sent him on."

Pretending to be angry, Elwood looked at Dean, "You'll pay for that one, Bud."

Elwood drove the Ford pickup into the Beauvais parking lot and shut off the engine. "Dean, I'll take you up on that bet you made earlier."

"What bet?"

"I'm going on a diet tomorrow, whether you quit drinkin' or not."

Dean said, "Okay, the bet is on. When I see you dietin, I'll quit drinkin'."

Dean looked at his brother. "You, know Elwood, it's 11 o'clock already. Our curfew is 10:30. I'm sure that Dad's got the door locked.

Now see, this is the kind of thing that bothers me, and tomorrow I'll have to hear Dad say that I lead you astray."

Elwood responded, "Maybe you're being too hard on Dad. He knows we were practicing music. Besides, Dad only does those things to show he loves us."

"How do you figure that, Elwood?"

"Well, Dad never had a father to set limits for him. I suppose he thinks we're fortunate to have a dad to set rules for us. He has always wanted to make sure his sons never felt the abandonment and isolation that he endured."

As predicted, the front door was locked. Elwood searched his pocket for a key. The boys entered through the side door that led them to their beds in the Bull Pen.

Pray that your loneliness may spur you into finding something to live for, great enough to die for. **Dag Hammarskjold**

Chapter 9

The inexpensive pine coffin lay at the front of the sanctuary. The two brothers sat silently in the pew of the small church in Springwater, Tennessee. It was 1901. Will Beauvais was eleven years old, and his older brother, John, was thirteen. Huddled together, they sat motionless between their two uncles, Pat and Newt Beauvais. Only about a dozen people were in attendance, most of whom were seated in pews toward the front in the old log structure.

As the elderly preacher stepped up to the pulpit, the brothers and their uncles gazed despondently at the wooden box that contained the deceased body of Robert Beauvais, the father of Will and John. In the sermon, the tall, bearded preacher who wore a grimy, black suit, used little time in consoling the bereaved. Instead, he spent a full hour railing against sin and its consequences. With threatening shouts, he vividly described the "molten pit of fiery hell that awaited transgressors at death."

After the preacher closed the service, the pallbearers carried the coffin to a wagon which was hitched to a single, aged horse. Since the cemetery was located in the church yard, it was necessary to transport the coffin only about 75 yards where an open grave ominously lay in wait for the body of their father.

It was a gloomy winter afternoon as the mourners gathered around the burial plot where their father was to be entombed. As the preacher prayed, the body of Robert Beauvais was consigned to the grave.

As friends and relatives expressed their condolences, Will and John said goodbye to each other. A dilapidated, squeaky buggy pulled by an old mule waited for John and his Uncle Pat. Will remained and watched sadly until the carriage disappeared from sight. He climbed into a wagon with his Uncle Newt, and the listless mare pulled the weather-beaten rig away in the opposite direction.

When he was dying, Robert Beauvais had summoned his sons to his bedside in order to give them instructions in regard to where they would be living after his death. His brothers, Pat and Newt, had each agreed to take one of his sons.

Robert Beauvais had been a share-cropper and a part-time carpenter. He was born in France, but in his infancy, his mother and father migrated to America and settled on land along the Tennessee River. Robert and his family had lived in a log cabin that he had built in Springwater Valley on a five acre piece of land, part of the same property that Will's grandfather had claimed years ago. Robert's first wife, Elizabeth, the mother of Will and John, died shortly after Will's birth. Two years after Elizabeth's death, he married a local woman named Hilda, who died of Typhoid fever, five years after their marriage.

The Beauvais family was poor. With the help of his sons, Will and John, Robert Beauvais scratched a meager existence from the over-worked land. Because it was a necessity that they work, his sons were denied a chance to attend school, and they acquired only a second grade education.

With a lowered resistance to illness because of malnutrition and over-work, Robert had contracted tuberculosis, which the rural people called "consumption". It was a well-chosen name for the disease, as it totally consumed the substance of Robert Beauvais. When he succumbed to the illness, his ravaged body weighed less than a hundred pounds. After Robert Beauvais married Hilda, the stepmother regularly abused both of her step-sons. However, John, although more mischievous than his brother, received less abuse than Will, who was her favorite target. Once, during a violent thunderstorm, she locked Will out of the house for the night. Sometimes, her abuse of Will became severe, but in fear of later repercussions, neither Will nor John ever reported the abuse to their father. Nevertheless, justice can have a sly way of serving itself; the typhoid fever that killed Hilda had stemmed from her contact with Will, for it was he who had been previously sick with the disease. Although John was apathetic in regard to the death of their stepmother, Will had strong feelings of guilt, mostly because he experienced absolutely no grief when she died—other than the sadness that he felt for his father's despondency.

With the stepmother gone, and with his own death looming before him, Robert realized that after his death, his sons would no longer have a home. It was then that he had made provisions for their future care with his brothers, Pat and Newt.

*   *   *

Will stayed with his Uncle Newt for less than a week. On an early January morning, Uncle Newt unceremoniously loaded Will and his puny belongings into his wagon. "Will," he said, casually, "I'm takin' you to stay with your brother over at your Uncle Pat's." During the long trip, those were the only words spoken by either of them.

Arriving at the house of his Uncle Pat, Newt deposited Will in the front yard and wordlessly drove his rig away. Soon after entering the house, Will discovered that his brother was no longer there; for shortly after his arrival at the home, he had promptly run away. Two days later, Uncle Pat performed the same procedure employed by Newt, by transporting Will to the house of his Aunt Tenny, dropping him off in her yard.

His Aunt Tenny was the sister of his father. A kind woman, she was overjoyed to see Will. She had no children of her own, and with her husband dying shortly after their marriage, she was a lonely woman. For the first time since his father had become ill, Will felt that he had found a home. He loved Aunt Tenny and spent many happy hours with her, helping her with many of the necessary chores.

It was during this contented time in his life that Will decided that he wanted to become an artist. It was easy to obtain pencils for sketching, and his creative abilities were shown throughout his drawings; however, the acquisition of brushes and pigments for painting required even more imagination. His imperfect solution to this problem was the use of commonplace elements that were available to him. For brushes, he used twigs, creating bristles by shredding the ends; also, he sometimes used his fingers. For pigments, he resorted to the use of ground-up leaves, shoe polish, flower petals, and crushed, wild berries. In his quest to find various colors, he experimented with the juice of numerous kinds of crushed vegetation. When not helping his aunt with work, he spent many carefree hours in the nearby woods and meadows, creating crude landscapes that were ardently praised by his Aunt Tenny. She loved his work, telling him that not only were his paintings original, but that he, too, was original since he was the first artist in the

114

Beauvais family. Like his Aunt Tenny, Will knew of no one in the family with the same creative ability. For years, he carried a restless energy inside, and at Aunt Tenny's he discovered that painting and drawing could soothe his disquieted nature. He could remember, however, this same restless energy in his father—an energy that work could not cure, but trying to feed a big family only left Will's father time to sleep, work and eat. Will felt a sadness when he realized that his father never had time to experience the healing abilities of painting and drawing. He cherished the time at Aunt Tenny's, and he wished that his father could have at least found a brief moment to discover a similar awakening. His idyllic days with his aunt, however, were short-lived. One evening, shortly after retiring for bed, Will overheard voices in the living room between his aunt and his Uncle Jim, who at the time was visiting Aunt Tenny. Assuming that Will was asleep, the couple was discussing him and his presence in her home. With his ear to the door, Will overheard the conversation, much of which included his uncle's admonition of Tenny. He was critical of her acceptance of the burdensome task of caring for Will, particularly since she was in failing health. Although, during the discussion, she defended her decision to care for him, Will was devastated. He felt that it was only a matter of time until she, too, delivered him to some new destination.

Will spent a sleepless night, thinking. Deciding that he could not endure another rejection, he realized, sadly, that it was time for him to move on.

Rising before daylight, he packed his art supplies into a cardboard box and gathered his skimpy belongings. After stuffing the articles into a pillowcase, he stealthily left the house. Crossing the front yard, he wistfully took a final look at his aunt's house, and after slinging the makeshift bag over his shoulder, he began his five mile walk to Springwater. He was to never again see his Aunt Tenny.

Will, at the age of eleven, was completely on his own. Not knowing the whereabouts of his brother John, and without the support of his aunt and uncles, he had no other relatives to which he could turn. To support himself, he ran errands and did odd jobs for some of the Springwater merchants. At night, he slept in hay lofts or stair wells, shivering in the cold during harsh winter nights.

On a particularly cold night, he discovered that he could keep himself warm in the train depot, which was managed by a man named Miles Craig. After a few nights of loafing in the building, he hid behind a bench in the large passenger area, with the intention of sleeping there.

Soon, the depot manager discovered him and chased him out of the building into the frigid night; however, when Will adamantly kept returning each night, the manager finally relented, and allowed him to sleep in the warm building. Miles Craig became very fond of Will and continued to provide a place for him to sleep and store his meager belongings.

As springtime was approaching, Will adapted to his lifestyle of living on the street. With money he had earned in the performance of menial tasks, he purchased some inexpensive brushes and paint and began to letter crude signs on the windows of some of the local merchants. In his spare time, he continued with his artwork by sketching and painting. Will's style of living began to take a turn for the better, but living alone with no friends except the station manager, Miles Craig, he felt isolated from the world. He wondered about the whereabouts of his brother John. Sometimes he would pass schools where children of his age were outside playing, which only increased his loneliness; however, because his past rejections had destroyed his trust in people, much of his isolation was self-imposed.

One late afternoon, Will watched as several boys were playing in front of a local store, *Henson's Grocery*, hoping that he might join them in their frolicking play. Suddenly, one of the more rowdy boys opened the front door of the store and threw a brick into the building, after which the entire group of laughing boys scattered in every direction, except for Will. Realizing that he wasn't guilty of the deed, Will simply stood motionless in front of the store, staring after the fleeing children.

Almost immediately, the owner, Mr. Henson, charged angrily from the building with a horse whip in his right hand. A huge, muscular man wearing a handle bar mustache, he bellowed, "You little bastard! I'll teach you to mess with me!" With his left hand, he grasped Will's scrawny wrist and proceeded to unmercifully beat him with the lash.

Will screamed with pain, trying to wiggle free of the huge man's vice-like grip, but to no avail. With all of his strength, he continued to lash Will's body.

Finally, breaking free, Will ran away with his back and legs dripping blood.

"Don't ever come back around here, you little son-of-a-bitch," shouted Mr. Henson, angrily.

Will could only manage to slink away, like a whipped dog, crying. Feeling cowardly, and with his self-esteem completely shattered, he crawled under a porch in the alley behind the store.

With his fingers, he felt the gaping wounds on his back and legs as he lay under a porch, sobbing. He stayed there for a few hours, and gradually, his whimpering subsided. Will by nature, was proud; but the rejection and isolation that he had endured had robbed him of his pride, making him feel like a worthless coward. As he thought of the whipping he had suffered, a terrible anger began to grow within him.

Since dark was approaching, Will realized that the grocer would soon be closing his business and climbing into his buggy that he had parked in the alley behind his store. Searching for a suitable weapon, Will found a portion of a tree limb about the size and weight of a baseball bat.

When Mr. Henson came out of the store in the semi-dark alley, Will sprang from behind the corner of the adjoining building. Enraged, he vigorously swung the club with all of his strength. With a sickening crack, the club connected with the side of the huge man's head, causing him to drop limply to the ground.

Tossing the club aside, Will said, triumphantly, "How did that feel, you fat bastard?" It was the first time in his life that Will had used such words.

Uncertain about his destination, Will ran from the alley into the street. Realizing that he may have killed the man, he grew terrified, deciding that he could no longer stay in Springwater.

Instinctively, he ran to the train depot where Miles Craig had provided a small cubicle in which Will kept his skimpy belongings. While the station manager was in the back room, Will gathered his belongings, crammed them into a mail bag, and slung it over his shoulder. Noticing that a southbound freight train had stopped at the depot, he crawled into the door of an empty box car and hid in a dark corner. The train left the station heading southward toward Chattanooga. Experiencing his first taste of the lonely life of a hobo, he soon drifted off to sleep.

While climbing a steep grade in Athens, the train slowed to a crawl, and Will jumped from the freight car. Making his way through a dense cornfield in the darkness of the night, he found a barn where he spent the night in the hay loft.

In Athens, he re-established his life style of sleeping in barns and stair wells. He was 12 years old now and took pride in doing a man's work by using his artistic talent by painting signs for the local merchants; although, there were times when he barely made enough money to eat. One day, when painting a sign on a store window in downtown Athens, he noticed an old, shabbily dressed street evangelist on the corner, preaching. He stopped his work and began to listen to the minister. Although the street congregation was comprised of only three or four curiosity-seekers, his message somehow warmed Will's heart.

After finishing his sermon, the preacher prayed, closed his Bible and slowly walked away without collecting an offering. Will had seen street preachers before in Springwater, but they always took a collection of money after their sermons. Because he was so touched by the unassuming manner of this man of the cloth, Will overtook him and gave the man his only coin, a dime.

Coincidentally, when he climbed into his usual hay loft that night, he discovered that the old preacher had chosen the same barn for his night's lodging. The old minister recognized Will and talked to him for much of the remainder of the evening. That night, Will experienced a spiritual conversion before he finally fell asleep. When he awoke the next morning, the old preacher was gone, and Will never again saw him.

After his religious experience, Will thought about the grocer that he had clubbed in the head in Springwater. He sincerely hoped that the man hadn't died; however, he felt that it would be fitting if his head bore a permanent scar, just as those inflicted on his own back.

His stay in Athens was brief, for he soon grew weary of the lonely, isolated life as a homeless boy of the streets. Suddenly, seized by wanderlust, but with no pre-determined destination, he boarded a freight train.

For the next two years, he roamed the country. From the flat country of Indiana and Ohio, through the coal mining mountains of West Virginia, through Tennessee and Alabama, he was always moving. The endless miles of lonely steel rails, the acrid odor of train smoke, and the countless small towns through which he passed, blended in his memory to a single montage of hardship, loneliness, and isolation.

In the twilight of an autumn evening, Will walked a lonely stretch of railroad near Anniston, Alabama. Looking ahead, behind the silhouetted leafy trees, he saw a glimmering fire. As he walked toward the illuminated, cozy glade in the woods, he realized that it was a hobo jungle. The tantalizing smell of stew pervaded the air. As he strode into the campsite, he noticed two shabbily dressed men sprawled on the ground. Eyeing them more closely, he recognized one of them: It was his brother John. The other man, who had the appearance of an albino, was introduced as 'Whitey'.

Will was immediately exhilarated. The brothers excitedly swapped stories for hours while John and his traveling companion took turns in sharing a bottle of whiskey. As the men consumed the stew, he listened to the conversation of John and his cohort. From Whitey's comments, Will decided that he was an unsavory character who, with his dominating nature, might lead John astray.

Late in the night after Whitey had fallen asleep, Will whispered, "John, why don't you dump that guy and trail with me? He'll get you into trouble...He's a bad influence on you."

"Will, don't preach to me," said John, who remained mostly silent until the brothers fell asleep. When Will awoke the next morning, John and his companion were gone. Sick at heart and lonelier than ever, he ruefully ambled down the desolate stretch of railroad. It was still early dawn when he heard the mournful whistle of a distant freight train. As the train came by him, it slowed its speed at a steep grade, and he jumped into a box car and headed for Tennessee.

Endless wandering over the thousands of miles of steel rail and countless stops at hobo jungles became his lifestyle for several months. He met his brother one other time in a small Ohio town; however, in the darkness of the winter night, John again abandoned him.

In his isolation, he yearned for companionship; however, the life of a vagrant was a lonely existence. Sometimes, in hobo jungles along the lonely miles of track, he made casual friendships, but they were fleeting because relationships between wandering people are usually temporary.

On a street corner in a small town in northern Alabama, he joined forces with a beggar, an old man who instantly developed a fondness for him. Will's pleasant personality and quick wit eased the gloomy way of life to which the beggar had been accustomed. During the few days they traveled together, Will lived much more luxuriously than usual, for the elderly bum collected rather generous daily sums of money through begging. In comparison, Will's contribution through his sign painting was meager. Sign painting was hard, honest work, which also contrasted with the beggar's lifestyle, for when Will was searching for more sign business, the old beggar was "panhandling". The drifter's favorite and most prosperous method of mooching was done when sitting on the sidewalk with a tin cup and wooden crutch at his side. To the citizens of each town, he was amazingly convincing about having a lame leg.

The partnership between the two men, however, was brief. After enduring Will's repeated lectures about his cursing and the thievery he employed in panhandling, the old beggar ultimately abandoned him.

Will's devout morality stood in sharp contrast to the unsavory character of most vagrants; consequently, their alienation from him made him feel even more isolated. Finally, by choice, he became a loner. Because of the past rejections he had endured, he neither trusted nor sought friendship with anyone.

His infatuation with wandering grew more intense; not because he enjoyed the life of being a vagabond, but rather, the opposite. He possessed a burning desire to be successful—if possible, as an artist. He wanted to find a place where he could ultimately put down roots.

For three more years he traversed the southern states. Now, at eighteen, he considered himself a man. In his travels, he had developed his artistic skills by painting signs in the numerous southern towns through which his journeys took him.

He found a home, of sorts, when he joined a carnival in Montgomery, Alabama. He went to work for *Howard Amusement Company*, a small side show that traveled throughout the Southeast. This opportunity was a God-send for Will because in addition to painting their necessary signs, he was able to improve his talents in pictorial painting. His large renditions of the Two-Headed Man, the Sword-Swallower, the Fire-Eater, and other illustrations of the carnival employees brought praise from the carnival owner.

Carnival workers, generally, are unscrupulous and notorious for cheating the public; however, in order to keep harmony in their small society, they adhered to a strict, unspoken code of honor in their dealings with each other. Consequently, they respected the moral code of Will. Although he learned from them how to juggle and walk the high-wire, he restricted his activities in the carnival to painting.

He traveled with the carnival for three years. His free room and board while employed by the show enabled him to save most of the money he had earned. When he was 21 years old, he left the carnival and established a sign shop in Knoxville where he began to prosper. No longer a drifter, he became less withdrawn and became involved in civic affairs. He began to have relationships with young women; he dreamed of settling down with the right woman and yearned to establish a home with children of his own. He particularly wanted a son.

After living in Knoxville for several months, he became engaged to a local girl named Kate Corrigan. Kate was a beautiful girl from a prosperous family. Her parents liked Will and saw in him an artistic and ambitious nature. Although he dated Kate for months, the couple had never set a wedding date.

Will's brother, John, was now living in Chattanooga, and Will often traveled there to visit. It was in Chattanooga that he first saw Sarah; and on more than one occasion, in their passing, they had glanced at each other. Each remembered the other's face, and the memory of their eyes connecting remained in their thoughts for several years.

One day in June, Will once again left Knoxville on a passenger train to Chattanooga to visit his brother, John. He was determined on this trip to not only see Sarah, but to also finally speak to her. Will and Sarah bonded almost immediately.

Although lacking in the physical attractiveness of Kate Corrigan, Sarah had an inner beauty and sensitivity that captivated him. Her understanding, gentle nature gave him a sense of belonging that he had never before experienced. Throughout his life, Will had felt an incompleteness in himself. With Sarah, he now experienced a feeling of wholeness. The void in him created by a lifetime of rejection was now filled by Sarah's acceptance of him.

Realizing that Sarah had all the qualities that he admired in a woman, Will broke off his engagement to Kate and began to concentrate on a future with Sarah.

In contrast to Will's life, Sarah came from a family with a strong bond. Although not affluent, her ancestry was rich in the tradition of teaching with an expansive knowledge of literature and music. Sarah loved to play classical music on the piano. Having one year of college, she wanted to be a school teacher, as was her father, Amos Thatcher. But, as a result of her father's meager wages from teaching, she was forced to drop out of school in order to help support her family. Through her hard work at the hosiery mill, Sarah helped to send three younger sisters and one younger brother through college.

Although Will quickly fell in love with Sarah, he knew that he was not ready for marriage. He felt a responsibility to "make something of himself" before being considered worthy of taking a bride and starting a family.

Again, he moved about over the country, hoping to discover or create a better opportunity for himself, and for a future family. During this time, World War I began and he was drafted into the U.S. Army; however, because of his sickly physical condition, he was deferred from fighting on the front lines in Europe. Unfortunately, after the war, he was assigned to an even more hazardous duty. During a global epidemic of the "Spanish Flu," it became his responsibility to work in the hospitals where thousands of soldiers were dying of the disease. Each day, he would remove hundreds of dead bodies from their hospital beds, depositing the rigid corpses in shoulder-high stacks, like cords of firewood. He performed this gruesome task for weeks; for after the war, 20 million people died during the flu epidemic—more than the number of soldiers lost in battle.

After being discharged from the army, Will came back to Knoxville where he was employed as a billboard artist in a sign shop. Although nearly ten years had passed since he last saw Sarah, she had rarely left his mind. Since so much time had elapsed, he feared that it might be presumptuous to assume that she still felt the same way about him. Now thirty years old and realizing that he would never earn a fortune, he left for Chattanooga once again—this time to ask for Sarah's hand in marriage.

She had waited for him.

*   *   *

May 1, 1920, was a beautiful, sunny day in Tyler City, Tennessee. It was the day that Will Beauvais was to wed Sarah Thatcher, his sweetheart of ten years.

Will drove to the house of Sarah's mother, Rachael, where they were to be married. Parking his Model T Ford at the curb, he stepped out of the car, accompanied by his brother, John, who was to be Best Man in the wedding. Will and Sarah had considered a church wedding, but they yielded to Rachael's wishes, taking their vows in the mother's home. Upon entering the house, Will and John were quickly ushered into a bedroom by Sarah's brother, Fred; for it was considered bad luck for the groom to see the bride in her wedding gown. However, Sarah's attire was only a simple, white dress.

Will and John, as well as the other male attendees wore dark suits, while the women were dressed in modest, ankle-length dresses, most of them light in color.

Since Sarah desired a simple wedding, only a few people attended the ceremony. The guests included Sarah's immediate family: Her mother and father, her three sisters, and her brother. An assortment of aunts, uncles, cousins, and a few friends completed the Thatcher assembly. John Beauvais, the Best Man, was the only guest invited by Will.

As the moment for the ceremony neared, the assemblage of witnesses claimed their places in chairs that the Methodist Church had provided. They sat rigidly stiff, looking awkward in their formality as they displayed an effort to show proper respect for the hallowed occasion.

When everyone was seated, an overweight, middle-aged woman began to sing,"Oh, Promise Me" in a highly-pitched operatic style, a mode of singing particularly despised by Will's brother, John. Upon hearing the first, ear-piercing note, he rolled his eyes, winced, and quietly cursed.

The female family members reverently listened, teary-eyed, their faces displaying a winsome smile as the song ended; however, Rachael's face revealed a grim expression, for although she liked Will, she didn't really approve of his marriage to her daughter. She disliked his past wandering ways that were vastly different from Sarah's steadfast nature. Sarah's father saw potential in Will, and because of his respect and admiration for Mr. Thatcher, he graciously accepted that as a compliment.

As the couple finally stood before the elderly Methodist pastor, Sarah lovingly smiled at Will, admiring his handsomeness in his navy blue suit. His blue eyes, brown hair, and pale complexion stood out in sharp contrast to Sarah's appearance. She wore her black hair at shoulder-length, and her snow white dress gave her brown eyes and olive complexion an even darker appearance by contrast.

On that beautiful summer day, Will Beauvais and Sarah Thatcher were joined in holy matrimony. Then, on February 14, 1921, Sarah bore her first child, a son, who was named after Will's father, Robert. They called their son "Rob".

Will cherished Sarah's gentle qualities that now enhanced their union. Her meek and nurturing disposition tempered the harshness and loneliness in him. She supplied the attributes that he found lacking in himself. The similarity of their moral convictions and values was the glue that bonded them together and balanced their complementary personalities.

In his youth, his passion for painting gave him his will to survive. Now, he had Sarah. It was she who directed that passion to make their life together plentiful.

Creativity is...seeing something that doesn't exist already. You need to find out how you can bring it into being and that way be a playmate with God. **Michele Shea**

Chapter 10

In the mid-fifties, Tyler City, Tennessee had a population of around 3,000. Essentially a farming town, it was nestled in the floor of the Tennessee Valley between the peaks and foothills of the Smoky and Cumberland Mountain ranges. Situated between Knoxville and Chattanooga, it was linked to these larger cities by Highway 11, which served as the main street of Tyler City as well as spanning half the country in providing the main route that connected New York to New Orleans.

Shipping and travel to distant destinations was still mostly by train; accordingly, the tracks of Southern Railway cut a path through the eastern edge of town, connecting Tyler City with other small towns in the valley. The steam-driven locomotives pulled a mile-long chain of passenger cars. From Tyler City travelers caught the "41" northward toward Knoxville and Roanoke, or rode the "42" to Chattanooga and other points to the south.

Located 25 miles southwest of Knoxville and hugging the north bank of the Tennessee River, Tyler City was the typical small southern town. Surrounded by rolling hills of diminishing forests and a patchwork of fertile, river-bottom land, the river stretched south to Chattanooga and beyond.

Typical of its neighboring towns and villages that sprinkled the valley, the local economy depended on revenue from farming and small businesses that offered little in the way of products and services. For more elaborate purchases, it was necessary for the potential customer to drive into Knoxville.

All of the small towns in the area shared common characteristics in their commercial activities, habits and appearance: On the main street, which consisted of only a few blocks, small businesses were stacked side-by-side like a row of dominoes, crammed into one large complex spanning the entire city block; a downtown movie theatre, where on Saturdays for 15 cents, children could enjoy double-feature westerns, a comedy and a cartoon; a couple of drug stores, each with an overhead fan and a soda fountain, a poolroom, a dry-goods business, two banks, two or three grocery businesses, small schools and churches, and a five and dime store. As the crime rate was minimal, most of the townspeople left the doors of their houses unlocked at night.

Since the introduction of the automobile more than 50 years earlier, garages and mechanics had replaced blacksmith shops. But the evolution had been gradual, because small-town southern people were usually slow in adjusting to change; for until the early forties, many farmers continued to deliver their produce to market in horse-drawn wagons.

As cars became more numerous, the era of drive-in movies and restaurants became knitted into the fabric of the southern small towns. Rock and Roll music replaced the "big band" sound of the Forties. The medium of radio featuring programs such as "Amos and Andy" and the western adventures of "The Lone Ranger" yielded to the modern miracle of television, which replaced the outmoded entertainment with actual moving images on the TV screen. More sophisticated programs featuring entertainers such as Jackie Gleason, Dick Van Dyke, Lucille Ball in "I Love Lucy" and James Arness of "Gunsmoke" gradually took the place of radio as the medium of family entertainment.

The horse and buggy era, although slow in its departure, had gradually faded away in the South.

In spite of the advanced mobility brought on by the increased number of automobiles, Tyler City continued to maintain its casual, slow-moving character. Generations of its residents had lived their entire lives and were buried in the isolated environment of the indolent southern town. Since, other than the local lock and key factory and a hosiery mill, the town had no industry to speak of, Tyler City had experienced little change in the past 25 years.

It was in this unpretentious, slow-paced community that Will Beauvais had put down his roots. Because of the city's simplicity and innocence, it was the place that Will and Sarah had chosen to rear their five sons.

After the Great Depression, Will established a relatively profitable sign business in Tyler City. *Beauvais Signs* was the typical small-town sign shop, serving Tyler City and the surrounding area by supplying every type of sign: Wall signs, murals, window signs, truck lettering, show-cards, banners, painted billboards, gold leaf lettering, and even neon signs, although Will found it necessary to order the neon tubing from a Knoxville shop that specialized in electric signs. By owning the only sign shop in Tyler City, Will had a corner on the market and could have built a very prosperous business; however, there were three factors that stifled its growth: His firm belief in keeping prices low for the customer, the radical behavior of most of his sons, and the wandering ways of Rob and Dean; for Will could rarely depend on either of them to stay with the shop for very long.

Sign painting is an unusual craft. It has a strong reliance on mechanics as well as a close kinship to art. Although every given style of lettering requires a prescribed formula in the forming of its characters, each craftsman, when hand-lettering a sign invariably leaves small imperfections of character in his lettering; thus, the hand-lettering of every sign painter reveals his distinct style in which he unintentionally leaves his indelible signature on the sign. A brief comparison of his sons' lettering told Will who the artist was.

In the craft of sign painting, Dean and Rob were the most talented of the sons, both having started working in the trade in their early teens. Although lacking in natural talent, Elwood had gradually become a good craftsman, but his style of lettering reflected a mechanical stiffness of characters, unlike the fluent, artistic lettering rendered by Rob and Dean. Alvin was not as talented in the visual arts; but in order to please his father, he doggedly kept trying to master the craft, but to little avail. Although his lettering satisfied the customer, it never reached the level of perfection to please his father. The superior talents of Rob and Dean were not unnoticed by Will, who was never reluctant to point our their matchless skill even in the presence of the other sons; for Will believed that the lack of excellence shown in the efforts of Alvin was because he hadn't diligently applied himself to the task of learning. Anyone who was a Beauvais ought to be a good sign painter. To Will, if a thing was so, he was blunt in the telling of it; hurt feelings be damned! He was never a man to mince words. Clay, however, was a different story. The youngest son in the family, he was an enigma to Will; for he steered clear of ever trying to learn the craft. When attending classes in school, he often displayed artistic talent by drawing cartoons instead of studying, but he showed absolutely no interest in sign painting. Apparently, he realized the futility of trying to please his father; consequently, he adopted the attitude of "to hell with it."

Will envisioned a family business in which all of his sons were involved. An unspoken prerequisite to his sons' working for him was his expectation that they live under the roof of the Beauvais household; as a result, there were few times that all five sons worked simultaneously for *Beauvais Signs.*

To a large extent, Will Beauvais was a man living in the past, for in business matters, he was twenty years behind the times. A man of rigid fairness (or what he perceived to be fairness), he tried to conduct his business with impeccable honesty. Although he already charged too little for his sign work, he sometimes felt that he had over-charged. On such occasions, he would reimburse the customers, even when the client was pleased with the initial price.

Conversely, when buying supplies in Tyler City, he sometimes complained about the prices charged by the local merchants; as a result, the store manager often adjusted the price of the goods to whatever Will considered to be fair. Although they understood his ways and held Will in their highest regard, they were often sad to see him coming into their stores.

The townspeople knew of Will's strict moral code and respected him for it. He was a religious man—a devout Christian, but not in the conventional sense. He believed that to be a Christian was to follow a difficult, but simple path. Although most of his friends were church members, and since he also sometimes attended church, he respected their views about religion; however, he felt that many of them were blind followers of tradition, much like sheep. In his opinion, many were enslaved by religious dogma—doctrines and creeds that were created by man, not by God.

Will understood the thinking of such people because he recognized that they found a sense of identity and meaning in religion only through a strict adherence to ritual and following prescribed disciplines. He refused to follow those who blindly exercised an unthinking obedience to orthodoxy, because *being his own man* was the essence of his spirit; for the integrity of spirit and the courage to be an individual were the qualities that he so desperately yearned to instill in the character of his sons.

*   *   *

Will squinted his eyes as he looked westward, watching the hazy orange sun disappear beneath the distant horizon. In early May, 1955, Will and Sarah were relaxing in lawn chairs on the patio adjoining the front of the Beauvais dwelling. It was a warm, early evening as they idly rested in their seats, absorbed in conversation. Their twilight discussions had become a common ritual, a conference between them that usually concluded in an assessment of the family. Elwood and Dean, having finished their work for the day, had gone to practice their music.

"Sarah," Will began, "I'll have to say that I'm very pleased, and also a little surprised that Dean is behaving so well. He's been here for over six months now, and he appears to have quit drinking… He hasn't gotten into any fights, either, and I noticed that he is working out with weights again…I saw him exercising yesterday."

"Maybe Elwood is a good influence on him," Sarah suggested.

"Well, I'm glad you talked me into letting him stay," continued Will, smiling at Sarah.

She returned his smile. "Will, I don't believe anybody ever talked you into anything in your life. You wanted him to stay, the same as I did. You just wanted to hear me say it."

Will responded, "I'm beginning to trust him a little bit, but I'm worried about Elwood. He must have lost at least 75 pounds. I think he's losing weight too fast."

"I'm concerned about him, too," Sarah's face reflected a worried expression. "But we've badgered him all his life about his weight. I guess we ought to be proud of him."

"Yeah, but he's losing it too fast," complained Will.

They sat quietly for awhile, enjoying the tranquility of the balmy evening. The radiance of the sun was now completely hidden behind the distant hills in the west as the evening atmosphere took on a veiled softness in the approaching shadowy twilight. The pungent aroma of honeysuckle blossoms ushered in by a gentle spring breeze permeated the surrounding air. It was Will's favorite season of the year.

Will finally broke the silence, "Sarah, I've always been puzzled by something. Why do all the boys have to be so extreme in everything they do? We wanted Elwood to lose weight, that's true. But does he have to lose it all overnight? Also, I've always taught Rob and Dean to produce good work. But do they have to be perfectionists? They distort everything I teach them. When they were young, I taught them to defend themselves… that a Beauvais never let another person push him around. But does that mean that they have to beat up everybody who doesn't agree with them?"

Unlike his sons who were given to excesses and extreme behavior, Will was a man of moderation. Once, as a child, when he showed the symptoms of constipation, his step-mother had commanded him to alleviate the ailment by drinking a dose of Epsom Salt. Rather than quickly swallowing the medicine, Will was more moderate in his consumption of the liquid, choosing instead to swallow the dosage in a series of small sips, each of which was followed by a bite of bread as a chaser, of sorts.

Even when swimming, he invariably chose to enter the pool gradually, rather than suddenly plunging into the water. And when warned by the family doctor that cigarette smoking was hazardous to his health, he stopped inhaling the smoke, and reduced his "puffing" consumption to four cigarettes a day. He always addressed the solution of difficult problems in a series of small increments. A creature of habit, he was rigidly dedicated to keeping his body trim and healthy, strictly adhering to a daily routine of rigorous exercise. Although he was a man of remarkable will power and tenacity, he had a single trait that contradicted his usual self-control: He had virtually no control of his temper.

Considering Will's remark regarding the harsh behavior of Rob and Dean, Sarah added, "You seem to only see the aggressive side of our boys, Will. They also have a tender, gentle side, too."

"I'll agree that Elwood has a tender side... and maybe Alvin. But I don't see much gentleness in Rob and Dean. Maybe not in Clay, either," Will replied.

"They show that tender side to me," continued Sarah, "Maybe they don't show it to you because they're afraid you'll see it as unmanly, or weak."

For a while, he pondered what Sarah had said. Trying to put his exact feelings into words, Will made an attempt to explain to her his stern attitude in regard to their sons.

"Sarah, I don't see tenderness as being unmanly. You know, Elwood is gentle, and he's a real man. But, you're right about one thing. I certainly don't want any of our sons to be weak. It's a tough, cruel world. If a man is weak and doesn't develop a hard crust on him, he's not going to make it. All of our sons have it pretty soft compared to the way things were for me when I was young. Do you realize how my brother, John and I celebrated Christmas? We got no presents; we expressed our joy by going outside at dawn and running around the house shouting, 'Whoopee'! While other boys were shooting fireworks, we tried to imitate the bang by slapping two boards together. Strangely enough, that was one of my best Christmases, because after that year I had many homeless holidays. And later in our lives... for you and me... when we had to struggle through the Great Depression."

Will's tenacity and determination were the by-products of his homeless existence as a youth. His iron will had been forged in the consuming fire of the Great Depression. After Will and Sarah were married in 1920, the country entered into an era of prosperity, a decade called *The Roaring Twenties*. For the first time in his life, Will prospered. He built a modest house, purchased a brand new family automobile, and accumulated a savings account at the bank. His business was flourishing, and his spare time was filled with his creative endeavors.

However, in October, 1929, with the crash of the stock market and a series of financial failures in the country, Will's house, which was financed by the bank, was worth only a fraction of the balance he owed on the building. Forced to sell the property at a huge loss, Will spent his savings account to pay off the remaining mortgage. Will and Sarah lost everything.

Many families were forced to depend on the local relief program for food; however, Will refused to accept a handout. One day, when two men delivered a large basket of food to the Beauvais front porch, Will politely, but firmly turned the men away. Throughout the Depression, because of his fierce pride, he never accepted any donated groceries.

Since the sign business had diminished, Will's creative skills rescued his family from starvation. Inside the window of a local furniture store, in plain view of the public, he set up a studio. As people curiously watched through the store window, Will rendered landscapes and still life paintings which he sold for a dollar each. Since he could finish the average painting in less than two hours, he sometimes made $5 or $6 dollars each day, which was an impressive amount of money during the Depression.

In 1935, with very little money, Will made a down-payment on a small, ramshackle house located on a five acre parcel of land, two miles north of Tyler City. In the ensuing years, Will and his sons enlarged and improved the house and built the sign shop, thus establishing the Beauvais sign business.

Knowing of Will's wretched childhood, and his struggles during the Great Depression, Sarah understood his rigid ways. She also had a great admiration for his fortitude and resilient character. She was proud to be married to this man of endurance.

Sarah looked lovingly at him. "Those years during the Depression weren't all bad, were they, Will? Sometimes I think those hard times brought us closer. They were also some of your most creative times…You were always working on one of your inventions."

Since his youth, Will had consistently been a dreamer. He was always striving to paint his masterpiece or to invent something of common use. He was an innovator, invariably in search of a better method of accomplishing everyday tasks.

One of his innovations was his installation of a bathroom in the Beauvais home. Since the family lived in the country, their only water supply was the collection of water on the roof, which ran from gutters into a huge underground storage tank. This cistern supplied the water used for drinking, as well as bathing, a chore that required filling a large metal tub with water. To offer the family the modern convenience of a shower bath, Will installed a showerhead in the bathroom. He then directed the rain water to a separate metal barrel that sat on the roof above the bathroom. The stored water from this large metal barrel was then heated by the sun, and with a turn of a valve on the shower head, the family could enjoy a warm shower.

Will's inventions did not stop there. When driving his car, his mind flowed with possibilities that could make travel safer. To offer better night vision on the road, he marked the edges and centerline with small reflectors, installing them on Highway 11 in front of the shop. He also designed and constructed the first turn-signal on an automobile. To avoid the awkwardness of extending his left arm out of a lowered car window, Will made a mechanical, crude contraption that worked by pulling a small cable by the dash panel. The cable, threaded through small screw-eyes, extended to the back of the vehicle—raising reflective cut-out arrows which pointed either left or right, according to which cable was pulled.

After installing this apparatus on his vehicle, his enthusiasm motivated him to install a similar device that raised a small sign above the back bumper, with the message, "You're Too Close," to be read by tail-gating drivers. However, Rob and Dean secretly employed their own creative skills in this invention. In order to pull a prank on their father, they substituted "You're Too Close" with a message of their own. It was several weeks before Will realized that the message given to annoying tailgaters actually read, "Let the Good Times Roll!"

Will never patented any of these inventions, but his creative ideas made life easier, and sometimes more entertaining, for the Beauvais family.

*　　　　*　　　　*

"That reminds me, Sarah. Remember some of the boys' inventions?

Elwood and Dean built a pretty good car. They were so excited about entering it in the *Soap Box Derby*."

"Yes, and after building it, they forgot all about the *Soap Box Derby*. They got all caught up in designing and building a glider." Sarah smiled with the memory.

Will laughed. "I think Dean got it off the ground a little bit when he ran down that big hill behind the property. But when Elwood tried it, his maiden flight turned into a colossal flop. He was only 12 years old, but after all, he weighed about 250 pounds at the time."

"They also built a boat that could be propelled by turning a crank," continued Sarah. "But they never put it in the water... I wonder why?"

"Sometimes the satisfaction comes from the development of the idea...the creation of the product, not the use of it. Maybe that's why I never got any of my inventions patented." replied Will.

"What about the secret language the boys invented?" Sarah smiled at the memory. "Nobody understood it but them."

Will returned her smile. "Maybe that's the only way they could cuss and get away with it."

It was now almost completely dark. They sat silently, listening to the incessant chirping of the night insects. Blowing softly from the south-west, a gentle spring breeze caressed them, carrying the fresh scent of springtime, cooling the air. Enjoying his conversation with Sarah on this pleasant spring evening, Will felt a trace of optimism about his sons.

"You know, Sarah, maybe things are looking up! Dean seems to have changed for the better, and Elwood is as steady as a rock. If Rob would straighten out his life, we could all have a real family again. Just look what a good sign shop we could have with all the boys working together. Even Clay and Alvin might develop into sign painters with the help of Rob and Dean. I'm giving all of them a piece of land right behind the shop, so they can build a house."

Sarah was hesitant in her answer. "Will, I'm afraid that idea will never work."

"Why not? If I give them a piece of property, it will give them a good start in life. Nobody ever gave me anything!"

Sarah patiently eyed Will. "When a mother bird feels that her babies are mature enough to fly, she pushes them out of the nest so they can try their wings. If you love them, Will, you have to let them go."

"What do you mean if I love them? Of course I do! I love them, and you, more than anyone on earth. It's because I love them that I want them to stay near to us, to maintain the family... the family that I never had." said Will, with frustration.

"You can't smother them, Will, the true test of love is to have the courage to let them go," replied Sarah. "Why do you think Rob and Dean have wandered all over the country? They're just a carbon copy of you when you were their age. They're searching for something, just as you were."

"But I was searching for a home," reasoned Will, "They already have a home, right here."

"Will, we're getting old, but the boys—they've got most of their lives ahead of them. They may want to make their homes someplace else. Then we can go and visit them in their homes. It would still be home to us, too, as long as our sons live there."

Will's face reflected his mood of sadness. "That may be true, I guess. Most of them might reject me, or reject my help. But not Elwood. I can count on him, for sure!"

"What are you going to do if Elwood finds a girl and gets married? He may not want to live here and paint signs for the rest of his life."

Will sighed, "Well, I was about to get into a pretty good mood until our conversation took a sudden morbid turn."

"Will, I don't mean to dishearten you, but some of the boys are torn between pleasing you and doing something else that gives them a life of their own. I know that Dean wants to be a fine artist, and Elwood wants a career in music. I wish all of our sons could've gone to college"

"Maybe they ought to be more realistic about life," suggested Will. "Most of life is just hard work. Anyway-in regards to college...our sons don't need it. It would be a waste of time for them, they already have a trade. Maybe they're just chasing a hopeless dream."

Sarah looked at Will and smiled, "If I'm not badly mistaken, it seems to me that you've been a dreamer all of your life! Maybe they're just a chip off the old block. Remember your dream of making living quarters on that old trailer chassis... And we were going to go to Florida every winter? It's rotting in that back field now, isn't it?" She smiled. "What ever happened to that dream?"

"Yes, Sarah, I may have been a dreamer, but I've had to sacrifice my dreams in order to survive when things got tough. As my dad always told me, 'when the going gets tough, the tough get going.'"

Sarah changed the subject. "I'm so glad that Dean is close to Elwood. I'm beginning to see some of Elwood's gentleness in him."

"Elwood wanted to help Dean," said Will, "Elwood has a generosity and a compassion for others who are hurting. I don't think Dean has those qualities."

Will and Sarah looked up as Elwood's truck pulled into the parking area. Elwood stepped out of the vehicle, limping toward them with a foolish sneer, in an imitation of Jim Burns. Walking up to his father, he deftly snatched a cigarette from Will's shirt pocket.

"How ya' doin', Cap'n?—Hi, Sairy."

They laughed and turned their heads toward the truck as Dean and another man were getting out of the vehicle. They watched curiously as Dean handed the stranger some money from his wallet. Then the man walked to the highway and extended his thumb.

Peering at his watch, Dean approached his parents and Elwood. He flashed a grin.

"Hi, Dad—Hi, Mom. Well, we beat curfew by a half hour."

"Dean, who was that man? And did you give him money?" asked Will, with a puzzled expression.

"Oh, I just gave him a couple of bucks. He's down and out. Elwood picked him up in Tyler City and gave him a ride. He said he was hungry."

"He'll probably just buy booze with the money, instead of food."

"Well, if I knew he was goin' to buy booze, I'd have given him five dollars instead of two." Dean replied, smiling.

"Why?" asked Will, in total bewilderment.

"Because a pint of whiskey costs more than a hamburger." He smiled at his father.

Dean knew that a man who was hurting for a drink was probably suffering more than a man who was in need of food.

The brothers walked to the front door. In unison they said, "Good night."

"Good night, boys," replied Sarah.

Will, still looking confused, removed his hat and scratched his head.

134

The most wasted day of all is that during which we have not laughed. Sevastian **R.N.Chamfort**

Chapter 11

Awakening with a start, Alvin Beauvais angrily reached to the table beside his bed and shut off the relentless reverberation of the alarm clock. It was 7:30 a.m., an unusually early hour for Al to begin his day. He awoke with a headache, the result of his consumption of a six-pack of beer from the night before.

In discouragement, he sat sullenly on the edge of his bed, dreading the prospect of working all day with his brother, Clay. He wondered how he had been foolish enough to become a partner with Clay in the house painting business.

Al's bad mood was a frame of mind that was not unusual for him on an early Monday morning. However, his moods were often transient; for he had a flighty temperament. He could quickly change his turbulent emotional state to one of affability.

In the Beauvais family, Al was an enigma. His usual personality was one of submissiveness, which stood out in sharp contrast to the aggressive nature of some of his other brothers. Alvin was content with blending into the background; as a result, his abilities and sensitivity were often unnoticed.

Because of his habit of daydreaming, he was inattentive to detail. This lapse in his alertness initiated many errors in his judgment; consequently, he was blamed with many bad circumstances, even those not of his making. He became the family scapegoat.

Since there was a sharp disparity between their temperaments, there existed a strong sibling rivalry between Al and Rob. He also had a personality clash with Clay, who had a fondness for ridiculing others.

Although Al found his brother's trait humorous, he became furious when Clay directed the derision toward him. Like Elwood, he had inherited most of his mother's characteristics, both physically and emotionally. His introverted, gentle nature was in direct opposition to the inherent aggressive nature of his father, a contrast that provoked a rebellious attitude toward his dad. When angry Al could be very unreasonable and belligerent.

Alvin enjoyed spending time alone. He was a loner who was one with nature. He had a deep yearning for his father's approval, which he felt that he never received. Like Elwood, Alvin was intellectually gifted, particularly in the area of literature; reading poetry and listening to classical music were a few of his favorite passions. However, because he displayed less interest in the visual arts, he was not as proficient in the craft of sign painting, which unfortunately, was the yardstick with which his father measured talent.

For most of his adult life, Al had seldom held a regular job; instead, he contracted small sign painting jobs or painted houses. Caring little about his appearance, he usually dressed in unstylish clothing. By nature, he was completely spontaneous; often abandoning his work to travel to the mountains in search of semi-precious stones, which was another one of his passions. He was a rebel at heart and shared his brothers' resentment of authority. A non-conformist, he was totally unconcerned about society's opinion of him; however, his independent lifestyle was costly, for it usually kept him and his wife, Amber, on the edge of poverty. Because of his emotional immaturity, he felt more comfortable with children than he did with adults.

Leaving Amber asleep in bed, Al grudgingly began his preparation to go to work. Without bothering to shave, he rinsed his face and ran a comb through his full head of hair. After putting on yesterday's clothes, he stuffed a stale doughnut into his mouth and drank a cup of coffee. Noticing the unusual chill in the spring air, he slipped into a light, paint-smudged jacket. Leaving his rented apartment, he drove away in his blue Chevrolet pickup truck.

Arriving at Clay's apartment, he pulled into the driveway and tooted the horn. Not wishing to get entangled in a useless conversation with Clay and his wife, Ellen, Al decided to wait in the truck for his brother. After a rather lengthy delay, Al again blew the horn, this time with several sustained honks; for patience was not one of his virtues. After another long wait, he again sounded a long blast of the horn, a continuous blare that lasted for several seconds.

As the peal of the horn subsided, Clay came out of his apartment with his face revealing a broad grin; for he derived pleasure from agitating Alvin.

"What's your hurry?" asked Clay, as he stepped into the truck cab. Al quickly drove away in the truck.

"I'd like to start workin' sometime before noon, if it's okay with you," Al replied, with sarcasm.

Clay laughed and asked, "Why are you wearing that jacket?"

"Because it's cold. Why does anyone wear a jacket?" asked Al, "Why are you not wearing a jacket?"

"Because it's May, not January," said Clay.

"Yeah, it's May, but it's also cold."

"But it'll be hot, before the day is over." Clay projected a derisive smile.

"Well, then I'll take the jacket off," countered Al, who was becoming more irritated.

"But it's warm inside the truck," reasoned Clay with a goading grin, "Why are you wearin' it inside the truck? Why don't you wait until you get outside to wear it?"

"Jesus!" yelled Al, angrily, "Will you please shut up about the damned jacket?"

Clay roared with laughter.

Suddenly, Al pulled the truck over to the curb and parked.

"Why are we stoppin'?" asked Clay. "I thought you were in a hurry to get to work."

"I am, but I'm also in a hurry to smoke." Reaching into his shirt pocket, Al pulled out a small cloth bag of *Buffalo* smoking tobacco. Extracting a cigarette paper from a small packet attached to the side of the bag, he proceeded to roll a homemade cigarette. After licking the edge of the paper to seal it, he lit the makeshift cigarette.

"Why do you smoke that cheap junk?" asked Clay, derisively.

"Because I like this cheap junk!"

"But why don't you smoke real cigarettes?"

"This is a real cigarette—see the smoke coming out of the end of it?" asked Al, sarcastically, as he pulled the truck back onto the road.

"Why don't you follow my example? I quit smokin'." Clay boasted, with a grin.

"I don't want to follow your example," replied Al, "I believe I'll keep smoking. Besides, you quit smoking, but you started chewing tobacco. What's the difference?"

"Al, you ought to quit that nasty habit," lectured Clay. "I'd hate to see the inside of your lungs."

"Well, I'd hate to see the inside of your mouth," said Al, who was becoming more agitated. "Look, I don't want to listen to your shit all day."

Clay again laughed.

"I've got to pull into that station and get some gas," said Al, "We're runnin' on empty."

Al pulled the truck into the *Esso* station by the gasoline pumps.

"Why don't you keep gasoline in your truck?" asked Clay. "Listen," Al cautioned. "Get off my ass, do you hear me? I don't feel good this morning!"

"It's those nasty old cigarettes that you smoke." Clay sneered.

"Okay. That's enough! I believe I'll just take the day off! I don't feel like workin' anyway. Not to mention, listening to your shit all day!" He inserted the key into the ignition of the truck.

Clay, realizing that he may have pushed Alvin too far, suddenly changed his attitude.

"Wait a minute, Al. I was just ribbin' you. Let's work… I need the money. Don't get pissed."

"Will you stay off my ass?" Al had completely lost his patience.

"Yeah… okay. It's just that sometimes I can't resist!" explained Clay, laughing.

A short, stocky service station attendant appeared at Al's truck window. "May I help you, sir?"

"How much is your regular gas?" asked Al.

"Thirty-one cents a gallon."

"Okay, put in two dollars worth of regular, and DON'T clean the windshield," ordered Al. He handed the attendant two dollars and rolled up the window.

Being exceptionally impatient with any kind of delay, Al was particularly irritated when he was forced to wait for someone to clean his windshield, regardless of its dirty condition.

The attendant obediently pumped the gasoline into the tank and replaced the gas cap. Then, since he apparently had forgotten Al's request, he pulled a small bottle of liquid window cleaner and a soiled rag from his pocket and walked to the front of the truck. Being very short in stature, it was necessary to hoist his feet off the ground in order to reach the windshield. He lay across the hood of the truck and began to clean the window. Nonchalantly, and with no warning, Al started the vehicle and drove away while the man's body was still lying across the hood. Finally, the attendant leaped backward, escaping his moving perch. Clay guffawed with laughter as he looked back and saw the man staggering down the street, trying to maintain his balance.

"Damn, Al, are you nuts?" asked Clay, still laughing.

"I told him, 'Don't clean the windshield'," explained Al. "He's the one who's nuts."

Concluding that Alvin was in a worse mood than he originally thought, Clay decided that it would be wise to restrain himself.

After several miles of silence, Clay spoke. "Al, do you see that old house on the corner, on your right? Stop there...I got us some cheap help for today. He'll work all day for a dollar an hour."

"Who is he?" asked Al, curiously. "We don't need any help, Clay."

"Oh yeah, we can use this guy. He can paint all the low stuff while you and I can use the ladders on the high work. Pull over and let's get him. He said he'd be ready to go."

"Tell me who he is," demanded Al.

"You'll see," Clay replied, as Al pulled the truck over to the curb and stopped.

"Just honk your horn. He'll come out." Clay continued.

Al gazed forlornly at the dilapidated house. Just looking at the run-down structure made him feel more depressed. The paint on the building was peeling and the yard was littered with trash.

Alvin sounded his horn, and soon a man came out of the house, limping toward them.

Al instantly recognized him as...Jim Burns.

"Ooooh, Hell!" moaned Al, "Are you out of your mind? You got Jim Burns to help us?"

Clay burst into laughter. "He's a pretty good house painter... Cheap, too!"

"Oh, dear God...Help me get through this day," Al groaned.

As Jim Burns limped toward the truck, Al said, "He's not sittin' in this truck cab. He'll have to ride in the back of the truck."

"Hell, you said yourself it's kinda chilly outside Al. He'll get cold. Maybe he could wear your jacket." suggested Clay.

"I wore this jacket because I wanted to wear it!" exclaimed Al. "Maybe a good cold wind will blow some of the odor off of him. Haven't you ever noticed how bad he smells? If he rode up front, I'd have to get the truck fumigated."

"Yeah, now that you mentioned it, he does smell kinda ripe." Clay again laughed.

"Ripe, Hell!" exclaimed Al, "You mean rotten!"

The brothers got out of the truck as Jim limped his way across the weedy yard, stepping clumsily around a pile of trash. He stopped directly in front of Clay and extended his grimy hand.

"Howdy do!" greeted Jim.

Clay winced as he grasped Jim's moist hand. After a very brief handshake, Clay withdrew his hand and vigorously dried his palm on the back of his pants.

"How's the Cap'n?" asked Jim, "Hain't seed him in a spell."

"He's okay," Clay replied. "Do you live here?"

"Hell no. I'm just visitin' my cousin that lives hyar. I just tol ye' to meet me hyar, cause it's handy fer ye' to pick me up. Shit, I could never afford a nice house like this-un." He was suffering from a head cold; consequently, his comments were punctuated with powerful sniffs. With each vigorous sniff, the sagging mucous disappeared into his hair-infested nostrils.

Jim was dressed in his customary garb of filthy overalls and worn-out brogan shoes. His usual grimy felt hat had been replaced by a dirty, red and white striped toboggan cap, which he had stretched to cover his ears. A lock of graying hair protruded from the front of the cap, covering most of his forehead. The neatly pressed tweed sport coat that he wore was completely out of character with his other attire. Clay concluded that Jim had probably found it on a coat rack somewhere and claimed it as his own.

"Nice jacket, Jim," complimented Al, as he moved a step further upwind from him.

"Yep… I like it. Figgered I'd need it since it's a little cool this mornin'." Jim grinned, exposing his yellow, decaying teeth.

"Jim, I'm glad you wore a coat because you're going to have to ride in the back. We don't have far to go," Clay explained.

"Hell, I don't mind, I like frash air," said Jim. He climbed into the back of Al's pickup truck, and the men drove toward the job site.

The house was a neat, well-kept, structure that hardly needed painting at all. Covered with weather-board siding, the two-story building rested in the center of a well-groomed yard with neatly-pruned shrubbery. A perfectly-aligned row of maple trees, all of the same size, flanked the front and both sides of the house. Considering the neat, orderly appearance of the property, it was obvious that the owners were fastidious people.

As Clay began to unload the scaffolding, Jim walked over to Al, who was opening a bucket of paint.

"Whar do ye' want me to start, pal?' asked Jim, as he closed his bad right eye and ogled Al with a one-eyed stare.

Al made an obvious gesture of stepping away from Jim's stench. "You don't have to start yet," answered Al, "Wait until we get set up, and I get the paint mixed."

"What did ye say? Ye' need to speak up, or else stand a little closer to me. I lost my hearing a few months ago."

Keeping his distance, Al yelled, "What happened to your hearing?"

"Dynamite!" he sneered.

Clay, showing interest in the direction that the conversation was taking, stopped working and walked closer.

"What happened to you with dynamite?" Al yelled.

"Well, it's like this, ye see. I got a contrac' to git rid of a houn'dog fer this guy over on East Side. He give me three dollars. Said the dog was killin' his chickens. Well, I don't own no gun, ye see. Could'a killed 'im with an axe, I guess. But I allus had a partic'lar likin' fer dynamite. Well, anyway, I tuck this houn' dog out in the woods and tied a stick of dynamite to his tail and lit it. I was lookin' forward to runnin' off about fitty yards an watchin' it blow 'im to hell. But that son-of-a-bitch follered me—musta liked me, I guess. I finally 'ad a climb a tree. When that dynamite went off, it blew dog guts all over me. Blast was sa' close, it done sumpin' to my hearin'. My ears been a ringin' ever since!" Jim's exhilarated cackle merged with laughter of both Al and Clay.

As Jim talked, his graying moustache became saturated with mucous, oozing from his nostrils. Exposing his saffron teeth in a repulsive smirk, he said,

"Watch this, fellers. See that daisy right thar?"

He placed his left forefinger over the left tip of his nose. From his right nostril, he propelled a volley of mucous. With amazing speed and uncanny accuracy, the slimy projectile struck the bloom of the daisy, dead-center. Then, using the sleeve of his sport coat, he wiped away the remaining slime from his nostrils.

"Bet you won't find many people who can do that!" he boasted, proudly.

"Who the hell would want to?" asked Al, with disgust. Clay laughed uproariously.

Finally, the men went to work. Al and Clay were on the scaffold, painting the siding on the second floor, with Jim working on the ground, brushing paint on the wall beneath them. Since the morning air had become warmer, Al had removed his jacket, tossing it carelessly in the yard.

As the brothers continued to work from the scaffold, Clay bit a large hunk from a plug of chewing tobacco, occasionally spitting as he worked. With an intense dislike of the habit, Al glared at Clay with loathing upon each expulsion of tobacco juice.

From the corner of his eyes, Clay took note of Al's disparaging stares. Rolling the quid around in his mouth, Clay suddenly discharged a large stream of ambier that landed on the ground, precariously close to Al's jacket.

Without a word, Al placed his paint and brush on the scaffold, climbed down the ladder, and moved his jacket about twenty feet further away.

Al then ascended the ladder and again started painting. Although Clay chuckled, neither of the brothers spoke. After working for awhile, Clay again issued a large volume of tobacco spit. A sudden gust of wind caught the substance, whipping it, end over end, carrying the russet blob within inches of his brother's coat.

Al again silently descended the ladder and retrieved his jacket. He was angry, and his penchant for exaggeration could prove it. This time he walked at least fifty yards to a neighbor's yard across the street where he neatly placed his coat on the lawn. Al fumed when he heard the sound of Clay's boisterous laughter.

While Al and Clay worked silently on the scaffold, Jim began to tire of painting. Setting his brush on the grass, he limped around the corner of the house, out of the brothers' sight. He stepped behind a large shrub and pulled a bottle of moonshine out of his coat pocket, then after a furtive glance in each direction, he tilted his head and swallowed an enormous drink from the half pint bottle.

Boredom overtook him. He regretted that he had agreed to work today, deciding that he would rather have gotten drunk. Filled with curiosity, he walked across the front yard and entered the adjoining garage. He began to prowl, looking for something that he might be able to take home.

In the corner of the garage, he noticed a ten gallon can. Curious in regard to the contents of the container, he stooped down and read the label— "Lacquer Thinner". He thumped his finger on the side of the can and noticed its hollow, empty sound. Baring his teeth in a gleeful smirk, he removed the lid from the top of the container and sniffed the fumes. Then, he rolled up an old newspaper and lit the end. Standing as far away from the can as possible, he stretched out his arm and lowered the flame to the opening in the top of the can.

An ear-splitting blast propelled Jim backward. The tremendous explosion rocked the house and echoed throughout the city block. People came out of neighboring houses to investigate the origin of whatever calamity had befallen them.

"What in the hell was that?" yelled Al, as he gripped the ladder.   "I don't know!" exclaimed Clay. When the detonation occurred, Clay's bucket of paint had spilled, oozing its contents down the wall of the house.

"Where's Jim?" asked Clay, suspecting his involvement.

Jim Burns limped around the corner of the house with an expansive grin on his face, just as the owner of the house emerged from the front door.

"How'd ye' like that little caper?" asked Jim.

"You damned fool!" shouted Al, in anger. Clay looked at Jim in amazement.

The home owner was a large, muscular, middle-aged man. His menacing demeanor bore testimony of his extreme anger.

"Did you cause that explosion?" he asked Jim, angrily.

"Yes sir, I shore did! Warn't she a beauty?"

Looking directly at Al, the man shouted, "Pack up your stuff and get the hell off my property! All three of you!"

After hurriedly loading their equipment on the truck, Al drove away in the vehicle. This time, however, Jim rode in the cab, lodged tightly between Al and Clay; for Al was too disheartened to protest the seating arrangement. He became totally obsessed with ridding himself of the company of Clay, and more importantly, Jim Burns. Holding his head out the open window for fresh air, Al turned the truck in the direction of home.

"We finished with that house sooner than I thought," remarked Clay. Al remained silent. Jim fished the half-pint bottle from his pocket and greedily gulped down another hefty drink of whiskey. Al turned and glared angrily at him.

"Don't drink that shit in my truck!" he stormed. "This is a dry county. We might all get in jail."

Jim responded with a cackling laugh, "Hell, I don't keer! I like jail. Shit, they feed better than a man can git at home!"

From his shirt pocket he withdrew a short cigar stub and clenched it between his stained teeth.

"Got a light?" Jim asked Clay.

"No, I don't smoke. Al might have a match."

Al suddenly pulled the truck into the driveway of the home of a known bootlegger. He parked the truck and lit a match for Jim's cigar. He then walked to the bootlegger's door and knocked.

"Damn!" said Jim, "Fer a while I thought he was peeved at me. And here he goes and lights my seegar fer me."

As Al drove away from the house, he reached across Jim's lap and handed Clay the bag containing a 7-Up and a fifth of vodka. Turning right at the next intersection, he drove slowly down an isolated country road. At the appropriate place, he turned left into a small lane. Because of the leafy overhanging limbs, the vehicle was almost completely hidden from the sight of anyone traveling the road.

"I felt like having a drink," explained Al.

Clay opened the vodka and took a lengthy drink, washing it down with a swallow of 7-Up.

"Aaah," he sighed, as he handed the liquor and chaser to Al.

Al took a drink and turned to Jim.

"Jim, do you want a drink of good liquor? If you'll wipe your nose, I'll give you one."

"Well, that's mighty white of ye'! But I like my moonshine better than that weak stuff. I'll jes drink my own. 'Course, when I run out of mine, I jes might take a swaller of your'n." Fetching the bottle of bootleg whiskey from this coat pocket, he proceeded to drain the remaining contents of the bottle.

Al began to feel the effect of the alcohol. The liquor had assuaged his anger and calmed his nerves. He began to feel mellow and was actually grateful that he was relieved of the responsibility of painting the house. He studied Jim's wrinkled face and suddenly felt a pang of pity for him.

"Look, Jim, I'm sorry I called you a fool. I had no cause to do that." He handed the bottle of vodka to him.

"Shit, I weren't offended! I am a fool," he said, with a raucous cackle. He wiped his nose on his coat sleeve, took a long drink from the bottle and spoke.

"That man that run us off from his place...I got a notion to dynamite his house. Ye know, I allus did have a fondness for dynamite. When I go to meet my Maker, that's how I'd like to go."

Clay laughed. "I got a feelin' that's how you'll go, Jim."

Al deposited the drunken Jim Burns at his cousin's house and proceeded to drive Clay to his apartment. It was now 5 p.m., and with the vodka bottle empty, it was time to go home.

"Where's your jacket?' asked Clay.

"Hell, I left it back in that yard. We got out of there so fast, I forgot it. After that explosion, I was afraid the police would arrest us."

"Why did you wear that jacket, anyway?"

"Because it was cold this mornin'." replied Al, with irritation.

"But this is springtime," added Clay.

"Yeah, it's springtime, but this mornin' it was also cold."

"But you wore it inside the truck, where it was warm," Clay smirked.

"Damn it, Clay, get off my ass!" Al replied angrily.

"And another thing, Al. Why do you smoke that cheap-ass tobacco?"

"Why do you chew that nasty wad of shit? That's the reason I lost my jacket." complained Al, angrily.

That day marked the demise of the *Beauvais Brothers' Paint Contracting* business. Their unlikely partnership had finally come to an end, going out with a bang and a whimper.

An eye for an eye makes the whole world blind.
Mahatma Gandhi

Chapter 12

On a stormy Saturday night in March, a relentless, drenching rain soaked Tyler City. Despite bad weather, a large crowd gathered inside the *Lazy Lagoon Lodge* where Elwood's band was performing. He had named the band *The Beauvais Brothers*. Elwood was the singer for the five piece combo, which was composed of saxophone, piano, bass violin, guitar, and drums. Dean had borrowed an electric guitar with an amplifier, which had really improved the sound of the band.

The club was built on the shore line of a deep cove on Fort Loudon Lake. Its patrons consisted mostly of people under 30 years of age, usually college students who frequented the place on Saturday nights. The repertoire of music was composed mainly of popular romantic ballads with an occasional rock-and-roll number.

Although the sale of liquor was illegal in Knox County, the *Lazy Lagoon*, being a private club, was allowed to serve liquor by the drink; however, the clientele of the upscale club had the reputation of being well-behaved.

The shallow platform where the band performed was nestled in the corner of the spacious room. The dance floor in the center was surrounded by an assortment of evenly-arranged tables. As customary in such establishments, in order to create a romantic atmosphere, the lighting was very dim.

In an attempt to give the place a modicum of class, the management required the musicians to wear suits and ties and to limit their consumption of alcohol. The club collected a $5 dollar cover charge that was used to pay each band member $20 dollars for an evening's performance which lasted from eight until midnight; however, Elwood, having organized the group, was paid $30 dollars. In addition to his singing, he sometimes played the saxophone. He had driven to the club alone since the car, which he had borrowed from his father, was filled with musical instruments. Dean had traveled to the place with his brother Clay, who wanted to see his brothers perform in the band.

During the band's intermission, couples danced to the music of the jukebox. A few couples scattered sparsely around the dance floor, danced to the romantic ballad, "Unforgettable," by Nat King Cole. The distant rumble of thunder intermingled with the soft music.

Elwood, Dean, and Clay sat together at the table near the dance floor, watching the dancing couples. Although Elwood and Dean refrained from drinking, Clay had consumed several beers, but appeared to be sober. As Dean peered across the dance floor to the opposite side of the room, he noticed an attractive female acquaintance waving to him.

"Excuse me, guys," he said to his brothers, "I want to talk to a lady friend."

Leaving his chair, he walked around the dance floor to the pretty woman's table. Her name was Virginia Christen. She and a female companion occupied two chairs at the table. They were apparently unescorted, since the other two chairs had been borrowed to accommodate other tables in the crowded club.

"Hi, Virginia," Dean cheerfully greeted them.

"Hi, Dean. I didn't know you played in a band." She displayed a friendly smile.

Dean had known Virginia for more than three years. For a short time he had dated one of her friends and had been on double-dates with her and her boyfriend. Shortly afterward, she was briefly married; however, the relationship was stormy, quickly ending in divorce.

Reared with two sisters by respected parents, she was a principled woman with a good reputation. A tall girl, pretty and dark-haired, her intelligence and amicable presence instantly attracted others to her. Dean concluded that she was non-judgmental since she was willing to openly associate with him. He liked Virginia and considered her a friend.

"Dean, this is Florence Adams. Florence, this is Dean Beauvais, a good friend of mine."

As she was introduced, Florence, a small blonde, took Dean's hand, and smiled.

"Hello, Dean. You sure play a mean guitar!"

"Thanks, I'm pleased to meet you."

147

"What are you doing these days, Dean?" asked Virginia, "I heard that you've been doing a lot of traveling."

Retrieving an empty chair from a neighboring table, Dean joined the ladies.

"I'm through travelin', Virginia. I'm workin' for my dad now, in the sign shop."

"Say, who is that good-looking guy who's doing the singing? He has a wonderful voice. He is really cute!" said Virginia.

Dean glanced across the room at Elwood, who was still seated at the table with Clay. Although he had never thought of his brother as 'cute', he suddenly realized that Elwood, dressed neatly in his suit and tie, was quite handsome. It was almost as if Dean had really seen his brother for the first time.

Since he had started his diet, Elwood had lost more than 100 pounds, weighing now about 220, an appropriate weight for a man of his height. Instantly, Dean conceived an idea.

"That 'cute' guy doin' the singin' is my brother, Elwood. How would you like to meet him?" asked Dean, smiling.

"Only if he's as nice as you are."

"He's a lot nicer than I am." replied Dean, "Look, let me bring him over here. Our break is almost over… I'll have to hurry."

Rejoining his brothers, Dean said to Elwood," Do you see that girl I was just talkin' to? She wants to meet you. Go over and speak to her. She said that you are 'cute'."

"I think you're cute, too, Elwood." Clay laughed, then drank another sip of beer.

"Which girl?" asked Elwood, "The brunette or the blonde?"

"The pretty one!" answered Dean.

"Then that would be the brunette." Elwood eyed Virginia.

"Well, I can see that you still have good eyes," Dean replied.

Looking toward Virginia's table, Clay made his assessment.

"Not bad," he complimented, "If you strike out, Elwood, let me take a shot at her."

"She's too old for you, Clay, and too nice, too," lectured Dean, "Besides, you're a married man, remember? Come on, Elwood, we've only got another five minutes before we have to start playin' again."

"What'll I say to her?"

"Say, 'Hello', for starters," Dean suggested. He turned and added, "Come on with me, Elwood."

When the brothers arrived at Virginia's table, the borrowed chair was gone, forcing the men to stand.

"Florence… Virginia, this is my brother, Elwood." said Dean, smiling at the women.

"Hi, Elwood," greeted Florence.

"Hello, Elwood," Virginia extended her hand, "You have a beautiful voice. It's so nice to meet a brother of Dean's. I guess he told you that we're good friends."

"Hello," replied Elwood. His face flushed as he began rocking back and forth.

"I would ask you to join us, but as you can see, there are no chairs." Virginia pointed out, apologetically.

"We've got to get back, Dean," interrupted Elwood, "the band is getting ready to start."

As the brothers returned to their band, Dean was slightly irritated at Elwood.

"You certainly weren't very talkative." he complained. Elwood looked embarrassed. "Well, at least you said 'hello,'" said Dean. "Look, during our next break, I think you ought to go back over there. She's interested in you…I wouldn't mislead you about something like this. Our next break is at 11:30, and after that, you don't have any more singin' to do. We close out the session doin' simple instrumentals. You can spend some time with her at her table."

"But what will I talk about? I don't even know her. I'm not very interesting, you know." Elwood said, with a downcast look.

"Elwood, just be yourself. Let her do most of the talkin'. She's a good conversationalist, and she's also a very sweet girl. This is a good chance for you to go out with somebody. By the way, did you fix it up with Dad so he won't lock us out of the house tonight? We won't get home 'til after 1:00. Maybe even later if you take Virginia home." Winking at Elwood, Dean smiled.

"Yeah, he understands that our engagement here is a special occasion. It's all okay. He'll be pleased when he sees that you're not drinking."

As the musical combo played, Elwood began crooning the romantic ballad, "Wanted", a song made popular by Perry Como. To his satisfaction, Dean noticed that during the entire song, Virginia kept her eyes glued to Elwood.

The crowd began to diminish at the 11:30 intermission. As Dean was returning to Clay's table, he urged Elwood to return to Virginia.

"Will you go over there with me?" asked Elwood.

"No—not this time. You have to muster up the courage to go over there by yourself. You don't have anything to worry about. Just be your-self. You've got a better personality that I have," said Dean.

"What about that other girl? What will I talk about with her?" asked Elwood.

"Hell, tell her to get lost." suggested Clay, "Send her over here to me. I know what to talk about." He was beginning to feel the effects of the beer.

With an understanding of Elwood's lack of confidence in regard to women, Dean felt compassion for his brother as he watched him walk to Virginia's table and take a seat in an empty chair across from her. He figured that Elwood would return in less than a minute, but to Dean's surprise, his brother remained at Virginia's table.

"Looks like he's makin' out," observed Clay, "but hell, if he takes her to a motel, he won't know what to do."

"He'd never get that girl to a motel, even if he was tryin'," said Dean. "But if he did, I believe he'd know what to do. There are some things you don't have to teach a man."

Near the end of the break, Elwood returned to the table with his brothers.

"What are you doin' back?" inquired Dean.

"She has to leave. Well, actually, she doesn't, but that girl she's with wants to leave, and since Virginia rode here with her, she'll have to leave, too."

"Man, what an opportunity!" exclaimed Dean. "Don't you see? That's an open invitation! Tell the other girl that you can take Virginia home."

"But I have to haul the instruments in my car. Virginia wouldn't have room to ride with me."

Dean remarked, "I'll get somebody to take the instruments. Go back and tell her you'll take her home."

As Elwood returned to Virginia and her friend, Dean, sitting lazily in his chair, glanced at his watch.

"I have to start playing again in about five minutes. We just have about 15 or 20 more minutes of makin' music, then we'll be going home. Better drink up, Clay."

Turning his head, Dean noticed a very pretty, dark-haired girl stand-ing close to him. Reaching out, she took Dean's hand. She was swaying her hips to the rhythm of the jukebox music.

"Dance with me," she cooed, with an elaborate smile. She appeared to be slightly inebriated. *Probably a college student*, thought Dean. She pulled him up out of his chair. Dean had discovered that girls were often attracted to band members. Earlier when he was playing with the band, he had noticed the girl looking intently at him from the floor as she danced.

"Oh hell," Clay griped. "It looks like I'll have to find a ride home."

"I'm sorry, Miss," apologized Dean. "I've got to get back to the band in about five minutes."

"Good, that will give you time for one dance." Peering directly into Dean's eyes, she smiled.

From the juke box come the nasal sound of Johnny Ray, singing, "Cry."

"Well, okay," conceded Dean, "one dance."

Taking the girl in his arms, he joined the scattered group of dancers on the floor.

When Dean rejoined the band for the final session, the combo livened up the place with "In The Mood." Looking across the dance floor as he played, he noticed Elwood escorting Virginia toward the front door. When Elwood turned to look at him, Dean stopped playing long enough to give him a "thumbs-up" gesture, as he smiled at his brother.

Many patrons had left the club daring the final half hour before closing time. Only a smattering of people occupied the dance floor. After the closing number, the musicians began to gather their instruments. As the lights increased their intensity, the clientele started to slowly move toward the exits.

Suddenly, seemingly out of nowhere, the pretty girl with whom Dean had been dancing ran to him.

"My name's Melinda," she purred. "What's your name?"

Before he had a chance to answer the girl, a large man approached Dean, savagely shoving him, sending him sprawling over a chair, onto the floor. Dean's initial reaction was one of surprise. Usually, Dean would have immediately retaliated; however, because he was a part of Elwood's band, he reconsidered.

"I'm gonna teach you to keep your slimy hands off of another guy's fiancée. I'll meet you outside, Romeo," roared the angry man. He was about 6'2", and weighed well over 200 pounds.

Clay quickly ran to Dean's side. "What's goin' on, Dean? What's up with that bastard? Aren't you goin' to clobber him? I mean, hell, he just shoved you down!"

"I'm meetin' him outside," explained Dean. He realized, since he would have to fight the man, that his musical debut at the *Lazy Lagoon* was also his grand finale.

Outside in the driving rain, as he faced the man, Dean realized that his adversary was accompanied by several friends, cheering him on. Clay stepped forward and spoke in a threatening voice.

"It's just between the two of them! Everybody else stay out of it—let them settle it."

A ring of bystanders surrounded the opponents. As the unabated downpour of rain soaked their clothing, flashes of lightning lit up the features of the combatants as they faced each other. Without hesitation, Dean quickly struck the man with several rapid punches that sent the antagonist reeling backward. Suddenly, Dean felt a stunning blow to the back of his head inflicted by one of the man's cohorts. In a split second, Clay entered the fray, whereupon several of the adversary's friends entered the brawl, one of which began beating Dean and Clay with a wooden club that he had found. As she witnessed the one-sided battle, the girl with whom Dean had danced, felt compassion for him. She pleaded with her boyfriend, who was wielding the club, to stop the assault. "Please don't hit him anymore—you're going to kill him!" Because of the girl's pity for him, Dean's fierce sense of pride created a deep feeling of shame within him.

With both brothers lying helplessly on the muddy ground, the fight was apparently over. Dean's tormentor tossed his club aside, and the group of attackers and their girlfriends got into the vehicles to drive away.

The storm's intensity increased as Dean and Clay unsteadily rose from the quagmire of mud. When Dean looked at the line of slow moving vehicles, he noticed that the car driven by the man who had wielded the club was momentarily delayed by the slowly departing vehicles in front of him.

Ashamed because he was pitied by the girl, Dean's temper again flared. Suddenly sprinting ahead until he was beside his adversary's car, he rapped on the driver's window. Failing to recognize Dean through the fogged glass, the driver unwisely lowered the window. Dean glared at him. "This fight's not over yet, you bastard!" With all of his remaining strength, he delivered a savage blow to the man's face, as Clay appeared by his brother's side.

Quickly, the entire group of assailants exited their cars in order to "finish the job" with the Beauvais brothers. Although Clay and Dean fought bravely, they faced overwhelming odds; at least seven or eight angry men surrounded them, pummeling each brother with savage blows. In a short time, in total exhaustion and nearly unconscious, Clay was lying helplessly on the rain-sodden lawn. Dean was moving about in a crouched position in an attempt to shield himself from the cruel kicks from two of his assailants while another man flailed him with a portion of a wooden fence post. The intervention of the managers of the club, who wielded guns, was the saving grace that kept Dean and Clay from serious injury, or possibly death.

During the melee, both Dean and Clay became covered with mud. Clay had lost both of his shoes in the deep sediment of mud, and his jacket and shirt were completely ripped from his back. Although both men were bleeding from their faces, their injuries were not severe. While Dean was driving home, he ruefully noticed the muddy interior of his recently-purchased used car.

"You should have clobbered that guy while inside the joint," commented Clay. "That way, we wouldn't' have gotten so muddy. Look what our muddy clothes have done to your car upholstery!"

"I'm not worried about the car, Clay. I'm worried about Elwood being humiliated because of me and another one of my fights. That place will probably never invite the band again."

"Hell, Dean, it wasn't your fault! You didn't even drink anything tonight. Anybody who calls himself a man would have hit that guy tonight."

"Yeah, sure, Clay. Try telling that to Dad. You're right, I didn't ask for it. But why is it always me? Do you think it's possible for a guy to be jinxed?"

Clay grinned at his brother, "That cute little girl sure took a shine to you."

"Yeah, well, if it hadn't been for that little bitch, we wouldn't have gone home lookin' like this!" Dean mumbled, through his swollen lips.

Suddenly, Clay began to laugh. Slapping Dean on the back, he said, "Don't worry about it so much, Dean. Hell, we had fun didn't we? You know, you've changed lately. You didn't used to give a damn when you got into a fight."

"Fightin' is a bunch of crap, Clay. I'm sick of it! And I'm sorry to see that you've started on the same path as I have. But I'll have to say, you saved my ass tonight. You know, you gave a pretty good account of yourself back there—you really showed some guts!"

"Hell, I'm confused," replied Clay. "Are you chewin' me out, or braggin' on me?"

"Both, I guess… Anyway, thanks."

Clay smiled. "Dean, I believe that you and I have more guts than we have brains."

From the west came the sound of rolling thunder as rapid flashes of lightning lit the dark sky. The unrelenting downpour became even more vicious, as Dean squinted his eyes to see the outlines of the road. The flailing windshield wipers worked furiously in a futile attempt to swab away the drenching rain.

As the brothers moved through the storm in silence, Dean looked over at Clay. A brilliant flash of lightning outlined his profile, revealing his bleeding nose and swollen lips. The strong odor of alcohol drifted from him, a scent more discernable to Dean since he had stopped drinking. Although he knew that Clay drank, tonight was the first time he had witnessed it.

Although Clay, since birth, had always had a terrible temper, he was well-behaved and obedient as a youngster. Moreover, he never smoked nor drank alcohol until he was about 20 years of age. As a young lad, he was aggressive when angry, but he had always abstained from fighting. In the past two years, however, his personality had undergone a radical change. Unlike his brother Al, who had a vacillating disposition, Clay's altered temperament seemed more permanent in nature. Also, peculiar to his brothers' distaste of war, and armed forces, Clay had a fondness for the military, an anomalous inclination that stood in direct contradiction to his contempt of authority figures.

As a youngster, without complaint, he had always adhered to his father's strict rules; however, he had recently rebelled against his father's rigid ways. Before his personality change, his behavior pattern was much like that of Elwood's; but now, in his manner, he was more like his brother Rob.

Finally, Clay broke the silence. "Dean, did you know that Ellen is pregnant?"

"Ellen—pregnant? No kiddin'? Congratulations! How far along?" asked Dean, excitedly.

"About three months, I think. She's startin' to show a little."

"Do Dad and Mom know?"

"No, I didn't tell them, yet. You know how Dad feels about me bein' broke. With not much money comin' in, I'm kinda hesitant to tell him. He'll think I can't support a kid."

"But he's gonna know in a month or two, just by lookin' at Ellen."

"Oh, I'll tell him before then, I just don't want to tell him right now," explained Clay. "By the way, Dad gave me a lot behind the shop. I'm goin' to build a house on it."

With a skeptical look, Dean said, "Good luck with that, Pal."

Dean pulled the car into the driveway at Clay's apartment. When he opened the car door, the interior light came on. As he turned, looking at Clay's appearance, he broke into a raucous laugh.

"Look at you! You ought to see yourself!"

Clay was a pitiful sight, indeed. His puffy lips oozed blood and his left eye was swollen shut. He had lost his shoes, jacket, and shirt, making his complete attire a pair of pants and a tie.

Dean followed Clay into the apartment where Ellen had been waiting up for him.

A petite lady, Ellen's slim face exuded a creamy complexion. Her green eyes complemented her auburn hair, which was arranged in a French twist on the back of her head. She was dressed in a terry-cloth robe, and her bare feet had the appearance those of a little girl's. She was a feisty woman and when not talking incessantly, she nervously popped her gum. Upon her first glance at the brothers, Ellen gasped.

"What in the world happened to you guys?"

"What do you mean?" asked Clay, nonchalantly, as if nothing had happened. As the brothers took a seat, with a casual expression, Clay smiled at her.

Ellen stared at Clay. "What happened Clay? Look at the way you're dressed!"

"What's the matter with the way I'm dressed? After all, I'm wearin' a tie, ain't I? A man can't dress any better than that!" Through his swollen lips, Clay painfully grinned.

*   *   *

It was after eleven when Dean awoke on Sunday morning. He looked across the Bull Pen to Elwood's bed, noticing that his brother had already gone. *He's probably in church with Mom and Dad*, thought Dean. Rising to a sitting position on the edge of his bed, he realized how badly his body ached. Gazing in the mirror, he noted his swollen lips and the gash in his right eyebrow.

He had not arrived home until after 3:00 a.m. the night before. After washing the blood from his face at Clay's apartment, he had driven home and surprisingly found that the front door was still unlocked. He had stealthily crept to his room, stashing his muddy clothes under his bed, grateful that Elwood was already at home, asleep. When he had arrived at home, his agitated state of mind prevented any apologetic explanation to Elwood; however, he would eventually have to explain his behavior to his brother.

Although he had little regard for religion, he had recently developed the habit of attending church with his parents and Elwood; however, when his brother awoke, having seen Dean's bruised and battered face, he must have decided that he was in no condition to attend worship services.

With no way to hide his swollen lips, Dean realized that it would be necessary to offer an explanation to Sarah and Elwood—and, even worse, to his father. Thinking of the unpleasant chore that faced him, he inwardly winced. He slipped into a tee-shirt and a pair of slacks and walked into the living room. To his surprise, his dad was sitting at his desk in the corner, reading the Sunday morning paper. Dean realized that his explanation would take place sooner that he had wished.

"Oh—Hi Dad," said Dean, trying to act casual. "I'm surprised you're not in church this mornin'."

Will looked up from his newspaper with a stern expression as he eyed Dean's swollen lips.

"And I'm surprised you're not in jail this morning," he replied, accusingly.

Dean curbed his anger, for in his opinion, he had committed no wrong. His remorseful attitude was suddenly replaced by one of justification. While he longed for his father's understanding, he decided that he would not grovel to him.

"Why should I be in jail?" asked Dean, calmly, suppressing his defiant attitude.

Will ignored the question. "Were you hurt badly? Is your hangover a bad one?"

"I don't have a hangover. I didn't drink anything last night. If you don't believe me, ask Elwood," retorted Dean, with a hint of defiance.

"Why should I ask Elwood? If you say that you didn't drink last night, then I believe you. I have never known you to lie to me."

"Well, then why should I be in jail? All I'm guilty of is defending myself. Didn't you teach your sons to do that? I remember when I was about five years old, you really knocked the heck out of a guy on our front porch."

Will remarked, "That's because he tried to force himself inside our front door after I warned him to stay out. His wife was scared of him, and she came running into our house, begging us to protect her from him. That was none of my business, of course, but it was my business to protect our home. I told him to stay out of here, but when he tried to force himself in, I hit him. A man has to protect his home; after all, a man's home is his castle."

"Well, you were defending your home, and I was defending myself. Ain't that kinda the same thing? I was minding my own business when this guy comes up, and—Oh, forget it...You wouldn't understand."

"Try me," challenged Will.

Will listened patiently as Dean explained the entire episode to him.

"So Clay got involved, too," said Will. "Was he hurt?"

"No, Dad, Clay wasn't hurt much. About like I was."

"Was Clay drinking?'

Dean's silence answered the question for Will. Dodging his father inquiry, he changed the subject.

"Dad, I can't figure it out. I must be jinxed. I used to think that my fights were caused by my drinkin'. But here I am, all beat up, and I haven't had a drink of alcohol in well over a year! Damn it!" Dean exclaimed with frustration.

Will overlooked the curse word; his son's anguish was more important.

"Dean—the guy you had the fight with—did you hit him first?"

"It wasn't a guy...It was several guys!"

"Well, did you throw the first punch?"

"Why, what does it matter?" asked Dean.

"Because it's a matter of honor, Dean. The guy that throws the first punch in the man that starts the fight...You don't hit a guy first if you want to keep your honor."

"Yeah, but that presents a problem, Dad," replied Dean, defiantly. "If I let the other guy hit me first, I might keep my honor, but I'd probably lose some of my teeth."

"Then you did hit him first," declared Will.

"Yes Dad, I did! When I see that the other guy is hell-bent on fighting, and challenges me, I don't stand around until he clobbers me! That first punch sometimes decides who wins the fight."

"Were you sure that the other man was intending to hit you?"

"Yes, Dad, I was."

"Well, I'm at least glad that you didn't let the guy push you around. I've taught you boys to defend yourselves, but I don't want you to ever start a fight."

Will's expression changed to one of compassion. "Dean, I'm not mad at you. If I had been placed in your situation, I would have done the same as you did. But I wouldn't have been in that situation in the first place."

"What did I do wrong? What was wrong with the situation that I put myself in? All I was doin' was playing music."

Will remained silent for a long while as he searched for the appropriate words.

"Dean, I don't believe that you start fights. I also believe that when you are challenged, you feel that you must fight, just to prove that you aren't afraid. But I want you to think of something. How come Elwood never gets into fights? Do you think it's because he backs down, or that he runs?"

"Of course not! Elwood is not afraid of anybody."

"Dean, it's the kind of lifestyle you've adopted…The kind of people you have always hung around with, the kind of places you go to. When it comes right down to the fight itself, I don't think you start it; but if you hang out with hogs, in a hog pen, you're going to get mud on you. Elwood avoids the circumstances that you seem to embrace."

"Yeah, but I was in the same circumstances as Elwood last night, the same place. But there I was…in a fight again." Dean lamented.

"First of all, I'm not too crazy about you and Elwood playing in places like you did last night. When you mix men and women, throw in alcohol and belly-rubbing dances…Well, that's begging for trouble. But even with that dangerous mixture, Elwood doesn't get into fights. He's been singing at places like that for a year, and he's never gotten into any trouble. But you, on the first night you play at a place like that, you get into a fight."

"It's true." replied Dean. "And it sounds crazy—even to me—I mean…I'm tired of wondering why I'm the one who always gets jumped, but last night….well, again…it just wasn't my fault. I mean…well, something is just wrong with this picture. It just happens too much, and I'm tired of it. Tired of hurting myself…and now I've hurt Elwood."

Will was direct. "For one thing, you start dancing with another man's girl. Elwood goes to places like that to sing, and that's what he does. He doesn't dance with other men's girls."

"But I didn't care anything about dancing with her…she approached me!" complained Dean.

"Then you've got to learn to walk away," said Will. "Look, Dean—I try to live a Christian life, but I haven't always been goody-two-shoes all my life. I've been around some. I was young once, too. Give your dad a little credit for having some acquired wisdom."

Will was always reluctant to talk about women to his sons; however, he felt that an example from his own personal experience would get Dean's attention and possibly have an impact on his future behavior.

"When I was about your age, working on the carnival in Alabama, sometimes in towns where we stopped, local girls were attracted to carnival guys. Well, you can bet that some local yokel who thought he owned the girl would be watching her like a hawk. It was a rule of the carnival that the workers were not to mess with the local girls, no matter how flirty they got with us. When they flirted with me, I ran in the opposite direction, because it meant trouble, every time."

Dean realized that his father was speaking to him man-to-man, rather than father-to-son; consequently, he felt that it was good sound advice, rather than a parental lecture.

"When you go to places to play music, then play music, and walk away from the girls. When you see a girl at a dancing joint, then it's almost certain that she went there with a guy. By the way, look back over the fights you've had. How many of them involved getting into a fight over a woman?"

Will studied Dean's face. "Am I making any sense to you?"

He considered what Will had said. Looking his father directly in the eye, he smiled. "Yeah, Dad. What you say makes a lot of sense."

"I'm not sore at you, Dean," said Will, as he rose from his chair. "And I want you to know that I'm proud of the way you have quit drinking."

"Thanks, Dad."

Without answering, Will folded his newspaper and picked up his felt hat from the top of his desk. After donning his hat and making his customary adjustment of the hat brim, he walked out the front door to his car and drove away.

Peering out the picture window, Dean watched Will's car disappear into the distance. For the first time, Dean began to recognize his father's wisdom and depth of understanding.

When Sarah and Elwood returned from church, Dean was waiting for them in the living room. Although he dreaded the confrontation, he wanted to give an explanation as quickly as possible and put the fighting incident behind him. When they entered the front door, it was apparent to Dean that they both already knew about his fight.

Sarah walked directly to Dean, who was nervously sitting stiffly erect on the living room couch. Placing her right hand beneath his chin, she gently tilted his head upward to inspect his face. With a worried expression on her face, Sarah spoke.

"My goodness, Dean, your face looks awful! Who did such a thing to you? I hope you aren't hurt bad."

"No, Mom, I'm not hurt bad at all. It was nothing. Now don't start worrying about me."

Reluctantly, Dean looked at Elwood, who, with a puzzled look on his face, stood beside his mother. Elwood put on his glasses and bent forward for a close examination of his brother's face.

"Well, at least you're not hurt bad. What happened, anyway?"

Dean noticed that the tone of the question appeared to be non-judgmental, having the sound of a simple inquiry rather than an accusation.

As Sarah and Elwood listened, Dean related the former night's violent episode, while omitting some of the gory details in order to spare his mother further worry.

Sarah asked, "Was Clay hurt?"

"No, Mom. He hardly got a scratch," replied Dean.

"Well," said Elwood, without anger. "It was the other guy's fault. He started it."

"That's right, Elwood, it wasn't my fault," said Dean. Then remembering the comments of his father, Dean amended his statement.

"No…That's not right, Elwood. It was my fault."

"How do you figure that?" asked Elwood, "After all, the guy attacked you. You weren't guilty of anything."

"Yeah, I was guilty of something. I was guilty of being stupid," said Dean. "It's strange that I haven't been able to see that, until now. I should have known better than to dance with that girl. Looking back, I can see where a lot of my past fights have been stupid on my part. Elwood, I'm really sorry about putting you in an awkward spot with the band. That club will probably never invite you back, all because of my stupidity. You won't be embarrassed by me anymore, because I quit!"

"Like heck, you will!" exclaimed Elwood. "I need you in the band! You're my guitar player. We don't need the *Lazy Lagoon*. To heck with them. There are plenty of places we can play. As a matter of fact, we have an engagement next Saturday night at the *Blue Moon* in Knoxville. You can't break a contract with me! You be there, or I'll sue!" he said, jokingly.

Smiling at Dean, Sarah ran her fingers through his thick shock of hair. "Dean, honey, please be more careful from now on. You're lucky that you weren't hurt worse."

Sensing Dean's remorse, Elwood grinned."Next Saturday night when the band plays, I'll talk to the manager of the club about hiring you as a bouncer during our breaks."

Pleased that Elwood was not angry at him, Dean laughed.

As Sarah walked toward the kitchen to prepare lunch, Elwood smiled, and in a hushed voice said, "Dean, I'm glad you introduced me to Virginia. I really like her... I think she kinda likes me too."

"I'm glad you like her. She's a nice girl. Did you kiss her goodnight?" Dean asked with a devilish grin.

"Getting a little personal, aren't you?" asked Elwood, as he took a seat on the couch, beside Dean. His face flushed as he smiled at his brother.

"Well, after all, you only gave her a ride home. No need to kiss her, if it wasn't actually a date," replied Dean.

"Actually, I did kiss her goodnight." Elwood's voice carried a hint of bravado.

"Man, Elwood, you're movin' fast!" exclaimed Dean.

"What's more, I've got a date with her for next Saturday night. I'm taking her to the club while we play music. Then, we're gonna go somewhere afterwards."

"Great!" answered Dean, "But you're going to be out really late. You better get Dad to change that curfew."

"Oh, he'll understand," explained Elwood. "I'll tell him."

The brothers looked up as the front door opened and Alvin walked into the room. After the brothers exchanged greetings, Al took a seat in the recliner, facing his brothers. Elwood then addressed Al.

"I was just telling Dean that I've got a date Saturday night."

"Oh? Will wonders never cease!" exclaimed Al, sarcastically. "You mean a date with a real, live, honest-to-goodness woman?" His question was dripping with sarcasm. He took note of Dean's swollen lips and bruised face, but made no comment.

Although similar in their non-aggressive nature, Al and Elwood each shared a mutual antagonism toward the other, most of which was based on Elwood's relationship with Will. Elwood's obedience and strong adherence to the wishes of his father disgusted Al, who felt that Elwood's ingratiating manner had motivated Will to favor him. Elwood was aware of Al's resentment toward him and enjoyed exaggerating his subservient attitude toward his father. He delighted in making Al believe that it was necessary for him to seek their father's permission in order to enjoy the slightest privilege. Al also disdained Elwood's innocence, an attitude that enticed Elwood to put even more emphasis on his chastity.

"Yeah," said Elwood, "I've got a date, but since I've never had a date

161

before, I don't know where to take her." He looked earnestly at Al, as if he were sincerely seeking his advice.

"Well, where you take her depends on what kind of a girl she is," explained Al. "Common sense ought to tell you that. If she's a real nice girl, take her out to dinner, and then maybe a movie. If she's a little on the loose side, take her to a motel."

"A motel?" asked Elwood, in feigned shock as he winked at Dean. "What would Dad say?"

"Jesus! Why in the hell would you ask Dad's permission for that?" He stormed out of the room toward the kitchen with his face reflecting a pronounced expression of disgust. Both Dean and Elwood simultaneously erupted into laughter.

After their merriment had subsided, Elwood became more serious, "Dean, I don't know how you feel about it, but Virginia has a date lined up for you, if you want it. That way, you and I could double-date. We could take the girls to the *Blue Moon*, then afterward, we could go somewhere else."

"A date for me? Who is she?"

"Florence Adams… The girl who was with her at the *Lazy Lagoon* last night."

"Oh, you mean 'Plain Jane'."

"Well, you don't have to go, if you'd rather not," said Elwood. "But I just thought we could have a good time, you and I being together with girls on a double date."

Dean noticed Elwood's disappointed expression. "Okay, Elwood, why not? Tell Virginia I'm willin' to go with Florence." Although the arranged date didn't appeal to him, he felt that his brother would need some moral support on his first date; anyway, he liked being with Elwood.

Al re-entered the room eating a sandwich. "Hey, Al." called Elwood, "How's the house painting business going with you and Clay?"

"We're out of business," replied Al. "When Clay hired Jim Burns to help us, that's when I decided to call it quits."

"Jim Burns?" asked Elwood, showing fascination. "You guys hired Jim Burns?" Elwood laughed.

"No, *we guys* didn't hire Jim Burns, Clay did." complained Al, with irritation.

"Didn't you hear about it?" Dean asked Elwood, "The customer ran them off!"

Elwood laughed, "Al, Clay, and Jim Burns! That must have been like a "Three Stooges" comedy."

"You mean Two Stooges," said Al, angrily. "I told you I didn't hire the damned idiot."

"Yeah, but I'll bet you furnished your part of the comedy." said Elwood, with a mocking grin.

"Well, I figured I'd get a bunch of shit out of you guys." Al swallowed the last bite of his sandwich, then turned and walked out the front door.

* * *

On the following Saturday night, the musicians left their station at the beginning of their first break at the *Blue Moon Club*. Dean set aside his guitar and walked toward the table near the dance floor where Elwood, Virginia, and Florence were seated. As the dancers began to scatter toward their tables, a plump red-haired girl approached Dean. She stopped directly in front of him and smiled.

"Hi! Do you guys in the band take requests for songs?" As she asked the question, she moved very close to him.

"Yes, we do," answered Dean, "What song would you like for us to play?"

The girl placed her hand on Dean's shoulder. "Well, I'd like for you to play 'Autumn Leaves,' that is, if it has a guitar part in it."

Looking to his left, Dean saw a large man walking toward him. *Here we go again*, thought Dean.

Stopping beside the girl, he said to Dean, "This is my girl that you're tryin' to make out with."

Dean smiled. He held up his opened hands at shoulder-height, in a non-threatening gesture.

"No problem, pal," he said, then turned and walked away. His submissive attitude and the fact that he was walking away emboldened the man, who called after him in a more aggressive tone.

"And stay away from her for the rest of the night!"

For an instant, Dean stopped, then slowly continued to walk toward the band. *Don't push your luck, pal.* Dean continued to walk away.

Chapter 13

Dean picked up speed as he headed toward home. Glancing at his watch, he noted the time to be 10:30; he had once again pushed the limit of his curfew. It was a crisp April evening as he and Elwood were returning home after their double-date with Virginia and Florence. The brothers had been dating the girls for more than a month, and while Elwood was smitten with Virginia, Dean viewed Florence only as a congenial friend.

Since they had been working together with their father for more than a year, the brothers had grown closer. When not working, they spent most of their leisure time together, either playing music, singing in their quartet, or double-dating the girls. They had become inseparable; often sharing their most intimate secrets; consequently, neither Dean nor Elwood could remember ever being happier.

Dean recognized his father's homemade highway reflectors ahead that designated the shop's entrance. He pulled the car into the driveway and parked the car. They found the front door unlocked and retreated to the Bull Pen.

"You know Elwood, this curfew of 10:30 that Dad imposed on us is kind of ridiculous. I'm almost 26 years old, and you're 28. I respect Dad's house rules, but after all, it's our lives."

Elwood responded, "Yeah, it's our lives, but it's his house."

"Yeah, well, I'm not complainin', but I just think it's a little ridiculous."

"Dean, speaking of Dad, I'm a little bit worried about something," Elwood said. "Dad and Mom know that I'm dating Virginia, but they don't know she's divorced. Mom might accept it, but I'm no so sure about Dad."

"It's none of Dad's business," said Dean. "It's your life. Are you gettin' serious about Virginia?"

Elwood didn't immediately answer. Finally, he replied, "Yeah, I am. To be honest with you, I think I'm in love with her."

"And how do you think she feels toward you?" Dean looked at his brother inquisitively.

"Well, she hasn't said so, but I think she loves me too. I know I haven't had much experience with women, but there are certain things you can feel, inside you."

Dean thought about Virginia and her relationship with Elwood. Knowing her sincere nature, he doubted that she would mislead his brother. Having observed their action when they were together, he believed that she did, indeed care deeply for Elwood.

"Do you think that you might marry her?" asked Dean.

"Well, I've thought about it, but it presents a real problem. What if Dad never accepts her? What would it do to my relationship with him? You know how close Dad and I are. I'd like to marry Virginia and work with you and Dad...Maybe build a house on the lot that Dad gave me behind the shop."

"Elwood, I'm pretty sure that Mom would accept her, and it's possible that Dad would. But even if he doesn't, you can't let him live your life for you. Sounds to me that you'll just have to make a choice, sooner or later."

"I don't know if I could ever make such a choice." Elwood's answer carried the tone of sadness.

"Would you let Dad's opinion of her keep you from marrying her?" asked Dean.

"No...I don't know...Anyway, I don't want to tell him about her being divorced, yet. I want to tell Mom, first."

"Give it a little more time, Elwood. You've only known Virginia for a couple of months. See what develops over time. Why don't you sleep on it tonight, and try not to worry about it right now. Let's get some rest, Elwood."

*   *   *

Although Dean spent most of his leisure time with Elwood, he occasionally spent evenings in the shop with his father where they were both engaged in painting pictures. Since returning home more than a year earlier, Dean had grown closer to his father, and a measure of mutual trust had developed between them. Will taught Dean many techniques in oil painting, a pastime that Dean found as enjoyable as music. On these nights, Elwood spent his time with Clay, or other friends, with Thursday evenings being the appointed night for Dean, Elwood, and Clay to practice their quartet music. Sometimes they practiced their singing on street corners, while passers-by stopped to listen to their harmony.

After dinner, on one of these evenings, Will and Sarah were seated in their usual lawn chairs on the patio in front of their living room. It was a particularly balmy early spring evening. The sun had dropped behind the western horizon as Sarah and Will began to discuss the family.

"Sarah, I'm really pleased with the way Dean has changed since he's been home. He is developing into a good artist. Have you seen the painting that he is working on? He really has talent in music, too. He loves playing in the band with Elwood."

"I know," replied Sarah. "I never saw two people any closer than those two…although Dean told me that he still misses Rob."

"Speaking of Rob, I'm glad that he left Ft. Wayne. Where in Indiana was it that he got that good job? Was it Bedford?" asked Will.

"Yes, it was Bedford. I hope Rob's doing well." said Sarah. "He and Dean write to each other occasionally. And Elwood said he got a letter from him yesterday."

"By the way, Elwood finally found himself a girlfriend." commented Will. "Do you think he's getting serious over her?"

"I don't know, but I'm sure she's nice if Elwood likes her. You know, Will, we have to face it. Someday Elwood may get married to somebody. If not this girl, maybe somebody else."

Since Elwood had started dating, Will noticed that his personality had slightly changed. Now that he had lost weight, he exhibited more confidence in his relationships with others, particularly with women. Will reasoned that prior to his weight loss, Elwood was too embarrassed about his obesity to ask a girl out. He realized, also, that someday a girl would come into Elwood's life and turn his head. Elwood was highly intelligent, but innocent—chaste, even, as far as Will could figure.

"Sarah, you're right, of course. It's possible that Elwood might marry. But it's also possible that he might not. After all, what would be wrong with him remaining a bachelor? And even living all of his life with us? He seems happy, here."

Sarah commented, "Will, I don't think that it would be natural for

Elwood to remain a bachelor, or live here all of his life. With his gentleness and understanding, look what a good husband and father he would make. He might even give us some grandchildren."

"See if you can find out what kind of woman he's going out with," said Will. "I think I'll ask Dean."

"Will, while we're on the subject of Elwood's dating women, I think you ought to do away with that curfew you imposed on the boys. Elwood's a good, level-headed man, and he's 28 years old."

"Sarah, every working man ought to be in bed before midnight, at least through the week. I don't think that's being unreasonable. The other night, Dean and Elwood came home together fifteen minutes late, and I didn't even get onto them about it."

Sarah hoped he would reconsider, but sensing the determination in his voice, she knew it was time to change the subject.

"I'm glad to see Clay going out with them some." she continued.

"Oh, did you know the contractors are starting on Clay's house tomorrow?" Will asked.

"Yes, I saw where they've got it marked off with string. It appears that it will be a cute little house."

"You know, if Elwood does ever marry the right girl, I would give him my blessing." said Will. "Then, he might want to build a house on the lot I gave him. Clay and Elwood could live side by side. But, Sarah, I'm worried about Elwood and the amount of weight he has been losing. He says he's below 200 pounds now. I think he looks skinny, and his face is looking gaunt."

Although Will considered Elwood's weight loss excessive, he understood his son's motivation. Elwood had been a large baby at birth and had suffered from obesity all of his life. On numerous occasions, Will and Sarah had tried to coax Elwood to diet, however, the attempts always proved to be unsuccessful. While his father often became angry at Elwood's inability to lose weight, his mother was more tolerant and understanding. Because she had also battled a weight problem since the birth of her first son, there was a bond of mutual empathy between Elwood and his mother.

During his elementary school years, Elwood had endured cruel remarks and harassment from school mates about his weight. During his high school years, however, the torment to which he was subjected was minimal because of the maturity of his fellow students and Elwood's quick wit and charming personality. Everyone liked Elwood.

He had always seemed to take the teasing in stride, not letting it bother him, but his unruffled demeanor was really only a facade. When anyone derided him, he was totally humiliated because hidden beneath his seemingly impregnable mask, Elwood was a sensitive, self-conscious man.

Will considered that Elwood's extreme determination to lose weight stemmed from the past suffering he had endured because of his obesity.

*   *   *

Will turned up the collar on his jacket as the evening grew noticeably cooler. He and Sarah shaded their eyes as the headlights of Elwood's truck swept the parking lot. Beating the curfew by 30 minutes, Dean and Elwood got out of the vehicle and approached their parents. Elwood, in an exaggerated imitation of Jim Burns, limped toward his father.

"Well, if it ain't the Cap'n." he said, as he ogled Will with a one-eyed stare. As Elwood plucked a cigarette out of Will's pocket, he turned to his mother.

"Hi, Sairy!" He leaned over kissing her on the cheek.

Sarah smiled. "Hello, boys. Did you have a good time tonight?"

"You're home early," said Will.

"Yeah, we've go a lot of work to do tomorrow." said Dean. "Early to bed, early to rise." He walked to the front door. "We're goin' on inside to bed. Gosh, Dad, you and Mom are turnin' into real night owls."

"We're going to bed, too," declared Will. "see you boys in the morning."

The next morning, Will met Dean and Elwood in the shop. The brothers began mixing paint in preparation of lettering the metal sign that rested on the large easel. Will lit a cigarette and casually handed it to Elwood.

"Elwood, Dean and I can letter this sign. I'd like for you to drive downtown and pick up a quart of red enamel. Also, go the post office and see if that package of brushes came in."

"Sure thing, Cap'n."

After Elwood had gone, Dean began to work on a layout for the sign.

"Why don't you take a little break, Dean," suggested Will. "I want to talk to you about something."

"Take a break? I haven't even begun to work yet." With his curiosity aroused, he stopped working, then lit a cigarette.

"Why don't you sit down?" invited Will, who remained standing.

Taking a seat in a nearby chair, Dean assumed a relaxed posture as he leaned back and crossed his legs, leisurely puffing on his cigarette.

"Dean, I'm worried about Elwood." Will's voice revealed anxiety.

"What are you worried about?"

"Well, for one thing, I'm worried about how much weight he is losing. He's well below 200 pounds now." Will began to slowly pace the floor as he spoke.

"Now that you mention it, he is getting' a little skinny, considerin' his big frame," said Dean.

"Also, I'm beginning to see a personality change in him," continued Will.

"Well, that's only natural, I guess. I think his personality change is probably for the good." Dean continued, "He has more confidence since he's slim. You know, his slimness is a new thing for him, and he feels that good things have been happenin' to him since he lost the weight."

"I notice that when he goes out at night, he dresses like a movie star, and he's beginning to act a little conceited," Will complained.

"Is that bad?" asked Dean. "He's proud of his new body. You know, Elwood has turned into a nice-lookin' guy."

"Yeah, but it doesn't seem to fit him. I miss the 'old' Elwood, with his sloppy clothes and his shirt tail hanging out." Will smiled at the memory of it.

"Dad, you may have to face the fact that the 'old' Elwood is gone for good. But we still have the 'new and improved' Elwood." Dean smiled at his father.

"Don't you think he has lost too much weight?"

"Yeah, Dad, I do. I think he ought to gain about 15 pounds—maybe even 20."

"You've got more influence on Elwood than anybody. I wonder if you'd talk to him about it. He'll listen to you."

"Sure, Dad. I agree with you. I'll talk to him, but he's pretty stubborn, sometimes." Assuming that the discussion was finished, Dean started to leave his chair.

"Wait a minute, Dean. I'm concerned about something else," continued Will, as Dean reclaimed his seat. "I notice that Elwood is seeing a lot of that woman. What kind of person is she? What do you know about her?"

"She's a real nice person, Dad. I've known her for several years. I think that she's good for Elwood."

"What kind of family does she come from?"

"She's from a real good family. They live over near Kingston," explained Dean.

"Well, Elwood is pretty innocent, you know. I'd hate to see some experienced woman make a fool of him, or break his heart. Where did he meet this woman?"

"I introduced him to her at the *Lazy Lagoon*, where we were playing music."

"He met her at a dance hall? A beer joint?" Will's face revealed his deep concern. "Was she with another man?"

"Dad, she's a nice girl!" explained Dean. "She went there with another girl. Anyway, that's a nice place where Elwood met her."

"Yeah, a real nice place! A place where you and Clay got beat up!" Will's expression now showed anger. "A lot of women that go to places like that are loose women with a shady past. Do you know anything about her past romances with men, or her past behavior?"

Dean hadn't lied to his father since childhood; however, his adherence to the truth was motivated more by pride than by virtue, for he felt that his lying to people carried the implication that he feared them. Although he loved his father, he was no longer afraid of him. Being torn between lying to his father or betraying Elwood, he dodged his father's question.

"Dad, I don't keep records on the romantic history of Elwood's girlfriend. Why are you asking me all these questions? And, unless you want to insult Elwood, I wouldn't ask him, either. Why are you makin' so much out of this? It's only a girlfriend of Elwood's. It's not like he is suddenly goin' to marry her. If I were you, I'd drop the subject and let Elwood enjoy his dates with her. It's the first time in his life that he's enjoyed a woman's company."

Dean was beginning to become annoyed with his father. He squelched the temptation to tell his father to mind his own business.

"I suppose you might be right," mused Will. "After all, Elwood's relationship with that woman may not amount to anything. I may have been makin' a mountain out of a mole hill. Besides, I know that Elwood would have more sense than to go out with an immoral woman. I'm just going to forget it."

"Yeah, I'd just let sleepin' dogs lie if I were you," advised Dean. "You won't find anybody with more common sense than Elwood." Looking at his father, he saw that Will's expression was no longer one of anger. Although Dean was relieved, he realized that Elwood had only been granted a temporary reprieve, for his awareness of Elwood's feeling for Virginia told him that his brother would eventually have to face his father in a showdown.

As Dean returned to his work, Will turned to him. "By the way, Dean, I've decided to do away with my curfew. You and Elwood just use common sense about whatever time you come home. I would appreciate it, though if you'd tell me in advance if you're going to come in past midnight, so your mother and I won't worry about you."

Dean smiled. "Thanks, Dad." Then, he resumed his work on the metal sign.

The front door opened, and Elwood entered the shop carrying the quart of red paint and a package.

"That package of brushes came in," said Elwood. "What do you want me to work on, Cap'n?"

"Help Dean on that metal sign. I got tied up with something else, and as you can see, Dean and I didn't get much done."

Will turned and walked through the doorway into the living room of the apartment.

Elwood joined Dean, as the brothers silently worked together on the sign. Finally, he reached into his brother's shirt pocket and filched a cigarette.

"Where are we goin' tonight with the girls?" Elwood asked.

"Oh, I don't know. To a movie, maybe?"

"What about the high school baseball game?" asked Elwood. "We could get a snack afterward. Just as long as we get home by 11:30."

"I'm not comin' home until 12:00," replied Dean, casually.

"Yeah, sure, and then you'll get Dad mad at both of us."

"Didn't you hear the latest? Dad did away with curfew. He told me a while ago. But we have to tell him if we're goin' to be out after midnight."

"Are you kidding me?"

"Nope. Ask Dad, he'll tell you."

"Great! Well, the first thing I'm going to do when we leave tonight is to tell him we'll be out until about one in the morning."

"Don't push it. We've gained a little ground, but don't overdo it all at once," cautioned Dean.

"By the way, Elwood. I've been dating Florence for a good while now, mostly just to be on double-dates with you and Virginia. I like Florence okay, and I'll go with her tonight, but I think I'll look around a little more for a girl that I'm really attracted to."

"Well, we could still double-date, even with your new girlfriend, couldn't we?" asked Elwood.

"Yeah, but I don't have a new girlfriend, yet."

Elwood noticed that Dean's mind became lost in thought. A long silence fell as the brothers worked to finish the sign.

"A penny for your thoughts," said Elwood.

"Huh...oh, I was just thinking. I saw a girl a few nights ago... well, her face just keeps coming to my mind. She sorta seemed to take to me. She was working in the ticket booth at the *Strand Theatre*, selling tickets to the movie. She's really pretty and real good-natured. I kept kidding her about lettin' me into the movie free. Then, the next day, as I was drivin' down Broadway past the theatre, she waved at me and smiled."

"Oh, really?" asked Elwood, "Who is she?"

"I've seen her around town a few times. Actually, the first time she caught my eye was when she was playing basketball in a Tyler City game. She told me her name the other night when I was kidding around with her about giving me a free ticket."

"What is it?" asked Elwood.

"Bobbie. Bobbie Summer."

"Pretty name. Does she know about you?"

"Does she know what about me?"

"You know... your reputation. Remember, you were saying that no nice local girl would ever date you because of your wild reputation. I don't really agree... but that's just what you've said several times."

"Yeah, well, just because she is friendly with me, doesn't necessarily mean that she'll give me a date."

"Why didn't you ask her for a date?"

"I just met her. Anyway, I asked around and a couple of people said she has a boyfriend."

"Well, that doesn't mean he owns her," replied Elwood. "She isn't married, you know."

"I don't know, Elwood. I may not pursue it. It was just an idea, anyway."

The door from the living quarters opened, and Will walked back into the shop.

"Boys, I just got some good news! Clay just called your mother and said that Ellen is going to have a baby." Will's face displayed happiness.

"Hey, that's great!" exclaimed Elwood, "Cap'n you're going to be a grandpa!"

"Yeah, and that'll make you and me uncles," boasted Dean. Pretending as if he had not heard the news before, he patted his brother on the shoulder. "Good old Uncle Elwood."

Elwood spoke, excitedly, "Dad, we ought to give Clay a job here at the shop. We're getting plenty of work now. I'm glad he's building a house. It ought to be finished just in time for the baby."

"I would offer him a job, Elwood, but Sarah tells me that Clay took a job yesterday at the airport in Maryville," replied Will. "It might be for the best, for now. Clay needs to get his life straight before he works here permanently."

"How does it feel to be an 'almost grandpa'?" Elwood smiled at his father.

"Well, Clay may be the only one that makes me a grandpa," said Will, smiling. "It doesn't look like either Rob or Al is going to give me a grandchild, and I doubt whether either you or Dean ever gets married."

The brothers finished their work for the day and took their girlfriends to the baseball game on that Friday evening. On Saturday night, however, Elwood dated Virginia while Dean worked on his painting in the shop with Will. Dean figured that since Elwood was getting serious about his relationship with Virginia, it would be wise to give the couple some privacy; besides, he was beginning to tire of spending so much time with Florence.

Elwood continued dating Virginia during the summer months, spending more time with her than ever as the couple became more enamored with each other. Sometimes they were accompanied by Dean and one of his casual dates; however, Dean had yet to find a woman to whom he was really attracted. Elwood hoped that maybe someday his brother could find the same happiness with a woman that he had found with Virginia. As for Dean, he had become comfortable with the possibility of remaining a bachelor for the rest of his life.

The meeting of two personalities is like the contact of two chemical substances: if there is any reaction, both are transformed. **Carl Jung**

Chapter 14

On a Sunday evening in September, Dean was aimlessly driving along Broadway in Tyler City. Earlier in the afternoon, he had washed and waxed his 1953 Plymouth hardtop, a sporty black and red vehicle that he had just bought. Since, in the past, he had driven so many dilapidated cars, he was proud of his late-model vehicle. He had no social plans for the evening, but the immaculate appearance of his car inspired him to dress in his sportiest clothing.

He drove slowly through town with no particular destination in mind, then casually steered his automobile into the parking area of *Shorty's Drive-In*, a local hangout for high school and college students. He parked his car and looked around him, observing the usual variety of sporty cars and hot rods. Several teenagers were outside of their vehicles, cavorting around as a nearby car radio issued the pulsating rhythm of Elvis Presley's popular song, "You Ain't Nothing but a Hound Dog." A young man had raised the hood of his car, proudly displaying his 'souped-up' engine to one of his friends.

After ordering a soda from the curb girl, Dean flipped on his radio and the soothing voice of Nat King Cole was crooning "That Sunday, That Summer." Lowering the volume of his radio, he took a sip of his drink and casually lit a cigarette.

Aimlessly scanning the parking area, he noticed a few feet to his left, a light blue 1954 Pontiac. Inside, apparently waving to him was an attractive blonde woman. Looking more intently he recognized the pretty girl. It was Bobbie Summer, the girl who worked at the ticket booth of the downtown theater.

Dean smiled and waved to her, "Hello, Bobbie. Nice evening, isn't it?"

Calling through the open window of the passenger side of her car, she answered, "Oh, yes, it's a beautiful evening. Isn't that a beautiful full moon?" She flashed a disarming smile.

Peering through his windshield, Dean studied the lush, glowing sphere suspending in the east, noting that it appeared to be swollen, larger than its usual size.

"Yeah, it's a beautiful moon. Are you having dinner?" asked Dean. Then, he regretted the stupidity of the question; for he remembered that it was past nine, and she would undoubtedly have dinner in a classier place than this drive-in.

"No, I'm just having a Coke," she answered.

"Nice car," commented Dean, "Yours?"

"No...not really."

"Goin' somewhere, in particular?" asked Dean. *Why did I ask that?* thought Dean, *That's none of my business!*

"No, I'm just having a Coke. I'm not going anywhere. Just home in a little while."

Dean considered ending the conversation because he couldn't think of anything else to ask except stupid questions; yet, he desperately wanted to get to know this girl. They both became silent.

Finally, Dean spoke, "Well, it's been nice seeing you again... and talking to you." He started to honk the horn to summon the curb girl to take away his tray.

Bobbie laughed, then repeated the question that Dean had asked her.

"Going someplace in particular?"

"Well, no, not really...I'm just killin' time, mostly." He noticed that she seemed to want to continue the conversation. So did he, but his usual quick wit had abandoned him as he found himself uttering stupid remarks.

"Do you work regularly at the movie theatre? I've always wanted to meet somebody in show business."

Bobbie laughed, "No, I worked there after school when I was going to high school. I just graduated last May. I worked full-time all summer, but I quit last Friday. I've enrolled at *Knoxville Business College* for the fall quarter. I start classes there next week."

"Well, that's good!" replied Dean. In spite of his faltering words, he wanted to continue the conversation; however, it made him feel even more stupid to engage in an extended conversation by shouting to each other from their separated vehicles.

Holding his tray to keep it from spilling his drink, he gingerly opened his car door. After getting out, he gently closed it. Summoning his courage, he walked to her car and opened the door of the passenger side. As he seated himself and closed the door, he felt like an intruder, for she hadn't invited him to join her.

"Well, hello!" she said, with a friendly laugh.

"Well, I...I felt that, if we're gonna talk, it would be better if we didn't have to shout back and forth at each other," said Dean, in an attempt to explain his boldness. "I won't stay but a minute, I'm not trying to force my company on you."

"Stay as long as you like. I don't have to be anywhere."

It was the first time that Dean had been this close to her. In his nearness to her, he suddenly became fully aware of her loveliness. Her beauty was not of the fragile, delicate type; instead, it exuded an aura of freshness and radiance that suggested durability and athleticism. She was wearing a short-sleeved pale blue blouse and white shorts that revealed her muscular bronze legs. Her blonde hair was cropped short around her ears and slender neck with a prominent, carefree shock of hair adorning the crown of her head. Its casual, ruffled style harmonized with her easy-going unpretentious personality. Her tanned skin indicated that she had spent much of her time outdoors. With her natural beauty, she needed little make-up.

Dean was so taken with her radiance that he became almost tongue-tied.

"I like your car," complimented Dean, in an attempt to keep the conversation moving.

"It's not my car; it belongs to my boyfriend."

"Your boyfriend? You must be goin' steady if he lets you drive his car."

"Well, you might say that."

"Are you engaged?" he asked.

"No...not exactly."

"Well, you either are, or you're not. Which is it?"

"That's none of your business!" she replied, but with an elaborate laugh, an indication that she wasn't offended by the question. Dean loved the sound of her uninhibited laugh.

"Well, I guess I was bein' a little nosy," he confessed. "Do you think he would be mad if he knew I was sitting here with you, in his car?"

"He'd be mad if he knew I was sitting with you in *any* car," she smiled.

"Would you rather I'd leave?" he asked.

"No," she answered.

"Then you don't care whether or not he gets mad?" asked Dean, cautiously.

"Well, I don't enjoy making him mad, but I don't like for him to feel like he owns me."

"Does he feel like he owns you?"

"Yes... sometimes." With a sad expression, she added, "I don't want to hurt him."

"Is he a nice guy?" asked Dean. He was becoming a bit more relaxed in his conversation; however, she seemed to be more comfortable than he.

"Oh, yes, Buddy's a real nice person, but he sometimes acts like he owns me."

Changing the subject, he commented, "I really like your hair—the way it's kinda fluffed up on top. It makes you resemble somebody, but I can't place who it is...Let's see—Doris Day, maybe. Or better yet, it kinda reminds me of Woody Woodpecker."

Oh, Lord, why did I say that? thought Dean, *I'll bet I just struck out.* Bobbie's melodious laugh flowed from deep inside her. It was obvious that she didn't take herself too seriously and had the ability to laugh at herself.

Usually, Dean felt totally in control when talking to any girl; however, he was puzzled about his inability to articulate his words with Bobbie. She exuded an innocence and tenderness that made him want to know her inner loveliness.

"Want to take a ride?" asked Bobbie, suddenly.

"Where to?"

"Oh, no place in particular. Just a ride."

Dean quickly felt more comfortable.

"Yeah, I'd love to take a ride," he replied.

"Well, you'd better get out and go park your car in the back of the drive-in. They won't like it if you leave it here."

Half suspecting that she would drive away and leave him, he got out of her car and moved his vehicle to the back of the parking area. He was mildly surprised to discover that she had waited for him.

Bobbie's relaxed manner and easy banter gradually restored Dean's confidence, and he soon felt completely comfortable with her. As she aimlessly drove the car on the unplanned course, the tone of their conversation became less trivial and they both began to discuss topics of a more personal nature.

She drove the vehicle for hours, sometimes parking for a brief period of time, then resuming her wandering journey as they talked to each other about many things.

It was now well after midnight. Noting the late hour, Dean asked, "What time do you have to be home? Do you live with your parents?"

"My Dad lives in Knoxville. I live with an elderly lady here in Tyler City. Her name is Mrs. Watkins. I don't have to be home at any certain time, but it is getting kind of late."

She pulled the car over to the curb in Concord Park. The romantic brilliant moon had risen higher in the star-studded sky as they sat silently for a long while, spell-bound by the magic of the soft moonlight and their unplanned intimacy.

Their conversation had taken an unexpected intimate turn and personal questions were no longer off-limits. Reaching across the seat, Dean took her hand. He hadn't attempted to kiss her, but he somehow felt a closeness to her.

"Do you know about my reputation?" he asked.

"Yes." she answered, without further comment.

He instinctively saw something wholesome and understanding about her, and he sensed that she detected a deeper side of him.

"Are you in love with him?" asked Dean.

"I don't know. I don't feel a passion about him, but he makes me feel comfortable." Dean felt that he and Bobbie, if the fates allowed, could develop a passionate relationship; for he felt an aroused passion for this woman that he never before experienced. *Please don't marry that man who makes you feel comfortable when you deserve a husband with whom you can share passion,* Dean thought to himself.

Although he had an intense sexual desire for Bobbie, he was entranced more by her inner beauty and honesty. He simply wanted to be with her, near her, and share his intimate feelings with her. He wished that this night would never end, and he believed that Bobbie shared his sentiments; however, he knew how fickle and fleeting such feelings can be when a couple of lonely souls are enraptured by the moonlight. He knew that he would feel the same way tomorrow, but in the revealing sunlight of the day, Bobbie's present tender emotions might fade away. He began to lose his confidence in hoping for a continuing relationship.

Dean took her in his arms as she nestled her head on his shoulder, but he still made no attempt to kiss her. They continued to talk, now more softly and intimate. Sometimes they fell silent, enjoying their shared closeness as they gazed at the soft, luminescent panorama of the lakeside park. His intuition told him that he and Bobbie had unknowingly altered the courses of their lives. On this magical night, they had sailed into uncharted waters.

It was 4:00 a.m. when Dean slowly drove the car away from the park toward home. After asking him to take the wheel, they had traded seats, and they both fell silent as he drove. As she gently snuggled her head on his shoulder, he became captivated by the intoxicating fragrance of her tousled, golden hair.

At last, Dean pulled the car into the deserted parking lot of the drive-in, beside his vehicle. When he got out of the car, he stood by the driver's side as he waited for her to slide over, under the steering wheel. Instead, she also stepped from the vehicle and walked around the car, facing him. When he viewed her in her standing position, he was enthralled by her voluptuous figure.

"I had a real good time tonight, Dean," she said.

"Yeah, me too." He again felt the awkwardness that he had experienced when he had first met her. He feared that this special night was probably the only one that he would ever spend with her; for, after all, she had been honest with him about having a boyfriend with whom she was 'comfortable'.

Facing Dean, Bobbie moved closer to him, so that their bodies touched. Instinctively, he wrapped her in his arms. He kissed her, affectionately; but it was more a kiss of tenderness than of sexuality. As he held her in his embrace, the soft, scented aroma of her graceful neck excited him.

With reluctance, he released her. "Well, good night." He smiled tenderly at her and turned to walk away. Abruptly, he whirled around. His voice trembled as he asked,

"Bobbie…would…would you see me again—sometime?"

She looked at him and smiled.

"Dean, I like you a lot, but remember, after all, I have a steady boyfriend. Maybe I need to think on this a while."

"Yeah, I know. I understand." He turned toward his car.

Bobbie had not intentionally led him on; for the evening rendezvous and the instant bonding of their natures had not been planned. Bound together by their kindred spirits in the lunar loveliness of the night, they spontaneously wandered wherever their feelings led them, powerless to resist the allure of their mutual attraction.

Suddenly feeling the risk of never seeing him again, she shouted, "Dean…wait a minute…do you like football?"

"Yeah, I love football." He walked back to her.

"U.T. is playing Ole Miss next Saturday. Are you going?"

"No, I don't guess so. Why?" asked Dean.

"Why don't you go?" she asked, smiling, "And take me!" Then she playfully ran her fingers through his thick shock of curly hair.

When Dean drove his car home that morning, his apathetic spirit had been rekindled, for he now felt the warm embrace of passion in his life.

Love is a fruit in season at all times, and within reach of every hand.
Mother Teresa

Chapter 15

Dean silently crept through the house to the Bull Pen. He found that Elwood was awake and concerned about him. It was now morning and as he related the past evening's experience to Elwood, the brothers made no attempt to sleep. Dean's excitement was keeping him wide awake, and for the first time in months, he felt totally alive.

Throughout the autumn months, Bobbie filled his every thought; however, his meetings with her were only occasional because she continued her relationship with her boyfriend, the suitor with whom she felt 'comfortable'. Although Dean yearned to see her more, he remembered her remark about her boyfriend who felt that "he owned her." Knowing the results of smothering love, Dean decided not to suffocate her with his frequent presence; he felt that his absence would offer her the freedom she desired. Deciding to leave the decision regarding her preference of boyfriends to her, he continued his relationship with other girls.   Sometimes when Dean and Bobbie dated, they were joined by Elwood and Virginia, as the foursome spent many lazy, autumn Sunday afternoons together. Bobbie and Elwood immediately liked each other and became good friends, for each had an admiration for the easygoing, unpretentious nature of the other.

The fall of 1956 was exceptionally beautiful. By mid-October, when the brilliance of the Indian summer foliage had reached its peak, meetings between Dean and Bobbie became more frequent; consequently, Bobbie began to spend less time with her other boyfriend. Dean became more enamored with Bobbie. She filled an emptiness that he had always felt within himself, and her insight into his true character gave him a sense of belonging. He had always held a skepticism regarding "love at first sight," but in remembering their first night together on the moonlit night in Concord Park, he realized that he had fallen in love with her on that evening.

From the time that Bobbie had met Dean, she had made no effort to hide her relationship with him, even to her other boyfriend. Dean's bad reputation had failed to deter her from associating with him. She had truly grown to love him; however, the closest she had come to telling him at that time was, "I could learn to love you". Knowing how serious she felt about him, she decided to introduce him to her family, particularly her father, of whom she was enormously proud.

Her father was an older man who had become a father to Bobbie at the age of fifty. He had once been a prosperous owner of two stores, but the Great Depression had stolen most of his wealth. As a result, his sustenance was derived from farming a few acres of land.

He had sired six daughters, one of whom was Bobbie, who, with her five sisters, grew up as farm girls. All of them knew the meaning of doing a man's job, often working from daylight until dark, farming the land.

Unfortunately, their mother had become an alcoholic and had deserted the family when Bobbie was eight years old, so the father, Benjamin Summer, having no sons, inherited the difficult responsibility of rearing six high-spirited daughters, without the help of a mate. Arriving at her father's small farm in Knox County, Dean and Bobbie walked into the yard of a small farm house. As her father stepped down from the front porch to greet them, Dean noticed that he appeared older than his age of seventy. The burdensome drudgery that he had endured over the years had taken its toll on his slender body, but not on his spirit. He was wearing a straw hat and overalls that were stained with dirt from the land on which he had worked that morning. His tanned, weather-beaten face was covered with perspiration produced by his recent labor of gathering corn from the fields.

Ignoring her own well-groomed appearance, Bobbie ran to her father, hugged him in a loving embrace, and kissed him on his sweaty cheek. She was totally unembarrassed and at ease with the unkempt appearance of her father, completely ignoring the dirt on his clothing that he had acquired through honest toil.

As Bobbie introduced the two men, Dean was deeply moved by her open display of affection for her father. She was immensely proud of him, as she was of Dean, and she wanted the most cherished men in her life to meet. After witnessing Bobbie's unpretentious gesture toward her father, Dean knew that she was a woman of unparalleled quality. At the moment, he knew that he wanted her to become his wife.

Dean was struck with the irony that Bobbie was reared in an all-girl family while his own family was comprised of only boys. Since having no sisters had deprived Dean of any significant knowledge of female behavior, he had wondered if Bobbie carried the same problem in her understanding of males. Dean found the answer when he saw how well she connected with Elwood and Alvin, and her father.

Bobbie then met Dean's parents, and shortly after introducing her, he deliberately left her alone with them. He invented a transparent pretext for his necessity to leave, in order for them to discover her positive qualities. He yearned for his parents' approval of her, and since he had never before introduced a girl to them, he assumed that they would understand the significance.

After he and Bobbie left his parents' home, Will asked Sarah, "I wonder why Dean brought that young woman here, tonight?"

"Will, it's obvious that he is getting serious about her. He wants our approval."

"Oh, Sarah, Dean never gets serious over any girl," said Will. "Why should she be any different from any of his other women?"

"Because she is different, Will. I don't know why you can't see it. She's a sweet little girl, and I can see that Dean is crazy about her."

Will said, "I know Dean like a book. He never wants but one thing out of a girl. He's got plenty of experience, but he's got no judgment when it comes to women. Now with Elwood, it's different. He'll pick a good woman when he decides to get married."

"Now see, you met Elwood's girl only once, and you've already made up your mind about her. Maybe you should give people a little more time. I just know that after seeing Dean's excited face and the way that little girl looks at him that they're crazy about each other. And I can really see the goodness and gentleness in her."

*   *   *

The glorious days of autumn passed too quickly, as the brilliant, multi-colored foliage fell from the trees, leaving them starkly naked, silhouetted black against the slate grey sky. The wind from the north whipped the land and threatened snow as the yuletide season rapidly approached.

Finally, a week before Christmas, a beautiful snowfall covered the area. Dean and Bobbie joined Elwood and Virginia as the foursome playfully frolicked in the snow; for they all loved snow and were excited about the approaching Christmas season.

Having done his holiday shopping early, Dean had already bought a lovely outfit for Bobbie, as well as presents for his parents and brothers. While decorating the family Christmas tree, Elwood and Dean were ecstatically happy, filled with the yuletide spirit. As Elwood placed ornaments on the tree, he began to rock. Excitedly, he said to Dean,

"Don't go snooping around in Mom and Dad's bedroom, especially in the bedroom closet."

"Why?" asked Dean.

"Because I bought you a little present and if you snoop around and find it, it would spoil Christmas."

"I hope you didn't buy an expensive gift for me because I really didn't spend a lot this year," replied Dean.

"Now, don't start thinking I got you something expensive, or you'll be disappointed," cautioned Elwood.

On Christmas morning, as the family gathered around the tree, Elwood could hardly contain his excitement. Of all members of the family, he was by far the most generous, often spending all of his money on others. As the gifts were unwrapped, both Sarah and Will received an appropriate expensive present from Elwood; for he never bought anyone a 'token' present, but was discriminating in his selection of gifts, always choosing the 'right' present for each family member. As Sarah unwrapped the necklace, Will was examining the assortment of tube colors and brushes that Elwood had given him.

Elwood gratefully thanked everyone for the gifts that he received, but he was really focused on the presents that he gave, along with the recipients' reaction.

Finally, all the presents had been given and unwrapped, with the exception of Elwood's gift to Dean.

Suddenly, Elwood, faking a shocked expression, exclaimed, "Oh, my gosh! I forgot to buy Dean anything!"

With the awareness that his brother was joking, Dean smiled at him, curious about what Elwood had selected for him.

"Dean, I want you to go into the Bull Pen and don't come out until I call you," requested Elwood.

"Are we starting a game of 'hide and seek'?" Dean laughed as he retreated to the bedroom. After a brief wait, he heard Elwood's voice.

"Okay, you can come back in here now."

As Dean walked back into the living room, he could scarcely believe his eyes. Positioned carefully against a chair by the tree was a brand new shiny electric guitar along with an alligator hide carrying case. Nearby, on a separate chair was an amplifier. Upon closer inspection, Dean saw the imprint on the guitar— "Martin." He knew that a *Martin* guitar was one of the finest instruments manufactured.

As he looked at Elwood in gratitude, he saw that his brother was grinning as he rocked nervously from side to side.

"Do you like it?" asked Elwood, excitedly. "Look here." He picked up the instrument. "Look at the quality of the finish," he said, with exuberance. He obviously wanted to savor the moment for which he had so long anticipated.

As Dean watched his brother's excitement, he realized that Elwood had spent more than he could afford for the guitar, but if Dean offered to help with the payments, his brother's Christmas would be ruined. He knew that Elwood's happiest moments were when he was giving, especially to Dean.

As he wrapped his arms around Elwood, Dean realized the breadth of his brother's love for him.

There are more pleasant things to do than beat up people.
Muhammad Ali

Chapter 16

It had been two years since Dean had tasted alcohol. He was feeling especially well now because he was exercising regularly in the gym. After a good work-out and hot shower, Dean and his friend, Tony Gilbert decided to cruise around in Tony's car. It was a bitterly cold, January evening, as the star-sprinkled winter sky held a full moon over the silhouetted trees in the east. The chill in the air enhanced the energetic feeling in the two men.

They had no definite plans, but since they had earlier discussed driving into Knoxville, Tony swung the car in that direction. Both men were casually dressed, and as Tony aimlessly drove around, Dean regretted that he hadn't stayed at home.

Ahead on the left, they spotted a popular restaurant. Although Tony was secretly hoping to meet a woman, Dean, who now was dating Bobbie, had no such desire. *The Volunteer Club* had a clientele consisting of mostly college students. The restaurant sold beer, but with the intent of its consumption as a beverage complementary to meals rather than as an intoxicant. Dean had been here before and knew the woman who owned the place.

"Why don't we pull in here?" asked Tony. "There might be some unattached chicks."

"I'm not lookin' for a girl," replied Dean. "I think they expect you to eat in there. You and I have already eaten. They might not appreciate us goin' in there and just hanging around. I don't want a beer, but if you want one, you can stop. You're driving."

Tony steered the car into the club's parking area and suddenly braked the car to a halt.

"Look over there at that mob, out on that side of the parking lot!" exclaimed Tony, "It looks like somebody's in a fight."

Dean quickly looked in the direction that Tony was pointing. He saw two large men, one who was beating the other man badly.

"Man, that guy is beatin' the livin' shit out of the other poor bastard," said Tony.

In order to get a closer look, Tony hurriedly parked the car, and the men got out. As they approached the fight, Tony blurted out, "Oh, Hell, Dean, that guy getting' beat up is Elwood!"

The two men hurriedly trotted to the scene of the fight. A large group of men and women encircled the fighting men.

"Pour it on him, Satch!" shouted one of the bystanders. As Dean made his way through the circle of people, he saw this man, Satch, land a crushing blow to Elwood's face.

Satch was a large, powerful man, weighing about 200 pounds, but rather slow and awkward. The rugged appearance of the man suggested to Dean that he was likely a local tavern brawler. The scars on his face proudly proclaimed that he had fought countless battles, probably at the expense of numerous hapless victims. His loyal entourage of cheering cronies surrounding the fracas indicated that he loved to show off and to display his masculine superiority over his adversary.

When seeing Elwood's bloody face as he bravely faced the sadistic bully, Dean's anger knew no bounds. Satch was toying with Elwood, punching him at will in the face. Although his punches were not particularly fast, they were much quicker than those of Elwood's, who, although clearly outmatched, courageously pawed at his tormentor in a fruitless effort to defend himself.

Aware of Elwood's gentle nature, Dean was certain that Satch had picked the fight with him, sensing that he was an easy victim. Elwood's extreme weight loss had weakened him, causing him to breathe heavily with fatigue.

"Aw, come on Satch," pleaded one of the bully's cronies, with pity, "I think the poor guy's had enough."

With a devilish grin, Satch responded, "I'm almost done with him; I just want to hit him one more time, for the road."

In order to protect Elwood from that final punch, Dean stepped into the center of the circle of people surrounding the fight. He had never before experienced such anger, but his face was an expressionless mask. He was itching to hit this sadist, but he wanted his extreme rage to come as a surprise to the man.

Raising his hand as a gesture to halt the one-sided slaughter, Dean gently pushed Elwood backward, stepping between the two men, facing Satch. Looking the man directly in the eye, Dean displayed a phony, friendly smile.

"Hey, pal—Satch is it? Hold up a minute. You look like a man who can really use his fists. How would you like to try me for a round?"

Satch looked at Dean with a puzzled expression. "Who are you?" he asked, "What business is this of yours?"

A grimace of anger gradually replaced his puzzled expression. Dean became excited with the anticipation of smashing his fist into the beefy face of this bully. Although adrenaline was racing through his veins, he feigned the appearance of being calm and relaxed, revealing no malice.

Because the man had humiliated and made sport of Elwood, Dean decided that in addition to punishing the man, he would also taunt and degrade him, the way the bully had tormented his brother. Because of his adrenaline and his intense anger, Dean had absolutely no doubt about the outcome of this fight.

Forcing a pleasant smile, he waited as Satch advanced toward him. Angrily Satch said, "Okay, asshole, I'll give you a dose of it too, just like I did him."

As the hefty man came within punching distance, his upper-body movement telegraphed his punch. Instantly recognizing the forthcoming blow, Dean easily beat him to the punch. His right hand shot out with a lightning-like movement. His fist struck the man's left jaw with such force that Dean felt the recoil of the impact all the way to the joint in his elbow.

Satch reeled backward, but Dean was quickly upon him. Following his initial blow, he delivered at least a dozen more, all to the head.

The man's face was gushing blood as he reeled unsteadily, attempting to maintain his balance. The feeble punches he threw had virtually no effect and went unnoticed by Dean.

Bleeding profusely, the man was barely able to stand.

"How does it feel, you bastard?" asked Dean, with a satanic grin. Using all of his strength and speed, Dean again brutally struck the bleeding face. The front of the bully's shirt was drenched with blood that spurted from his mangled nose.

"It hurts, don't it?" mocked Dean, cruelly taunting the man.

One of Satch's cronies stepped forward and pleaded, "Please don't hit him anymore, buddy. He's hurt bad. What more do you want?"

"I want to hit him just one more time," gloated Dean, "one for the road."

He threw another vicious punch into Satch's face, the force of it causing the man to stagger backward, sprawling on the ground.

As the beaten man was being helped to his feet by his followers, Dean walked over to Elwood to see how badly he was injured. When he got very close to his brother, he was shocked. On closer inspection, Elwood's injuries were worse than he had expected. His left eye was already almost swollen shut; there was a large horizontal cut along his left eyebrow, so severe that it looked as if the skin would fold down over his eye; his nose was bleeding badly, maybe broken; and his left jaw was swollen. The front of Elwood's shirt was soaked with blood, and his glasses were lying broken in the street.

In an attempt to appear undaunted, Elwood grinned at his brother, exposing teeth that were coated with congealing blood, some of which spilled over his lower lip, trickling down his chin.

"Damn, Elwood!" exclaimed Dean. "That son-of-a-bitch really messed up your face! I've got to get you to a doctor. You'll need some stitches."

After seeing the damage that the bully had inflicted on his brother, all for the sole purpose of bolstering his ego at Elwood's expense, Dean again became livid with rage.

He suddenly turned and shouted, "Where did that cowardly bastard go?"

In the parking lot, the crowd had thinned, with only a few curious onlookers remaining. A man standing nearby said, "I think he went inside the club to get away from you." He stared at Dean curiously.

Dean quickly ran to the front door of the restaurant. Trying the door, he discovered that it was locked. Fearing that Dean wasn't through punishing the man, the woman who owned the business had allowed the beaten man to come inside and had locked the door to keep Dean from entering.

The front entrance was a French door of the type that contains fifteen small glass panes, with a moulding between the panes that held them together. In a rage, Dean lowered his shoulder and dove through the door, sending shards of glass and splintered moulding in all directions. He then lunged through the opening into the interior of the dining room.

The dining guests were completely awestruck, many of them scattering in all directions in order to escape the inevitable mayhem, most of them making a run for the exit in the rear.

Dean had now abandoned any pretense that he was not angry; his eyes revealed a satanic gleam. As the room emptied of customers, Satch no longer could use the crowd to hide himself from his tormentor's view. Realizing that Dean now saw him, he tried to escape into the kitchen, only to be tackled by Dean, the action causing a table and several chairs to be upended. He managed to wiggle from Dean's grasp, crawling under a table with his buttocks protruding from underneath the table. Dean repeatedly kicked him, once savagely in the testicles.

Noting the complete helplessness of the man, Dean's anger began to subside. His adrenaline was spent, as was his strength. Breathing heavily, he leaned against the wall for support, resting his exhausted body.

When Satch realized that Dean had finished with the assault, he slowly crawled from beneath the table, looking up at his adversary with fearful eyes. Dean glared at his victim with contempt. Bending down, he spat in the man's face.

Except for Dean and his victim, the room was now empty. Even the manager and the employees had evacuated the building. Dean turned and left the dining room through the gaping hole in the front door that he had destroyed.

He walked over to Elwood, who was now standing by his car. A few curiosity seekers were standing around in the parking lot. Dean noticed that Tony Gilbert was also gone. *Probably scared of getting into trouble*, thought Dean.

"Come on, Elwood, get in the car—I'll drive. The police will be here soon, and I've got to get you to a doctor."

The brothers climbed into Elwood's car, and Dean drove rapidly as he rushed his brother to the doctor. The handkerchief that Elwood pressed to his left eye had stemmed the flow of blood, and it now appeared that his nose wasn't broken after all. However, holding his left hand to his mouth, he discovered that he had two loose teeth.

"Has it stopped hurting so much?" asked Dean.

"Yeah, it's not bad. I sure wasn't much competition for that guy."

"Oh come on, Elwood, you showed a lot of bravery back there." Dean attempted to reassure Elwood. "You're going to be okay. A couple of stitches and a good night's rest will fix you up fine."

Elwood looked fondly at his brother.

"You did even a better job on that guy than he did on me. Anyway, I'm a better lover than I am a fighter," joked Elwood.

"From what I've heard, you ain't worth a damn as a lover either," Dean quipped, in an attempt to be light-hearted.

"Dean, on a more serious note, I sure do appreciate what you did for me. I want to tell you how proud I am of you." Elwood said sincerely.

Dean suddenly felt sick at his stomach. He felt that he might throw up. "Hell, it was nothing. All in a day's work." Dean said, trivializing the incident.

Dean was proud of his brother. Elwood, showing no fear in spite of having absolutely no fighting skill, had bravely stood up to a man who could beat him to death if he chose. Not wishing to point out Elwood's ineptness as a fighter, Dean refrained from telling him this.

Dean parked the car in front of the home of Dr. Spiegel, their family physician. He left his brother in the car and quickly sprang up the front steps of the doctor's house. After rapping on the front door several times, the front porch light came on, and Dr. Spiegel's pajama-clad figure finally appeared in the doorway.

"Hi, Doc," greeted Dean, "My brother, Elwood's been beat up pretty bad. I was wonderin' if you could look at him."

Dr. Spiegel's face mirrored extreme anger.

"Do you know what time it is? It's 1:30 in the morning! I'm not getting out of bed to patch up one of the Beauvais boys every time one of you gets the hell beat out of him! Go to the emergency room!"

He punctuated his last comment by slamming the door in Dean's face. While the intern in the emergency room was attending to Elwood's injuries, Dean used a phone in the lobby to call home. Knowing that his parents would be worried about Elwood, who was accustomed to being home by midnight, he wanted to assure them that Elwood was with him and would be home soon.

When the brothers entered the front door of the Beauvais home, both parents were waiting for them in the living room. When they saw Elwood with his bandaged face and bloody clothing, Sarah gasped, then her eyes turned to Dean.

"Did you get Elwood beaten up somewhere?" Her eyes displayed anger.

Dean was troubled. His mom had given him such a look of accusation only rarely in his lifetime.

He looked at his father, whose expression was one of anger.

"What happened, Dean?" he demanded.

Dean was so physically and emotionally exhausted, he didn't attempt to explain. Avoiding the angry stares of his parents and turning away from them, he said wearily,

"Let Elwood explain it to you." With that, Dean walked out the door.

That night, he spent the night in a cheap motel room often used as a lovers' rendezvous. Although completely drained, he slept fitfully, his sleep invaded by bizarre dreams. Consequently, when he awoke, he still felt depleted of energy. Feeling pain in his left hand, he noticed for the first time how badly swollen it was. Other than that, he escaped the violent brawl with only a few superficial cuts and bruises.

He decided to return home to check on Elwood. When he arrived there, his brother was still in bed, but his mother and father were sitting in the living room.

Sarah quickly came to meet him. Hugging him tightly, she smiled, "Elwood told us what happened, and although I don't believe in fighting, I appreciate what you did for him." Knowing how loyal Dean was to his brother, she continued, "I hope you didn't hurt that other fellow very much. You didn't, did you?"

He knew from her question that Elwood hadn't elaborated on the cruelty of the fight, thus sparing their mother from hearing the gory details.

"Nah, Mom, I just slapped him around a little bit, that's all. He saw the error of his ways and apologized to Elwood. Everything ended up fine," lied Dean.

His father said nothing, only looking at him. Dean noticed that Will's expression projected no animosity.

Sounds came from Elwood's bedroom, indicating that he was awakening. His mother turned and walked quickly in that direction to attend to him.

When she was out of earshot, Will stood, starting to follow her. Suddenly, he stopped and turned to face Dean.

"Dean, if you get into any trouble over that little ruckus you got into last night, just let me know. Don't hesitate to call on me."

Though his father didn't vocally approve or disapprove of his actions the night before, Dean noted that this was the first time his dad had ever offered his help in getting him out of trouble.

There is only one admirable form of the imagination: the imagina-
tion that is so intense that it creates a new reality, that it makes
things happen. **Sean O' Faolain**

Chapter 17

In the aftermath of the altercation at the *Volunteer Club*, Elwood's injuries rapidly healed. Although Dean sustained no physical injury other than a swollen hand and a few minor cuts, his emotional psyche suffered. It had taken two years of exemplary behavior to partially rebuild his damaged reputation, but a 15 minute fight had completely destroyed the headway he had made. A complete account of the brutal fracas with all its gory details was common knowledge to the people in Tyler City.

During the two years that he had been home, Dean mistakenly felt that he had learned to control his terrible temper, but his behavior during the brawl proved him wrong. He wondered how Bobbie would feel about dating him now, or if she would be embarrassed to be seen with him in plain view of her friends. However, when she learned the cause of Dean's behavior, she defended his actions because her knowledge of Elwood's gentleness and the closeness of the brothers convinced her that Dean's behavior was justified.

Hoping for the best, Dean tried to put the incident in the past.

The brothers grew even closer to each other since they spent most of their time together, both at work, and during their leisure time. Their band was booked regularly in different clubs around the area as Dean proudly played his new guitar. Their quartet was also flourishing as they joined their brother, Clay, and Ray Houser, singing in area churches and women's social clubs.

Dean and Elwood sometimes escorted Virginia and Bobbie to their band performances. The presence of the girls helped keep Dean out of trouble with jealous boyfriends of women patrons. Although Bobbie quickly recognized the attraction of women to the musicians, she was amused when she realized that other girls were attracted to Dean. Bobbie felt no insecurity in her relationship with him, for by nature, she was not a jealous woman.

Dean and Bobbie were now deeply in love, but neither of them had talked of going steady or of marriage. Because of his uncertainty and renewed tainted reputation, he somehow felt unworthy of her. He recognized that Bobbie's forthright character was far superior to those of the fickle, conceited women in his past. He feared that the euphoric relationship with her would be short-lived because due to his past disappointments in life, he had developed a cynicism, telling him that his wonderful experience was too good to be happening to him. He kept dating her with the firm belief that she truly loved him; however, knowing how she disliked feeling owned, he was reluctant to bring up the subject of going steady.

He also knew that some of Bobbie's female friends were aware of his reputation, and that they viewed her relationship with him as unacceptable. When it became apparent that Bobbie was infatuated with him, one of her close friends, Betty Bosworth, had pleaded, "Please, Bobbie, don't marry that man!"

However, such negative remarks had apparently failed to sway Bobbie's opinion of him. He could see that, cloaked in her easy-going, gentle nature was an independent streak similar to that of his own. To make sure that she didn't see him as controlling, he had given her free-rein, even telling her to date others if she so desired; however, she had ultimately chosen to date only him.

*   *   *

Despite the reassurance given by those he loved, Dean began to feel that his life was going nowhere. Work at the shop had diminished for the time being, and Will, now 65 years old, was thinking of asking Elwood to run the business. Dean began to feel that he was simply marking time, not only in his job, but also with Bobbie. Wanderlust, once again, began to eat at him. He treasured his relationship and his shared musical experience with Elwood, but he had a longing to do something more creative with his life. He wanted to marry Bobbie, but he felt that working in his father's shop and living in Tyler City would not be rewarding enough for him. At the same time, it occurred to him that Bobbie, with her headstrong nature, might choose to never leave Tyler City.

The recent fight and his re-tarnished reputation added fuel to his burning desire to once again leave his hometown. Sadly, he also thought that his attachment to Bobbie and his relationship with Elwood both needed a change of pace; also. he saw them as factors that stunted his ability to roam.

It was during this disquieting time that Dean received a phone call from a company of previous employment in Miami. The company manager offered him a position as a pictorial artist, a job that provided not only more creative opportunity, but more than twice the money he was currently earning. Remembering his past experiences in Miami, with its balmy, winter climate, he became excited. The Florida shop owner gave him a week to consider his offer, and as Dean hung up the phone, his mind was in a turmoil.

After spending a near-sleepless night, he made his decision. With a desire to talk with Elwood before discussing the matter with Bobbie, Dean postponed his Saturday night date with her until the following night. On Sunday afternoon, immediately after church, he confronted his brother.

"Elwood, let's take a ride, I need to talk to you," said Dean.

"What's up, Dean? Is something wrong?"

As the brothers drove through Tyler City, they engaged in small talk. Finally, Dean pulled into the City Park at the picnic grounds and parked the vehicle at the curb.

"You seem worried about something," observed Elwood, apparently anxious.

"I've made a decision about something, and I wanted to tell you about it first," replied Dean.

"What is it?"

"I've decided to take a job in Miami."

"What? You're leaving here again? Why?"

"Well, Elwood, that's why I wanted to talk to you. I hope I can make you understand." Dean struggled for the right words.

"If you've already made up your mind, then why are you discussing it with me?" asked Elwood, with slight irritation.

"It's a real opportunity for me, Elwood. I'll get to paint murals on my new job, and the money is great! I'll have a chance to be more creative. I'm an artist. There's not much of a real future here in the shop, at least, not for me. I'm trying to be true to myself."

"What about our music? Dean, since you came back home, it's been the happiest two years of my life." Elwood's expression revealed his inner sadness.

"Elwood, I'll miss it as bad as you will, but music is a hobby of ours, not a way of life. If I stay here all my life, I'll just become a complacent, mediocre local yokel. I can't be happy with just being comfortable—I want to feel alive. I'd never be able to really support a wife or raise a family."

"Well, speaking of supporting a wife, what does Bobbie think of your decision?" asked Elwood. "What about her?"

"She doesn't know about it yet. I postponed our date last night. I wanted to talk to you about it first."

"Are you going to just leave here—leave Bobbie? I thought you were in love with her. I thought you had found your soul mate."

"I've decided to ask her to come with me."

"But what if she won't?" asked Elwood, "She's still just a girl, really, and she was raised here. Her family lives here…She may be glued to this place. She may not want to just pull up stakes and go, the way you always like to do. Are you going to ask her to marry you?"

"Yes, I am."

"How long do you have before you have to report to that job?"

"A week—well, actually five days, now. It's been a couple of days since he called me."

"You expect Bobbie to make up her mind to marry you, and be living in Miami with you in five days?" he asked, in amazement. "Same old Dean!" Elwood appeared to be slightly disgusted.

"Elwood, she'll have to make a decision about what she wants to do. I just know I can't pass up this chance."

"Well, that's putting Bobbie in a heck of a spot. It's either-or, with you, is that it? She has to decide to marry you immediately, when you haven't even talked about marriage, or you leave her, and she loses you. And, you'll be losing her. Have you thought about that? Dean, you're taking a hell of a risk."

"Elwood, a famous man once said, 'Never taking a risk is the biggest risk a man can ever take'."

"Dean, I don't understand you. You've got everything here… Bobbie, Mom, Dad, and us—and our music! As for me, all I'd ever want is to marry Virginia and take over the shop for Dad. Maybe build a house on that lot that Dad gave me. I'd be content for the rest of my life! We could have a life together, and a family…Maybe raise our kids

196

together."

At the risk of hurting Elwood's feelings, Dean cautioned, "Elwood, even if Dad turns the shop over to you, he will still always be running it. In my opinion, with your intelligence you should have gone to college years ago like you wanted to, instead of working for Dad as a sign painter. As long as you're here in the shop, you'll nothing but an extension of Dad. You and I are alike in many ways, but there is one big difference between us. You are not a risk-taker, and—right or wrong, I am," declared Dean. "You would be content with what you have here, so you belong here. I sometimes wish I was that way, but I'm not. But here's something else you ought to think about. You need to make a decision about whether or not you're going to marry Virginia. She won't wait forever for you to make up your mind. Don't you think that's taking a chance, too?"

"Yeah, but I still don't know if Dad will accept the fact that she's divorced." Elwood lamented.

"Well, that's another difference between us," pointed out Dean. "I'm willing to make a choice, and you can't seem to be able to do that. You may have to make that choice between Dad and Virginia."

"You're right, Dean. I'm not willing to make that choice…at least, not yet. But what about Bobbie? You don't seem to give her much choice in the matter."

"Yes, she has a choice, the same as I have. She'll have to make that choice. I've never talked to her about marriage because I'm afraid she won't marry me…at least I'm not sure. Also, I feel that I need to have a good job before I have the right to ask her to be my wife. Anyway, I figure this is a good way of finding out if she wants to marry me. It's decision-making time for Bobbie."

"When are you going to ask her to marry you?"

"Tonight."

"What if she says 'no'? Will you still leave for Florida then?"

"Either way, I'll be on my way to Miami on Thursday morning. If she says 'no', it'll break my heart…But if I stay here, it'll break my spirit."

"When are you going to tell Dad?"

"Tomorrow, after I talk to Bobbie."

They were silent as they drove back home. Noticing his brother's sadness, Dean almost regretted the heart-wrenching decision he had made.

When he met Bobbie at her door that evening he thought about how this night with her might be his last. He again was overwhelmed by her loveliness, making him realize that he had for months taken her beauty for granted.

Her disarming smile captivated him. He felt in a strange way that since she was unsuspecting in regard to his plan, he was somehow betraying her with the hidden knowledge of his decision, for as far as she knew, this was just another Sunday night date.

"What would you like to do?" she asked, with a smile, "Want to go to a movie?"

"I don't know. Why don't we just ride around?"

"Ride around where?"

"No place in particular," he said, "just ride."

"Okay, let's just ride around." She smiled at him.

Dean became silent as she excitedly chattered about her progress in *Knoxville Business Colleg*e, an involvement of Bobbie's that he had failed to consider when making his decision to leave for Florida. Sadly, he realized that he had been thinking about his own dreams without really considering those of hers. Her attendance at the school would probably be the factor that would prevent her from leaving Knoxville. As he considered this, he began to lose his courage. *What right have I to ask her to abandon her education, her family and friends, to suddenly leave for Miami with me? How could she possibly love me that much?* thought Dean.

He suddenly decided that he would never have the brazenness to make such a request of her. It would be simpler to tell her that he loved her, and ask her if she would wait for him… that maybe someday they could start over again; however the prospect saddened him.

"Dean! Dean…! Where in the world is your mind tonight?" asked Bobbie, laughing. "I've been talking to you, and you act like your mind is a thousand miles away! What are you in such deep thought about?"

"Oh, I'm sorry, honey, I guess I was just day-dreaming."

They were both silent for a long while as Dean drove aimlessly through the suburbs of West Knoxville. Having a keen perception of his moods, Bobbie looked at him and smiled.

"Honey, you're not yourself tonight. Is something wrong? Do you want to share it with me…maybe I can help, if you're worried about something."

"Bobbie, I…I want to talk to you about something." He found himself nervous and almost tongue-tied, the same emotions he had experienced on the first night that he had met her.

"Is something wrong?" She was beginning to feel concern.

He wheeled the vehicle into Concord Park, stopping the car in the same place that they had parked on their first night together. This time, however, there was no romantic harvest moon smiling down on the couple; instead, the surrounding park was dark and cold, as the biting north wind buffeted the car. The gloomy darkness of the park and the mournful cry of the wind coincided with his despairing mood.

In an attempt to escape his melancholia, Dean sat erectly in his seat displaying an optimistic smile.

"Well, Bobbie, I've got some good news and some bad news. Which do you want to hear first?"

She looked at him as she displayed a puzzled smile.

"Give me the good news first."

"Well, the good news is that I am taking a great job in about a week," said Dean, with a confident grin. "It's a real creative job, and I'll make about twice what I've been making."

"That's great news, Dean! I'm so proud of you. I'll bet you're excited."

"Yeah, I'm real excited about it."

"Okay, what's the bad news?" asked Bobbie, cautiously.

Dean swallowed hard before he answered.

"The bad news is that it's in Miami, Florida." Out of the corner of his eyes, he looked at her.

For a moment, she sat silently, then she said with phony optimism. "Well, I'm so happy for you. Are you sure you're going to take the job?"

"Yeah, I'm sure. It's such a great opportunity, I can't turn it down." *Well, I've said it. Now she knows.*

"When do you have to leave?"

"Thursday."

"Oh," she said, sadly.

Suddenly, they both stopped talking, and Dean began to feel uncomfortable.

Strangely, his feelings for her were much like the emotions he had felt on that first night, for that was the beginning of a magical relationship, and this night was possibly the end of it. Again, he felt that they were about to alter their courses and sail into uncharted waters; however, he feared that their journeys might take separate paths.

As he had done on their first night, he gently took her hand. He tenderly pulled her warm body against his as she nestled her head on his shoulder. For a long while they sat quietly as they listened to the moan of the lonely wind as it whipped the leafless trees. The outside cold had begun to invade the interior of the vehicle, the coolness contrasting sharply with the warmth of her lovely body, snuggled against him. *I'm about to lose her*, thought Dean. He began to consider abandoning his plan to leave as he envisioned what his life would be without her.

"Will I see you again before you leave?" she asked as she pressed her body closer against his. The question, though innocent, carried the ominous tone of finality.

"I don't know…I have a lot to do before I leave. Anyway, it would just make it harder for me to leave you," he said, sadly.

They cuddled together, without speaking, while the inside of the car grew colder. Finally, he started the car, and as they wordlessly drove out of the park toward Knoxville, he silently said goodbye to this special place where he had fallen in love with her.

They both felt an awkwardness, neither of them knowing what to say, as Dean drove the car in silence, back into the city.

"Are you taking me home?" asked Bobbie.

"I'll take you anywhere you want to go." He turned onto Cumberland Avenue and headed toward downtown Knoxville.

"Well, is this the end of it?" she asked.

"Bobbie, I don't know how I can handle not seeing you anymore. Maybe if I took the job and worked for maybe a year or so, would you wait for me? I could always come back."

"Come back for what? For a date, and then you'd go back to Miami? What's the point in that?" she asked, innocently and without anger.

Dean realized how foolish his question had sounded. He knew that he wanted to marry her, but his fear of rejection made it impossible for him to utter the question. Anyway, how could he ask her to give up her education?

Slowly, he turned the car left on Henley Street. Mustering all of his courage, he asked her, hesitantly, "Bobbie, do you think you could leave school for a while?"

"No, I wouldn't want to leave school. Why are you asking me that, anyway?"

His heart sank. *Of course she doesn't want to leave school, you idiot!* He tried to explain his foolish question.

"I'm not saying I want you to quit school. I just thought that when I go to Miami, maybe you could come down there and live, and we could keep seeing each other. You could enter Business College down there, and we wouldn't have to part. You're a grown woman now, and you can do whatever you want."

"Do you mean I would ride down there by myself, and then get a place of my own after I get there?" she asked. She was aware of Dean's insecurities and suspected at the moment that in his clumsy way, he was asking her to marry him; however, she wasn't completely sure of his intentions. Deciding to come to his aid in his bumbling attempt, she took the chance that he was unable to take.

"Dean, I'd really like to go down to Miami with you so we could continue being together. I'd even be willing to drop out of school in order to be with you. But I could never follow you down there unless I knew that someday you would marry me." She looked at him to see his reaction.

"I'd marry you, I promise you that! If you feel that way, why don't we just get married before I leave—then you could go down with me?" In order to not appear over-eager, he made a futile attempt to hide his excitement.

"All right, why don't we just do that?" With a radiant smile, she took his hand in hers.

Finally, Dean drove into the driveway of her father's home where she was now staying.

"You'll have to ask my daddy, but he'll be in bed now, so you'll have to ask him tomorrow," she said.

"Listen Bobbie, sleep on it. I don't want you to feel like I pressured you into this. After you are awake tomorrow, I'll call you, and you can tell me if you still feel the same way."

He passionately kissed her good night. As they ended their embrace, she looked at him with a puzzled expression.

Oh. Lord, why did I say that...? It was all settled and now she probably thinks that I feel unsure about our decision.

The next morning, after packing his clothing, he called her. Her first statement that came over the phone was—"I still feel the same way."

He hurriedly drove to her house. After receiving her father's blessing, Dean and Bobbie were married in the Knox County Courthouse with Bobbie's older sister, Ruby, as a witness to the ceremony.

After the couple arrived at the Beauvais home, Dean told his family goodbye. Sarah hugged him and said, "You have an adorable wife." She and Bobbie held each other, cheek to cheek, as Sarah told them how proud she felt of them.

Elwood squeezed Bobbie tightly, then tousled her hair as he said goodbye. His arms reached for Dean, and they held each other in a lengthy embrace. After Dean opened the car door for Bobbie, he and his father shook hands, with Will wishing them the best.

With a sense of adventure and excitement in their hearts, Dean and Bobbie drove away, as Elwood stood in the Beauvais parking area, waving to them until his brother's car disappeared from sight.

Any change, even a change for the better, is always accompanied by drawbacks and discomforts. **Arnold Bennett**

Chapter 18

Elwood awoke with a splitting headache. After the departure of Dean and Bobbie, he had been awake for the greater part of the night. During his brief periods of sleep, his unconscious mind had been invaded with unsettling dreams of abandonment. His melancholy, nocturnal visions alternated between Dean's impulsive desertion of him and vivid images of being forsaken by both Virginia and his father, Will.

He sat up, his sleep-deprived eyes gazing forlornly at Dean's empty bed. He longed for his brother's companionship. Since Dean had been back at home for two years, Elwood had assumed that his brother had found a measure of peace in his life, and that his years of aimless wandering were now behind him.

As he analyzed his brother's behavior, he thought about when Dean came to his rescue in the recent fight. Looking back, he could see that the incident coincided with his brother's altered attitude, and that it was probably the catalyst that re-kindled the flame of unrest in Dean. Knowing his brother's regret of his past aggressive behavior, he felt that perhaps Dean concluded that he could never repair his blemished reputation. Since Dean's decision to leave may have been initiated by the brawl, Elwood now felt responsible for his departure. There was one positive aspect of the recent events that Elwood felt good about— and that was Dean's marriage to Bobbie.

Smelling the toasty aroma of freshly-brewed coffee, he knew that Will and Sarah were starting their morning chores. Without bothering to groom himself, he halfheartedly got dressed and dejectedly walked into the kitchen where his parents were having breakfast. They looked up as Elwood walked listlessly toward the pot of coffee.

"Good morning, Elwood," they said, almost in unison.

"Morning," replied Elwood, without emotion.

"Sit down and have some breakfast with us," invited Sarah, attempting to appear cheerful.

"No, I just want coffee." He poured the steaming brew into a large mug.

"You need to start eating something," lectured Will.

Without answering, Elwood took a sip of coffee, then seated himself at the table.

"I don't feel like working today, Dad. I didn't get much sleep last night. We don't have much work anyway...That's one reason Dean left."

Will looked at Elwood.

"No, Elwood. Dean left for the same reason that he always leaves. He will always be nothing but a drifter. You just can't count on him. I hate to think about the lonesome, aimless life that he will put that little girl through. I wonder why in the world she married him. I'll give that marriage about six months."

"I don't agree with you, Dad. Dean and Bobbie really love each other. I think that getting married was the best thing that they both ever did. Dean left because we don't have enough work in the shop to keep him, and he didn't see any future here. His reason for leaving wasn't because he's a drifter...It's just the opposite. He wants to establish a good life for himself and his new wife."

"Well, I'll tell you something Elwood," said Will. "He won't find what he's looking for by traveling all over the country. In a way, I know how he feels because I used to think that the grass was always greener in another back yard. But that woman he married will get tired of that, and I don't think she will stick with him. What kind of girl is she, anyway?"

Sarah stopped eating as she looked directly at Will.

"She's a fine girl with a lot of character!" she said, with a trace of defiance in her voice. "That young woman has a lot of spunk. She'll be good for him. She has an independent side to her, and it's refreshing to see that around here...refreshing for Dean too."

"And you can tell that much about her, just from the few times that we've met her?" asked Will.

"Yes, I can!" answered Sarah. "A woman knows these things. It doesn't matter how long we talked. It was the content of what was said, and the way she acted, and how she looked at Dean. Didn't you even listen to the conversation? Maybe you need to open your eyes and ears, Will."

Will realized that this was the first time that Sarah had dared to question his judgment when in the company of a family member.

"Well, anyway...Is it okay with you if I take the day off, Dad?" asked Elwood.

"Yeah, it's alright with me, but you're making a mistake by loafing around, brooding. Right now things are tough for you. That's when you need to go to work and do something positive," said Will. "Come on, let's go into the shop. I need to talk to you about something that's been on my mind."

When Sarah began to clean away the breakfast dishes, Will and Elwood left the table and walked into the shop. Reaching into his shirt pocket, Will drew out a cigarette and handed it to his son.

"Let's sit for awhile and relax, Elwood."

Elwood lit his cigarette as the men took seats, facing each other.

"Elwood, you're going to have to get into a better mood. Just because Dean's gone for awhile doesn't mean it's the end of the world. I'll guarantee you that he'll be back here in less than six months, because he'll miss your company, just as you miss his."

"Do you think so?" asked Elwood, his face displaying a hopeful look.

"I know so, because I know Dean. Elwood, I'll tell you what we ought to do. We ought to lure him back here. You know, I feel partly responsible for Dean's leaving here. I realize that work has been slow around here, but since I've had it in my mind to retire, I've lost some of my enthusiasm about the shop. Because of that, I've sort of let my feet drag in selling work. If you're interested, I'd like for you to take over the business. That would give me time to sell work. I could keep us covered up in sign jobs. We'll let Dean make the winter in Florida, and then we'll get him back here in the spring when we're loaded with business."

"But Dean wants to do something more creative than just painting signs," Elwood declared.

"When I retire, Elwood, I'm going to build me a room on the side of the shop and start a studio where I can paint. I'm sure Dean would like to paint pictures in his spare time," said Will.

"You know that's a good idea, Dad." Elwood grinned at his father.

"Then let's make some long range plans together," suggested Will. "I was thinking about the acreage behind the shop. Clay's house is almost finished. It's going to be real nice on that lot I gave to him and Ellen. Dean already picked a lot too, and I was hoping he would someday build him a house. So, when are you going to pick a lot for yourself, Elwood?"

"Well, Dad, until recently I always figured that I'd live here with you and Mom."

"But you've got a girl now," Will pointed out. "Someday you may want to marry. And, if you do, you may want to build a house on your lot, too. Why don't we walk up the road behind the shop and you can pick out a lot for yourself. So far, there are still three lots left. You can have your pick of the three."

They walked around the building and started a leisurely stroll up *Beauvais Lane*. The road, which carried the family name, flanked the Beauvais property and provided access to the adjoining neighboring houses atop a sloping hill behind Will's parcel of land. They strolled past the first lot where Clay's house was rapidly taking shape. Then, as they continued to walk up the lane, Will pointed out the location of the remaining four lots, all of which were located to the left of the road. Finally, after reaching the rear boundary of the Beauvais property, Will halted.

"This last lot is the one that Dean claimed," Will said, as he laughed, "I guess he wanted his lot to be as far away from me as possible."

"I want that lot, right there," Elwood pointed, "the one next to Dean's lot."

"Okay, it's yours. Also, if you want it, the shop is yours. Maybe Dean will come to his senses and come in as your partner before too long. You could just give me a small percentage of the profit, and we'll figure out a time when you can take over. Is that okay with you?"

Elwood's mood quickly brightened.

Displaying a broad smile, he replied, "Yes, Dad…It's fine with me. As soon as I hear from Dean, I'm going to start to try to get him to come back to us."

"You don't need to rush it," cautioned Will. "Let him work in Miami for awhile. It won't take long for him to get bored with it…You know, he's worked there twice before. He'll come back here, I'll guarantee it. Your problem will be in trying to figure out a way of keeping him here."

"I think that Bobbie will keep him here, Dad. She's really a good woman, and she'll settle Dean down. I'll bet he'll build a house on his lot, now that he's married."

Following his talk with his father, Elwood began to feel much better. He arrived back at the shop with a renewed spirit and started to work with enthusiasm. As he considered his father's offer, he began to make an assessment of his future. Since he had chosen his lot, he decided that he would follow Clay's example by building a house. He and Virginia had already discussed marriage; however, the unresolved problem of his Dad's possible reaction to Virginia's past divorce weighed heavily on his mind.

As he watched his father drive away, Elwood stopped working. Putting his paint brush aside, he walked into the living room quarters where Sarah was relaxing in an easy chair, reading the Saturday Evening Post.

After grinning at his mother, he took a seat on the couch, facing her. Noticing his warm smile, she put her magazine aside.

"Well, Elwood, you seem to be in a better mood than you were in at breakfast."

"In a way, I am, Mom… But in another way, I'm anxious about something. Can we talk?"

"Elwood, you know that you can always talk to me," she answered. "Is something worrying you?"

"I don't know where to start," he said. "I'm happy that Dad wants me to run the shop. And he seems to think that maybe Dean and Bobbie will come back …Do you think Dean will come back, Mom?"

"Yes, I do, Elwood," she said. "Dean has a wife now, and I believe he will be back, mostly because he loves you so much. Have you and Virginia been thinking about marriage?"

Elwood hesitated before he answered.

"Mom, what do you think of Virginia? You've met her. Do you think that we're right for each other?"

"Yes, I do, and she must be a good woman if you are in love with her. She seems like a very nice person. I think she would make a good wife. What's the matter, honey? Are you having second thoughts about her?"

"No, Mom, but I'm afraid Dad might have second thoughts about her."

"Why do you think that?" asked Sarah. "He met her when you brought her here. He seemed to like her. Anyway, you know how Will is. He never seems too enthusiastic about any girl that goes out with one of you boys. Look at how he acted about Bobbie when she married Dean. But he'll eventually like Bobbie when he sees how genuine she is. And I'll bet he'll like Virginia, too."

"Mom…There's something about Virginia that I didn't tell you or Dad," he said hesitantly, as he began to rock. "Virginia has been married before."

Sarah was shocked, and for a long time she didn't respond. Finally, she looked sadly at him.

"Elwood, after meeting Virginia, I'm sure that if her marriage didn't work that it was not her fault. You'll have no problem with me, but I'm afraid that you'll have a real problem with Will when you tell him."

"What can I do, Mom? If I tell him and he doesn't accept her, what will it do to my relationship with Dad? You know how close we are. I don't want to lose my closeness with him, but I could never give up Virginia. We've even talked about marriage."

"Then you might have to make a choice."

"Yeah…that's the same thing that Dean told me."

"Do you want me to talk to your dad for you?"

"No, Mom. I'll have to talk to him myself. Dad would be even more disappointed if I let somebody do my talking for me. I'll just have to think about it for awhile before I can tell Dad."

"Elwood, I love your dad with all my heart, but I know sometimes he's a hard man."

"Mom, I wonder why Dean felt like he had to move so fast when he decided to leave? When he made up his mind to get married and to move away, he was out of here like a whirlwind."

"Elwood, that's his nature. Neither Dean nor Rob, when they decide to do something, let any grass grow under their feet."

"Mom, I just can't be that way. I've been trying to get the guts to talk to Dad about Virginia for over six months."

After considering her son's remarks, Sarah replied, "I'm not saying you should be that way…As a matter of fact, I think Rob and Dean are sometimes too impulsive in their actions. You've always been more patient and put more thought into your decisions, but Elwood, you also have a mighty good heart—and it has always kept you and those who love you happy; so it seems to me that there is only one thing that you need to do….Follow your heart."

There came a time when the risk to remain in the bud was more painful than the risk it took to blossom. **Anais Nin**

Chapter 19

The pastel shades of pink and white Dogwood sprinkled the hillsides of Tyler City. The slow, dreary months of winter were over, and Elwood welcomed this spring more than any other season of his life. Will had gradually relinquished the sign shop's management responsibilities to Elwood and assigned himself the role of salesman for the company; as a result the shop was filled with sign orders. Although Elwood, on occasion, employed the services of Alvin, he nonetheless found himself working many overtime hours.

It was an eventful time for the Beauvais family. Clay's house had been completed and his wife, Ellen, had given birth to a son, Terry, who became Will's pride and joy. After having been laid off from his job, Clay enlisted in the U.S. Army and was sent to Korea at the end of the war. Consequently, in Clay's absence, Will became a second father to his first grandson, Terry.

At the beginning of his retirement, Will's brother, John died of tuberculosis. For the period of this sadness, Will began construction on the addition to the shop building, a structure that he intended to use as his art studio.

During this time, Elwood and his father grew emotionally closer. More than merely father and son, they were also pals. Elwood was one of the few people in his life that his father had ever allowed to get emotionally close to him. Will's prejudices were overlooked by Elwood, who felt that his father's moral character and love for his family outweighed his flaws; Will truly worshiped his family.

Recognizing a need for additional help in the shop, Elwood began to make plans to coax Dean to return to Tyler City. Perhaps, he thought, if Dean and Bobbie returned, he could marry Virginia, and the brothers could again work together and build houses on their adjoining lots. In dread of a confrontation about Virginia's divorce, he began to consider the possibility of concealing it from Will. In his inability to make a final decision, he decided to postpone marriage with the hope that Dean would come home to offer advice and moral support.

As his father worked at his desk in the shop, Elwood was lettering a sign on the large easel. He was in a talkative mood as he enthusiastically discussed the possibility of building a house on his lot.

"Cap'n, if I build a house, where should I place it on the lot?"

"I'd put it fairly close to the hedge row in the back of the lot. It will give you a bigger front yard. By the way, when are you planning to get married? If you stay single, you won't need a house...You can keep on living right here with Sarah and me."

"Oh, I'm in no hurry to get married. I'm not impulsive like Dean or Rob. I like to think about things instead of rushing into them."

Putting his lettering brush aside, he strolled across the room to his father and reached into Will's shirt pocket for a cigarette.

"Dad, I'm a little worried about Dean. I was getting letters from him regularly, but now I haven't heard from him in at least two weeks."

"I wouldn't worry too much about him, Elwood," replied Will, as he shuffled through his papers. "How was he doing the last time you heard from him?"

"He said he was doing fine, but that he was lettering signs more than painting pictures. I need help here in the shop. Don't you think I should call him and ask him to come back home?"

"No, let him make up his mind. If he decides to not come back, then I'll hire somebody else to help you. You can never be sure of what Dean will do. You might be better off without him." Will put on his hat. "I've got to go to town for a few things, Elwood." He walked out the front door to his car as Elwood went back to work on the sign.

During his lunch break, Elwood strolled up the hill to examine his lot. Walking near the back edge of the property, he looked to the western horizon toward the distant blue silhouette of the Cumberland Mountains. A huge oak tree beside the lane bordering the south boundary of the lot offered a large expanse of shade to the future front yard. As he viewed the gradual slope of the adjoining lots, his eyes fell upon a hollow that had once been a pond, located in a low elevation behind one of the lots. Remembering the pond from his childhood, Elwood vowed to replace it. In the depression were the remains of a decomposing trailer chassis upon which Will had once intended to build a trailer that would transport the family on a yearly winter trip to Florida. Will had bought the chassis new, twenty years earlier, with the annual pledge that next year his car would pull the trailer to southern Florida where the family would spend the winter. Elwood felt a twinge of sadness as he viewed the deteriorating framework with the rotting rubber tires; for the dilapidated chassis was a symbol of his father's restlessness and unfulfilled dreams.

After returning to the shop, he completed the sign, then walked to the desk to make a few phone calls. Idly peering out the window as he chatted on the telephone, he noticed an unfamiliar car drive into the parking area in front. It was a new, 1957, gold and white Fairlane Ford convertible. *A classy vehicle*, thought Elwood. As he curiously eyed the car, both doors opened and out stepped Dean and Bobbie.

Elwood hung up the phone in the middle of his call and suddenly bolted through the front door to meet his brother. Bobbie was dressed in a tee-shirt and white shorts. As Elwood ran to meet them, Bobbie clutched him in a vigorous embrace as he playfully ruffled her hair with his fingers and exclaimed, "Well, if it isn't my favorite sister!"

Dean, dressed in casual clothes and wearing sunglasses, quickly walked to meet Elwood, and the brothers enveloped each other in a spirited hug.

"Dean! It's great to see you! Are you home to stay?" asked Elwood, excitedly.

"Hi, Elwood! Am I home to stay? You know that I could never answer a question like that!" he laughed as he playfully slapped his brother on his shoulder. "Why would I want to stay in this one-horse town, anyhow?"

"Don't let him kid you, Elwood," said Bobbie, projecting a happy grin, "He's here to stay, and I'll see to that!"

"Do you see what you get into when you get married?" asked Dean, "I no longer have a choice in the matter. I guess maybe I am here to stay."

"Is your mom home?" asked Bobbie.

"Yeah, she's inside," answered Elwood.

"Then, I'm going in the house to see her! Nice to see ya again, Elwood." exclaimed Bobbie, as she ran happily into the living quarters.   Dean laughed, "Well, now that we're rid of her, maybe we can talk a little bit."

Both men took a seat at the desk. "Are you really here to stay, Dean? I sure need some help here in the shop."

"Yeah, Elwood, I'm here to stay, although considering my past, I doubt if anybody will believe me."

Elwood displayed an expansive grin as he began to vigorously rock from side to side. "And I'm going to build Bobbie and me a house on my lot," Dean declared.

"That's great, Dean! Dad gave me a lot, and I chose the one right beside yours. I'll build Virginia and me a house there."

Excitedly, Elwood reclaimed his seat, then leaned forward, close to Dean.

"So you're really going to put down roots this time? What makes you sure that you're through rambling?"

"Elwood, I've been running away from, or toward something for years now. But I've learned life is not a question of where you are, but who you are. You won't find the answers out there somewhere, but in here," he said as he gestured with his thumb toward his chest, "Except for the scenery or climate, every place you go is just a carbon copy of the last place you've been. You know, I've always said I wanted to have a career in art or music…Well, maybe I can find it here. Anyway, for some reason, I always seem to find my way back here."

"Dad's building a studio on the end of the shop, and he wants you to start painting pictures with him," said Elwood.

"Is that what he's building, there? I noticed it when we drove in here."

"Yeah…and we can get back into our music," said Elwood, as he began to energetically rock.

"Elwood, if you are going to build a house on your lot, who's going to live in it? Just you? When are you going to marry Virginia? I figured that you would have married by now!"

"Well, I'm getting around to it."

"You're a slow mover, Elwood. I've seen snails move faster than you do."

From habit, Elwood reached into Dean's shirt pocket for a cigarette, but found the pocket empty.

"Sorry, Elwood…I quit smoking when I was in Miami."

"That's good, Dean. You quit drinking, now you've quit smoking. Come to think of it, I don't remember you cursing for a long time. Are you turning into a saint?"

Dean laughed, "No, I'm just trying to be healthy. I've started to work out in the gym pretty regularly. By the way, where's Dad?"

"He went to town for something. Come on, let me show you some of the jobs we'll be working on. Let's take tomorrow off and maybe do something with our women. I can make those kinds of decisions, now that I'm running the shop." The brothers quickly stood and Elwood proceeded to show Dean around the shop, occasionally stopping to rock.

*   *   *

In order to accommodate Dean and Bobbie for the evening meal, Sarah had decided to serve dinner in the dining room rather than in the usual setting at the small kitchen table. Being in a festive mood, Sarah selected her best china, silver, and cloth napkins. Together, Sarah and Bobbie set the table and chatted. An immediate bond developed between them as they shared friendly conversation, much of which related to the future plans of Dean and Bobbie.

At last, the family was seated for dinner. As the roast beef and stewed vegetables were passed around the table, Dean helped himself to large portions of the food, for after his long drive, he was famished; however, Elwood served himself only a small portion.

"You're not still dieting, are you Elwood?" asked Dean.

"No, not really," replied Elwood. "I'm just not very hungry tonight. I'm just excited, I guess."

"He still won't eat enough," said Will, "By the way, Dean, do you plan to stay around for awhile? Elwood could sure use some help with the sign shop."

"Yes, Dad... I know, considering my track record, you probably don't believe that I'll stay, but I really intend to. As a matter of fact, I plan to build a house on that lot you gave me."

"How are you going to pay for both a house and that fancy convertible?" asked Will.

"Dad, I got a fantastic deal on that car. I can manage it. I plan to settle down and work hard... now that I'm married."

As the conversation continued, Will exchanged comments with everyone at the table except for Bobbie. Noticing that Will's coffee cup was nearly empty and craving his affection, Bobbie smiled and asked, "Mr. Beauvais, can I pour you some more coffee?"

"Why, yes, thank you," replied Will, clumsily.

As Bobbie poured the coffee in his cup, Will looked timidly at her while displaying an affectionate, but shy smile.

Dean noticed the brief exchange between his father and Bobbie. It suddenly occurred to him that Will didn't dislike her, but only felt bashful when in her presence. Having no memory of his mother, and with no daughters, his only exposure to women had been his wife, Sarah. In his world of male-dominance, he had developed an awkward and constrained attitude toward the female gender.

As Sarah passed another serving of roast beef to Dean, she looked affectionately at Bobbie. "Bobbie, Dean tells me that you're from a family of all girls…aren't there six of you? I always wanted a daughter, but I ended up with five, mischievous boys."

"Yes, Mrs. Beauvais, there are six of us. I guess it's kind of odd, marrying into a family that has five boys."

"You mean five men," corrected Dean, with a smile.

"I'm sure glad that you and Dean are going to build a house and live here." said Sarah. "You know what the next step is, don't you? You need to bring me a little granddaughter."

Dean and Bobbie traded glances, both of them exhibiting a trace of a smile.

Displaying a bashful grin, Will said, "Now, Sarah, how do you know it will be a granddaughter? If I know Dean, he'll follow the Beauvais tradition of giving me a grandson. That way, Terry would have a playmate." His face became radiant with the mention of the name "Terry".

After finishing his coffee, Will got up from his chair and said, "That was a great meal, Sarah, but I ate too much. Why don't you and I go outside and relax and let these young people visit together for awhile?"

"You go on outside, Will. I can't just eat and run like you, I've go to clean off the table." Sarah smiled at him.

"No, Mrs. Beauvais, you go on outside with Mr. Beauvais and rest…I'll clean up in here… I insist," said Bobbie.

Sarah smiled. "I've got a better idea, honey. This is a special day! Let's both forget about cleaning up the table for now, and you and I will do it together later. Come outside with Will and me. I haven't had a chance to talk to another woman, except Ellen, in a long time."

"Yeah, scat, honey!" said Dean. "Elwood and I have some serious catching-up to do. And don't reveal our little secret."

Finally alone in the dining room with Elwood, Dean replenished their cups with hot coffee as Elwood casually fired up a cigarette.

"When did you start carrying cigarettes?" Dean asked.

"I always do. It's just that I always lay them down somewhere and can't find them."

Dean smiled. "Put me up to date on the family, Elwood. What's everybody been up to lately?"

"Well, Rob is doing okay. He's working at a good job. And Al is still painting a few signs...Sometimes he works a little for me. Clay...well, you know how he always had a fondness for the military."

Dean took a sip of his coffee. "Clay and I are alike in some ways...But man, he's different from me when it comes to liking the armed services. They demand so much discipline, and Clay is totally undisciplined. And I can't believe they sent him to Korea. What a hell-hole. He probably won't get a furlough for a year or more."

"Yeah, I worry about him," said Elwood. "Ellen is doing okay, I guess. The army takes care of her financially."

"Well, I haven't seen their baby—little Terry—yet. I'll have to go up and see him tomorrow."

As Elwood puffed on his cigarette, he began to sway, to and fro, in his chair. He sipped his coffee. "Man, you do things on the spur of the moment, Dean. When did you decide to come home, and what instigated you to do it?"

Dean grinned at his brother. "Well, for one thing, I kinda started missing you." He punched Elwood on the shoulder. "No, really, something very important brought me back. Elwood, you're going to be an uncle again."

"You mean...?"

"Yeah, Bobbie is going to have a baby. She's probably about three months along now. Not really showing much, yet."

Elwood began to forcefully rock with excitement.

"When are you going to tell Mom and Dad?"

"Not for awhile. I want to surprise them when the time is right. You see, that's why I feel that this time I'm putting down some roots. I don't take it lightly, becoming a father. Anyway, I could tell Bobbie was homesick for her family, and it's really fitting that our baby will be raised around kinfolks. This time my rambling days are over for good."

"Dean, that's great!" Elwood rocked furiously.

"So, when are you and Virginia going to marry? I hope you have kids, too, so our children can grow up together."

"I've been thinking of not even telling Dad about Virginia's divorce...Maybe I will just go ahead and marry her."

"Well, that's your decision," said Dean. "After all it's your life, not his. But if it were me, I'd tell him, and then I'd marry her, no matter what Dad thought."

"Sometimes, I wish I was like you, but I'm not. If I marry Virginia, and Dad won't accept her, I could never stay around here…not if he did-n't accept my wife. I couldn't call myself a man if I did that." Elwood's face showed sadness.

"Elwood, why do some things have to be so final with you? Everything can't be perfect. I'd hate to see you leave here just when I got back. Marry her and stay here, too!" Dean hated the thought of losing Elwood.

"Do you want me to talk to Dad about it for you?"

"No, Dad would never respect me if I let you do that," said Elwood. "I'm going to tell him sometime this week."

Elwood changed the subject. "Dean, where are you and Bobbie staying tonight?"

"Oh, we'll get a motel somewhere."

"No, Dean. You and Bobbie stay in the Bull Pen tonight, and I'll sleep on the couch. I'll call Virginia and we'll all go for a ride somewhere, right now! Then, we can spend the day together tomorrow."

"Elwood, I'd love to do that, but I'm kinda tired. I've just finished a 20 hour drive. Anyway, if we go out tonight, we'll be getting home late. Dad might lock the door and Bobbie and I would have to sleep in the car." The brothers broke into a boisterous laugh.

"Dad finally gave up on curfew a long time ago," said Elwood.

*   *   *

As the days quickly passed, the brothers adjusted to the routine of the sign shop. Although Elwood asked Dean to become his business partner, Dean, feeling that he hadn't yet earned the right, declined the offer.

After hiring a carpenter to help him, Dean had started construction on his house. When not at work in the shop, he spent each evening and every weekend on the project, often laboring until late into the night. In order to eliminate car payments, Dean traded his new convertible for a used sta-tion wagon, enabling him to invest more money in the construction of his house.

Elwood and Dean had resumed their participation in music, both in their band and with their singing quartet; however, with the absence of Clay, it was necessary to replace him with another first tenor.

Seeing the excitement of Dean and Bobbie about their future baby, and the progress being made on the construction of their house, Elwood decided that the time had come for him to marry Virginia, who had been patiently waiting for him to set the date.

As the brothers started to work one morning, Elwood said to his

216

brother, "Today's the day, Dean. I'm going to marry Virginia right away. We're going to set the date tonight, for sure."

"Great, Elwood... Man, you're a fast mover!" said Dean, with benign sarcasm.

"Now, I wonder who I can get to be my best man?" asked Elwood, as he cupped his chin in his hand, as if pondering the question.

"I'd be honored!" Dean replied.

"I'm going to take the bull by the horns and tell Dad about her divorce tonight after dinner." Elwood's voice carried the tenor of resolution.

"It will work out okay, Elwood. Think positive."

*　　　*　　　*

Will was silent as he walked through the front door into the shop. Upon seeing his father, Elwood stopped working and walked toward him with a limp and a one-eyed stare in an imitation of Jim Burns. Placing an arm around Will, he fished a cigarette from his father's pocket. Will stood in stony silence, with a gloomy expression.

"Elwood, come outside with me. I want to talk to you." Elwood was worried, but also puzzled. *What bad thing has happened?* he wondered.

Once outside, both men remained standing. "Elwood," Will began, "I just found out when I was in town something that disturbs me. That woman that you've been going with has been married before. A woman that used to live next door to her told me. Why didn't you tell me that woman was divorced?" His face appeared more disappointed than angry.

Elwood was devastated.

"That woman, as you refer to her, has a name. Her name is Virginia, and I intend to make her my wife, Dad, because I love her."

"Do you mean to tell me that you'd marry that woman and live in adultery for the rest of your life?" asked his father.

Will had a contradictory personality. Although in his habits he was a man of moderation, in his view of moral behavior, he was extreme. In the area of aesthetics, as an artist, he saw a multi-colored world of subtle nuances, with countless shades of gray.

However, in his evaluation of moral behavior, his thinking was more like that of an accountant, where there exists only one correct answer at the bottom line of the column. In all ethical matters, his judgment was rendered with uncompromising certainty. His moral world was painted in black and white: An attitude, circumstance, or deed was either right, or it was wrong. There was no middle ground.

Elwood's resolve began to crumble.

As he became nervous, he began to rock and hang his head. He stammered as he answered his father.

"Dad, I ...wouldn't be living in adultery...She's...legally divorced, by law."

"There's a higher, moral law that says different," countered Will, with a look of accusation.

"But, Dad...It wasn't her fault... Her husband mistreated her and was unfaithful to her." Elwood was beginning to tremble.

"Elwood, I'd like for you to marry someday, but find you a *good* woman. That woman has a living husband. Please don't marry a woman like that!" Will pleaded, "I could never accept her in this family."

Suddenly, Elwood bolted away from his father and walked rapidly through the shop into the living quarters. Dean stared in puzzlement as Elwood wordlessly hurried through the shop. Laying aside his lettering brush, Dean quickly followed his brother into the living room of the house.

"Elwood... what's wrong?"

"Everything's wrong!" explained Elwood. "Dad found out about Virginia's divorce. He said he could never accept her into the family. Now, I don't know what to do!"

"I thought you had made up your mind to marry her," said Dean. "Calm down, Elwood."

Dean grew more concerned as he sadly watched his brother pace the floor. Suddenly, Elwood stopped and began to nervously rock from side to side.

"I've got to get out of here for a few minutes, Dean...I don't know what to do—about getting married, or staying here, or anything! I'm going to take a ride." He walked through the front door toward his truck.

Dean followed behind. "Want me to go with you?"

"No...I have to be by myself, to think."

Dean stood silently as he watched Elwood's truck disappear toward Knoxville.

*   *   *

Elwood drove slowly into the wooded lane, parking his truck under a large oak tree. His windows were down, for the beautiful spring day was unusually warm. In deep thought, he sat silently, idly gazing at the winding lane in front of him, tracing its path with his eyes as it disappeared into the deep, dark woods. Lazily, he studied the sun-drenched meadow to his right, with its display of scattered goldenrod. Gradually, his emotions began to calm. As he sat in the comforting shade of the massive oak, only the occasional sound of a wayward, whining bee intruded upon the silence of the forest. The heady aroma of honeysuckle invaded the air as he listlessly rested in the seat of the truck.   Slowly, his subsiding agitation was replaced by a brooding melancholia. As he thought about his father, rather than feeling anger, he only experienced sadness, an emotion that was compounded by a deep feeling of loss. Gone was the close relationship with his dad. Also, he realized that he would never live with Virginia on the lot next to Dean and Bobbie where their children could play together.

A gentle breeze from the west carried a hint of the fresh smell of rain as the faint rumble of thunder interrupted his concentration. Looking in the direction of the muted sound, he watched the flickers of lightning playing among the darkening cumulus clouds in the distant western horizon.

As he lit a cigarette, he smiled at the fond memory of the countless times he had playfully stolen a cigarette from his father's pocket.

His uncertainty grew more intense as his mind began to grow weary of struggling for a solution. He considered getting drunk, in the hope that oblivion would offer a brief respite from the despair he felt in his heart. However, he quickly reconsidered, for the decision that lay before him demanded clear thinking.

Suddenly, he looked upward. A flapping noise from somewhere high in the oak tree had captured his attention. Almost hypnotized by the serenity of the forest and the sound from above, he peered intently in the direction of the clamor. As he looked more closely, he saw that the fluttering movement was caused by a small bird. He watched it fall from a high limb, only to be cushioned as it landed on the leaves of a lower branch. At first, he thought that the bird had a broken wing. Upon closer inspection, he noted that the wings of the tiny fowl were in perfect working order as it frantically flapped them in an effort to stay aloft. Watching the desperate struggle of the flailing bird, he became mesmerized as it fluttered to an even lower leafy arm of the tree. Finally, the feathered creature hurled itself from the lower limb, then after swooping low and grazing the mossy forest floor, it flew away, rising high into the sky. Elwood watched, spellbound, as the tiny bird flew free, disappearing into the distant southern sky.

A man travels the world over in search of what he needs and returns home to find it. **George Moore**

Chapter 20

Welcome to the Great State of Tennessee. The message became visible and quickly disappeared as Rob Beauvais finally crossed the border into his home state. Energized by the fact that he was closer to home, he increased the speed of his vehicle. He noticed that Madge was napping, so he lowered the volume of the radio and repositioned the fallen cushion that had cradled her head.

Reaching into his shirt pocket, he retrieved the last stick of spearmint gum from the package. Since he had stopped smoking more than a month earlier, he had developed the habit of incessant gum-chewing to alleviate his craving for nicotine. He lowered the sun visor to shield his eyes from the western sunset while he began to estimate his time of arrival at the Beauvais home. He wanted to get there before everyone went to bed.

He was driving his first brand-new car, a red and white Ford sedan, which he had purchased only a week earlier. He enjoyed the sound of the soothing hum of the V-8 engine and the clean, pleasant aroma of the new interior.

Realizing that his unannounced visit would take his family by surprise, he wondered what the initial reaction of his father would be. Rob had been kept abreast of family activities through exchanged letters with his brothers and Sarah, but he had yet to communicate with his father.

The sun had now descended beneath the western horizon, and with the increasing envelopment of dusk, the surrounding atmosphere became bathed in an eerie, orange glow. Looking to the fields as he traveled, he noticed standing water in the low-lying areas, an indication of a recent drenching thunderstorm.

As the twilight darkened, he switched on his lights and raised the sun visor. He thought about the many changes that had taken place within the family since he and Dean lived together in Ft. Wayne three years earlier, but mostly he reflected on the recent radical change that had occurred in his own life. As he reminisced about his family, he realized how much he had missed them. In excited anticipation of arriving home, he increased his speed even more as the new vehicle pushed westward toward Knoxville.

"Where are we?" Madge's voice interrupted Rob's thoughts.

"Oh! I'm glad you woke up, honey. I was getting kinda lonesome. We're about an hour out of Knoxville, I guess. We'll be at Mom and Dad's in a couple of hours."

"I'll be glad to see your Mom and Dad—your brothers, too," said Madge. "I'm glad to hear that Dean is doing so well. I can't wait to meet Bobbie. I wonder what she's like?"

"I can't picture Dean being married," said Rob. "And what about Elwood? Mom says he's really serious over—what's her name, again—Virginia?"

"Yes…Virginia," said Madge. "And I just can't believe that Elwood is slim, now."

Rob lowered the window and spat the wad of gum from his mouth, for the constant gum-chewing had tired his jaw muscles.

After driving through Knoxville, he glanced at his watch. "We'll be home by 9:30. They should still be awake."

"Do you think your dad will be glad to see us?"

"Well, maybe not at first," Rob said, "but he'll mellow after we've been home for awhile."

Another hour's drive delivered Rob and Madge to the Beauvais home. After Rob opened the unlocked living room door for Madge, they both entered the house. Will and Sarah looked up, staring at the couple in bewilderment.

"We're home again!" said Madge, as she ran to Sarah, who quickly looked up from her easy-chair.

As Madge embraced Sarah, Rob smiled at his father, who was seated in the corner at his desk.

"Hi, Dad," greeted Rob, as he walked slowly toward his dad. Rising from his chair, Will cautiously eyed his son while Rob awkwardly extended his hand to his father.

As they shook hands, Will said, "Well, you sort of caught us off-guard…We didn't know you were coming."

Rob hoped that the mood of sadness reflected by Will's eyes was not indicative of his disdain for his and Madge's return; however, being perceptive about his father's moods, Rob sensed that something else was amiss.

"Is something wrong, Dad?" asked Rob, with concern.

"Oh, I'm sorry Rob…It's good to see you. I didn't give you much of a welcome, did I? I'm worried about something, that's all. What made you come home? Is everything okay?"

"Everything's fine, Dad, but I've got a feeling that everything is not fine here. What's wrong?"

"Elwood's gone!" said Will, sadly.

"Gone? Gone where?"

"He went to Miami. He suddenly married that girl that he's been dating, and left here without even telling me goodbye."

"I'm sorry to hear that, Dad."

Aware of the bond that Elwood also shared with Sarah, he turned to his mother and hugged her compassionately.

"I'm sorry, Mom. How long has he been gone?"

"He just left here yesterday," answered Sarah, who now had tears in her eyes. "You just barely missed him."

"What made him leave so quickly?" asked Rob. "I thought he was running the business for you, Dad."

Sarah looked at Rob, then cast a disapproving glance toward Will.

"He left because your dad didn't approve of Virginia! He came and told me goodbye, and I begged for him to stay, but he wouldn't. He wanted to tell Will goodbye, too, but as usual, Will put on that hat of his and left before Elwood got here. I'm worried about him. He's never lived in other places, like you and Dean."

Rob hugged his mother again. "Don't worry, Mom, Elwood will be fine. You know how smart he is."

Will interjected. "I didn't want him to marry that woman who had been divorced. I only had his best interests at heart."

During the discussion, Madge, feeling like an intruder, sat silently on the sofa. Rob, who was tired from the long drive, decided to change the subject, for he feared that further discussion of Elwood's departure might lead to a quarrel with his father. He forced a smile as he attempted to brighten the somber mood by asking about Dean.

"How's Dean? I hear the rascal got married. What's his wife like?"

"She's really pretty and a fine little girl," said Sarah. "And she's going to have a baby, too."

"Are you serious? Dean's going to be a 'dad'?" asked Rob, "Looks like you're going to have a house full of grandchildren! How's Clay's new baby doing?"

For the first time, Will smiled. "That's the one bright spot in my life. Since Clay's gone, I'm just like a daddy to little Terry."

"What do you hear from Clay?" asked Rob.

"Well, we get a letter every now and then," said Sarah. "He's in Korea, you know...It'll probably be several months before he gets a furlough. He's doing all right, I think."

"And Al, what's he doing?"

"He works here some, but he's still painting houses, too. I just can't figure him out," said Will.

"Where do Dean and Bobbie live? When can we see them?"

"They have a small apartment in town. He'll be working here in the shop tomorrow," replied Will. "Right now, Dean's kinda confused about the shop. He was working for Elwood, but now Elwood's gone...Just left here with no advance notice."

"I'm worried about Dean, too," said Sarah. "He's awfully sad about Elwood leaving."

Rob finally took a seat on the sofa beside Madge as Will turned to face them.

After a brief silence, he said, "Rob, you're sure looking good. You look like you've lost quite a bit of weight."

"Yeah, Dad, I've lost more than 20 pounds... I only weigh a hundred seventy-five now. Also, I've quit smoking," Rob replied, proudly.

"Rob, I don't know how to say this tactfully, so I'll just spit it out. I'm really glad to see you, and I'm proud that you've lost weight and quit smoking. But I may have already lost Elwood, and I don't want to lose Dean again. I want to ask you, Rob...Please don't get Dean back into drinking or in a rambling mood. He's been really behaving well for the last couple of years, and that girl he married seems to have settled him down. He's different from the Dean you used to know."

"Looking back, maybe I wasn't the best influence. Well, maybe I'm different from the Rob you used to know," said Rob, as he smiled at his father.

"Have you quit drinking?" Will's face expressed skepticism.

"Yeah, Dad...I gave that up too."

"I'm glad to see that you've turned over a new leaf."

"Actually, I've done more than turn over a new leaf, Dad. I've turned my life over to God. I've had a spiritual conversion, or as most people say—I've been 'saved'. In fact, although I'm not sure of it yet, I think God is calling me to become a minister."

Appearing to be in total shock, Will looked at his son in utter disbelief. His mouth fell open as his transparent emotions reacted to the incredulity of Rob's statement. Will was speechless, as Sarah ran to her son, encircling him in her arms.

"Glory be!" she cried out through her tears. "Thank you, God!"

Finally, Will spoke. "Rob, you'll never know how proud I am of you! You know, I always knew that there was something special about you! Ever since the day you were born, you have shown an independent spirit that made you different. If you only knew how many times we've prayed for you!"

"Well, maybe God answered some of your prayers. By the way, I've already preached a couple of times at the church where I was baptized. I was only a guest speaker, of course, and I guess my delivery was a little weak, but God helped me to say the right words."

"When did this spiritual conversion happen?" asked Will.

"A couple of months ago. I didn't tell you because I wanted to come home and surprise you with the news."

For more than an hour they continued to discuss Rob's recent spiritual conversion. Noting the late hour, Sarah spoke.

"I know both of you must be very tired. Why don't you sleep here tonight?"

"Yeah, you can sleep in the Bull Pen. It's empty now, with Elwood gone," said Will.

After Madge and Sarah retired for the evening, Rob and his father sat in the living room for most of the night, talking. As he struggled to comprehend the radical change in his son, Will's emotions were infused with ambivalence; for while Elwood's abandonment had left an emptiness in his soul, Rob's redemption and reunion with the family had partially filled the void.

*   *   *

The next morning, Dean was unusually late in his arrival at the shop. His sadness over Elwood's departure had produced a sleepless night, leaving him to feel as slow and sluggish as the next morning's sunrise. As he pulled his car to the curb, he noticed the new red and white Ford parked in front of the building. He cringed at the thought of greeting the customer who was apparently waiting inside. *I don't need this...Let Dad deal with it...It's not my problem, anyway.* With that thought, Dean suddenly realized that Elwood's rapid departure had left an unforeseen problem. *Just whose problem is it, then?* Dean wondered if this had crossed his father's mind. *So, wonder who I am working for?* thought Dean. The whole thing seemed foolish, but it angered Dean when he thought of the seriousness of it, for he knew how a single, disagreeable act could knock a person from his father's pedestal forever. Sadly, Dean thought of the one person who could make things as final as his father—and that was Elwood.

To his surprise, Dean found the front door locked. After unlocking the door, he entered the dark, empty room of the shop and flipped on the light. The bright red letters on the sign that rested on the easel caught his attention. He recognized the style of lettering on the sign—it had been hand lettered by Elwood. The recognition of it saddened him.

The locked door had aroused his curiosity. *Could it be that Dad had closed the shop until further plans could be made?* As he pondered the ambiguity of the situation, he heard someone enter the shop from the living quarters. Expecting to see his father, he turned and suddenly stopped in his tracks. Unable to believe his eyes, he recognized the somewhat slimmer, pajama-clad figure of Rob.

"Rob! Is it you?" yelled Dean.

"Yeah, Pal...It's me!" Rob walked swiftly to his startled brother. After a brief handshake, they spontaneously came together in a partial embrace.

Stepping back from his brother, Dean exclaimed, "Rob, you look great! You're so slim, I hardly recognized you! What are you doing home?"

"Well, I started missing you, ole' buddy...and Mom and Dad, and the rest of the family, too."

"Where's Madge?"

"She's still asleep. So are Mom and Dad. We stayed up pretty late last night."

"Are you on vacation? How long can you stay?"

"I can stay as long as I wish. I quit my job." Rob laughed and said, "Only this time, I gave my boss two-weeks notice."

Dean joined him in laughter, then asked, "Why did you quit? Do you have another job lined up?"

"No, not really. I may look for something in a few days, though."

"Is that your new car out front? That nice Ford? You better get a job soon if you want to hold on to that beauty." Dean remarked.

"Well, maybe the Lord will provide," said Rob.

Dean looked at Rob curiously, and then laughed.

"I guess Mom and Dad told you about Elwood," said Dean.

"Yeah, I was shocked. And Dad's taking it kinda hard...I guess Elwood is too. As close as those two are, they should find some way to mend their relationship." Rob carefully placed a stick of gum into his mouth. "Tell me Dean—when did Elwood get married?"

"The day before yesterday. I was his best man...or you might say, I was the witness. It was only a civil ceremony performed by a justice of the peace. Elwood wanted to get married quick, and get out of here. It's totally unlike Elwood to do something in a hurry like that."

"What was his big hurry?"

"He was mad at Dad...He didn't approve of Elwood's girlfriend—Virginia."

"He got married in a hurry because he was mad at Dad? What kind of reason is that to get married?" asked Rob.

"Oh, he was going to get married, anyway. He'd been planning to marry for months. He just wanted to marry her quickly so he could get away from Dad as fast as possible."

"Where is he going? Does he have a job?"

"He's going to Miami. I called *Morris Sign Company*, where you and I used to work, and Moe gave him a job. By the way, Moe asked about you...He wanted to know if you still drank wine for breakfast."

The brothers laughed, and Rob said, "Sounds like he still has a sense of humor. He's a good boss, and I'm sure that Elwood will get along great with him."

"Yeah, but Dad's really torn-up about Elwood leaving. And to make matters worse, a terrible storm raged for most of the day. You know how Dad reacts to storms...I've never seen him so upset!"

The door sprang open, and Sarah entered the room, smiling. "Dean...Did you hear the news about Rob?"

"What news?" asked Dean.

"Didn't he tell you? Rob's a preacher!"

"Rob's a *what?* Dean's face registered a shocked expression.

"He got saved awhile back, and now he's preaching!" Sarah walked to Rob and hugged him.

Dean's emotions were running amok. He hadn't yet adjusted to Elwood's sudden departure, and now he had to deal with another inconceivable circumstance. He felt that he might have just entered the "Twilight Zone." Speechless, Dean took a seat in the nearest chair.

"Well, you finally did something that shocked me!" Dean exclaimed. Rob laughed, then his expression changed to one of seriousness. "Yeah, Dean…Mom's right. I've had a religious conversion, and I think God is calling me to the ministry…But, I'm not sure. I'll have to continue to pray about it."

"I…I don't know how to act around you!" said Dean. "I've never known this side of you."

"Oh, just be yourself, Dean," said Rob, in a comforting tone. "I've always kinda liked you just the way you are."

"Dean is going to be a daddy…Did he tell you that?" asked Sarah.

"Oh, yeah! Congratulations, Dean!" said Rob, "You know Madge and I have been talking lately…We both wish that we had children. Maybe if we'd had a couple of kids a long time ago, things would have been different."

After recovering from his initial shock, Dean said, "I just hope I can make a good dad. Bobbie and I really want this baby. Say, you haven't met Bobbie. Maybe you and Madge can come over and meet her!"

"I'd like that," said Rob.

Dean curiously studied Rob in an attempt to determine the possible changes in his brother's nature. In the past, his closeness with Rob had been based, in part, on their mutual appreciation of frivolity; however, if his recent religious experience had rendered him humorless, Dean feared that their relationship would now be awkward.

Sarah turned toward the door. "I hear Will poking around inside the house. I'll need to fix him some breakfast. He's in a bad mood this morning since he didn't get enough sleep last night. He's as angry as an old hornet…He woke up with his stinger sticking out!"

Sarah disappeared through the door. Then, with a mischievous grin, Rob whispered to Dean. "That's a pretty good feat for a man Dad's age."

Dean laughed. He felt relief to see that Rob had not lost his earthy sense of humor, after all.

The door suddenly opened, and Madge appeared, wearing pajamas and house shoes.

"Dean!" she yelled, and after running to him, the two embraced.

"Hi, Madge! The last time I saw you was when I told you 'goodbye' in the kitchen of that awful apartment in Ft. Wayne."

"And the last time I saw you, Rob was pushing you in that old pile of junk you called a 'car'."

They both laughed.

"I hear that you're married," said Madge, "and that you're going to be a daddy! Congratulations! When can I meet Bobbie?"

"Well, it doesn't look like Dad's going to open the shop today. Why don't you and Rob get dressed, and I'll take you both to meet her."

"That sounds great!" said Madge. "Come on, Rob, your mother made us some breakfast."

Dean sipped on coffee as the others had their morning meal. They engaged in a cheerful banter about family matters, but since Will was in a somber mood, he remained silent throughout breakfast.

*   *   *

The three exchanged stories as Rob proudly drove his new car to Dean's apartment. When they pulled into the driveway, Bobbie, clad in shorts, was sitting outside in a chair, sunning herself. With her right hand, she shielded her eyes from the morning sun as she curiously eyed the strange vehicle. Recognizing Dean as he stepped from the car, she smiled and rose from her chair; however, as her eyes moved to Rob and Madge, her puzzled expression returned.

Dean introduced everyone, and the foursome engaged in friendly conversation. Rob and Madge offered congratulations, ending with the topic of the new baby.

After patting Bobbie affectionately on the stomach, Dean suggested, "While you two girls get to know each other better, maybe Rob and I could take a ride and engage in a little bit of man talk."

"That's fine with me," said Bobbie.

"Yeah," Madge included, "you guys get lost, so we can have a little bit of girl talk."

Rob wheeled the car out of the driveway. "Where to?"

"Let's drive over to the City Park," said Dean. "It's quiet and peaceful, and we can relax and talk there."

Rob drove ahead until he reached the park. After parking the car, he looked at Dean and smiled. "This is the exact spot where we parked about three years ago. Remember? We sat here and shared a pint of moonshine whiskey."

Dean laughed, "Yeah, and as I recall, we finished that bottle and drove back to the bootlegger for another one."

For awhile, the brothers sat in silence, absorbing the beautiful view

228

of the shimmering lake in front of them. After fishing a stick of gum from his pocket, Rob said, "I guess you feel pretty bad about Elwood leaving, don't you pal?"

"Well, right now, I've got mixed feelings. I'm really glad to see you and Madge, and I'm happy about what's happened in your life, but I'm really sad about Elwood. I didn't think I would miss him this much. Now, I know how he felt all those times when I left."

"Maybe it's for the best, Dean. Elwood's been under Dad's control for too long. I guess it took something like this to happen before Elwood could be his own man."

Dean agreed. "Yeah, and although I'm mad at Dad for having a stubborn attitude, I feel sorry for him, too. I know how much he loves Elwood…and I don't know what he's going to do now."

"Dean, there's one thing I've learned in life," said Rob. "The tighter we cling to something, the more it eludes us. Although Dad may have lost Elwood's closeness, Elwood gained something…He stepped out to independence. You know, sometimes Dad's stubbornness really costs him. He can be as stubborn as a mule."

"Speaking of mules…Did you hear about Dad and Luke Sanford's mule?" Dean smiled as he continued. "Luke lets his mule run loose, so one day, it came down *Beauvais Lane* and walked into the open door of the shop. Dad was so mad that he grabbed a paintbrush and painted a sign on the side of the mule that said, 'Keep me at home'. I had a heck of a time holding the mule for Dad. Most everybody in Tyler City laughs about it."

The brothers chuckled.

After a few moments of silence, Dean's mood became more serious. "Rob, why don't you talk to Dad about Elwood? Maybe Dad will ask him to come back home."

"I'll talk to him later, when the time is right," said Rob.

"I just got home…and I don't want to get chased away the first day after I get home." Rob started the car and slowly pulled away from the curb. "By the way, Dean, Elwood wrote me a letter about the fight you got into the night that you helped him. He said that you had to pay quite a bit of money for the damage done to the door. How much did that cost you?"

"Five hundred dollars. The door didn't cost that much, but the lady who owns the place said most of the money was to cover the amount that she lost from customers who had ordered food. Dad and Elwood offered to pay it since I was helping Elwood, but I didn't feel right letting them pay for it."

"Good thing the owner didn't have you arrested. I bet she was pretty upset, though."

"Well, she said the customers were upset. I asked her what they were so upset about....Didn't they enjoy a little entertainment with their meal? We sure gave them a good floor show!" Dean flashed a mischievous grin.

Rob's robust laughter indicated that he had retained his fondness for the ridiculous.

"Oh, by the way, did you hear about Dad and his social security?" asked Dean.

"No, what happened?"

"Well, it's just another example of Dad's stubbornness. When it came time for him to draw it, he refused to take it! He said he didn't want to take a government handout. The agent came back to Dad and told him that he had about a year's back-pay coming. But Dad refused to take it. The agent didn't know what to do...said he had never encountered such a situation before. Dad had so much pride that he wouldn't take money that was coming to him."

"So, what was the final outcome?" asked Rob. "Did he ever take it?"

"I told the agent that I would try to talk Dad into taking it," said Dean. "I've explained it to Dad over and over. I think I finally have him convinced to accept it."

Rob shook his head and chuckled. "That's Dad."

In the following months, Dean heard from Elwood several times. He and Virginia had rented a small house on the northwest side of Miami, close to the place where Virginia had found a job as a waitress at a nearby restaurant. Elwood liked his job and was promoted to foreman of the shop where business was so good that Elwood had given Alvin a job; consequently, Al and Amber had journeyed to Miami and moved in an apartment close to Elwood and Virginia. Although he hoped that Al would soon be back, Dean was saddened by Elwood's continued resolve to never move back to Tyler City.

In the absence of Elwood and the other brothers, Rob and Dean were now operating *Beauvais Signs*. The family had heard Rob preach in several small area churches, and although his initial efforts were timid, he gradually began developing his speaking skills, with the substance of his messages growing more profound.

It was obvious to the Beauvais family that God had, indeed, called Rob into the ministry. He realized the time had come to prepare himself for full-time service to God; therefore, he enrolled at *Southern*

Wesleyan College to study for the ministry, while he worked at the shop for Dean on a part-time basis.

Dean and Bobbie had now moved into their unfinished house, which Dean decided to complete while living there. Rob and Madge took up temporary residence in the Bull Pen. Bobbie's pregnancy was now very obvious; its advancement was revealed by both her girth and her physical and emotional radiance. While Sarah was excited about the approaching birth of the new baby, she became more depressed over the severed relationship between Will and Elwood. Because she perceived Will's attitude as one of stubbornness, Sarah began to pressure him to reconcile with his son. Since Will had developed a great respect for Rob's sincerity and judgment, he decided to seek counsel in regard to Sarah's discontentment.

One afternoon, with Dean was working on a sign in town, and the women visiting with Ellen and little Terry, Will had an opportune time to speak to Rob in private. He seated himself in the living room of the empty house and waited for Rob's arrival. When Rob finally entered the living room where Will was waiting, he could easily discern his father's uneasiness by his facial expression.

"Hi, Dad."

"Rob, could we talk for a few minutes?"

"Sure, Dad. What's on your mind?" Rob placed his books on the coffee table and took a seat in the rocking chair, facing his father.

"Rob, I'm worried about your mother. She's upset over Elwood and keeps putting pressure on me about trying to get him to come home. She's really been putting the ice on me lately…but I can't condone adultery. You're a preacher, now. You know the stand that the Bible takes about committing adultery."

"Who's committing adultery?" asked Rob, with feigned innocence.

"Elwood is…since he married that woman!" declared Will, with frustration. "It's right there in the Ten Commandments."

"Well, yes, the Bible does say that adultery is wrong. The Ten Commandments also say that killing is wrong. War is also evil. But I helped kill men in the war. Was I sinning?" asked Rob.

"You were protecting your country. God expects us to protect our own. No! You weren't sinning!"

Rob responded, "But how can you be so sure? Everything is not that simple. The Ten Commandments is a set of rules, of sorts, that presents a general pattern for us to live by. They deal in generalities, but it's when we get into specific instances that we run into trouble. In what situation is it okay to go to war? Or to kill another human being?"

"But you're a preacher. You should know what's right or wrong!" said Will.

"Dad, I'm just beginning to learn how little I know. I used to see the 'right' and 'wrong' as black and white, but now I realize most of the world is rendered in multiple shades of gray."

"Don't you preach against sin? Don't you point out to a man that he is living in sin?" asked Will.

"No, Dad, I would never do that. I preach the gospel, hoping that my message will open the man's eyes so he can see his own sin. It's not my job to point out a man's sin to him. If I did, I'd lose any influence I had over him. He'd completely reject me. It's human nature..."

"Well, was I wrong in telling Elwood that he would be living in sin if he married that girl?" asked Will.

"Dad, I can't tell you when you do right or wrong! You're asking me to be your conscience. Also, I would never tell Elwood whether or not he's right...I can't be his conscience either. When you try to be another man's conscience, you're playing God! I know I fall short of the mark, but I try to make my decisions by asking myself, *what attitude would Jesus have?*"

"Well, some things are right, and others are wrong!" lectured Will. "I can't compromise with sin!"

Rob thought for a moment, then said, "You know, if there was a set of rules that we could follow that could ensure that we'd never be wrong, then life would be simple. We'd be like robots... we wouldn't have to think or agonize over difficult decisions. But life is complex. I believe that God created a mind in man so that he could use reason in his struggle to determine what's right."

Slowly, Will rose from the couch and reached for his hat.

"Thanks for talking to me, Rob. Tell Sarah I'm going to town. I'll be a little late for supper." Then he walked out of the room to his car.

At the beginning of dinner, Will had not yet returned as Rob said a blessing over the evening meal. Just as the family began to eat, the front door opened, and Dean rushed into the dining room.

"I just got a call from Virginia," said Dean, displaying an ashen face. "Elwood is in the hospital in critical condition!"

Sarah's abrupt rise from the table was quickly followed by Rob and Madge.

"Oh, dear! What's wrong with him? Did she say?" asked Sarah, with an expression of agony on her face. "Was he in an accident?"

"No, but...Mom, I hate to tell you this—he's real sick with something. Virginia said that Elwood wanted me to fly down there immediately...if I want to see him again...I've already called the airport and scheduled my flight to Miami. I leave at 6:30 in the morning."

"Should we all drive down there?" asked Rob.

"No...not yet. Let me fly down and I'll call you as soon as I find out how bad it is. Don't worry, Mom...He'll probably be all right. I'll help him all I can."

Rob and Dean both walked to their mother and embraced her. Encircling the table and joining hands, they all bowed their heads as Rob prayed.

Nothing is so strong as gentleness and nothing is so gentle as real strength. **Ralph W. Sockman**

Chapter 21

Dean shielded his sweating face from the torrid, Florida sunlight and headed for the row of taxi cabs parked in front of the airport. He tossed his small suitcase into the back of the nearest cab, then slid into the seat behind the impassive cab driver.

"Where to, sir?" droned the cabbie.

"*Jackson Memorial Hospital,*" said Dean, "and get me there fast!"

"You got it, pal." The driver sped away from the airport.

The three hour flight to Miami had seemed endless, and now the heavy stream of traffic surrounding the cab tested Dean's patience. Sitting apprehensively in the back seat of the taxi, Dean fidgeted nervously as the cab driver expertly maneuvered the vehicle through the moving congestion with seemingly minimal effort, enabling Dean to arrive within twenty minutes at the front entrance of the hospital.

After paying the driver, he sprinted up the four marble steps into the lobby where he feverishly glanced around in search of the information desk. Then, on his left, he spotted the receptionist and quickly trotted in her direction. His stomach was now a hard knot, and when he was only two feet away from hearing the news about Elwood, a student nurse entered from the right and stepped into his place. With agitation, Dean impatiently tapped his foot as the young lady asked the receptionist a myriad of jumbled questions.

"Did you say she was in Room 201? I followed your directions the first time, and I ended up in the snack bar. I've been all over the second floor and I can't find that room anywhere! Oh, so I need to take a different elevator? Well, where is it? Over there...oh, I see it now.... You just wouldn't believe where all I went. First, I turned left... then ... well, anyway, somehow I ended up in the second floor snack bar...Can you believe that?"

My God, girl! Get your head out of your ass! thought Dean. *I'm waiting to find out if my brother's still alive, and you can't stop talking about the snack bar!*

As the girl continued her useless questions, Dean felt like he was on the verge of a panic attack. He was desperate to learn of Elwood's condition, but he also feared hearing it; after all, hours had passed since he had received the news from Virginia, and the despair he had heard in her voice would not leave his mind. *Is it possible that my brother may die? Could it be that he is already dead?*

Finally, the student nurse moved away from the desk. Dean quickly stepped up, and as he blurted out the question, his voice trembled.

"Excuse me, Ma'am! What room is Elwood Beauvais in?" *Please don't say that he passed away during the night!* thought Dean.

The woman scanned the patient list, a simple task that seemed to take forever. "Room 321, in the west wing. That's the critical care unit. You can take that elevator over there on your right. But, in order to see him, you'll have to check in at the nurses' station upstairs."

He's alive! thought Dean. He pushed the 'up' arrow by the elevator door, then inwardly squirmed as he restlessly waited. Finally, the sliding doors slowly opened and several people spilled out into the lobby. Dean hopped into the elevator and pushed the button for the third floor as another man entered, pushing the number two button. The stop at the second floor seemed endless. Eventually, the door slid open, and the departing man was replaced by two nuns, each pushing buttons for different floors.

When he arrived at the third floor, he prepared to dash through the slowly opening doors, but his attempt was thwarted by a man boarding the elevator in a wheelchair, pushed by an assistant. At last, he entered the hallway and quickly strode straight ahead to the nurses' station.

"I'm here to see Elwood Beauvais...Room 321."

"Are you a relative of his?" asked the head nurse.

"I'm his brother. How's he doing? How bad is he?"

"He's holding his own, but he's in very critical condition. You may go in and see him but please limit your visit to twenty minutes. He needs rest. His room is the second door on your left." She pointed in the direction of Elwood's room.

Hastily, he walked the short distance to his brother's room, then abruptly stopped.

The closed door displayed the sign, "Caution. Oxygen in Use."

Now that he was standing at the door, he was hesitant about entering the room. His heart raced, and he was sweating profusely. Fearing that he might faint, he leaned against the wall for support as he drew in deep breaths of air. He was eager to see his brother, but he dreaded the first glimpse of him. *Would he be awake? Alert? Could he possibly be in a coma?* He fervently hoped that his own reaction to Elwood's appearance would not reveal shock. Assuming a pretentiously casual demeanor, Dean braced himself and entered the room.

Elwood was awake, and upon his brother's entrance, he turned his head toward Dean. His gaping, bulbous eyes expressed the fear within him; however, as his gaze recognized Dean, his fearful expression softened to one of relief, and he smiled. The tube in his nose supplied his oxygen from the tank in the corner of the room, and his arms were inundated with needles and tubes attached to intravenous bottles beside his bed. Dean grinned, straining to maintain a cheerful composure.

"Hi, Elwood. What happened to you, man?" Dean moved to the bedside and gently took his brother's hand.

Elwood's mode of speaking was spasmodic, his rasping voice delivering intermittent phrases between breaths of oxygen. "I—don't know exactly—what happened. I coughed up—a lot of blood…I'm glad—you came."

"Don't try to talk Elwood. Just lie there and relax." His pallid complexion and sunken eyes suggested a face of death, deeply disturbing Dean as he helplessly watched his brother struggle for air.

"How is everyone—at home?" asked Elwood.

"Everybody's fine…I'm not so sure you should be talking."

"How long—can you stay?" Elwood continued.

"I'll stay until you're okay again. And don't worry…I'll be right here with you, and I'll take care of you. Get some rest…Now stop talking."

The door opened and a small, stocky nurse walked briskly into the room. Her right hand was shaking a thermometer, and her face bore a stern expression.

"I'm sorry, sir, but you'll have to leave for awhile. The patient needs attention and some rest. You can go to the lounge… down the hall to your right."

"What's wrong with him?" asked Dean.

"I'm sorry, sir, but you'll need to talk to his doctor or the head nurse to get that information. All I can tell you is that he's a very sick man," said the solemn nurse, with a dispassionate air of professionalism.

Dean grinned reassuringly at Elwood, "I've gotta leave for awhile, Elwood. Don't worry, I'll be back soon, and I'll be here until they say you're going to be okay."

Elwood returned the smile.

"I'm awfully glad—you came...I'm sorry—to worry everybody."

"Who's worried?" joked Dean. He winked at his brother, then left the room.

Quickening his stride, Dean walked to the nurse's station. A seated, middle-aged nurse peered upward at him through thick-lensed glasses.

"How may I help you, sir?"

"Are you the head nurse?"

"Yes sir, I am."

"Elwood Beauvais...Room 321—what's wrong with him? What's his condition?" asked Dean.

"He's a very sick patient." she replied. "In fact, his condition is listed as critical." Quickly she looked to her left. "There goes his doctor now, making his rounds...Oh Dr. Stein!" she called to him.

The tall grey-haired doctor turned, and Dean hurried to him. "Dr. Stein? Are you Elwood Beauvais's doctor? Room 321."

"Yes, I am. Who are you, sir?" asked the doctor.

"I'm Dean Beauvais, the patient's brother. Doctor, could you tell me what's wrong with..."

"Who pays?" interrupted the doctor, sternly. "Who's responsible for paying his bill? He isn't covered by insurance—who pays?"

Dean suppressed his mounting anger, for he feared a verbal retaliation might inhibit Dr. Stein's treatment and care of Elwood. "Sir, I'm sure that your services will be paid for by someone...but at the moment, my first concern is limited to the survival of my brother. Surely you can understand that... can't you, sir? What's wrong with my brother, and what's the prognosis?" Dean stared directly into the eyes of Dr. Stein.

"Your brother has tubercular pneumonia. Yesterday, he hemorrhaged quite a bit of blood from his lungs. He almost drowned in his own blood."

"How sick is he, now? What are his chances?" asked Dean.

"I'm sorry to tell you, sir...His chances are not very good at the moment, but of course, we'll do what we can." Dean was surprised to note a trace of concern in the doctor's expression.

"Should I call the family and get them all to come here?"

"Where does the family live?"

"Knoxville, Tennessee."

"I wouldn't advise that—at least not yet. Let me work with him for awhile. He's still holding his own. I'll be looking in on him again, soon."

"Okay, thank you, doctor."

"No problem," said Dr. Stein. He then turned and hurried away toward Elwood's room.

Dean returned to the head nurse. "When can I return to see my brother?"

"After Dr. Stein examines him... Come back in about 15 minutes." She glanced around to ensure that no one heard her and then added, "When you come back to his room, you can stay as long as you like. Just promise me that he doesn't talk too much. He needs rest."

"Thank you," Dean answered wearily.

Disheartened, he walked slowly to the waiting area where he discovered Alvin and Virginia sitting in the corner, talking.

Virginia saw him first. Quickly, she left her seat and ran to Dean. They hugged each other tightly. "Oh, Dean! Thank God you're here! Have you seen him yet?"

"Yes…I saw him, just for a minute, then they ran me out."

Using her pet name for Elwood, Virginia said, "You were the first one Woody asked for after it happened."

"Exactly what did happen, Virginia?"

"We were just sitting there in the living room, and all at once Woody suddenly bent over and hemorrhaged about a quart of blood onto the floor! He had been feeling sick for a while, but we never expected this."

"My God!" said Dean.

Al appeared at his side and took Dean's hand. "It looks bad, Dean." Al's unshaven face and blood-shot eyes confirmed his distressing all-night vigil in the hospital waiting room.

"Man, it's good to see you again, Al. Only I wish it was under better circumstances," said Dean. "How long have you and Virginia been here?"

"Since it happened, yesterday. Amber just left awhile ago."

"You and Virginia both need some rest, Al. Go home—both of you. Besides, you have jobs. I'll stay with Elwood as long as it takes."

Al and Virginia nodded as Dean spoke.

"Al, I'll need your address. Write it down for me because I'll eventually need a place to shower and shave. After I talk to the doctor again,

I've got to call home."

They continued talking as Dean followed them to the lobby. "I'll call you both, tonight. Get some rest if you can," suggested Dean. He obtained Al's apartment key and address, and watched as they walked away.

The doctor's report was not optimistic. The best news was that Elwood's condition had not worsened, and that he was still 'holding his own'. After calling home, Dean returned to Elwood's room where his brother was asleep. With each breath, a gurgling rasp emanated from his lungs as he exhaled. Dean noticed the diminished strength of his lungs and wondered if his brother would ever sing or play the saxophone again. After standing for awhile by the bedside, Dean ambled to the door on the south side of the room that led to an outside balcony. He walked through the doorway and sat in a chair on the small, screened porch—a portico structure that was imitated by every room on the south side of the building. As he looked across the city toward the Atlantic Ocean, he remembered his happier times in Miami, particularly his most recent visit which marked the time of when his new life with Bobbie began. She was now miles away, carrying their first child, and he longed to be with her. For Dean, Miami had now become an empty place.

*   *   *

As Dean began his extended vigil, he was filled with uncertainty about what lay ahead. Dr. Stein's daily reports were generally the same, with the only positive aspect being that Elwood's condition remained stable. Elwood slept most of the time, only awakening sporadically for brief periods with limited ability to talk. Morning activities became a ritual of brushing teeth, shaving, and combing hair—first grooming himself, then doing the same for Elwood. Minutes became hours…days…then a week. Al, Amber, and Virginia, all holding full-time jobs, came by each evening, offering relief to Dean's bedside vigil; however, Dean vowed to stay by Elwood's side until he received better news from the doctor.

The passing of the repetitious days became a blur in Dean's mind as he stayed with his brother twenty- four hours a day. His own sleeping became a series of brief catnaps. He ate sparingly, and because of boredom and worry, he again took up the habit of smoking. As the lonely days passed, he became intimately acquainted with the balcony, the hospital room, the hallway, the drink machine, the cigarette vender, the bathroom, the cafeteria, then back to the balcony again. His days became a blurry mélange of idleness and meaningless activity, with the monotonous action of each day a replica of the day before.

In the early morning, around the eleventh day, as Dean was sleeping in a chair by his brother's bed, he was awakened by a tap on his shoulder from the bespectacled, head nurse.

"Your brother is better, Mr. Beauvais. The doctor just checked him, and his vital signs are much improved. He just went back to sleep, so I wouldn't awaken him for awhile." She smiled at Dean. "Since he's better, why don't you go home and get some sleep...? You've been here for so long, you must be exhausted."

"Thank you, Nurse...thank you." For the first time in several days, Dean grinned.

After calling Bobbie and his parents with the good news, he caught a cab to Al's apartment, where he found no one at home. He opened the door with Al's extra key, and then curiously wandered around the apartment, which revealed his brother's personality and style of living. Even though the place was nice and adequately furnished, several of the rooms were in disarray. In the larger of the two bedrooms, Al's discarded clothing was tossed on the unmade bed. By the living room couch, a plethora of books and magazines was scattered on the floor, and in the kitchen, the sink was filled with dirty dishes. As Dean's eyes studied the apartment from the living room, he concluded that Alvin's preoccupation with Elwood had caused him to be even more messy than usual. He then retreated to the bathroom for a long shower. After getting dressed, he stretched out on the living room couch and quickly descended into a deep, peaceful sleep.

He awoke to the sound of Al talking to Amber as she prepared dinner in the kitchen. Sitting up slowly, Dean sleepily peered at his watch...8:16...He had slept all day.

"Hi, Amber," said Dean.

Surprised that he was awake, she turned from her cooking chores and smiled timidly at him.

"Hi, Dean," she said, as she walked to meet him. They embraced, but only briefly, for Amber was a shy, modest person. She was small and pretty, but her outmoded attire and hairstyle gave her an ordinary appearance that belied her attractiveness. Contending with Al's vacillating nature had molded her personality into one of patience and tolerance.

"Hello, Dean," greeted Alvin, as he shook Dean's hand. "We didn't mean to wake you. You need sleep. How's Elwood—anything new?"

Dean grinned. "I've got great news! The doctor says that he's much better."

"Elwood's better? Boy, that is great news! Dean, you stay here and rest. Amber and I will go over to the hospital and sit with him tonight."

"No, Al…You and Amber have both worked all day. I've had enough sleep. I'll go over there and spend the night. You both need your sleep. Besides, I can't wait to talk to Elwood."

"Well, let's all sit down and eat," suggested Al. "It's time Dean had a good home-cooked meal."

They talked as they ate, with most of their conversation consisting of a discussion of Elwood and the family.

"Dean, I guess you're right…Amber and I are both tired. A good night's rest would be nice. But how are you going to get back over there? I'll need my truck early in the morning," explained Alvin.

"I can get back over there in a cab," said Dean. "That's how I got here today…I can be there in ten minutes."

As he left Al's apartment, twilight was descending upon the city, and in the eastern sky, an oversized full moon hovered over the Atlantic Ocean. Dean strolled to the corner of 36th Street where he hailed a cab. In less than a half hour, he was back at the hospital.

When he walked into the room, Elwood was sitting up in his slightly elevated bed. Upon seeing Dean, he ogled a one-eyed stare, cocked his head to one side, and sneered at Dean in an imitation of Jim Burns. To emphasize the foolish gesture, he made a feeble effort to scratch his crotch, but without success since the contraptions hooked to his arms thwarted the attempt.

Dean laughed happily, for he knew that Elwood was, indeed, feeling much better.

"Hi, Dean," greeted Elwood, "did you get some rest?"

"Yeah, I feel like a new man!" said Dean, cheerfully.

Dean noticed that Elwood's speech was less erratic, and that he was breathing much better.

"Tell me, Elwood, how do you feel?"

"Well, I couldn't play a game of football right now," joked Elwood, "but I'm doing okay."

The small, stocky nurse entered the room with her usual stern expression. Again, she was vigorously shaking a thermometer in her right hand.

"Time to get some sleep, Mr. Beauvais," she ordered, as she stuck the thermometer in Elwood's mouth. Silently, she eyed her watch while checking the pulse rate in his wrist.

After she removed the thermometer, Elwood grinned. "Hey, Nurse…I'll tell you a good trick that you could play on a patient."

"Why would I want to play a trick?" she asked, solemnly.

"Whenever you bring the patient an oxygen tank, you could fill it with mustard gas, instead. Now wouldn't that be a good trick?"

Both Dean and Elwood laughed, but the humorless nurse only eyed Elwood with a vapid stare.

"Go to sleep, Mr. Beauvais," she said in a robotic tone. "And you," she pointed at Dean, "you need to let him sleep. Mrs. Kirk, the head nurse, said you could stay with him, but you'll have to let him get some rest." She turned and walked briskly from the room.

"I call her the 'Wicked Witch of the West Wing'," said Elwood. "She's not a bad sort, but she's got absolutely no sense of humor."

"The head nurse is nice, though," replied Dean.

Elwood agreed. "Yeah, I call her 'The Angel of Mercy'. She's really lenient about the rules, and she's always cheerful."

"You'd better do as she says, Elwood…Go to sleep. You'll get well faster if you'll get enough rest."

A brief moment of silence overpowered Elwood's energy, and when he fell fast asleep in less than a minute, Dean realized the extent of his brother's weakness. Dean walked out onto the balcony and took a seat. With trembling hands, he lit a cigarette and cursed himself for adopting the habit again. Propping his feet on the railing, he leaned back in his chair and drank in the beauty of the radiant full moon in the east, suspended over the city. As his brother slept, he wondered what lay in store for Elwood; also, he thought about his own future, and what it held for him—and Bobbie. He wished he could be with her during these last weeks of her pregnancy.

In the days that followed, Elwood continued to improve, but gradually. During the day, he was awake for longer periods of time, allowing the brothers ample time to talk about many things. Sometimes they would laugh together over past ridiculous behavior of their brothers; other times were spent sharing intimate feelings in conversations more serious. On alternating nights, either Al or Virginia would relieve him, and Dean would sleep at either Al's apartment or Elwood's house where Virginia and her mother were staying. But on the other nights, as well as every day, he stayed by Elwood's bedside. Al and Dean phoned home frequently to inform their parents of Elwood's condition. Each day, Will and Sarah considered driving down to Miami, but since it was a long, arduous drive from Tennessee, Dean pleaded with them to stay home for now.

Since Dean was constantly present, the overworked nurses left most of Elwood's non-medical care to Dean. In addition to the usual morning grooming, Dean now fed solid foods and liquids to his brother. Also, he assisted him with the bed pan, along with the usual necessities required. All in all, Dean regularly kept his brother clean and comfortable with the use of warm sponge baths. At first, both men felt somewhat awkward; however, Elwood's cleaning and feeding needs changed very slowly, and so it was with Dean's care of Elwood. The gradual, consistent help from Dean conditioned Elwood to feel at ease with his brother's care. Without Dean, the comfort and dignity of daily living skills would have been impossible.

As the days passed, the brothers spent more time talking and usually with the topic being about the family.

"You know, Dean, I really do miss Mom and Dad," said Elwood. "I wish there was some way I could make up with Dad."

"Mom misses you, Elwood. Don't judge Dad too harshly. He misses you, too, and I predict that you'll make up soon. Dad is just stubborn, you know. He really loves you."

"Tell Dad I am asking for his forgiveness," said Elwood.

"No need for me to do that, Elwood. You can tell him yourself. Besides, you didn't do anything to be forgiven for."

For a moment, Elwood seemed lost in thought. "Dean, when I get well, I can't continue to paint signs...It's too hard physically. And besides, I want to do something more rewarding. Do you think I'm too old to go to college? I'd like to study music. After all, Rob went back to college and is doing great!"

Dean smiled. "Elwood, you're not too old! And you're by far the smartest one of us. That's what you ought to do!"

Elwood appeared excited. "See if you can get me some literature about it. I've been thinking about it a lot, and I've kind of made up my mind."

Elwood's mood grew more serious. "I've really missed you, Dean. I miss all the good times we had together."

"Yeah, and we'll have many more good times, pal." Looking at his watch, Dean said, "Elwood, I need to leave now to shower and shave and get a little shut-eye. I'll be back in the morning. Virginia will be here soon to stay with you."

"Dean...before you leave, I want to say something to you. Do you remember when I told you that I was proud of you…the time you whipped that guy who was beating me up? Well…I was proud of you, and I still am. But, you know, beating a guy up doesn't make you a man. The actions that make you a man are the things that you have done for me…right here in this hospital. I've always admired you, but never as much as I do at this very moment. I want you to know that you are a *real man.* I always knew you were, deep down inside of you."

Reaching to his standing brother, Elwood took his hand.

Dean was slightly embarrassed. "All in a day's work, pal," he said. He patted his brother on the shoulder. "I really appreciate what you said, Elwood. Look, get some rest, and I'll see you tomorrow…Okay, Pal?"

As he left the room, Dean considered Elwood's praise of him—*he was a real man.* It was the first time anyone had ever told him that. He thought it was strange that the tribute came about as a result of his nurturing and gentleness, rather than an act of aggressiveness.

Before leaving the hospital, Dean met with Dr. Stein. "Your brother's progress has been amazing, Mr.Beauvais, but he's not out of the woods yet. When he improves a bit more, you need to get him transferred to a tuberculosis sanitarium. Do you have one in mind?" asked the doctor.

"What about *East Tennessee Tuberculosis Hospital* in Knoxville, Tennessee?" asked Dean. "Our family lives close to it."

"Good," remarked Dr. Stein. "We can fly him there. I'll continue to monitor his progress closely, and I'll tell you when the time is appropriate for moving him there. You might want to call the hospital up there and tell them to prepare a bed for him in the next couple of weeks."

Dean's mind raced at the thought. *The next couple of weeks!*

"Thank you, Dr. Stein!" said Dean, excitedly.

Dean called his parents and Bobbie with the good news. Then, with a bounce in his step, he walked out of the hospital and caught a cab to Elwood's house. That night, he slept better than he had in several days.

When he arrived at Elwood's room the next morning, he was shocked to see the frenzied activity around his brother's bed. Elwood appeared to be semi-conscious as Dr. Stein and two nurses were frantically attending to him. The rasping noise from his throat had returned. Each of his laboring breaths was accompanied by a gurgling sound from his lungs.

"What's wrong?" asked Dean. The doctor turned from Elwood's bed and led Dean from the room.

"He had another massive hemorrhage this morning. He's lost a lot of blood. His recent extreme weight loss has weakened his immune system."

Dean's heart sank.

"How bad is it?"

The doctor looked solemnly into Dean's eyes. "It's very bad. His vital signs are getting worse. You'd better call the family. I'm sorry, Mr. Beauvais."

"May I see him?"

"Not now, we're still working with him. He wouldn't know you right now, anyway. Come back in a few hours. Call the family as soon as possible."

The ensuing thirty-six hours became a blur of frantic activity for Dean. After calling the family in Tennessee, he finally succeeded in notifying Clay, in Korea. Dean assembled with Virginia, Alvin and Amber in the hospital lounge, as they all began their depressing vigil, hoping in vain for some encouraging news about Elwood.

The twenty-four hour drive from Tennessee had taken its toll on Will and Sarah, who were exhausted and fraught with worry. With the exception of Al and Clay, the members of the immediate family met at Alvin's apartment. Al had elected to stay at the hospital with Elwood, while Clay had not yet arrived from Korea. Bobbie and Ellen had been unable to make the trip.

Grief-stricken, Will called Dean aside. "Dean, do you think Elwood will recognize me? Can he understand anything? I want to tell him that when he gets well, to come on back home...Back to the shop. Talking with Sarah changed my mind about a lot of things."

Feeling compassion for his father, Dean said, "That's good news, Dad. You can tell him that when we go over to the hospital. Even if he doesn't respond, I'm sure he can hear you."

Sadly, Dean feared that his father's change of heart had come too late. Before leaving for the hospital, the family gathered in a circle for prayer. Bowing his head, Rob prayed: "Dear God, if there be any other way, let this cup pass...But, if there be no other way but that we drink from it, thy will be done."

Rob and Dean led the way to the hospital in Alvin's truck, followed closely by the other family members in Elwood's car. As Dean and Rob hurried down the hospital hall, they met Alvin, trudging toward them from Elwood's room. He walked with slumped shoulders and in an unsteady gait. As he came near to them, his ashen face foretold his dreadful message:

"Dean...Elwood's dead!"

The Moving Finger writes; and, having writ, Moves on: nor all your Piety nor Wit Shall lure it back to cancel half a Line, Nor all your Tears wash out a Word of it. **Omar Khayyam—translated by Edward Fitzgerald**

Chapter 22

The long stretch of highway seemed endless as the exhausted Beauvais family journeyed homeward. Amber and Alvin drove their truck while the remainder of the family crowded into Rob's car. Will and Sarah, who sat in the back seat with Clay, tried to nap occasionally, because only two days earlier they had made the same arduous journey; now with virtually no rest, they were retracing the same 900 miles.

Arrangements for Elwood's funeral had been made earlier by Dean, who had called a funeral home in Tyler City. The family would receive friends on the evening after their arrival at home, and the funeral and burial were scheduled for the following day. While in Florida, the family waited for Clay to arrive; however, in keeping with Clay's continuous bad luck, a mix-up in Army red tape caused him to depart late from Korea. Sadly, he arrived too late to see Elwood alive.

The brothers hid most of their grief from their parents, who were practically inconsolable. Realizing Sarah's previous bond with Elwood, the brothers were particularly concerned about her. Immediately after Elwood's death, Dean had hugged his mother, vowing to her that he would try to fill the void that Elwood's death left in her heart.

Since the delay in leaving had pressed the family for time, the brothers alternated shifts behind the wheel, traveling continuously and stopping only for food and gasoline. This was particularly exhausting for Will and Sarah. And to make matters worse, because of the unmerciful heat, the car windows had all been lowered, causing the noise of the inrushing, hot air to hinder any attempt of conversation.

In the relentless swelter, they drove northward taking Route 27 through the shimmering mirage on the heated asphalt, past Lake Okeechobee, then through the orange groves north of Orlando where they stopped briefly for a meal. Continuing northward, past Gainesville, and finally crossing the border into Georgia, and when the light of day was gone, so was Florida. Car windows went up as darkness brought cool air, but the family did not talk. Then northward along the southern Georgia flatland, through the town of Perry, a landmark where Dean and Bobbie spent the first night of their honeymoon. Soon it was Macon, where red dirt replaced the sand, and the pine trees were now in abundance; the sun rose over northern Georgia, and they could see the rolling hills, then the car dipped and climbed into their home state. Next, came Chattanooga, and they ate breakfast, until finally, northeast on Highway 11, and homeward toward Knoxville.

The mid-morning of the second day, their car finally glided into Tyler City. As they drove down Broadway, they hardly noticed the row of stores on their left, for it was the train running on their right that caught the family's attention. Moving at the same speed, in the same direction, the train ran side-by-side with the Beauvais family. The family was in awe as their tear-filled eyes caught sight of the casket that lay in an open freight car. Elwood had joined the family in Tyler City at precisely the same moment.

Early on the morning of the funeral, the Beauvais family was awakened by the deafening clap of thunder. Leaving his bed, Will separated the curtains in the bedroom window and gazed eastward. The usual golden glow of the early spring morning was now eclipsed by the pitch-black sky casting a dismal darkness over the area. A blinding flash of lightning that was instantaneously accompanied by the sharp crack of thunder indicated that the storm was upon them as the torrent of rain fell on the roof with a sudden, deafening roar.

What a wretched day this is, thought Will.

The storm violently raged, with the blinding veins of lightning flickering incessantly as the constant rumble of rolling thunder shook the foundations of the house. Rivulets of water gushed rapidly down the sides of the road on *Beauvais Lane*, depositing a spattering of gravel in the parking area.

The storm lasted all morning, and although the sun briefly peeped through the clouds at noon, the sky again grew darker as the family left for the funeral.

Large crowds of people gathered at the church to pay their last respects to Elwood. Sarah wept openly, and Will was teary-eyed, but the Beauvais brothers sat stoically through the heart-wrenching funeral, for they felt that it was their responsibility to keep the family from falling apart. At the cemetery, when the funeral director dismissed the family at the end of the graveside service, Will paused and placed his hand on top of Elwood's casket.

"I'll be seeing you, Elwood," he promised.

As the family left the cemetery, the reverberation of thunder echoed from the dark clouds in the west. The remainder of the day was invaded by intermittent storms.

Two days after the funeral, Virginia left Tennessee and returned to Miami. Al and Amber decided to stay in Tennessee since Elwood's death had soured their memory of Florida. Clay had been granted a 30 day furlough which enabled him to stay with Ellen and little Terry for three more weeks. Bobbie, who was in the last weeks of her pregnancy, comforted Dean, sharing his grief, because she, too, had learned to love Elwood. All of the brothers shared what time they had in comforting Sarah.

After the friends of the family had gone, the Beauvais family was left alone to contend with their suffering. In dealing with emotional issues, Sarah found comfort in discussing her feelings with others with whom she felt a closeness. Like her sons, she faced debilitating consequences head-on, without hesitation. After a death, there is a measurable amount of sadness that one has to endure; it was her nature to plunge into her anguish quickly, thus shortening its duration. With the death of Elwood, the bitter river of sorrow flowed before her, its decadent breadth separating her from the serenity found only on the opposite shore. Intuitively, she knew that only an unflinching leap into the cold, morbid stream of despair would deliver her to the peaceful haven on the other side.

In contrast, Will chose to suffer alone, rarely expressing his feelings to anyone. He isolated himself, either by sitting in a chair on the patio or driving away in his car, often parking in a lonely spot for hours. His method of dealing with grief was identical to his technique in handling all problems of severity. He only tip-toed into the river of despair, choosing to swallow the remedy in small doses; as a result, his sadness was prolonged.

A full week had passed since Elwood's death. Upon recognizing his father's suffering, Dean pulled a chair beside him, as he sat alone on the patio. Without speaking, Dean and his father watched the evening sun hide its face behind a purple cloud on the western horizon. The soft echoing call of mourning doves added to their feeling of melancholia. Finally, Will spoke.

"Did you ever read that poem, *The Raven,* by Edgar Allan Poe?" The question puzzled Dean. "Yeah, Dad—I've read it. Why?"

"When I remember Elwood, and think of that word 'nevermore'....It haunts me."

Dean remained silent.

"It's strange," said Will, "But do you know what I miss the most? It's the way he used to put his arm around me and steal a cigarette from my pocket..."

Dean looked at his father with compassion, but still said nothing.

"I'd give everything I own if I could just see him walk through that door acting like Jim Burns...Remember how he did that?" asked Will.

"Yeah, Dad...I remember," said Dean.

For a long while, they remained quiet. Twilight had descended and the silence was only interrupted by an occasional passing vehicle.

After several minutes had passed, Dean assumed that his father had ended his discussion of the subject. Thinking that further expression from Will might assuage his grief, Dean asked, "Dad...Would you like to talk some more? I know it's painful, in a way, but it might help both of us."

Slowly, Will rose from his chair. "Dean, I've got to get something else on my mind for awhile. I can't stand anymore of it right now. I'll deal with it later." He walked into the shop.

Aware of his father's method of grieving, Dean realized that in order for his father to achieve true peace, he needed to purge his soul of the terrible guilt that he felt over his rejection of Elwood. Perhaps the guilt had been temporarily buried deep in his unconscious mind, for there are some feelings that the conscious mind cannot bear to examine, except perhaps in small increments.

Dean was exhausted, both physically and emotionally. He had been strong during both the illness and death of Elwood. Even during the drive home from Miami, he had been a pillar of strength in helping hold the family together. He had yet to shed a tear, but his emotions were spent. Because of his past ordeal, he had lost 20 pounds. As he lit a cigarette, the tremble in his hands exposed his emotional bankruptcy.

With a sudden, desperate desire for solitude, he walked to his car and drove away. Turning toward Tyler City, he drove aimlessly for awhile, then turned into the driveway of a local bootlegger. From past experience, he knew that the illegal booze was dispensed by way of the back porch. After rapping on the rear door, he waited until a porch light came on. An overweight, balding man poked his head through the doorway.

"What do you need, buddy?" he asked.

"I want two fifths of vodka."

The man obediently went inside, then reappeared with the two bottles, handing them to Dean. After paying the man, Dean turned to leave, then abruptly whirled around.

"I'm sorry to trouble you again, but maybe you'd better give me another fifth."

The bootlegger repeated his same routine. "You must be throwing a party." He handed Dean the vodka.

"Yeah…A party for one," said Dean.

*   *   *

The cheap motel room reeked of stale cigarette smoke and disinfectant. He switched on the bathroom light, leaving the door slightly ajar to offer a limited amount of light to the bedroom. After closing the blinds in the single window, he placed two of the bottles of vodka on the small table. Carrying the other fifth with him, he sat on the bed in the small, semi-dark room, opened the bottle, and swallowed an enormous drink. He then placed the liquor on the night stand by the bed.

He had called Bobbie before checking into the small motel, explaining to her his compulsion to be alone in his grief. Knowing his nature, she reluctantly accepted his behavior, but pleaded with him to "please be careful, and don't get into any trouble." He felt guilty over leaving Bobbie in her late stage of pregnancy; however, he knew that Sarah would be with her. He only knew that he had to be alone, to sort out his feelings and to experience the temporary oblivion that the alcohol would provide. Until now, he had thought mostly of others; but at the moment, he was obsessed with his own needs.

Reclining on the bed, he was aware that a major portion of his grief was laced with guilt, for he realized that but for him, his brother would probably still be alive, working in the shop with his father. It was Dean who had motivated his brother to embark on the diet that weakened his endurance, thus contributing to his death. In addition, his introduction of Elwood to Virginia had caused his brother's broken relationship with his father; he had encouraged his brother to take a risk and had even arranged employment for him in Miami. Now Elwood was gone—along with his dream of attending college. He thought of his own life in Chicago, *Why did I come back here? Life would have been better for everyone if I had stayed there. And Rob...giving his life to God...What kind of God would permit this horrible, senseless catastrophe to happen?*

The enormous sob that emanated from his soul echoed through the small room like a resounding bark, and he began to cry bitterly. Quickly, he took another drink from the bottle, gagging at the biting taste of the liquor, then lit a cigarette for a chaser. In the pit of his stomach, he began to feel the tingling relief that he sought as his nerves began to calm.

Hours became days, as he became oblivious to the passage of time. His total activity alternated between drinking and sleeping, and his awareness of reality became a meaningless blur, as disturbing dreams of Elwood invaded his tortured mind.

A vigorous shake awakened him. Looking up from his bed, he saw Alvin's tall figure standing over him.

"How do you feel, pal?" asked Alvin.

For a few seconds, Dean lay silently on the bed, trying to comprehend his surroundings. Gradually, his awareness of reality returned.

"How did you get in?" asked Dean.

"I got a key from the manager."

"Why?" asked Dean. He rose to a sitting position, cradling his aching head between his hands.

"Because you've been gone for three days, and everybody's worried about you."

"Is Bobbie okay?" asked Dean.

"Yeah...She's fine, except for the fact that you worried the hell out of her." Al said, calmly.

Dean started to rise from the bed, but Al restrained his effort.

"Lie back down for a few minutes. You need some food. I brought you some soup."

Wordlessly, Al poured a cup of chicken soup into the cap of the thermos bottle and handed it to his brother. Upon smelling the steaming liquid, Dean gagged and pushed the cup away.

"Come on, pal... Drink it," said Al. As Dean tasted the soup, Al smiled at him. Then, he walked into the bathroom and returned with a paper cup filled with water.

"Here," he said, "You'll need some water—you're probably dehydrated."

Dean quickly gulped down the liquid. Immediately, he regurgitated the clear liquid onto the carpet. He noticed Al was non-judgmental in his demeanor—even gentle. Dean sensed the compassionate, nurturing side of his brother and realized how similar it was to Elwood's nature.

Stooping down, Al picked up the two empty bottles from the floor, then placed them in the waste can. From the night stand, he retrieved the half-full bottle, walked into the bathroom, and poured most of it down the sink, saving only enough for a couple of drinks.

"I saved you a little drink to help you through the withdrawal. Come on, drink your soup...I want to take you home."

"But what about my car?" asked Dean.

"Don't worry about it. Rob and I will come back and get it."

"How did you find me?"

"I drove around until I spotted your car," explained Al.

Slowly rising to his feet, Dean picked up the bottle and with Al's help, he walked unsteadily to the door. After helping Dean into the truck, Al drove his brother home.

Dean stepped out of his car and thanked his brother. Al smiled and drove away.

Bobbie met Dean at the door, and without saying a word, she hugged him.

"I'm sorry, honey," he said. Then, he walked into the kitchen and poured the remaining vodka down the sink. For three days, he had joined Elwood in death; now, he was ready to rejoin his family, once again embracing life.

One does not consent to creep when one feels an impulse to soar.
Helen Keller

Chapter 23

Soon after Elwood's funeral, the sorrow of Bobbie and Dean was compounded by the unexpected death of Bobbie's father. Following a brief illness, Benjamin Summer died of kidney failure, a misfortune that required Bobbie and Dean to attend two funerals in the same month. During their deep sadness, the couple spent most of their time attempting to comfort one another.

Through it all, even in the darkest hour of the night, there resides hope in the approaching dawn; for although the sunset ushers in a night as black as ink, the sun also rises. Dean and Bobbie walked into the brilliant, redeeming sunrise in the birth of their first child, a baby girl whom they named, "Deana Sue."

It was a difficult, dangerous delivery, a "breech birth," the doctor called it, a condition necessitating surgery to extract the baby. When Bobbie was finally out of danger, she and Dean were ecstatic. Dean was bursting with pride because he had fathered the first girl in the Beauvais family. They found it only appropriate to give her the name "Deana Sue" – *Deana* after her father's name and *Sue* after her mother's middle name. Dean spent countless hours with their little daughter, admiring her dark complexion and jet black hair, and when he noticed the same protruding ears that her grandfather had, he couldn't help but laugh.

Deana's birth gave new life to Sarah, helping to soothe her wounded spirit. She immediately bonded with her granddaughter.

"I knew that you would bring me a little girl!" she exclaimed to Bobbie as she held Deana in her lap, gently rocking her. Sarah became so enamored with Deana that she became a second mother to the child, and as the attachment grew stronger, the severity of her grief over the death of Elwood began to gradually diminish. She discovered new meaning in her life, for Sarah found her purpose in the nurturing of others. By the time Deana took her first steps, Sarah had once again begun to display a radiant spirit.

Will was slower in recuperating from the sting of Elwood's death. However, in his close relationship with his grandson, Terry, he gradually began to find the same solace that Sarah discovered with Deana. The degree of Will's clinging was in direct proportion to his severity of his former loss; therefore, Terry was the object of Will's affection and with his father's frequent absence, Will became a surrogate father to him. The closer his relationship was with Terry, the less he felt the pain of Elwood's passing.

This possessive love of Terry often caused friction between Will and Clay. Terry was a mischievous child, but when his father attempted to punish him, Will often came to his rescue, censuring Clay.

"He's a good boy," Will would say, "I won't stand by and see you spank him!"

Since Clay was on the eve of reporting back to his army base, he suppressed his anger, although he found Will's protective love of Terry inconsistent with the former punishment he had meted out to his own sons, particularly Rob, whose headstrong nature was like that of Terry's.

After Clay returned to his military duties, Will spent even more time reading to Terry, painting with him or taking him to the park; in contrast, because of the separation imposed on them, Terry and his own father failed to bond with one another. During Clay's last months in the army, Ellen gave birth to a second son, Eldon. Soon after that, Clay was discharged, and he returned home.

The period following Elwood's death was a time of transition for the Beauvais family. Grandchildren had entered their lives, but many more changes were taking place. Rob and Dean operated the sign shop, but Rob was beginning to grow impatient in the pursuit of his education. He was attending college on a part-time basis, but he felt his academic progress was moving slowly. In September, he relinquished his role in the family business and enrolled in college as a full-time student, moving with Madge to the location of the school in Athens.

Clay had returned home at an opportune time, for upon Rob's departure, he began to work for Dean. With the sporadic help of Al, the business continued to operate routinely. Things were now going well for Dean. He had finished the construction of his home, he and Bobbie had a beautiful daughter, and the shop was functioning reasonably well. In spite of these positive elements in his life, he once more began to experience a growing discontentment. He felt strangled by the bonds of mediocrity; for he felt no passion for his life style. He had once advised Elwood to take a risk, but with the predictable mundane routine in the sign shop, he found his life totally without excitement. For Dean, the sign shop was now dull and lifeless. At one time, his guitar could soothe his emptiness, but his creative drive for music was now lost. It was as though all the harmony in music and all the vigor in the shop were locked somewhere in Elwood's spirit.

To make matters worse, he was smoking heavily and had developed an incessant cough, and although he had quit drinking completely and was eating healthily, he had failed to regain his lost weight.

When Deana was three, Bobbie again became pregnant. With the knowledge that he would soon be the father of two children, Dean began to long for a better life for his family, as well as a more exciting existence. He found temporary relief from the monotony in his life after making acquaintance with Bud Scott, the husband of a close friend of Bobbie's.

Bud was an intelligent, creative man with an adventurous spirit, and Dean was immediately drawn to him. As both men discovered their common interests, the relationship quickly blossomed into a close friendship. Bud was a *University of Tennessee* graduate with a major in geology. He was a good cartoonist, a private pilot, and one of the pioneers in the new sport of skydiving.

Since Dean was seeking a spark of passion in his life, he joined the skydiving club that Bud had organized and soon began to satisfy his hunger for excitement by leaping from airplanes. On countless weekends, Dean and Bobbie would join Bud and his wife, Mary Ann, and other club members at *Roane County Airport* for an all day session of skydiving. Without fear, Bud quickly became skilled in the sport. Dean soon dispelled his fear, but he was never able to overcome his anxiety. After making several jumps, it became obvious the he had absolutely no aptitude for the sport. In contrast to Bud's graceful, controlled free-fall from the airplane, Dean's uncontrolled descent reflected the agility of a pregnant elephant. The only notable aspect of the sport that he mastered was his adherence to the law of gravity, as he awkwardly plummeted from the plane with the grace of a crated piano. Dean soon realized that the dexterity needed in skydiving was different than that for boxing and football. While Bud was truly a skydiver, Dean was only a parachute jumper—and a clumsy one at best. Because of his apprehension, however, the excitement he derived from the sport probably equaled that of Bud's because it was in taking the risk and overcoming his anxiety that Dean discovered the thrill. Unfortunately, his experience with skydiving was short-lived; for when the Scotts moved to Nashville, the local skydiving club was relocated.

Now that the adventure of leaping out of planes was behind him, Dean became even more lethargic in regard to his role in the family business. During the day, he was listless and his workouts in the gym had begun to sap his energy. He had given up smoking, but his cough persisted. Occasionally, he awakened from his sleep with night sweats, his pajamas drenched with cold perspiration. Will urged him to have an examination by the family doctor. Instead, Dean took a short vacation from work. Soon, he began to feel better, and his coughing spells became less frequent.

As the months passed, Bobbie's pregnancy became more evident. Dean was happy that their first child had been a girl, but now he fervently hoped for a boy. With another child on the way, he began to worry about his finances, especially since the business was not flourishing. Both Al and Clay were discontent with working in the shop, and Dean considered that Rob was the wise brother for returning to college.

At the end of the summer quarter, Rob graduated Summa Cum Laude from *Southern Wesleyan College*. He was valedictorian of his class and planned to enroll in graduate school at *Emory University* in Atlanta at the beginning of fall quarter. Will and Sarah were immensely proud of him.

In order to finance his education, Rob had become a circuit preacher, conducting services each Sunday in five small country churches. The Beauvais family had heard him preach on numerous occasions, and they were all amazed with his creative sermons and the improvement of his skill as a preacher.

Although Al was apathetic in regard to Rob's achievements, both Dean and Clay envied him for having the courage to take a risk; for, at nearly 40, he had abandoned a secure job in order to pursue his dream. Dean wished he had done the same, but now with a wife and children, he felt that he could never afford the time and expense of college. His past behavior at *Southern Wesleyan* haunted him, and he had to accept the fact that he had thrown away a chance for a college education.

Clay, now the father of two children, shared the same regret as Dean. In his thoughts of becoming more ambitious, he vastly improved his sign painting skills, and considered taking a correspondence course in cartooning.

"Dean, you said that you wanted to be an artist—maybe even a musician, but you never paint pictures anymore...or play your guitar," said Clay.

"Since Elwood died, I haven't picked up my guitar...It makes me too sad," replied Dean. "And I don't feel like painting either. I've just lost all enthusiasm for it, I guess."

"Why don't you go to art school?" asked Clay. "I know that's what you really want to do. And it would be good for you right now."

"I can't afford it, Clay. You would like to go to school too, but hell, I'm in the same boat that you're in."

"Well, Rob did it, so it's not impossible."

"Yeah, but Rob doesn't have any kids...Besides I'd have to close the shop...And that would break Dad's heart."

"Dean, sometimes you have to follow your own heart."

Summer blended into fall, and in late September, Dean's cough became chronic. He lost his appetite, and the night sweats worsened. One early morning, a coughing spasm awakened him, and just as he rose from his bed, bloody fluid from his lungs overflowed from his mouth. Later that day, x-rays confirmed his worst fears: He had been infected with the malady that had claimed the life of his brother: He had tuberculosis.

Sanity calms, but madness is more interesting.
John Russell

Chapter 24

Deana put her Barbie Doll aside and picked up her baton. As she proudly pranced across the living room in a regimented strut, she flashed a pretentious, 'movie-star' smile at Sarah.

"Look, Mamaw," she said, "Look how good I can twirl."

"That's good, honey! You look just like a grown-up majorette!" Sarah scooped her granddaughter into her lap and hugged her. Deana returned the hug and kissed her on the cheek. Her white, radiant smile contrasted sharply with her bronze complexion and her thick, dark hair. The tip of her nose was identical to that of her mother's, but her eyes, skin color, and physique mirrored the characteristics of her father.

Sarah looked fondly at Deana. "Lord, honey, you've sure got your Papaw's ears!" Grinning toward Will, she added, "Poor little girl."

Will felt uncomfortable in Dean and Bobbie's house, as he sat erect in the easy chair, facing Sarah. They had come to keep Deana while Al had taken Bobbie to the tuberculosis hospital to visit Dean. With no intent to baby-sit, Will sat anxiously and waited for Al to deliver the news of Dean's condition.

Bobbie was nearly full-term in her pregnancy, with the baby due in less than a month. Remembering the previous difficult birth of Deana, Sarah was concerned for Bobbie in the delivery of her second child.

Sarah's cheerful demeanor was in sharp contrast to the pessimistic mood of Will's.

"Sarah, when we saw Dean yesterday, what did you think of his condition? They won't tell us anything at the hospital about his chances. Why is that? I'm worried... Dean appeared to be awfully depressed."

"Will, I can understand his depression. You know, he won't even be here when Bobbie has her baby…And poor Bobbie, she'll have to go through it without him. We'll just have to pray about Dean, and put his fate in God's hands. I'm not going to start feeling downcast about it…I'm going to think positive."

Will intervened. "Yeah…We thought positive about Elwood, too…Remember? And look what happened. This TB disease has turned out to be the biggest enemy of my whole life. I have buried my dad, my brother, our son, and now we may have to bury another son. A man is not supposed to bury his sons…sons should bury their parents." Will's expression was one of total dejection.

"Now don't you start predicting the worst. I'm worried too, but sitting around and talking negative is not going to make anything better," lectured Sarah. "I'm going to make us a pot of coffee."

Immediately, Deana tossed her baton aside and picked up a children's book. Then she ran to Will and jumped into his lap.

"Read to me, Papaw," she said, gleefully.

Will suddenly stiffened, slightly recoiling from Deana's embrace. His awkwardness in the expression of physical affection toward the female gender had obviously extended to include his granddaughter.

"Honey, I can't read to you right now," Will scooted Deana from his lap. "I'm worried about your daddy."

"What's wrong with Daddy? When will he be back home?" Deana ran into the kitchen, waiting for her grandmother's answer.

"Honey, he's sick," said Sarah, "But he'll be back with us soon!"

The front door opened, and five-year old Terry, who had walked the short distance from Clay's house, quickly ran to his grandfather.

"Hi, Papaw!"

Will's gloomy mood instantly changed to one of delight.

"Well, there's my little buddy!" He pulled his grandson into his lap. Handing the children's book to Terry, he said, "Read to us, Terry… Sarah, I want you to listen to how this kid can read! He's been reading for almost a year, now!"

As Terry began to read from the book, Sarah came back into the living room, carrying a tray with two steaming cups of coffee. After placing the tray on the coffee table, she handed a cup to Will. Deana quickly followed Sarah and crawled into her lap.

"Deana can't read, and I can!" boasted Terry, proudly as he stuck out his tongue at Deana.

"Yes, I can, too!" fibbed Deana. With a pouting expression, she returned Terry's gesture.

"Well, she's not old enough, yet," explained Sarah, "But she'll be able to read too, in a year or two, just like Terry."

"She might be able to," conceded Will, "I'd bet that all of our grandchildren will be smart, but Terry can outdo any kid I've ever seen for his age."

Peering through the picture window, Sarah saw Al's truck pull into the driveway.

"They're back." She released Deana and walked to the door, opening it, as Al and Bobbie strolled up the walkway.

"How is he, Alvin?" she asked.

"He's okay, I guess," replied Al, as he and Bobbie entered the house. "You can't find out anything at that hospital…They won't tell you anything. Dean's pretty depressed, but he was awfully glad to see Bobbie. He's worried about her, with the baby coming soon."

Bobbie held her protruding stomach and awkwardly positioned herself on the couch. Deana jumped on the cushion nearby and wrapped her arms around her mother's neck.

Sarah looked at her. "How do you feel, honey?"

"Just tired, Mamaw," answered Bobbie, wearily. "I feel like I need to lie down for awhile."

"Come on, honey," said Sarah, "Come into the bedroom and lie down. Get some rest. Try not to worry about Dean…He's going to be just fine. I'll be with you when you have the baby, and we'll take good care of Deana for you, too. You can't afford to worry right now." Bobbie followed Sarah into the bedroom, with Deana tagging behind.

Will looked at Al. "What do you think, Alvin? Is he getting any better, or do you think he might take a sudden bad turn, like Elwood did?"

To spare his father from further worry, Al said, "Dad, I believe he'll be okay…Dean's a tough bird." However, Al had his doubts.

"He's been in the hospital for two months, already," complained Will, despairingly, "How long will it be before we know something about his condition?"

"Well, at least he's not in critical condition like Elwood was," reasoned Alvin, "And they don't have him hooked up to any gadgets. You know, Dad, recovery from TB is a slow process…Sometimes it takes two or three years."

Alvin was sporting a black eye, and Will quickly called it to his son's attention.

"Did Clay give you that shiner?" asked Will, accusingly.

"I guess he must have. I haven't been in a fight with anybody else."

"Can't you guys get along for awhile, at least while Dean is in the hospital? He turned the shop over to you and Clay while he's out of commission, and all you two ever do is argue and fight like children," complained Will. "I heard the two of you arguing in the shop, yesterday...It sounded like you were about to get into a fight, then." Will eyed Alvin.

"Talk to Clay about it, Dad...Not me. He won't stay off my—rear end. He's always raggin' me about something. Anyway, I've got to go to work. I'll see you all later." Pouting, Al suddenly abandoned his chair and left for the shop.

Terry crawled down from his grandfather's lap and ran into the kitchen with Sarah and Deana. The children sat quietly, watching Sarah peel potatoes, while in the living room, Will reflected on the radical behavior of his sons. He was aware that environmental influences contribute to behavior patterns, however, he was beginning to wonder how much of a role genetics played in it all.

In the black and white world of Will, there always had to be a reason for everything. Unable to accept the possibility that certain things simply are what they are, he found it necessary to assign blame for undesirable characteristics. From whom did his sons inherit this crazy streak? Who was to blame for Alvin's vacillating moods and Elwood's predilection for ridiculous behavior? Since he was unable to recognize this tendency within his own heritage, he began to consider the possibility that his sons' propensities for the inane might have come from Sarah's side of the family. As he pondered the question, an incident from the distant past came back to him....

*   *   *

On an unseasonably warm day before Thanksgiving while Will and Elwood were working in the shop, Clay and Dean were playing in the front yard. With youthful curiosity, they looked toward the highway as a Greyhound bus stopped in front of the shop. As the bus pulled away, they saw a lone figure, whom the bus had deposited, standing by the road.

As the boys watched with interest, the man suddenly raised his right arm over his head and fired a pistol into the air. The blast of the weapon instantly brought Will and Elwood to the door of the shop. Sarah, who had also heard the report, came into the front yard, and Clay and Dean stared incredulously at the man wielding the gun.

Crossing the highway and walking into the parking area in front of the shop, the man gradually became recognizable: It was Uncle Fred. As he crossed the lot, he fired three more shots, each in a different direction. Puzzled, the Beauvais family considered taking cover; however, they merely stood, motionless as Uncle Fred, grinning, walked into the yard.

Having heard the shot, a neighbor, Pete Walker, who lived across the highway, ran into the yard. As he approached, he slowed his pace. Uncle Fred turned and quickly walked to him.

"Let me show you a nice pistol. Here! Take it and shoot it! Give it a try!"

"I don't want to fool with that damned thing!" yelled Pete.

"Then, you're nothing but a big baby. You're nothing but a cowardly son-of-a-bitch!" yelled Uncle Fred.

Instantly realizing that Uncle Fred was mentally disturbed, Pete Walker retreated toward his home, anxiously looking back at Fred, his expression a mixture of confusion and terror. Rather than feeling angry, he felt thankful that he had escaped with his life.

Uncle Fred was Sarah's brother, a large man, standing six-feet two and weighing over 200 pounds. In his facial features, he was a replica of Sarah, and when sober, he displayed her gentle disposition. He was an intelligent, scholarly man who had once held aspirations to be a writer, and because of his sentimental nature, he often quoted poetry, particularly when he was drunk. He loved children, and since he was extremely generous toward them, all of the Beauvais boys looked forward to his visits.

Uncle Fred was a binge drinker. He only drank about once every year or so; however, on the rare occasions that he imbibed, he drank continuously, to the point that he became mentally unbalanced. Physically, he didn't appear to be intoxicated, never staggering or slurring. It seemed to affect only his mind. When drinking, his mood changed instantaneously. At one moment, he might be quoting poetry, in tears; but in the next instant, he would suddenly tell a raucous joke, bellowing with insane laughter at the grand finale of the vulgar anecdote. This erratic behavior angered Will.

During his binges, he would always leave his home in Virginia and travel to visit Sarah; for she was the one person in the world who understood him. Will was fond of Uncle Fred when he was sober, but when he came to visit the Beauvais family, his unstable behavior would worsen as his consumption of alcohol increased.

By the same token, Uncle Fred liked Will. He understood his nervous, skeptical nature; consequently, in his drunken, deranged state, he enjoyed irritating Will with his demented behavior.

One evening, as the family was finishing dinner, Will was still seated at the table, drinking his last sip of coffee. Fred left the table and stood directly behind Will. In his right hand, he brandished an eight inch butcher knife. As Will turned his head to look at him, Fred moved the blade of the knife within inches of Will's throat. Uncle Fred then turned the knife from side-to-side and when he spoke to Will, he gracefully stroked the razor-sharp blade.

"You know, Will, this is a nice knife." As the eyes of the two men met, Fred grinned fiendishly. Immediately, Will retrieved his hat and quickly left the house.

Soon after, Sarah, for the third time, had him committed to a mental hospital.

Sharing his Uncle Fred's penchant for irritating Will, for years following his visit, Elwood occasionally flourished a butcher knife when at the dinner table.

"You know, Dad, this is a nice knife," he would say, with an idiotic sneer.

*   *   *

Terry jumped back into his lap, and Will's mind returned to the present. He turned his head toward the kitchen and yelled, "Sarah, I think I know where our boys got that crazy streak. It comes from your side of the family."

I know God will not give me anything I can't handle. I just wish that He didn't trust me so much. **Mother Teresa**.

Chapter 25

Deana took a bow and blew a big kiss toward the fourth story window. It was the end of her baton routine—her favorite part when the man in the window returned her kisses. He was a prince, her knight in shining armor. Without him, her tea parties were drab and empty. She yearned to touch his face again, to squeeze his ears, to rub her nose against his.

"Come on, honey. We have to go now." Bobbie shared her daughter's sadness. "Daddy will be coming home soon."

Since children were not allowed inside the patient's rooms, Deana would perform on the front lawn of the hospital. When she finished her routine, the viewing patients on the entire west wing of the hospital clapped their hands in applause. Because of their monotonous life in a tuberculosis sanitarium, all the hospital occupants looked forward to her occasional twirling act. As if it were an off-Broadway play, they longed for an encore performance.

As time passed, the Beauvais family continued their visits with Dean. The remaining autumn leaves yielded to the persistent November wind, laying the dark limbs stark and bare against the gloomy gray sky. Just before Christmas, a cold front from the north converged with the blowing moisture from the Gulf, blanketing the area with a heavy snowfall. Although not shared by the Beauvais family, the spirit of Christmas was in the air.

The snow was falling heavily as darkness fell on the cold December evening. A howling wind from the west whirled huge snowflakes against the window panes while Bobbie looked out the front door at the blowing snowstorm. Feeling thankful that her baby wasn't due until Christmas day, she only hoped that she wouldn't be snowed in when the time arrived. Sarah had assured Bobbie that starting tomorrow she would be staying with her until after the delivery of the baby.

As she prepared Deana for bed, Bobbie listened to the fierce winds whipping the eaves of the roof, moaning in a mournful refrain, as the heavy snow blew in from the west. She held the pajama pants as Deana stepped into them. Then, pulling her daughter's hair back, she brushed it gently and secured it with a clip.

"When does Santa Claus come, Mommy?"

"Just four more nights...It won't be long, now!"

Bobbie looked at the small Christmas tree in the corner of the living room that she and Deana had decorated only two days earlier. It was a cedar tree, skimpy in size, but beautiful in symmetry and lavishly decorated. Al had spotted it on the side of a mountain road and stopped to cut it for Dean's family. A few gifts, beautifully wrapped, lay scattered beneath the tree. The pungent aroma of cedar that permeated the room piqued Bobbie's nostalgia of past Christmases when she was a child. Without Dean, this would be a sad Christmas for her, but because she wanted to make it special for Deana, she displayed a pretentious holiday spirit.

Deana was excited about the snow. "I want a sled for Christmas, Mommy. Will Santa bring me a sled?"

"I thought you wanted a Chatty Cathy doll, honey."

"I do! But, I want a sled, too, since it snowed so pretty! When can we make a snow-man?"

"We'll see. Maybe tomorrow...Now let's get to bed, Mommy's tired."

"Can me and Uncle Al make some snow cream?"

Bobbie laughed. She knew Uncle Al's fondness for playing in the snow and making snow cream. "Yeah, honey...I can almost guarantee that."

She switched off the living room lamp and then pulled the plug that led to the tree lights.

"Mommy! Leave the Christmas tree lights on...! Don't turn them off! Santa may be outside right now, looking at our house. He may think that nobody lives here!" Deana was almost panicky.

Bobbie smiled. "He knows where we live. I gave him directions to our house in your Santa Claus letter." She turned the Christmas tree lights on again, anyway.

She placed her daughter in bed. "Will Santa Claus bring Daddy anything? Does he know where to bring presents to Daddy?"

"Yes…He knows where to take Daddy's gifts. I'm sure Santa will be good to him."

Because of her swollen belly, Bobbie awkwardly twisted herself into bed beside Deana, and then turned off the table lamp. The glow of a small night light illuminated the corner of the bedroom.

"Honey, why don't you scoot over here and keep Mommy's back warm?"

Deana snuggled with her mother in the cozy bed, as the unrelenting groan of the wind played its wintry melody against the window. The warmth of their coupled bodies offered a feeling of safety from the harsh, wintry elements outside.

"Goodnight, honey."

"Goodnight, Mommy…Do you think Mamaw will play with me in the snow tomorrow?"

"Yes, I'm sure she will…Now go to sleep. Mommy needs some rest." Bobbie pondered the approaching delivery of her baby as she tried to adjust her body to afford more comfort to her bulging abdomen. In spite of the difficult birth of Deana, she was not afraid, nor did she particularly dread the pain associated with childbirth; for she possessed the same mind-set held by most expectant mothers: the muted memory, or sometimes the mysterious forgetfulness of the terrible pain they suffered in the birth of their last child.

She wondered what Dean's thoughts were at this moment, as he lay in his hospital bed. She longed for his presence and realized that Deana missed him, too. Since marrying Dean, Bobbie had become keenly aware of his faults, the worst of which was his attitude of male-dominance, similar to that of his father. Sometimes on certain evenings he would leave home for hours without explanation, usually to play pool at *Tyler City Billiard Parlor*. She had never experienced this with her own father, so at first, she found Dean's disappearances puzzling and shocking. Although he was never unfaithful to Bobbie, his unexplained departures irritated her. With her easy-going, forgiving nature, however, she rarely remained angry at him for long; for she realized that in his heart, he was a loving husband and father.

As she was falling asleep, she was suddenly awakened by a sharp pain from her lower abdomen. Sitting up in bed, she wondered if it was a true contraction. She looked at the clock on the small nightstand. If it was a labor pain, she needed to measure the length of time between each contraction. She rested her head on her pillow. *No need to worry,* she thought, *Sarah is just a phone call, and a hundred yards away.* Eight minutes later, she was stabbed by another pain—this time with more severity. Trying to calmly reassure herself, she waited to see if other pangs followed. In just under seven minutes, a severe contraction caused her to rise to a sitting position. *Could the baby be coming early? I better get dressed and call Sarah.*

Rotating the circular dial on the telephone, she dialed the number. *The line was dead!* She jiggled the receiver, hoping for a dial-tone, but she heard only silence. The snowstorm had rendered the telephone useless. She became alarmed. *Oh no, what can I do now?*

The next contraction struck with a vengeance, causing her to cry out in pain. Suddenly, the vivid memory of the unbearable pain of Deana's birth returned to her. The force intensified, and her stomach tightened into a large, hard knot. *Go away! Go away!* Her fingers gripped the blankets as she pushed powerful puffs of air from her lungs. Finally, the contraction began to soften, and her clear thinking returned. *I have to wake Deana...And get dressed now...We'll have to walk to Sarah's...Now, before the next pain begins!*

She put on her thickest socks and rushed to the closet.

Suddenly, the next contraction caused her to kneel in agony. Her heavy panting returned as panic filled her mind. *I've got to go now...I can't take Deana...I've got to get help...* She lay still on the floor, until at last, the pain ceased. Then, donning a night gown, she hurriedly slipped her feet into a pair of Dean's combat boots and made her way to the living room. After opening the front door, she discovered that a deep snow drift blocked the outside storm door. Within seconds, the pain would consume her body again. At that moment, she pushed the door with such a force that it finally surrendered and swept the mound of snow into the empty flowerbed below.

Once outside, Bobbie met the ferocity of the storm. She battled the icy, savage wind while she waddled across the front yard, pulling each leg out of the snow as high as her abdomen would allow. Her face was pelted by the sting of tiny pellets of sleet and snow, each biting into her skin like grains of sand. Leaning against the howling wind, she slowly struggled along, tugging her body down *Beauvais Lane,* under the snow-laden Maple trees, each one a milestone that led to Sarah's house. The angry winds had deposited an uneven blanket of snow over the area—the hilly, front yards and back fields displaying only a sparse coating, while houses, trees, and fence rows had wind-swept snowdrifts more than two-feet deep at their bases. From the northwest the ferocious wind blew in repeated gusts, and the powdery dust melted into her eyes and swirled up her nightgown.

About half-way to Sarah's, another contraction stiffened her body. Her arms swept at the night air as she tried to keep her balance in the deep snow. She stumbled and fell to her knees, then, after struggling to an upright position, she felt a warm, flowing liquid gush down her thighs and into her boots. She feared that she would faint as she struggled onward, bracing herself against the merciless gusts of wind. Finally, she fell into a deep snow drift, swept by the wind, piled against the outside wall of Sarah's bedroom.

Another excruciating pain seized her as she called out weakly, her voice competing with the screaming wind:

"Mamaw! Mr. Beauvais…Help me…Mr. Beauvais…"

To-morrow, and to-morrow, and to-morrow, / Creeps in this petty pace from day to day, / To the last syllable of recorded time; / And all our yesterdays have lighted fools / The way to dusty death. Out, out, brief candle! / Life's is but a walking shadow; a poor player / That struts and frets his hour upon a stage,/ And then is heard no more; it is a tale / Told by an idiot, full of sound and fury, / Signifying nothing.
William Shakespeare—Macbeth(V,v,19)

Chapter 26

"Mr. Beauvais! Mr. Beauvais! Wake up," said the nurse. Dean's eyes opened quickly, for he had been sleeping only lightly. Suddenly, he raised upward in bed.

"You're a daddy again, Mr. Beauvais!" she grinned, obviously happy for him.

Dean was now excited and completely awake. "The baby came early! What is it—a boy, or girl?"

"A little boy…Seven pounds and eight ounces." She smiled and turned on the light.

"Oh! Thank God…How is my wife?" he asked, anxiously.

"She's doing just fine. Your mother called us with all of the news. Congratulations!"

Dean looked at his watch: *6:15 a.m.* "What time was he born?"

The nurse reached into her pocket for a small note. She looked at the paper. "5:44…Just about a half-hour ago." She handed Dean the small paper that gave all the news about his new baby son.

Relieved and ecstatically happy, Dean sprang from his bed. Although hospital rules had confined him to his room, he excitedly walked down the hall, peering into each room, and shouting the good news to every patient who happened to be awake. The sympathetic nurse allowed him free rein to roam the hall and spread the glad tidings, her only admonition was "Sssh…Don't be so loud, you'll awaken everyone in the hospital. By the way, what did you name the baby?"

"Vince Elwood," Dean smiled. "Vince Elwood Beauvais. It has a nice ring to it, don't you think?"

"It certainly does. Now, try to be a little bit quieter."

Since entering the sanitarium, Dean had been plagued by anxiety and depression. His apprehension about Bobbie's pregnancy and discouragement over the lack of any prognosis in regard to his illness had left him sick at heart. With the birth of his son, however, he was temporarily relieved of his depressed mood. Realizing that children were not allowed in the hospital, he wondered how long it would be until he could hold his son in his arms.

This was Dean's third month in the hospital, and he was still as uninformed about his condition as he had been upon entering the facility. During the first month, he had been given a bronchoscopy, but even after the surgeon probed and peered into the diseased lung with the slim instrument, he was still left without information. He only knew that X-rays had confirmed that he had 'moderately advanced' tuberculosis.

His room was on 'Fourth West', as the nurses called it. His fellow patients occupying the other rooms of the wing were in various stages of recovery, ranging from those only slightly afflicted, to the patients in the last stages of the diseases who were in critical condition. Dean learned that there is no cure for tuberculosis; however, its progress can be arrested, partly with the use of drugs, but mostly by months, maybe even years, of bed rest. He became deeply depressed upon learning that some of his fellow patients had been in the facility for more than two years.

The hospital staff was reluctant to discuss patients' conditions with them for fear of either totally discouraging them, or offering false hope. When the hospital physician decided that a patient was sufficiently well and his disease was not longer communicable, he was, with no advance notice, released from the hospital. Discharge from the hospital worked much like the process of being paroled from prison: Every six weeks, a patient's condition was reviewed, and a determination was made whether or not he was to be released. If not discharged at that time, he was 'condemned' to another six week's wait before his condition could again be evaluated. Because recovery from the disease was abysmally slow, it was especially difficult for a patient with Dean's active and impatient nature.

Two patients were assigned to each room. Dean's roommate, Fred Parkinson, was an uneducated friendly man who was married to an obese, domineering woman named Alice. The couple had two daughters, who, along with their mother, frequently came to visit Fred. Dean liked Fred's easy-going, soft-spoken manner, but he soon began to tire

270

of his roommate's incessant talking. Often, when Dean was attempting to read or listen to music, Fred would launch into an endless monologue, delivering his vocal ramblings in a monotonous drone. With absolutely no inflection in his low-keyed tone, his repetitious stories became an unending stream of inaudible mumbling. Although he learned to ignore the muted murmuring of Fred's dreary voice while listening to music, he found it impossible to concentrate when attempting to read or watch television.

Dean had been accustomed to an exceptionally active lifestyle; consequently, he found the idleness of each day maddening. His roommate had assumed control of the television, and on rare occasions when he wasn't engaged in mundane mumbling, he was watching "Rawhide" or "Bonanza."

To escape the withering grip of boredom, some of the patients took up the hobby of doll-making, a chore in which the hospital furnished the bare rudiments for constructing the figurines. Upon completion of the doll, the patient could then sell it to visitors for perhaps a couple of dollars. It was a time-consuming diversion that helped many patients while away the long, dull hours, but Dean found the pastime even more boring than doing nothing at all, so he made only one doll before retiring from the doll-making business.

He was finally rescued from the stagnating boredom when he started drawing cartoons. Clay had assembled the necessary drawing supplies and packed them into a kit. In addition to the tools, he brought a drawing board which Dean propped against his knees while lying in bed, enabling him to draw while in a reclining position.

Enthusiastically, he began to draw caricatures of the nurses and his fellow patients, with each cartoon displaying one or more of the fellow-residents in a humorous situation. The renderings were then passed around to the hospital rooms, where the patients often roared with laughter at Dean's comical portrayal of them. His daily display of nonsense not only boosted the morale of the staff and patients, but it also lifted him from the depths of despair, as it revived his withered spirit.

Poking benign fun at his fellow-patients with his cartoons enabled them to laugh at themselves; as a result, Dean became the most popular resident of the entire west wing. His revitalized spirit, however, fluctuated between lofty peaks and deep valleys, because some of the new friends surrounding him died shortly after their friendships began. The strictness of the daytime nurses mandated that all patients stay inside their rooms; they were not allowed to either walk the hallway or visit others. On the other hand, the leniency of the evening nurses enabled the healthier patients to intermingle on a limited basis, a privilege that kept Dean from going insane since it gave him a brief respite from his garrulous roommate.

One morning when Dean awoke, a small boy was seated by his bed, peering intently at him. Apparently, the lad, who appeared to be about 10 years old, had been sitting in the chair for quite awhile, patiently waiting for Dean to awaken. He was a new patient, for Dean had never before seen him.

"Hello, Mister," he said, "I want to l'arn to draw, like you. Can you l'arn me?"

"Hey, kid…You'd better go back to your room. The nurses will chase you out."

"She said I could come and talk to you. She said that I kin come in here anytime I want to."

"Why does she allow you to do that?" inquired Dean. "Nobody else can visit anytime they want to."

"I dunno. She jus' said that I could. What's your name, mister?"

"My name's Dean. What's yours?"

"My name's Tim…Tim Stewart."

"How old are you, Tim?"

"Fourteen, but some people think I'm younger."

Dean studied the boy carefully. His skin reflected an unhealthy pallor, and a closer look at his sunken eyes indicated that he was indeed, older than he appeared to be at first glance. He was a scrawny youngster and less than five feet tall. Considering his demeanor and illiterate speech, it was obvious that he was uneducated.

"I'll help you to draw, if you really want to," remarked Dean. "What would you like to draw?"

"I'd like to draw funny people, like you do," Tim replied.

"Okay." He handed the boy his drawing board, a pencil, and a sheet of paper. "Draw me something, and let me see how much talent you've got."

"I'll draw a pitcher of you," said Tim, smiling.

The finished drawing was crude, but to Dean's surprise, the youngster appeared to have a bit of talent. After talking with Tim for awhile, Dean gave him several sheets of paper and a couple of drawing pencils, and the boy went back to his room.

The next morning, Dean again awoke to the sight of Tim sitting by his bed, waiting for him to awaken. From inside the leaves of a magazine, he pulled out several crude drawings that he had rendered, and proudly displayed them to Dean, who lauded the lad's efforts.

"What are you doing here this early, Tim? They're about to serve breakfast. You'd better go back to your room."

"I've done et. Let me show you whut my pa giv' me, afore he died last year." He pulled a small pocket knife from the shirt of his pajamas and opened the blade. Carefully handing the knife to Dean, he boasted, "Look at her! She's a genuine Barlow knife. Pa carried her fer years, then when he passed on, he giv' her to me."

"That's a pretty knife," remarked Dean. Then in jest, he asked, "What would you take for it? You want to sell it?"

"Sell her? Lord no! I've been offered ten dollars for her, but I turned it down. This knife is the most pracious thing I own…It was my pa's knife—a genuine Barlow!" Tim seemed outraged at Dean's joking offer to buy the knife.

"I was just kidding you, Tim," replied Dean. "I can see how much it means to you. And it really is a nice knife."

Each morning, Tim, with more of his drawings, would be sitting by Dean's bedside, waiting for him to awaken. Sometimes Dean would tell him many stories of his adventures while Tim would sit, wide-eyed, idling away the time sharpening his genuine Barlow knife on a whet stone. As the weeks passed, Dean grew very fond of him, although, at times he wished that the youngster would give him more privacy.

One day as Tim was watching Dean draw more caricatures, he turned and spoke.

"You know, Dean…I wish that you was my pa. If you was, jes' look at the fun we could have together when we git out of this here hospital."

Dean was deeply touched, for he had become emotionally attached to Tim.

Dean awoke one morning, and was surprised to find that little Tim wasn't waiting by his bedside. When Minnie, the nurse's aide, entered the room with his breakfast tray, he decided to ask about Tim. Dean had made friends with Minnie, and although she was breaking hospital rules, she often confided in him about matters pertaining to the hospital.

"Minnie, where is little Tim Stewart? He didn't get the flu or something, did he?"

"I'm not supposed to tell anybody, Mr. Beauvais, but they sent him off to another hospital."

"Why? Why didn't he tell me?" asked Dean.

Minnie responded, "He didn't know about it. They just came and got him about six o'clock this morning. He came by your room to tell you goodbye, but you were still sleeping. He didn't want to wake you. To tell you the truth, they just sent him away to die."

"How do you know that? What's wrong with him that could make him die…He didn't seem to be that sick!"

"Mr. Beauvais…Don't you tell anyone I told you this…I'm only telling you because I know how close you were to him, but little Tim has lung cancer, and the TB had gotten into his bones, too. I'm awfully sorry, Mr. Beauvais."

When Minnie left the room, Dean quickly got out of bed and began to pace the floor. Looking at the small table in the corner, he saw what appeared to be a note. Picking it up, he read…

"Deer Dean, thank you for teeching me to draw. I wont you to have my nife. Good by. Your frend, Tim."

As his vision blurred, Dean picked up the genuine Barlow knife. He sat down in a chair, and for a long while, he looked at the gift and thought about the unfairness of life.

With a sudden departure of Tim, Dean again fell into a deep depression; in addition, he again 'failed' his six weeks' evaluation, which meant at least six more weeks of waiting, maybe even longer. Although he received regular visits from Bobbie and the other members of the Beauvais family, his sadness worsened. He hadn't even a vague idea how much longer he would be hospitalized, and he was yet to see his son, Vince, except to view him from the fourth floor of his hospital window as Bobbie proudly displayed him from the sidewalk below. When his family was visiting, in order to cheer them up, Dean would fake an optimistic attitude, an act that failed to convince Bobbie, who could quickly read his frame of mind.

In April, with no warning and little fanfare, Dean was finally released from the hospital after having been in treatment for six months. Upon his discharge, he was given a list of specific instructions: Continue medication for 18 months, stay confined at home with plenty of bed rest, and abstain from work for at least two years. Furthermore, the doctor advised him to permanently abstain from weight-lifting.

He cherished this new time with his family, particularly his reunion with Bobbie and his first physical contact with Vince. He resumed the regular tea-parties with Deana, but for the first week, she could only follow him from room to room, watching him in disbelief with a speechless stare on her face.

Before long, Dean started to develop a feeling of uselessness.

Sometimes he would visit the sign shop where he talked with Al and Clay; occasionally he would spend time with Will and Sarah, then he would return home to be with his family. Since he hadn't worked in months, the lack of money began to be a problem, prompting Bobbie to talk of getting a job for herself. The prospect of his wife being the family bread-winner humiliated him further, and he again was consumed by a pervading depression. The assistance from friends and family members was appreciated, but time after time of needing and relying on others made him feel worthless. He had come home to a new, beautiful family, yet he could do nothing but withdraw himself from their needs. He had endured enough of this nasty illness, and before long, his gloom was replaced with anger, and the one to blame was God.

What kind of God would allow all this to happen to my family? Hell, maybe there is no God. But, there has to be a God, thought Dean, *or else, who is it that I keep cursing?* He became consumed with negative questions and thoughts: *How unfair and cruel is this meaningless existence called life! In an attempt to give life meaning, we struggle and set goals, only to fail and abandon our efforts; we reach out and take risks to love others, when we know that those we aspire to love will die and leave us; we make elaborate plans for the future, only to discover that existence is only temporary, and all will ultimately return to dust. What is the meaning of it all? Our struggle in life is all vanity, and much ado about nothing.*

Thinking about his past, he was filled with remorse in regard to his pitiful contribution of goodness to the world. If our short span of life on this earth is all we will ever be given, with the chance of passing this way but once, and with no hope for an afterlife, then that is even more reason to contribute to the goodness of mankind.

He considered the cruelty of man, and realized that he had been part of that brutality…His mind drifted back to the sadistic actions of the bully who had viciously beaten Elwood, and his own heartless behavior in his savage retaliation against the man. He was filled with sadness that either of the incidents had to happen. In addition, he felt indirectly responsible for Elwood's death; and he deeply regretted his past behavior that had brought heartache to his parents. Having no sense of direction for his life, he found himself in complete despondency.

For Dean, these negative thoughts invaded his sleepless nights. Early one Sunday morning, he left his home and began to drive aimlessly through Tyler City. As if obeying some hidden instinct, he set his course toward Decatur, Tennessee, where Rob and Madge now lived.

At 11:45 a.m., he walked into the small country church where Rob was in the middle of preaching a sermon about the "Prodigal Son." At the conclusion of the sermon, Rob always gave an altar call, an invitation for those who are burdened to dedicate their lives to God, receiving new life.

Slowly leaving his seat in the pew, Dean walked to the altar. As he arrived at the front of the sanctuary, Rob smiled and took his hand.

"Kneel down, Dean," he whispered kindly.

Dean knelt, and prayed softly, "God...Help me! Show me the way...Give me direction for my life."

As he felt the tender touch of his brother's hand on his head, he sadly remembered the times that both he and Rob had lifted their hands to each other in anger. Then he rose from his kneeling position, and Dean and his older brother held each other in a vigorous embrace.

In nature, nothing is perfect and everything is perfect. Trees can be contorted, bent in weird ways, and they're still beautiful.
Alice Walker

Chapter 27

"Lord, Vince, you're getting heavy!" Sarah stooped and placed her grandson's feet on the front porch.

Deana pulled at Sarah's dress. "Mamaw, can I ring the doorbell?"

"Yes, honey, but only push it one time."

Deana carefully and firmly pushed the small, gleaming button. Bobbie was now working as a waitress in Knoxville, and Sarah had eagerly agreed to keep Deana and Vince while she worked. It was a chore that she relished, and today she had brought them with her to the home of Irene Woodley, a lonely, middle-aged widow who, with her son, lived next door to Dean and Bobbie on the lot adjoining the Beauvais tract of land.

Waiting for a response, Sarah stood at the door with her grandchildren. After a brief while, she looked down at Deana.

"Honey, ring the bell one more time."

Deana gladly complied, when at the same time, the door opened and Irene Woodley appeared. Tall and slim, she was a homely woman but with kind features. Her hair was pulled into a bun, making her slender face appear even smaller, and her thick-lensed glasses magnified her already-bulbous eyes. The vertical stripes of her neatly-pressed house dress gave her slim figure an even more willowy appearance.

"Well, I'll swear, if it ain't Sarah...! Come in, Sarah! I see you brought the little ones with you."

"Hi, Irene." Sarah then squeezed Deana and Vince's hands. "Say hello to Mrs. Woodley, children." Smiling shyly, they both greeted her.

Sarah spoke as she and her grandchildren entered the living room.

"How have you been, Irene?"

"I've been fine…You have such beautiful grandchildren!"

"Thank you. They are pretty, aren't they?" Sarah boasted. "Are we interrupting you with anything? We came to see Lamar. I baked some cookies for him."

"Oh, thank you, Sarah…No, I wasn't doing anything. I hope you can stay for awhile. This will make Lamar's day! He's in his room. I'll get him." Irene left for her son's room. From the hallway, she called, "Lamar…Lamar. You've got company. Three people are here to see you!"

Mrs. Woodley returned, pushing Lamar in his wheelchair. The boy was twelve years of age and afflicted with cerebral palsy. His contorted hands were drawn grotesquely toward his chest, and his head and arms gyrated with involuntary tremors. Immediately upon seeing Sarah, his face displayed a broad grin as he began to vigorously stomp his feet in delight. His voice, although discernible and normal in volume, was spasmodic, and exuded a droning monotone. His unusual demeanor and the noisy clamor of his stamping feet frightened Deana, who quickly hid herself behind Sarah. Vince only stared at the handicapped boy in bewilderment.

"Oh, boy…Hello Sarah! You came…to see me!" As he laughed, foaming saliva dripped from the corners of his mouth. Mrs. Woodley reached into her apron pocket for a clean handkerchief and dabbed it across Lamar's mouth. She then gently tucked the handkerchief into his tightly-clenched fist.

"That's right, Lamar, we came to visit you!" said Sarah, "and we brought you something! Give him his present, Deana."

While still hiding behind Sarah, Deana reached around her grand-mother and handed her the paper bag filled with cookies.

"Oh, boy…oh boy," yelled Lamar, as he accepted the cookies from Sarah. The agitation of his hands became more intense with his sudden excitement, as his head wobbled wildly. Because the undulation of his arms prevented him from taking a cookie from the bag, Sarah selected one for him. Laughing, he stuffed a cookie into his mouth. As he chewed on the confection, he placed the bag in his lap, then with his quivering, outstretched arms, he met Sarah's embrace.

"Thank you, thank you, Sarah," he said, excitedly. With each sound of this voice, Deana retreated further behind Sarah, finally burying her body into the back of her grandmother's dress. Before releasing Lamar, Sarah kissed him gently on his forehead.

Lamar looked up at his mother, "Mom...do you think...I should show Sarah, now?"

Sarah inquired, "Show me what, Lamar?"

Lamar smiled, "Well, you gotta keep your eyes on my hanky." With concentration, he slowly moved the handkerchief in his right hand closer to his face. In order to stabilize his shaking upper limbs, he pulled his arms into his chest as he braced one with the other. As he slowly leaned forward, his involuntary shaking maneuvered the waving handkerchief, until eventually, his chin was patted dry by the cloth's unsteady strokes, an accomplishment that he had always been determined to master.

"Lamar! That's great!" Sarah spoke with loud praise. "I know how much you have practiced doing that. I'm so proud of you!"

Lamar gleamed with pride, for he had used his spasmodic movements to accomplish his purpose.

Sarah smiled at Mrs. Woodley. "Irene, that is wonderful! This is a big step in his independence. I know this will be helpful... for him, and for you."

Deana had partially recovered from her initial shock. Thrusting out her head from behind Sarah, she finally summoned the courage for a wide-eyed peep at the boy.

"Pretty little girl!" gargled Lamar, with a wide grin, "Want a cookie?" With a quivering arm, he extended the bag toward her. As quick as a titmouse, Deana darted back into her hiding place. Vince, however, ambled over to the boy and pulled two cookies from the sack, then stepped back and stared at Lamar while munching on the sugary treat. Lamar again bellowed in laughter and energetically stomped his feet in approval.

"Lamar likes little kids," said his mother.

"I'm sure they like him too," remarked Sarah, "They're just bashful. Sarah turned to Lamar. "Honey, would you like for me to read to you? I brought The Adventures of Tom Sawyer with me. Have you read it?" asked Sarah.

Lamar's head oscillated violently. "Read it to me...Yes—oh, thank you Sarah."Seating herself in a rocking chair, Sarah pulled the book from her jacket pocket. The children curiously watched while Lamar rolled his wheelchair through the living room. When he came closer, Deana quickly scurried behind Sarah's chair, slowly elevating her head slightly above eye-level over the back of the chair and ogled the handicapped boy with a fixed stare. Abandoning his former bravery, Vince joined his hiding sister where he could get an occasional peek from his haven of safety. Lamar's mother smiled at them from her seat on the living room couch.

Softly, but with dramatic expression, Sarah read the first two chapters of the novel. While Lamar attentively listened, his erratic motions began to subside. Sarah's reading voice captivated her small audience as she brought the characters to life with her skillful imitation of their colorful dialect. Before long, the mischievous Tom Sawyer was in the very presence of them all, making Lamar's mysterious, dark world change to a place of playfulness. Deana and Vince slowly crawled out of their hiding place, and soon everyone in the room delightfully connected with Mark Twain's energetic misfits.

When Sarah finished reading, Deana and Vince became restless. The children were still leery of Lamar, but they had come close enough to play with the wheels of his chair.

"We have to go now," stated Sarah, "But I'll be back in a day or so, and I can read some more of it to you. I'll bring you another surprise, too."

"Oh, good! Thank you, Sarah." Lamar's intensified jerky movements revealed his excitement.

Everyone said their goodbyes as Sarah and her grandchildren left Irene Woodley and Lamar's home.

"Are we going home now, Mamaw?" asked Deana. "Let's not go home yet…Let's go see Daddy and Papaw in the shop."

"Okay, honey, we can go for a little while, but not for long. Your mommy will be home from work soon." Sarah held Vince's hand as she strolled with the children down *Beauvais Lane*.

As they walked across Sarah's back yard, Deana suddenly cried out, "Look, Mamaw, There's a horsey! Oh no…He's eating the flowers we planted yesterday! And it looks like he broke down all of your grape vines!"

"That's not a horse—it's a mule! Luke Sanford's mule! Oh my! And we worked so hard. Will's going to be mad when he finds out that Luke's mule is here again."

After running to the mule, Sarah delivered a vigorous slap to the animal's rump. "Shoo! Get out of here!" The animal expelled a forceful bray, then galloped away.

Quickening her pace, Sarah strode through the kitchen and into the living room, closely followed by her grandchildren. Will, who was keeping Clay's children, was seated in his favorite chair with Terry in his lap while Eldon was playing in the corner toy box.

"Will, guess what happened! Luke Sanford's mule ate those beautiful flowers that Deana and I planted!" complained Sarah. "I chased him away, but now my flowers are ruined! What are we going to do about that pesky mule?"

"Yeah, and I'm not surprised." replied Will. "That blasted thing is always running loose!" With irritation, Will scooted Terry from his lap and reached for his hat. "It looks like I'll have to paint another sign on the side of that danged mule."

"Don't trouble yourself, Will. I've already chased the animal away. He's gone."

"Sarah, you might as well forget about planting more flowers, with that crazy jackass running loose."

Sarah quickly retorted, "No, I'm going to have flowers, mule or no mule!"

"You're wasting your time. I swear, Sarah, sometimes you can be as stubborn as that old mule out there."

"I'm not stubborn! I'm just determined! That mule is not going to whip me!" said Sarah, emphatically. "This isn't the first time I've had to deal with that mule. I've been putting up with it for a long time. Every year it eats up my cabbage patch—but I just always plant more!"

"Well, I'm eventually going to have to do something about that mule," said Will. "Come on, Terry; let's go into the shop with Dean and your dad. You and I will paint us a picture."

Sarah watched as Will and Terry went into the shop. Discarding his toy, Eldon trotted after them. Deana watched as her cousins followed Will into the shop. "Mamaw, why doesn't Papaw ever ask me to paint pictures? Why doesn't he teach me?"

"Deana, it's hard to explain, but you're the first girl born into a family of all boys. They all pal around together, and well…they have a problem because they think that a girl is very different from them. It's hard to understand, but it's all they know. But now, with you in the family, they are finally going to learn. It just takes a little time. And I will always be here to help you."

On rare occasions in life, fate is indeed kind; for sometimes the intersection of two lives at a given moment fills the needs and yearnings of both. When Deana came into Sarah's life, she helped fill the void that Elwood's death had created, and gave her a renewed passion for life; for she was the daughter that Sarah had previously been denied. When Deana was born as the first female in an all-male family, Sarah became her advisor and protector. Shielding her from the strangling control of masculine power, she became a buffer between Deana and the remainder of the male-dominated Beauvais family. Their love and dependency was reciprocal; for each became a hero, a rescuer on the other's behalf. Sarah was the master, the expert in survival amid a world of men. As a mentor to her granddaughter, she taught Deana that the attainment of any measure of influence and self-worth in such an environment depended upon discretion and ingenuity.

"Mamaw, if we plant more flowers, they're just gonna get ruined again," explained Deana.

Sarah squatted down and looked into Deana's eyes. "Deana, do you want to plant more flowers?"

"Yeah, I really do."

"Then, we will plant more flowers," replied Sarah. "And they may get eaten by an animal, mowed down, or killed by frost, but we will plant them again."

Vince pulled at Sarah's dress. "Mamaw, can I go into the shop and play with Eldon?"

"Yes, honey…Just don't get in the way of those working. Oh, and Vince… if you want to plant some flowers too, then, you can join us."

"No, thank you, Mamaw," said Vince as he walked toward the shop entrance.

Sarah sat down in the rocking chair and pulled Deana into her lap. Slowly, she began to rock as she softly sang to her granddaughter. For awhile Deana sat silently, then she asked, "Mamaw, what was wrong with that boy we went to see?"

"Honey, he's sick. He was born that way. He has something called cerebral palsy."

"I was scared of him," said Deana.

"No need to be scared of him…He's a sweet little boy. He needs all the love he can get."

"Why do you have to go see him, Mamaw?"

Sarah answered. "Well, I don't have to visit him. I want to visit him."

"But why?" asked Deana.

"Well, you know how much pleasure your daddy and Papaw get from painting pictures, don't you? And how you like to help me plant flowers?"

"Yes."

"Okay, I get the same kind of pleasure when I visit little Lamar. That's my favorite thing in life—bringing a little bit of happiness into someone's life, like Lamar's. He may not be pretty on the outside, but inside, he's just as pretty as you and Vince. Inside he's beautiful. Didn't you see how happy we made him?"

Deana quickly responded, "Yeah, and he was really happy when he wiped that spit off his mouth. Did everybody clap when I learned to wipe my mouth?"

"Maybe. But we expected you to do that, Deana. You don't have problems with your muscles and your body like Lamar has. Wiping his own face was one of the big things that he really wanted to learn. We all have different things that we would like to do, at different times in our lives, and we have to be like Lamar, and never give up on it. Is there something that you would like to do, but it seems impossible?"

"Yeah, I wanna read books like you, and I wanna paint like Daddy does."

Sarah took a deep breath. "Well, just keep working on it, honey. And you and I can be best friends while you do it, okay?"

Deana arms reached around Sarah. "Okay, Mamaw."Sarah continued, "And Lamar would like to be friends with you, too. The next time we go see him, maybe you can talk to him a little…okay?"

For a long while, Deana considered Sarah's remarks. Then she smiled, "Okay, I'll try."

Inside the shop, Clay was lettering a metal sign while Alvin was in Tyler City painting a store front for the *Security Mills Company*. Dean was at the drawing table, sketching a design. Although he was not yet supposed to be working, he nonetheless spent four hours a day at the drawing table in order to supplement his family's meager income. Vince slid into a chair beside Dean and immediately began to vigorously rock, for he had inherited Elwood's predilection for the habit. With aroused curiosity, he watched his father work.

Terry was seated on a tall stool facing an easel, and with the aid of his grandfather, was attempting to render an oil painting.

"Dip your brush into that blob of umber, right there, Terry, and just roughly sketch what you want to paint, right there on your canvas." Standing directly behind Terry, Will gave him instructions as he squeezed tiny globs of paint from an array of tube colors onto a pallette.

Pausing from his work, Clay looked over at his father. "Dad, Terry is wearing an almost new pair of pants. If he gets that oil paint on them, it will ruin them."

"Don't worry about it, Clay. If he gets paint on them, I'll buy him some more," remarked Will. "Terry loves to paint. You ought to be encouraging him."

"I do encourage him. I just don't want him to ruin his new pants."

"We'll be careful, won't we Terry?" Will smiled at his grandson.

Eldon pulled up a stool behind Will and Terry and sat down behind his older brother to watch him paint. Upon discovering the stool's rotating seat, Eldon began to amuse himself by singing and spinning around repeatedly on the stool.

As Will praised Terry's efforts, the crude painting began to take shape.

"Clay, you and Dean should come over here and look at this painting," remarked Will, "This boy's going to be an artist."

"I can't put my brush down right now, Dad. I'll look at it when I get a convenient place to stop working," replied Clay.

Just as Eldon was nearly spinning out of control on the stool, Deana opened the door and entered the shop. She dodged Eldon as she walked to the other side of Terry's easel, and as she watched her cousin paint, she became spellbound by the artistic enterprise.

"Papaw, can I paint too? Help me paint a picture."

"Honey, you're too young to paint pictures. Besides, little girls don't work here in the shop…You'd just make a mess, and you'd get paint all over your pretty dress. Why don't you and Eldon go play somewhere together?"

At that moment, Eldon came tumbling to the floor. Quickly, he got up, but since his vertigo thwarted his attempt to walk normally, he reeled and staggered around the shop, only to again lose his balance and tumble into a waste can.

"Damn!" exclaimed Clay. "Dad, do you have to bring all the kids into the shop when we're trying to work? Eldon, get out of here!"

"Yeah, you too Deana," added Dean, "Go play with Eldon for a little while. Mommy will be home soon, and we'll go home for supper. Vince, you can stay here with me. I don't want you out there unless a grownup is with you."

"Those kids weren't hurting anything, Clay," protested Will. "They weren't bothering your work."

Clay responded, "Dad, when we were growing up, you wouldn't allow anybody in the shop unless they were working. Man, you sure have softened in your attitudes."

Terry had stopped painting. He longingly looked through the window at Eldon and Deana laughing and playing in front of the shop.

"Come on, Terry," instructed Will, "We might be getting in their way. Let's go over to the park at the lake and feed the ducks. I'll buy us an ice cream cone at the drive-in."

"Dad, we're going to have supper soon," said Clay. "I don't want him eating ice cream before he has his evening meal. Anyway, he should really stay here because Ellen will be home from work right away."

"Ice cream is good for him," replied Will. "When we get back from the lake, he can eat supper with his Mamaw and me."

"Dad, you don't listen to what anybody says anymore!" yelled Clay. "He's my son, and I think I know what's best for him."

Will turned and looked at Clay with a pleading expression. "Clay, Terry and I have become best buddies...He's the greatest joy in my life. I would never do anything that I thought was bad for him. You ought to be glad that I love him so much."

Clay stood silently for a moment, as his irritation was replaced by compassion for his father. "Okay, Dad...But don't keep him out too long. As soon as you are finished with supper, send him home."

"You know, Clay, it's summertime, and he doesn't have school tomorrow, so what's the rush about getting him home so quick?"

"None, I guess," sighed Clay, with resignation.

"Hey, Dad," said Dean, "As you're leaving, tell Deana and Eldon to go back inside the house with Mamaw. Clay and I can't watch them very well while we're working."

After his father was gone, Clay stopped working and walked over to the corner where Dean was sketching. He fished a cigarette from his pocket and lit it, remaining silent for awhile. Then, in deep thought, he slid into a nearby chair and leisurely crossed his legs. Finally, he spoke.

"Dean, my living here, next door to Dad, is not going to work. Can you see what's happening? I'm losing control over Terry...Dad totally controls him."

"Well, Clay, that's because you were gone for so long in the army. Dad and Terry got close during that time, but now that you're back, you'll re-connect with Terry. Just give it a little more time." Dean then turned to Vince, "Say little pal, run inside and play with Deana and Eldon—okay?" He playfully ruffled his son's shock of curly hair.

As Vince obediently left the room, Clay sat silently, puffing on his cigarette.

"Giving it more time won't do any good," retorted Clay. "I'm afraid that Terry will end up just like Elwood—being smothered under Dad's thumb for all of his life. But that's not the only reason I can't get along with Dad. He's always butting into my business, trying to control me."

"Oh, I wouldn't say that, Clay. You're too assertive to ever let that happen."

"Well, I need to leave here, sometime, and find a job. There's not future in working here at the shop, for either of us—or for Al either, for that matter. Of course, for Al, it's probably ideal for him. No kids, no worries, no ambition."

Dean was hesitant in his response. "Clay, I didn't mean to tell you this yet, but I'm pretty sure that I'm going to enroll in art school this coming fall quarter."

Clay suddenly sat upright in his chair. "Where? What art school?"

"*Atlanta Art Institute.* I sent off and got a brochure from them. They mostly feature fine arts, but they also have a good graphic design program."

Dean had suddenly gained Clay's attention. "But how are you going to swing that financially?"

"I think I can get my tuition paid by the vocational rehabilitation program, since I'm recovering from T.B."

"Damn! That's a chance of a lifetime. If you're going for sure, then I'm going, too!"

"How can you afford it?" asked Dean.

"I'll figure a way. Can I look at that brochure you got?"

"Sure. I'll give it to you, tonight."

At that time, the front door opened and Bobbie walked in wearing her white waitress uniform.

"Hi, Bobbie," greeted Clay.

"Hi, Clay—who's that handsome guy with you?"

"Hello, honey. Are you tired?" asked Dean. He walked over to Bobbie and embraced her.

"Not too tired. I had a good day. Look at the money I made in tips!" Opening the white apron she carried, she dumped a large mix of bills and change onto the nearby table.

"What a pile of money!" said Dean. "How much did you make?"

"Almost $16 dollars!"

"Hey, see if you can't get me a job as a waitress where you work," Clay joked, as Dean and Bobbie laughed.

"Well, I've got to drive up to the house and start supper. I better go inside and get the kids."

"Clay and I are about finished for the day. Do you want me to just bring the kids up with me?"

Bobbie walked to the door leading to the house. "No, I'll take them with me now. I'm eager to see them, and I'm sure Sarah is ready for a break. Come on home soon. Dinner will be ready in about forty-five minutes."

When she was gone, Dean looked sadly at Clay. "That's the reason I want to go to art school and amount to something. To see Bobbie work like a slave and take care of the family...and I'm not even supposed to work. What kind of a man did she marry?"

"Hell, how do you think I feel? I *am* working, and Ellen is still the bread-winner in our family. I feel like a bum," Clay spoke as he rinsed his brush in the paint thinner and wiped it clean. "Let's go in and see Mom. I've got to get Eldon and take him home. It's time for Ellen, too."

Inside the house, Eldon was in the rocking chair, watching "Howdy-Doody." As Dean and Clay walked toward the kitchen, they heard their mother singing happily in the bedroom. Clay grinned at Dean, and with a wink, said, "Let's execute our favorite football play."

Dean laughed, and after the brothers walked into the bedroom, they faced Sarah and suddenly squatted down, pretentiously assuming the body positions of football offensive linemen and calling signals, "Ready...Set...Hike!"

"Oh, no!" cried Sarah, laughing, "Surely you're not going to tackle me again!"

In unison, they sprang toward their mother, gently picked her up, and dumped her into the middle of her soft bed.

"Oooo," she squealed as she laughed hysterically. "You boys are going to kill me yet!" Then, after gently lifting her from her bed, Clay hugged her and kissed her on the cheek.

"Why did I have to end up with a bunch of roughnecks for sons?" she laughed.

"You know you like it, Mom!" said Clay.

"Well, it brings back memories of the way Elwood used to tease me...He teased me a lot..." Sarah smiled at the fond remembrance. "But Elwood used to talk to me about serious things, too. I sure miss some of our conversations."

Dean sadly realized that his mother, surrounded by men, had little opportunity to share her deepest feelings, especially since Elwood was no longer in her life.

Clay interrupted the thought. "Eldon and I are going home for supper. Dean, don't forget to give me that brochure."

"Okay, I'll bring it to you tonight," replied Dean. "Mom, I'm going home, too. I'll see you later...Oh, by the way, Mom...I really appreciate you keeping the kids for Bobbie and me. I don't know what we'd do without you."

"Dean, you don't have to thank me. Keeping your children is my greatest joy."

After dinner that evening, Dean returned to visit his parents. While Sarah was cleaning the kitchen after the evening meal, Dean and his father were in the living room, engaged in trivial conversation. Will rested in his favorite chair while Dean carelessly sprawled on the couch. At the break in their casual discussion, Dean left the couch and sat in the rocking chair that faced his father.

"Dad, I really came down here tonight because I need to talk to you about something."

Taking note of his son's somber expression, Will sat erectly in his chair, eyeing his son with curiosity. "What's on your mind, Dean?"

"Dad, I know how much this shop has always meant to you…And I also realize that you always dreamed of your sons carrying on the tradition of the shop…" Dean hesitated.

"What are you trying to say? Spit it out!" Will was never a man to mince words.

"Okay Dad, I'll just get to the point. "I've decided that I'm going to art school in Atlanta. I'm going to start this fall—in September. I can get my tuition paid by vocational rehab."

In frustration, Will looked at his son for a long while. Finally, he spoke. "Well, that will just leave Alvin and Clay to run the shop again. And neither of them can paint signs like you and Rob can… and like Elwood could."

"But Dad, Clay says he's going to art school too."

"How in the world can Clay go?" Will asked. "Where would he get the money?"

"I don't know, but he said that if I go, then he's going, too."

"Then that would just leave Alvin!" Will was stunned. "I can't depend on him! Besides, he doesn't even want to work in the shop."

"Dad, sometimes we just have to face things. It's not your fault, but there's really no future for the shop anymore. Times are changing. You're from a different era, Dad, when small businesses were doing great. But now, big corporations are taking over. In a few years, it will be impossible to operate a small shop like ours and make any money."

Will's face bore an incredulous expression. "Big corporations? I never thought I'd see the day when you, with your independent spirit, would ever even think of going to work for a big corporation!"

"Dad, I don't like the idea of working for a big corporation any better than you do, but I'm married now—with two kids. I want to give my family nice things! I want a nice house for them. I want them to wear nice clothes…And I'm tired of seeing my wife come home from working in a restaurant ten hours a day…worn out…with her hair smelling like hamburger grease."

Will's eyes silently screamed with disbelief. It was the response that Dean expected, and dreaded.

"Dad, I'm sorry, but corporations are offering things that our small shop can't give. They have paid insurance programs, vacations, sick leave…My family has to have all of those things."

"So, you're willing to sell out? You're willing to let some corporation buy you!"

"If it were just me, and I didn't have the responsibilities of a family, I'd stay right here in the shop, just to keep from destroying your dream. And anyway, I may not even go to work for a big corporation. I just want to be an artist and make a good living somewhere."

Sarah entered the room, but upon noticing the intensity of the conversation, she said nothing and took a seat on the couch.

"Well, what am I supposed to do now?" Will asked. "I had plans to have a good business here, just for you boys. I gave all five of you some land, so you could live here…and look how it all turned out. Rob became a preacher, and I'm proud of him, but he'll always be living somewhere else. Alvin doesn't want to live here or work here either. Now you and Clay are both talking about going in some other direction. And Elwood…"

Will's dejected expression became one of desperation. Dean felt a deep compassion for his father, and a moment later, he watched him pick up his hat, and wordlessly walk out the front door to his car.

Slowly, Dean turned to face his mother. "What am I supposed to do, Mom?"

Sarah smiled lovingly at her son. "I'll tell you what I once told Elwood," she said, "Follow your heart."

Every child is an artist. The problem is how to remain an artist once he grows up. **Pablo Picasso**

Chapter 28

When Dean and Clay enrolled at *Atlanta Art Institute*, they both instantly felt at home in their new surroundings. Located on North Peachtree Street, the school was relatively small, consisting of a large, main building bordered by two smaller additional structures. Next door to the art school was the *Atlanta Museum of Art*, and although a separate entity, it actually functioned as a part of the entire complex, as art history was taught there. Students had easy access to each building by way of the hardwood walkways that connected them.

The main building was a large, two story colonial style brick structure. Four white columns standing like sentries, rising from a large front porch embellished the main entrance. The old mansion had obviously once been an elegant dwelling, probably having been occupied a century earlier by an affluent Atlanta family. The large building stood atop a sloping hill, its elevation accentuating the majestic appearance of the edifice and reflecting the antiquity of the Old South. The different architectural style and newness of the adjoining buildings gave an incongruous appearance to the overall complex. The additional buildings had been constructed later to accommodate the growing enrollment of art students.

Leaving their families in Tennessee, Dean and Clay settled into a small apartment located on the top floor of a dilapidated, three story apartment building. The first and second levels were used for storage, and the basement floor housed a dark, shabby bar called *The Bottom of the Barrel,* an appropriate name for the decrepit tavern, which was frequented mostly by art students and hippies.

Two features had attracted the brothers to the apartment: It was only three blocks from the art school, and many other art students lived in the immediate vicinity. Since it was a ramshackle, empty space that hadn't been used for any purpose in months, the brothers obtained the run-down apartment at a bargain price. After an enormous cleaning effort, and a couple of coats of paint on the walls, they furnished the apartment with items from a used furniture store. Their beds were two mattresses thrown carelessly on the 'bedroom' floor, and their cooking was done on a hot plate in the combination living room and kitchen area. The area was also used for their weight-lifting workouts, since, in spite of his doctor's advice, Dean had begun to work out with weights again.

The kitchen window gave easy access to a large, flat asphalt roof where Dean and Clay often worked on paintings when the weather was favorable. At night, the expanse of roof offered a place where the brothers and other students often went to drink wine and discuss art, sprawling on blankets as they viewed the starry sky.

In order to afford the expense of attending art school, Clay had taken a second mortgage on his home, and because Dean was recovering from tuberculosis, his tuition was paid by the vocational rehabilitation program. Financially, the brothers were in dire straits, and only by developing extremely frugal habits were they able to survive.

The conglomeration of students was composed of an unlikely blend of personalities from an incongruous social strata. One faction was comprised of middle-aged, affluent women who were either genuine patrons of the arts, or simply older, wealthy women, who had become bored with their garden clubs and bridge parties. The main group, however, was a clique of bohemian type students who were dressed like hippies, some of whom sometimes went barefoot and wore beads to class, and enjoyed sitting in the floor, even when a chair was available. Many of these people were exceptionally talented; however, they were interested only in fine arts, and living the life of an artist. The remaining students, who were in the minority, were majoring in graphic design, a field of study that would someday enable them to earn a living in the advertising business with their developed skills. They usually dressed in conventional style garb and were sometimes looked upon with disdain by the "bohemian" students who were majoring in fine arts.

Strangely, because of their close association in the small school and their similar interests, the drastically divergent types harmoniously blended in almost every instance, whether it was during class, study sessions, or parties. In any other setting, it is highly unlikely that these radically different types of people would have ever mingled with each other.

With their bearded faces and unkempt clothing, many of the fine arts students tried desperately to project an image of non-conformity; ironically, in their strict adherence to a corresponding mode of dress and behavior among their ranks, they, themselves became trapped in a kind of strict conformity. Dean was aware that the fine arts students considered the field of graphic design a crass profession and a vulgar prostitution of art. Matching their contempt for him, he felt equal disrespect for their contrived image of non-conformity; for he saw in their hypocritical attitudes an inconsistency: A simultaneous rejection and embrace of uniformity. Dean considered his father, Will, to be the authentic non-conformist, for he harbored absolutely no desire to adhere to either the mode of dress or behavior pattern of any group, even to those of his fellow artists.

Atlanta Art Institute was a two-year school. During the freshman year, the curriculum for both fine arts and graphic design majors was identical: Basic courses in perspective and figure drawing, elementary painting, basic design, and art history. In the second year, advanced, specialized courses were directed toward the students' major area of study.

Other than the middle-aged, wealthy women who dabbled in painting, Dean and Clay were older and more experienced in life than their fellow students. Because they were both veterans of the armed services and had previously engaged in contact sports, their male-dominant attitudes stood in sharp contrast to some of the more effeminate types commonly associated with art; nonetheless, the brothers' sense of humor and affinity for ridiculous behavior made them extremely popular with the instructors and students.

The brothers' previous exposure to the multi-faceted world of art had been limited; therefore, they had tunnel vision in regard to the essence of the broad spectrum of visual images and ideas that constitute art. Dean, in particular, questioned the necessity of studying art history and abstract painting as prerequisites to becoming a graphic designer. On the other hand, Clay, who was less proficient than Dean in graphic design, felt that design courses were unnecessary for him since he had a desire to become an illustrator. Even so, the brothers plunged into all their art assignments with great fervor. Clay had always exhibited little aptitude for sign painting, so Dean was surprised by Clay's enthusiasm and talent in the drawing and painting classes; for Clay was only second to Dean in the praise he received from the art instructors.

Dean's work, especially his drawing, was admired with envy by other students. His former vocation as a sign painter had developed his talents, and honed his skills to a certain extent. His past experience in painting pictures on billboards had given him an advantage over the other students in painting class, for he was one of the few students who had actually done professional work.

During painting classes, Dean and Clay experimented with various media, methods and materials, appropriate tools, complementary colors, and techniques. Most of the actual painting was limited to rendering simple objects, while experimenting with color. Given the fact that the brothers had been exposed to these same elements since childhood, they felt totally at ease in the painting classes. Moreover, the pungent aroma of turpentine and paint gave the classrooms the odor of a sign shop, filling Dean and Clay with nostalgia.

The painting instructor's name was Harrison McCrea, a large muscular man with a craggy face, who had developed a fondness for the Beauvais brothers, and found their attitude of male-aggressiveness sometimes disturbing, but humorous. At age 40, his rugged appearance suggested anything but a sensitive artist; but his paintings reflected a delicate, emotional quality that contradicted his demeanor.

McCrea, as he was called by the students, was a very perceptive man who was able to quickly recognize potential in students. Also, by studying a painting, he could usually determine the emotional attitude of the artist.

Realizing that his students were becoming bored with the routine of practicing the basics, McCrea gave them a more exciting challenge. "Alright, class. I've got a project for you. You've been working on dull, routine assignments for a long time, and you've all mastered the basics of painting," he said, with a friendly sarcasm. "Now I'm going to release the chains of bondage and let you paint your masterpiece."

"What'll we paint, McCrea?" asked Clay.

"Anything you wish to paint," replied McCrea. "This is just a one-time assignment because next week you will resume the torture of basic, same old stuff, even though you are all accomplished artists already," he jested. "Actually, I'm curious in regard to what you come up with. Have your painting done by Friday, and we'll critique them in front of the class."

When the class met again on Friday, Dean and Clay proudly brought their paintings to class. Dean had painted a still-life: an arrangement of flowers, fruit, and books resting atop a table on a wrinkled tablecloth. Clay had painted an old pair of army boots, positioned carelessly in a chair.

McCrea had all the students place their work on lightweight easels, arranged in a semi-circle around the students, some of whom were sitting on the floor while others sat on low stools.

As they compared the paintings, Clay whispered to Dean, "Yours is the best in the class…Man you really know how to use color." Clay's painting had remained a mystery. Not wanting Dean to see his work until it was finished, he had rendered his painting at a fellow student's apartment down the street.

When Dean finally viewed Clay's painting for the first time, he was amazed at the work. With a limited use of color, Clay had captured the rustic character of the worn-out boots with rough, indelicate strokes of his brush. The honestly and simplicity in the presentation of the subject captivated Dean.

"No, Clay, my painting is not the best in the class, yours is," Dean remarked, feeling a tinge of envy.

When Dean again compared all the paintings in the room, he could see that his own work displayed the most generous use of color. In the area of color, Clay's work was a deep contrast with Dean's. His rendition was probably the most colorless in the class, but he had skillfully used the few colors as part of his technique in capturing the essence of his subject matter.

"Okay, let's start out critique," said McCrea. "I want comments from the students, first. I'll add something whenever I think it is appropriate."

A male student quickly gave his opinion. "Dean Beauvais has produced the best painting in class. I like his use of color."

The instructor quickly interjected a comment. "We're not interested in whose painting is *best*. After all, that's a relative term. *'Best'* from what standpoint? Try to confine your comments to qualities of each painting. However, I do agree with you that Mr. Beauvais has used color very effectively. Also, the overall composition of the painting is good."

The students continued making comments about the paintings on display, most of them complimentary of Dean's and Clay's paintings. Finally, a student named Randall Ramsey, who had been silent, spoke for the first time.

"I think Dean Beauvais failed to capture the essence of his subject. There's a kind of hardness about the character of the flowers and the table cloth."

"A very astute observation," said McCrea.

Dean was embarrassed. "Well, Ramsey, your painting completely leaves me cold." He clearly detested the student's pretentious scholarly demeanor.

Looking at Dean, McCrea said, "Don't be so touchy, Beauvais. I happen to agree with Mr. Ramsey. Your painting is lacking in the necessary softness and sensitivity of the subject matter."

Dean sat in silence for the remainder of the class period. Finally, the bell rang, ending the session, which was the final period of the day. Dean and Clay gathered their paintings and supplies and left for their apartment.

With school closed until Monday, Dean and Clay decided to stay in Atlanta over the weekend. They were financially strapped, so the thought of going to Tennessee was out of the question.

On Saturday evening, they attended an informal get-together that was held in *The Bottom of the Barrel*, and was comprised of a blend of students, a couple of instructors, and others who felt at ease fraternizing with students. When Clay and Dean walked down the steps into the dark tavern, they saw McCrea, who was seated in the corner booth with a pretty, but sloppily-dressed female art student named Cynthia Holland. She and McCrea were both drinking wine from a half-empty bottle on their table. Upon seeing the brothers' entrance, Mc Crea beckoned them.

"Join us," invited McCrea, as he and Cynthia slid to one side to make room for them.

Dean sat down by McCrea while Clay claimed the seat by the girl.

"Bring us two more glasses," McCrea bellowed to the bartender.

As the burly bartender brought the additional glasses, Dean eyed the interior of the bar. It was a medium-size, run-down, establishment with sawdust scattered carelessly on the floor; the right rear corner on the large mirror behind the bar had been shattered, leaving a jagged crack across its entire surface, and the atmosphere reeked with the strong, stagnating odor of stale beer and cigarette smoke; the plastic upholstery on the back of the seats was worn and faded, its color bleached away by years of absorption of sweat from the backs of countless drinkers. Fortunately, the interior darkness helped to conceal the overall deteriorated condition of the pub. Dean felt that the "hippie-types" admired the shoddy environment because frequenting such a place made them feel more "arty."

About a dozen art students were scattered about the room, a couple at the bar, sitting on stools, with the remainder of them dispersed at tables and the two other booths. A passed-out vagrant sat on the barstool with his head resting on his hands on top of the counter. The condition of the sleeping derelict filled Dean with anxiety, for he feared that the unconscious man might fall from his stool at any moment.

McCrea picked up the bottle and poured wine into the empty glasses. As Clay took a sip of the wine, Dean gently pushed his glass toward the wall of the booth. "Thanks, McCrea, but I don't drink. I'll get a Coke in a few minutes."

"You're a wise man, Beauvais," declared McCrea, "It's best to steer clear of the devil's brew."

"I'll drink his share," volunteered Clay. McCrea and Cynthia laughed.

As the foursome engaged in idle conversation, an art student, Chuck Brymer, walked over to McCrea's booth, carrying a stein of beer. Following close behind him was Randall Ramsey, the student who had criticized Dean's painting.

"Hi, McCrea," greeted Brymer, "You don't care who you associate with, do you?" He laughed as he winked at Dean and Clay. He was a large man, dressed in the customary hippie attire, identifying him as a fine arts major.

"Hi, Brymer," said McCrea, "You're in one of my classes with Cynthia, so you obviously know her, but do you know the Beauvais brothers…Dean and Clay?"

"Yeah…I don't have any classes with either of them, but I know who they are. Dean is the *Atlanta Art Institute* Prima Donna. His work's not too bad, I hear. Too bad he can't take constructive criticism."

His remark was saturated with antagonism toward Dean.

Looking the man directly in the eye, Dean countered, "Look. Pal…I don't know you well enough for you to take verbal jabs at me, even if you're disguising your dislike for me with a chicken-shit grin. Let me give you some advice that might save your ass from a hard lesson. Don't say anything else to me, or about me…Do you get my message?"

Without answering, Brymer heeded Dean's advice. He smiled, then shrugged.

"See you later, McCrea," he said. Then he and Ramsey ambled away, joining some of their friends at the bar.

"Damn, Beauvais! For a minute there, I thought you might clobber Brymer!" exclaimed McCrea.

"Dean's gettin' soft in his old age," said Clay, who was beginning to feel the wine. "A couple of years ago, he would have mopped the floor with that guy's ass."

After ordering another bottle of wine and a soft drink for Dean, McCrea spoke. "Dean, why are you and Clay so damned aggressive? I know that Brymer's a smart ass, but that's not a reason to beat the hell out of him. Maybe there's a grain of truth in what he said about you not being able to take criticism."

"You're right. I'll admit that I'm not too fond of criticism. I also don't like a guy who criticizes me, and then is so cowardly that he hides his dislike for me behind a chicken- shit grin. Anyway…what's wrong with being aggressive? Submissive people are usually losers!"

"Well, aggressiveness is not always bad…on occasion, it's neces- sary," said McCrea. "But, sometimes, when people are habitually aggressive, it inhibits any tender feelings that they might otherwise have…and tenderness and sensitivity are valuable assets to an artist."

"Well, I wish Dean had kicked that bastard's tender ass," said Clay. McCrea and Cynthia laughed, then McCrea looked at Dean. "Beauvais, why did you get so mad at Ramsey in class yesterday? He wasn't being a smart ass—he was just making an honest observation."

"I wasn't really that angry. I was a little pissed off because of who the criticism came from. I wasn't angry when you said it. It's just that Ramsey pretends to be such an intellectual. And to me he's a big fake. It's typical that he would be the one to make a comment about the *essence of flowers.*"

"Beauvais, I think that he was correct in his comment. And what is this hang-up you have with Ramsey? Why do you feel threatened by his sensitivity? It doesn't make him less of a man, you know. We've all got a sensitive side to us—even you, Dean."

Dean spoke up. "Well, for one thing, I guess I always thought of sen- sitivity as a female trait."

McCrea answered. "That's the problem—because females openly display traits like sensitivity and gentleness, men are all afraid to show those traits. But when they do, they don't have to be perceived as less of a man."

"Ramsey certainly shows that he retains some of the female side in him. To my way of thinking, he's not much of a man," remarked Dean.

"Perhaps he's more of a man than you think," suggested McCrea, "Because being a whole man requires that we incorporate the traits the you refer to as 'feminine' into our personality, to achieve balance.

Ramsey has more sensitivity than you have, Dean. Unfortunately, he doesn't have your skill in painting, so he's not able to convey that sensitivity in his work."

"Are you saying that I need to show a female side? That's not who I am, McCrea. I don't really need a psychological analysis...Just tell me what was bad about my painting."

"At the risk of making you angry, I'll give you my honest appraisal of it. Your use of color was good, so was the composition of the painting. But your painting didn't capture the essence of the subject. It lacked feeling and sensitivity. The texture of the flowers displayed a hardness, almost as if they were made of stone or concrete. Surely, that's not how you see the world! When you look at the delicacy of a flower—let your eyes caress and feel the softness of the petals. Look at the paintings of Degas, and Renoir, for instance. Try to feel the texture of the flower."

The foursome sat in silence for several minutes. The gathering of students was beginning to disperse, and only about half of the original group remained in the bar. Cynthia peered at her watch in the muted light.

"Well, guys, it's getting late...Anyway, the bull is getting deep in here—no offense, McCrea."

The others laughed, as Clay stood, and she scooted out of her seat. "Bye, Guys," she said, then strolled toward the door.

A few minutes passed, then McCrea poured himself and Clay another glass of wine and lit a cigarette. After a brief silence, Dean responded to McCrea's earlier analysis.

"Maybe I don't belong in art school, if I have to behave like a half-woman. I still like manly things, like football. But I guess you wouldn't understand that."

"Well, about 20 years ago, I was one helluva line backer in college. I was a mean bastard," McCrea laughed and playfully flexed his biceps.

"Really?" Dean suddenly developed a new respect for the man. "How'd you get into the art field?"

"Actually, I got my master's degree in psychology...I wanted to be a psychologist, but then I got involved in art and went back to school to study fine arts. It's now my passion in life."

"Well, I want to know more about this female side we're supposed to have, McCrea," said Clay.

"Actually, we shouldn't really refer to these different qualities as 'male and female,' for that reference implies that aggressiveness is totally a natural male characteristic, with gentleness and sensitivity being exclusive female qualities. In fact, it's very unnatural for man's nature to be devoid of tenderness and sensitivity. The natural state of a man's and woman's personality is the balance of the two extremes. Look at the gentleness and sensitivity of the real men in history: Jesus Christ, Mahatma Gandhi, Martin Luther King. The balance in their personalities gave them the passion, and compassion that made them great. By referring to these divergent qualities as male and female, we infer that men and women are in opposition to each other. Actually, one complements the other, each bringing out the best qualities of the other. The reason we refer to these characteristics as 'male and female' is because man has rejected these tender qualities, so we see only the aggressive side of him; therefore, we have come to think of his almost total aggressive nature as natural, when actually it's only an imbalance in him. When a man has lost his sensitive side, he's really only half a man. Now take a baby, for example, he is born with a balanced personality because he retains the complete range of characteristics, including assertiveness as well as gentleness and sensitivity...or rather what you refer to as 'female traits'."

"Yeah, but don't we grow out of that as we get older and face the world?" asked Clay.

McCrea took another sip of wine. "Unfortunately, in many cases, we do. But a sustained retention of some of these characteristics that we see in the opposite sex is vital to a person's personality."

Dean was skeptical. "Why is it vital?"

"To ensure the wholeness of the personality," answered McCrea. The topic had sparked Clay's interest. "Do you mean that as we mature, men and women shouldn't lose that part the opposite gender—or rather, those traits that we have labeled 'opposite gender'?"

McCrea responded. "Well, ideally, this blending of male and female characteristics, within one's self, should be sustained throughout life. This ensures the ongoing completeness and balance in the personality." Dean asked, with puzzlement, "If I've lost this balance, why did it happen?"

"If you have lost it, maybe it's not entirely your fault," answered McCrea, "Society's traditions play a role. Look at the kinds of toys we give our male children—G.I. Joes, toy guns, bows and arrows...All suggesting aggressiveness. Girls receive Barbie Dolls, baby carriages, and doll clothes—playthings that encourage gentleness and nurturing."

"But isn't that only natural?" asked Clay, "Men have to fight wars, and women have babies...What's wrong with that?"

McCrea explained further. "There's plenty wrong with it. Because it's a man's world, this distortion is weighted heavily toward bolstering male characteristics at the expense of the female. This creates an imbalance between the two. Women also fall victim to this distortion. For fear of appearing manly, women sometimes reject the assertiveness that is needed to assure a balanced personality."

Dean protested, "But surely the type of toys we get as children don't play that big of a role in the imbalance in our personality. We don't remain children...We eventually grow up."

"That's true, but as we grow up, this 'man's world' mentality becomes a continued bombardment that further represses the 'female' side of a man's nature. As a boy becomes a man, he is indoctrinated by society that violence and force are natural inherent characteristics of the male, while tenderness, love, and sensitivity are instinctive qualities of the female."

"Alright, but how is this detrimental to an artist?" asked Clay.

"Because a person must be aware of his vulnerability to feel the emotions necessary to an artist. Man has been programmed to believe that vulnerability is an inborn female trait; but a man is perceived to be invulnerable and impervious to emotion. For instance, for a man, crying is recognized as weakness."

Clay interjected, "I think I'm going to cry if you don't order us another bottle of wine."

McCrea laughed. "I don't think we need a whole bottle. I'll just order us a couple of beers and a Coke for Dean...how does that sound?"

As the bartender placed the drinks on the counter, the melodious voice of Nat King Cole drifted from the jukebox through the darkness of the tavern, "Rambling Rose..." Dean's remembrance of his former rambling ways gave him an affinity for the song. Only a few people remained in the bar, as the intoxicated man at the counter staggered to the recently vacated corner booth, placed his head on the table, and immediately resumed his drunken sleep. The men sat silently, listening to the music of the jukebox. When the ballad ended, Dean continued the conversation.

"Are you saying that if a man can't achieve this balance in his personality, he can't be creative?" asked Dean.

"Well, it would be less likely that he could," answered McCrea. "Since tenderness and sensitivity are perceived as feminine traits, man's repression of this 'female' side leads to a reluctance to express emotions. This inhibits the emotional feelings that are necessary in creativity. But, you know, everyone can't be an artist, so what we're really talking about is *passion*. When we have that balance, that completeness in our personality, we are able to develop a passion within us, a passion for life. As a whole person, we can become better carpenters, better engineers, better nurturers, or better husbands and wives, because then we are better people. I feel that I have that passion, and in my case, it's art."

Trying to better understand McCrea's approach, Dean asked, "Well, just assuming that I have repressed my 'female' side. Am I permanently disabled in my unbalanced personality?"

"Maybe not," replied McCrea, "I'm not suggesting that your creative impulses have been completely erased, but important parts could be better developed if they weren't lying dormant within you. It's just that some of the needed requirements have been buried beneath the stifling layers of insensitivity and aggressiveness." McCrea wiped the beer's foam from his upper lip and continued, "As children, we haven't yet been exposed to those suffocating influences. Children are born with a completeness of personality...That's why they are the only true artists. Sometimes I even feel that art schools also contribute to further destruction of a person's inherent creativity. I don't think the dean of our school would be too thrilled to hear me say this, but I think that many schools can often destroy the uniqueness within a person, and create stereotypes. Anyway, with a modified attitude regarding gender roles, creative awareness can be revived in you."

"McCrea, what you say makes a lot of sense," said Dean, "But I'm pretty much entrenched in who I am. What you see is what you get."

"You know, Dean, I really don't believe that. I believe that deep inside you and Clay, too, that there's much more that what we see. Most of the instructors here are talking about how much potential you both have. I've seen your drawings. Some of them have shown a great deal of sensitivity. There's someone else inside you just dying to be unleashed. I'd like to help you two guys find that other half of yourselves."

Dean responded. "Well, how do I discover this other half of myself? To be honest, I really didn't grow up around females."

Clay interjected. "Dean and I both have wives, but I'll have to admit, we don't understand them."

"You don't have any sisters?"

"No, just all boys in the family," said Clay.

McCrea replied, "It figures. Not only a male-dominated society, but also a male dominated family. Is you dad a dominating person?"

"Yeah, pretty much." Dean answered, irritated at McCrea's prying about his father. "Hey, can't we just talk about art? I didn't enroll in art school to get a psychology lesson."

The idea of the Beauvais brothers coming from a large family, exclusively all male, made them all the more interesting to McCrea. Despite Dean's request, McCrea's added, "But you see, that's the whole point of this discussion. You can't separate art and psychology. All the arts in which we engage reflect who we are inside; they are an extension of us—they reveal our feelings about our perception of the world."

"So you feel that if I had the correct balance in my personality, my paintings would look better?" asked Dean.

"Well, probably. But even if they didn't, I guarantee that your life and your perception of the world would be better. This balance would awaken your passion, and you would be more sensitive to the feelings of others, as well as your own."

Dean responded. "Yeah, maybe so, but I still get angry when somebody who's not as good as I am criticizes my work. I know that's not good, but when it's someone like Ramsey…well, I just can't help it."

"Difference in opinion is often good," said McCrea, "Often, one side is a complement to the other. Together, they form a healthy balance."

"In what way?" asked Dean.

"Since you are good with colors, let me give you an example that you'll easily understand."

Clay, who was now obviously feeling the alcohol, smiled sarcastically and asked, "What does color have to do with it… I mean, after all, we're only here attending *art school.*"

McCrea laughed, "Okay, Clay. We're groovin' now."

With a grin, Clay mocked the same lingo. "Cool, man…now lay a little color on me."

The look on McCrea's face grew serious. "When an artist puts down a color on a painting, sometimes he will place, in close proximity to that color, either a harmonizing, or a complementary color. Placing harmonizing colors side-by-side—let's say two shades of blue—can create delicate distinctions between the two. They are slightly different in hue or value, but they are both members of the same family. There is a close kinship, just as when people of common interests and opinions mingle with each other. They 'harmonize' with each other in their ideas and opinions. This can reinforce their beliefs and values, but also, possibly their prejudices."

"That makes sense, but what about complementary colors…Colors that are directly across the color spectrum from each other, like violet and yellow? How do they harmonize?" asked Clay.

"Well, they don't harmonize with each other—they're opposites… They *complement* each other. When placed side-by-side, each color enhances the other, giving each hue a dazzling brilliance they wouldn't otherwise have. The same phenomenon is true when male and female are complements to each other—as in a good marriage."

Clay smiled, "Maybe you ought to be a marriage counselor instead of an art teacher."

"Maybe, I should, at that," laughed McCrea. "But the same is true of our other relationships. If we connect with people whose views differ from ours, or who can critique our ideas, we are complementing each other. Just as an art student displays his artwork to be critiqued by his instructor and fellow students, the infusion of other ideas expands his creativity. This complementary atmosphere provides a rich soil from which creativity can grow. So you see, when Ramsey critiqued your painting, he was only being honest. Actually, he was doing you a favor."

"And I forgot to thank him," said Dean, sarcastically.

"What's your mother like?" asked McCrea. Again, Dean resented the prying question. "She is the gentlest, most sensitive woman I ever knew."

"Don't you think you have some of your mother's qualities in you?"

"Yeah, maybe somewhere, down deep inside me. But tell me this…Clay came from the same background that I did. How come his painting showed sensitivity, and he captured the essence of his subject?"

McCrea answered. "For one thing, Clay chose a rather safe, masculine subject—a pair of old worn-out army boots. Also, he chose a simpler subject with fewer textures to deal with. However, Clay's painting also showed some insensitivity, just as yours did. Unfortunately, or maybe *fortunately*, you chose a subject that reveals insensitivity very easily. I say fortunately because it initiated this very interesting conversation we're having. By the way, Clay, your work shows a lot of talent, also."

"Thanks, but I don't necessarily agree with you about aggressiveness." Clay swallowed the last drink of his beer. "Sometimes it's essential to be aggressive in order to protect yourself. A man who won't do that is a damned wimp."

"Aggressiveness is a trait, just like any other trait," said McCrea.

"Sometimes it's very valuable and necessary for survival, or protection. But when societal influences distort it to the extent that it overpowers the emotions of compassion and sensitivity, terrible things can happen. Carried to the ultimate, aggressiveness can evoke monstrous passions in man that can result in mayhem, and war, while suffocating creativity. You know, war is creativity's opposite."

"What makes you say that?" inquired Clay. "I know war is bad, but how would it stifle creativity?"

McCrea answered, "Creativity is the process of starting with nothing and making something. War is the process of starting with something and reducing it to nothing. If people could grasp the importance of creativity, then maybe the world would be a more peaceful place. But our country's way of thinking is way off track; for example, during a budget cut, the first things eliminated from the school's curriculum are the art and music courses."

"Then how do we get on the right track...to awaken the passion in us, or to be more creative?" asked Clay.

"You need to get into the habit of making a conscious effort to rid yourself of some of your male-dominant attitudes. To attain completeness in our personality, we must re-capture the innate tenderness and sensitivity with which we were born. Our aim should not be to merely become more creative, but to become a whole man—a better person. It is only when we develop a sensitivity to the plight of others that we become a real man."

Clay thought about what McCrea said. "Well, we brothers didn't show much tenderness and sensitivity when we were younger. Mostly, we raised hell, got drunk, an pulled shitty tricks on each other." "That's not surprising," said McCrea, "Creativity is an energy that must be released in some direction. When men and women are forced into stereotyped roles that society demands of them, their passion is stifled, or misdirected. When we inhibit its expression, we either stifle the impulse to create, or misdirect its application; it may be released in the pursuit of frivolous or destructive behavior. Alcohol abuse, drug addiction, extra-marital affairs, vandalism, and other misbehaviors are often products of misdirected creative energy."

Dean interjected. "If a man needs those so-called 'female' traits in him in order to have the sensitivity necessary, how do you explain my dad? I don't see any of those characteristics in him, but he's the most creative man I've ever known."

"There's nearly always an exception to every rule, I guess. Perhaps he attained that balance through his wife. You said that your mother was gentle and sensitive. Maybe, together, their unity, the merger of their complementing personalities, gave your father the completeness he needed to make him a whole man. Some men don't find completeness as a man until they marry the right woman. Together, they bond to form the necessary balance."

Clay was becoming intoxicated. He looked at McCrea and projected a silly grin. "McCrea, tonight I've learned that we're supposed to be half-female. That gives new meaning to the well-known directive—'Go screw yourself'."

McCrea expelled an uproarious laugh. "Clay, I find your sense of humor very creative—but I'm still not sure of your sensitivity. Maybe in your case, sensitivity and creativity are not tied together."

"Hell, McCrea, I was just teasin' you. I think what you say makes a lot of sense, even if I'm not able to abide by it."

It was now past midnight, and other than the bartender and the sleeping drunk in the corner booth, the tavern was now empty of everyone except the threesome in McCrea's booth.

"Drink up, guys...Closing time," said the bartender.

Dean still worried about the man in the corner booth. "What about that guy over there? How are you going to get him to leave?"

The bartender answered, "Hell, I'll just let him stay there for the night. He'll sleep it off. He's my brother-in-law."

As the three men left the tavern, Clay was showing the effects of the alcohol, both in his speech and his unsteady gait, for his consumption of the wine had exceeded that of McCrea's.

"Where are you guys headed? I've got my car—I'll drop you off," offered McCrea.

"We live right here, McCrea, on the third floor apartment," replied Dean.

"Must be an elegant place," McCrea sarcastically laughed.

"Yeah, *Modern Living Magazine* is going to do a feature article about our place," laughed Clay.

For a brief time the men stood silently on the sidewalk in front of the tavern. Towering over the brothers as he stood between them, McCrea affectionately draped his arms around their shoulders. A sudden gust of late autumn wind chilled them and issued a scattering of crispy leaves swirling around their feet, forewarning the inevitable approach of winter.

"If I wasn't so drunk, I bet I'd be cold," muttered Clay.

McCrea laughed as he released the brothers. "I didn't mean to preach you guys a sermon tonight...I guess I got carried away."

"Hell, I talk like that myself, sometimes, especially when I've had too much wine," remarked Clay. "You know, McCrea, you'd make a pretty damn good preacher."

Again, McCrea laughed. "You guys both show a lot of promise in your work. Goodnight guys...I'll see you in class Monday."

"Goodnight, McCrea," replied the brothers, then they walked up the two flights of stairs to their apartment.

The pain passes, but the beauty remains.
Pierre Auguste Renoir

Chapter 29

As their first year of art school quickly passed, the brothers became more skilled in their artwork, for they put forth more effort than that of the other students. Both of them were consistently on the honor role, and at the end of the school year, in May, Dean won the honor of "Best First Year Student," an award that created some sibling rivalry between the brothers.

Earning the tribute instilled a renewed life in Dean because he felt that if he exerted sufficient effort, the future offered unlimited possibilities. Clay, on the other hand, felt that Dean was having "delusions of grandeur." While Clay had a passion for painting, he expected no accolades for his efforts; the satisfaction of performing the art of painting was reward enough. If necessary, after graduation, he would supplement his income by working in some other line of work.

Prior to their attendance of art school, Dean and Clay had spent little time together. Now, with a kinship in their personalities and their mutual interest in art, Dean and Clay had become emotionally close. Although similar in many ways, they were vastly divergent in their view of circumstances. Clay was an agnostic realist, often displaying a fatalistic outlook in regard to the outcome of events. He wasn't necessarily pessimistic: He expected that a good consequence was as likely as a bad one. He believed that the result was mostly a matter of mere luck. If the outcome was bad, he accepted the consequence without complaint.

Conversely, Dean was an idealist. Much like his father and his brother, Alvin, he was a dreamer, believing that wonderful things could happen if only he properly applied himself to a task. When the dream was unfulfilled, however, he complained in frustration about the unfairness of the result, a trait that caused both Clay and Rob—who were more fatalistic in nature—to tease him about being a constant griper.

During the summer between school years, Clay worked in the sign shop with his father and Alvin. Dean was still recovering from tuberculosis and was not supposed to work for another year; however, to supplement the meager income that Bobbie was earning from her waitress job, he took in less physical work, doing free-lance design jobs for other sign shops. During Bobbie's absence, Sarah became a second mother to both Deana and Vince. Her baby-sitting chores injected new life into her, diminishing the pain of Elwood's death. Since Clay and Ellen were both working, Will kept a watchful eye on their children.

Although they struggled financially, both Dean and Clay returned to art school the following fall quarter. When they enrolled, Dean continued in his graphic design studies; however, Clay changed his emphasis to fine arts, with a major in painting. The brothers returned to their shabby apartment above *The Bottom of the Barrel* tavern and resigned themselves to another year of hard work and study.

As the months passed, Dean became one of the best graphic design students in the school, and Clay was making great strides in his painting efforts.

Clay was becoming a first rate artist, as his talent in painting exceeded that of Dean's. As Clay became enamored with painting, he yielded to the temptation held by most of the student painters: He grew a beard and began conforming to the 'non-conformists' in both his mode of dress and attitude. His compliance was short-lived, however, because in his nature, he had inherited his father's abhorrence of pretentiousness: Ultimately, he shaved his beard and returned to wearing more nondescript clothing.

In spite of their success in art school, both Dean and Clay held deep feelings of guilt about their wives supporting their families. By the end of the school year, the brothers were deeply in debt.

Occasionally, Clay and Dean had dinner with Rob and Madge, who were also living in Atlanta. Rob was earning his master's degree in theology at *Emory University,* and he too, was struggling financially. On Sundays, he still worked as a circuit preacher, serving five churches, which required him to drive and preach in five different locations. Madge held a job in the *Emory University* cafeteria.

As graduation approached, both Dean and Clay realized how much they had progressed since enrolling in art school. They learned to appreciate constructive criticism of their work, and in turn, their paintings displayed much more sensitivity. Two years had passed since Dean and Clay had the discussion with Harrison McCrea in *The Bottom of the Barrel,* and McCrea's explanation of the pitfalls of male aggressiveness had impressed Dean. When he thought of gentleness and sensitivity, he realized that Elwood and his mother had consistently displayed the balanced personality that McCrea had described. As he thought of tenderness, he only hoped that he could somehow become more like them; for he was now convinced that in order to be creative, man must reawaken the tender emotions that lie dormant within him.

Dean and Clay graduated from *Atlanta Art Institute* with high honors. Only one week later, Rob graduated from *Candler School of Theology* at *Emory University.* He was valedictorian of his class and was selected in "Who's Who in American Colleges," an honor that awarded him an expense-paid trip to Washington, D.C. Shortly after, he joined the Civil Rights Movement and participated in several protest marches.

After graduation, Clay moved back to Tyler City and took a job near Knoxville in a sign shop, and Rob became the associate pastor of *First Methodist Church* in the same city. In Chattanooga, two hours away from his brothers, Dean re-located his family and accepted a job at *Charles Thompson Advertising Agency.* Although his duties were routine in nature, involving little creativity, he believed that the job presented a great future opportunity for him. On many weekends, he took his family to visit Will and Sarah in Tyler City.

Will had closed *Beauvais Signs,* replacing the former business with a modest studio and gallery where he sold a few paintings and picture frames. Although he missed the activity of the sign business and the presence of his sons, he seemed moderately content in his retirement, operating his part-time studio.

In mid-November, Bobbie received some shocking news. Her mother, Lily, who lived in Ohio, had suddenly died of a heart attack. Once again, the Beauvais family was in mourning. Three days later, the entire country mourned, for on November 22, 1963, the day of Lily's funeral, President John F. Kennedy was assassinated.

It was a surrealistic time for Bobbie and Dean, as it became difficult to comprehend such a compound loss. It was an especially troubling time for Bobbie. Because of her mother's former abandonment of the Summer family, Bobbie found it even more difficult to deal with her mother's death.

As Christmas approached, Bobbie's spirit began to gradually heal as she became more involved with her children. On Christmas Eve, Will and Sarah drove through a heavy snowstorm in order to spend the night and celebrate Christmas with Dean and his family in Chattanooga. When they pulled into the driveway of Dean's home, Deana and Vince were in the front yard in a laborious process of constructing a huge snowman. Immediately upon seeing Sarah step out of the car, Deana excitedly ran to into the arms of her "Mamaw."

The exceptionally beautiful snowfall ushered in the first white Christmas that East Tennessee had experienced since the birth of Vince, three years earlier. The spectacular multitude of enormous flakes fell so heavily that it obscured the definition of faraway objects. In the distance, sky and landscape merged into a single, misty image. Except for the tiny tracks of a few unidentified animals, the carpet of snow was undisturbed. As the snow grew deeper, it covered the land like an unblemished blanket.

Across the street, two stray dogs, invigorated by the frosty air, frolicked in a nearby field, their joyful barks muffled by the thick mantle of unspoiled snow. As Deana and Vince trudged through the deep drifts, the huge fluffy snowflakes accumulated on their coats and toboggan caps.

Their rosy-red cheeks and delighted squeals reflected their excitement as they gazed at the darkened sky over the distant woodland; the sky that would deliver Santa Claus to their home on this very night. Laughing with delight, the two children opened their mouths, catching the downy snowflakes on their tongues.

On Christmas morning, Deana received her first bicycle—a bright red beauty with training wheels. Vince, who was only three, got a tricycle and several games. Deana, being more excited over the presence of her grandmother, spent more time in Sarah's lap than with her toys. "Lord, Bobbie honey, you can't imagine how much I miss this child," said Sarah.

"She misses you, too. Why don't you and Mr. Beauvais come and live with us? We miss you and Papaw."

Will cast an indignant look at Bobbie. "Do you expect us to abandon our home? I spent my life creating a home, and you expect us to just up and leave it? Why don't you and Dean move back to Tyler City? You both built your house on *Beauvais Lane* together, but now you just let some strangers live there and pay you rent for it. Why don't you all come on back there? Dean could find a good job in Knoxville… just like the one he has here…We do appreciate your offer, though,

Bobbie."

Dean looked at Will. "Dad, there's a great opportunity for me here. I have a good job with the promise of a great future. I can't give up this chance for happiness."

"Things sure do turn out strange, sometimes," remarked Will. "I used to have dreams of a profitable sign shop with all my boys working there and living side by side on *Beauvais Lane*...Now, look how it's turned out. The shop is deserted and nobody's living on the property except Clay and Ellen, and now they're talking about moving to Knoxville. It looks like it will be just me and Sarah, all alone...No sons...no grand-children....just us. Anyway, I'm really doing a lot of artwork now, Dean. You ought to see some of my paintings."

"Dad, we're just a stone's-throw away. We'll visit you often. I want Deana and Mom to continue their close relationship. I wish you would re-consider and move in with us. You and Mom could go back to the house and to your studio on weekends...or whenever you wanted to."

"I could never do that, Dean," answered Will, sadly.

The next day after Christmas dinner, Will and Sarah left. Deana cried and clung to her Mamaw, begging her to stop. Sarah, through her tears, pleaded, "Don't cry, honey, I'll be back to see you, real soon—and your daddy will bring you to see me."

As the family stepped onto the front porch and continued to depart, Deana, now with both hands, gripped at Sarah's dress. With each step, Sarah paused and stroked Deana's raven hair.

Following the footprints in the snow, Will walked to the car. "Let's go, Sarah. We need to make it home before dark."

As Sarah stepped into the snow-ridden yard, she felt Deana's released tug.

Dean yelled, "Dad, please drive carefully. The roads are still gonna be slick. And they'll get worse tonight."

Will backed the car out of the driveway and Dean and Bobbie stood on the front porch, waving to his mother and father. As they pulled away, in Dean's last glimpse of the car, he saw Sarah waving to them. She was glancing from side to side, hoping to also wave goodbye to her grandchildren, but both had retreated under the Christmas tree in the warm living room. While listening to the diminishing sound of the car motor, Vince rocked back and forth, crying as he watched his sister curl in a ball and whine as she rubbed her bare, cold feet.

The car disappeared into the misty, wintry distance. As Dean stood motionless for several seconds, he felt a deep sadness for his parents.

As darkness falls on Christmas day, an indescribable gloom begins to seep into one's soul. There is no relief in trying to escape it with sleep, knowing the next day's dawning will not be healing. And so it was with Dean and his family. The thrill of anticipating Christmas was over... the holiday spirit was gone. Compounding his sadness was the departure of his parents, and the lonely life they were living. He ached with compassion for his father, who had reluctantly given up his dream of having his family to be his island.

The day after Christmas, Dean struggled with his emotions in order to feel better. In the kitchen he could hear Bobbie preparing dinner. He wished that he too could have the same necessary chores. He entered the room with Bobbie, opened the kitchen cabinets, and removed the plates.

"What do you think you're doing?" she asked.

"Well, I thought I would set the table."

"Look, Dean, I can't make it any faster than this!"

"Okay... Well...I..." Dean didn't know what felt more uncomfortable—the plates in his hands, or helping his wife in her territory. He felt lucky to retreat to the living room to play with the kids and their new toys. Soon, he was on the floor by the family Christmas tree, wrestling with Deana and Vince, and eventually, the sadness that had enveloped the house gradually dissipated.

The ringing telephone interrupted his play. "I'll get it," he yelled to Bobbie, "It's probably my boss."

When he picked up the phone, he recognized his father's voice.

"Dean...something's wrong with your mother."

"What is it, Dad? What's wrong?"

"Well, I...I don't know what's wrong with her." Will's voice quivered.

"What do you mean, you don't know?" asked Dean.

"Well, she went to the bathroom, and then...when she didn't come out....I waited for a long time...I finally called to her several times, but she wouldn't answer me...and she wouldn't come out, either." Dean could hear the desperation and confusion in his father's voice.

"Well, did you go into the bathroom and see what was wrong?"

"Yes...I finally went in there, but she didn't respond to me...Maybe she just fainted, or something..." Will's voice trailed off.

"Dad...Did you check to see if she was breathing? Did you check her pulse?" Dean impatience was beginning to show.

Will tried to explain. "She doesn't appear to be breathing...she's just lying on the floor...She's been in there for about a half hour."

"Dad...Is she...?"

"I don't know...I called an ambulance. I'm waiting on it now...But, yes, I believe she is..."

Although neither of them could utter the words, Dean knew that his mother was dead.

There is really nothing more to say—except why. But since why is difficult to handle, one must take refuge in how. **Toni Morrison**

Chapter 30

Dean and Bobbie gazed ahead at the darkness, silent, as if in a trance. As big, moist snowflakes splattered against the windshield, Dean flipped on the wipers and dimmed the headlights, softening the hypnotizing illumination of the multitude of swirling snowflakes ahead. Just yesterday, they had cherished the fall of snow, now it was only one of the many unpleasant obstacles that lay before them.

Fate had once again played a capricious prank when it dealt a double-dose of despair to Dean and Bobbie; for Sarah's instant death from a massive stroke occurred only one month after the death of Bobbie's mother.

Dean had called Rob soon after receiving the bad news from his father, and Will had called Clay and Alvin. There were funeral arrangements to make, with friends and relatives to call, pall bearers to choose, and other dreadful tasks to perform. Dean was almost grateful for these unpleasant chores that filled his thoughts, temporarily holding at bay the terrible grief that would ultimately invade his mind.

Bobbie slid over in the seat, touching her body to Dean while he continued their drive to Tyler City. Vince was curled up in the back seat, asleep. Deana sat silently beside him, awake, and like her mother, stared straight ahead. She knew that something was terribly wrong, but was puzzled about the mysterious situation, because neither Dean nor Bobbie had garnered the courage to tell her.

"Daddy? Is something wrong?" Deana asked timidly, as if she instinctively knew that the question was forbidden. Dean hesitated, then looked at Bobbie, uncertain in regard to the best way to break the news to his

daughter. He knew that, other than her parents, Deana loved her grandmother more than anyone in her life. Realizing that his daughter had
never experienced the heartbreak of death, he worried about her reaction to it.

Reluctantly, Dean said, "Honey…Mamaw has gone away…"

"Gone away? Where?" she asked.

"Well…Mamaw has gone to heaven," answered Dean.

"Oh. Well, when will she be back?"

Without knowing how to answer, Dean tried to explain. "She probably won't come back. But don't you worry about it because we'll all see
her again someday."

"When?" Deana inquired, innocently.

"Well, nobody knows that for sure. She may not ever come back to
see us, but we will all go to live with her again, someday, with God, in
her new home in heaven." He glanced back at his daughter to determine
her reaction.

Deana continued to peer straight ahead into the swirling snowflakes.

"Why did she go away?" asked Deana.

Dean answered. "She was tired, she's gone to rest for awhile."

"Well, when can we go to be with her?"

"Honey, I can't tell you when, exactly, but I can promise you that we
will someday. Now, don't you worry about it anymore. Lie down and
get some sleep."

"Okay, Daddy." She then lay down, cuddling beside Vince.

"Daddy?"

"What is it, Deana?"

"Does God laugh?" Deana loved to see her Mamaw laugh.

"Yes, God likes to see you laugh and play."

"Do you think that Mamaw feels sad that she's not with me, Daddy?"
asked Deana.

"Well, it's different with her, honey. She can see you, but you just
can't see her. Deana, honey, when we get to Mamaw and Papaw's
house, don't ask Papaw where Mamaw is."

"Why, Daddy?"

"Because…Right now, he's sad because she went away. So don't ask
him. Okay?"

"Okay, Daddy."

As Dean drove silently through the snowstorm, he dwelled on the
relationship that he and his brothers had previously developed with
their mother. There had been a closeness, a bond in which each brother

had unique connections to her. Because of their similar natures, Elwood had established the most cherished association with her; but the discernable intimacy between Sarah and her other sons was based more on a teasing, light-hearted affection. Dean regretted that he had seldom engaged in serious discussions with her; for being surrounded by males who were insensitive to feminine interests, Elwood had been the only son who shared personal feelings with her.

The strangling clutch of guilt began to squirm its way into his sorrow because he realized that taking Deana away from Sarah had broken his mother's spirit. Dean began to understand that for every risk taken, for every positive change we make, there is a price to be exacted; for the lives of all people—like the links of a chain—are bound together. To toss even a tiny pebble into undisturbed water has a rippling effect on the entire surface. All choices have consequences.

Dean slowed the vehicle to compensate for the accumulating film of snow that had begun to reclaim the surface of the highway. Traffic was sparse as Dean cautiously proceeded through the thickening snow blanket. The children were now asleep, and except for the rhythmic flap of the windshield wipers, a muffled quietness pervaded their world.

Dean broke the silence. "Bobbie, how do you think Mom's death is going to affect Deana?"

"Well, she doesn't understand it right now. But she does know that something very strange has happened. We'll have to help her to understand."

"This has been really tough on you, honey. First your mother, and now, Mom. I know how much Mamaw meant to you, too." Dean realized that Sarah was to Bobbie the mother that she had been previously denied. "What's going to happen to Dad?" Dean continued. "He's going to be all alone in his home. Of course, Clay and Ellen live next door…And he still has Terry."

Bobbie responded. "But he's getting old. He'll need somebody to take care of him. Who's going to cook for him, wash his clothes, clean the house? Maybe he'll move in with us in Chattanooga."

"That's fine with me, but he'll never do it," said Dean, "Can you picture him ever leaving the 'Beauvais Empire'?"

"Maybe Ellen could help take care of him."

Dean thought about Bobbie's idea. "No, that wouldn't work. Ellen has her hands full already. She works, you know. Well, let's not worry about it right now. We'll have to figure out something, though."

The final leg of the journey was difficult as the accumulating snow had made driving hazardous. As a result, it was past midnight when Dean finally pulled his vehicle into the Beauvais parking area. To avoid awakening Vince, Dean gently lifted him from the car, as Deana, who was now awake, took her mother's hand as they gingerly made their way through the snow to the front door. When they entered the house, only Will and Rob were present. Madge was sleeping in Sarah's bedroom, and Ellen was in her house next door. Alvin had not yet arrived since he was snowed in at his home in Kingston. Clay, falling prey to his habitual bad luck, had skidded off the road as he returned from his job in Knoxville. He was unhurt, but his car had to be pulled from a ditch by a wrecker.

Rob sat facing his father, vainly attempting to comfort him. Will's demeanor was one of utter despondency and confusion. His usual erect posture had given way to an exhausted slump, and his appearance was that of a broken man.

After somber greetings were exchanged, Dean gently placed his sleeping son on the couch, as Deana crawled into her mother's lap on the other end of the sofa. Aware of Will's aversion to physical expressions of emotion, Dean resisted the urge to embrace him.

Deana sat silently, staring wide-eyed at her grandfather. Suddenly, she jumped from her mother's lap and walked over to Will, directly facing him.

"Where's Mamaw?" she demanded.

Although Dean inwardly winced, he was unable to suppress a smile because he realized that his daughter's disobedience was innocent. She merely wanted an answer to a simple question that she had every right to ask.

Will looked at Deana with sadness. "Did you explain it to her, Dean?"

"Yeah, I did the best I could. You know, she'll eventually see the true significance of it, but after all, sometimes kids can handle things better than we can."

When Bobbie and her children eventually went to bed, Will and his sons made no attempt to sleep, sitting up all night, grieving. Sometimes they talked about Sarah, and occasionally, as a brief respite from their sorrow, they engaged in routine conversation. At other times, they sat in silence, thinking.

Dean's concern about his father's survival without Sarah still plagued his mind.

"Dad, I don't want to worry you more at a time like this, but we need to talk about some things. The house will be full of people tomorrow, and we won't be able to have privacy. This seems like a good opportunity to discuss some things. What are your plans after we bury Mom? I mean, where do you plan to live? You can't stay here by yourself. Why don't you come and live with us in Chattanooga? If you stay here by yourself, you won't have anyone to take care of you."

"I don't need anybody to take care of me!" said Will, indignantly. "But Dean, I do appreciate the offer. Anyway, I could never leave Terry. He's about all I have left in my life."

Finally, Rob spoke. "Dad, I believe you should either stay with Dean, or me. Of course, if you stayed with Madge and me, you'd have to move around to different parsonages whenever the church relocated me."

"Thanks, Rob, but I'm going to stay right here. This is my home. I never had a home in my life until I married your mother, and I've dedicated my life to making a home. I could never live with somebody else, and obey the rules of their house. I plan to live right here until I die."

With an understanding of their father's uncompromising nature, Dean and Rob temporarily dropped the subject. By daybreak, Al and Amber had arrived, although it was two hours later when Clay reached home. After the wrecker had removed his car from the ditch, his vehicle ran out of fuel, a misfortune that necessitated a four-mile walk in the snowstorm. As a result, he almost developed a case of frostbite on his toes.

After considerable effort, the four brothers persuaded their father to retire to his bedroom since he was exhausted from his all night sleepless ordeal. Bobbie and Amber neatened the house while Ellen and Madge made coffee and cleared the large dining table in preparation for the variety of food that friends would soon be bringing. In mid-morning, while the women mingled with visiting friends, the brothers drove to the funeral home to choose a casket and a grave stone.

The reception of friends took place as a preliminary part of the funeral. The service was sad, but an affair that boasted a large attendance, for Sarah was loved by many. On December 29, 1963, Sarah's body was planted beside Elwood in the snow-covered family plot at the cemetery.

Two days after the funeral, it was time for the brothers to return to their usual routines. After his brothers had gone, Dean sat down with his father.

"Dad, come home with Bobbie and me. I don't feel right leaving you here by yourself."

"Dean, I just simply can't do it. How can you expect me to suddenly change my whole life? Just look at what's happened. Clay is talking about selling his house and moving to Knoxville near his job. Now, if he leaves, it'll just be me, all alone in my house and my little studio…But I don't know any other home but this one."

On the drive back to his home in Chattanooga, Dean was low in spirit. Although he grieved for his mother, he worried more about his dad. He feared that since his father had lost both Elwood and Sarah, his spirit would die, soon to be followed by his body. Will still had his grandson, Terry; but if Clay moved away, he would have nothing. Dean decided that he couldn't leave his father alone and still live with his conscience. After talking it over with Bobbie and his employers, Dean gave his two-week notice at the company where he worked, then moved his family back to his father's house. He stayed in a hotel in Chattanooga until he worked out his notice, then he, too, moved in with his dad.

Dean was now unemployed. With heavy heart and in need of an income, he again began to paint signs in his father's studio. It was no inconvenience to Will, for he never used the studio area since he had lost all interest in painting following the death of Sarah. He tried to stimulate an interest in his father, but to no avail. With a dying spirit, Will had apparently given up on his dream.

As the months passed, Will's interest was confined mostly to his grandson, Terry. In deep concern over his father's apathy, Dean consulted with Clay.

Together, they concocted a plan to re-ignite his flagging spirit. Choosing their best paintings from art school, they displayed them on the walls of the shop. Then, in the evenings, after work, the brothers began to paint. At first, Will ignored their efforts, but one evening he idly ambled into the shop, watching his sons as they painted. Clay was working on a landscape, with which he seemed to be having difficulty in capturing the essence of a sunset.

"I can't seem to get these colors right," complained Clay, "Dad, what am I doing wrong here?"

With aroused interest, Will studied the painting. "You're using the wrong hue of red. Here, use this red instead." He took Clay's brush, dabbed it into his recommended color, and began to correct the painting. Clay grinned and winked at Dean.

In the ensuing evenings when Clay and Dean painted together, Will joined them to offer advice. One night when the brothers came to the shop to paint, Clay was unable to participate because Will had claimed his easel, working on a painting of his own. Ultimately, the lure of art had captivated him. As his creative pursuit of painting had done in the past, it once again had brought him out of the depths of despair and given him new life.

Both Dean and Clay knew that it was only a matter of time until their father rebounded from his despondency; for they had never known anyone with courage and resiliency of their dad. He wasn't a quitter, but the ultimate survivor.

While Dean and Bobbie were living with Will, Dean continued to work in the shop. As Sarah had done, Bobbie did the cooking and household chores, as Will became part of the family. Gradually, he began to appreciate and feel more at ease around her. Since Clay and Ellen were both working, Will kept Terry and Eldon, and sometimes Dean's children. A few months later, after Will's grief began to subside, Dean and Bobbie moved up the hill into their own house. Their proximity to Will enabled them to nurture him while allowing him to retain a measure of his own independence.

Slowly, Will began to resurrect his flagging spirit. Although he still missed Sarah, Terry had helped fill the void that the deaths of Elwood and Sarah had created. He had even regained his enthusiasm for painting and was now doing some of his best work.

His affection for Terry, however, had again begun to cause friction between him and Clay, for it seemed that Will had almost claimed Terry as his son. One day when Clay was attempting to discipline Terry, Will interceded. Will's admonition of Clay resulted in a terrible quarrel between them. The antagonism between them escalated, ultimately resulting in a deep bitterness. Because of the similarity in their unyielding natures, each of them began to avoid any association with the other. Although Dean made attempts to reconcile them, their mutual hostility only worsened and remained unwavering for weeks.

In June, Dean took his family to the mountains on a week's vacation. Since Will saw an opportunity to paint the beauty of the wooded ridges, he decided to go with them. A week later, upon their return home, they discovered a SOLD sign on the lawn in front of Clay's house. Peering through the front picture window, Dean saw that the house was empty of furniture. When he called Clay's place of employment, Dean was told that he had resigned. Clay was gone. His departure had been swift, and no one knew his destination.

Go confidently in the direction of your dreams. Live the life you have imagined. **Henry David Thoreau.**

Chapter 31

For more than a year, Dean continued to work in the shop, and during that time there had been no word from Clay or of his whereabouts. Will had made several inquiries around Tyler City in the hope that someone would know where to locate his son. He had asked Ellen's kinfolk and Clay's closest friends, but apparently Clay had told no one of his new location.

It was now in the turbulent 60's. In the autumn of 1964, David Michaels became a part of the Beauvais family. The lad was the 14 year old son of Bobbie's sister, Bernice, who had recently moved to Indianapolis, Indiana.

David had begged to stay in Tennessee in order to finish high school with his friends, and Bobbie and Dean had agreed to take him into their home. The Beauvais family treated him as one of their own, and although Deana and Vince were only small children, David quickly bonded with them. He became like an older brother and protector of his younger cousins. An affectionate, obedient youngster with the gentle nature of his mother, he was provided for and nurtured by Dean and Bobbie. Intimately bound together with the Beauvais kinfolk by a mutual love, he became an integral part of the family unit. He stayed with Dean and Bobbie until he graduated from *Tyler City High School*, then joined the U.S. Marines. Unfortunately, he was immediately sent to Vietnam.

Again the horrible specter of war had severed the ties of family members as the entire Beauvais family was saddened by David's commitment to the controversial war.

America's involvement in the Vietnam War had divided the country. The separation grew more pronounced as American casualties mounted. Violent war protests became commonplace occurrences in many cities, disputes that were further exacerbated by the Civil Rights Movement. Organized peace marches were prevalent as the country was embroiled in constant turmoil. On April 14, 1968, Martin Luther King was assassinated in Memphis, Tennessee. In black communities, riots broke out in the slums of Washington, D.C., and Chicago, while across the country, many stores were looted and burned to the ground.

The spirit of the unrest was also reflected in the music of the era. Carefree love ballads of Nat King Cole, Perry Como, and The Platters gave way to the protest songs of Bob Dylan, The Beatles, and Peter, Paul, and Mary.

The turmoil that pervaded America was in keeping with the divisive nature of the Beauvais family. Will again became depressed after Clay moved away because once more he had been abandoned—this time by Terry. Having endured countless rejections, he developed a cynicism in regard to relationships, an attitude that caused him to withdraw even more from involvement with people.

Because of Will's emotional withdrawal, Dean's attempts at encouragement fell on deaf ears. His father had simply lost interest in re-establishing a meaningful life, or even any involvement with the shop. Dean was struggling financially because painting signs in the shop brought a meager income; therefore, when he was offered a job at *Paul Winthrop Advertising Agency* in Knoxville, he quickly accepted. Will made no attempt to influence Dean's decision, and because of his father's debilitating apathy with the family business, Dean, with sadness, closed the doors.

Ultimately, Will's cynicism grew into a smoldering anger. As it increased in intensity, because he felt that his past rejections were unjust, he became more vocal in his protests against unfairness. This outrage translated into an abhorrence of all injustice in the world; thus he began to verbally champion the causes of downtrodden people who had been victimized by inequity. He became angry about the Vietnam War as well as the high price of prescription drugs. At first, he restricted his protests to spoken complaints; but as his indignation grew stronger, he began to express his feelings in writing. He began to submit angry forum letters to the *Knoxville News-Sentinel* and the *Tyler City News*. As a daily ritual, he sat at his typewriter, tapping the keys, venting his anger.

After Dean proved his abilities at the advertising agency, he was promoted to Creative Director, a position that offered more creativity as well as a large increase in pay. Since his children were growing up, he decided that his family needed a larger house, but he dreaded broaching the subject to his father, and when he did, Will's reaction was just as Dean predicted.

"You're going to leave *Beauvais Lane*? You're going to sell the property I gave you?"

"Dad, I hate to sell the house because I have a sentimental attachment to it, but I need to move on. My kids are growing up, and we don't have enough room. I found a brand new house at a good price over in Tyler Estates that has plenty of room…It even has an extra bedroom for you," explained Dean.

"Dean, you can forget that idea. I'll never leave this place. It looks like I'm going to be deserted again!" His face displayed his anger. Dean tried to reason with him. "Dad, we don't want to abandon you, we want you to come with us. You can live with us, and it won't cost you a cent!"

"Dean, you're making a big mistake! Please don't do it!" Will's tone was almost pleading.

"I'm sorry, Dad…Bobbie and I have already made up our minds. We want you to move with us, but if you won't, we're moving anyway."

Slowly, Will stood erect, donned his hat, and left the room with his expression transparently revealing his sadness. Although Dean and Bobbie were excited about their new home, leaving the house on *Beauvais Lane* was a sad affair. Dean had labored hard on the construction of the dwelling, and it had been his and Bobbie's first real home. It had been built with concrete blocks, covered with stucco, and painted pale green; accordingly, to all the Beauvais clan, it became known as the "Green House." Embedded in its walls were many happy memories, and when they bade the house goodbye, they felt as if they were abandoning an old friend.

Vince, in particular, didn't want to leave the house because it had been the only home he remembered. When they pulled out of the driveway, Deana said to everyone in the car, "Turn around and say goodbye to our house." The whole family waved farewell to the Green House.

Will, true to his promise, refused to move with them, but after a week of living alone, he finally visited their home and spent the night. Then, five days later, he again came for an overnight visit. In keeping with his moderate nature, he haltingly eased into the relationship with a series of baby steps, cautiously testing the waters. After increasingly frequent overnight visits, he finally made a commitment and moved in.

The Green House sold immediately, and although he welcomed the money, it saddened Dean to realize that since Clay's house had already been sold, the "dynasty" of the Beauvais family was disintegrating.

Their new home had four bedrooms, two baths, and a two-car garage. The all brick structure rested in the center of a large, level lot in a middle-class neighborhood. The most attractive and useful focal point of the new house was the expansive brick fireplace in the den. The complete interior wall was constructed of bricks, with the fireplace boasting an unusually large mantel and hearth.

Having moved into the new house with Dean and Bobbie, Will made the reluctant decision to sell the shop; after all, he reasoned, the sale of Clay and Dean's property had fragmented the original Beauvais homestead. The lonely remnants of the remaining property embodied too many ghosts. It was the place of Sarah's death, and the cradle of Elwood's passion. In his mind, the happy sound of his sons' laughter during happier times reverberated from the walls of the shop.

Will had already located a buyer for the property, but before the deal was made, Dean interceded and bought the old Beauvais estate from his father. Although Dean actually had no practical need of it, he believed that Will would ultimately regret the decision. After all, Dean had his own sentimental attachment to the place.

His decision to buy the property was ultimately a wise one. With the shop living quarters intact, it became a place for Will to spend his days while Dean was working in Knoxville. At first, because of the loneliness of the empty building, Will was reluctant to spend time there; but with the passage of time, he discovered that the phantoms of the past that haunted the building held a certain allure for him. Gradually, his spirit was renewed. He again opened his studio, where he spent his days painting and writing. In the evening, after work, Dean often joined his father in the studio where they sometimes painted for hours.

After Dean and his family settled in their new home, the years passed quickly. Both Bobbie and Dean became active in civic affairs and volunteer work. Bobbie developed a passion for helping with the care of the elderly in nursing homes, volunteering her services at least once a week; also, in keeping with her nature, she became involved in athletics, playing softball for the church league and coaching a youth softball team. Because of a mutual interest in youth activities, Dean and Jake Stone joined forces as volunteer football coaches for the *Little League* program.

The whereabouts of Clay and his family was still a mystery, and although Will's pain over the loss of Terry was less severe, he still suffered. His enduring grief over his past rejections instilled in him a reluctance to nurture relationships; as a result, he avoided any close attachment to Deana and Vince. In order to alleviate the pain of being forsaken by others, Will now found solace in endless hours of writing. Before long, to compound his despondency, his vision became impaired. A visit to the family doctor resulted in the dreadful confirmation that he had glaucoma. Treating this degenerative disease required his utmost attention; otherwise, blindness was inevitable. As a result, Will had to abide by a strict schedule of placing drops of medicine into his eyes at various intervals during the day.

Visits from Rob and Madge were less frequent as the Methodist Church Conference had assigned Rob to a church in St. Paul, Virginia. Dean often received letters from Rob, and in his most recent correspondence, he revealed that he and Madge had adopted two boys: ten-year old Dennis, and Ronald, who was eight.

Since Alvin and Amber had moved to Tyler City, their visits to the home of Bobbie and Dean became more frequent. Al only worked when the mood struck him, and as result, many of his days were spent in spontaneous, carefree activities. Because of his love of the mountains and geology, he often stopped working in the middle of the job, heading for the Smokies to dig for semi-precious stones. On other occasions, he and Amber would unexpectedly show up at Dean's house to have dinner and spend the night. Such surprise visits caught Bobbie off-guard in her dinner preparation, but because of her fondness for them, she never complained. They usually arrived at Dean's home in the afternoon when no one was there. On certain days when Vince and Deana got off the school bus, Uncle Al's truck was parked in the driveway. They would eagerly run to the house, because they dearly loved Uncle Alvin.

Because of Al's affinity for children, he often played games with them. His nature was similar to that of a child's—playful and uninhibited. When Deana and Vince thought of Uncle Al, they brightened at the prospect of spending time with him. Part of Al's playful nature included childish pranks, some of which were downright silly, and others that were destructive in nature and could have landed him in jail. It was the behavior of the latter that proved to be a bad influence on Vince. Sometimes Vince would go along to help him work. Once out of sight of the house, with Amber driving the vehicle, Al stood in the back of the truck with Vince and taught him the skill of good marksmanship. From the bed of the truck, with dozens of empty soda bottles as a cache of ammunition, Al and Vince would hurl their streaking missiles at highway signs, with Alvin usually scoring a direct hit.

On a straight stretch of highway, in order to avoid a stray cat, Amber swerved the vehicle—a maneuver that caused Alvin to miss his target.

"Damn it, Amber!" he angrily screamed, "Can't you drive any better than that? Damn, another bottle wasted!"

It was an unusual form of recreation for a man in his late forties. The discretion of Vince spelled good fortune for Al since Vince never tattled to his parents. It was many years before Dean and Bobbie learned of the childish capers.

On a late afternoon summer day, Dean arrived home from work. As he approached his driveway, he noticed Alvin's truck parked at the curb. He smiled because the mere presence of Al always lifted his spirits. His brother's visit was unexpected—as usual. Dean parked his vehicle behind Bobbie's car and went inside.

In the large den, Will sat erectly in his favorite chair in front of the television set, absorbed in the six o'clock evening news. Since the Vietnam War was going badly, he was in a sour mood. Alvin, Deana, and Vince sat casually on the floor. With contracted knees and crossed legs, they sat in a circle, surrounding the *Monopoly* game.

After greeting everyone, Dean removed his tie and smiled at Alvin.

"How's it going, Al? Where's Amber?"

"She's visiting her mother in Kingston."

"Staying for supper?"

"Well…if you'll have me."

"Good," replied Dean.

Dean walked into the kitchen where Bobbie was preparing dinner. He greeted her with a hug.

"How was work? Are you tired?" Dean asked.

"Not too tired," she answered, "Working as a secretary has its good days and bad days. Today was a good day."

"Better set an extra place at the table. Al's staying for dinner." Bobbie laughed, "Well, that's unusual…! By the way, I have a softball game tonight for the church league at 7:30. I'll have to be through with dinner quickly."

After dressing in more comfortable clothing, Dean returned to the den, waiting for Bobbie to call the family to dinner. He sat on the couch and began to read the newspaper. As he relaxed, he was distracted from his reading by the spirited activity of the *Monopoly* game in progress on the floor. Alvin took the game seriously. His goal was always the same: Win!

"You cheated!" Al said to Deana, "You only rolled a six on the dice, and you moved seven spaces!"

"No, I didn't!" protested Deana, "I only moved six spaces! Now, I'm on Boardwalk."

In order to satisfy Al, she recounted the spaces for him. Al was beginning to become frustrated.

When Vince took his turn, his careless toss of the dice knocked Al's hotels from the board.

"Jesus!" Al whispered, then loudly he said, "Vince, watch what you're doing! Now I don't know where these hotels were!"

The heated activity and Al's bellowing voice hindered Will's ability to hear the news. He glared at Al, but said nothing. Fascinated by the spirited commotion, Dean laid aside his paper and intently watched the game.

Al rolled an eight, a number that placed his game piece on property owned by Vince.

"You owe me $200 dollars," gloated Vince, jubilantly, "Pay up!"

In order to stay in good favor with Vince, Al smiled at him. "Vince, old buddy, how about waiting to collect off me. On my next roll of the dice, I'll pass 'Go' and collect a bunch of money…I'll pay you then."

"I can't do it, Al," protested Vince, "You already owe me $300 dollars."

"Come on, Vince," Al pleaded, "I promise I'll pay you on my next roll."

"But you already owe me! That's just not good business!"

Alvin exploded with anger.

"Are you so blasted tight that you can't give me credit?" he shouted. Will again glared at Al. Slowly, he stood and increased the volume on the television set.

"Dean, Al's being a poor sport again," he announced.

His father's accusation angered Al even more. Suddenly, he turned the *Monopoly* board upside down, scattering pieces around the floor.

"That's it! I quit!" He looked to Vince, "Deana cheats and you're so danged stingy with your money that it takes all the fun out of the game. You're both just big babies! I'll never play *Monopoly* with you again."

"Dinner's ready," called Bobbie, from the kitchen.

Bobbie placed a pan of corn bread and a large bowl of steaming beef stew on the table, as the family claimed their customary seats. As usual, Alvin sat between Deana and Vince. Having no children of his own, Al had developed a special love for them, almost as if they were his own children. He even had a pet name for Vince, often calling him "The Feller."

After filling his plate with beef stew, Al said, "Pass the corn bread, please." Because of the presence of food and the fellowship at the dinner table, he had recaptured his good humor.

For a while, they ate in silence. Then, Al smiled at Vince.

"Did anything new happen lately, Feller?" asked Al, as he dished up a second helping of stew.

"Well, Queenie bit Barney Headrick on the butt yesterday," answered Vince. "It brought the blood, and I'm glad too, because he's been mean to Deana!"

Al erupted with a cackling laugh. "Do you mean she bit that little pest that lives up the street? That's the best news I've heard in days!"

Dean frowned. "If that collie of yours is going to start biting people, Deana, we'll have to keep her tied up when other kids are playing in our yard."

Will spoke up. "I saw what happened, and Queenie didn't really know any better. Deana and Vince were playing football with a bunch of kids, and Barney Headrick tackled Deana. Queenie thought that he was hurting her. That's a good trait in a dog...protecting those they love."

"I think it's a good trait for Queenie to bite that little punk even if she's not protecting Deana," said Al, "I'd like to sic her onto him."

When dinner was finished, Deana helped her mother clean the dishes from the table.

Will's eyes lit up as he ogled the home-baked apple pie that Bobbie placed in the center of the table. "Now that's more like it, Bobbie," he said with an elaborate grin.

She smiled back at Will. "I knew that it was your favorite when I baked it, Papaw."

"You must be trying to get on my good side," said Will, "What did I do to deserve this treat?"

"You'd better cut yourself a piece first, Papaw," cautioned Dean, "Before Al gets his paws on it."

Except for Alvin, everyone laughed.

As they feasted on the pie, Al looked at Deana and smiled, "I brought you and the Little Feller a present." From his shirt pocket, he fished out a couple of semi-precious gem stones that he had polished. "I dug these up over at Fontana Village."

"Thanks, Al," said Deana, as she held the translucent stone up toward the light, peering at it.

"Wow, that's pretty, Al" exclaimed Vince. He breathed on his stone, then polished it against the leg of his pants.

"Let's play some more *Monopoly!*" suggested Alvin.

"I'm kinda tired of *Monopoly,*" replied Deana.

"Then how about some *Crazy Eight?*" asked Al, with excitement. "I'm going to Jill Grayson's house, and Vince promised Chris Jackson he'd go to his birthday party," explained Deana, "But maybe we can play some when we get back." Al appeared disappointed, but answered, "Okay—we'll play some other time."

After dinner, Bobbie dressed for her softball game while Will took his newspaper out to the deck under the shade trees. With Deana and Vince gone, Dean and Al had the air conditioned den to themselves.

Dean claimed the couch facing the empty fireplace, while his brother stood in front of him, rolling a homemade cigarette. Al was dressed in his customary dark blue, cotton clothing; both his short-sleeved shirt and his trousers were identical in color, giving his attire the appearance of a work uniform. As he eyed his brother, Dean figured that Al must own several sets of duplicate outfits, for he had seldom seen him wearing anything different.

Al struck a match on the fireplace bricks and lit his cigarette while resting his right foot on the hearth.

"Stay all night with us, Al," invited Dean, "I think the kids will be home early if you want to play some more games with them."

"I can't tonight Dean. Amber is expecting me to come home. But we'll both come over tomorrow night—maybe for supper and to stay all night."

Dean smiled, knowing that Al's plans could change in an instant. Al puffed on his cigarette as he claimed a seat in Will's favorite chair.

"How's your job going, Dean?"

"Okay, I guess. But lately, I'm getting a little restless. I'm thinking seriously of going back to school."

"And quit your job?"

"No, I couldn't afford to do that. Anyway, I like my job, okay. I can go to school at night and take some correspondent courses."

"Where would you go to school...the *University of Tennessee?*

"Yeah, I could take some classes there and work too. My job's pretty close to U.T."

"You've already been to art school. Why do you feel that you have to go back to school?" queried Al, as he tossed his unfinished cigarette into the fireplace.

"I don't feel like I have to go back. Art school was great, Al…I learned a lot about art and about life, too. But what I learned about life just whetted my appetite to learn more. Art school is focused on art. I'd like to get a more well-rounded education…history, philosophy, science…and especially literature. I might want to write someday."

"Well, you better make up your mind because you're not getting any younger," said Al.

Alvin pulled the sack of *Buffalo* tobacco from his shirt pocket, rolled another cigarette, then after striking a match on the leg of his pants, lit up. For a long while, he pondered as he smoked.

"You know, Dean, I wish I had gone to college when I was young…But back in those days, most people didn't go to college as much. When a fellow graduated high school that was it…unless he was going to be a doctor or lawyer— or a teacher, maybe."

"Yeah, I messed up my first chance, way back when I was 20 years old." Dean remarked, sadly.

Al removed the cigarette from his mouth and spat a grain of tobacco, then continued to smoke. He became silent, in deep thought. Finally, he said, "Maybe…Maybe, I could still go to college."

With the realization that his brother had always been a dreamer, Dean assumed that it was only a passing thought of Al's.

"I know I'm getting a little age on me, but why couldn't I go back to school? Rob did it. Do you think I could still go back?" asked Alvin.

It saddened Dean to think that Al had never been able to realize his potential. Of the five brothers, Alvin and Elwood were the ones most suited for college; ironically, they were the two who had never attended.

"Al, I know that you're smart enough, but man, it takes a lot of self-discipline. Especially if you're working while you go to school." Dean realized that Alvin was short on self-discipline as well as steadfastness.

"Are you sure you're going back?" asked Al.

"Yeah…I'm pretty sure. I'm going to check on it next week and get my transcript from art school sent to them."

Al got up from his chair and crushed his cigarette in the ash tray. He walked back to his previous spot in front of the fireplace, and replaced his foot on the mantel. Then he turned to Dean and spoke.

"Do you know what I'd like to do? I'd like to go to college and get a degree in education. I'd really like to teach!"

"Well, just like you said to me, you'd better make up your mind because you're not getting any younger." Dean smiled at him.

Al remarked, "All of us brothers are late-bloomers...even Dad didn't find his sense of direction until he was in his thirties."

Placing his hands on his hips, Alvin began to pace the floor. With the thought of attending college, he was becoming animated.

"Dean, I'd like to teach English and literature. Maybe in high school. I guess you know that I've always loved poetry...I love any kind of literature. You said you might take up writing...Well, I'd like to do the same. It must run in the family. Have you read some of the stuff that Dad writes? His grammar is not perfect, but the content of what he writes is great! He has a strong opinion and a great ability to put his feelings in writing."

"Yeah, he does. I've been trying to get Dad to write a column in the local paper," said Dean.

"I've made up my mind!" exclaimed Al. "I'm going to college. I'll tell Amber tonight!"

Dean knew that Al was serious; still he wondered about the duration of his brother's resolve.

*   *   *

In late August, after Dean had his transcript of grades sent to U.T., he reported to the admissions office. To his surprise, the office of admissions at first refused his entrance. He was told that, although he had graduated from art school with honors, his grades from that school were not admissible because the institute was not accredited in the state of Tennessee. Instead, they only considered his academic performance from *Southern Wesleyan,* where he had flunked out, many years before. Once again, his past mistakes had come back to haunt him.

After an elaborate persuasion and many promises, he was finally admitted to the university on the condition that he maintain a grade point average of not less than a 3.0. Indirectly, his outstanding record in art school helped him in getting admitted, for it indicated that an attitude change had taken place in him.

In September, Dean enrolled in the liberal arts program, majoring in fine arts, with a strong emphasis in graphic design. Since his completed courses in art school were not transferable, he had to begin his college career as a freshman; furthermore, his fine arts curriculum required the repetition of some of the same basic courses he had already taken in art school.

His job at the advertising agency was demanding; as a result, he was only carrying a half-load of courses in evening school. As he began his first class, he made an estimate of the number of years until he graduated; if he attended school on a year-around basis, he could possibly finish in six years. With steadfast resolve, he embarked on the arduous journey.

Arguably, no artist grows up: If he sheds the perceptions of child-hood, he ceases being an artist. **Ned Rorem**

Chapter 32

It was after 11:00 P.M. when Dean arrived home. His day at the ad agency had been grueling, requiring that he stay late to complete an urgent job. With no time for dinner, he had hurriedly driven to class, arriving late. After a four hour class in geology, he wearily drove home, dreading the additional two hours of study awaiting him before retiring to bed. Exhausted from the hectic activity of the day, he considered the years ahead of him that would require this frantic pace; nonetheless, he continued to maintain his unwavering resolve.

The pleasant aroma of burning logs enhanced the chill October evening as Dean slowly stepped from his car. As he made his way into the den, he noticed Alvin, clad in his usual blue uniform, sitting on the hearth with his back to the shimmering coals in the fireplace.

The remainder of the family had already gone to bed, and apparently Al was waiting up for Dean. The hour wasn't late for Alvin, for he didn't live his life by the clock.

"How's it going, Al?" greeted Dean.

"Ah, pretty good. Amber and I came to stay the night. She's already asleep in the spare bedroom. I was waiting up to talk to you."

Dean tossed his books on the couch, then removed his jacket, draping it across the back of the easy chair.

"What's on your mind?" asked Dean.

"I enrolled at U.T. today, for the winter quarter…in evening school."

"Great, Al!"

"Amber's mother thinks I'm crazy."

"You don't care what she thinks, do you?" asked Dean.

"No…I don't care what she thinks as long as she doesn't poison Amber's attitude about it. Her mother says that a man is born to work, not to play school."

Alvin left his seat at the hearth and claimed the easy chair as Dean took a seat on the couch.

"I'm excited for you, Al."

"Yeah, well…I just hope I can swing it financially."

"I'll help you any way I can, Al. I'm proud of you for enrolling, but I feel I should warn you…It's tough to go to school and hold a full-time job."

Noticing the dying embers of the fire, Dean strode to the fireplace and removed the screen, then tossed another log onto the glowing coals. As he jiggled the log with the poker, the fire rekindled, responding with resounding pops and flying sparks. He replaced the screen and remained in front of the fireplace warming his extended hands. He then turned to face his brother.

"What are you going to major in?"

"Education, I guess."

"You need to talk to an advisor, Al." Dean returned to his seat on the couch.

Alvin was excited. He got up and began to pace the floor. "Dean, did you have any problem with getting back into the routine of studying?"

"Well, a little, at first," answered Dean, "There are a lot of distractions…But you just have to learn to shut them out of your mind. I do my best studying late at night, here in the den, after everyone else is in bed."

"Studying is going to be a problem for me. Over at my house, there's always some kind of distraction…some nuisance. Amber's brothers are always hanging around. And Amber's mother hates the idea of my going to college. She'll do anything to disrupt my study."

"Then, you'll need to have a special place where you can have some privacy," answered Dean.

Alvin resumed his pacing. "Dean, if it's okay with you and Bobbie, maybe I could do some of my studying here, at your house."

"Al, you know you and Amber are always welcome…anytime."

Al took a seat in Will's easy chair and lit a hand-made cigarette.

"Are you hungry?" asked Dean, "I've got to eat a sandwich—I haven't had anything to eat since lunch."

"Yeah, I could eat a sandwich."

As Dean left for the kitchen, Al threw another log on the fire. He then

334

returned to his seat and excitedly studied his class schedule.

Dean returned with a tray containing three ham and cheese sandwiches and two glasses of milk. He placed the tray on the coffee table and selected a sandwich.

"Help yourself, Al," he invited, as he swallowed a sip of milk. "I made you an extra sandwich." Dean was aware of his brother's hearty appetite.

"Thanks, Dean."

The brothers sat in silence, chewing on their food. The light in the room was limited to the flames of the fire. Dean switched on the corner lamp.

"Al, I've got to hit the books for a couple of hours. Help yourself to something else to eat, if you want. Anyway, I'll need a little privacy so that I can study."

"No problem. I understand. I'm going to bed, anyway...Goodnight."

"Goodnight, Al."

As Alvin walked from the room, Dean called to him, "Al...Don't let anyone discourage you in what you've set out to do. Come to my house anytime you want. We can study together. Maybe we can help each other. By the way, I'm proud of you."

Dean feared that Al's college experience would be short-lived, in view of his vacillating nature. To Dean's surprise, however, his brother's determination grew stronger as his enthusiasm caught fire. The adventure of attending college had become his obsession, and his personality became more animated. Attending college was now his mission in life, and literature his passion.

As the months passed, the brothers spent endless hours studying together at Dean's house. Sometimes he brought Amber, but mostly, Al was alone in his visits. He practically became a member of Dean's family, as he and Amber often ate and slept in his brother's home. His frequent presence instilled a strong bond between Alvin and the children, with Deana and Vince growing more fond of him and looking forward to his visits.

Just before Christmas of the following year, East Tennessee experienced its first big snowfall. It was the kind of fluffy snow that clung to tree branches and covered the area like a thick, downy blanket. Although Deana and Vince were growing up, the Beauvais family carried on the same yuletide traditions as they did when the children were small. Sentimental, and set in their ways, Deana and Vince insisted on adhering to the identical ritual of past Christmases: Going together to select the perfect tree, which the entire family elaborately decorated; listening to their father tell bedtime Christmas stories, and opening only one gift each Christmas Eve night, saving the remainder for Christmas morning.

Another tradition in the family, which happened throughout the year, was joyously anticipating Uncle Alvin and Aunt Amber's "unexpected" visits. Getting off the school bus on cold, winter days and seeing smoke drifting from the chimney meant only one thing...Uncle Alvin was home! Uncle Alvin and Aunt Amber enjoyed participating in the Beauvais Christmas festivities, and they were always there for Bobbie's Christmas dinner. When the children were small, Alvin was genuinely interested in what Santa had brought them. He would enthusiastically glance around at the toys until he spotted a plaything or a game of interest. Then the action would start.

"Hey, Deana...Vince! Break out that game called *Sorry.*" Then Al would play games with the children for the remainder of the Christmas morning.

Apathetic in regard to Christmas shopping, Alvin always gave money to the children. He would take it out of his wallet and hand it to them just as he would have done on any other day, but they knew that it was a big part of his Christmas. Having no children of their own, Alvin and Amber vicariously enjoyed the holidays through their intimate attachment to Deana and Vince.

Although Christmas was only a week away, because of Dean's hectic schedule, the Beauvais family hadn't yet put up their tree. Filled with the spirit of Christmas, Deana and Vince became anxious and began pressuring their father about it.

"We'll all go, first thing in the morning," promised Dean, "We'll pick out the prettiest short-needle pine on the lot."

The next morning while they were preparing to leave, the back door opened and in walked Uncle Al and Aunt Amber. In their usual manner, Amber sat down on the couch and Alvin walked to the fireplace, placed one foot on the hearth, and rocked back and forth with his arm resting on his knee. His eyes sparkled with excitement.

"I've got a surprise in the truck," remarked Al. Deana and Vince became animated.

"What is it?" asked Vince, "Go get it!"

When Al returned, his arms were hugging a big Christmas tree. As Deana and Vince examined the tree, they noticed that it was quite unique in appearance. It was a tall, thin—really thin—cedar tree. Alvin looked at Bobbie. "Where do you want it, Bobbie?" He displayed a proud grin.

Deana's heart sank, for decorating a beautiful tree had always been one of their most important traditions of Christmas.

Dean secretly winked at his daughter. Expressing disappointment, Deana blurted out, "We usually get the other kind of Christmas tree." Al's beaming smile disappeared. "Oh," he said.

Although Deana was disappointed, she suddenly felt sorry for Al. In an attempt to cheer him up, she said, "I really do like this one, though." Al's smile quickly returned.

Reluctantly, Bobbie helped Alvin place the tree in the stand as Deana and Vince retreated to the bedroom.

"I wonder where he got that tree," asked Vince, "It's kinda ugly, isn't it?"

"It's too skinny," Deana added, "How will we put decorations on it?" When they returned to the den, their Uncle Alvin was still glowing with pride. He walked back to his spot by the fireplace and hiked his foot to the hearth. Deana and Vince watched him as he proudly admired his pick of the crop. It was then that Deana noticed the heady, cedar aroma that saturated the room.

Will walked into the room and instantly noticed the tree. "Kinda scraggly, ain't it?" he asked.

"It'll look great when we finish decorating it," said Dean, "Al brought it for us. Isn't it pretty?" Dean winked at his father.

Will joined the others as the entire family began to place decorations on the tree.

As he worked, Al beamed with excitement.

"It needs something on this side," he commented, with the proud awareness that this was his tree...his sentimental gift to the Beauvais family.

As the days passed, the house became permeated with the fragrant aroma of the fresh cedar tree, a smell that the Beauvais family, forever after, associated with Christmas. As a result, Al's Christmas tree initiated a new tradition within the family: A cedar tree became the official symbol of future Christmases.

Christmas Eve finally arrived. In the evening, in keeping with their tradition, the family exchanged one gift each. Since his children had outgrown Santa Claus, Dean's annual Christmas Eve bedtime stories had evolved from tales of Santa and his elves into stories of a more mature, but often silly nature. Shortly before bedtime, Al and Amber joined the family in the den for the story-telling session. In the darkened room, only the glowing coals of the fireplace and the multi-colored tree lights offered illumination, giving the shadowy den the eerie glowing atmosphere of Christmas. On the tree, each big light tucked inside the branches left a beautiful warm glow of its own color, filling the family with nostalgia of long-ago Christmases.

Most of Dean's Christmas stories were spontaneous tales in which he originated the plot as he told the story; others were repeated nonsensical tales that he had related to them on past Christmases. The Beauvais family never grew weary of the rehashed fables, for it reinforced the family tradition.

Grinning at her father, Deana made the request: "Tell that funny story you told last year, Dad!"

"Which one is that?" asked Dean.

"That story about how Uncle Fred tried to shoot Santa Claus!" The family responded with joyful laughter.

"Poor Uncle Fred," commented Will.

"I want you to tell the one about how Uncle Fred tried to stab Santa with a knife!" exclaimed Vince, as the family again laughed.

"That's getting a little bit bloodthirsty, Vince," lectured Will.

Alvin erupted with uproarious laughter.

As Dean told ridiculous stories with foolish conclusions, the darkened room was filled with happy laughter, with Alvin's high pitched cackle reverberating louder than the others. Dean's nonsensical stories were followed by Will's tales of adventure, describing his youthful years as a hobo and his long-ago adventures on the carnival. In the darkened room, a feeling of family closeness, a spirituality blossomed in their souls as the embers slowly dimmed and the howling wind outside thickened the blanket of snow.

The family sat in silence, enjoying the rare feeling of intimacy that engulfed them, entranced by the dying fire and the tree lights in the twilight atmosphere of the room. The falling snow and the shared spirit of Christmas enhanced the mysterious and magical night. Finally, after wishing each other a Merry Christmas, the family retired to bed, with Al and Amber claiming the spare bedroom.

On Christmas morning, the family awoke to a winter wonderland. The glistening blanket of snow was at least a foot deep, covering every blemish of the land with an unspoiled mantle of fluffy purity.

Still clad in pajamas, Deana, Vince, and Uncle Al hurried to the tree in the den in eager anticipation of opening the gifts. As they waited for the remainder of the family to join them, Al anxiously paced the floor. Finally, when all the family had gathered around the tree, Al smiled at

Deana and Vince. For the first time, instead of giving them money, Al had bought gifts for them. As he handed them their presents, his eyes revealed his excitement. Al had bought each of them an expensive, leather-bound copy of their favorite fairy tale: *Sleeping Beauty* for Deana, and for Vince, *The Emperor's New Clothes*. After receiving their gifts, they each hugged him and gave him his presents from them: A new shirt, and the classic novel, *The Grapes of Wrath.*

The adults exchanged gifts and then retreated to the kitchen for breakfast.

"We'll eat later," announced Al, "We're going outside to build a snowman." Al, Deana, and Vince, bundled in heavy coats, pulled toboggan caps over their ears, and hurried outside through the sliding door of the dining room.

After Will and Dean finished their breakfast, they moved to the glass door to watch the outside activity. Before the snowman was completed, Deana and Vince began to vigorously pelt Alvin with snowballs. Al's retaliation was swift, and soon a full-scale war had broken out between the three. Dean and his father broke into laughter as they watched the melee.

"Bobbie, Amber…Come in here, you need to see this," called Dean to the women, as they tidied up the kitchen. With aroused interest, Bobbie and Amber came into the dining room and peered through the glass door.

Will chuckled. "You know, Alvin is a bigger kid than Deana and Vince…Look at him! He's having a better time than either of them!"

Amber laughed. "Al really loves your kids, Bobbie. He feels almost like they're his children." She smiled as she watched Al ward off a barrage of snowballs from both Vince and Deana.

The women laughed, then returned to their chores in the kitchen. As Will intently watched the raging battle, he turned to his son.

"Dean, I know that Alvin loves your kids, but sometimes I think he might be a bad influence on them…especially Vince."

"Oh, I don't think so, Dad. They know to do the right thing. How do you think he is a bad influence?"

"Well, for one thing, sometimes when he comes here, he's had a few beers. Sometimes he's kinda high."

"I don't think you'll see much of that now, Dad…now that he's going to college. He's really a new man. I've never seen him so passionate about anything before."

Will chuckled, "You know, Dean, that snowman makes me think of

339

that time that you and Rob rolled up that big snowball on top of the shop roof, and you were going to let it drop onto Al's head as he walked out of the building."

Dean smiled. "We abandoned that plan…and it's a good thing we did! That snowball was about four feet in diameter, and must have weighed three or four hundred pounds. I don't think we realized how that big thing could have killed him. It seems that we picked on Al a lot back then."

The snowball fight had ended; evidently, Al had called a truce to the activity. Vigorously rubbing their hands together, the three combatants hurried to the door in preparation of re-entering the house. Bobbie opened the sliding door, and as they rushed into the house, the wintry air invaded the room.

"You kids wipe your feet…Don't track snow all over my new carpet!"

"We kids?" retorted Al, resentfully.

"You too, Alvin," Bobbie corrected herself.

Without responding, Al cleaned his feet, then re-entered the house, pouting. His mood quickly changed, however, when Bobbie rewarded him with his favorite dessert—Snow Cream!

Later that night, without any warning, Al and Amber said their good-byes. After installing chains on his tires, he and Amber drove away to his favorite place…the Smoky Mountains. Deana and Vince soon forgot what was under the tree that year, but they never forgot the wonderful tree and the way that Uncle Al's spirit warmed Christmas.

*   *   *

When the holidays were over, both Al and Dean began their winter quarter at the university. Attending school while working full-time was a rigorous way of life for Dean, but Al's schedule was less demanding. A free spirit with few financial obligations, Al only worked occasionally. Since Amber held a full-time job, Alvin was able to pursue his education while engaging in his hobby of hunting rocks in the Smoky Mountains. Because of this carefree lifestyle, Alvin had ample time to attend college on a full-time basis; even so, he only wanted to keep pace with Dean in order for them to graduate together.

Although they majored in different fields of study, whenever practical, they scheduled evening classes together. On nights when their classes were separated, they usually met for dinner at a restaurant near the school. On many evenings, they studied together at the library, and often during the day when not in class, Al studied at Dean's house.

In their junior year, they attended an English class together. Requirements of the course included both the study of great literature and an abundance of writing assignments. It was while attending this class with Alvin that Dean began to recognize the full extent of Al's sensitivity. When given a writing assignment, Dean usually submitted short stories of everyday occurrences; however, Al almost invariably wrote poetry, some of which Dean found exceptionally moving. Dean had always felt that, hidden beneath his rough exterior, Al had a gentle, perceptive side; but not until Dean read his poetry did he fully realize how inaccurately his brother's sensibilities had been judged. Dean began to recognize in Al some of the same compassionate qualities of Elwood and his mother.

The six years in which the brothers attended school together wrought many changes in the country as well as within the Beauvais family: Man walked on the moon, the Vietnam War ended, and the Watergate scandal resulted in the resignation of President Richard M. Nixon, an event that thrust the nation into even more trauma.

Deana and Vince were now in their teens, and although Will's glaucoma had worsened, he had become even more active in his painting and writing. His humorous column in the local newspaper had begun to contain undertones of protest, stirring mixed sentiments in local residents. In his personal life, Will had become more trusting in his relationships with Bobbie, and had begun to develop a strong bond with his grandchildren, particularly Vince.

During his senior year, despite his heavy load, Dean accepted a temporary teaching position at the university in which he taught design courses in evening school. Dean and Al continued to study and attend classes together.

Al's mother-in-law habitually cast aspersions on his efforts to continue his education. In her efforts to dampen his spirits, she often ridiculed him. Instead of discouraging him, her disdain of his ambitions only reinforced his resolve, for it presented a challenge, creating a goal to which he became stubbornly dedicated.

At last, the brothers reached the threshold of graduation, a ceremony that they had vowed to experience together. As the time approached, however, Dean became reluctant to participate in the formal functions of the graduation ceremony.

"Al, why go through with all the formality of renting a cap and gown and standing in line to receive our diploma? We'll still have our degrees…What difference does it make?"

"It makes a lot of difference, Dean. I worked my ass off for that diploma, and I'm proud of it. Hell, I'm 50 years old now, and this will be the greatest achievement of my life. And the same goes for you."

A few nights before graduation, Dean was in his den studying for his one remaining final examination. He desperately wanted to make an "A" in his last Spanish course. As he was in deep concentration, Al jauntily strolled through the door into the den. He was in a giddy, garrulous mood as he greeted Dean.

"Hey, Dean." He walked to his favorite spot in front of the fireplace. After placing his right foot on the hearth, he lit a cigarette and turned to face Dean.

"Well, we're finally graduating next week, old pal," Al flashed a happy grin. "I have a few more finals to take, and then I'll be all finished." He was bursting with pride.

"Well, you'd better study for those exams, Al. That's what I'm doing right now. I'm trying to study for my final exam in Spanish," Dean firmly hinted.

Al was beside himself with excitement. "I'm going to study all weekend. Amber and I are going over to Fontana Village where it's quiet. Nobody will bother me there."

Bobbie and Will came into the den, and Alvin immediately began an excited monologue, discussing his upcoming graduation. Turning to face Dean, Al continued his to talk.

"You know, Dean, I'm gonna kind of miss school…You and I in the same classes and studying together. Remember how hard it used to be to find a place where we could study without some kind of disturbance?"

"Yeah, I remember," answered Dean, "Kinda like I'm trying to study now," Dean hoped Al would finally take the hint.

Engrossed in his enthusiasm, Al was oblivious to his brother's allusion. He became even more animated, as he began to pace the room. With child-like exuberance, he began to skip as he paced, a gesture that brought laughter to Bobbie and Will.

Unnoticed by Al, Dean resentfully gathered his notes, and without a word, retreated to his bedroom to continue studying, feeling a trace of guilt for snubbing his brother.

After poring over his notes for an hour, Dean closed his book and returned to the den where Will and Bobbie were watching television.

"Where's Al?" Dean inquired.

"He left about 15 minutes ago. He went to get Amber. They're going to Fontana Village," replied Bobbie.

"You know, I feel a little guilty walking out of the room and ignoring Al. He was just happy and excited…But when he gets into one of his playful moods, you just can't study around him. And this final exam is very important to me."

"Oh, he wasn't offended," answered Bobbie.

While Dean was lying in bed that night, he felt a rush of happiness about his accomplishments. At the age of 43, he had completed college! He also felt joyous for Alvin, who at the age of 50, was graduating with him. He was proud of his brother. He smiled as he said goodnight to Bobbie, then he drifted into a peaceful sleep.

*   *   *

The persistent ringing of the telephone awakened Dean. From habit, he glanced at the ticking clock on the nightstand…*3:28*, he noted. Who would be calling at this hour? He thought of Rob and Madge and hoped nothing bad had happened. As he picked up the phone, the tangled cord raked the clock to the floor.

"Hello."

"Hello…Is this Dean Beauvais?"

"Yes sir, it is."

"Do you have a brother named Alvin Beauvais?"

"Yes sir, I do…Why? Has something happened?"

"Mr. Beauvais, my name is Neil Wilson. I'm the security officer at Fontana Village Resort in North Carolina…Mr. Beauvais…I'm awfully sorry to tell you this…but your brother passed away about an hour ago. He was in one of our vacation cabins. He seems to have had a heart attack. I'm awfully sorry, sir."

The telephone fell from Dean's hand as he stared ahead into the darkness of the room.

You must take personal responsibility. You cannot change the circumstances, the seasons, or the wind, but you can change yourself. That is something you have charge of. **Jim Rohn**

Chapter 33

Alvin's death devastated the Beauvais family. The unexpected event was underscored by its cruelty, for it struck at the happiest moment in Al's life. Because of their special affection for him, Deana and Vince were particularly grief-stricken since many of their playful childhood memories included their Uncle Al.

Although Dean was deeply saddened by the sudden death of his brother, he no longer harbored the feelings of bitterness he had experienced following Elwood's death. He had blamed God for the past tragedies in his life, but the lessons of life had instilled in him a revelation that dawned on him with a profound clarity: With God's priceless gift of man's free choice comes the obligation of responsibility. Dean realized that all men are bound by natural laws, many of which are crucial to survival. He knew that Al had lived his life in defiance of these laws by neglecting his health, for he was a heavy smoker, never exercised, and had seldom visited a doctor. His death was not a punishment for disobedience, but a consequence of his neglect. If God spared even one irresponsible person from death, where would his intervention end? Such an act would render man's behavior irrelevant.

Alvin had died of a massive heart attack, a myocardial infarction, as the coroner referred to the mishap. According to the family doctor, Al had probably suffered little pain since the event occurred during his sleep. Death was instantaneous; however, having knowledge of the facts did nothing to lessen everyone's grief.

Before Al's funeral, in his effort to locate Clay, Dean had made several phone calls, one of which finally revealed his whereabouts. One of

344

Ellen's brothers who lived in Atlanta finally released Clay's St. Petersburg, Florida phone number. Upon receiving Dean's call, he promised to catch the next plane to Knoxville.

Characteristic of his pattern of misfortune, Clay arrived too late to attend the funeral, only making his appearance at the Beauvais home a full day after the burial. Flying in from Tampa, his plane had encountered severe thunderstorms in the Knoxville area; as a result, his flight had been redirected to Cincinnati where he had endured a layover of several hours. Finally, he had managed to board a plane that experienced engine trouble before takeoff, forcing the pilot to abort the flight. After another lengthy wait, he eventually had managed to catch a flight home. To compound the ordeal, the airlines had lost his luggage.

At 8:55 a.m., Dean picked up his brother at *McGhee-Tyson Airport*, and after exchanged greetings, Dean swung the car onto Alcoa Highway, and they began the hour's drive home toward Tyler City. Although he hadn't seen Clay in years, Dean noticed that other than a weight gain of about 15 pounds, his brother's appearance had scarcely changed. Dean had feared that their initial meeting would be awkward, but soon found himself completely at ease in their reunion. He was relieved when he discovered that Clay's congenial personality had remained intact.

"Man, this flight has been hell, Dean," he complained, "After I called you from Cincinnati, I had to wait several more hours to get a plane. Now, since they lost my luggage, I won't even have a change of clothes while I'm at your house."

"I may have something you can wear, Clay."

"Hell, I'm too fat to wear your clothes, Dean." The brothers laughed. Clay lit a cigarette, deeply inhaling the smoke.

"God, I sure hated to hear the news about Al," he said, "And, didn't you say that he was about to graduate from U.T.?"

"Yeah…We were going to graduate together. He was happier than I've ever seen him." Dean face expressed sadness.

"When do you graduate?" asked Clay.

"Next week. I wish you could come."

"I wish I could, too, but I have to go back in a couple of days. Speaking of college, I graduated from the *University of Tampa* last year," said Clay.

"Really? That's great, Clay! What did you major in?"

"Marketing."

"I thought if you ever went to college, you might major in art."

Clay remarked, "I love art…and I still paint, but I had to major in something that will help me make a living."

"What are you doing for a living?" asked Dean.

"I'm creative director for the company I work for," answered Clay.

"Are you serious? Me too! I'm creative director at the company where I work, too."

With a desire to keep their conversation pleasant, the brothers shared a mutual reluctance to elaborate on Al's death. They also postponed any discussion of the former breach in the relationship of Clay and Will.

"How's Ellen…and Terry and Eldon?" asked Dean.

"Well, Ellen's working. We have three kids now…We also have Adam. He's eight years old."

"Wow! You have another boy? Congratulations!"

Clay continued. "Terry and Eldon are grown men now. They're both in college. How about Deana and Vince?"

"Deana will be starting college this fall, and Vince is a sophomore in high school."

"Is Vince still playing football?" asked Clay.

"Yeah…And he's a real good player, too."

"How's Bobbie? Is she working?"

"Yeah…She's a secretary at *Tyler Utility Company*. She has a good job."

Clay lit another cigarette and cracked his window. "How's Rob doing?"

"He's doing great. He and Madge moved to St. Paul, Virginia. He was assigned to a church there. Did you know that they adopted a couple of boys…? No, of course you didn't. We haven't communicated in years. Anyway, the boys—Dennis and Ronald—are in their teens now. Rob had to get back to work today, so they left early this morning. You just missed them."

"Gosh, I wish I could have seen them," replied Clay. "By the way, what about Bobbie's nephew, David Michaels? Did he make it through Vietnam okay?"

"Yeah, he's been back in Knoxville for several years now. He's going to college."

The brothers lapsed into silence as Dean drove the car into the southern suburbs of Knoxville. The only family member they had left out of their former discussion was their father. Finally, Clay cautiously broke the awkward intermission.

"How's Dad doing?" Clay cast a furtive glance at Dean.

"He's doing okay," answered Dean. "Al's death hit him pretty hard, but you know how Dad is. He'll bounce back. He's a survivor."

Again, the brothers became quiet as Dean turned left on Kingston Pike toward Tyler City. They were both hesitant in any continued discussion of the broken relationship between Clay and his father. Eventually, Clay spoke up.

"I guess you think it was pretty shitty of me to suddenly leave Tyler City the way I did and stay away for years without contacting the family. I imagine that it was especially hard for Dad...the way he was attached to Terry."

"Yeah, it was hard for Dad. The rest of the family missed you, too. Why didn't you write to me? You and I weren't mad at each other about anything." Dean struggled to maintain a non-judgmental tone in his voice.

"Well, when I left I was kinda pissed-off at everybody. I wasn't getting' along with Alvin, and I felt like I was in everyone's way, especially with you and Dad—and the shop. But I got over all those grievances, pretty fast. One reason I left with no forwarding address was the way that Dad had taken total control of Terry. You know how Dad is. He completely dominates everybody around him. I guess the main reason I left is because Dad tried to control my life. His dominating attitude completely takes your balls away from you! It was impossible to feel like a man when I lived close to him...and he really got his claws into you, too! How did you stand it?"

"Dad means well, Clay. His only crime is that he loves people too much. His fear of abandonment causes him to hug people too tightly so they won't desert him. He's sorta like a little kid who loves his puppy so much that he squeezes him so hard he kills it."

"But his influence over Terry got so extreme that I no longer had any control over my own son. Terry acted like Dad was his father, instead of me. I figured that I'd better get him away from Dad's control for a long time...until I could regain some kind of relationship with Terry."

"How many years does that take, Clay? If Al hadn't died...would you ever have contacted any of us? Would we have ever seen you or your family again?"

"Dean, I really meant to contact you before now. But after a couple of years, the time just kept sliding by, and, well... you know how we get settled into a certain life style. I just kept putting it off."

"Didn't you ever wonder about us...and how we were doing?" asked Dean.

"Many times, Dean. But you don't realize how deep my resentment of Dad was. He had no confidence in me. His words and actions were proof of that…to me and to everybody else. I really resented him. I forgive him now, but he took my balls and he almost destroyed my relationship with my own son. Terry and I are still not as close as we should be."

"Maybe you ought to make your peace with Dad while you're home," suggested Dean.

"I don't know… what's his attitude toward me?"

"Well, he was hurt for a long time. He desperately tried to find out where you went. He missed Terry a lot, but he missed you too…you and the rest of your family. Right now he's so sad about Al's death that it probably obscures any other feeling that he might have."

"I can imagine…poor Dad," said Clay sadly.

"Clay, our immediate family is dying off. Elwood, Mom…and now Al. We all need to forgive each other and forget past hurts. Life is too short for any of us to be alienated from our family."

"I'm not mad at anybody," declared Clay, "Maybe from now on, we can get together a few times a year. By the way, Dean, I've got to call Ellen pretty soon. What time is it?"

"It's 9:45. You can call her from my house if you want to. We're almost there." Dean looked at Clay's watchless wrist.

"When did you quit wearing a watch?"

Clay glanced at his left forearm, which had been bronzed by the Florida sun. The white band of skin encircling his left wrist bore evidence of the missing wrist watch.

"That's an interesting story," he replied. "You know how prone I am to having bad luck."

Dean laughed. "How could I forget?"

"Well, a couple of days ago, I was driving down a crowded freeway, and I was preparing to make a left turn, but when I switched on my turn signal, it didn't work. So I stuck my left arm out the window to give a hand signal. I guess I didn't have the leather band fastened too well, because my watch fell off my wrist and into the street."

"Yeah, that sounds like your luck." replied Dean.

"I stopped the car and ran back to pick it up, but before I got there, a motorcycle ran over it. There wasn't much left of it after that. Then, when I started to leave, my car wouldn't start. I had to walk about a mile before I could get to a phone."

Dean broke into laughter. Somehow, it comforted him to know that some things never change; Clay was the same brother that he had always known.

At last, Dean swung the car into the driveway of his home. Noting that the only other cars there belonged to Bobbie and Deana, he realized that sympathetic, visiting friends had gone, leaving the Beauvais family alone in their grief.

Dean held the door open for Clay as he walked into the den. Immediately, Deana ran to meet him. "Uncle Clay!" she exclaimed, as they embraced one another.

"Hi, Deana!" greeted Clay. He then pointed to Vince. "And who is that big guy over there? Vince, I can't belief it! You're a man, now."

"Hi, Uncle Clay," said Vince. He grinned as he walked up to Clay and shook his hand.

Bobbie entered the den. "Is that my long-lost brother-in-law?" she asked with a grin. After hugging him, Bobbie asked, "How was your flight?"

"It's a long story," he remarked.

"You really don't want to know," said Dean, sarcastically.

"How's Ellen...and the boys?"

"Ellen's fine and still working as hard as ever. Terry and Eldon are in college...And we have another boy now—Adam. He's eight years old."

"Oh, I can't believe it. That's great! Congratulations!" Bobbie continued. "We're so glad you came. I'm sorry you missed seeing Al. It's been so sad around here...and especially hard for Deana and Vince, since they were so close to him...and your poor dad..." Her conversation was smothered by a sob, as she began to softly weep.

Clay again hugged her. "I know, Bobbie...I'm sad too."

Embarrassed by her emotions, Bobbie retreated to the kitchen.

"Sit down, Clay...Make yourself comfortable," Dean invited. Clay claimed a seat next to Vince on the couch.

"What's Papaw doing?" Dean asked, as he slid into the recliner.

"He's asleep in his room," replied Deana. "He hasn't had much sleep since...since we heard about Uncle Al."

"Yeah, I can understand that," remarked Clay. His face mirrored his sadness.

The silence that followed was evidence of their reluctance to discuss Alvin; later, they would speak of him, but for now, it was too early. Clay quickly changed the subject. "Well, Vince, your dad tells me you're a sophomore now...and still playing football. You were always a good quarterback."

"Thanks, Uncle Clay. How are Terry and Eldon?"

"They're fine. They both like college."

Vince smiled. "Did I hear you say that I have a new cousin?"

"You sure do, kiddo. His name is Adam." Clay continued. "They all wanted to come, but we couldn't work it out this time."

"I really would like to see them." Vince continued. "Hey, Uncle Clay, Deana and I are going down to arrange the flowers on Uncle Al's grave. You're welcome to come with us if you want to."

"Thanks, but I'm not up to it right now. I'm going to go later."

"We'll be back in a little while...Bye, Mom," Deana and Vince shouted in the direction of the kitchen.

"Bye, kids," yelled Bobbie. "Deana, drive carefully."

After they had gone, Clay reclaimed his seat on the couch as Bobbie came into the room carrying a tray with two steaming cups of coffee. "I brought you guys some coffee." She placed the tray on the table. "I need to go out and water my flowers. Clay do you want me to get your suitcase out of the car while I'm out there?"

"No, thank you," replied Clay, "I don't have a suitcase. That's another long story."

"They lost it at the airport," said Dean.

As she left the room, Bobbie suppressed her laughter and only smiled.

Dean sipped on his coffee while Clay lit a cigarette.

"I wonder when Dad will wake up," said Clay, "I'll be glad to see him, but I kinda dread facing him. You know I really do love Dad, and I admire his guts and tenacity. He's much of a man. It's too bad he's so controlling. He's tried to control all of his sons...and even his grandchildren."

Before replying, Dean thought for a long while.

"Clay, I used to really resent Dad for having that trait, but now I'm beginning to understand him a little better since I'm a father."

Clay changed the subject. "Dean, both of your kids have grown up to be nice-looking people. That Deana's a knockout! She looks like both her dad and mom; she has Bobbie's pretty face and your dark hair and complexion. I noticed she's real outgoing like Bobbie, too."

"Yeah, we're real proud of her. She's worked hard with dance and baton. She was head-majorette in the high-school band."

Dean said with pride. "I'm going to miss her when she goes off to college next year. Sometimes I wish she could stay with us forever; although, it already seems like I never see her...She's always running off someplace with her friends."

Clay smiled and continued. "And Vince...he's a carbon copy of you!

Or should I say when you were about 30 years younger. He even walks like you, and his body language is like yours. Also, I noticed when he was sitting on the couch that he still rocks just like Elwood did."

"Yeah, I guess he's going to do that all his life...like Elwood did," responded Dean.

"Well, I'm sure you're really proud of both of them. I bet they have lots of friends."

"Man, that's an understatement! There are usually two or three kids around here all the time... and usually spending the night."

Dean laughed, "Sometimes they're here for days."

"Well, you're sure not like Dad when it comes to your kids having friends," said Clay, "Remember how Dad used to chase away all our friends? As a parent, you're very different from Dad—as different as night and day."

Dean stood and began to pace slowly across the room. Then, he stopped and took a seat on the hearth, facing his brother.

"Clay, I'm not so different from Dad, when you really compare me with him," he said, thoughtfully. "I'm different in some ways, but just like him in other ways."

"How are you like him?" asked Clay.

"In my controlling ways," replied Dean. "In fact, I think a lot of parents have the same trait. Even Bobbie has tried to control Deana."

"In what way?" Clay lit another cigarette and leaned forward in his seat.

"Well, Bobbie and I are extremely proud of our kids, and we got totally involved in their school activities. Bobbie was a great basketball player in high school, but she always wanted to be a majorette. So when Deana became a majorette, Bobbie began to push her...She even wants her to be a majorette in college when she enrolls. She has pushed her until Deana is sick of it."

"Did you push Vince in football?"

"Yeah...I'm sorry to say that I was a lot worse at trying to control him than Bobbie was with Deana."

"But pushing Vince has paid off," reasoned Clay. "Look what a good football player he is now."

"Yeah, in high school after I got off his back, he took more interest in it. He started playing the game more for himself."

"He's played football for a lot of years, hasn't he?" asked Clay.

"Yeah...ever since he was six years old. I was even his *Little League* coach...Jake Stone was my assistant. I probably should have listened to Jake a little more. He warned me about pushing Vince so much. That's what got Vince sick of it—*Little League*. He was always small, and football has turned into a big man's game. I drove him until he hated it."

"Hell, Dean, I was the same way with Terry and Eldon. I wonder why we push our kids that way?"

"Well, I don't know what your motive was, but I guess I expected Vince to complete the football career that I abandoned when I quit college. You know, our kids are not supposed to be an extension of us. They're not put here on earth to fulfill their parents' dreams. So you see, in a different area, I have committed the same sin that I condemned Dad for. He always tried to force me into carrying on his dream by operating the shop, and I've done the same thing to Vince in football."

Clay took another sip of his coffee, which was now as cold as tap water. Captivated by the conversation, he leaned forward and placed his elbows on his knees.

"Dean, at least you realize the error of your ways. You are aware of the mistake you made with Vince, but I don't think that Dad ever realized the way he controlled his sons." Clay crossed his legs and leaned back into the soft fabric of the couch.

"I'm not so sure, Clay. I believe Dad does realize some of his mistakes. When I was pushing Vince in football, Dad told me to back off. He said that Vince might not want to play football... that I should let Vince choose what he wants to do. He warned me that Vince was so small that he might get hurt."

"Well, but Dad was always cautious. Vince didn't get hurt did he?"

"Yes, he had his arm broken twice," said Dean sadly. "So you see, we are often destined to make the same mistakes that our parents have made before us. Maybe we've been too hard on Dad about his controlling nature. It took me years to forgive Dad. I just hope that our kids can forgive Bobbie and me."

"I've been guilty of the same things, too," said Clay. "I feel bad about leaving here years ago; Al and I were not on the best of terms...and now, he's dead, and I'll never get a chance to make up with him. I guess the funeral was pretty sad, wasn't it?"

Dean got up from his chair and began to slowly pace the floor. Finally, he took a seat on the hearth and faced Clay.

"The body...lying there in the casket didn't look much like Al...not the Al that I remember. I mean, his face looked like him, but for one thing, his hair was all slicked down, perfectly combed...and he was dressed in a suit and tie. You know, I don't believe I ever saw Al in a tie in his entire life. If I hadn't known that it was Al, I would have thought he had been a corporate executive, or a preacher. There was only one small tell-tale sign that told me it was him—when they cleaned up his body, they missed a tiny fleck of white paint on his right thumbnail…You know how Al always had paint on his hands."

The door from the kitchen opened, and their father walked into the room. Both Dean and Clay stood as Will suddenly stopped and stared intently at Clay.

"Hi, Dad." Clay walked toward his father, extending his hand.

Will took his hand. "Hello, Clay. When did you get here?"

"A little while ago," answered Clay. "I'm sure sorry about Al."

"Yeah…we all are. You missed the funeral. How did that happen?"

"The same way that weird things always happen to me. This time there was a storm, then a foul-up with the plane, and…well, it's a long story."

"I get the picture." Will walked to the rocking chair and took a seat. To afford them the opportunity to mend their broken relationship, Dean decided to give the two of them some privacy.

"Excuse me, Dad…Clay…I've gotta go help Bobbie make some lunch," he lied. "Would either of you like some coffee?"

"No." They both answered.

"But thanks." Clay responded, as he reclaimed his seat on the couch, facing his father.

After Dean had gone into the kitchen, Clay and his father sat silently as Will massaged a cigarette between his fingers and then stuck it in his cigarette holder. Clay flicked his lighter, holding the flame to the tip of his father's flaccid cigarette while Will clenched the stem of the holder between his teeth.

"How are your boys doing?" asked Will.

"Fine. We have another son now…Adam. He's eight years old. Ellen gave birth to him shortly after we went to Florida."

"You mean I have another grandson? Too bad we haven't ever seen him. What grade is he in?"

"He's in the third grade."

"How's Ellen doing?"

"Fine. She's working at Sears, there in St. Pete."

The limp cigarette fell from Will's cigarette holder onto the floor. With irritation, he quickly picked up the smoldering butt and tossed it into the empty fireplace. He placed the holder into his shirt pocket, and with the heel of his shoe, he ground out the glowing tobacco sparks that remained on the floor. In order to conceal the burn marks on the tile floor from Bobbie, he covered them with the small throw-rug near his feet.

Although they continued to talk, each had an uncertainty in regard to the other's attitude, thus confining their dialogue to trivialities. Both men felt compassion for one other but were strangely too embarrassed to express their sentiments. Finally, garnering the courage, Will spoke.

"Your youngest son…Adam, is he smart?"

"Yeah, he's very smart."

"How's Eldon doing in school?"

"He's doing very well. He really likes college."

Will hesitated before continuing. Although he was consumed with curiosity about Terry, he saved his questions about him until last, posing them as if they were an after-thought.

"And Terry…how is he?"

"Good…Terry's doing well. He's in college now, too."

"Does he ever talk about the way that he and I used to be such good buddies?" Will smiled at the memory.

"Yeah, Dad. He's often talked about it."

As he looked at his grieving father, he was overcome with regret and compassion; for Clay's experience as a father had been accompanied by a measure of understanding and wisdom. Realizing Will's reluctance to openly express emotion, he restrained his impulse to embrace his father or to tell him how much he loved and admired him as a man.

Accordingly, Will felt a tenderness toward Clay, but being uncertain about his son's feelings, he was hesitant to express his emotions. As a result of their mutual reluctance, and in accordance with the masculine Beauvais tradition, their words of tenderness were left unspoken.

Two days later, as Clay was preparing to return to Florida, he took his father's hand, but he never expressed remorse to his dad. As they walked toward the door, Clay placed his arm around his father's shoulders. It was not a complete embrace, but considering Will's reserved nature, the gesture was bold, indeed. While Al's death had stolen a son from Will, it had restored the life of another in the resurrection of Clay.

After telling Clay goodbye at the airport, Dean was depressed as he drove homeward. Upon his arrival, his grief was compounded when he received additional news of sadness: Bobbie's older sister, Bernice, had died suddenly of a massive heart attack; a myocardial infarction, the identical heart trauma that had claimed Al's life.

The death of Bernice marked the third time that Dean and Bobbie were forced to endure double-tragedies within their family. The unusual series of simultaneous misfortunes was incomprehensible to Dean; as a result, he wondered if he and Bobbie were plagued by some kind of jinx. Again, they attended two funerals within the span of a week.

As the date of his college graduation approached, Dean was still in the throes of grief. The thought of going through the graduation ceremony, wearing cap and gown, made him heart-sick since Al would no longer be standing beside him. He related his feelings of sadness to his father.

"Don't let these hard times whip you!" said Will. "You promised Alvin that you'd go through the ceremony. If he could see you now, he would be proud of you for doing it. Remember how you told me to show courage after your mother died? Well, I'm telling you the same thing now! I'm not going to let hard times whip me! When the going gets tough, the tough get going."

In the first week of June, wearing his cap and gown, Dean graduated from the *University of Tennessee* with high honors. As the diploma was handed to him, he remembered the harsh words of the Dean of *Southern Wesleyan College*, twenty-three years earlier: "You should drop out of school and stop wasting your time, and more importantly…ours!"

*   *   *

Responding to his father's advice, Dean decided to get busy. In an effort to overcome their grief, Dean and Bobbie became more active in *Central United Methodist Church*. Since they loved their association with young people, they accepted jobs as youth counselors, a responsibility in which they coordinated religious and recreational activities of teen-agers in the church.

Temptations facing the youth during the turbulent 70's were greater than those that were prevalent during Dean and Bobbie's teen-age years. Returning veterans of the Vietnam War had introduced illegal drugs into the American fabric; consequently, drug abuse in schools began to increase. In addition, young people were consuming alcohol at an alarming rate, and with the increase of the number of students driving cars, adolescent death on the highways became more common. Teenage pregnancy was on the rise, and to make matter worse for the adolescents, schools became over-crowded, a situation that was exacerbated by a shortage of quality teachers.

The absence of organized youth activities in Tyler City magnified the unrest of the young. With little to do in their idle time, they often drove their vehicles around town at night in search of some type of recreation. Easy access to drugs and alcohol, idle youth with raging hormones, fast automobiles, adolescent boredom, lack of parental supervision, and an absence of organized youth activities combined to create a breeding ground for trouble.

With children of their own, Bobbie and Dean were particularly concerned with the environment in Tyler City, along with the healthy development of young people. They both were imbued with a youthful spirit, a quality that endeared them to the youth in the program. Drawing on the temptations and frustrations of his own wayward youth, Dean was well-qualified to guide young people away from the pitfalls that had plagued his younger life.

Their fondness for working with the youth inspired Dean and Bobbie to employ their maximum effort to the project. They designed a dynamic format for the program, which included not only discussing the moral dilemmas of the times, but an energetic schedule of recreational activities, in which they engaged in many overnight trips involving unique adventures. As a result, the youth membership grew to gigantic proportions. Their involvement as youth counselors revitalized the lives of Dean and Bobbie, for it had become their passion. Dean also teamed with his father in the development of an art studio and framery, with both producing dozens of paintings. During this time, Will's weekly column in the *Tyler City News* grew more vociferous in his protests against injustice.

In late summer, Dean received his first letter from Clay since the death of Al. In the lengthy message, Clay related the commonplace events experienced by the family, then launched into his latest mishap: While driving his car in Downtown Tampa, he was stricken with a gall-bladder attack. After driving his car to the nearest hospital, he hurriedly parked his car and painfully got out. Writhing in agony, he limped along the parking lot, whereupon he was attacked by a pack of vicious stray dogs—something that rarely occurs in a city, but apparently there was something about Clay they didn't like.

His letter reassured Dean that he had completely recovered from the attacks of both the wild dogs and the gall bladder surgery. The best part of the letter, however, was the last paragraph, for in that portion he confessed recognition of his own faults as a father, traits with a similarity to those of Will's. With that realization, he stated, he had developed a better understanding of his dad which he thought was the initial step in the process of forgiveness. As a postscript, he added that he intended to invite his father on an expense-paid visit to his home in Florida.

With the knowledge that the healing process had begun, Dean smiled.

Storms make trees take deeper roots.
Dolly Parton

Chapter 34

Deana wheeled the car into the *East Broadway Gulf* station and parked in front of the large roll-up door. After placing the stick shift in neutral, she engaged the emergency brake and lowered the volume of her radio. The single car parked outside the station indicated that business was slow. Vince, who was seated beside her, was in an impatient mood.

"Deana, why do you insist on getting the car serviced right now? And could you at least play some decent music?"

"Okay, hand me that Paul Simon tape, then."

Vince reached into the glove compartment, pulled out the requested tape, and handed it to his sister. Deana slid the tape into the cassette player and increased the volume.

The bouncing vibrations of "Fifty Ways to Leave Your Lover" blasted from the speakers as Vince adjusted the sound to a more moderate level.

"Look, let's go ahead and return these Christmas gifts and you take me home. Then, you can get your car serviced."

Directly in front of her, the sliding door began to slowly ascend. A young man appeared, pulling downward on the chain, hand-over-hand, in a manner of a man climbing a rope. Upon seeing the attendant, Deana lowered her window.

"Hi, Jeff! How long have you been working here?"

"Oh, hello, Deana!" Jeff smiled. "I've been working here for more than a year."

Sporting an afro-hair style, the young man, Jeff Bowman, was wearing a faded oil-stained cotton jacket and a soiled pair of denim bell-bottom pants. He had graduated from high school two years prior to Deana, and had once had a secret crush on her.

"Oh, man! What a loser that guy is!" whispered Vince. "I'll bet he's one of your...old flames! Let's get this over with and get out of here." Jeff grinned at Deana. "What ya' been doing since you got out of school? "

"I've been going to U.T. I'm on Christmas vacation right now."

Jeff walked over to Deana's car window and thrust his head inside. "Hi Vince. How's football been going for you?"

"Pretty good" answered Vince, "I'll get to dress out for the varsity next fall."

"That's great, Vince!" commented Jeff. "Say Deana, when did you get this classy car?"

"Mom and Dad gave it to me for Christmas," she said smiling, "It's nice isn't it?"

The car was a white 1974 Mazda, a vehicle that Dean had originally bought for himself; but since his employer now furnished him a company car, he had decided to give the Mazda to his daughter as a Christmas present.

"Is it a straight shift or automatic?" asked Jeff, as he stepped back to admire the vehicle.

Rolling his eyes with impatience, Vince increased the volume on the tape.

"Straight shift," smiled Deana, "I've always driven Dad's Volkswagen Bug, so this car is pretty easy for me to drive."

Jeff smiled, "Well, what can we do for you today?"

"I called Mr. Letner earlier and made an appointment to have my car serviced. Where do you want me to park?"

The assistant hesitated, then remarked, "Since you haven't been driving this car for very long, maybe I better pull it onto the grease rack for you."

"Wow. Big deal." Vince commented dryly.

At that moment, the owner Ray Letner, a tall, thin, older man with a thick shock of gray hair walked up to the car.

"Jeff, you go ahead and work on that Chevy over there. I'll take care of this car." Mr. Letner looked at Deana. "If you and your buddy want to slide out of there, Miss, I'll pull your car onto the rack for you." Vince turned the music off and got out of the car as Deana slid out of the driver's seat and stepped out onto the pavement.

"Aren't Dean and Bobbie Beauvais your parents?" asked Mr. Letner.

"Yes sir," answered Deana.

"They're good people" he remarked, as he smiled, "You know, Dean's daddy painted that sign up there for me more than 20 years ago!" He pointed at the sign on the roof of his business.

After Deana had stepped from the vehicle, Mr. Letner started to enter the open door, then he suddenly stopped. As Deana looked back, she saw the cause of the man's hesitation: a half-full bottle of vodka had slid from beneath the front seat onto the floor of the driver's side. For a moment, the eyes of Mr. Letner met those of Deana's as Vince covertly peered into the car from the passenger side. Deana's face paled.

Oh, God...He saw that bottle! Thought Deana. *How could I forget about leaving that in the car?*

Mr. Letner said nothing, but slid the bottle back under the seat. He then got into the car and drove it onto the grease rack.

Jeff called from the other side of the garage. "Deana, you and Vince can wait in the office where it's warm. There's a couch in there."

As Deana and her brother walked toward the door of the office, Vince cast an incredulous look at her.

"Was that a bottle of whiskey in the car? My God, Deana! This is a dry county! They could put you in jail for that! And we're not of age, either."

"No, Vince...it was not a bottle of whiskey!"

"It was too! I know a bottle of whiskey when I see one! I saw the label on it."

"Well, I swear it wasn't a bottle of whiskey. It was...it was vodka."

"Oh, well...Well... that's okay, Deana," said Vince sarcastically. They walked into the small office and took a seat on the couch. As Deana hung her head, Vince stared at her, his expression a mixture of worry and anger.

"The owner of this place knows Mom and Dad. What would Dad say if he found out you had booze in your car?"

"I don't plan to tell Dad...or Mom either," replied Deana.

"Surely you don't drink that stuff when you drive, do you?"

"No, I would never do that! Do you think I'm nuts? I just bought that bottle for a little party that Marian and I had at my apartment. We finished our final exams and felt like partying. That's all. And I forgot to take the bottle out of my car."

After they sat silently for several minutes, a police car drove into the parking area and a policeman stepped out of his vehicle. Immediately, he walked to the front door and entered the office. Without hesitation, he looked at Deana and Vince.

"Are you Deana Beauvais...and Vince?"

"Yes sir," answered Deana, meekly.

"Oh, brother," whispered Vince.

"I want you to come with me, please...Both of you." Deana attempted to detect his tone of voice, but it displayed no discernable emotion.

At the same instant, they both stood.

"What's wrong, officer?" asked Deana, her voice trembling.

Peering angrily at his sister, Vince rolled his eyes. "What's wrong, my ass!" he whispered to Deana. "Mr. Letner called him about the booze. That's what's wrong."

"Did we do something wrong?" She asked the officer. Her voice carried the tone of innocence.

"Just come with me, please." They walked out the door toward the police car.

"My car is here, being serviced...What about my car?"

"Don't worry about it right now. Would you step into the car please?" Deana and Vince clumsily bumped into one another. "Should one of us get in the front?" Deana whispered to Vince.

Vince answered, bitterly. "No, I don't think you get that privilege when you get arrested."

Together, they slid into the back seat. The officer closed the door and pleasantly smiled at both Deana and Vince. As Deana eyes scanned the different gadgets in the police car, she thought about her brother's words. *Arrested...arrested? Oh, how could I be so stupid...This is gonna really kill Mom and Dad.*

The officer quickly drove the car onto the highway, then turned right toward Martel Road.

"Are you both students?" he asked kindly.

They glanced puzzlingly at each other. His pleasant attitude was confusing...Actually, it was beginning to become scary to both Deana and Vince.

"Yes, sir," Vince answered. "I go to high school , and Deana goes to U.T."

He stopped at the intersection, then turned left onto Martel Road. "This isn't the way to jail," Deana whispered to Vince, "This is the way to our house."

Softly, Vince returned an answer. "Maybe he is going to tell Mom and Dad about it first."

Deana muffled her words as she put her hand to her lips. "Shit, I think I would rather head in the direction of the jail."

The officer increased his speed as he drove away from the city. After a brief silence, his face revealed a sad expression and he turned to look at them.

"I'm sorry to tell you this, but your house is on fire."

"What? Are you sure? When did it start? We just left there a few minutes ago!" screamed Deana. "How bad is it?"

"It's pretty bad, ma'am. When we round this curve, you can see smoke."

"Oh, God, Deana!" cried Vince, "Mom and Dad were at home."

"Oh, please, God! Don't let Mom and Dad be in the house!" prayed Deana.

"Don't worry," remarked the officer, "I know your parents, and everybody I've talked to said they were at work today. I'm sure that the house was probably empty when the fire started."

"No, no!" screamed Deana, "You don't understand! Mom and Dad took some vacation time for Christmas…They don't go back to work until next week!"

The policeman pushed the accelerator to the floor and turned on the siren. After adjusting the channels on his CB radio, he relayed a message to the fire department: "I've got the children with me…They say the parents were at home! You'll have to check inside there! We'll be there in less than two minutes."

They rounded the next curve. Although they were still almost two miles from the burning house, they could see a thick column of jet-black smoke rising straight up, towering hundreds of feet into the air.

"Oh, dear Jesus! Please don't let Mom and Dad die!" cried Deana, "And where is Papaw? Did Dad take him to the shop this morning?"

She looked at Vince. His pallid face bore evidence of the severity of his distress; nonetheless, he pulled his sister close to him in a reassuring embrace.

"Don't worry, Deana," he said, with feigned composure in his voice, "You know that Dad wouldn't just sit there and let him and Mom get burned up! And I'm sure that Papaw is at the shop. He always is at this time of the day."

They clung to each other as the police car turned into Tyler Estates. When they turned the final corner, the burning house was in full view, revealing a terrifying scene of complete mayhem. Because of the frantic activity surrounding the fire, the officer was forced to park his car a half block away. Several vehicles and dozens of people ringed the house from a distance of at least a hundred feet away from the fire. The intense heat made a closer position impossible.

The furious, hungry flames had burned completely through the roof, leaping skyward with a roar to a height of at least thirty feet. Windows exploded, sounding like shotgun blasts as the intense heat inside the house sent shards of glass flying into the yard. Two fire trucks spewed thousands of gallons of water into the hellish inferno, but with little effect. As the fire grew more intense, it became obvious that it would ultimately consume the entire house.

Deana and Vince sprinted from the police car toward the house, winding their way through the crowd of onlookers, looking at their faces, in a frantic search for their parents. As they reached the front edge of the ring of people, they were suddenly restrained by two firemen. Although they were still a considerable distance from the fire, the heat was almost unbearable.

"Get back! Get back!" yelled the firemen, as Deana and Vince struggled to wiggle free from their grasp.

"Our Mom and Dad may be in there!" exclaimed Deana.

"Don't get any closer!" shouted one of the firemen, "We looked earlier and didn't see any evidence of them. It's useless to go in there now…Nobody could be alive in there! They are probably somewhere among this crowd!"

Vince broke free and bolted toward the burning house, but the unendurable heat drove him back. *The fireman was right,* he thought. *Nobody could be alive amid such hellish heat.*

Again Vince and Deana searched the crowd for their parents. As they moved through the gathering of people, many friends and neighbors expressed their condolences. At last they spotted their mom and dad, trotting up the hill toward the fire.

"Mom! Dad!" shouted Deana. Her tears of heartbreak now blended with tears of thanks.

"Thank God you're alive!" yelled Vince.

The family came together in a long, reassuring embrace.

Finally, they turned toward their burning house and huddled together as they silently watched the fiery holocaust mercilessly devour their home. The flames had now burst into a raging inferno, completely out of control.

Over the raucous sounds of the chaotic bedlam, they heard a voice yelling to them.

"Dean—Bobbie!" It was Papaw, making his way through the crowd toward them. His frantic frame of mind was indelibly written on his face. Both Deana and Vince ran to him, and as they embraced him, he shouted over the tumultuous noise.

"Dean, I was worried to death! I was afraid that you and Bobbie or the kids were in the house!"

"No, thank God we weren't, Dad," exclaimed Dean, "How did you find out about it?"

"Rob was visiting me at the shop when someone phoned and told us about it. Rob's here somewhere searching for you...He brought me over here. Where were you when it started?"

"Bobbie and I were having lunch downtown when someone came running into the restaurant and told us." He turned to hug Bobbie as she hung her head and wept silently. Dean held her tightly and tried to comfort her as Deana and Vince stepped in and embraced both of their parents.

"Do you see Rob anywhere?" asked Dean.

"No...last time I saw him, he was in the crowd looking for you all...He's pretty worried," Will replied.

"Thank God I found you!" shouted Rob, as he trotted out of the crowd. Immediately, he embraced Bobbie, then his brother.

"I know it's tough, Dean, but we should be grateful to God that no one was inside when it happened."

Suddenly, Deana began to cry. "Someone was inside!" she exclaimed, between sobs. "I left Poochie inside when I left this morning. Do you think there is anyway that he could have gotten out, maybe?"

"I doubt it, honey," said Dean sadly, "We can get you another little dog."

"I don't want another dog...ever! I just want Poochie...and what a horrible way to die! He burned to death!"

"I doubt he suffered at all," said Rob, as he wrapped his arm around Deana's shoulders. "The smoke put him to sleep. Don't cry...I'm sure he didn't suffer."

Will looked sadly at Dean and his family, huddled together in front of their burning house. He thought of the long years they had struggled in order to buy a place that they could call home; and they had made a place for him in their family, an act of love that he had never been shown in his early life. The losses they had suffered were horrendous:

The house itself, with all its memories; the furniture, and all of their personal items; photographs and films of babies and happier times, the guitar that Elwood had given Dean; dozens of paintings done by family members; and even the family dog, Poochie, who was as old as the home, itself. When Will considered the magnitude of their loss, he was overcome with compassion for Dean and his family. Slowly, he moved to Dean's side and placed his arm around his son's shoulders. Despite the tears that streamed down Will's cheeks, he smiled at Dean.

"Don't let hard times whip you, Dean. We'll be okay, we still have each other. That's all that counts. We'll be okay."

Deana and Vince moved close to him as Rob draped his arms around the shoulders of Dean and Bobbie. Huddled together, the entire Beauvais clan watched the remaining section of the roof collapse. For a long time, they stood, silent and motionless, until the home they had loved was completely gone. The only thing left standing was the expansive fireplace that on many dreary winter days of the past had once cradled the glowing embers of happiness.

Our greatest glory is not in never falling, but in rising every time we fall. **Confucius**

Chapter 35

It was before sunrise when Will awoke from a fitful sleep. The motel room was semi-dark, its only light being a small lamp that rendered objects in the room barely discernable. Having no pajamas or clean underwear, he had bedded down the previous night in his clothing, which still bore the acrid odor of smoke. The scent of sooty fumes had once rekindled pleasant memories of steam driven trains during his years as a hobo; but now he was repulsed by the odor. The sensation that had once been an aroma to him had forevermore been altered to be remembered as a stench. He realized that he would never again find the scent of smoke pleasurable.

Fidgeting with unrest, he looked over at Vince, who was sleeping beside him. Fully clothed, his grandson was lying on his back, expelling vigorous rasping snores from his open mouth. As he studied the boy, he experienced a deep feeling of empathy for him. The long-ago childhood of his own gave him first-hand knowledge of the hopeless feeling of being deprived of a place to call home.

Nonetheless, he was comforted by the awareness that the Beauvais family was still intact. A house is an integral part of a family, but the shared love of the people who inhabit the dwelling is the true essence of a home. In spite of the sadness he endured over the enormous loss, he felt his heart strangely warmed; for Dean and his family had given him the one thing that had eluded him for much of his early life: a home. The family welcomed him and he no longer experienced the feeling of isolation and abandonment. As he pondered yesterday's catastrophe, his emotions were ambivalent—a mixture of sadness and overwhelming gratitude.

The slight chill in the room prompted Will to gently spread a blanket over his sleeping grandson. He adjusted the covers and Vince suddenly stirred, but then he rolled over onto his side and continued to snore. He studied his grandson and began to realize how emotionally attached he had become to the boy. As a music-lover, Vince had owned countless recordings of music from a multitude of contemporary artists, along with many antiquated songs from the 40s and 50s. He smiled in fond remembrance of the numerous sessions that he and Vince had shared in the Beauvais home, listening to music. Will was not particularly fond of Rock and Roll; however, he did share Vince's passion for certain ballads, especially those with lyrics about rambling: "Walkin' Man," "Carolina in my Mind," "Walking Down a Country Road," and "Fire and Rain," were his favorite James Taylor tunes. He liked the Beatles— despite the fact that they were all "overdue for a haircut," and he was especially captivated by "Fool on the Hill." Now, it saddened Will to think that his grandson's music had all been destroyed by the fire.

Dean had rented adjoining rooms at *Riverview Inn* immediately after the fire. Because of the major disruption in their lives, the family was fraught with confusion and anxiety; as a result, it was after midnight when they finally went to bed. Exhausted and nervous, Will began to make an assessment of the family's predicament: The fire had completely destroyed the home and all its contents, including personal items necessary for ordinary cleanliness and daily routine; clothing, underwear, and toilet articles. It would be necessary to immediately purchase the bare necessities of personal grooming before they were able to brush their teeth, shave, or even comb their hair. As he considered the enormous tasks that lay ahead, Will was suddenly filled with a feeling of unrest.

Rising from his bed, he squinted his eyes as he peered at his watch in the dimly-lit room, but his deteriorating eyesight prompted him to move closer to the lamp. It was 6:30, he noted. *Would Dean be awake yet?* He rapped softly on the door of the adjoining room where Dean, Bobbie, and Deana were staying.

The door opened and Dean's unshaven face appeared. He, too, was fully-dressed, and with his entrance into Will's room, his clothing reintroduced the depressing odor of smoke.

"Hi, Dean…Did I awaken you?"

"No. I've never been asleep. I've been too worried. What do I do now, Dad? How do we survive this? I don't even know where to start."

Will was worried about his son's expression of hopelessness; he was aware of Dean's resiliency and courage, but he feared that the severity of this recent setback would defeat him.

"I'll tell you where to start," said Will. "You start at the beginning...You start by taking just one step—then you take another. Just put one foot in front of the other until you're walking again...walking with Beauvais pride and confidence. I'll take these steps alongside you!"

Dean slowly walked to the bed and wearily sat down beside Vince, who was still asleep. Reaching down, he tousled his son's curly hair.

Will took a seat on the bed. "Is Deana handling it pretty well?"

"Yeah, okay...but she's really grieving over her dog. How's Vince taking it?" asked Dean.

"He's doing okay. That kid has a lot of guts! He's a lot like his Dad and Mom!"

"And his grandpa, too. So, what are we going to do first, Dad?"

"Well, we start by buying some of the things that are essential for living...toothbrush, razors, soap, shaving cream, and another change of underwear, and...well, you get the picture. Let's get dressed and go shopping for these things!" said Will.

"Get dressed? We're already dressed." The remark provoked a laugh from both men.

"Are Bobbie and Deana asleep?" asked Will.

"Yeah, they finally went to sleep about two this morning. Maybe we ought to just let them all sleep while you and I go out and buy some things we need."

Dean walked back into the semi-darkness of his own room and found Bobbie asleep, but their daughter had awakened.

"Good morning, honey." He faked a cheerful grin.

"Hey, Dad." She walked to her father and hugged him.

"Deana, Papaw and I are going to a store to buy some personal items that we all need. Can you think of some special things that you need?" Ignoring the question, Deana said, "Dad, I want to go back to Tyler Estates and look for Poochie. He may have gotten out of the house when the fire broke out."

"Deana, you can go over there and look for him, but don't get your hopes up, honey." He hugged her again. "You might have to face the fact that he's gone."

"I've already faced it, Dad. But I just wanted to make sure. Maybe one of the neighbors rescued him...It's worth a try, isn't it?"

"I guess so. No harm in checking."

Having been awakened by the conversation, Bobbie stirred in her bed, then slowly assumed a sitting position.

"Good morning, Sleeping Beauty," greeted Dean, with simulated cheerfulness. He took a seat beside her on the bed and cuddled her.

"Good morning, honey," she said as she smiled weakly at him. "What's on the agenda for today?"

"Well, I can't decide on whether to schedule a cruise to the Bahamas, or book a flight to the French Riviera," joked Dean.

Bobbie laughed briefly, then her sad expression returned. "I've got to finish working on my list."

"What list?" inquired Dean. She pointed to a pad of paper on the night stand, upon which she had scribbled several items.

"I have to list everything we lost in the fire…for insurance purposes." Dean cringed when he considered anyone taking on such a gargantuan task; however, he felt that such a time-consuming chore might actually be helpful to Bobbie. It would not only serve the purpose of keeping her busy, but it would also help her in taking a positive step toward ultimate recovery.

"Deana wants to go look for Poochie," remarked Dean. "Can you take her? I won't be able to because I've got to go with Dad and buy some things we need. Is there anything special that you want us to pick up?"

"Oh, no, I can't think of anything that I might possibly need," she answered sarcastically. "I've got everything in the world that I need. After awhile, I want to go through my elaborate selection of clothes and pick out a party dress for the ballroom dance tonight!"

Dean laughed as Bobbie looked at him through teary eyes. Then she smiled. "I'm sorry I sounded bitter. You know, we really do have everything we need. We have each other, and that is everything in the world we should ask for!"

When Dean saw the spunk in Bobbie's character, he knew that the Beauvais family would indeed rise from the ashes of hopelessness. Because of the insufficient insurance coverage, Dean and Bobbie suffered an enormous financial loss, but monetary losses are replaceable, and ultimately forgotten. More profound and always remembered were the personal items and tokens of family love that were forever gone. Also the fire had destroyed dozens of Dean's paintings, as well as the extravagant collection of cartoons that he had drawn while a patient in the tuberculosis hospital. Although he was saddened by the loss of these items, he realized that they were only objects, products that bore proof of the process involved in their production. Still etched in his memory was the joyful experience of rendering the paintings, for that had been his salvation...the medication for his soul.

With a strong will for survival, the family was determined to overcome their misfortune, but sometimes, individual perseverance and tenacity are not enough. Regardless of our strong resolve, there are times when we cannot, within our resources, resurrect ourselves. On occasion, it is only through the combination of our own efforts and the loving acts of others that brings about rebirth. So it was with the revival of the Beauvais family when their friends in *Central United Methodist Church* offered help in their resurgence.

At first, because of his pride, Dean was reluctant to accept the rescuing efforts of his friends, particularly when they offered money. When an emissary of the church offered assistance to the family, Dean was uncertain about accepting the help that they desperately needed. Torn by the emotional conflict in his mind, he discussed the matter with Rob.

"I guess I must have a lot of Dad's independence inside me. I just can't seem to accept something free from people."

"I understand how you feel," answered Rob. "But giving of ourselves and of our money is what Christian love is all about. If the shoe was on the other foot... If the same happened to one of your friends...Would you try to help him?"

"Why, yes...I guess I would."

"I know that you would, Dean. And that would make you feel good, right?"

"Yeah...I guess so."

"Why do you think it would make you feel good?" asked Rob.

"Well, I would be fulfilling my duty as a Christian..."

"Do you want to deprive your church friends from feeling good about doing their duty as a Christian? Those people love you and your family."

Dean became silent, slowly considering Rob's remarks.

"Dean, I know how you feel, and I used to feel that way, too. It took a long time for me to rid myself of some of the Beauvais pride. But do you know what makes people cling to that kind of pride? It's ego. We feel good when we are the giver, and not the receiver. Sometimes, being the giver makes us feel superior to others. We need to learn to be a grateful receiver, to be humble enough to allow others to help us when we need it. Jesus had that humility. He never owned anything except the clothes on his back. You've helped a lot of people, Dean, and in helping them, it also helped you become a better man. Now it's time for you to be man enough to let other people help you... To show their love for you."

Dean heeded his brother's advice, and in doing so, he had never before experienced such an outpouring of love from his fellow church members, particularly from those in his Sunday school class. People responded in droves with offers of help: They rented a house for the family and provided furniture, working tirelessly to ready the house for immediate occupation; many donated money and articles of clothing; cooking utensils and food were also contributed. Hurley McIntyre, a church member who managed a local clothing store gave Dean's family several new outfits.

In witnessing this unified expression of love, Dean was overcome with gratitude and developed a new understanding of the acts of giving and receiving, for he felt that there was an element of the divine in a group of people working together in a concentrated effort to lift up a fellow being in distress.

The fire had been terrible—a monstrous event that had reduced their dreams to ashes; but out of the blackened rubble sprang the brilliant blossom of love that gave a sense of meaning to the tragedy.

Although Deana never found her dog, she and Vince began to rebound from the calamity. Displaying the typical resilience of the young, their recovery was more rapid than that of the remainder of the family, particularly when Dean quickly purchased a new house in an adjoining neighborhood.

The two-story residence was larger and more elaborate than their previous dwelling, boasting four bedrooms and three full bathrooms. An all-brick structure, it rested on a full acre of land in an upscale suburban neighborhood. Like their previous home, the den sported a large brick fireplace that covered the entire wall.

Once more, with the aid of beloved friends, the Beauvais family was able to take the initial steps toward restoration. Complete recovery from a loss of such magnitude requires a lengthy passage of time; however, the open wounds left by the dreadful event began to gradually heal.

*   *   *

The tragedy of the fire had given the Beauvais family an even closer emotional bond with one another, and although Deana and Vince had an abundance of teenage friends, their attachment to their parents and grandfather remained strong. Both had inherited the independent spirit of their parents and the creative talents common to the Beauvais family. Dean and Will were amazed at the artistic skills of Deana and Vince.

In personality, Deana was a blend of her parents; the outgoing nature that she had inherited from her mother was interwoven with the risk-taking tendencies and sense of humor of her father. Like her grandfather, Will, she sometimes rebelled against conformity. Although she felt an emotional closeness to her dad, she had developed an even stronger bond with her mother, because since Deana's childhood, Bobbie had been involved with her in school activities, dance lessons, Girl Scout meetings, and majorette camps.

Vince had a consuming desire to please his father. Easy-going, but moody, he was a curious composite of his parents and uncles. Like his mother, he was small-boned and slim, but he was incredibly strong for his size, and quick. In his appearance and mannerisms; he was almost a carbon copy of his father. Although at times he had the explosive temper of his Uncle Clay, he was quick to forgive; for embedded in his spirit was the inherent gentle nature of his Uncle Elwood. With his quick wit and penchant for ridiculous humor, he often displayed many of Elwood's behavior patterns and tendencies, including his restless habit of rocking.

Vince loved everyone in the Beauvais family, but he truly idolized his father. The intimate bond that developed between Vince and his dad reflected a similarity to the closeness that had existed between Elwood and Will. They were also true friends, each of them having the ability to read the feelings of the other.

On the rare occasions when he was angry, however, Vince was unlike Elwood; for in those instances he often displayed the former sensitive yet aggressive nature of Dean and Rob. Sometimes he became engaged in fights, usually as a result of some slight criticism that one of his peers had directed toward a member of the Beauvais clan, for Vince shared the traditional Beauvais' fierce loyalty to the family.

Each of Vince's fights was followed by a confrontation with his father. When Vince was twelve-years-old, after an altercation with one of his friends, Dean took him to task for his actions. Seated at the kitchen table, they faced each other. Projecting a puzzled expression, Dean began to question Vince.

"What were you fighting about this time? What made you hit Ricky Swain? I thought he was one of your best friends!"

"He is my friend...But I felt honor-bound to hit him, Dad."

"Why? What did he do to you?"

"He didn't really do anything to *me*. He insulted Papaw." Vince displayed an expression of anger.

"How did he insult Papaw?" Dean was curious.

Vince shifted in his chair and began to rock.

"Well...you know how Papaw is always taking naps in the car when he is parked in the driveway? When Ricky drove me home and pulled into the driveway he looked at Papaw and laughed. He asked me, 'Who is that old man who sleeps in his car all the time with his mouth open? Look how he is slobbering!' So, you see...I hit him. What else could I have done? I'm not going to let anybody make fun of Papaw, friend or not."

With an understanding of Vince's loyalty, Dean saw a peculiar logic to his son's rationale; consequently, after delivering a short lecture, he let Vince off the hook. In pondering his son's aggressive behavior he wondered if it was somehow a part of the genetic makeup of the Beauvais family. The occasional aggressiveness of Vince worried him; he now had a better understanding of his own father's concern in regard to the past combative behavior of Dean and his brothers.

Vince had his first fight when he was eight years old, an incident that ended with his adversary crying and running away. After dinner that evening, Dean called his son into the den to discuss the fight.

"Vince, your mother tells me that you got into a fight today. Fighting very seldom solves any kind of problem...Where did it happen?"

Vince hung his head. "Well..It happened in front of our Methodist Church downtown."

"Who did you fight with and how old is he?" Dean took a seat directly facing his standing son.

"It was Marty Williams. He's not a very nice boy, Dad. He's nine years old and bigger than me."

Dean cast an accusing look at his son. "What caused the fight?"

"Well–actually, Dad, it's kinda complicated...Let's just say that he had it comin' to him."

"Why did he have it coming? Did you hit him first? The boy that hits first is the one who starts the fight, you know."

Vince remained silent.

"Well, did you hit him first?" Dean was becoming impatient.

"Why does it matter, Dad?"

"It just does. Well, did you?"

"I forget...I might have," stammered Vince.

"Well, why did you hit him?" Dean stared into Vince's eyes.

"He had it comin' to him, Dad. We were walking up the hill to school...and just as we were passin' the church, he says this awful cuss word right in front of the House of the Lord!"

Dean stifled a smile. *How can I fault Vince for being so reverent and loyal to the Church?* In the past, Dean had used a multitude of excuses to his own father for fights in which he had been involved, but the rationale offered by Vince was unquestionably more original; for he had based his defense on the grounds of "righteous indignation."

Unlike his father whose youth had been punctuated with violent fights, Vince had relatively few physical confrontations, however, he held within his spirit the Beauvais predisposition to stand up for himself, his family and his beliefs.

During their teenage years both Deana and Vince were popular in school with both of them having many friends. As he matured, however, Vince gradually began to adopt the private reclusive nature of his father and grandfather. While Deana shared her Uncle Al's creative penchant for literature and classical music, Vince had inherited his father's talent in graphic design and painting as well as his Uncle Elwood's passion for all types of music.

In spite of their hectic work schedules, Bobbie and Dean spent countless hours with their children. Because of shared interests and similar personalities, Bobbie and Deana spent a lot of time together. Vince, when not in school or with his friends spent most of his time with his father. Dean coached Vince in *Little League* football as well as engaging with his son in a multitude of shared activities: painting, listening to music, attending sporting events, working out, watching football games—all these activities they experienced together. As their friendship grew stronger, they became almost inseparable. While other teenagers grew apart from, and were sometimes embarrassed by their parents, Deana and Vince remained emotionally close to Dean, Bobbie and Will. They were proud of them, even in the presence of their teenage friends.

*   *   *

As the first Christmas in their new house drew near, Dean and Bobbie had already beautifully wrapped the Christmas gifts and hidden them in the bedroom closet. Will also had purchased his gifts, inexpensive items that would remain unwrapped, as usual, and presented to the recipients in paper bags on Christmas morning. They had waited for Deana and Vince to come home before putting up the tree, because total family involvement in the ritual had become a Beauvais tradition.

Filled with the yuletide spirit, Dean built a cozy fire in the fireplace, then brought in the tree from the garage. While Will watched the activity from his favorite chair, Dean, Bobbie, Deana and Vince began to decorate the large, symmetrical cedar tree. The fragrant aroma of the tree invaded the room, evoking memories of the long-ago Christmas that Alvin had given them.

While placing the shiny ornaments on the tree, Deana and Vince were ecstatically happy. With the voice of Nat King Cole filling the room with "The Christmas Song," Vince began to rock from side to side.

"Don't go snooping around the hiding places in the house, Dad."

"Oh, really. And why is that?" Dean smiled.

"Because I bought you a little present, and if you snoop around and find it, it would spoil Christmas."

Since Vince was only fourteen-years-old, Dean knew that he had little money. The past summer, he had helped a local farmer harvest a hay crop, but Dean figured that Vince had already spent the money.

"I hope you didn't buy an expensive gift for me because I didn't spend a lot on you and Deana this year," said Dean.

"Dad, don't start thinking I got you something expensive, or you'll be disappointed. I didn't have a lot to spend, so don't expect something wonderful," cautioned Vince, as he winked at Deana.

On Christmas morning, as the family gathered around the tree, Vince could hardly contain his excitement. Being generous by nature, Vince often spent most of his money on others. As the gifts were unwrapped, both Deana and Vince had appropriate presents for everyone, for they never bought "token" presents, but were discriminating in their selection of gifts, always choosing the "right" present for each family member.

Finally, all the presents had been given and unwrapped, with the exception of Vince's gift to his father.

Grinning at his dad, Vince said, "Dad, I'm sorry, but I forgot to buy you anything!"

With the awareness that Vince was joking, Dean smiled at his son, curious about the gift that Vince had selected for him.

Reaching underneath the skirt of the bottom of the tree, Vince retrieved a tiny package, no bigger than a match box. Although small, it was beautifully wrapped with the attached bow larger than the present.

With his curiosity aroused, Dean unwrapped the gift, only to find a hand-written note inside.

Look in the hall closet for your gift.

Immediately, Dean hurried to the hall closet, where he found a second small present. After opening it, he discovered another note. *Go upstairs and look in the spare bedroom closet.* By this time, the entire family had become curious. Laughing, they followed Dean and Vince to the upstairs bedroom closet. As Dean picked up the small gift, Vince grinned and nervously rocked with excitement. Again, inside the small box, Vince had placed another note. *Go back downstairs and look under the bed in my old bedroom.* Everyone roared with laughter, then joined the procession to the downstairs bedroom.

As the other family members looked on, Dean reached under the bed, and then pulled out the gift. It was a shiny, new guitar, and although not an expensive instrument, it was priceless to Dean. He looked at Vince in gratitude and saw that his son was grinning as he rocked nervously from side to side.

"Do you like it, Dad? As soon as I get a little more money, I'll buy you an amplifier to go with it. I wanted to replace the guitar you lost in the fire—the one Uncle Elwood gave you."

As Dean witnessed his son's excitement, he realized that Vince had spent more than he could afford, but if Dean offered to help pay for the instrument, his son's Christmas would be ruined. He knew that Vince's happiest moments were when he was giving, especially to his father. Dean embraced his son. At that moment when he received the gift from Vince, he realized the breadth of his son's love for him.

*   *   *

Although the emotional impact of losing their former home to the fire had been devastating, involvement in the ordinary business of living slowly swept away the ashes of sadness, and in the five years following the disaster, the Beauvais family began to fashion new memories.

The children were now grown. Vince had graduated from high school and was a freshman at the university. Although he had received all-county honors in football, he declined to pursue the sport in college.

Deana had married while a senior at U.T. In September, on a glorious late summer day, she and her groom, Kevin Lansing, became husband and wife in an outdoor wedding ceremony held at the lakeside of *Tyler City Park*. Deana's Uncle Rob united the couple in an elaborate ceremony that included a large group of guests. In the two years following the wedding, Deana had graduated and the couple had moved to Louisiana.

The Methodist Church Conference had relocated Rob from Johnson City to a Knoxville church—a move that afforded Rob and Madge more frequent visits to his brother's family in Tyler City.

The departure of Deana and Vince necessitated an extreme adjustment in the marriage of Dean and Bobbie as they began to cope with the "empty nest syndrome." Except for occasional weekend visits from Vince, the household now only consisted of Bobbie, Dean, and his father.

Will was now in his 80's. He still exercised regularly, and although his overall health was excellent, his eyesight had worsened. At regular intervals during the day, in order to alleviate the pressure in his eyes, he treated them with droplets of medicine. As his eyesight deteriorated, he became night-blind, and his diminished driving skills precipitated his involvement in a series of minor automobile accidents. His car was a second home to him. When not driving, he often spent hours in his parked car, reading, or writing notes for his newspaper column.

In the small town of Tyler City, the Beauvais family was well-known, a familiarity that made Will's banged-up car easily recognized by other local drivers; as a result, upon seeing the approach of his vehicle, they began to take precautionary measures to avoid any proximity to him.

Will's accumulating accidents and mounting complaints from local drivers induced a growing concern in Rob and Dean regarding their father's driving, but their attempts to persuade him to stop operating a vehicle fell on deaf and stubborn ears. With sadness, they realized that by depriving him of his driving privilege would be taking from his last vestige of independence and dignity; consequently, in their efforts to prohibit his driving, they only achieved a compromise: Their father finally agreed to confine his trips to those of only absolute necessity. With resignation, both Dean and Rob realized that this arrangement with their father, though not ideal, represented a major milestone in their relationship with him, for it was one of the few times in his life that he had ever made a concession to anyone.

In spite of his advanced age and failing eyesight, Will became even more zealous in his creative pursuits. His passion in life became a combination of painting and writing, an irony indeed, since adequate eyesight is a prerequisite to both professions. Nevertheless, because of his strong desire and perseverance, he accomplished his finest work during these twilight years of his life.

Influenced by the painting methods with which Dean and Clay had become acquainted in art school, Will's style of painting began to slowly evolve. For most of his life, his painting fashion had been rooted in realism, reflecting the dark, somber characteristics of the 19th century Barbizon painters, the old masters, and Gustave Courbet, a painter of simple, realistic landscapes of the same period. As he became more involved, his painting style gradually changed, displaying qualities of impressionism similar to the works of Monet, Renoir, and Degas. Some of his paintings bore a resemblance to the work of Van Gogh and Cezanne, of the post-impressionist movement. As his mode of painting expanded, his technique of subtly blended colors yielded to a new approach in which he applied rough strokes of pure color, creating a heavy texture on the canvas. He finally abandoned the safe, sameness of his former technique and became totally absorbed in experimentation. The smooth, sedate appearance of his prior paintings began to be replaced by more carefree, colorful, spontaneous images. Because of his endless hours in the studio, Will could have accumulated hundreds of paintings, but he only amassed a few. He sold some and gave many away; however, his sparse collection was mostly due to one of his unusual habits: After finishing a painting, he often painted another directly on top of the previous image, for his interest in painting was the process of doing the work, not the product.

Likewise, the theme of his writing underwent a transformation. His weekly newspaper column, which had once been totally comprised of humorous stories and satire, became slowly infiltrated with articles of protest, in which he made sweeping indictments of various forms of injustice. As his outrage grew, so did the frequency of dissent in his columns, as it gradually became a vehicle solely for his remonstration. The altered tone in his weekly column pleased many of his readers, but disappointed others who enjoyed his former humorous writing; in addition, his articles began to generate criticism from those who had opposing opinions to his own.

When the editor of *Tyler City News* approached him in regard to the complaints of readers, Will refused to compromise his beliefs and continued to write his controversial column. He was surprised when the newspaper allowed him to continue his disputable writings.

He became obsessed with leaving behind him a legacy of good works. A rebel at heart, he became a crusader, possessing the inherent uncompromising nature that is characteristic of all who are hell-bent on reformation.

The focus of Will's anger was directed mostly toward injustice to the elderly, particularly in the exorbitant cost of prescription drugs. He wrote several articles on the subject, and even produced circulars of protest, which he placed beneath windshield wipers of cars. When the price was suddenly drastically increased on his glaucoma medication, he painted several signs in protest of the cost. Taping the banners to his vehicle, he parked the car directly in front of the drug store where he marched back and forth carrying a protest sign. After a large crowd had gathered, the owner of the pharmacy, feeling that he was being persecuted, phoned Dean.

"Mr. Beauvais, your father is in front of my store with signs all over his car. He's protesting the cost of drugs. But my prices are identical to the other two drug stores in town. Why is he picking on me?"

Dean laughed. "Because your store is the place where he bought his medication." Feeling embarrassment for his father and fearing that he might get into trouble, he told the pharmacist, "I'll drive down there and talk to him...But I can't promise you anything."

After considerable persuasion, Dean finally succeeded in luring his father away from the drug store, but at the expense of Will's anger toward him. Dean felt that his father was fighting for a just cause, but since the three pharmacies had identical prices, Will's focus was misdirected.

In keeping with his desire for the common good, Will was also active in bringing about positive changes in the community. Since the incorporation of the city a hundred years earlier, many rural areas were still without running water. After knocking on hundreds of doors, he obtained countless signatures on a petition that he presented to the city officials. As a result of his efforts, a new water utility board was established, which furnished water for the formerly deprived areas. He was asked to serve on the board, but true to his nature as a loner in which he didn't work well in concert with others, he declined.

Although Will was a man of independent spirit, he had, by necessity, developed a dependency upon Dean and Bobbie. He felt that he was a part of the family and began to feel comfortable in the home of his son. In years past, when people spoke of the Beauvais homestead, they were referring to Will's home, on *Beauvais Lane*, but now, the family headquarters was the home of Dean and Bobbie. When Rob and Madge, and family friends came there to visit, they considered it to be Will's home. While Dean was the head of the house, Will was still considered the head of the family.

Will missed the presence of Deana and Vince, but their absence brought him emotionally closer to Dean and Bobbie. Although a creative director, and involved in a different type of art, Dean still spent hours in the studio, painting pictures with his father. Their father-son relationship grew stronger, although sometimes their mutual stubbornness caused temporary friction between them.

A modest man, Will's awkwardness and shyness in the presence of women had often caused him to maintain an emotional distance from them, but in recent years, he had begun to develop a trust in Bobbie. Since his youth, he had been a good judge of character, and in Bobbie, he began to recognize a woman of unsurpassed quality. Aware of her sound judgment, he often sought her advice. Because of his pride, he was reluctant to do so with Dean, for he was hesitant to reveal any weakness to his sons.

Accordingly, Bobbie recognized Will as a man of high principles; he became a father figure to her, a man for whom she felt a responsibility to nurture. Also, she had become keenly aware of his peculiar ways, and in her ingenuity, she had learned how to manipulate him, usually for his own good.

When Will was ill-tempered or depressed, she brightened his spirit with a freshly-baked apple pie—his favorite dessert. She felt the responsibility to care for him as she would have done with her own father, had he lived. Although she was careful to be diplomatic, she attended to his appearance, often dusting the shoulders of his gray flannel suit as they left home for church. Will had a penchant for ugly ties, some of which were tattered and food-stained—flaws that his diminished vision was unable to detect. He was sensitive about his choice of ties, however, and refused to wear any article of clothing that someone else had chosen for him.

Noticing the threadbare condition of his ties, Bobbie presented him with a new one on a night before Sunday morning church services. Reluctantly, Will accepted the tie, but with an expression of disdain, he placed the object in his dresser drawer. Upon witnessing the exchange, Dean grinned and whispered to Bobbie.

"This time you've gone too far. The one thing that he won't tolerate is someone choosing a tie for him."

To Dean's surprise, the next morning when his father walked into the den, fully dressed for church, he was wearing the tie that Bobbie had chosen for him. Strutting in his customary proud fashion, he thrust out his chest and smiled bashfully at Bobbie. At that moment, Dean grinned, for he realized that his father and Bobbie had truly bonded.

I shut my eyes in order to see. **Paul Gauguin**

Chapter 36

The unbroken stream of time crept relentlessly onward, measured only by the passage of the changing seasons. The merging years were linked together by the chain of milestone events within the Beauvais family. In the span of six years, Deana had given birth to three children—John, Sarah, and Daniel.

Their family resided in Buras, Louisiana, a small town outside of New Orleans, where Kevin's commercial fishing business kept the family busy. Deana fulfilled her dream of becoming a teacher and was now teaching English at the local high school.

Vince finished college with a major in art and was now a graphic artist in Oak Ridge. A year after accepting the job, he married a beautiful auburn-haired girl named Carmen. True to the solitary nature of Vince, the wedding was a simple, private affair held in a local Baptist Church and attended by family members and friends of both the bride and groom. It was a bittersweet event for Bobbie and Dean since the marriage of their youngest child marked the end of an era for them; for the baby bird had flown from the nest, leaving a void in their lives. As the newlyweds drove away from the church on their way to Myrtle Beach for their honeymoon, Dean and Bobbie stood motionless in the parking lot, watching and waving until Vince's car disappeared from sight. Then Bobbie hugged Dean tightly, and softly cried.

After returning from their honeymoon, Vince and Carmen made their home in Tyler City, only a mile from the home of Dean and Bobbie. Soon after, Vince and Carmen had their first child, a boy whom they named Jordan.

Will was now almost 90 years old; and yet, except for his rapidly failing eyesight, he appeared at least ten years younger. As he had grown older, the difficult lessons of life had tempered his disposition. Like a vintage wine, his spirit had mellowed with his aging; but the diminished harshness of his nature was overshadowed by his increased stubbornness. He was a complicated man.

Will had long ago made his peace with Clay, who wrote to his father regularly. In Clay's last letter, he had invited Will to visit him and Ellen for a month at his home in Florida. Will had accepted his son's invitation, scheduling his visit for February. Because of his distrust of airplanes, he caught a *Greyhound* bus to St. Petersburg, Florida.

Dean and Bobbie were now alone at home, and although they missed Will, his absence afforded them an opportunity to enjoy some private time alone.

In the celebration of Valentine's Day, Bobbie prepared a special evening meal for just the two of them. The candlelight dinner was a prelude to a romantic movie that they planned to see on this rare, private evening together. With the final course of food on the dining table, Bobbie lit the three candles, then switched off the ceiling light. A dim romantic radiance barely illuminated the room, casting ghostly shadows onto the wall behind Bobbie, as she seated herself at the table.

Dean smiled at her. "Isn't this romantic? What a wonderful atmosphere…Here, I've got something for you." Reaching across the table in the muted candlelight, he handed her a valentine card. "I bet you forget to get me one!" he said in a pretentiously accusing voice.

"Well, I cooked this steak for you. I think that's better than a valentine!" she playfully chided him.

"I'll take a steak instead of a valentine, any day!" said Dean. "Mmmm…Look at all this good food. Did you bake me an apple pie too, like you do for Papaw?"

"No, I didn't. You should be satisfied with what you have!" She scolded him, then displayed a grin.

"Well, I'm kinda tired of apple pie, anyway." Dean said.

She smiled. "I made you banana pudding instead…with whipped cream on top."

"Wow!" exclaimed Dean. "That's my favorite dessert. You must be trying to seduce me!"

Bobbie smiled. "If I am, you'd better take advantage of it while we've got the house to ourselves. Besides, you're not getting any younger…Although, you're not bad for a man pushing fifty."

"What do you mean, I'm not bad! I'll be going strong when I'm eighty."

"Yeah…You wish!" Bobbie chuckled. "Neither of us will think about such a thing when we're 80."

"Speak for yourself, babe," said Dean.

Without answering, Bobbie rolled her eyes in mockery, then laughed. The couple lapsed into silence as they busied themselves with the meal. As he munched on a piece of steak, Dean finally said, "I hope Dad enjoys his time with Clay. Do you think he will?"

"He'd enjoy it a lot more if Terry and Eldon were there," she answered. "Where did Clay say they are now?"

"Terry has a job in New York, and Eldon just recently moved to Tallahassee, Florida."

"But Adam is there with Clay and Ellen…isn't he?" asked Bobbie.

"Yeah, but Dad hardly knows him. He'll probably feel awkward around him."

"Well, this is an opportunity for your Dad to get to know him. Maybe they can become close, like Papaw was with Terry."

Dean smiled. "The trouble is, Dad is a slow mover. It'll probably take him about ten years to feel close to Adam…By that time, he will be a hundred years old! It took him ten years to marry Mom. And look how long it took Dad to trust you. How much time did it take? Ten or twelve years?"

She laughed and silently continued her meal. "You know, Papaw and I are close now, aren't we? He seems to really trust me now, and he relies on me to do things for him…and the grandchildren love him. He's still shy around me, though, but I can tell he likes me."

"Yeah, Dad's always been shy," said Dean. "He's extremely modest. I don't think Mom ever saw him in the buff."

"Oh, come on, Dean! He couldn't have been that modest! After all, he fathered five sons."

"Yeah, that's true. I guess the bedroom had to be as dark as a cave before he made love to her," said Dean, as Bobbie laughed.

Without further conversation, they finished their steaks.

"Man, what a meal!" remarked Dean. "I may not be able to hold any of that banana pudding. In fact, after that wonderful meal, I may be too drowsy to watch that video you rented."

"You'd better not be too full! You're going to eat banana pudding and then we're going to watch that movie…or else!" she threatened, jokingly. Then she smiled at him and said, "Your valentine is under your place mat."

Dean pulled out the valentine. Unlike the humorous card he had given to her, Bobbie's was romantic in nature. He opened the card and read the sentimental message.

"Thank you, honey," he said, "The card is beautiful. I knew you hadn't forgotten me! You always remember to give me a valentine."

"Oh, yeah? Well, next year it may slip my mind." She smiled. "Now eat your banana pudding."

As Dean watched Bobbie stack the dishes in the sink, he noticed she had that same beautiful radiance that she had on the first night they met.

"Honey, you're just as beautiful as the first day I saw you." Dean blushed as he spoke the words.

"And look at you." Bobbie smiled and pointed at Dean. "You're just as shy as the day we met. Good thing I finally asked you for a date...Look at all we would have missed." She swept her arms, gesturing their surrounding home.

"Me... Shy?" Dean's face reddened. "Well, I just didn't want to be a pushover. I wasn't sure how you felt. Anyway, now I can see how much you adore me...so being a pushover is the least of my worries tonight."

Finally, Bobbie blushed. "Come on, big talker. Let's go watch the movie."

Dean strolled to the fireplace and agitated the glowing coals with a poker until the logs rekindled, popping sparks onto the oversized hearth. With the resurgence of the fire, he replaced the screen and walked to the couch and took a seat. Bobbie remained in front of the television, jiggling the VCR and methodically pushing its buttons.

"What movie did you choose for us?" asked Dean.

"Well, it's a romantic movie...Cary Grant and Deborah Kerr...Can you guess what it is?"

"Oh, yeah...Let's see...That's the one where they plan to meet in New York City... *An Affair to Remember!* "

She claimed her seat beside Dean. "You're right. That's it."

Dean reached to the end table and switched off the lamp while Bobbie cuddled closer to him. The only light in the cozy room was provided by the television screen and the fireplace.

"This is so romantic." said Bobbie.

Dean agreed. "Yeah, this is great. Just the two of us, with no one to disturb us."

It was an amorous night as they snuggled together in the romantic atmosphere of the shadowy room.

"Do you know how long it's been since we've been alone like this together?" asked Dean. "Do you realize that we have four generations running in and out of here…And sometimes all at the same time? I mean, I miss everybody, but this sure is nice, tonight."

"Yes, it's wonderful." remarked Bobbie.

The ring of the telephone startled Dean. He gently pushed Bobbie away from him and reached for the phone. "Well, so much for that," he remarked.

"Hello."

"Hello—Dean? This is Clay. How are you guys doing?"

"We're fine…We're just watching an old movie. How's everything down there? Is Dad all right?"

"Oh, yeah. Dad's fine. Actually, that's what I called you about," Clay said, "Tell me, how in the hell do you handle this stubborn man? What's your secret?" Clay's frustration was obvious.

"Why? What's wrong?" asked Dean.

"I can't seem to please him—no matter how hard I try! You know what's he's doing right now? He's sitting on the couch in the living room with his suitcase completely packed. He's demanding that I take him to the bus station…"

"Can he hear what you're saying right now?".

"No, I'm on the phone in the bedroom."

"Have you had a quarrel with him? Did he get mad at Ellen…or Adam?"

"No! Everybody's been completely kissing his butt to get along with him!" Clay's frustration was mounting. "You and Bobbie have done this for a long time. Please, tell me what to do. I'm at my wit's end. I don't want him to go back home, to your house. He's supposed to be here for three more weeks."

"Is he mad about something? Or does he just want to come home?"

"He just seems lost here with me. For months I've looked forward to having him here. But, for one thing, he got off to a bad start on his trip down here. When his bus arrived here, in St. Pete., he was asleep, so when the bus pulled out, he was still on it. Then, when he woke up, he was halfway to Miami. I had a hell of a time locating him and getting him back here."

"Gosh, I hate to hear that. And he's getting along okay with Adam?"

"Yeah, fine. Adam is hardly ever here. You know how teenagers are…when he's not in school, he's gone somewhere with his friends. I don't know what to do. Dad just sits here in the house all day, sulking."

"Well, get him out of the house. Take him sightseeing. You know how he has always loved Florida."

"I can't do that either, Dean. Let me give you the complete picture…First of all, as I've already told you, Dad got lost on the way down here. Then, on his first day here, it starting storming—you know how he hates storms. Well, it's been storming ever since he got here. In fact, it's flooding here. You know I live on this little island, and the flood has washed out the bridge, so we're marooned here with no way out. We can't even buy groceries. We're running out of everything to eat! We couldn't even go to church Sunday."

Dean was surprised. "When did you start going to church, Clay?"

"Oh, we've been going for a couple of years now."

"That's great, Clay."

Dean carefully considered the situation. "I'll tell you how to make him happy. Get him started on a painting…You know how he loves to paint. Don't you have some art supplies you can let him use? Or better yet, get him a tablet, and he'll probably start writing something."

"I can't do any of those things either," said Clay. "The storm knocked the power out, so the house is completely dark inside. Since we don't have electricity, we can't watch television or read. Also, the food is going bad in the refrigerator."

"Maybe you and Dad can just sit around and talk until the power comes back on. You know how he likes to re-tell those hobo stories and those stories about his years on the carnival."

"We can't do that either, Dean, because Dad's hearing has gone bad. Haven't you noticed that he can't hear anymore?"

"Yeah, you have to speak up if you want to talk to him. Maybe you can take him for a drive around the island…He likes to ride around in a car," suggested Dean.

"That's impossible too. Yesterday, I took him for a drive, and as I tried to drive through standing water on the street, the motor was drowned out. The water finally rose all the way up to the car windows. Wringing wet, we had to get out of the car and leave it…It's still there. We're lucky we didn't drown. Now, we're stranded in a dark house with no electricity. Just Ellen, Dad and me…And it's still raining!"

Again, Dean considered the situation. "Well, since you're without power, you can't read, you can't watch television, and Dad can't paint, and since you can't talk very well because of Dad's hearing, I guess that just leaves one thing you can do…Just sit around in the house and stare at each other, and starve!" Dean was beginning to be sarcastic.

"Nope, we can't do that either because it's so dark in the house that we can't see each other…and speaking of seeing, I've noticed that Dad has become almost blind."

"Yeah, Clay, his glaucoma has gotten a lot worse since you last saw him. It won't be long until he completely loses his eyesight. He's almost 90 years old now, you know."

There was a momentary silence on the telephone line. Then Clay spoke up. "I'm not too worried about the electricity being off because they'll soon restore the power…I'm just concerned about how to get along with Dad. He doesn't seem to feel at ease around Ellen. She is trying hard to please him. She is always bragging on him and flattering him, but he just stays unhappy. Adam is good to him, too."

Before answering, Dean carefully pondered Clay's dilemma.

"Clay, maybe you all are trying too hard to please him. As you already know, Dad is a strange man. If you don't give him enough attention, he feels slighted…but if you're too nice with your comments, he thinks you're insincere, and it pisses him off. You'll have to learn to be *just right* when you're dealing with him."

Dean sensed Clay's irritation.

"And how in the hell am I supposed to know when I'm *just right?*"

"It just takes a lot of practice," answered Dean.

"Do you mean that I'm supposed to sit around all day, just practicing ways to behave *just right* toward my father? That's bullshit!"

"Well, you asked me, Clay. So I'm just telling you how to get along with Dad. He's been living with Bobbie and me for about 15 years, and I'm finally beginning to understand him. He knows that he's living in your home now, so he feels like an intruder. You've got to make him feel at home."

"Dean, we've rolled out the red carpet for him. Ellen is always trying to talk to him…We always tell him how welcome he is. We even asked him to come and live with us."

"I understand how you feel, Clay. But let me give you a suggestion about Dad. Instead of saying nice things to him, *do* something nice for him. Dad is not much of believer in talk…He appreciates *deeds.* Instead of gushing over him or trying to please him with compliments, just be yourself and just let him be himself. Let him do whatever he wants. Also, tell Ellen to make him an apple pie."

"I bought him an apple pie last week, and he wouldn't even eat it! So that won't work either!"

"He doesn't like store-bought apple pie. Ellen needs to bake one from

386

scratch. As I said, when you're dealing with Dad, you have to treat him…"

"Yeah, I know….*Just right!*" Clay finished the sentence for his brother.

"Another thing, tell Ellen not to butter him up too much, and not to agree with everything he says."

"Does Bobbie ever disagree with him?"

"Yeah, when she feels like he's wrong."

"Oh, I get it. Then he gets pissed off and Bobbie bakes him an apple pie in order to kiss-up, and make up with him!" said Clay, accusingly.

"No, Clay, you've got it all wrong. He might get pissed off at Bobbie, but she bakes him an apple pie because she loves him. When she disagrees with him, he might get angry at her for awhile, but he always gets over it. He is perceptive enough to know that Bobbie cares for him, and he finally feels at home here."

"Well, Ellen cares for him, too!" said Clay, with irritation, "and we want him to feel at home with us!"

"Then just treat him like a member of the family…no better, and no worse. As long as you treat him like a privileged guest, he won't feel at home. It's kind of a delicate thing. You have to learn to treat him just…well, you know."

"I wish he would bond with Ellen the way he has with Bobbie. Why does he have such a hard time relating to women, anyway?"

"Clay, it took several years for Dad to really learn to love Bobbie. Dad's a slow mover, and besides Mom, Bobbie is the first woman he's ever trusted or gotten close to. He'd learn to love Ellen, too, if he was around her for a long time."

"Dean, I appreciate you giving me the advice because I want to be close to Dad, just like you are. I worry about him a lot…Did you know that he's starting to forget things? Sometimes I think he's losing it!"

"Yeah, I've noticed. But after all, he's pushing ninety. I only hope I can make it to that age."

"Well, Dean, I'll give it another try with Dad…Man, he's odd!" Clay laughed as he made the statement.

"Anyway, changing the subject…Dean, I think we're going to move back to Tennessee."

"Great, Clay! I wish you would. The family is dying off, and Dad isn't getting any younger, you know. When do you plan to move up here?"

"As soon as I can get my affairs in order. I think I already have a job up there."

Clay and Dean continued their conversation, most of which had switched to the subject of Clay's possible relocation. By the time they hung up, Bobbie's sentimental movie was over, and she had retired to bed, leaving Dean alone in the den.

So much for our romantic evening, he sighed.

*   *   *

In early March, Will left Florida and returned to Tennessee. On his first night home, he sat in the cozy den relating the experience to Dean. In recalling his visit, he told a multitude of stories concerning Clay's bad luck. He spoke fondly of Clay, but he was disgruntled in regard to the misfortunes that plagued him.

"Clay seems to be jinxed," protested Will, "and his bad luck rubs off on everybody near him."

"Yeah, both of you had plenty of bad things happen to you while you were visiting him…That storm you had, and the flood. Typical event in Clay's life." He walked to the easy chair and took a seat facing his father.

Will continued. "Well, believe it or not, he had other episodes of bad luck while I was visiting him. After the electricity came back on and the floodwater receded, Clay decided to drive us over to visit *Disney World.* Immediately after we left town, one of his tires blew out.

After we put on the spare and drove on, his car engine broke down. We had to get the car towed in and catch a bus back to St. Pete. We never did get to see *Disney World.*"

"Wow, Clay does seem to be jinxed. Did you do anything else for fun while you were there?"

"Well, Clay wanted to rent a boat and take us out fishing, but I didn't want to risk something like that with him," said Will.

Dean laughed. "The only way I'd go out in a boat with him is to be wearing a deep-sea diving suit—in case the boat sank."

"Did Clay tell you that he might move back to Tennessee?" asked Will.

"Yes, he told me. I hope he does. Maybe the three of us can get back into our painting. Rob may want to paint some, too. His paintings are really good."

Will fetched a cigarette from his shirt pocket. After routinely massaging it between his fingers, he lit up, clenching the holder between his teeth.

"Did Clay say where he wanted to live?" asked Dean.

"Yeah," said Will between puffs of his cigarette, "he wants to live in

388

Knoxville."

"Great!" said Dean, "Since Rob lives in Knoxville, that'll mean that the whole family will be close together again!"

The limp cigarette fell from Will's holder onto the floor. Hurriedly, Dean bolted from his chair and retrieved the lit cigarette from the carpet, then gently handed it to his father. Embarrassed and irritated at himself, Will angrily snuffed out the butt in the ashtray.

"I'm sorry, Dean. I didn't see that cigarette fall onto the floor. Did it scorch a place in the carpet?"

Dean looked at the myriad of cigarette burns that defaced the carpet area surrounding the coffee table. "Don't worry about it, Dad. It didn't burn a hole in the rug," he lied. Realizing the extent of Will's failing eyesight, he feared that his father's smoking might eventually cause a fire. A concern of equal magnitude was his driving since he had recently been involved in several minor auto accidents.

Dean had begun to notice a more rapid deterioration in Will's general health: His eyesight had worsened, and his hearing had degenerated; moreover, his forgetfulness appeared to be more than simple absent-mindedness, for on occasion, he had absolutely no memory of recent events. Although he continued to paint and write, the quality of his weekly newspaper column had declined; also because of his impaired vision, his paintings had begun to exhibit a weird appearance. He was no longer able to discern the subtle distinction between colors. On one of his recent paintings, Will had rendered a landscape with blue trees and a bright green sky, a combination that gave the painting an eerie, surrealistic appearance.

The subject matter of his paintings also changed. His interest in producing impressionistic landscapes had yielded to a preoccupation with painting scenes of fantasy, with dream-like images of people and objects portrayed in incongruous circumstances. Although his faculties were rapidly failing, he refused to give up his passion, as he steadfastly pressed on with his work.

Dean had never witnessed a person with such dogged determination; consequently, he felt that only total blindness would ever deter his father from pursuing the passion that, during his entire lifetime, had repeatedly lifted him up from the strangling clutch of despondency. He looked at Will with sadness. Reluctantly, he called attention to his father's failing eyesight.

"Dad…It seems that your glaucoma is getting worse. Are you able to see well enough to continue driving a car?"

"Yeah, Dean, my eyesight is getting worse. But if I have to give up driving, I might as well be dead. Because when I give it up, I'll be giving up my last little bit of independence. If it will make you feel better, I'll cut down on my driving even more."

"Dad, you know that Bobbie and I will take you anywhere you want to go. You don't really need to drive. But I think I know how you feel about your independence. After all, I'm a whole lot like you in my personality."

Will smiled. "No, Dean, I used to think you were just like me…but in the last few years, I've come to see that you're more like your mother instead of me. I don't know why I couldn't see it years ago…And Rob— he's more like Sarah, too. I may be going blind, but in many ways, I can see better now than I ever could before. One of the things that I can now see so clearly is what a wonderful person I had in your mother. She was the kindest, most gentle person I have ever known…But when I was a younger man, because of my hard ways, I didn't appreciate her enough. I always honored her and respected her, but I was just not gentle enough with her. And the same is true for Elwood—he was just like Sarah, and I was really hard on him. And golly, how I regret the hard whippings I gave Rob. And I can see now that I never really recognized the talents of Al and Clay. If God could just let me go back in time, I'd show some gentleness—if I just had it to do over."

"Dad, don't be so hard on yourself. You've been a good man—both to Mom and all of us boys." Dean stopped short of telling his father that he loved him.

The door from the garage opened, and in walked Deana and her oldest son, John, who was now five years old.

"Hi Dad…! Hi Papaw…!" greeted Deana.

Dean walked to the door. "Hi Deana! And who's that little guy tagging along behind you? Is that little John?"

After briefly hugging his daughter, Dean immediately scooped up his grandson. Cradling the small boy in his arms, he turned to Deana. "What are you doing here? When did you get home? Is Kevin with you? Where are Sarah Beth and Daniel?"

"My gosh, Dad! One question at a time!" Deana laughed. "Sarah Beth and Daniel are with Kevin. They're visiting Kevin's family. We'll be here for a couple of days. John and I couldn't wait to get over here. I've been missing you all so much."

Deana walked to her grandfather and hugged him. Dean followed behind with John still in his arms.

"Dad, you remember your little great-grandson, don't you?" Dean smiled. "Here's little John."

Will had an affinity for children, and upon seeing John, his face instantly brightened. Displaying a timid expression, the small boy returned his smile.

"He sure is a handsome young man!" stated Will, "I'll bet he would like to sit on my lap!"

"Well, I don't know, Papaw," said Deana. "He's a little bit shy... John, go hug your great-grandpa!" John reluctantly obeyed his mother.

"Let's see you dance!" requested Will.

Displaying a look of anxiety, John took a step backward, but continued to smile.

"I know how to get him to dance!" said Will, "I'll play some music!" Will had formerly brought his antiquated 78 RPM record player to Dean's house and placed it in the corner of the den. Quickly, he slid a record on the turntable and turned on the machine. Soon, the harmonizing voices of *The Sons of the Pioneers* quartet filled the den with the old ballad from the 40s: "Tumbling Tumbleweed." Unabashed, Will took Deana's hand and began to slow-dance with her. In spite of his advanced age, he moved smoothly around the floor with Deana while Dean and John smiled and watched the graceful couple.

When the number was finished, he replaced the record with an even older, but peppier number, "The Dark Town Strutter's Ball." This time he took the hands of both Deana and her small son as he began to move clockwise with them, cavorting to the pulsating beat, moving in a circle as he held their hands. Although John was initially reluctant, his enthusiasm quickly mounted and he smiled as the dance progressed. Dean laughed and clapped his hands to the swinging number.

When the music ended, they all roared with laughter, and the dancers breathlessly took seats in various places in the room.

Will looked at little John, who was standing directly in front of him, eyeing his great-grandfather with curiosity. Suddenly, Will's expression changed to one of acute recognition.

"Terry, I can't tell you how much I have missed you! I'm so glad you came back to see me! Remember when we used to feed the ducks over at the lake?"

At first, Deana and her father were dumbstruck that his mind had wandered so far into the past, but their initial shock was quickly replaced by sadness, for they knew that with his imaginary recognition of Terry, Will's perception of the world had forever changed.

If we had no winter, the spring would not be so pleasant: if we did not sometimes taste of adversity, prosperity would not be so welcome.
Anne Bradstreet—*Meditations Divine and Moral*

Chapter 37

Clay readjusted the reclining lawn chair to a more upright position. Sitting erectly in his makeshift easy chair, he turned the page of his newspaper from the editorials to the advertising section. Across the empty room, Ellen was relaxing in a lawn chair of her own. Clasping small, wooden hammers in each hand, she was beating out the monotonous tune of "Chopsticks" on a toy xylophone. Annoyed by the distraction of the repetitious ditty, Clay turned from his newspaper and looked at Ellen.

His gentle expression masked his irritation. "Honey, do you have to play that thing right now?"

Ellen flashed a disarming smile. "Is it bothering you, Clay?" Her expression was one of total innocence.

Clay's head dropped as he looked over his glasses; with compassion he reconsidered his complaint.

"Oh, it's okay if you want to play it, honey…But why don't you play it a little softer—not as loud? And maybe you could play a different tune for awhile."

"Am I disturbing your reading?"

"No, but I'm looking in the furniture ads…I'm trying to see if I can find us some bargain furniture."

A rap at the front door captured Clay's attention. Setting his newspaper aside, he strode to the door and opened it. He immediately recognized the figure of Rob, silhouetted against the bright sunlight of the morning.

"Anybody home?" shouted Rob, in a booming voice that seemed even louder as it reverberated through the empty rooms of the apartment.

"Hi Rob…Come in!" greeted Clay. The brothers embraced as Ellen lay aside her toy xylophone and walked to Rob, also hugging him.

"Hi, Ellen!" said Rob, grinning. "My, don't you look pretty!" His compliment was sheer flattery because Ellen's pink house robe gave her a nondescript appearance. Although she was a small woman, her French-twist hairdo made her appear much taller.

"Rob, it's so good to see you! Did you bring Madge?" asked Clay.

"No, she stayed home. She's full of excitement about starting a new quilt."

"Well, come on in and pull up a …box!" Clay invited, "You can take that box there, or there's another crate over in the other corner…although it's not too strong. I would hate for it to cave in with you."

"Oh, I see that your furniture is not here yet. When will it be here?" asked Rob, as he took a seat on the most comfortable-looking box. Ellen returned to her lawn chair and continued to play her toy instrument, only this time softer.

"My furniture? Well, that's an interesting story! I no longer have any furniture," answered Clay.

"What happened to it? Did you sell it?" Rob laughed.

Clay was piqued by his brother's curiosity.

"No, I didn't sell it. I know a guy in St. Pete with a big truck, and I hired him to haul it up here for me. Anyway, he got drunk and wrecked the truck, so somewhere south of Atlanta my furniture is demolished and scattered along the side of the Interstate. He called me from jail this morning and gave me the news."

Rob shifted his weight as he sat on the box. "Well, won't insurance cover the loss?"

"No, the guy didn't have any insurance, and my insurance won't cover it for that kind of thing." Clay's dispassionate attitude indicated his acceptance of his continued ill fortune.

"So, what are you going to do about furniture?"

Clay answered, stoically. "Buy some more. What else can I do?" Changing the subject, Rob asked, "How was your drive to Tennessee?"

"Not too bad…I only had one flat tire. I must have run over a nail on the other side of Chattanooga."

"How does it feel living back here in Tennessee?"

"I feel good about it. It will be nice to be around you and the rest of the family…How is Dad?" Clay's face expressed sadness.

"Dad's not doing too well. He seems to be slipping pretty fast. He had to quit driving, you know," said Rob.

"I'll bet getting him to quit driving was as hard as pulling a tooth!"

"No, it really wasn't. He just kinda forgot that he ever drove. I'm not so sure he knows what a car is. He did the same way about his smoking…He just started forgetting that he ever smoked. Occasionally, he seems to remember it." Rob changed his seat to a more comfortable box in the corner and continued his conversation.

"I'll tell you a story about his smoking…It's sad, but it's also humorous. A few weeks ago, he reached into his wallet and pulled out a $20 dollar bill. He started rolling it between his fingers—you know how he always did that before he smoked. He finally rolled it into a cigarette shape, then stuck it in his mouth and lit it!"

"My gosh!" said Clay," What happened then?"

"Dean saw it and quickly jerked it out of his mouth. I told him that kind of smoking was too expensive. If he's going to smoke money, he should at least choose one choose $1 dollar bills instead of $20s."

In his awareness of Rob's penchant for finding humor in dismal situations, Clay eyed his brother curiously, then chuckled.

Rob hung his head. "Sometimes you have to laugh to keep from crying, Clay." He then awkwardly shifted his position atop the box. "This is not the most comfortable seat that I've had the pleasure to use."

"Here, take my seat…I'll swap with you." Clay abandoned his lawn chair and the brothers traded seats.

"Where's Adam?" asked Rob.

"He's out trying to make new friends. He took his basketball with him. He sure misses Terry and Eldon. I hope they come and visit pretty soon."

The repetitious plinking of the xylophone abruptly stopped. Clay turned to Ellen.

"Honey, why don't you make Rob and me some coffee?"

Ellen left her chair and headed for the kitchen.

Clay looked back at Ellen. "Honey, can you remember all the steps we went through this morning, or do you need me to help you make it?"

Rob appeared to be puzzled by the question.

"Of course I can do it! Don't ask me a silly question like that!"

Clay repositioned himself on the box. "It's a good thing I packed the kitchen utensils and TV set in the car."

"Where are you going to sleep?"

"On the floor, where else?" Clay's answer was nonchalant. "We've got blankets and pillows."

Rob got up and slowly began to pace the floor. "Take your chair back, Clay. I've got to be going before long. When I got your call and you gave me your address, I just thought I'd come over and see if Dean and I can help you get moved in…But I see that you don't have much to move. Dean said you already have a job lined up."

"Yeah, I'll be going to work next week over at *Benson Plastics* as a graphic designer. I had to take a cut in pay, but I think I'll be happier, being here in Tennessee."

Clay reclaimed his seat in the lawn chair.

From the kitchen, Ellen returned carrying a dinner plate containing the two cups of steaming hot beverage. Grinning coquettishly, she announced, "Well, guys, here's your coffee."

To provide a table beside Clay's chair, Rob dragged an empty box upon which Ellen placed the improvised tray. Looking at their cups, the brothers simultaneously discovered that the liquid was clear. Raising the cup to his lips, Rob cautiously tasted the contents: The clear fluid was merely hot sugar water.

"What is this stuff, Ellen?" asked Clay.

"Why, it's coffee, just as you asked for!" answered Ellen, "It's just perfect! Isn't it Rob?" She looked at Rob and smiled innocently.

"Ellen, you used that bag of sugar again instead of the can of coffee. Just take these cups back to the kitchen. Don't worry about it, honey."

After retrieving the cup from Rob, Ellen wordlessly retreated into the kitchen with the containers. Soon, the repetitious pinging of the tune, "Chopsticks" drifted from the kitchen.

Rob reclaimed his seat on the box across from his brother. "What's wrong, Clay? Is Ellen okay?"

Clay eyed Rob, and his eyes echoed the sadness within him.

"I guess you can tell by now. Ellen is in the beginning stages of Alzheimer's. What am I going to do?"

Rob stood and walked to his brother. Gently, he placed his hand on Clay's shoulder. "I'm so sorry, Clay. I wish I could utter some profound words, like a lot of preachers do. Words like, 'it's God's will,' or 'things could be worse.' Those are hollow comments, but the truth is, we don't know why these things happen."

Clay looked up at Rob.

"Do you think Dad has this too…Alzheimer's?"

"I don't know," answered Rob, "It may be. Or it may be hardening of the arteries… or he may have had a small stroke. But he's getting worse every day. Eventually, I think that Dean and Bobbie will have to put him in a nursing home. I know it sounds cruel, but it's getting to the point that it's impossible to give him the care he needs."

"I guess he's had to give up painting?"

"That's the one thing that he still tries to do," answered Rob.

"Although he's nearly blind, and he gave up his writing—he still makes an effort to paint. He's unwavering in his efforts, although some of his paintings are really pretty weird. I guess he'll quit painting only when he can no longer function, or goes completely blind."

For a long time the brothers were quiet while the plinking melody from the kitchen continued.

"I've got to go see Dad right away," said Clay. "Tomorrow I've got to go shopping for furniture, but as soon as I get situated here, I'm going to go and see him."

"Well, if he's having one of his better days, he'll know you. But if he's having a bad day, he may not. Either way, he may not remember that you even came. He's quickly losing his short-term memory."

"That's so sad…What have I got to look forward to, Rob? Ellen being the way she is, and Dad…"

Having no answer, Rob didn't respond.

"I've got to be going, Clay. But before I go, I wanted to tell you that Madge and I are joining Bobbie and Dean for a trip to the mountains. We're leaving early in the morning, and we'll be back in a couple of days. Dean and I would like for you and Ellen to come with us…Can you?"

"Who will take care of Dad?" asked Clay.

"Well, tomorrow's Saturday, so Vince is staying with him. Dad feels closer to Vince than anybody in the world right now…You remember how he felt about Terry…Well, he's that close to Vince. He's really good at taking care of Dad."

A soft smile of relief covered Clay's face. "I'm so glad."

"Will you go with us?"

"No, I can't Rob. I've got to go shopping for furniture. Anyway, I don't feel well. You wouldn't believe the stress I've been under lately. After I get my furniture moved in, I just want to rest for two or three days. I don't have to be at work until next Wednesday."

"Well, I don't have to be at work anytime! I just retired!"

"Congratulations!" Clay playfully punched his brother on the shoulder.

"Clay, I'm going to talk to Dean and see if we can put off our trip to the mountains until Sunday, so we can help you move your furniture."

"No…I won't need you. We only bought a few pieces, and the furni-

396

ture store will move it in for me. Adam's real strong, and the couple who live next door have volunteered to help us in anyway they can. Besides, it may not even come this weekend; I still have to find bedroom furniture. You and Dean go on to the mountains and have a good time. I'll see you guys when you get back."

Rob leaned toward the kitchen and yelled. "Bye, Ellen. I'll see you in a few days."

The music stopped and Ellen came into the room displaying a happy grin. She hugged Rob and smiled.

"Let's have a little prayer, Clay," said Rob. The three bowed their heads as Rob said a prayer for deliverance and of thanks.

The excursion to the mountains had been planned as a brief respite from their troubled circumstances. The long and arduous care of Will had sapped their emotional strength; and now with their additional worries about Ellen's affliction, the family needed a rekindling of their spirits. Following a two-day escape from their burdens, the two couples returned to their homes.

After dropping off Dean and Bobbie, it was near midnight when Rob pulled the car into his garage. As he and Madge stepped from the car, the ringing of the telephone hastened their entry into the home. Hurriedly, Rob picked up the phone.

"Hello."

"Hello...Uncle Rob?" It was Adam, and he was crying.

"Adam? Is anything wrong?"

"Uncle Rob, it's Dad. He's in the hospital...He had a stroke."

I wanted you to see what real courage is, instead of getting the idea that courage is a man with a gun in his hand. It's when you know you're licked before you begin but you begin anyway and you see it through no matter what. **Harper Lee—*To Kill a Mockingbird***

Chapter 38

Rob bounded up the four marble steps to the entrance of *West View Hospital*. The automatic door swung open, and he stepped inside the lobby. Hurrying down the empty hallway, he checked his watch for the time: *12:45 a.m.* The trip to the hospital had taken less than 30 minutes. Dean had not yet arrived since he had further to drive.

Being a pastor and intimately familiar with the layout of the hospital, Rob had no need to inquire about Clay's whereabouts. Quickening his pace, he stepped into the elevator, pushed the desired button, then got off at the third floor. Briskly, he walked through the swinging doors into the intensive care unit toward the nurse's station where he saw only two attendants on duty. Glancing around, he noticed the minimal activity in the unit.

"Good morning.I wanted to inquire about the condition of Clay Beauvais. He was admitted here last night."

The nurse flipped through the patient list and studied the information on the chart.

"He's in room 316. His doctor is with him at the moment…His condition is listed as critical, but stable. You can go to the waiting room at the end of the hall and sign in. The doctor will come to give you a report on him in a little while."

"Thank you, ma'am," said Rob.

He turned and walked to the waiting area. Upon his entrance, he noticed a half-dozen people in the room; some sleeping from fatigue and others pacing with anxiety, waiting to receive information about a family member.

A pot of coffee and a stack of Styrofoam cups were set up on a table in the corner. In the back of the room in one of the center seats sat a young man who was a replica of Clay at the age of 15. Although Rob hadn't seen the boy in several years, he instantly recognized the youngster as Adam. It amazed him to see that his nephew was now a young man—even more amazing was his size: He was at least 6 feet 3 inches tall and weighed well over 200 pounds. His ashen face reflected anxiety, and as he glanced toward the door, his worried eyes displayed a sudden recognition of his Uncle Rob.

As Rob embraced his nephew, Adam flashed a friendly grin; but his show of bravado was betrayed by his jittery demeanor.

"It's good to see you, Uncle Rob... I'm glad you could come."

"Hi, Adam... Man, I can't believe it! You're even bigger than your dad!" Rob kept his voice at a low level. "Have you heard any report on his condition yet?"

"Not since they examined him when he first came in. All they told me then was that he had suffered a bad stroke."

The tremor in Adam's voice revealed his fear.

Each of them took a seat, facing each other. Sensing his distress and feeling compassion for him, Rob reached over and gently placed his hand on Adam's shoulder.

"Try not to worry so much, Adam. These doctors really know what they're doing."

Adam smiled, then hung his head.

"Where's your mom?" asked Rob.

"She's at home...The woman next door is staying with her."

"Was it obvious that he had a stroke? How did it happen, anyway?"

"Well, he was taking a nap before dinner, and when Mom and I had dinner ready, he just couldn't get up from the couch...He couldn't move. He couldn't talk either. He made sounds, but he couldn't form words. I called 911... Then, I tried to call you and Uncle Dean, but I didn't get an answer from either of you until you finally answered about midnight."

"Yeah...We all went to the mountains together. It was late when we got home. Anyway, I called Dean and told him what you had told me. Did you call Terry and Eldon?"

"Yes, I finally got in touch with them. They'll be home as soon as they can get a flight."

Adam looked toward the door as Dean walked into the room.

"There's Uncle Dean," said Adam. Both walked to the door to meet him.

Dean's smile belied his somber mood as he rapidly walked to Adam and hugged him.

"Hi, Adam… Man, you're bigger than I thought you'd be!"

"Yeah…That's what Uncle Rob was just telling me," said Adam, forcing a casual grin.

"Do you have any news about your dad?" asked Dean.

"Like I told Uncle Rob, I haven't heard anything more than what they told me when he first came into the hospital. They just said that he had a bad stroke."

As the three stood talking, the doctor came into the room carrying a chart. He was a tall, balding man with a stethoscope dangling from his neck. He walked directly to them.

"I'm Dr. Richardson. Are you the family of Clay Beauvais?"

"Yes, we are," replied Rob. "How is he?"

The doctor glanced over Clay's chart, then looked at Rob. "Are you his brother?"

"Yes sir," Rob responded.

"Your brother has suffered a stroke… A cerebral embolism, a rather severe one. There has been a cessation of the blood supply to part of his brain, causing an infarction—or death of brain tissue. He is in critical condition, but he's holding his own for now."

"What are his chances? Do you think he will live?" asked Dean.

"I don't have a crystal ball, but I'd say that he is definitely not out of danger. Things could go either way."

"Will he be paralyzed?" ask Adam, now on the verge of tears.

"There definitely will be some paralysis, but at this time, I can't predict the extent of it. He may suffer some intellectual impairment… And the stroke could affect his speech."

"How long does the intellectual impairment last?" inquired Rob.

"Unfortunately, it is often permanent. However, with time and therapy, he may partially overcome some of his paralysis. Although, we aren't able to offer a definite prognosis at this time, he could very well learn to walk. We're just not sure yet. For now, we are watching him closely and giving him anticoagulant drugs to prevent another stroke."

"When can we see him?" Dean asked.

"You may go in and look at him, but he's asleep. I'd advise you to wait a few hours until he's awake—and until we know more about the prognosis. Why don't you all go home and get some rest?"

Rob responded to the doctor's advice. "We just got here… We only heard about it an hour ago. I'm a minister. Is it okay if I go into the room and have a prayer?"

"Of course. Just don't disturb him."

"Thank you, Dr. Richardson," said Rob.

"You're very welcome." The doctor shook hands with the three men, then left the waiting area.

Rob led the way into Clay's room, with Dean and Adam closely following. With his mouth agape, Clay was lying unconscious on his back. The abundance of gadgets attached to his body indicated the severity of his condition. The tubes inserted in his nostrils were attached to a ventilator in order to maintain his breathing. His right wrist was inundated with tubes and needles to enable the intravenous drip to control his body fluids, blood sugar, and medications. For a long while, they stood quietly, watching Clay and curiously eyeing the monitoring equipment.

Standing between Dean and Adam, Rob took their hands and prayed: "Lord, lay Thy healing hand upon Clay. If it be Thy will, let this cup pass... But if there be no other way except that we drink from it, Thy will be done...Amen."

Hearing the prayer and seeing Clay in his desperate situation reminded Dean of the long-ago vision of Elwood's death bed. Reaching over to his brother, he gently patted Clay's arm.

After leaving Clay's room, they returned to the waiting area to begin their despondent early-morning vigil. The debilitating hours passed slowly, punctuated by frequent trips to the coffee pot and apprehensive conversation between Rob and Dean. Exhausted by trauma, Adam had yielded to his weariness. With his huge physique draped across two seats, he fitfully slept. Six other waiting visitors were dispersed about the room, their lives temporarily suspended in weary expectation and anxiety.

*   *   *

Rob and Dean quickly stood as Dr. Richardson entered the room.

"How is he doing, doctor?" asked Rob.

"His condition is stable. He is no worse than when you last saw him. The scan showed that the stroke occurred in the right cerebral hemisphere of the brain, so there will definitely be some paralysis in the left side of his body. At the moment, we are not able to determine the extent of the paralysis. He is scheduled for more blood tests and an MRI. We should be able to examine the extent of brain damage then."

Adam had awakened and was now standing beside Rob as the doctor

401

gave his report.

"Is he awake?" he asked, anxiously.

"Yes…You may visit with him, only very briefly. I'd advise you to stay with him for not more than five minutes, and then go home and rest until we run more tests on him. I'm very sorry about your misfortune. We're doing all we can do, and he's in good hands."

"Thanks for your help, Dr. Richardson," replied Adam.

Clay was conscious when the three entered his room; however, he was initially unaware of their presence as they stood at the foot of his bed. His muscular frame seemed inconsistent with his critical condition.

"What happened to you, pal?" asked Rob, as he gently patted Clay's foot.

Clay struggled to elevate his head, then when he looked in the direction of Rob's voice, his expression reflected bewilderment. When the image of his family finally came into his focus, he displayed a crooked smile, with the left side of the face showing little response to the gesture.

"Hello, Guys…I'm glad you came. I don't know…exactly what…happened to me."

The indistinct pronunciation of his faltering words bore proof of his speech impediment.

Moving closer to him, Dean and Rob advanced to one side of his bed. When Adam eased to the opposite side, Clay feebly clasped his son's extended hand.

"I'm just so tired," he said, lisping the words.

Immediately, he repositioned his head and fell asleep.

Realizing that Clay needed rest, Rob said a brief prayer before they left the room. Deeply concerned, they returned to their seats in the waiting area and proceeded to make plans.

Dean fidgeted nervously. "How long do you think it will be until we know more about his prognosis? Should we wait here until we hear something?"

"You have to go to work, don't you?" asked Rob.

"No…I'm going to take a week off. I'm busy with Dad right now, too. Vince stayed with him over the weekend and took the day off to stay with him today. I've hired a man to stay with him starting tomorrow."

"Then. Dean, why don't you go home and check on Dad? And Adam, you should go home and be with your mom for awhile. I'll stay here with Clay, and I'll call you both as soon as I hear something. Okay?"

They all agreed, but before parting, Adam embraced each of his uncles.

While driving home, Dean's mind was teeming with worry. His concern regarding the unclear outcome of Clay's dilemma was compounded by the deteriorating condition of his father. Since Will's mental capacity had recently declined, Dean had accepted the inevitability of hiring someone to care for him. As a result, a retired widowed neighbor, Frank Shields, had agreed to be his caregiver. He would start tomorrow, and then on Monday through Friday, while Dean and Bobbie were working, he would keep Will company and attend to his needs.

Dean arrived home from the hospital and found his dad and Vince sitting in the den, listening to music. Upon seeing Dean, Vince immediately stood.

"How's Uncle Clay?" he asked, anxiously.

"Clay's holding his own—I'll tell you more in a few minutes... Have you told Dad anything about it yet?"

"No," answered Vince. "I don't think he'd understand what's going on."

Will looked up at Dean, "What's that you say about Clay? It's a long drive from Florida, but I hope he'll come and visit. I sure miss him. Maybe he'll bring Terry..."

Will's face reflected a puzzled expression as if he were attempting to capture an illusive thought from his memory. "You know, I haven't seen Clay in about twenty years...

The statement saddened Dean, for only recently his father had spent a month at Clay's home in Florida. Now, Will had no memory of the trip. The strange disease that mercilessly steals from so many, had magnitude enough to overpower even the mind of Will Beauvais. But although years of memories had been discarded from his mind, all the joyful feelings lived on in his heart. It reminded Dean of his father's love of painting. He could so easily throw out the finished product, but his passion for painting never died.

Dean poked Vince on the shoulder and motioned for his son to follow him into the bedroom and out of the hearing range of Will.

"I don't want to talk about Clay in front of Dad. Clay is in bad shape, but the doctor says he's in stable condition. The stroke was pretty bad." Vince hung his head in despondency.

"Is he going to live, Dad?"

"I don't know…The doctor was vague about it. He implied that his chances might be 50-50."

"I'm going to the hospital to see him." said Vince.

"Go ahead, Vince…They'll only let you see him for a short time. Call me if there's any change in him."

After embracing his father, Vince told his grandfather goodbye and left for the hospital to see his uncle.

For the next several days, Dean juggled his responsibilities between attending to his father's needs and spending time at the hospital with Clay. Terry and Eldon had arrived and stayed with their father in alternating shifts. In early evening hours, they were often relieved by Rob, Dean or Vince. Gradually, Clay's condition improved enough for him to begin therapy.

During their visit, Terry and Eldon spent some time with their grandfather, but to little avail, for Will didn't recognize either of them. His remembrance of his grandsons was his image of them twenty years earlier. They eventually returned to their respective homes in New York and Florida as Clay's condition continued to improve. He was now at home using his own exercise equipment and resuming his physical rehabilitation.

On a snowy winter day in February, Rob went to Clay's house for a visit. After letting himself in, he encountered Clay sitting in a wheelchair in his living room. The smile he projected was no longer skewed, indicating the he had regained much of his facial muscle control; also, his speech had vastly improved.

After an embrace by his brother, Clay grinned and said, "Let me show you what I can do now!"

While seated in his wheelchair, he reached to the table top with his right hand and picked up a walking cane. Shifting his weight forward, he placed the tip of the staff on the floor, then slowly began to push himself up from the wheelchair. When he had risen halfway to a standing position, his entire body began to quiver as he gathered his determination. His face displayed droplets of perspiration when he struggled to stand erect. Fearing that his brother might lose his balance and fall, Rob rushed to his side, only to be rebuffed by Clay.

"Don't help me! Don't help me! I've go to do this on my own!" he commanded.

At last, Clay was standing in an upright position with a portion of his weight supported by his impaired left leg.

Rob was dumfounded at his brother's miraculous feat. "That's wonderful, Clay!"

"Wait a minute...I'm not finished yet."

For a brief moment, he stood motionless. Then, with his right foot, he took a tiny step forward, maintaining his balance with the cane. Stopping momentarily, he slowly dragged his left foot forward, bracing himself with both hands as he pushed downward on the supporting cane. Applying all of his will and strength to the grueling effort, his body shuddered violently as he struggled to continue his forward movement. Inch by inch, he walked to a small table four feet from where he had started his arduous journey. While sweat dripped from his face, he bellowed triumphantly, "I did it! I walked!"

Rob was immensely proud of his brother; however, the expression of fatigue that was etched on Clay's face revealed the cost of the torturous journey. Realizing that he would be unable to make the return trip, Rob quickly rolled the wheelchair to his brother, who, quivering with exhaustion, slowly lowered himself to the seat.

"Clay, you just made a giant leap!"

The expression of exultation of Clay's perspiring face indicated the extent of the reward for his perseverance. At the moment, Rob realized that Clay possessed the raw courage of their father. Clay was a Beauvais; like his father, he was a survivor.

Rob pulled up a chair beside Clay and tenderly patted him on the shoulder. In viewing his muscular physique, Rob realized that the debilitating stroke had not yet diminished his athletic appearance. Clay, like his brother, Dean, had always taken pride in his muscular body. As young men, the brothers had often worked out together, lifting weights, a routine that initiated a friendly rivalry between them. With pride in his brother, Rob realized that Clay was not yet willing to give up his passion.

From the bedroom, Ellen walked briskly into the room. She was wearing her favorite pink house robe, and her hair was done up with a towel. Her brilliant smile and vivacious spirit belied her mental impairment, for Ellen was a rare blossom who perpetually exuded happiness. Pretty and outgoing, she had the appearance of a much younger woman.

"Clay, honey...why didn't you tell me we were having company?" Her lilting voice carried a child-like tenor.

"Oh, hello honey...You remember Rob, don't you?" Clay's voice was gentle and patient.

"Sure I remember Rob...Hi Rob! I've just had my bubble bath."

"Hi, Ellen. My, don't you look pretty today!" As Rob hugged her, the

405

essence of perfumed soap emanated from her body.

Pointing to Clay, she exclaimed, "This is my husband—Clay. Do you know him?"

"Sure, I know him." Rob answered, gently. "I'm his brother."

"Well, he's my husband…and I have three sons—Terry, Eldon, and Adam…Adam is my baby son. Have you met him?"

"Yes, I've met him, and he's a fine young man."

"Well, it's good to meet you, Rob…I'll see you again before you leave. I've got work to do." Ellen displayed a cheerful smile and peppily walked toward the kitchen.

Rob reclaimed his seat beside Clay, and the brothers became momentarily quiet.

Clay spoke softly, "I'm not sure what to do about her. I love her dearly, but her mind is getting worse. I'm afraid to leave her alone anymore. I'm home with her now while I'm recuperating, but what will happen to her when I go back to work? Adam can't do much. He's still in school."

"Will you be able to work again?" asked Rob.

"Yes…I'm determined to go back to work."

"You may have to hire somebody to stay with her during the day. Dean has hired a man to look after Dad during the day."

The opening front door ushered in a gust of wintry air as Adam's large physique appeared in the doorway. Before entering, he stomped his feet to rid his shoes of snow. On his head, he wore a snow-speckled toboggan cap pulled over his ears, and the collar had been turned upward on his fur-lined jacket. Between his mittened hands, he was carrying a large blob of snow that he had gathered from the front steps. His rosy, wind-blown face displayed a disarming grin.

"Hello, Uncle Rob!" he bellowed. His booming greeting revealed his gregarious mood. "I saw your car parked outside."

"Hello, Adam—it's good to see you."

"Hi, Dad! They let school out early because of the snow. Did you have a good day?"

"Yeah, I had a great day! Come on in and close the door…You're letting all the heat out."

Adam was munching on the hunk of snow in his hands. Before closing the door, he removed his toboggan cap and slapped it against his thigh to remove the accumulated snowflakes. He handed the lump of snow to Rob, then removed his coat and threw it on the couch.

"Let me have that ball of snow, Rob," said Clay.

Clay held the frozen, fluffy substance with both hands and studied it for a while.

"You know, this is the first snow I've touched in about 20 years!" A portion of the snow fell onto the floor as he lifted the remainder and nibbled from it.

"I've always loved snow." Then vigorously massaging the snow between both of his hands, he proved that the grip was returning to his left hand when he molded a firmly packed snowball. With a mischievous grin, he hurled the snowball across the room at Adam, who was barely able to dodge the streaking missile.

The sound of the activity lured Ellen from the kitchen. "What on earth is going on? Is somebody in a fight?" The innocence of her question, and her shocked expression drew hearty laughter from the others in the room.

*   *   *

Dean also visited Clay on numerous occasions, but with the recent drastic improvement of his brother, he turned most of his attention to his father, whose dementia had become more obvious. Since Rob was now retired, he often attended to Clay's needs, and on occasion he still came to check on his father.

The bleak winter days gradually relented to the persistent progress of springtime, but the advance of the radiant season matched the decline of Will's senses: The degeneration of his eyesight, hearing, and awareness reduced his world to a shrunken halo of existence; for he was oblivious to any reality beyond his limited field of sensations.

As his mental condition worsened, he also began to lose his physical strength. His caregiver, Frank Shields, was doing a good job, but lately he complained about Will's stubbornness and his refusal to eat or take his medication. He also needed help with simple physical activities, particularly when he attempted to walk.

From somewhere deep within Will's consciousness, he realized that he needed assistance; however, he was very selective in regard to whom he would allow to help. With Bobbie, he developed a complete trust, and with Vince, he had become best friends. Only in them did he feel comfortable in accepting help. Vince regularly gave him baths and dressed him. Bobbie cooked for him, gave him medicine, and shaved him. Although, he loved his sons, he felt uncomfortable in receiving physical aid from them, for he disdained their possible perception of weakness or vulnerability in him.

The good news within the Beauvais family was that Deana was pregnant with her fourth child, and Clay's condition had drastically improved. He was still confined to home, but to his doctor's surprise, he was now walking regularly; although he needed a cane for support and moved about with a pronounced limp in his left leg.

On a summer Saturday morning, as Dean and his father were watching television, the doorbell rang. Upon opening the front door, Dean was surprised to see his brother, Clay. Dressed in natty attire, he flashed a slightly skewed grin as he stood in the doorway, steadying himself with his cane.

"Hi, Dean. I came to see you all...especially Dad!"

"Come in, Clay!" Dean carefully embraced his brother in fear that he might lose his balance.

"Dad and I are the only ones here. Vince is putting up hay, and Bobbie is volunteering at the nursing home today. Who drove you down here?"

"I drove myself! I bought myself a new car...Look out in the driveway."

Dean stepped outside. Peering around the corner of the house, he saw a new white Dodge Neon parked in the driveway.

"Wow! Nice car. And better than that—you driving it! Let's go look at it!" suggested Dean.

"Not right now, Dean. I'll take you for a ride in it before I leave...Let's go inside and see Dad."

"Can you drive okay? I mean, do you have any trouble physically?"

"Oh, maybe a little—not much. I'm working out regularly. I can bench press 50 pounds now."

"Man! That's wonderful, Clay." Dean was amazed; nevertheless, he was saddened by his remembrance of his brother's former strength when he was able to bench press over 300 pounds.

The brothers went inside with Clay leading the way, limping along as he steadied himself with the cane.

Will looked up from his easy chair as the brothers entered the den. His blank expression bore evidence of his impaired vision, for in the semi-dark room, he was nearly blind. Dean flipped on the overhead light and turned off the television.

"Dad, Clay is here to see you," said Dean cheerfully.

"Who?" Will's face reflected a puzzled expression.

Dean spoke louder. "Clay...He's here to see you."

Will's eyes widened as he strained to see the figure of Clay standing before him.

"Hi, Dad! How have you been doing?"

Upon hearing Clay's voice, Will's eyes communicated recognition. His glowing facial expression revealed his transparent mood of joy.

"Well, I swear! Clay, is it you?" He reached out and clasped his son's extended hand.

"Yeah, it's me." Clay took a seat on the couch facing his father. "Have you been feeling okay, Dad?"

"I've been doing fine. Let me tell you who I saw yesterday, Clay! Gomer Pyle came to see me! We talked right here in this room!"

Clay smiled sadly at his father. "Are you sure you didn't fall asleep and just dream about seeing him?" asked Clay.

"No, I didn't dream it. I talked to him! Dean was here too…He knows that Gomer Pyle was here."

Dean smiled and sat down on the couch beside his brother.

"Have you seen my newest painting?" asked Will.

"No, I haven't, Dad," answered Clay. "But I would like to see it."

"Okay. You know, I don't like that man that's here most of the time," said Will.

"What man?" asked Clay.

Dean spoke up. "He's talking about Frank Shields…The guy I hired to stay with him."

Clay looked at his father. "Why don't you like him, Dad?"

"He's too bossy. Every time I turn around he's trying to get me to eat and take medicine. Did you bring Terry with you?"

"Not this time, Dad. Maybe he'll come to see you soon," Clay answered sadly.

"Tell him to come and see me, and we'll go get us an ice cream cone. Then, we'll go over to the lake and feed the ducks."

Dean changed the subject. "Clay, you look like you have lost quite a bit of weight. Have you been dieting?"

"No…not really. But I'm glad to lose a few pounds because I was getting a little too heavy."

"Well, you sure have made a lot of progress in your rehabilitation," said Dean. "Have you been feeling okay?"

"Yeah. I feel fine…except my stomach has been giving me some trouble lately. Up here, in the right side." Clay rubbed his ribs. "With my luck, I probably have an ulcer."

"Who has an ulcer?" asked Will.

"Nobody, Dad," said Clay. "I have a stomach ache, but I'm fine."
Clay patiently continued the disjointed conversation with his father for
at least two hours; then, with heavy heart, he said his goodbyes and
drove away.

For a long while, Dean sat in the den with his father, in silence.

*　　　*　　　*

For the next couple of months, Will's condition stabilized, although
his stubbornness increased. His caretaker, Frank Shields expressed
doubts about his ability to care for him. His reluctance became a growing concern for Bobbie and Dean.

They continued to care for Will as Dean began to spend more time
with him. On occasions, Will had his lucid moments—instances that
were cherished by everyone, for it temporarily brought back the father
they remembered.

The sweltering dog days of summer yielded to a golden autumn. On
one of these crisp afternoons, Dean received a phone call from Rob.

"Dean, Clay is back in the hospital."

"Did he have another stroke?" asked Dean.

"No, he's having a lot of pain in his upper abdomen. He's back in
West View Hospital. I'm going to drive on over there now."

Dean exhaled a long sigh of worry. "I'll be leaving right away. See
you up there shortly."

Courage is being scared to death—but saddling up anyway.
John Wayne

Chapter 39

Dean stepped off the elevator and onto the fourth floor of *West View Hospital.* As the doors closed behind him, he wondered about Clay's latest affliction. Since the pain was in his abdomen, Dean considered the possibility of a gall bladder attack. Then, he suddenly remembered that Clay's gall bladder had recently been removed.

The word displayed on the overhead sign sent a chill through him: "Oncology." The arrow pointed in the direction of room 424—the number given to him by the downstairs receptionist. Although his knowledge of medical terminology was limited, he knew the word oncology was synonymous with cancer.

With an increasing dread pervading his mind, he stepped up his pace, briskly walking the short distance to Clay's room. The door was open, and he could hear Rob's voice coming from the room. Upon entering, he found Clay lying in bed on his back with his hands tucked behind his head. He was dressed comfortably in pajamas and appeared to be relaxed. A baseball game played on the television, but the volume had been lowered. Clay casually crossed his legs and smiled as Dean walked to his bedside.

"Hi, Dean. I'm glad you could come. Rob's been keeping me company."

Dean greeted both of his brothers. "What's wrong, pal? Is your stomach still giving you trouble?"

"Well, it gave me a fit yesterday, but it's better today."

"Have they been doing anything to help you here?" asked Dean.

"They're running some tests on me. They did some ultrasound scanning yesterday, then they did a liver biopsy. I'm just waiting on the results. I'm not too worried…As I said, I feel better today."

Dean eyed his brother's reclining figure. "Clay, haven't you lost more weight?"

Rob spoke up. "That's what I was just asking him. It looks like he's lost quite a bit of weight."

"Oh, you guys worry too much," replied Clay.

Although the three brothers understood the connection between the words oncology and cancer, none of them dared utter their suspicion. Changing the subject, Clay said, "By the way, Dean, Vince called me a while ago. He said you told him I was here. I was glad to hear from him."

"Yeah…He's been kinda worried about you," said Dean. "What did he have to say?"

"He made me promise to call him at work as soon as I find out something from the tests. I don't know when that will be… It may be tomorrow or the next day. Why don't you guys go on home? They probably won't tell me anything today."

"We'll wait around for awhile, Clay. I'm in no hurry." Dean took a seat by Rob near the foot of the bed.

"Stay as long as you like. I don't feel bad, so the nurses won't be running you out."

An hour passed, during which the subject of their conversation changed from Clay's medical tests to a discussion of their father. Outside the window, the light of day was waning. Rob casually glanced at his watch.

Slowly, Rob stood and walked to the bedside of his brother. "Clay, it does appear that they're not going to give you the tests results today. I've been here for most of the day, so I need to get home. I'll be back tomorrow."

Clay grinned and returned Rob's embrace. "Okay, Rob. I'll call you at home if I find out anything."

Dean and Clay peered through the open door, watching the elevator door close behind Rob.

After a brief silence, Dean spoke. "Clay, how are you doing financially?"

"Not too bad. I had some money saved up that we're living on right now. Anyway, I'm going back to work next week."

"Are you sure you'll be able to work?"

"Yeah, I can sit at a drawing table and make designs. I'm learning to render computer graphics now, so I can easily do that. Do you do computer graphics yet?"

"Yeah, I think everybody's on computer now. I wonder what Dad would think of computers?"

Clay laughed. "I'm surprised that Dad didn't invent the computer."

The doctor casually walked into the room and closed the door behind him. He was a young, swarthy man who appeared to be Hispanic. He stopped by the foot of Clay's bed and busied himself in the study of information on the clipboard he carried. Finally, he looked up from the chart and smiled.

"Good afternoon, gentlemen. I'm Dr. Sanchez. How are you feeling, Mr. Beauvais?"

"I feel much better today than I did yesterday," answered Clay.

The physician's relaxed demeanor was puzzling to Dean. Nonchalantly, the doctor turned and looked at the television set.

"Enjoying the baseball game? You think the Red Sox will win?"

"Oh, I don't know…I really don't keep up with baseball. Football's my sport."

"I like football too. Did you play football when you were young?" The doctor claimed the seat that Rob had vacated.

Clay's attitude was also casual. In a relaxed tone of voice, he addressed the doctor.

"Doc, I believe you must have some news for me…and from the way you're trying to be so easy-going about it, I believe that the news is bad, and maybe you're trying to sugar-coat it for me. Do me a favor. Just give it to me straight, okay?"

The physician was young, and probably had little experience in the delivery of bad news. The expression on his face indicated his reluctance.

"Clay, the news is not good…In fact, it's very bad. The biopsy shows that you have a malignant tumor in the liver."

"How bad?" asked Clay. His tone reflected an indifference to the tenor of the message.

"As bad as it can get, Clay. I'm sorry."

"Then it's terminal?"

"Yes…I'm sorry."

There was momentary silence between the three men as Clay reflected on the bad news.

"How much time do I have?"

"Well, that's difficult to say, exactly. We have some excellent anti-cancer drugs now. At least we may slow the progress of the disease, and…"

Clay interrupted. "I've suspected for a long time that I have liver

413

cancer. And I've done a lot of reading on the subject. Medical books say that a guy with liver cancer lives from three to six months. Is that an accurate assessment?"

The doctor's expression was one of sadness. "Yes...I'd say that you have learned the prognosis quite well."

"Which time allotment would you say is more accurate, Dr. Sanchez? Three months? Or six months?"

Dr. Sanchez looked directly into Clay's eyes. "From our evaluation of your liver damage, I would say that you're looking at the lower figure."

"Three months?"

"Somewhere in that neighborhood." The doctor walked to Clay's bed and shook his hand. "I'm very sorry, Mr. Beauvais to bring you such news."

Clay grinned, "It's not your fault." Then his expression became serious. "Thank you for being honest, doctor."

Dr. Sanchez turned and walked away from the room, closing the door as he left.

Dean was stunned. At a loss for words, he sat in silence as he witnessed his brother's calm demeanor. Casually, Clay sat upright and picked up the phone from the table beside his bed.

"I promised Vince that I'd give him the news as soon as I knew something. I also need to call Rob... and then my boys."

Still in a mild state of shock, Dean remained quiet as Clay began his conversation with Vince.

"Hello, Vince? This is Uncle Clay. I promised to call you as soon as I heard something. Well, the doctor just gave me the news...I'm a goner, Vince. It looks like I have about three months, or thereabouts."

As the conversation between Clay and Vince continued, Dean experienced a feeling of awkwardness in regard to a continuation of his discourse with Clay. Because of his brother's casual attitude of acceptance, Dean was reluctant to express his despairing feelings; and yet, he couldn't bring himself to display an unruffled demeanor. However, when Clay hung up the phone, he came to Dean's rescue, resolving his brother's dilemma.

"I know how you feel, Dean. You're shocked by the doctor's prognosis. Just be yourself...You just got the news, but I've really known it for a long time...All the symptoms were there."

*   *   *

Dean was in deep thought during his drive homeward. In robotic fashion, he moved along the highway as if he were in a trance, and upon his arrival at home, he had no remembrance of landmarks he passed during the journey. Reluctantly, he began to focus on the tasks that lay ahead for the family. *Breaking the news would be difficult, especially to Ellen. With her state of mind, how would she react? It would be sad for everyone, but mercifully, Dad's mental impairment will spare him the burden of grief.*

Terry and Eldon returned to Tennessee and joined their brother during this sad time. Vince supported his Uncle Clay as often as possible, while other nephews and his niece arrived from out of state to visit.

Dean began to feel the strain of the constant pressure that had been thrust upon him, because not only was his job more demanding, but the dismal outlook for Clay and Will was disheartening. Since there had been a steady and unrelenting decline of his father's mental and physical condition, he found it necessary to place emphasis on his needs. When Bobbie and Vince nurtured him, he was very obedient—even docile; but with Frank Shields, he had become almost totally uncooperative. He often refused to eat or drink, and when given oral medication, he promptly spat it from his mouth. Finally, in total frustration, Mr. Shields resigned as his caregiver.

Dean and Bobbie were now caught in a serious dilemma. For most of his life, Will had only trusted and accepted favors from his wife or from people with Beauvais blood lines; however, he had slowly developed a deep trust in Bobbie, who had become the daughter that he never before had. As a result, Bobbie and Vince became his temporary caregivers—Bobbie during the day, and Vince in the evenings.

Will's noncompliant attitude worsened, finally resulting in his refusal to cooperate with family. His defiance to take medication for an enlarged prostate gland soon resulted in bladder and kidney problems. The family doctor urged them to hospitalize Will. He had an urgent condition that would require catherization and others treatments. During his entire life, Will had never been hospitalized; and his strong-mind was determined to keep it that way. Several times Dean and Bobbie had attempted to get him out the car in the hospital area, but in total exasperation, they would drive him back home.

The situation rapidly became an emergency. After receiving a phone call from Bobbie, Dean came home from work with the determination to personally admit his father into the hospital. On the pretext of taking him for a pleasurable joy ride, Dean drove him to a medical facility; but upon his recognition of the building, he again refused to get out of the vehicle. With the help of hospital attendants who brought out a wheel-chair, he forcefully wrestled his father from the car. Will grasped the door of the car, and his strength amazed Dean. As he vigorously placed his dad in the wheelchair, guilt consumed his mind. Only moments ago, Will's face gleamed during the "joy ride" with his son. Now, he was slapping and screaming. As he looked directly into Dean's eyes, his expression revealed his emotional torment; for in his impaired mind, he felt that once again he had been betrayed and abandoned.

A complete physical examination of Will confirmed his decrepit physical condition. In the opinion of the doctors, he now needed con-stant care from a complete staff of attendants. Dean was urged to admit his father to a nursing home where he could receive the care he needed.

At first, Dean resisted because he had once naively promised his dad that he would never place him in a nursing home, but he now realized that such a promise could not possibly be kept. Dean's family could no longer provide for him: If Will returned home, he would surely die.

Reluctantly, Dean had his father placed in *Southern Haven Health Care Center* upon his release from the clinic.

*   *   *

Ellen displayed a friendly smile as she opened the door for Rob.

"Hi, Ellen. I thought I would come to visit. How is everybody?"

"Did you come to see my husband?" she asked pleasantly.

"Well, yes…I also came to see you and Adam."

"Come on in…Clay's in the bedroom. Adam's not here. He's not home from school yet."

Dressed in her pink robe, Ellen was vigorously towel-drying her auburn hair, and she once again emanated the aroma of perfumed soap.

"I bet you just had your bubble bath," said Rob, as he entered the liv-ing room.

"Yes, I did…How did you know?"

"I can tell because you smell so good!"

"Thank you! Make yourself at home. Clay! Somebody's here to see you!" She then walked toward the bathroom as she energetically scrubbed her hair with the towel.

The acrid odor of turpentine pervaded the room. Resting on a large easel in the corner was a half-finished oil painting which would ulti-mately be a rather abstract portrayal of the crucifixion. From a bedroom came the unmistakable clanking of barbells in use. Upon entering the bedroom, he saw Clay seated erectly on a workout bench, executing arm curls with a small dumbbell. Clay's face was sprinkled with perspiration as he looked up at Rob. Noticing the expression of puzzlement on his brother's face, Clay smiled and explained.

"I know what you're thinking…and I guess you're right. You're wondering what a dying man with three months to live is doing working out. Well, I'm not dead, yet! And I'm going to keep doing the things I love to do as long as God will let me do them! That's why I started another painting."

Rob was amazed at Clay's attitude.

"Great, Clay," said Rob, "I admire your grit!"

"Well, I'm not fooling myself. I know I can't work out for very long…And I may not even be able to finish that painting, but I'm going to paint as long as I'm able. If we quit doing things because we are going to die, then we might as well not ever do anything. Because we are all going to die…We've been under a death sentence since we were born. The only difference in my case is that I know approximately when I will leave this world."

Clay wiped the sweat from his face, then set aside the barbell and slowly stood.

"Let's go into the living room and have a cold drink."

Rob took a seat on the couch while Clay limped from the kitchen carying two soft drinks.

"How do you like the start I made on my painting?'

The brothers eyed the unfinished picture of Christ.

"It's taking shape," commented Rob. "It's not going to be rendered in a realistic style, is it?"

"No…I didn't want to try to depict what Jesus looked like. I just wanted to convey the idea, and the drama."

As he viewed the painting, Rob realized that Clay had become devoutly religious; however, his profession of faith had not been initiated by his diagnosis of terminal cancer, for he had been religious for years.

In admiration of his brother's faith and courage, Rob asked, "Clay, you're not afraid of death are you?"

"No…I'm not particularly happy about it, but I don't view it with fear. I trust God to take care of my soul. I'm sure glad that I'm not agnostic like I was years ago."

Clay viewed his impending death with the stoical perspective that was characteristic of his nature; he had always accepted the consequences of fate without complaint.

Rob was disheartened by the outlook for both Clay and his father. He took a sip of his drink, then place it on the coffee table.

"Dean and Bobbie sure hated to put Dad in a nursing home. It nearly broke Dean's heart…And I think Bobbie cried for days. I'm glad you and Dad make peace with each other years ago."

"Me too, poor Dad. When I was younger, Dad and I were sure hard on each other. I guess that we're basically too much alike."

Rob reached for his drink, then crossed his legs, relaxing. As he looked at his brother, it occurred to him that Clay's personality had begun to reflect many of his father's characteristics.

"You know, Rob, I didn't used to understand Dad. But now that I'm older, I can see what a real man he has always been. He is honest, sincere, and loyal. Sometimes he has been hard…but that just shows how he never wavers about his convictions. He loved all his sons with a passion and always wanted the best of us. He feared no man, always looked every man in the eye, and you could put his word in the bank. When life got tough, he never ever thought of quitting; he was steadfast, dependable, and always courageous…Also, he always honored Mom. I just hope I'm half the man that Dad has always been. I honor him more than any man I have ever known."

Rob was touched by Clay's testimony, and realized that Clay had these same qualities.

Clay slowly stood and walked to the small table in the dining area. "Let me show you what I'm working on." He pointed at the stack of papers on the table. Rob joined him as the two claimed seats at the table.

"What's all this stuff?"

"Well, these are papers I have to get into order," Clay answered.

Rob peered at the neatly arranged array of documents and lists displayed on the table top.

"Here's my will. And here are all the insurance papers…and this list itemizes all the things I have to take care of before I get too helpless to function."

Clay was systematically preparing for his death in the unemotional manner of a man preparing to embark on a journey.

"I'm going to be a busy man for the next few weeks, Rob… and if I get too weak to function, I'll need for you and Dean to help me. My biggest concern, of course, is Ellen. I want Eldon to take care of her and to be the executor of my will."

Clay's deterioration was unmerciful and relentless. As his cancer worsened, his body wasted away, but not his spirit; the fountain of courage within him remained intact. The rapid increase in the disintegration of his health was accompanied by almost unbearable pain though he never complained. With a constitution like his father's, Clay felt that he was somehow honor-bound to bear his pain unflinchingly.

During his decline, he became too weak to function on his own; consequently, Rob, Dean, and Clay's sons attended to his needs, doing his shopping, sitting with him for hours at his home and taking him to the clinic for his chemotherapy treatments.

Autumn was Clay's favorite season, and when the brilliant October leaves peaked in their multitude of colors, Rob drove him to the mountains for his final, awesome view of the breathtaking spectacle, for he knew that this would be the last autumn that he would ever see. Systematically, Clay talked to each to his sons, one at a time, making his peace with each of them for any past misunderstandings or grievances. After affirming his love for them, he felt that he had now completed his preparation for death.

Accompanied by Rob and Madge, Clay and Ellen spent Christmas Day in Dean and Bobbie's home, although he had become too sick to enjoy the holiday dinner. Suddenly, in January his condition took a sudden turn for the worse, and when he was again taken to *West View Hospital*, the cancer had consumed the substance of his body. He now weighed only 125 pounds.

He lapsed into a coma, and his sons were summoned to his bedside. They were soon joined by Rob, Dean, and Vince, who took alternating shifts in caring for him. While sitting by his hospital bed, Dean once again listened to the gruesome gurgling tone of his breathing, a sound that Elwood had made many years ago as he struggled for life. To Dean, the noise was a death rattle, for it unmistakably foretold the onset of death. After four days of struggling for life, Clay gave up his gallant fight.

Clay was buried in a military ceremony, accompanied by volleys of rifle fire as a salute to his honorable service in the army.

Because of his mental impairment, Will was spared the grief of Clay's death, and Ellen was unable to comprehend the full significance of the sad event. Because her mental deterioration was accelerating, she moved in with her son, Eldon, who became her caregiver as well as assuming the responsibility as executor of his father's will.

Since the three prior deaths in the Beauvais family had been duplicated by an almost simultaneous death in Bobbie's family, Dean and Bobbie half-expected another family member of Bobbie's to suddenly die. After several weeks of anxiety, however, their apprehension gradually yielded to relief. Apparently, the Beauvais double-death jinx had been mercifully lifted.

The family gradually began to recover from Clay's death, but respite from worry was brief; for on a late August night, Dean received a phone call from Deana's husband, Kevin. Deana had been rushed to a hospital in New Orleans. Although her baby was not due for seven more weeks, she was experiencing severe contractions.

Flowers grow out of dark moments. **Corita Kent**

Chapter 40

Throughout the endless night, Deana lay unmoving. She felt no after-birth pains or postpartum blues; instead she suffered only grief, as it slowly bled into every corner of her being. She didn't take her baby home and worry about the soft spot or umbilical cord. As other babies were being rolled into their mothers' rooms, an ambulance was rushing her baby to another hospital for emergency surgery. The day's exhaustion had softened Deana's loud weeping, and a deep sadness now replaced her earlier hysteria.

That night, Deana spent some of the most painful hours of her life. Her mind kept flashing back to the baby's birth: the soft kitten-like cry, the pale solemn look on everyone's face, and that horrible remark from the doctor… "She has something wrong with her spine."

After her Caesarean section, Deana was wheeled into the hallway where the nurses apologized for the lack of space in the recovery rooms. There had been fourteen babies born that evening (a normal occurrence they said, of what happens during a severe thunderstorm, such as the one that night). When the hallway became overcrowded, Deana was lodged into a tiny, dark cubicle to wait for a room on the maternity floor. It was during this time that the intercom blared, "Code Blue…Code Blue…Third Floor...!"

Deana screamed, "That's our baby! She's dying!"

"That's not about us, Deana!" Kevin tried to console her.

In disbelief, she yelled, "Go see, go see, now!"

While Kevin was gone, Deana prayed to God for help, yet at the same time, she screamed out to Him for allowing this to happen. Between her time of prayer and silence, she looked around the small room and suddenly realized that she was in the hospital's third floor linen closet. Kevin returned with a nurse who informed them that their baby was being stabilized. Soon, Deana was taken to a room on the maternity floor where the shock joined with grief. She had not seen her baby and without her to hold, a most indescribable emptiness filled her heart.

Grieving in the small linen closet was now a preference to this new room, for hearing the nearby cries of the healthy newborn babies was unbearable to Deana. She thought of the barren feelings a mother must experience after having a stillborn baby.

After Deana and Kevin signed the necessary papers for their baby to have surgery, Dr. Norris, a pediatric neurosurgeon, phoned the room to explain the specifics of the surgery. Deana heard the words *myelomeningocele, spina bifida, lumbar region, hydrocephalus, shunts, skin graphs*…Words that would become part of her vocabulary for years to come.

In a daze, she hung up the phone, glanced over at Kevin and realized that he had been staring at the same wall for hours. Suddenly, she felt sad, but also selfish. During the periods of trying to comfort her, he had remained calm and supportive, but not until now did Deana realize that the ordeal was just as painful for him as it was for herself.

When it was time for their baby to be leave for another hospital, a nurse rolled a small glass box to the side of Deana's bed. Inside was a tiny beautiful baby girl with ten perfect fingers and toes, delicate little features, and a head of thick-black hair. Only one problem: the dime-size opening in the small of her back had left her with the birth defect of myelomeningocele, or more commonly known as *Spina Bifida*.

Deana ached to hold her; however they had been informed that the baby girl could not be touched due to the chance of infection to the spine's opening. The nurse handed Deana a Polaroid picture of her baby, and as her baby was rolled away, she cradled the photograph hoping to relieve the emptiness that she felt in her arms.

Kevin followed the ambulance to the hospital and promised to keep Deana posted. Dean and Bobbie called again to say that they would be leaving immediately. Their original plan of coming to help when the new baby got home had changed. To Deana, everything had changed. She pondered the thought that things like this in life always happened to others, but could not grasp that she, too, was now one of the others.

Deana remained alone in her hospital room. Through the walls, she could hear the other newborn-babies cry. Deana's pain intensified…*Can my baby cry like that? What if she dies? Oh, God, is she hurting right now???* Her voice then echoed loudly throughout the room, "Why…God, Why…? A little innocent baby! How could you! To her? To our family?" She prayed to God to change it all. She prayed to Him to lift the sorrow from her heart. But as the hours passed, and at her highest peak of emptiness and feelings of isolation, she asked herself, *Just who is it that am praying to? The God who I thought I knew, doesn't even exist.* Deana's finger pressed the bedside control. The mechanical bed stretched her body into an uncomfortable flat position until she finally remembered that she had the option to stop it herself.

Deana drifted away, finally entering into a deep sleep.

The next morning, an employee from Records Department came to obtain information for the birth certificate. With the shock of everything that had occurred, and happening seven weeks earlier than planned, Deana had still not chosen the baby's name. Previously, she and Kevin had narrowed their choices down to either Maggie or Emily. Now, all alone, and with other worries on her mind, Deana had to make the decision. As the employee pressed her for the baby's name, Deana's mind struggled in an attempt to choose one or the other.

"I'm sorry, I just can't decide right now. Can you please come back later?"

The employee retorted, "Well, I can come back at 2:00, but if you don't know by then, the birth certificate will read, 'Baby Girl Lansing.' I have to get all of the records sent to the state department by a specific time."

The warning filled Deana with guilt. She burst into tears and promised, "Okay, I'll know by then."

Later that day, Kevin called again, this time to tell Deana that the baby was out of surgery and doing all right, but that another surgery would be required in a few days.

"Kevin, it's just up and down. This is getting so hard to handle. And what are we going to do about the baby's name? That woman is coming back for it any minute."

Kevin remarked, "That's another thing I called about. One of the nurses was putting a name tag on her incubator, and she asked me for the name. I didn't tell her our choices, but I told her that we had been doing some hard thinking about it. And Deana, get this! Out of the blue, the nurse said, 'She looks like a Maggie to me'."

"Kevin! I don't believe it! And you had not told anyone our choice of names?"

"No!"

An indescribable relief came over Deana. Through this strange occurrence, her baby had been named. And through this strange occurrence, she felt that an angel had been sent to name her.

The next day, Deana was released from the hospital, and she and Kevin headed straight to Children's Hospital. Before entering the unit, they scrubbed their hands and arms and covered themselves with the paper protective clothing. They still could not hold the baby.

As they entered the small room, there was that same sweet face, and on the side of the glass crib, read the sign, "MAGGIE."

After three surgeries and eight weeks of living on the neuro-intensive care unit, Maggie seemed to be out of danger and ready to come home. Before leaving the hospital, they had to meet with an orthopedist, a neurosurgeon, and a urologist. Each doctor went into specific details about kidney function, catherization, urinary tract infections, shunt malfunctions, leg braces, hip braces…and the list went on.

Having Maggie home and away from the sterile environment of the hospital was wonderful. The family no longer had to scrub and wear protective clothing. Deana had only held her twice, now she had Maggie in her arms forever. She bathed her, fed her, rocked her, and slept with her. Despite her healing wounds and the connecting wires from the sleep monitor, Deana's time with Maggie was as heavenly as the time she spent with her other children after their birth.

On the third night of having the new baby at home, Deana began preparing Maggie for bed. Two hours later, after giving medication, inserting monitor wires, and changing bandages and diapers, Deana placed the baby down to sleep. Exhausted from nurturing the new baby, she trudged into the living room and sank into the recliner. The realization of how much care Maggie needed was beginning to sink in.

Scattered papers covered the floor. Deana watched her three children roll and wrestle, while they carelessly crumpled their homework. Suddenly she was consumed with guilt. The turmoil of the past few months had left her neglecting many of the individual needs of her other three children. It was now bedtime for all the children, yet homework was still not done, and baths were still not taken. Deana's fears had been confirmed, but scorning what lay ahead only filled her heart with more guilt.

Since Kevin found it necessary to work extra hours, the children's needs became solely Deana's responsibility. Making the task even more arduous was the fact that both sides of their families lived in Tennessee, nearly 600 miles away.

In order to meet their financial needs and to have a successful business, Kevin often worked from six o'clock in the morning until midnight. Deana was basically doing the same, only her job took place at home. When not there, she was running the children to doctor's appointments, baseball practice, karate lessons, physical therapy…. and other activities, often with two or more occurring at the same time. Resentments began to consume Deana, and her anger did not stop with hospitals and insurance companies, but it grew even more to Kevin, to herself, and to God.

"Kevin, I need to talk to you." Deana had stayed up late, awaiting his return from work. "I can't do this anymore."

"Can't do what?" asked Kevin.

"I can't keep taking care of the kids like this! You've got to help me more!"

"Deana, I'm doing all I can. I can't keep leaving at work. It's hurting my business! Besides, we have lots of bills to pay."

"Kevin, you have no idea! Maggie alone requires more than the other three kids combined. This is taking a toll on me...and the kids too!"

"Well, I'm sorry," remarked Kevin. "Things will get better though."

"You're *sorry?* All you can say is *'sorry!'* I guess this looks easy to you! Well, you don't know what it is like to hear the bad news from Maggie's doctors, over and over again…and you don't have to dress her, and wonder what she is crying so much about. But today I was thinking about all of my anger and depression over this…and well, I think that the way that we feel about Maggie's disability is how she will feel about it, too."

"That's exactly right, Deana," responded Kevin. "That's why we need to shed a positive light on all of this."

"Oh, really? Well, I guess that I forgot my feelings have an off-on switch!" Deana reacted with bitter sarcasm. "Excuse me while I reach inside and flip it over to positive! Kevin, I can't do this anymore, and trying to pretend will not help anyone. Don't you see…? This is something that I will never get over."

Life without love is like a tree without blossoms or fruit.
Kahlil Gibran

Chapter 41

The sweltering heat of the summer sun aroused a shimmering mirage on the asphalt surface of *Beauvais Lane*. The imaginary grassy lawns adjoining the road were in reality only fields, speckled with dandelion and thistle. Then the parching sun yielded to the clear blue skies of autumn, whose chilling winds swept dancing leaves across the languishing lots that were never claimed by the Beauvais brothers. The parcels of land that were reserved for Elwood, Alvin and Rob lay fallow, their thick weeds and vines obscuring the phantom homes that had once been a hopeful reality to Will Beauvais.

The former homes of Dean and Clay still bordered the road, but were showing signs of neglect by the owners. At the entrance of *Beauvais Lane* was the shop where Dean occasionally painted, but had mostly abandoned.

The lively activity and optimism that once pervaded the atmosphere of the homestead had slowly drifted into a legacy of empty dreams. The decaying Beauvais Estate represented a lifetime of struggle for Will; it was his mark of achievement, a legacy to his sons. Born in the 19th century, he envisioned a world of permanence, an existence in which hard-working families could put down roots and find strength in togetherness and unity; but he had failed to take into account the winds of change, the irresistible force that directs the course of lives and events. Man conforms to the authority of change or he atrophies, and ultimately dies; for the laws of change are uncompromising. Although Will had outwardly yielded to the inevitability of change, he secretly never surrendered his penchant for permanency; for inwardly, he had nurtured the dream of somehow physically reuniting the family.

Ironically, fate was kind to him, for in the winter of his life, his impaired mentality had rescued him from the sad memory of the abandonment of his life's dream. As the months faded away, so did Will's mental and physical stamina; his overall presence had been reduced to one of feebleness and unawareness.

The family celebrated Will's ninety-fourth birthday in the nursing home. Instead of the customary birthday cake, Bobbie brought him a home-baked apple pie upon which Dean placed a single candle.

Dean paused in the hallway and peeped inside before entering his father's room. Following closely behind him, Bobbie placed the apple pie on the night stand beside Will's bed. As they approached his bed, his near-sightless eyes fixed on them in an incomprehensible stare. His white gown, which spread apart at the bottom portion, revealed his bare condition. With his pronounced sense of modesty, Will would have been mortified by the exposure. Dean reached to the open garment and gently covered his father's nakedness.

Dean and Bobbie stood on opposite sides of the bed, as Bobbie gently straightened the tangled tuffs of gray hair that grew wildly above his protruding ears.

"Hi, Dad," greeted Dean, cheerfully, "Have they been treating you pretty well?"

Will stared at his son in bewilderment; his muddled expression indicated his confused state of mind.

"We came here to wish you a happy birthday," continued Dean.

"When can we go home, Dean? Do you like for us to live here? Why can't we go back to our real house?"

"Maybe we can, someday Dad."

"Happy birthday, Papaw!" said Bobbie, "Look what we brought you!" When she held the apple pie close to his face, an expression of recognition slowly appeared in his eyes, and he displayed a child-like smile.

"Hi Dad…Hi Mom," said Vince, who suddenly appeared at the door carrying a small package. "How's Papaw doing?"

Bobbie smiled at him. "He's doing better since I showed him his apple pie. I'm glad you came, Vince." She set the apple pie aside and hugged her son. Vince stood at the foot of the bed and smiled at his grandfather.

"I wouldn't have missed Papaw's birthday party for anything. I brought you a present, Papaw."

Vince tore the paper from the gift, revealing Will's favorite treat of vanilla wafers. He squinted his eyes as he peered at Vince. His gradual recognition of his grandson prompted a broad grin, and for a brief moment, his expression was one of comprehension.

"Hello, Vince. Are we going to listen to some music?" His voice was weak and raspy.

Vince grinned. "Papaw and I have had some wonderful times together listening to music...Haven't we, Papaw?"

Dean walked to his son. "Vince, we need to have his little birthday get-together in the dining room. He needs to get out of bed for awhile. Let's put him in his wheelchair and roll him in there."

Dean rolled the wheelchair to the bedside, and Vince lifted the emaciated body of his grandfather and gently placed him in the seat of the chair. Bobbie picked up the pie and vanilla wafers, then they walked through the open door and down the hall toward the dining area.

"Where's Deana?" inquired Vince.

"She's going to meet us here. She left Louisiana early this morning," answered Bobbie.

Vince pushed the wheelchair to the end of the long table, enabling Will to see the whole family. Everyone took their seats and Will eyed them curiously.

"Where's Rob? Where's Clay? Is he coming?" He was unaware of Clay's recent death. "Dean, let's all go home," he pleaded.

The door to the dining room slowly opened, and Deana peeked through its narrow gap. She entered and projected an elaborate smile. "Hello everybody!"

Deana held the door open, and Maggie swirled into the dining room. She rushed ahead of her mother as her small arms vigorously rolled her wheelchair toward the family. Echoing her mother's smile, Maggie looked like a miniature clone of Deana. Her raven hair, dark complexion and hazel eyes mirrored the image of Deana when she was four years of age.

"I'm so glad to see you all!" greeted Deana. Maggie only smiled and waved because her partial paralysis had denied her the ability to speak. Everyone hugged Deana, then kissed Maggie on her pudgy cheek. She responded with a boisterous laugh as she gleefully clapped her hands together.

Deana and Vince embraced. "Hey, Uncle Vinney! I sure missed you. Where's Jordan and Garrett?"

Vince answered, "Carmen took them to the creek again. You know how they love it there. I hope Jordan watches over Garrett. The last time we were there, Garrett chased a snake up a tree. That boy has no fear...He's always taking risks. Speaking of taking risks, where's Daniel?"

Deana laughed. "He's skateboarding with some friends. I guess all that risk-taking is in their genes."

Deana turned and kissed her grandfather on the forehead. "Happy Birthday, Papaw! I bought you a present!" Reaching into the bag she was carrying, she pulled out a bunch of ripe bananas and placed them on the table top. Will smiled and reached for the fruit.

Bobbie smiled at Deana "It's so good to see you! How was your trip up here?" asked Bobbie.

"Everything was fine. We've really missed you all!"

"We'd better get on with the little party," suggested Dean. "If he keeps eating these bananas, he won't have any appetite for the apple pie."

Bobbie placed paper plates and forks on the table and lit the candle. The family took seats surrounding Will, who was munching on a banana.

"Blow out the candle, Papaw," said Dean.

Will's eyes slowly reflected lucidity, and he smiled as he obediently blew out the flame. The family applauded his efforts as Bobbie cut into the pie and placed slices in the plates.

Will munched on the pie as the family engaged in casual conversation that alternated between a discussion of family matters and simple chit-chat. Will reached for another banana and clumsily attempted to remove the peeling. Gently, Bobbie took the fruit from his hand and peeled away the top half of the banana, then handed it back to him. He flashed a broad grin, then bit into the treat.

The small party ended, and Deana cleared the table. Dean stood and smiled at his father.

"It's a beautiful day outside. Vince, why don't you and I take Papaw for a walk around the complex...? Maybe we can show him the fountain in the front yard."

"Sure, Dad," He smiled at his grandfather as he stood. "Want to take a ride, Papaw?"

Dean called to the others as they walked away.

"We'll be back shortly."

Deana and Bobbie sat idly at the table, facing each other. Deana studied the tired expression on her mother's face.

"Mom, I have never told you how much I admire you and Dad."

Bobbie smiled at the statement. "Well, thank you…What have we done to deserve so much admiration?"

"The way you and Dad have cared for Papaw…I especially admire you Mom. For several years you have made a home for him, treating him like he's your own father…and now that he's sick, and completely vulnerable, you continue to show your love for him. You and Dad have sure faced a challenge."

"Well, your dad and I have a lot of admiration for you, too. You've been presented a huge challenge with Maggie…How do you do it?"

Deana became quiet as she considered her mother's question.

"I'll tell you how I do it, Mom. I have come to look at it differently. When she was born, I asked myself the same question: How can I ever do this? I viewed her disability as a cruel misfortune…as something that my family could never endure; but now I feel that I have been presented a magnificent gift. Inside Maggie's soul is a beauty that is beyond belief. She is an angel. I consider it a privilege to be entrusted with the responsibility of nurturing such a precious gift. Every day I thank God for her, for she has shown me a beautiful side of life."

"I'm so glad things are working out for you, Deana," said Bobbie.

"Mom, it's really just the opposite of what I thought it would be. Despite her disability, she has enriched the lives of others. She reminds me a lot of you, Mom. She has that same bubbly, vivacious optimism that you have. Her sense of humor and rosy outlook are contagious and have a humbling effect on those around her who complain of the trivial hardships of life. She has a special affection for you, Mom, and it is so funny to see how she laughs and claps her hands when you playfully nag Dad. She is a rare blossom…You wouldn't believe the friends she has."

Bobbie's voice interrupted her thoughts. "The doctors prepared us for so many things, but they told us that she would be able to talk. She's almost five now, but let's not give up on her speaking."

"I believe some day she will. There's no physical abnormality that can keep her from talking. But even if she never talks, we'll still be able to communicate. She is doing pretty well with sign language."

Maggie tugged at her mother's sleeve, then signed that she wanted to go into the hallway.

"I guess so, honey" said Deana. "But don't go too far away, okay?"

Maggie nodded as she rolled her wheelchair toward the swinging doors.

Bobbie smiled, "I guess she's getting bored."

"Yeah, probably…By the way, Mom, I not trying to always paint a pretty picture of our difficulties. As you know, we've had some hard times too. It's scary sometimes because a lot of my fears have been confirmed…the shunts, catherization, surgeries, wheelchairs, and on and on…I've prayed so many times for her life to be free of all that. But my prayers aren't always answered, and things happen anyway. And remember one of my worst fears…that terrible vision that I've told you about before?"

Bobbie asked, "You mean the one about the playground?"

"Yeah, the vision of seeing all the children running and playing, but with Maggie sitting over to the side, just watching, all alone."

Bobbie placed her hand on Deana's leg. "Don't worry about that Deana."

"Mom, when she started kindergarten this year, I was so nervous. For one thing, they move so fast academically, but I worried about that 'playground' thing, too. I couldn't resist, so I walked by the school several times during her recess period. The first time that I did it, I didn't see her anywhere. It was very upsetting. I had spoken to Maggie's teacher earlier, and I told her how social Maggie was. You know how much she loves people!"

"Yes, I do. She needs to be outside with the others, Deana."

"Well, there's more to this story, Mom. As I looked around, I suddenly noticed a small huddle of children, and between their tiny arms, I could see Maggie…right in the center of it all. She had the biggest smile on her face. When I observed the exchange of love between her and her classmates, I saw God's love at its highest level. They weren't playing kickball, or dodge ball…or the games that kids usually play. Instead, without any supervision from the teacher, they spread out into a circle, and slowly passed the ball from player to player, making sure that Maggie got her turn too. They had given their recess time and had created a game that Maggie could play. I could see that the other kids did not pity her, but instead they expressed admiration and love for her. And in doing so, there was an exchange of love among them. I felt the presence of God that day, and I saw an energy of love among them that fulfilled God's highest purpose—*His perfection of love.* I spoke to the teacher later, and she called Maggie a 'social butterfly'. She said everyone adored her."

"Deana, that's wonderful!"

"I wish you could see it all. The kids are so helpful. They love to push her wheelchair, and if she drops something, they literally run to pick it up for her. They always make sure that she gets her turn and is never left out. They become totally unselfish. They remind me of little angels, so perfect and so good. And the last few surgeries that she's had, Mom, you wouldn't believe the visits from her friends, the presents, and cards and letters she received!"

Bobbie responded, "Deana, that just makes my day! I'm so glad to hear that!"

"You know, Mom, I used to ask myself, what was God's purpose in creating a handicapped child? But I no longer believe that God caused her to have a disability. Perhaps he could have prevented it from happening, but I just don't know. I think that God takes what we consider imperfection, and changes it into His perfection.

Bobbie frowned, "I guess so, but sometimes there's a lot of sadness in it all."

"Yeah, but gone is that terrible fear of seeing her all alone. God has taken her disability and turned it into a wonderful example to further his purpose. I can now see a profound meaning in Maggie's disability. She brings out the best in people."

Bobbie said, "I can understand the fear you had, but I knew that everything would be okay. I have seen how she lights the spark of love in others."

"Yeah, she's like a courageous little candle glowing in the dark, with her aura lighting up everything around her."

Maggie entered the room with an apple and a shower cap that she had collected from other residents in the home. She then rejoined the others at the table.

Deana turned to Maggie, simultaneously speaking and signing.

"Say something to Grandma, Maggie."

Maggie quickly made several gestures, then pointed her finger at the table.

"What did she say?"

Deana laughed. "She says she wants a banana."

Joining her daughter in laughter, Bobbie retrieved the last piece of fruit from the table and handed it to Maggie. She smiled at the realization that Papaw had eaten all of the other bananas.

The noise from the side entrance drew their attention. Dean held the door open as Vince pushed Papaw inside the dining room.

"We had a good walk. Papaw really liked the weather outside. I think we better get going though…He seems to be getting pretty tired."

Vince pushed the wheelchair through the door and down the hall as the others followed. When they arrived at his room, Dean asked his father, "Dad, do you want to sit in your wheelchair, or do you want to go back to bed?"

Will looked up at his son, his eyelids were drooping. "I'm tired."

Vince lifted his grandfather into bed, then rolled the wheelchair aside. With the exception of Dean, everyone hugged him and told him good-bye.

"You all go on ahead of me," said Dean, "I'll be there in a few minutes."

After the others had gone, Dean stood by his father's bedside, observing him. Sadly, he studied his wrinkled, weather-beaten face, and sunken blue eyes, which no longer exuded their characteristic brilliance. His body had wasted away, as had his personality; for he now saw the world through the eyes of a small child. He had become completely vulnerable to any element that might threaten his well-being; his helplessness was totally out of character with his former pride and strength.

As he looked up at his son, the stupor reflected in his eyes deeply saddened Dean. Reaching out to his dad, he gently placed his hand on his father's shoulder and looked him directly in the eyes.

"Dad…"

His father's dazed expression indicated his impaired perception.

"Dad…I love you," he whispered as he tenderly hugged the limp frame of his father.

Will's recent rapid decline had made Dean realize the imperative nature of the expression; if he waited, he may never again have the opportunity.

He released his father from the embrace.

"Goodbye, Dad. I'll be back to see you soon." When he was walking out of Will's room Dean suddenly felt cowardly because he had never mustered the courage to express his love for his father when he was rational enough to comprehend the gesture. He had played it safe, avowing his love only when there was no risk of awkwardness or rejection. The expression had done nothing to sustain his father; it only served to assuage the guilt and negligence of Dean.

In the months that followed, both Dean and Rob brought their families to visit Will. His deterioration was relentless, finally reducing his sensibilities to the mentality of an infant. In addition, his physical strength had gradually ebbed away, confining his existence to one of bedridden infirmity. He no longer had episodes of mindfulness, but now displayed a constant insensibility. With a deep sense of foreboding, the remaining Beauvais family looked to the future with sadness.

*　　　　*　　　　*

The moving van turned off of Highway 11, and the driver shifted to a lower gear as the heavy truck slowly proceeded up *Beauvais Lane*. The brakes squealed as he came to a stop in front of the cedar-shake covered house. Slowly, the clumsy vehicle backed into the gravel driveway, coming to a stop beside the small dwelling.

Deana and Kevin stepped out of the truck and walked to the house. Kevin unlocked the door and the couple walked inside. It was the former home of Clay Beauvais, which had been listed for sale for several weeks. Yielding to Deana's longing to move back to Tyler City, she and Kevin had bought the house and had brought a load of furniture in the large van.

The home was located directly behind the Beauvais shop building, and Deana looked forward to improving the house as well as refurbishing the entire Beauvais property. Kevin and Dean began to overhaul the condition and appearance of the original "Beauvais Empire": Deana and some friends replanted Mamaw's flowers in the backyard of the shop; Vince repainted the shop and built a ramp for Maggie. Together, they reinstalled the old pond which adjoined Elwood's lot, and that still cradled the decrepit remnants of Will's rotting trailer chassis. They created a path to the pond and adorned its sloping banks with an elaborate display of flowers.

Vince and Carmen had just been blessed with their third child, a baby girl whom they named Carly. They decided to build a house on the lot that was never claimed by Elwood, which was now owned by Dean. With the renewed activity on the Beauvais property, the dying dream of Will Beauvais once again began to show the spark of life. In keeping with the creative nature of their grandfather, Deana and Vince embraced the hobbies of painting and writing, often working for hours in the shop building.

Deana was hired as an English teacher at Tyler City High School while Vince heightened his career as a graphic designer. Living side-by-side on *Beauvais Lane* would enable their children to spend time together, thus realizing the unfulfilled dreams of Elwood and Dean, who had once wished for their children to grow up together.

As he neared his retirement years, Dean began his preparation for the

434

milestone in his life. He gradually refurbished the interior of the shop and installed computers and design equipment with plans of operating his own design business upon his retirement.

*   *   *

The golden days of Indian Summer grew cooler, and the multicolored mélange of foliage yielded to the late autumn wind. The rustling leaves loosened their tenuous grasp, laying the branches bare, as they floated away like a horde of fluttering bats, shrouding the fields with a bronze blanket of discarded leafy apparel. The winter winds ushered in the gray days of December, followed by the bleak, hopeless days of January; and on one of those dreary days Dean received the news that his father had been taken from the nursing home to the county hospital. He had developed pneumonia, and his condition was listed as critical.

When the Beauvais family reached the hospital, Will was unconscious. Lying on his back with his mouth agape, his left arm was impregnated with intravenous needles, and the tubes in his nostrils provided his oxygen.

Dean and Rob painfully watched their father struggle for air, as the now-familiar gurgling sound sent an ominous message of the impending outcome. Will had once been a healthy, vibrant man; now his ravaged body was almost unrecognizable, for he weighed less than a hundred pounds.

The family stayed with Will in alternating shifts. Since Rob was now retired, he and Madge took the day shift; then, Dean and Bobbie relieved them at 5:00 p.m., staying with him until midnight. Deana and Vince took turns spending the remainder of the night with him.

Dr. Sanders, the family physician was amazed at Will's endurance, for in spite of the doctor's prognosis that he would probably last only about 24 hours, he continued to cling to life. As his weakened lungs struggled for air, the rasping noise grew more pronounced.

Several dreadful days passed as the family continued their depressing vigil by Will's bedside. On the sixth day of the ordeal, Dean and Bobbie came at five o'clock to relieve Rob and Madge.

"How's he doing?" asked Dean.

"The same," answered Rob, "He's still struggling. Man, Dad is sure tough. I don't see what's keeping him alive."

For a long while, the two couples stood and studied Will as he gasped for air.

435

"It sure is hard to watch him struggle like that," said Rob. "I wish I could take his place and breathe for him for awhile so he could get some rest."

Because of their weariness from sadness, Dean changed the subject. "Have you had dinner?"

"No…Do you want to go eat? We can leave him for an hour…don't you think so?"

"I hate to leave him," replied Dean. "But we need to have dinner before we stay with him. Let's go to the cafeteria and eat a bite, and then Bobbie and I will relieve you. I know you and Madge must be tired."

"Oh, I'm not that tired," said Rob.

They all left for the cafeteria, and after eating a hasty meal, they made their way back toward Will's room. In the hallway, they were intercepted by an approaching nurse.

"Mr. Beauvais," she said to Rob, "I'm sorry to tell you, but your father just passed away."

"When?" asked Rob.

"Just a few minutes ago. I'm sorry sir."

Dean and Bobbie led the way to Will's room, followed by Rob and Madge. They stood at the foot of his bed, watching him for a long while. The medical attachments had been removed from his body, and he looked peaceful for the first time since entering the hospital, for he no longer struggled for breath.

Rob bowed his head in prayer, while Dean walked to Will. Reaching down, he took the slim, still-warm body of his father in his arms. He hugged his dad tenderly and whispered into his ear.

"I love you, Dad."

Strangely, Dean felt that unlike his prior expression of love, he had not been too late in uttering the words. This time he felt that his timing had been just right; for he believed that his father had just passed to a better existence, a place where he was once again sound of mind and could hear the words with complete clarity.

Sometimes our fate resembles a fruit tree in winter. Who would think that those branches would turn green again and blossom, but we hope it. **Johann Wolfgang von Goethe**

I'm not sure exactly what heaven will be like, but I don't know that when we die and it comes time for God to judge us, he will NOT ask, How many good things have you done in your life?, rather he will ask, How much LOVE did you put into what you did? **Mother Teresa**

Epilogue

The patchwork of passing seasons pressed onward in an unrelenting cadence, melding into years; then clusters of years became the changing seasons of life. The ghostly, blossoming memories of the springtime of youth were gathered up, then swept away by the soft breezes of life's summer. They rode the crest of the gentle wind, collecting phantom playmates on their melancholy flight across the unbroken annals of time; then, after breathing warmth into the frost-laden autumn years, they alighted at last, coming to rest in the welcoming embrace of the lonely soul of winter.

So it was with the surviving Beauvais brothers, who in the winter season of their lives, found solace in the fond remembrance of their family.

On a cold winter afternoon in late March, several years after the death of their father, the brothers relaxed on the back porch of Dean's home, enjoying the sensation of the cool air. Rob swayed lazily in the porch swing while Dean sat facing his brother in a rocking chair. The conversation was sparse, and sprinkled with intervals of silence, reflecting their contemplative moods.

The brothers had entered their years of retirement. While Dean appeared younger than his age, the passage of time had been especially kind to Rob, who was ten years his brother's senior, but appeared to be about the same age. Both men remained extremely active. Rob worked as a bereavement counselor and occasionally preached at church revivals. As a retirement venture, Dean had established a part-time graphic design business in the old shop building. Both were still involved in physical fitness, working out regularly at a health club. As their father had done before them, they spent their spare time painting and writing.

The secluded nooks of the fields displayed spotty remnants of a recent late-winter snow; but in defiance of the unseasonable cold spell, early blossoms had begun to spring forth, bravely enduring the menacing chill. The blooming of buttercups, the chatter of songbirds and the budding willow trees heralded the promise of rekindled optimism. Easter was rapidly approaching, and its arrival would replace the bleakness of winter with the resurrection of life and hope, a metamorphosis that characterized the lives of the Beauvais family.

The brothers had just returned from the cemetery where they had placed white carnations on the graves of their deceased family members. On Clay's grave, however, they had difficulty in finding a spot for their placement of the flowers; for a load of dirt from a recently dug grave had been heaped atop his burial site.

Because honoring the family with flowers was a very personal gesture, the brothers had taken no one with them on the mission of remembrance.

Although the thought was unspoken; the brothers felt the need to discuss family members, particularly their father, partly as an informal, unrehearsed eulogy to him but mostly as an attempt to clarify their relationship with him.

Their initial conversation had been limited to casual topics, but now it seemed appropriate to expand their dialogue to a discussion of their family.

"What did you think about that pile of dirt on Clay's grave? Isn't that typical of the things that always jinxed him? Tomorrow, I'll call the funeral home and get that dirt removed," said Dean.

Rob woefully shook his head. "It seems that his bad luck follows him even after he's buried."

Dean's face expressed curiosity. "Rob, there's something I've always wondered about our family. Why were we all late bloomers? You and I …as well as our brothers, were all middle-aged before we found our direction in life. Even Dad…he was a late bloomer, too. He did his best painting when he was in his eighties."

Rob agreed, "Yeah, we all got off to a slow start…but the important thing is that we always kept moving. We had to find our passion in life. I believe that Dad's smothering love was a negative force that kept us from blossoming. Also, I think that our hostile, aggressive attitudes sometimes took us down the wrong road. As we encountered more positive experiences in life, we began to gradually soften and develop a more balanced personality."

Dean replied, "Going to college was a great positive influence for us...involvement with the church also helped. But the greatest influence of all was our mother. She was a perfect example of sensitivity and understanding..."

Rob interrupted, "It's too bad, but most men feel that showing gentleness is a threat to their manhood."

"You're right, Rob. Dad probably felt that way until he met Mom, but she gradually made him gentler in his nature. Man, Dad sure had a hard shell on him when he was young."

Rob smiled. "Well, it's probably a good thing that he was so tough, or he wouldn't have survived his earlier years. But I think he recognized his own one-sided nature. I believe Mom's gentle nature attracted him. He admired that in her, and he knew he needed more of that in his life...something that would balance his own personality. And with that, he could gradually discover his passion in life."

Dean stopped rocking in his chair. "To have a passion in life is our purpose for living. You know, I just wonder how many people really ever find that passion?"

"Sad to say, not too many," replied Rob. "Most people just muddle through life in a kind of numb existence. I think that God wants everyone to be passionate about life. God has a purpose for each of us. He lets us know that we have found his purpose by making us feel *alive.* Most of the Beauvais family found their passion in the arts."

Dean responded, "Unfortunately, some people feel that the arts don't contribute much to the necessities of life."

"Well, their thinking may be off-track." Rob answered. "All of the arts—painting, literature, music, or whatever form of artistic expression—are some of the most important necessities because they are food for the soul. After all, is there anything more important than the soul?"

Dean nodded. "But some people don't seem to be able to express themselves artistically; they aren't very creative in their nature. It's hard to understand what their passion would be...take for example, a plumber or an electrician."

"But if you think about it, any job takes an amount of creating. It's just that some people expand on it more than others. Take plumbers...some had to work feverishly to create ways for us to wash our hands—or better yet…to flush a toilet!"

"Yeah, thank God for that one!"

Both men laughed, then Dean continued. "Anyway, back to the subject of finding a passion in life. Sometimes it's not related to their occupation, but it is found in other areas of life. Regardless of what they do for a living, life presents all people with creative, passionate opportunities. Jesus Christ was a carpenter by trade; the Apostle Paul was a tent maker…and Simon Peter was a fisherman, but they may not have found a passion in doing those things. Some people find it in activism, or in crusading for a cause. Others find it in altruism, or nurturing, such as doing volunteer work to help others. Look at our mother…her passion was in caring for others—that's what made her feel alive. It might have taken a long time for the rest of the family, but I truly feel that we all found our passion."

Rob answered, "I think we did, too. I found mine in the ministry. Clay discovered his in painting, and you also had Dad's passion for art. Al discovered his in literature, and Elwood's was in music."

"Maybe Dad was the most creative member of our family," remarked Dean, "He was an inventor, painter, and writer…And he finally finished his book about his life. He never had it published, but it's in manuscript form."

"Yeah, and to think that he only finished second grade in school! He had to educate himself—what an amazing man! Where is his book? I'd like to finish reading it."

"He gave it to Vince a couple of years before he died. Vince loaned it to me…I've got it here at home. I'll let you borrow it."

"Good! I really enjoy reading his work. He wrote some wonderful articles, too, but I think his talent in painting was even better."

"Well, that may be true, but Dad never felt that he was successful as a painter," said Dean.

"I believe that he was a great success," answered Rob, "Success isn't always measured by fame or making money. Painting made Dad feel alive and made him a better man."

Dean replied, "Yeah Rob, I think you're right. It doesn't matter that he never became well-known or made much money from it. Look at Vincent Van Gogh…he never acquired any wealth or recognition in his lifetime. He died believing that he was a failure; but now his paintings bring millions, and he is remembered as being one of the greatest artists in history. The fact that he died a pauper doesn't define his passion or diminish his talent."

Rob rocked gently in the swing as he listened intently to his brother's comments. Dean continued, "Jackson Pollock, the famous abstract expressionist had an interesting theory about painting and the act of creating. He never cared very much about his finished painting. He was only interested in the *doing* of it. He said that the product is not important—only the process. He believed that once the creative process is over, the product is not art anymore."

Rob smiled. "Dad felt that way, too. Remember how he used to render a new painting on top of another one...right on the same canvas?"

Dean laughed. "He lost interest as soon as he finished painting it."

Rob's face reflected intense interest. "You know, Dean, maybe Jackson Pollock had something there. Perhaps, without realizing it, he touched on the meaning of life. Maybe it's the journey that's important—not necessarily the destination. We may not ever reach our destination, but as long as we're moving toward it—maybe that's the purpose of life. The life of a Christian is a journey. It begins at the moment he turns his life around and heads in the right direction. His goal is perfection. Although it's impossible for a Christian to reach that goal, he continues the journey, anyway."

"Yeah, but aren't people happier in life when they feel that they have completed something?"

"Not necessarily." Rob answered. "For instance, take the case of Alvin. He enrolled in college at middle age and died only a month before he graduated, so he never reached his destination...But he was the happiest I'd ever seen him. He was alive with passion!"

Dean interjected. "That may be so, Rob, but I think at first we need a *vision*. Al started back to college because he had a clear view of the prize that awaited him at the end of the journey. It might not be so important that we finish, but without a vision, we often won't even start. And sometimes the road gets bumpy, but if we keep our eye on the ultimate goal, we'll keep moving ahead, whether or not we reach it."

Rob nodded. "Al was a success because he was moving toward it. I think that it's the journey that God wants from us—ever moving forward."

Dean reclined in his chair. "The same is true of Elwood...He never had a chance to enroll in college, but he made the decision to begin...So actually, with that simple decision, he had begun the journey."

Rob replied, "I don't think the distance we've traveled on the journey matters as much as the direction we're headed."

Dean commented, "Finding passion often means making major

changes in our lives, which requires taking risks…and most people are afraid of that." His face revealed sadness. "Unfortunately, because of my influence, Elwood took a risk and it cost him his life."

"Sometimes taking a risk is costly," replied Rob, "but maybe Elwood's risk didn't cost him his life. It's possible that by taking a risk he discovered his life…Maybe a short time on earth feeling alive is worth more than a long life of bleakness. I think God wants us to be excited about our lives because it's his most precious gift to us…He wants us to be happy."

Dean replied, "You know, sometimes happiness doesn't depend on our circumstances. Take Deana's daughter, Maggie. She is one of the happiest people I know, in spite of the fact that she will never be able to do some of the things that she would like to do. She doesn't gripe about being permanently bound to a wheelchair. I've never heard her complain about life's unfairness…She just keeps moving ahead and smiling at life. But maybe Maggie, somewhere along in her journey, will have a life free of physical pain, and hopefully she will be able to walk or do the other things she would like to do. Somehow, I don't believe the journey is over when we die. I'm inclined to believe that we will continue our journey in another existence. I'm amazed at the courage that Deana has shown in dealing with Maggie's disability."

Rob considered Dean's opinion. "My own beliefs are a lot like yours. I believe that Heaven is simply a continuation of the journey. In another life, maybe we'll continue to grow, helping to create God's master-piece, moving forward toward some purpose that God has for us. I think maybe that the sin is to drop out—to never take part in the journey or make any headway."

Dean nodded. "I agree. I don't think that God will ever finish his masterpiece. God is eternal, so his process of creating will go on for-ever. If he ever finished his masterpiece, then he would have to quit 'painting'… and if he did that, it wouldn't be art anymore…If Jackson Pollock's theory is correct, the act of creating is the art…the journey itself is God's masterpiece."

Rob added, "Do you remember when you once told me that you never felt more alive than when you were creating something? Well, I believe that God is pleased when we feel alive. I believe that when we are cre-ating, we are more God-like—we are closer to God. He wants us to be like him.."

The men sat silently, listening to the chirping of the birds as they her-alded the approach of spring. In the west, the reddish sun completely

443

hid its face beneath the distant horizon. Dusk descended on them, and the setting sun was accompanied by an increased chill in the air.

While engrossed in their intense discussion, the brothers had become unaware of the gradual advance of the evening. Now, in the temporary lull in their conversation, they had become uncomfortably chilled.

Leaving his rocking chair, Dean suggested to Rob, "Why don't we go inside and get away from the cold? I think Bobbie and Madge have a small fire going in the fireplace and a pot of hot coffee brewing. It'll be cozy in there."

Leaving their seats, the men strolled into the adjoining den, and Rob comfortably positioned himself on the couch. Dean walked to the kitchen, then returned with a tray of two steaming cups of coffee, which he placed on the coffee table.

"You still take yours black, don't you, Rob?"

Rob smiled. "Yes, thanks, Dean. This hot coffee will hit the spot."

Dean reached for his cup and commented, "Remember how we used to always make sure that the amount of booze in our cups was equal? Well, now, I believe my cup of coffee is fuller than yours."

Rob took a sip of his coffee. "In the old days, I probably would have whipped your ass for that."

The brothers laughed.

Noticing the dying embers of the fire, Dean strode to the fireplace and removed the screen. Using the poker, he agitated the glowing coals until they flamed up again. He threw another small log onto the awakening flames, and as the tongues of fire licked hungrily at the surface of the wood, the fire flared again, emanating sparks and resonating with a raucous staccato of angry popping sounds. As the fire intensified, Dean replaced the screen and stood facing the fireplace, warming his extended hands. He turned to face Rob.

"Rob, it's ironic that we had it tougher than the other brothers, but we outlived all of them. Of course, a lot of the hardships that we went through, we brought on ourselves. We're like Dad in regard to our longevity. Dad had to overcome tremendous hardships in his lifetime, yet he lived to be ninety-four. Maybe adversity does make for a longer life."

Rob smiled, "Dad was the great survivor. And I think that our hardships have made us survivors, too. When the journey got tough, we kept going...But sometimes we lost our sense of direction."

Dean added, "When we were growing up and went astray, Dad would always forcefully put us back on course. Particularly in your case," Dean grinned at Rob as he spoke the last words.

"Yeah, he really put the belt to my butt quite a few times."

"Well, Rob, let's face it. You were downright mean!"

"You mean *high-spirited.*" Rob displayed a playful grin. "You know, Dean, I believe that some of our past mischievous and destructive behavior was caused by misdirected creative urges we had as younger men."

Dean returned his brother's smile. "It sure seems surprising that you, the meanest brother in the family, became a preacher."

Rob replied, "Well, it seems rather odd to me that you, after being the biggest wanderer in the family, would be the only one of us who would come and settle here in Tyler City."

Dean smiled. "I guess it took me a while to find my way home."

He returned to his chair and continued, "You know, Rob, Dad knew that you and I would be the risk-takers of the family. He felt that he had to keep a tight rein on us and from bad outside influences. He wanted to keep us in his world."

Rob responded, "There's an old saying that says if you try to capture a butterfly, it will fly away, but if you just let it fly free, it will return to alight on your shoulder. Those are not the exact words, but that's the gist of it."

"You know, if I had been dealt Dad's hand of cards, I don't believe I could have played them as well as he did. He was honorable and forgiving, in spite of the rejection he endured. Unfortunately, he was also as stubborn as a mule."

"Well, the word *'stubborn'* is sort of negative," said Rob. "If you wanted to put it in a more positive way, you could say he was determined and tenacious. In fact, the most important thing he left us was the legacy of courage and unwavering perseverance. Look at the way Clay faced death. I've seen many men die in the war—many of them faced death bravely. But I've never witnessed a stronger show of courage in facing certain death than that shown by Clay."

"Man, I really admire Clay. I miss him, too." Dean changed the subject. "Speaking of journeys, does that also pertain to the hare-brained type of journeys that you and I made throughout the country many years ago?" Dean chuckled.

"Well, you laugh because some of those journeys we took had comical aspects to them," answered Rob. "But those journeys were important, too. We were searching for something because we knew that something was missing in our lives. Without being aware of it, we were trying to discover who we were, and what our purpose in life was."

Dean replied, "Those were hard times, but I think those experiences helped us to become better men. I'm not saying that we are better than anyone else. I just know for certain that we are better men than we were."

The log in the fireplace had burned away in the middle, causing it to collapse and break into two chunks. The pieces fell, propelling a shower of sparks onto the fireplace screen. Dean left his chair and walked to the hearth. Pulling the poker from the rack, he removed the screen and began gently stirring the glowing embers. He idly toyed with the glimmering coals, and then slowly turned to Rob.

"Looking back, I would have to say that Dad—and Mom, were two of the most successful people I've ever known. Mom was a smashing success because she succeeded in what I consider God's greatest calling—being a mother. She was a great peace-maker. She was the glue that held our family together. Mom was as gentle as a lamb...But she was also plenty tough! Putting up with Dad showed how tough and resilient she was."

Rob laughed, "That's true. And I agree with you about their success. Dad turned his early misdirected life into a home and family."

The discussion between Rob and Dean had given them a mellow frame of mind; their moods reflected a warm and cozy feeling. The dying embers in the fireplace had darkened the room, causing the brothers' features to be barely illuminated by the light from the glowing coals.

Dean spoke from the semi-darkness. "When Dad began painting, he even had to make his own canvas and brushes. But Mom and Dad, by passing on their values and genes to us, prepared our canvas for us. Dad was always striving for the perfect painting. Too bad he never painted his masterpiece."

Rob reflected on Dean's comments for a long while, with the dying firelight now barely making his features discernable.

"But, don't you see...? Dad did paint his masterpiece. His masterpiece was his journey in life. He started with nothing and created his painting of life—his home and his family. You and I are part of his masterpiece. No man ever finishes his painting...It's up to us to continue the work he began, then pass it on to other generations. The contribution of every man is just a small piece in this giant mosaic of God's."

Dean thought about Rob's comments, then said, "I guess you could say that our time on earth is like running a relay race. We don't complete the race ourselves—we just run our lap and hand the baton to someone else who then runs his lap in a continuation of the journey. Dad left a great legacy. He passed the baton to his children, grandchildren, and even to his great-grandchildren, through his genes and his teaching. All of Dad's sons and grandchildren are somehow involved in something creative, either in the arts, or in teaching. Did you know that Deana's oldest son, John, is a musician? He organized a rock band, and they perform at places in New Orleans. And her daughter, Sarah, studies and speaks several languages. All of her children are involved in music or painting. Vince is a very good artist and though his kids are still young, they are also showing a lot of creativity. And Clay's sons are good artists. Eldon is a painter and sculptor."

Rob smiled. "We also pass the baton to others outside our immediate family, Dean. Think of the other lives you and Bobbie have influenced, and I hope my 40 years in the ministry have somehow influenced some lives along the way. Mom also passed the baton, Dean. She passed the nurturing baton to you, for you have been the caregiver to the Beauvais family.

"You flatter me, Rob. How can you call me a caregiver?"

"Because you are the 'hub' of the family, for you're the only one who had equal intimate ties to all of the others. You've opened the doors of your home to all of us... and that has brought the family together. You and Bobbie made a home to Dad for many years. He wouldn't have lived with any other son, or any other daughter-in-law, because he truly learned to love Bobbie."

"Thanks, Rob. It would make Bobbie feel good to hear you say that."

Seeing that his brother was apparently embarrassed by the comment, Rob changed the subject. "You know, the journey is never-ending. We won't know how long man will exist in this life. Scientists tell us that the sun will someday burn out. Maybe man will have to continue the journey in another existence."

Dean added. "Well, maybe man will be smart enough to migrate to other planets...or it's possible that intelligent beings already exist somewhere else in the universe who can continue God's journey. God's canvas is the entire universe. It doesn't make much sense to me that God, with such a large canvas, would confine his great masterpiece to a tiny corner of it."

The fire had almost completely died by now, the embers glowing a faint light orange in the fireplace. The facial features of the brothers were almost completely obscured by the darkness in the room.

Rob peered at his watch. "Dean, I need to be going home soon. What are you going to be doing tomorrow?"

Dean answered, "I'm thinking about doing some writing. I may start

447

writing a book about the family."

"Oh, really, that's great Dean!"

Dean grinned. "I have an outline for it, but I'll probably have to use fictitious names."

"Why is that? It seems like you'd use our real names."

"Well, Rob, I'm afraid that the statute of limitations hasn't expired on some of the insane things that we did when we were young. I wouldn't want this book to land us both in jail."

Then, Rob remarked, "Well, then you better leave some of the worse things out of the story. Just tell them the good things...like how handsome I am."

The brothers joined in laughter.

Suddenly, the door from the kitchen sprang open and a light came on, temporarily blinding the men. Vince's twelve year old son, Jordan came into the room, pushing Maggie along in her wheelchair.

Dean turned toward the door and smiled. "Jordan, you're a spitting image of your dad when he was your age."

Jordan grinned, "Hi, Papa! Dad says I'm a spittin' image of you, too!" He turned to face Rob. "Hi, Uncle Rob. What are you two guys doing sittin' here in the dark?"

"Oh, were the lights off?" asked Rob, "I didn't even notice."

Dean, Jordan, and Maggie all laughed, with Maggie laughing the hardest.

Dean smiled and greeted his grandchildren.

"Hi, Papa—Hi, Uncle Rob," said Maggie, cheerfully.

"I love to hear you talk, Maggie!" said Rob. "Are you going to give me a kiss?"

"Yes, and Papa, too," replied Maggie with a gleeful laugh.

Jordan grinned, rolling Maggie's wheelchair over toward Rob, who met her and bent down and kissed her.

"What about mine?" asked Dean, as if he were offended by Maggie going first to Rob for the kiss. Dean stood up and walked to Maggie and collected his kiss, which delighted Maggie. She was fondly clutching a white carnation between her hands.

Noticing the flower, Dean asked her, "Maggie, where did you get that pretty flower?"

She flashed a mischievous smile at her grandfather. "Jordan pulled it out of that bunch of flowers before you took them to Mamaw's grave and gave it to me. Isn't it pretty?"

"Why, that little sneak!" replied Dean, with a laugh. He then turned and hugged Jordan.

"Papa, we've been coloring Easter eggs all afternoon," said Jordan.

Slowly, the kitchen door eased open and Jordan's little sister, Carly, poked her head through the opening.

"Come on, you all!" yelled Carly. "Are you and Maggie going to help us finish coloring the eggs? Garrett's already making his prize egg!"

"We'll be there in a minute!" yelled Jordan. "Papa, they said that Maggie's surgery is gonna be next Tuesday. I'm staying out of school to go stay with her in the hospital," said Jordan.

"Is Maggie going to have another surgery?" asked Rob, with a concerned expression. "That must be about a dozen she's had. She's sure had it tough!"

"Yeah, I'm a little bit worried about her surgery this time," Dean continued.

Jordan opened the door that led to the kitchen, then held it open for Maggie, who rapidly propelled her wheelchair to the entrance. Suddenly she stopped and wheeled half-way around, facing Dean and Rob. As she inserted the single, white flower from Sarah's bouquet into her curls, she said, "Don't worry about me, Papa! That operation's not gonna bring *me* down!"

When Dean looked at his grandchildren, he felt a deep sense of pride, because he realized that some of his Dad's blood was flowing through their veins. They had inherited his father's tenacity, his will to survive and his steadfast courage to move forward on the journey. Dean loved his grandchildren's playfulness... and tenderness. It was that of his mother's. It too was embedded into their spirits, and in this blending, Dean could see Will's greatest masterpiece. Seeing these qualities in his grandchildren, he realized that his father's dream lives on.

Then, as she turned to leave the room, Maggie displayed a glowing smile, its radiance echoed by the lovely white carnation that adorned her locks of raven hair.

The withering vine of despair that causes the faint-hearted to kneel in submission inspires and challenges the courageous to rise and stand tall. **Don Pardue**

Blossoms of Winter
by Don Pardue

Orders may be made by phone or mail to
the address/phone number below.

Please send me the novel of *Blossoms of Winter* by Don Pardue.

_____ @ $14.00   = _____
(quantity)

Shipping and handling* = _____

Total enclosed   = _____

*Please enclose $4.00 to cover shipping and handling, or $6.00 if order is more than $20.00.

Please pay by check or money order and make payable to:
Blossoms of Winter.
Sorry, we do not accept charge cards at this time.

Send your payment with the order form above to:
Don Pardue/Blossoms, P.O. Box 521   Lenoir City, TN 37771
865-986-8812 or 865-988-6644.

Prices subject to change without notice. Please allow 4-6 weeks for delivery.